The President's Daughter

Other Books by Barbara Chase-Riboud

From Memphis to Peking

Sally Hemings

Validé

Portrait of a Nude Woman as Cleopatra

Echo of Lions

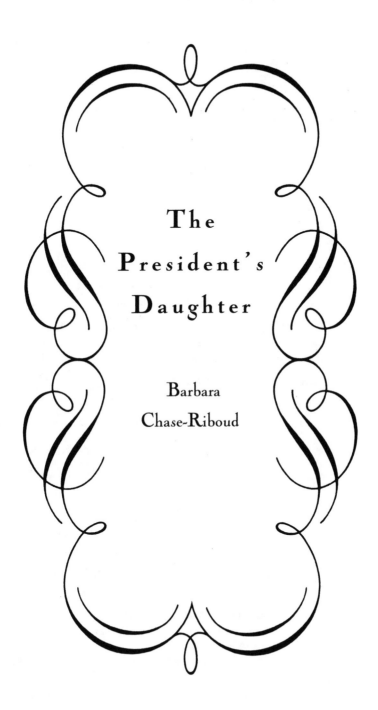

The President's Daughter

Barbara
Chase-Riboud

Crown Publishers, Inc.
New York

Published by Crown Publishers, Inc., 201 East 50th Street, New York, New York 10022. Member of the Crown Publishing Group.

Random House, Inc. New York, Toronto, London, Sydney, Auckland

CROWN is a trademark of Crown Publishers, Inc.

Manufactured in the United States of America

Design by Linda Kocur

Library of Congress Cataloging-in-Publication Data
Chase-Riboud, Barbara.
The president's daughter/by Barbara Chase-Riboud.—1st ed.
1. Young women—Pennsylvania—Philadelphia—Fiction.
2. Jefferson, Thomas, 1743–1826—Family—Fiction.   3. Children of presidents—United States—Fiction.   4. Illegitimate children—United States—Fiction.
5. Mulattoes—United States—Fiction.
I. Title.
PS3553.H336P7   1994
813'.54—dc20   93-42499
                                                                CIP

ISBN 0-517-59861-2

10 9 8 7 6 5 4 3 2 1

First Edition

*To the historical enigma of Harriet Hemings
and to Thenia Hemings, 1799–1802, of Monticello*

Her complexion was not brown, but it rather appeared charged with the color of rich blood, that seemed ready to burst its bounds. And yet, there was neither coarseness nor want of shadowing in her countenance that was exquisitely regular and dignified, and surpassingly beautiful.

—*James Fenimore Cooper,* The Last of the Mohicans, *1826*

By the fiction created by herself . . . deceptions intended solely for others gradually grew into self-deceptions as well; the little counterfeit rift of separation between imitation-slave and imitation-master widened and widened, and became an abyss, and a very real one—and on one side of it, stood Roxy, the dupe of her own deceptions, and on the other stood her child—her accepted and recognized master.

—*Mark Twain,* Pudd'nhead Wilson, *1894*

—*Make upon the window the fingerprints that will hang you.*

—*Mark Twain,* Pudd'nhead Wilson, *1894*

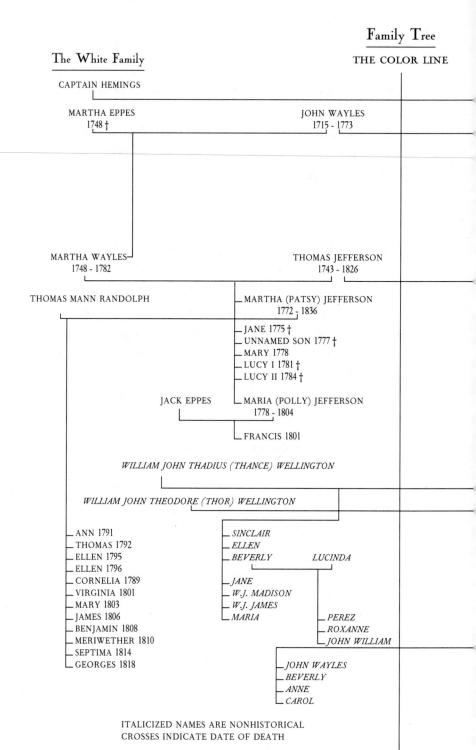

Family Tree

The White Family   THE COLOR LINE

CAPTAIN HEMINGS

MARTHA EPPES   JOHN WAYLES
1748 †   1715 - 1773

MARTHA WAYLES   THOMAS JEFFERSON
1748 - 1782   1743 - 1826

THOMAS MANN RANDOLPH   MARTHA (PATSY) JEFFERSON
                                         1772 - 1836

                                        JANE 1775 †
                                        UNNAMED SON 1777 †
                                        MARY 1778
                                        LUCY I 1781 †
                                        LUCY II 1784 †

JACK EPPES   MARIA (POLLY) JEFFERSON
                                         1778 - 1804

                                        FRANCIS 1801

           WILLIAM JOHN THADIUS (THANCE) WELLINGTON

       WILLIAM JOHN THEODORE (THOR) WELLINGTON

ANN 1791   *SINCLAIR*
THOMAS 1792   *ELLEN*
ELLEN 1795   *BEVERLY*   *LUCINDA*
ELLEN 1796
CORNELIA 1789   *JANE*
VIRGINIA 1801   *W.J. MADISON*
MARY 1803   *W.J. JAMES*
JAMES 1806   *MARIA*   *PEREZ*
BENJAMIN 1808   *ROXANNE*
MERIWETHER 1810   *JOHN WILLIAM*
SEPTIMA 1814
GEORGES 1818   *JOHN WAYLES*
                                    BEVERLY
                                    ANNE
                                    CAROL

ITALICIZED NAMES ARE NONHISTORICAL
CROSSES INDICATE DATE OF DEATH

The Black Family

THE AFRICAN *(BIA BAYE)*

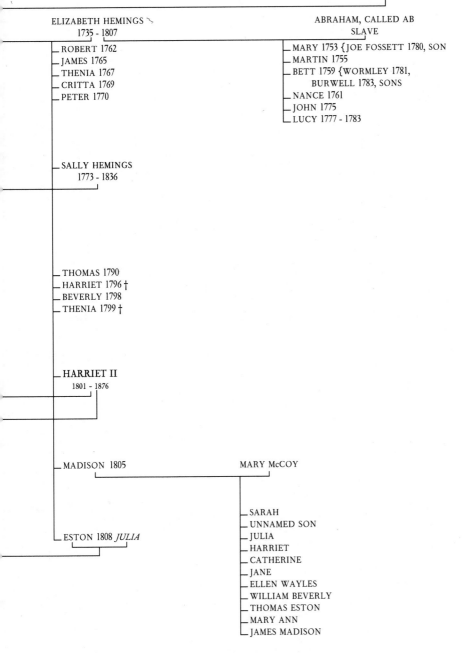

ELIZABETH HEMINGS
1735 - 1807

ABRAHAM, CALLED AB
SLAVE

— ROBERT 1762
— JAMES 1765
— THENIA 1767
— CRITTA 1769
— PETER 1770

— MARY 1753 {JOE FOSSETT 1780, SON
— MARTIN 1755
— BETT 1759 {WORMLEY 1781,
        BURWELL 1783, SONS
— NANCE 1761
— JOHN 1775
— LUCY 1777 - 1783

— SALLY HEMINGS
1773 - 1836

— THOMAS 1790
— HARRIET 1796 †
— BEVERLY 1798
— THENIA 1799 †

— HARRIET II
1801 - 1876

— MADISON 1805

MARY McCOY

— ESTON 1808 *JULIA*

— SARAH
— UNNAMED SON
— JULIA
— HARRIET
— CATHERINE
— JANE
— ELLEN WAYLES
— WILLIAM BEVERLY
— THOMAS ESTON
— MARY ANN
— JAMES MADISON

1822

1

God, from the beginning, elected certain individuals to be saved and certain others to be damned: and no crimes of the former can damn them, nor virtue of the latter save them.

Thomas Jefferson

The day I ran away from Monticello as a white girl, I left my mother standing in a tobacco field filled with moths and white blossoms, a good way beyond the peach orchard and the mansion. My one thought was that her only daughter was leaving her forever, and all she did was stand there facing east, leaning into the wind as I had seen her do so many times, as I imagined explorers did, her skirts whipping around her, staring toward the Chesapeake Bay as if she could actually see the ships, in this year of 1822, quitting the harbor, leaving port.

My mother was famous in Albemarle County, and had been ever since I was born. People as far away as Richmond knew her as my father's concubine, mistress of his wardrobe, mother of his children. I was one of those children and my father, a celebrated and powerful man, had hidden us away here for twenty years because of a scandal they called "the troubles with Callender." I was never told any more about it then, except that it made my mother the most famous bondswoman in America and put me in double jeopardy. For despite my green eyes and red hair and white skin, I was black. And despite my rich and brilliant father, I was a bastard.

As I approached, my mother remained as quiet and immobile as a monument. I walked around her as if she were one. She was the most silent woman I had ever known. Only her famous yellow eyes spoke and they spoke volumes. Her eyes had always given her face the illusion of transparency, as if one were gazing into a lighthouse beam. Those eyes were gold leaf in an ivory mask, windows onto mysterious fires that consumed everything and returned nothing to the surface. She was caring and kind to us children, but she surrounded herself in a shell of secrecy and disappointment that we were never able to penetrate, try as we might. We loved her, adored her, but we often wondered if she loved us.

"Mama?"

"*Laisse-moi.*" My mother spoke in the French she had taught me and which we used between ourselves all our lives.

"Maman, the carriage is waiting."

"I know. *Laisse-moi,* please leave me."

"*Au revoir, Maman.*"

My mother remained staring toward the bay.

"*Je t'écrirai, Maman . . .*"

"*Oui. Ecris-moi, ma fille.*"

"*Tu viens, Maman?*"

My mother looked at me as if I were mad. The yellow light of her eyes struck me like a blow.

"*Non, je ne viens pas.* I'm not coming," my mother said.

Last night, my mother had closed my trunks readied for Philadelphia, filled with my "strolling" trousseau.

"Promise me," she said, "that if you ever reveal your true identity to your future family, never tell your own children. Choose a female of your second generation, a granddaughter. Grandchildren are easier to talk to than your own children, and any secret is safer with your own sex."

"Why is that, Maman?"

"Women carry their secrets in their wombs," she said, "hidden and nourished by their vital fluids and blood, while men," she continued, "carry their secrets like they carry their genitals, attached by a thin morsel of mortal flesh unable to resist either a caress or a good kick."

I'm not sure what passing for white meant to me in those days, except fleeing slavery and leaving home. In reality I was doing it for other people. For Maman. For Grandma. For Papa. I had no yearning for freedom because I had no specific definition of it. I hadn't even known I was a slave until I found out I couldn't do what I wanted to. And freedom was a vague and indiscriminate thing: neither animal nor mineral, neither real nor phantom. It wasn't solid like a field or a tree or a snap of cotton. I only knew what I'd seen and what my grandmother had said: "Get that freedom . . ." It became a possibility, or rather an enticing and kind of limitless labyrinth of possibilities, all of which I intended to explore, precisely to see what would happen. This was the prize, and I had had my eye on it ever since my grandmother had told me that once I had it, I would no longer be invisible. Once I set foot in Philadelphia, I had all my moves figured out down to a tee—the steps of a complicated dance in which I was the principal dancer and the ballet master all in one.

That morning I had already said good-bye to my youngest brother, Eston.

"You might have waited, Harriet. Mama hasn't gotten over Beverly's leaving yet."

"Wait for what, Eston? Today, tomorrow, yesterday, what difference does it make where and when I go since I'm going? I won't stay here one day longer than I have to. Besides, Mama is never going to get over Beverly's leaving . . . he didn't even tell her . . ."

"Didn't tell Master, neither. Father expected him to stay."

"He *did* stay, Eston—two years beyond his twenty-first birthday! What more did Father expect? That he wait around to be sold by his own kin like Fennel's baby? Was that what he was supposed to wait around for? Another slave father howling down Mulberry Row with a hatchet ready to kill the white man who just sold his child?"

"I think he thought Bev would stay with him . . . to the end."

"And what exactly would that have gotten him? More freedom? An inheritance? A citation for bravery? Beverly should have left the day he turned twenty-one. Even before, like Thomas did."

"Well, it wouldn't have been for very long, Harriet. Our father's an old man—a real old man."

"Fiddle-dee-dee, Eston. Father is as strong as a mule—still looking out for him, aren't you?"

"I still ride out behind him—keeping my distance, of course," Eston said defensively. "Just making sure he doesn't get thrown by Old Eagle on those wild rides he takes every morning."

"Oh, Eston. Why?"

But I knew the answer. Eston loved the father who despised him, with a wrenching, desperate love that knew no bounds and no humiliation. He was, in this sense, like me.

"I would never forgive myself if I let something happen to him—he's strong, but he's stubborn and old and Mama still loves him so. . . ."

I contemplated Eston tenderly. Of all my father's sons, Eston most resembled him physically, although of all his children I was his replica. Eston had my father's aquamarine eyes and wavy red hair. His voice, too, was high-pitched and had a feminine sweetness about it. He was as short on words as our brother Madison was long, and he had a slight stutter when upset. At fourteen, he was almost six feet, with huge hands and wide Virginian shoulders. And he still expected some kind of love, some kind of recognition, some kind of reward he was never going to get from Father—just like Madison, who had raced down to the southern boundary and beat his head against the white birch fence until blood came because he couldn't understand why our father didn't love him.

"Maybe I can find Beverly," I whispered, changing the subject.

"Aw, Harriet. Beverly's *gone*. He's gone clean to Papa's Louisiana Territories—as a white man. You know he always dreamed of going with Meriwether Lewis on his expedition. And he's always had land fever. He craves land. He lusts after it, and out in Louisiana is the only place he's going to get any—buy it, grab it, steal it from the Indians. And it's rough out there. There's no place for a woman unless you want to be one of those mail-order brides. . . ." He laughed, but I didn't think it was funny.

"I know," continued Eston. "You're going to be married in a church, with music, and flowers, a preacher, and witnesses, in a white dress and you're still going to be a virgin and you're going to choose your husband . . . and he's going to be your darling—the love of your life.

"That's what I want for you, too, Harriet," he persisted. "And honey, you'll get it. You're so surefired set on whatever you want, you'll get everything out of life—once you're free."

He looked at me tenderly for a long, long time, his soft youthful eyes holding mine in a kind of covenant. He loved me and I loved him.

"I can't believe I'll never see you again."

"Never is a long time," I replied.

"Up the river or down, Harriet, it still means I'll lose you forever. You're a maroon—a fugitive slave."

"Until I get to Philadelphia. Then I'll be a nice white girl."

"With a price on your head."

"Better a bounty price than an auction price."

"Father would never sell you."

"Madison doesn't think so."

"Don't listen to Madison."

"I don't intend to. I'm going north."

"And then?"

"Well," I said romantically, "maybe abroad—Paris, London, Florence."

"Where?"

"Well, Paris anyway. I've promised myself that."

"How?"

"I'll work. I'll marry. I'll manage."

"It seems that black people starve up north."

"I'm white."

"Not if they catch you."

"They won't catch me, Eston. I'm too smart."

"What if Master sends slave catchers after you?"

"He won't. He promised Mama long ago."

"Well, that's one promise he kept at least."

"Only because of my color."

"Don't count on it, Harriet. If Martha Wayles inherited Mama, then Martha Randolph can inherit you," said Eston. "They can hunt you right to your grave. They can send slave catchers after you in Philadelphia as soon as Father takes his last breath. It's been done. This slavery stuff is for good."

"I'd shoot the first slave catcher who tried to take me back to Monticello. And I'd kill the kin that ordered it as well."

"Someday we'll meet again, Sister," Eston said quietly as he hugged me for the last time. "I promise . . . maybe white and maybe not," he added, "but certainly free."

The night before, I had stood in the amber light that filtered out through the tall windows from the glowing chandeliers of the ballroom at Montpelier, a neighboring plantation belonging to James Madison. I stood amongst the assembly of maids, valets, outriders, lackeys, and mammies; every shape, age, and color of slavehood. In less than twenty-four hours, I would be twenty-one years old and free to follow my brothers Beverly and Thomas into white oblivion. My father had sworn and decreed this long ago in Paris, according to my mother, and we had all played the game. In my mind's eye was always the knowledge of my special position. I was a slave about to be free, a girl about to become a woman, an individual about to be given a future. All for my birthday.

I hummed to myself as the music of the slave orchestra wafted out over the damp frosted lawn hedged with jasmine, banks of roses, and flowering magnolias. The circle of light flickered as laughing, dancing couples drifted by like Chinese-lantern shadows. The slave orchestra broke into a sprightly quadrille to the melody of "The Ballad of Gabriel Prosser," the slave rebel. The crowd outside began to snicker as the whites continued to dance on. Wasn't it typical of white people to dance to a tune they didn't know the words to? They swung and looped, turned and skipped, grouped and re-grouped, forming circles that broke the light like moving lace.

Suddenly, someone caught me from behind and swung me around and we too began to dance in the yellow circle of light. The servants outside continued to dance as long as the ball lasted, far into the night, laughing and flirting, cooler outside than those sweating within. We would outlast them and then drive them home, undress them if they were drunk, wash them if they had puked, pick up their clothes where they had dropped them, and put them to bed. The words of Gabriel's song wafted out beyond the silhouettes in motion.

> And then they called for a victory dance,
> And the crowd, they all danced merrily.
> The best dancer amongst them all
> Was Gabriel Prosser who was just set free.

I was the best dancer, I thought. I was the ballet master. And I was soon to be free. I was going to choose my husband. I was going to be married in a church. And I was going to the altar a virgin.

The cunning caress of cold steel touched my thigh. Since the age of sixteen, I had carried a razor-sharp stiletto deep in my petticoat pocket. It had belonged to my uncle James. Mama had given it to me for protection. No one would ever chase me up a tree again.

⁀

My dark reverie was broken by my brother's condescending voice.

"You strolling, Harriet?"

Madison, my seventeen-year-old brother, sauntered up, his tall rangy body looming out of the darkness. I could hear the suppressed anger in his voice, the rage, see his anguished expression in the candlelight. People sensed his suppressed violence, and it bothered people, black and white.

"Yes, Madison. I am leaving tomorrow." I tried to face Madison's anger calmly.

"You going to pass for white?"

"Yes, Mad, I am going to pass."

"Father knows you strolling?"

"Yes. He's arranged everything. He's sent for Adrian Petit to come and fetch me."

"You got any money?"

"Papa gave me fifty dollars."

"You know how much you worth on the slave block, Harriet?"

"Oh, Madison, don't."

"You're worth a pile of money, sweetheart! You don't know it, but you're a fancy. Fancy that! My sister is a fancy!"

"Madison."

"I tell you, Father could get five thousand dollars for you in New Orleans! Five thousand dollars from some white gentleman . . . at one of those quadroon balls."

He grabbed my wrist with his strong brown hand. "I hear tell that the test of acceptance at those balls is that your veins should show blue under the skin of your wrists. Just like yours, Harriet."

"Is that what you want for me, Mad?" I spit out the words, flashing my eyes into his.

He let go.

My flesh burned where he had held it, and the pain radiated up my arm. There were tears standing in his gray eyes.

"Oh, Madison, don't cry; I love you. Do you think it's easy to leave you? If I don't take this chance, what other chance will I ever have?"

"You'll have no family, Harriet, no kin. It's the end of Mama. It's oblivion, Harriet; it's death."

"It's not death! Not mine or hers. Don't put Mama on me, Mad. Anyway, I'll always be a part of her, of you. I am you, I am your sister, I'm your flesh and blood, and I'll always be, no matter what happens. That can't change. No matter how far away I go, I'll never forget you."

"Yes, you will."

"Madison, don't be so hard. You know what a slave woman can expect. Your turn to stroll will come; perhaps then you'll understand better. Wait until then."

"Never. I'll never pass. It's worse than being sold. Selling yourself for whiteness."

"It's Papa's doing, not mine."

"You should love your color."

"I would love my color if I knew what color I was. Perhaps when you turn twenty-one, Madison, you can have *your* freedom without stealing it!"

"Five thousand dollars you're worth to some white man . . ."

"Whose fault is it that I am a slave, Madison? Whose fault?"

"A five-thousand-dollar fancy!" he mocked.

I stared at my bare wrists with their fragile crisscrossing veins so vulnerable, so slim that Madison had reached out and encircled them with one hand. In them coursed the warring bloods that mutually polluted each other. Whose fault is it? Whose fault?

I stood leaning weakly against the trunk of an oak tree. I felt the rough bark against my face and shoulders. One false move, I thought, and I could peel the skin right off my forehead. With one false move, I could skin this whiteness right off myself, and bleed . . . The old haunting fear came back just as the music, which had stopped, began again.

～

There had been a white carpenter at Monticello named Sykes who had tipped his hat to me one day in the presence of my cousin Ellen Randolph. I was on my way from the mansion to the weavers' cabins, and Ellen was standing on the south veranda. I was fifteen. Ellen was almost twenty.

"How come you tipping your hat to a nigger, Mr. Sykes?" she had said, laughing. Sykes had stopped in his tracks.

"A nigger, Miss Ellen? I thought she was your sister!"

"That'll be the day!" replied Ellen as she flounced by him, flinging *day* over her shoulder.

I was trying desperately to slip by the astonished man, but he caught me by the arm.

"How come you didn't say nothing, gal? I've been doffing my hat to you for months!" Without answering, I tried to squeeze by.

"Answer me or you'll get a taste of your mistress's switch, by God."

"There's nothing to answer," I said, my eyes pleading with Ellen, who was snickering behind her hand.

"You sassing me?"

"No, sir."

"Master!"

"No, Master."

"If you spoke like a nigger, I wouldn't have mistaken myself, ain't that so?"

"Yes, Master."

"So I think you should say you're sorry you deceived me."

"Deceived him," sneered Ellen, ready to collaborate in my humiliation.

"I'm sorry," I whispered.

"Louder, gal."

"I'm sorry."

"Sorry who?"

"Sorry, Master."

"And from now on, talk like a nigger."

His touch made my skin crawl and his words made my blood boil. But my true outrage was directed toward Ellen, my erstwhile playmate. She averted her eyes from my gaze, her thin mouth set in a face flushed with contempt.

A few days later, I was walking the deserted road leading toward the nearest of my father's plantations, Edgehill, when Sykes approached, driving an empty buckboard. This situation was ideal. To his advantage he had superior speed, his sex, and his horsewhip. He could run me down with the wagon or abandon the wagon and come after me on foot. My heart accelerated; I weighed my chances.

"Hee, little Snow White," he called down from the driver's seat, "climb on up here! I got a present for you."

I stared straight ahead, trying to decide if I should keep to the road in hope that a gang of returning field hands would pass—no, they could hardly stop a determined white man—or take to the woods where he would have to find me before he caught me. I knew those woods like the back of my hand. My brothers and I had tracked rabbit and squirrel, run races, picked berries, played hide-and-seek in them since childhood. And, if I could outrun Eston and Beverly, I could outrun Sykes. I kept to the edge of the road while he followed, ordering me again and again onto the buckboard.

"You deaf or something, white nigger? I said to get your butt up here!"

He quickened his mules to a trot; I broke into a sprint. Sykes laughed as he gained on me. Suddenly, I veered off the road and darted into the woods, clutching up my skirts and attaching them to my apron strings as I ran. I heard him crashing through the bushes behind me. "Hee, Snow White," over and over. I picked up speed as he closed in behind me, and I heard the sudden crack of the horsewhip. The sound rode through me as if the lash were actually laid on my back. I reared. The *whoosh* and *snap* of it seemed to fill the whole woods, then the whole world. I bounded like a gazelle, leaping hurdles, gasping for breath, my heart thumping out of my chest as the sickening knowledge dawned on me that capture meant not only the pain and defeat of rape, but the end of safety, of wholeness, of childhood, forever. I would never dance again.

The low branches caught at my clothes and hair as I abandoned the trail and plunged into the underbrush. Sykes followed, laughing, cursing, and threatening. He gained on me as my strength ebbed. I was drenched in cold, acid sweat; tears and dirt streamed down my face. I had neither time nor force to wipe them away. Sykes's heavy boots smashed into the scattered dead leaves along the trail I left. I could smell him and measure his breathing.

"Goddamn it, Snow White, when I catch you, I'm going to ram your ass, you whore!"

My skirt was torn and my hands and forearms were scratched and bleeding like an overworked plough horse. A white ball of saliva had formed at the corner of my mouth. Had I been running ten minutes? Twenty? My stomach turned; green bile rushed into my throat; a pain in my chest cut off my breathing. I had to stop. I gagged, my legs giving way under me as I pitched forward. My head struck a rough, gnarled tree root growing out of the moss-strewn glade. I looked up at the lowest branches. It was my only hope. I scrambled up the tree, the way my brothers had taught me, scraping my cheek and thigh against the jagged bark just as Sykes crashed into the light beams of the clearing. His whip shot out and caught my ankle. The pain seared so I thought he had taken off my foot. I screamed, hanging by the upper limbs just out of his reach, and pulled myself up into the dome of the leafy sanctuary. The whip slid off my ankle, tearing the skin and bloodying the tree trunk. With one wrench, I pulled the crippled leg out of his reach and crouched twelve feet above his head, hissing like a cornered wildcat. The whip fell back, then sliced into the trunk of the tree, shaking it, as Sykes repeatedly slashed the tree itself in anger, tearing off the bark, each blow pulling back strips as wood shavings flew and the tree bled sap. Again and again the whip fell in rhythm to Sykes's curses, tracing white streaks along the dark crescents of the weeping hickory.

With each blow, I shuddered as if the lash had been laid on my own body. I covered my ears against the mournful screams of Sykes's victim, which were perhaps my own.

"Come down from there, you little white nigger! I'll show you how to obey an order!"

I crouched lower in the arch of the tree and watched as Sykes took out his sex, brandishing it like a weapon against the tree. I screwed my eyes shut.

"Come down and see what I got for you!"

All at once, there was an explosion of sound that I felt more than I heard. It scattered the perched birds and shook the leaves free around my head. Sykes had aimed his gun into the branches and fired wide. I must have lost consciousness, for a few seconds later, when I came to, still clutching the torso of the tree, Sykes had disappeared.

It was night before they found me. I could see the procession of lighted torches drawing closer and closer and hear my name being called over and over. It wasn't long before I looked down at a circle of fire beneath me. Mr. Treadwell, the overseer, was there. My uncle Robert, my uncle Martin, Isaac, and my father were staring up at me. I began to whimper.

"Harriet," Martin called softly, "Harriet, it's all right, it's me, Martin. What the devil has happened to you, darlin'? I'm coming up to get you. You don't have to move. Hang onto the limb. You don't have to talk, just hold on, Sweet Jesus, hold on. . . . Lord Almighty," he whispered as his hand touched the blood on the tree trunk. "What happened to you, Harriet?"

I looked down at my father. He towered over the rest of the men, and his face was drawn. I saw him with a whip in his hand for the first time. Our eyes met in the flickering torchlight, mine pleading, his glacial. He blamed me! He blamed me, as if I had provoked and planned his humiliation. But I was his creature! His! And he didn't love me for it. Instead of love, I had inspired only pity. The fury and disgust in his face were directed at me. In my misery, I reached down toward him, still unable to utter a sound. Martin had me now by the waist, and his touch provoked a storm of bitter tears. He was handing me over gently to Beverly below, when almost in exasperation, my father pushed Beverly aside and took me from Martin's arms. I felt the rough shaft of the handle of the whip he still held against my back. He swept me up and carried me back to where everyone had left the horses and sat me upon Jupiter. He mounted, his back to me, pulled my arms around his waist, and started off toward the mansion. Timidly, I pulled myself closer to the broad, navy blue back. I could hear his heart through the rich wool. I sighed, then sniffled and closed my eyes. I had almost had to die to get his attention. When we arrived home, he lifted me roughly from Jupiter and carried me into the house up to my mother's room. He stopped a short distance from her inside the door, and I felt his trembling as his shoulders hunched forward in an effort to master a monumental tantrum:

"See if she is hurt or not." Then slowly he turned, his voice clear and temperate, as if he were giving early-morning orders for the fields. "A mother should know where her child is at any moment. I beg you remember that. If you ever let her out of your sight again, you will have me to answer to. I have told Martin I want the name of the man, and I want to know what he was doing tampering with my property."

For a split second, his eyes met mine. I saw no tenderness nor comprehension, only a deep shame. I had felt it in his arms, and it had struck me mute.

I remained dumbstruck. It was weeks before I could speak without weeping. Finally I stammered . . .

"It was Sykes." That was when my mother gave me the long slender stiletto with the silver handle that had belonged to my uncle James.

"Keep it with you at all times. Keep it hidden deep in your skirts. Remember you were not raped. Nothing happened to you. You are still intact. It is hard to kill a man, Harriet, too hard probably. So if you can't kill, then maim. Aim low. Draw blood. That's enough to stop most men. Never hesitate. It's your life against his lust. Rape is murder in disguise. If you hesitate, Harriet, you're dead."

Sykes was banned from the premises of Monticello and ordered never to set foot on its soil again. My father never again allowed me to walk on the roads of the plantation alone, and my mother escorted me from the big house to the weavers' cabins and back again.

Was it, I wondered cynically, because Father cared for me or because he distrusted me around men? But Father never let Mama forget it. Was it our fault we were Negro wenches?

My ankle healed, but the thin line of the whiplash remained, a pale, slightly raised scar which encircled the joint anklebone as if I had worn a shackle or had caught my foot in a squirrel trap.

◈

I stooped down a moment and touched the scar, then straightened and stared at my mother. The tobacco field, which surrounded us, was a good way beyond the mansion and stretched in a wide highway of feathery waves, so vast the eye couldn't take it all in. The heat had reduced everything else to wavelets of sepia and black, and the blossoms, which reached our hips, glowed iridescent, parading in long lines like soldiers to the horizon. With amazing grace, they floated in the sun-spoiled daze of light, at times gathering into small foams of purple as I stood there gazing at my mother's burnt umber figure, my skirts caught in the stems and thistles.

Early this morning I had searched for him. I had decided to ask him, beg him, to free me—legally. What if I refused to be transported out of the state like a bale of cotton with the master's ticket on it, his indigo stamp, but not his recognition? I had saddled up Ripley, an old bay nobody rode, and gone out to find him. I knew I would find him in the saddle at that time of the morning, and I was determined to have it out with him. I had vowed to look him in the eye and force him to see me for what I was, his daughter. The bastard daughter who was trying to say good-bye, trying to get him to call me by my name.

I found him over by the west frontier, near the stand of woods that divided the rise of the mountain from the first planting fields. There was a birch fence that enclosed a pasture and a narrow bridge spanning a clear-running creek. He had just taken the fence, and he sat there immobile on Old Eagle—a tall horse with wide shoulders and a heavily muscled chest—as still and luminous as a marble sculpture. The light broke all around him, shining in a domelike configuration, reflecting long yellow dashes of light, and enclosing his profile. I screwed up my courage. I was going to ask him to give me my manumission papers as a freedwoman. He could do it. I knew he could.

Old Eagle shied away as Ripley blocked his path. Both horses were steaming and their flanks touched. I drew in my breath; the cobalt eyes cut through me as if to ask how I dared interrupt his early-morning ride.

"Master . . ."

"Harriet." He gestured, then waited patiently for an explanation.

I shivered. I wanted to turn Ripley around and gallop off, but I forced my mount to stillness and trained my eyes level with his. Jade met sapphire.

"It's my birthday," I said stupidly.

"Yes, Harriet." Still his voice carried a question.

"My last day at Monticello."

His horse began to sidestep impatiently, trying to avoid me. It wasn't Old Eagle, it was my father's knees doing it. He didn't want to listen. He didn't want to talk.

"I don't want to run, Master. I don't want to steal myself. . . ."

For a moment, his eyes seemed to flicker with a recognition or a reminiscence, I couldn't tell which, as if he had heard this plea, this desperate boast, before. He looked away from me, then, toward the mountains. I stuttered on.

"Papers, Master. I need papers to prove I'm free . . . otherwise I'm a fugitive slave, a criminal." *You can't want your own daughter to be a felon.*

"You don't need any papers, Harriet. You're white. You must live your life without them. It's your only chance. I've arranged everything. Petit is coming to get you."

"But what about my freedom? Mother promised me I'd be free."

"You are free, Harriet. As free as I am. No one will challenge you. No one would dare."

"But what if they do? What if they . . . ask?"

"Hasn't your mother told you what to do? That's her duty."

"She said men can't keep secrets."

"She's wrong. I've kept your secret, haven't I? I've hidden and protected all of you all these years. I've shielded you from the newspapers and a vicious campaign against all of us by our political enemies. I kept my silence. I didn't send you all away after the troubles with Callender. I resisted all sorts of pressures in order to keep the promise I made to your mother in Paris. I risked . . . everything, for you. Here at Monticello you were safe."

"But . . ."

"I've done all I can."

"But papers are important! Without identity papers as your slave, or recognition as your daughter, I'm twice illegitimate. I'm nobody's . . ." My complaint had cost me all my strength. I watched helplessly the frown of disapproval on my father's face. I had learned this silent language fluently. I knew by his look of petulance that I was being told to get on my way, that I had stepped beyond an invisible frontier. He pulled in Old Eagle's reins, cutting me off, and galloped off in the opposite direction.

I watched him as he fled, taking the two-foot-high barrier in a savage jump, his whip coming down heavily on Eagle's flank. He beat his horses cruelly. It was a well-known fact about him. Nobody knew why. In his panic he would have flown, I thought, if he could have, not to answer me. And now I would never have an answer. For the rest of my life. I would live in dread, on guard against a slip, a chance encounter, a keen eye, or a sentimental confession. I was a runaway slave, in danger of recapture and sale, even if I had stolen myself. Madison had been right. It *was* worse than being auctioned on the block. I could meet my kin and would not be allowed to acknowledge them. I would never be able to stand over my father's grave and weep. I could no more recognize my white family than my black one. This was the price I had to pay for freedom.

My tears began to fall, as quiet as ashes.

"Papa . . . ," I whispered into the early-morning mist.

Suddenly my heart began to behave strangely. It set off like an explosion, like gunpowder, and began to leap around unevenly in my chest. It began to pound in a most alarming way, then stop irresponsibly, hitting some sort of inward nerve, mocking like Madison's laughter. Then all at once, I couldn't hear it at all. As if my heart had simply stepped outside my body. And my tears stopped.

Flight had always been my father's answer to everything. Maman had told me that. Now I studied her as a breeze ruffled her black skirts. She hadn't moved. If *flight* was my father's name, *immobility* was my mother's. I felt tears of frustration and hopelessness start in my eyes. They were going to leave me all alone in this world, both of them. The blind injustice of it gripped me like a fist.

"Oh, God, *Maman, je pars*. I'm leaving. Petit is here with the carriage. Aren't you . . . even happy for me?" I cried.

"It's no victory for me, Harriet, only justice."

Oh, Maman, tell me you love me, I begged wordlessly. Tell me he loves me, please. I think I'm dying of not being loved. But to my mother out loud I simply said, "*Adieu, Maman.*"

My father was waiting for me by the time I had walked back from where I had left my mother. I saw him long before he saw me, and so I studied him from afar with all the confused loathing and yearning he had evoked in me that morning. I hated my mother for hiding. She should have come to stand beside him this once in a proper farewell to me. Instead, Petit, my father's old majordomo, was standing there. The Frenchman with his bald head and extravagant mustache had left Monticello just before my birth, but my mother had nurtured the legend of the indomitable Petit in Paris, Petit in Philadelphia, Petit at Monticello.

For the first time, I noticed the frailness under the imposing height of my master and the new physical suffering beyond his proud exuberance. My father was old, nearly eighty, and I might never see him again. Now I was standing close, looking up into his eyes. I caught his scent of old wool, lavender, ink, and horseflesh. For a moment he seemed not even to recognize me. Then he swayed slightly, clutching his left wrist. He reached down and picked up a wicker basket and held it out to me.

"Do you want one of these Monticello pups, Harriet? Clara just gave birth to a litter. She might keep you company and remind you of home."

He held out the basket of squirming Dalmatian puppies as if it were a peace offering.

"Choose one for I shall drown the rest. I consider all dogs the most afflicting of all the follies for which we tax ourselves."

He reached down into the basket and took out an adorable black-and-white bitch. Father seemed to recognize the necessity and utility of dogs, I thought, as he did of Negroes, but he still begrudged their existence.

For my mother's sake, I swallowed this last humiliation, matching his smile, which he never lost, and suppressing an overwhelming desire to wring the poor puppy's neck. How, I wondered, could I love and despise my father so much at the same time?

I looked down at the animal squirming in the huge outstretched hands. An apology for this morning? I wondered.

"She's beautiful."

"Think of a good name for her."

"I'll call her Independence."

I took Independence in my arms, clutching her to me in the same way my father clutched his wrist against his chest. I noticed that a tear had rolled down my father's cheek. I looked away. WHITE PEOPLE! Why was he crying now? Now, when it was too late? What had he expected? That because he was the President he wouldn't have to pay someday? I turned and held

Petit's horrified gaze in a silent command to take me away from this place. I would not throw away the gift of freedom in exchange for any man's promise . . . especially white men, who never kept their promises. Had Captain Hemings married my great-grandmother? Had John Wayles freed my grandmother? Had my father ever called me daughter? Was this parting gift of Independence an acknowledgment? Well, I thought, grab it and run. Freedom, that is. Leave everything you have ever loved, start your new life as an orphan: nameless, homeless, and friendless. White. White. White.

I drew his eyes to mine. *You're asking a lot of a daughter,* I thought.

"Papa," I whispered. "You could still change things."

But I kept my eyes as hard as the precious stone they resembled, my thoughts tight in my womb. I wouldn't cry anymore. I was free. I was white; I was twenty-one. I had nothing to cry about.

Petit and I drove down the mountain in broad daylight. Everyone knew we were leaving. My uncle Burwell drove the carriage, which headed toward Richmond. Another uncle, Fossett, was the outrider. People deserted the slave quarters and drifted toward the road that traversed all my master's plantations to have a last look at Harriet Hemings leaving home. Inside the vehicle, I turned back to look only once, but that was enough to see that my mother had come to stand beside the tall stooped figure of Father, who had stepped through a hole in the rotting steps and fallen from the veranda to his knees. Steps my uncle Robert was supposed to have fixed months ago.

2

It is difficult to determine on the standard by which the manners of a nation may be tried, whether Catholic, or particular. It is more difficult for a native to bring to that standard the manners of his own nation, familiarized to him by habit. There must doubtless be an unhappy influence on the manners of our people produced by the existence of slavery.

Thomas Jefferson

My boot went through a rotten plank in the veranda as the lilac phaeton disappeared down the mountain. I pitched forward to my knees, falling on my bad wrist and fracturing it again. I cursed Robert for not having repaired the step as I had told him to. I cursed Sally for not having made sure her brother did it. I cursed Harriet, for without her, I, Thomas Jefferson, wouldn't have been standing out here in the first place. I cursed all the Hemingses and their abominable, secretive burden. The pain was exactly as it had been that long ago day in June 1787, in the Bois de Boulogne, when another phaeton containing another forbidden woman had ridden out of my life. I hardly heard the jerky cry of pain my fall exacted from me, unbidden and humiliating—an old man's cry for help. I sensed rather than saw my slave wife hovering over me. I squeezed my eyes shut to make her invisible. I hated her. I hated Harriet, who had forced me to relinquish a part of myself against my will.

Despite myself, I thought about a June afternoon in 1805, after the trouble with Callender and my reelection. I was home from the President's House,

free of all the fracas of Washington politics and happily astride my old bay
Jupiter. I had swept four-year-old Harriet into my arms and tossed her high
in the air, while her mother screamed with fright and the child with delight.
The perfectly weighted little body had risen in the air like a painted *putto* in
an Italian fresco, her arms outstretched, her wings the Blue Ridge Mountains,
a halo of fluffy clouds around her head, displacing the tepid air which
approached the temperature of the human body. Harriet hovered overhead,
static, immobile, her golden curls bobbing, her fern green eyes shining, her
laughter babbling like a brook before she came rushing down toward me like
a whirlwind, sure of my waiting arms. At that moment, I saw Harriet's life
beyond Monticello. I kissed the incredibly fresh puckered lips, the blond
tendrils of hair, the warm cheeks.

"This one will live," I boasted to her mother, thinking of our dead infants
Harriet the First and Thenia.

That had been the same year I had written Francis Gray from Washington
about when black became white. The letter, which I had mistakenly shown
to Petit this morning, glowed before me in the darkness.

THE PRESIDENT'S HOUSE
1805

MR. FRANCIS C. GRAY

Sir,

You asked me in conversation, what constituted a mulatto by our law.
And I believe I told you four crossings with the whites. I looked afterwards
into our law, and found it to be in these words: "Every person, other than
a Negro of whose grandfathers or grandmothers anyone shall have been a
Negro, shall be deemed a mulatto, and so every such person who shall have
one-fourth part or more of Negro blood, shall like manner be deemed a
mulatto"; L. Virga 1792, December 17: the case put in the first member of
this paragraph of the law is *exempli gratia*. The latter contains the true
canon, which is that one-fourth of Negro blood, mixed with any portion
of white, constitutes the mulatto. As the issue has one-half of the blood of
each parent, and the blood of each of these may be made up of a variety
of fractional mixtures, the estimate of their compound in some cases may
be intricate, it becomes a mathematical problem of the same class with those
of the mixtures of different liquors or different metals; as in these, therefore,
the algebraical notation is the most convenient and intelligible. Let us
express the pure blood of the white in capital letters of the printed alphabet,
the pure blood of the negro in the small letters of the printed alphabet, and
any given mixture of either, by way of abridgment in MS. letters.

Let the first crossing be of *a*, pure negro, with *A*, pure white. The unit of blood of the issue being composed of the half of that of each parent, will be $\frac{a}{2}+\frac{A}{2}$. Call it, for abbreviation, *h* (half blood).

Let the second crossing be of *h* and *B*, the blood of the issue will be $\frac{h}{2}+\frac{B}{2}$, or substituting for $\frac{h}{2}$ its equivalent, it will be $\frac{a}{4}+\frac{A}{4}+\frac{B}{2}$, call it *q* (quarteroon) being $\frac{1}{4}$ negro blood.

Let the third crossing be of *q* and *C*, their offspring will be $\frac{q}{2}+\frac{C}{2}=\frac{a}{8}+\frac{A}{8}+\frac{B}{4}+\frac{C}{2}$, call this *e* (eighth), who having less than $\frac{1}{4}$ of *a*, or of pure negro blood, to wit $\frac{1}{8}$ only, is no longer a mulatto, so that a third cross clears the blood.

From these elements let us examine their compounds. For example, let *h* and *q* cohabit, their issue will be $\frac{h}{2}+\frac{q}{2}=\frac{a}{4}+\frac{a}{8}+\frac{A}{4}+\frac{B}{4}=\frac{3a}{8}+\frac{3A}{8}+\frac{B}{4}$, wherein we find $\frac{3}{8}$ of *a*, or negro blood.

Let *h* and *e* cohabit, their issue will be $\frac{h}{2}+\frac{e}{2}=\frac{a}{4}+\frac{A}{4}+\frac{a}{16}+\frac{A}{16}+\frac{B}{8}+\frac{C}{4}=\frac{5a}{16}+\frac{5A}{16}+\frac{B}{8}+\frac{C}{4}$, wherein $\frac{5}{16}$ *a* makes still a mulatto.

Let *q* and *e* cohabit, the half of the blood of each will be $\frac{q}{2}+\frac{e}{2}=\frac{a}{8}+\frac{A}{8}+\frac{B}{4}+\frac{a}{16}+\frac{A}{16}+\frac{B}{8}-\frac{C}{4}=\frac{3a}{16}+\frac{3A}{16}+\frac{3B}{8}+\frac{C}{4}$, wherein $\frac{3}{16}$ of *a* is no longer a mulatto, and thus may every compound be noted and summed, the sum of the fractions composing the blood of the issue being always equal to unit. It is understood in natural history that a fourth cross of one race of animals with another gives an issue equivalent for all sensible purposes to the original blood. Thus a Merino ram being crossed, first with a country ewe, second with his daughter, third with his granddaughter, and fourth with the great-granddaughter, the last issue is deemed pure Merino, having in fact but $\frac{1}{16}$ of the country blood. Our canon considers two crosses with the pure white and a third with any degree of mixture, however small, as clearing the issue of the negro blood. But observe, that this does not re-establish freedom, which depends on the condition of the mother, the principle of the civil law, *partus sequitur ventrem*, being adopted here.

But if *e* emancipated, he becomes a free white man, and a citizen of the United States to all intents and purposes. So much for this trifle by way of correction.

Th. Jefferson

I wanted to stay as I was, my eyes screwed shut in this blackness which was the corollary of blindness. What else was there, really, to see? The lilac phaeton had already turned the bend out of sight. If I opened my eyes now, I would see only my reflection in the eyes of my slave wife, and I didn't want that. Perhaps this obscurity I experience now is forever. Perhaps I've fallen off my back porch and killed myself. Perhaps if I open my eyes, I won't see Sally Hemings's golden eyes, but the red-rimmed hollows of the Devil's. And what would I say to him? That he made me do it?

I finally opened my eyes and rose from my knees, cradling my injured wrist against my chest. I shrugged off Sally's offer of help. I could see the lilac phaeton again, the wing of a tropical bird in the dense greenery, speeding away in a cloud of dust, winding its way down the mountain toward my plantation of Pantops, which had already been seized by my creditors.

Why were daughters so unforgiving? Oh, Harriet was an armed camp, cautious, secretive, proud. She'd been that way ever since Sykes. She'd carried that grudge against me, against the world, since she was knee-high. I do believe my daughter drank in all that bitterness and anger with Sally Hemings's milk. She had been conceived the summer that, ballot-by-ballot, I was being elected President of the United States. The scent of fear, power, and machinations had swirled around her infant head. Fear because of James T. Callender. Power because envious men like John Hamilton coveted the highest office in the land. Machinations because of my own naiveté and the ambitions of my old enemy, Aaron Burr. Then, too, Harriet had been born in the shadow of death. First Jupiter, my body servant of fifty-seven years, then my nemesis Callender, which at least shut him up. And finally my slave wife's favorite brother, James's.

Her infant ears must have heard her mother's screams when Thomas Mann Randolph announced that James Hemings had hanged himself in Philadelphia. She might even have heard Meriwether Jones's hoots of joy as he danced a jig on the front lawn upon hearing that Callender had been silenced forever. Or perhaps her little face had shriveled in the heat of my slave wife's curses when our eldest son, Thomas, was banished from Monticello to dampen the gossip surrounding his birth.

All these truths Harriet had grown up with, and she had taken them with her in the lilac phaeton. But what exactly was the truth? Truth in Virginia had to be cultivated like a blossom: it grew from long-forgotten seed. A fact like assassination or suicide had scarcely happened before the genuine historical kernel of it had disappeared; annihilated by fabrication, rhetoric, imagination, pride, contempt, and self-interest. The passions, self-delusions, and fantasies of the South, both black and white, simply flung themselves over poor truth and devoured it. That's what happened to truth around here. Virginians honored virility over skepticism, which is the essential to clear thinking. It was for that reason that a realistic appreciation of life did not exist. That is to say we were constantly driven back upon our own imagination, and our belief was limited only by our capacity to conjure up the unbelievable.

And so, although everybody knew Harriet was a bastard, knew she was a slave, knew she wasn't by fact or fiction white, knew she would have to annihilate all these facts by *fraud* if she were ever to be free, that little grain of veracity had disappeared into the lilac carriage. A whole race of liars lived down here in Virginia: black, white, and mulatto liars whose only subject of conversation was Truth and Beauty. They were the ones, including myself, who had set up our greatest pillar of falsehood: that with every gesture and emotion, with every breath we took, with the very pollen we inhaled, we had not entered into black people as deeply as black people had entered into us.

It was the most tremendous lie we had ever told ourselves in the South: that one drop of black blood was enough to condemn an individual to slavery, which in turn protected the incredible, invincible, overwhelming myth amongst us that the crime of miscegenation had never occurred—that the purity of the two races, but especially the white race, had been preserved, forever separate, forever untainted.

Harriet was the killing field and the blood victim of these two strains. She was an enduring vessel, immutable and enigmatic, in which the poison and its antidote checkmated one another. Silently, I watched the lilac phaeton become smaller. Within sat my daughter, who had begun her slavery even before she had begun her existence, and who could not dispose of her life without committing some kind of fraud.

I the undersigned, Thomas Jefferson, third president of the United States, author of the Declaration of American Independence, of the statute of Virginia for religious freedom and Father of the University of Virginia, age seventy-nine, father of thirteen children (six deceased), grandfather of thirteen children (one deceased), tobacco planter, scientist, naturalist, musician, politician, widowed husband to Martha Wayles, erstwhile lover to her half sister Sally Hemings, head of a household containing eight free white males, eleven free white females, and ninety-three slaves, do hereby attest that I did allow my daughter Harriet to run away on her twenty-first birthday and disappear into the white population of the United States. What I felt about the destiny of my illegiti-

mate daughter I can reveal to no one, not even my slave wife. It had too much to do with blood ties and the intemperance of passion, of rage, really, which tarnished the image that I cultivated of Olympian detachment and a magisterial view of the world: to have been brought low by a mere snip of a girl, my own issue at that. However, I did record her departure in my farm book on this day, May 19, 1822.

THOMAS JEFFERSON

3

The whole of time moved on with a rapidity of which those of our carriage have but a faint idea . . . and yet in the evening, when we took a retrospect of the day, what a mass of happiness had we traveled over.

Thomas Jefferson

We drove all night, not stopping until we had crossed the Mason-Dixon line. Petit, who had taken my cold hands in his, kept up a running conversation to keep us awake as Fossett and Burwell sped us north. Fossett was the son of my mother's half sister Mary, a dark Hemings. And Burwell, my uncle, had served my father as valet for thirty years. What, I wondered, was in their minds? Shame and derision at this charade in which we were all locked? Envy or compassion for a Hemings going up the river instead of down? Petit, the ex-valet, seemed to be struggling with some overwhelming dilemma. Then, like the breaking of a great dam, he suddenly blurted out:

"Although it's hard for you to believe, Harriet, I was young once upon a time. Your mother must have told you a lot about your father's days as the American ambassador to the court of Louis XVI. We lived quite a bit of history during those years from eighty-four to eighty-nine, including the most glorious Revolution. We were all young then. Even your father. He was a tall, handsome, rich widower in his forties and an exotic American like the adored Benjamin Franklin. I was in my twenties at the time and had been in service for over a decade. Your uncle James, your father's body servant, was a year younger than I, Martha and your mother were fifteen when your mother and Maria arrived from Virginia in 1787 on command of your father,

who wanted Maria, his only other living child, with him. I believe sending
your mother, who was hardly more than an adolescent herself, as her nurse-
maid to Paris was your grandmother's idea. And just as I am escorting you
to Philadelphia, I was sent to London by your father to bring back Maria and
your mother to Paris. I found them installed in the American embassy in
London under the surveillance of John Adams and his wife, Abigail, a stern
yet compassionate American couple of such dignity, affection, and rectitude
as to have enlisted my admiration for all times. I was an unpleasant surprise.
Mrs. Adams had expected your father to come and fetch his daughter in
person, and she was furious that a servant had been sent instead. But your
father was waiting in Paris for a lady, Maria Cosway, and I had the task of
cajoling Maria, consoling your mother, whom Mrs. Adams wanted to send
straight back to Virginia when she realized she was a slave, and mollifying
Ambassador and Mrs. Adams. Mrs. Adams especially was appalled at having
under her roof what she called a 'white slave,' a term I had yet to understand.
Mrs. Adams was an abolitionist, and she knew how white Negroes were
created. I was the only one who didn't know.

"Then Maria refused to leave with me, a stranger, to join still another
stranger, the father she didn't remember. Mr. Adams agreed that Polly, as she
was called, would never leave with me without your mother, Sally Hemings,
and that in any case they had no authority to dispose of Mr. Jefferson's
property, regardless of their stand on slavery.

"It was three weeks before little Polly agreed to leave with me, and those
three weeks I had spent amusing, teasing, and escorting her and your mother
around London. What a wonderful time we had. It was my second time in
London. I had gone the first time with the Comte d'Ashnach as his page and
had been introduced to the gambling, racing, and womanizing life of the
English aristocrats. I knew every nook and cranny of London, every elegant
shop, restaurant, and theater, from Covent Gardens to Cambridge! The girls
adored my excursions with them, and one of their favorites was Hyde Park.
Your mother was a very beautiful girl. She stopped traffic and was admired
by everyone. There was something that no one could put their finger on
which made her special beyond her spectacular looks. A gentleness, an
otherworldliness, an aura of enormous spirit—a kind of life force which
bewitched you and held you in its spell. And the voice . . . It was the voice
of an angel—low and sweet and honeyed—your voice, Harriet. Your mother
could charm the birds out of the trees.

"Maria was a fragile, beautiful child of nine, your mother almost a young
woman with golden eyes and ivory skin and raven hair—the picture, I was

told, of her half sister Martha. I remember how astounded Mrs. Adams was at the resemblance.

"We left London on April twentieth, 1787, and had a fair crossing. We arrived by public coach at the Hôtel de Langeac, your father's embassy, in the late afternoon of April twenty-fifth. I'll always remember that trip from harbor to city, through Brittany and Normandy to the Ile-de-France, the modest carriage—for your father hadn't yet bought this lavish one—rumbling through the most beautiful countryside in the world, although I'm personally from Champagne . . . and prefer that landscape. . . .

"Your father and James were awaiting us in the courtyard. Maria didn't recognize her father at first, and James was hard put to realize that the young woman who descended from the carriage was his little sister. But your father remembered Sally Hemings as the daughter of Betty Hemings and from her days of nursing and running errands for his wife. It was your mother who brought welcome news from Virginia and Monticello. Your mother was very good at delivering southern gossip, and your father soon became addicted to, as he put it, 'who has died, who has married, who has hanged themselves because they cannot marry.' They became a regular two-person salon, with your mother holding forth in dialogue and imitations, dramatic monologues, and cruel invasions of privacy. She knew something about everyone, a feat she had learned, I found out later, from another expert, your grandmother.

"But I'll never forget the moment we rolled into the courtyard of the Hôtel de Langeac and the girls rushed from the confines of the carriage. Your mother was scooped into the arms of her brother James, who was now an apprentice cook in the embassy kitchens, while poor Maria cowered behind the carriage not recognizing her own father! Thomas Jefferson was mortified. He finally picked his daughter up in his arms despite her protests and dragged her into the mansion, leaving your mother and James to their tearful reunion."

Petit paused, if only to catch his breath. It seemed to me as if this last service to my father had opened an ever-widening breach in his legendary discretion, or that in escorting me to Philadelphia he had deployed his last reserves of servitude to my father.

"You're going to tell me everything, aren't you?"

"One day. Perhaps. I think I've said enough for now."

"Mr. Petit, you're going to talk all the way to Philadelphia. I know it."

"Call me Adrian."

"Mr. Adrian."

I sat opposite Adrian Petit in the dark green interior, in my yellow plaid "strolling" outfit, my back flattened in panic against the leather upholstery, my hands clenched in my lap to stop their trembling. I watched Petit closely. The irises of his smallish eyes invaded even their whites and shone pantherlike from his face, half-hidden in the shadows. More than any other white man, he knew what had happened between my mother and father during those years they had spent in Paris. He had known my uncle James in his prime, Maria as a little girl, Martha as a young, shy convent intern. He had received the mysterious Maria Cosway on her secret visits to my father. I leaned forward, caught in the fascination I felt for the knowledge he held of my parents' past.

On that day and every day at Monticello, there existed light Hemingses and dark Hemingses. We were all the grandchildren of Elizabeth Hemings, who had died in 1807. Betty Hemings, as she was called, had had two families, just like my grandfather John Wayles; one black and one white. My grandmother's white Hemingses were my grandfather's black ones. They had together as master and slave produced six children, the last of them being my mother, Sally Hemings. John Wayles had also been the father of Martha Wayles, my father's first wife, making my mother her half sister and me her niece. I had learned the secret of my white family in bits and pieces, in whispered asides and shattering looks, but I had finally pieced it all together with a little help from my grandmother. My mother, like most slave women, had never told me anything of my origins.

The reason we were all called Hemings was that my great-grandfather, Captain Hemings, fell in love with an African named Bia Baye and they had a natural daughter together, who was my grandmother Elizabeth. The poor Captain Hemings wanted to buy Bia Baye and his daughter from John Wayles, who owned them both, but he refused to sell them since amalgamation had first begun to be studied and he wanted to see how Elizabeth would turn out. The captain tried to steal his wife and child but was betrayed by a treacherous slave. Bia Baye and Elizabeth were locked away in the big house and the captain sailed without them. The legend is that Bia Baye's wails could be heard all the way to the Chesapeake Bay and that the captain, hearing them, rang the ship's bells in response. The clearness and stillness of the night mingled the two laments into a song which the Virginia bluetail heard and copied, and so, on a clear still night, Bia Baye and her whaling captain can still be heard. Bia Baye ran away from John Wayles's plantation so many times that he finally decided to have her branded on the cheek with the *R* for runaway. But the story has it that when the hot iron of the brand came close to her flesh, he knocked the iron out of the overseer's hand and it fell upon her breast.

John Wayles took Elizabeth Hemings as his concubine after his second wife, who had given him two legitimate daughters, died. And so it was that Elizabeth remained in the big house, which she ran, and gave birth to six children by her master. But before that she had been given to a slave named Abe, by whom she had had six children. These would become known as the "dark" Hemingses, while her children by the master were the "light" Hemingses. Then Thomas Jefferson married John Wayles's white daughter Martha. After John Wayles died, he inherited all of Martha's half brothers and sisters, the light Hemingses. The irony was that before it was all over, Thomas Jefferson, my father, had loved and married two half sisters, one white and one black, both with the same father and different mothers. This bonded the Wayleses and the Jeffersons and the Hemingses in an infernal blood tie which still ruled Monticello, for eventually Elizabeth's dark Hemingses became my father's property as well, and my grandmother, who had raised his white wife, his housekeeper.

The twelve Hemings children all married, reproduced, and remained as slaves at Monticello. I had two favorite cousins, one the daughter of a light Hemings, Critta, and the other the daughter of a dark Hemings, Nance. Critta's daughter Dolly was as white as I, and Nance's Marie was as black as the ace of spades. But only my mother's children, Thenia and Harriet I, who had died in infancy, Thomas, Beverly, Madison, Eston, and myself, had been promised freedom at twenty-one. The rest of my family remained slaves and children of slaves.

Petit removed his hat, and revealed a matted halo of hair around a bald spot. As I leaned forward, I caught the odor of lavender, fresh bread, and wine. His strongly accented voice was alarmingly loud in the quiet of the moving vehicle, and it broke not only that silence, but the silence of years and years. Adrian Petit spoke perfect English but with a heavy French accent that he cultivated, he confessed to me, to make himself more exotic. He was in a way as much a counterfeit as I was—a lackey, passing for an aristocrat.

"Ah, Harriet. If only I could explain. This could be a quarter of a century ago . . . this is the diligence that arrived with your mother and Maria, rumbling into that sunny courtyard."

Petit, I calculated, had spent almost fifteen years as my father's majordomo. The five years in Paris must be added to the years he had spent at Monticello when he rejoined my father's service, and the years he had served him in Philadelphia and at the White House. Petit was a walking gold mine of information!

I found myself thinking of Petit's fortune. He was a relatively rich man— at least richer at the moment than my debt-ridden father—who, in a strange reversal of roles not unlike my own, found himself in the position to judge his ex-master.

"Your father seems to think that the greatest privilege an American can have is to be born white."

During that night as we rumbled across the Maryland state line, Petit took me back to the days of the French Revolution, days when my mother had discovered she was free on French soil. It had not only been my uncle James, but also Petit, who had slowly led my mother through the intricacies of Parisian life and the manner in which it was lived. And there had been others: Mr. Perrault, who taught her French; Lucy, who taught her sewing; Madame Dupré, who taught her fashion; and my father, who taught her love.

"One thing I learned years later when I came to America to work for your father at Monticello. It was not only your mother who found herself a liberated woman in France. Your father, too, found relief for a few short years from the stifling oppression of the Virginian slave society that he had grown up in and which owned him. Do you understand?

"Imagine, he had never been beyond Philadelphia before his trip to France and he was over forty years old. Any nobleman worth his salt had seen London, St. Petersburg, Vienna, Berlin, Paris, Barcelona before the age of twenty-five! Yet he had known only the American civilization of the back-woods plantations of Virginia. True, this society believed itself to be the very height of sophistication and planter aristocracy when they were really nothing but a bunch of provincial burghers.

"So he, too, found a kind of freedom . . . a kind of escape from slavery. For what happened in Paris could never, Harriet, have happened at Monticello. By the time your parents returned to Virginia, it was too late to change anything except to hide their secret cruelly. Most cruelly."

My mother had never spoken to me of the things Petit recounted that night. It was as if they were memories she no longer owned or wished to transmit to any of her children. Shocked, I listened to anecdote after anecdote, some funny, some sad, of my mother's education in France. Petit seemed to have been my uncle James's only friend. And between them there seemed to have been a genuine love.

"I loved James," Petit continued. "He was born on his father's plantation in 1765 and was twenty when I met him. He had accompanied his master to Paris in eighty-four, as his body servant, but was quickly apprenticed to be trained as a master chef for Monticello. He was a beautiful boy. Very tall and muscular, with a light beige tawny complexion and wiry black hair that he wore long and straight back in a queue tied with a ribbon. He had eyes of a strange gunmetal gray flecked with yellow and disgracefully long and thick eyelashes which gave the impression that he wore kohl, as many of the aristocratic dandies of the day did. His cheeks were as rosy as if they'd been rouged, and he had a natural beauty mark high on one cheek which had never seen a razor's edge. How I envied him that. Dressed in the livery of the Hôtel de Langeac, he was a naturally elegant, even remarkable, figure. He had long graceful hands which were in constant motion and long legs which were never still also. There was about him the aura of a forest animal, not jungle, I insist —his grace and stealth were of a pattern and shadow of cool and wooded places, not the sultry tropical jungle so mythically attributed to anyone who had African blood in his veins. He was pale enough so that none of the French aristocracy suspected he was what they would have called a blackamoor. Neither your mother. Otherwise, they would have been the talk of Paris, blackamoors were so coveted and in vogue. Maria Cosway had one, a little boy attached to her household in London.

"I can only describe the expression in James's eyes as ironic resignation. Oh, there was anger and envy and rage and malice, too, but the overriding tenor of his face was that of a very young lion, golden and tawny, posed and patient, waiting for the moment to step onstage as a king or at least a prince. That was James's nickname in the kitchen, 'King Jimmi,' for he had turned out to be a natural cook and a natural kitchen aristocrat. He was an inventive, intelligent, talented cook, and the food that passed through his hands bore the mark of a future master chef. I suppose," sighed Petit, "that is why everyone put up with him.

"We got on famously from the very start. I might even say we fell into each other's arms. I felt a brotherly love and protection for the younger man, and I introduced him to the entrails of high and low life in Paris. We spent almost all of our free time together, me feeling half of the time like his father and mentor and the other half like his accomplice and younger brother in a series of the most adolescent and outrageous *sottises* possible. We became in all ways inseparable, and the bond forged between us lasted until death parted us.

"Your uncle James was as close to a younger brother as I possessed. I loved him. James's tragic end was one of the greatest sorrows of my life."

"And what of . . . my mother's tragic end—a slave whose children steal themselves away from her in the name of whiteness?" I murmured.

Petit looked shocked, and indeed I was shocked by the bitterness in my voice. Did I despise my mother, I wondered.

Petit must have sensed my unspoken question, for he looked sternly at me and said, "There are reasons under the sun for everything. Things that are unfathomable. I have never underestimated the force of love, loyalty, or passion. I have seen them work in many men and women, including your father and mother and uncle."

The long journey into the night continued. We had decided not to stop until we had crossed the Mason-Dixon line into the free state of Delaware.

"There was a fashionable convent for girls in Paris, L'Abbaye de Pan-thémont, where Martha was already in school. Your father allowed your mother to attend briefly. He also had her tutored in French and music at home. The tug-of-war between James and your father for your mother's soul began the day she set foot in that courtyard of the Hôtel de Langeac. What was most important was that we all loved your mother. James loved her. I loved her. Monsieur Perrault, her tutor, loved her; Monsieur Felin, her music teacher, loved her. Polly loved her. John Trumbull, the painter who lived at the embassy, loved her and drew portraits of her. Only poor unhappy Martha, jealous of her father, began to hate your mother. But in the scale of love, nothing would balance the weight of your father's love. Not even your mother's own desire for freedom and emancipation. Almost at once she realized, thanks to James, that on French soil she was free. But love held her. The more they struggled against it, the more it held them fast. It was a terrible thing to see. When your mother realized she was carrying your brother Thomas, she ran away from the embassy and stayed away for almost two weeks. I thought your father was going to lose his mind. He came down with one of his violent migraines, which left him in darkest pain for days. She finally returned of her own accord, after hiding out all that time at her old landlady's boardinghouse. They had a discussion and came to an agreement. Not even I know what went on behind those closed doors that day. But your father did promise to free all their children at age twenty-one. And he promised to return with your mother to France one day. Perhaps they both finally realized the awful improbability of their transgression. In the end, I tell you, it was a struggle of life and death. James couldn't live without your mother's freedom, and your father couldn't live without your mother. Her seduction, if you want to call it that, was more like two mighty oaks falling . . . and crushing a slender pine tree—my poor James. I knew or guessed everything. Men have few secrets from their valets, and I was a cynical young man. It was James, so much more vulnerable than I, who suffered. All James's hopes had been in your mother, and she betrayed him. All your father's hopes for happiness after his wife's death were in his half sister-in-law, your mother.

"Just before we left, President Jefferson said only one thing to me. He said, 'I loved two sisters, one white and one black, to my everlasting despair.' "

"You mean my father's first wife was my aunt . . . then?"

"Yes."

By this time night had fallen, and the dark woods and bluish trees sped by in moonlight. My mother had told me little of her life before my birth. The image I had of her had been one of a proud, secretive woman, with a room full of mysterious treasures, disillusions, and unrealized dreams. Seeing her, I had vowed that I would not live a life of imagination but of reality. I would live a life of facts, plain and simple, filled with action and decisions. A heroic life. My father had kept none of the promises he had made to my mother in Paris. Wasn't that the only thing that remained of all of Petit's stories? Broken promises? My eyes began to get heavy, but I had to stay awake until we crossed the Mason-Dixon into Delaware, I told myself. It was like crossing the Rubicon; there would be no turning back after that.

"First thing I knew, Harriet, Sally and James Hemings, your father, and Martha had left for Virginia. And in less time than it takes to shake a stick, your father was Secretary of State, then Vice President and then President of the United States. By this time I had rejoined him in America. You, Madison, and Eston were all born while he was in the White House. . . . Looking back, I think that witnessing your father's passionate attachment to your mother inoculated me forever against fatal love. I have remained an unattached, unrepentant bachelor for all these years, in love with neither women nor marriage. In a way, I suppose you are as close to a daughter as anything I possess on this earth, Harriet. I was at Monticello when you were born. I held you in my arms. Your father celebrated your birth as if you had been white."

Petit hesitated as if he were trying to decide to tell me one more horrible, fateful thing. The perfect maître d'hôtel warred with the dawning guardian angel.

"He was in the grips of one of his monumental migraines when I walked into the office. You see, I had already spoken to your mother. When I congratulated him on your birthday and your majority and freedom, he flew into a rage, the same kind of tantrum he threw in Paris when your mother left him. His last words to me about you were: 'Since she's white enough to pass for white, then let her be white.'

"Your father showed me the most extraordinary letter he had just written to a gentleman called Gray, an ironic choice of name, but anyway this gentleman, English I think he was, had asked your father where the line between black and white was drawn, and to my total amazement, your father showed me his answer: an algebraic equation which filled a whole page and which boiled down to when he, Thomas Jefferson, decided. And Thomas Jefferson decided that a person with one-eighth black blood was no longer a Negro. And that is you, Harriet. You had a white great-grandfather, a white grandfather, and a white father. You had an African for a great-grandmother, a mulatto for a grandmother, and a quadroon for a mother, which makes you, Harriet, an octoroon. In this way he willed you white with a mathematical equation."

I bowed my head, imagining the sonorous, high-pitched voice of my father searching for a way out of three generations of miscegenation. Meanwhile, we passed the Mason-Dixon line. I could not even be angry with him. I felt only a profound and enduring sense of solitude.

4

Power always thinks it has a great soul, and vast views, beyond the comprehension of the weak and that it is doing God's service when it is violating all His laws. Our passions, ambition, avarice, love, resentment, etc. possess so much metaphysical subtility, and so much overpowering eloquence, that they insinuate themselves into the understanding and the conscience and convert both to their party.

Thomas Jefferson

It was incredible that the dusty, dilapidated God walked around his desk to shake hands with me, Adrian Petit, his ex-valet, the morning I was to escort Harriet Hemings from Monticello. His pale eyes, tinged with melancholy and aquamarine, had swept across the top of my head with the same expression they had held for the past eighty years: autocratic and desperately willed serenity.

"A final service to an old friend" was all the curt invitation had said, the invitation that had resulted in my taking a public coach all the way from Philadelphia to Virginia and my now being seated opposite Harriet in this carriage. And even that invitation had been stated in terms that suggested that the writer's requests had of late been more than often refused.

And it was true that the man who had stood before me earlier this day was a man no longer either sartorially or politically in fashion. He was tall, almost six feet three, and his lined handsome face was still lightly freckled, and his mouth was stern, a narrow ridge between the deep, vertical valleys of his cheeks. His eyes were his finest feature. They were an astoundingly glacial shade of blue, hooded and surrounded by a map of fine lines. They were fascinating eyes, full of assured and irreproachable intelligence, which looked down upon one and indeed the world itself from the Olympian heights of good birth, good breeding, and power.

My former master had been dressed in thin, soft leather shoes with pointed toes, and heels which ascended in a peak behind. He wore very short quarters and red worsted stockings and a black-and-white-checked frock coat with oversized, comic buttons of hand-carved horn. Under this was a blue waist-coat of stiff, thick, coarse material, badly manufactured from the wool of his own merino lambs and surely slave woven, and corduroy small clothes.

However, my French sensibilities were most offended by his shirt, which was made of homespun flannel and incongruously bound with red velvet. Moreover, nothing fitted. The long bony figure with the broad shoulders of a true Virginian spilled out of every item of clothing as if he were nineteen and still growing. His navy blue silhouette danced like a hinged skeleton, seemingly taking up all the space in the room as he shuffled around the cluttered writing table. I then noticed that his legs were terribly swollen and his right hand, which he absently massaged with his left, was atrophied. He held it cradled against his chest.

I had the impression I faced an absolute reliquary of pain. Not only were the twice-broken wrist throbbing and the water-logged limbs aching, but the cloud of one of my ex-employer's famous migraines flickered in his eyes.

The reason for the President's migraine and the reason I, Adrian Petit, had been called there, I decided, were the same. Startled, I had seen them lurking just outside the room, standing side by side: the Mother and, a full head taller than the Mother, the Daughter, a female version of the Father. She had his nose, lips, and eyes, and that same trick of his frown, his high, wide forehead and milk-white freckled complexion, even the valley and famous dimple of his chin. She had his smile. She even had the same mold and frame of his hand. But slender, young, and undeformed. Tall like him. Big-boned like him. Redheaded like him. She so resembled the troubled Father before me, you did not even have to ask her name.

She was the President's daughter.

The Daughter had eyes which were the perfect combination of the blue of her Father's and the yellow of her Mother's, producing a limpid emerald with tawny irises edged in gray. The preternaturally pale and milky skin hid a blush of penny copper which seemed to reflect a darker core under its translucency. Her nose was long like his, and narrow, but her mouth was just the opposite: generous, full, and wide, with an upper lip that was slightly fuller than the lower. Her high cheekbones pulled her eyes, bright with running away, upward toward temples that were stretched taut by a lavish coil of basket plaits the color of red corn. As I said, she was almost as tall as her father, with wide shoulders and a fine bosom, a waist that was no more than a hand span, and hands that were long, narrow, and had never seen hard work. She had a densely luminous, astoundingly compelling smile that seduced both men and women indiscriminately. But what was strange was an inexplicable and hypnotic charisma that hovered about her, wholly different from that of an ordinary young girl; it was an aura that surrounded the rich, famous, or notorious. It was as if Harriet, having been born at the height of the national scandal over her mother and father's liaison, had absorbed with her mother's milk all the sexual innuendos, lewd vibrations, and obscene accusations of that maelstrom of controversy. She exuded the faint perfume of transgressions that she had never committed and that had nothing to do with her, which, in the face of her innocence, gave her a provocativeness and an unnerving sexual duality that might have been explained away if she had been black, but she was white. Like demons the epithets of those awful days that had engulfed her mother and father, and us all, seemed to cling to her: *Black Asparia, Lower-World Nymph, Dusky Sally, Blackamoor, Monticellian Sally, Negro Wench, Sooty Sal, False Ethiop.* This innocent and sequestered girl trailed the shreds of secondhand celebrity like shrapnel clinging to a magnet.

Yet Harriet seemed completely unconscious of the effect this produced on men.

The President had stood framed by the low window out of which I could see the shady lawns of Monticello and, in the distance, his Blue Ridge Mountains, which the soft promise of summer had turned a deep mauve. The stillness in the room had seemed to echo the silence of the landscape before everything suddenly darkened with the rush of swift clouds passing across the sky. I heard a cough and then the palsied hand lifted as if in benediction as the good one shot out so abruptly that it was all I could do to restrain myself from falling to my knees in the old-fashioned obeisance of the ancien régime. He shook my hand.

His Excellency had changed. But hadn't we all? Thirty years was, after all, a long time. Thirty-five if one went back to the Paris of '87. My former master was now nearly eighty, his presidency fourteen years behind him, his ambassadorship more than thirty. Burrowed into the thin ascetic face were the lines of his uncommon destiny, blunted by the passage of time into an expression of benevolent sovereignty and self-entitlement. But I was not

duped. No man is a hero to his valet, after all. The fifteen years that I had
served the President in that capacity had made me an expert in discerning the
rage and despondency that had brought on the pain he was trying to hide.
He was angry with the woman standing beside her daughter outside in the
hallway: the Mother who had stopped me outside the door and who had not
changed from the first time I saw her in the drawing room of the Adamses'
London home thirty-five years ago. It was as if every line on the President's
face had, at the same time, been spared from her own, leaving only a patinated
oval of burnished ivory, impassive as a moon, yet thrillingly omnipresent.
And it was clear her imponderable power over the man standing before me
was still intact after all these years.

I continued evaluating the President, noticing the new glaze of encroaching
cataracts in his eyes, remembered how the mane of snow white hair, which
now rose in tendrils like a field of corn silk standing on end, had once been
the wild, burnished vermilion of the young girl standing just outside the door
beside the Mother.

I smoothed my own shiny cranium in honest envy. Once, in the old days
before the Revolution, it had been covered with unruly dark curls. Now I
compensated for my baldness by cultivating luxuriant sideburns which I
combed forward toward my eyebrows and which gave me the distinct allure
of an extremely handsome chimpanzee. I was short, not even five feet eight,
and slender almost to gauntness. I had the blue-tinged chin of a twice-a-day
shaver, and the livid complexion of a man whose profession is good food and
wine. Since leaving the President's service some twenty years ago, I had made
a fortune in Washington as a caterer to the political elite of that city. My great
success was based on my French accent, which I used as a prop for my
impersonation of an aristocrat swept from fortune and power by the famous
events of 1789.

I, too, had been not much more than a slave for the first eighteen years of
my life. Set to work at seven or eight (I never knew which, for I never knew
my exact birthdate), I had been sent by my parents to the Château de Landry,
where I learned the menial duties of the lowest lackey, coal boy, and even bed
warmer. By nine I had been buggered by the master, his son, and the head
groom. By twelve I had bedded the scullery maid and the master's illegitimate
daughter. My monies, if they could be called that, were sent directly to my
father, and so I stole in order to have pocket money of my own. Being
attractive to both sexes, I rose in the servant hierarchy of the château to
second butler, and it was then I decided to try my luck in a Paris kitchen,
only to be told that I had been sold by my prince and could not leave the
boundaries of the estate on pain of whipping, prison, or death. I was the

merchandise which carried itself, so I promptly stole myself, changed my name, and escaped to Paris. I was taken into the service of Prince Kontousky, who eventually recommended me to the new American ambassador. I quickly made myself indispensable in his service and gained his esteem. I must say I loved my new master and did everything I could to make his life more amenable. His way with servants was new to me, based as it was on the plantation system, and I marveled at our imagined intimacy. He actually conversed with me, even to asking my opinion in certain matters. This quaint American custom soon went to my head, and I vowed undying devotion to such an egalitarian.

The familiar room at Monticello served as both bedroom and study for the man who finally signaled me to sit down. The walls were upholstered in red, and red draperies trimmed with gold tassels hung at the windows and enclosed the bed, which was built inside an alcove in the middle of the room that separated it into a distinct bedroom on one hand and a study on the other. Built into the alcove was a door which opened onto a miniature staircase leading to an entresol over the President's bed, which led to the second-floor corridor. Three bull's-eye windows in the passageway looked down upon the scene below. For years, this was how the Mother had left and entered the President's chambers without being seen by the prying eyes of hordes of servants and visitors. The staircase, which had been invented for her and built in her image, was so minuscule that the President's wide shoulders would not fit into its width, and so cleverly disguised, it seemed a portrait of the woman herself. It, like she, took up no space at all, and if one did not know for a fact of its existence, it would be the easiest thing in the world to dismiss it as a figment of one's imagination.

I knew the room itself by heart. Disorderly piles of letters overflowed the large writing table, and columns of stacked books lined the walls along which were artifacts, maps, and marble portraits of Franklin, Lafayette, and Washington. The bust of the President that the French sculptor Houdon had carved in Paris thirty-seven years earlier stood in mild reproach to lost youth, fierce intelligence, and the suppressed sensuality of his forty-second year. The handsome features were lost under a layer of dust, the hooded eyes fixed on dreaming some impossible dream. There were unopened crates marked WINE, or stamped with the addresses of Boston and Philadelphia publishing houses. The worn Persian rugs glowed in the half-light, the lemon-scented French furniture gleamed, the Italian paintings winked from the walls, and the expensive, polished brass scientific instruments glowered uselessly from a forgotten corner. To my highly educated nose the atmosphere reeked, like its occupant, of ink, horseflesh, and mildew while a Franklin stove blazed in the center of the room despite the balminess of a May day.

"Can you believe, Petit, that this year alone I've received one thousand sixty-seven letters—not counting, of course, dunning letters from all my creditors? I spend all my time answering other people's questions. I often wonder if this is life. At best it is the life of a mill horse who sees no end to his circle except in death."

The President's high-pitched, youthful voice had reverted to the easy familiarity of our former master-servant relationship.

Money, I thought as my eyebrows rose in distress. When a man spoke of creditors and death in the same sentence, he was getting ready to ask for a loan. I had heard through the Washington grapevine that the old man was in dire straits. The President had mortgaged his plantations and had sold Monticellian slaves to his son-in-law. He had bankrupted himself to build his new university in Richmond. A note of twenty thousand dollars he had endorsed out of friendship for the governor of Virginia had fallen due on the eve of the governor's death, which had left him obligated for the entire sum. Moreover, I knew how costly the President's life-style (not counting his slaves) was. His sumptuous and openhanded hospitality was legendary. The plantation of Monticello was run as the equivalent of a London club and a Paris hotel. I, who had risen from valet to caterer in Washington City, whose first industry was eating in restaurants and sleeping in hotels, calculated that if I were paying for my own services, my former employer's household expenses would be enough to break my catering business in less than a year.

I immigrated to the United States thirty-one years ago, in 1791, at his invitation, to serve as his majordomo at his seat at Monticello, just as I had served him between '84 and '89, at the American embassy in Paris. Then I followed him to Philadelphia, then to Washington when he was elected President, and served him at the White House. After the President left office I remained in Washington and made a fortune speculating in real estate, thanks to the tips of the political figures I catered to. And, if the truth were known, I was at this moment a great deal richer than my former master. But the President continued as if money was not at all the subject of discussion.

"Consider this letter," he said as he held up a sheet of paper covered with algebraic equations. "A curious northerner named Francis Gray wrote me and asked me what constituted a mulatto in our country, or more simply when black becomes white. I have written Mr. Gray that three crossings with white clears the issue of Negro blood."

My eyes blinked and I almost rose from the shock of having guessed correctly. So it was the girl, the Daughter, and the promise made in Paris so long ago! My eyes drifted toward the staircase and then back to the President.

"Which brings us to our problem, Petit. You see, Petit, she is white enough to pass for white."

"Who?" I asked, as if I didn't know. But I knew.

"This . . . member of my family. . . . I promised . . . another member of my family in Paris . . . if you remember, that is . . . That is that all of my . . . of her family, would be allowed to 'stroll,' as we call it in Virginia . . . at the age of twenty-one as free white persons. And tomorrow is . . . her birthday. Two of her brothers have already left. . . . Since she is white enough to pass for white, I say let her go."

The violence in the old man's voice had been like an odor in the room. I half rose, sniffing in alarm. The President's twilight eyes were steadfast as evening stars, blinking in the dusky, gray silence. The great mass of silver hair was backlit with mauve and stood on end, while the tumultuous voice rose and fell hypnotically. All I could think of was a cartoon I had seen recently in the *London Observer* of a wild-haired, raving alchemist stirring a bubbling tub of magic potions, searching for the equation of the elixir of life. The only difference was that this was the President of the United States searching for a way out of the crime of miscegenation.

"I remember you held her in your arms right here at Monticello. You know her mother and loved her uncle James. Because you know . . . all the parties involved, I am asking this service of you, Petit. Escort her to a free state where she can disappear into the white population. Find her a home or a school and take care of her until she finds a husband who can offer her protection in your stead. I ask this in the name of her mother, who has always had a place, I believe, in your affections. I have made out the necessary papers for Burwell and Fossett. If you want to take the phaeton, it will be cheaper and safer than a public stage, and you will not have to stop until you cross the Mason-Dixon line. I have made out a letter of credit for fifty dollars, which is as much as I can afford at this time of great financial difficulty. I beg you, Adrian, accommodate me in this. Please."

I did rise then, as if my movements were a lighted match in a room full of explosives. With horror I realized I was to escort the daughter out of slavery just as in Paris I had escorted the mother out of slavery thirty-five years before.

"Where shall she go, Your Excellency?"

"To Philadelphia."

The name was like a knife in my heart.

The old man stared bleakly at me without further words. The President, who had never once said please to me in his whole life, was begging. His bastard children were leaving him one by one. His legitimate ones, Maria,

Lucy I and Lucy II, Jane, and his unnamed son, were all dead. His grandchildren, Francis, Thomas, and Meriwether, were at loggerheads with one another. His only living legitimate daughter, Martha, was unhappy in marriage, living apart from a brutal, half-crazed husband, the drunken ex-governor of Virginia. Thomas Mann Randolph refused to live under his father-in-law's roof. The whole refuge of family life that my former master had so carefully nurtured had crumbled down around him.

"I'm too old to have a predicament," he had said when I had commiserated with him. "At this stage in my life, Petit, I am only allowed a 'situation.' My predicament, like my life itself, is a long way behind me. And that was that I loved two sisters, one white and one black, one my better half and the other my slave, one my wife and the other my sister-in-law, to my everlasting despair."

"I beg your pardon?"

"Despair, Petit. Like praying to Jesus Christ from the same rock of Abraham that Mohammed ascended into heaven from.

"When I look over the ranks of those whom I have loved, it is like looking over a battlefield. All fallen . . . away," the small voice had said.

"There are few men I could trust with this."

There are few men, I thought, who would understand why such a thing was necessary. "Consider this my last duty to you as the majordomo of the Hôtel de Langeac."

"L'Hôtel de Langeac. Promises go back a long time, don't they?"

I, too, I thought, have obligations and promises to keep, have ghosts from the past to assuage. All because of the Mother. And that sunlit Parisian courtyard.

"I have seen her, Your Excellency," I said, finally. "How can you bear to part with her?"

"Because I always lose everything I love. I've always lost everything I've loved.

"Oh God," a half-sob, half-groan exploded out of the looming, shadowy figure, now caught in the delitescence of his own ominous mountain, "since she is white enough to pass for white, then let her be white."

Thomas Jefferson turned away from me then, almost eagerly. From the cluttered desk he drew out an oversized ledger bound in red leather, which I recognized as his farm book. The turning of the pages, his heavy old man's breathing, and the fluttering sigh of a lighter more breathless beating, which could have been my heart or the hearts of the Mother and Daughter just beyond the door, were the only sounds in the room. The President found what he was looking for, as he absently massaged his crippled wrist, holding it close to him like a gift. Then he wrote her name with his left hand, laboriously and deliberately in his fine, clever calligraphy: *Harriet. Sally's. Run. '22.*

⌒

I had good reason to wonder at the strange ways of Virginians. They had their own world, and in a sense I had been excluded from it by caste and color, something I realized at Monticello the day of James's emancipation, Christmas Day, 1795.

Sally Hemings had been holding an infant in her arms that Christmas afternoon. That child symbolized her lost dream of Paris: its happiness and promise, of which she no longer spoke. As if she sensed what I was thinking, our eyes met. Affection? Pity? Horror at this Monticellian "family" with all the inhabitants and servants of the big house circled around the tree? I didn't know what to think. I had never understood the "crime" of miscegenation up until that moment. I shrugged and, with a wry smile, looked slowly to my right, following the circle from dark to light, from slave to free, from cradle to old age. So intricate and so intimate were all those different shades of color, caste, and blood that I flushed with embarrassment. It was the most naively promiscuous assembly I had ever attended. There was no way that these intertwined families could unravel or disengage themselves from all the unspoken obligations that I felt emanating from each in one resounding, melodious chord.

The Mother stood next to my beloved James, holding Martha's first Ellen in her arms, the five-year-old Thomas Hemings clutching her skirts. Spreading in a circle were nine of his eleven aunts and uncles, five of them fathered by John Wayles and the others by a slave, including Martin the majordomo. Sally Hemings was either daughter, stepdaughter, sister, half sister, aunt, niece, or half sister-in-law to practically everyone present.

The white side of the circle consisted of two of her white half sisters, Tabitha Wayles Skipwell and Elizabeth Wayles Eppes. There were Polly Jefferson, and her fiancé Jack Eppes, her cousin, and Martha, already married to Thomas Mann Randolph, who stood next to her. Then came James Madison, small, birdlike, insignificant, and his unexpected prize, the widow Dolly Todd, whom he had captured from the attentions of Aaron Burr and who, as Dolly Madison, would have a resplendent career as First Lady. Next to Dolly stood George Wythe and his mulatto son, Michael Brown.

I winked at my black equivalent, Martin, one in the net of blood ties that wove itself in and across and around the two parts of the circle, binding one half to the other in arabesques as twisted and complicated as the hanging strands of silver on the tree.

Then I, the indomitable and imperturbable Petit, joined the circle, unwittingly attaching the white half of the circle around the Christmas tree to the black half. It was at that moment that Thomas Jefferson offered James Hemings the manumission James had extracted in writing from him in Paris.

Watching those faces at that moment, I finally understood those convoluted family ties so completely that I could calmly sit there facing a weeping fugitive named Harriet Hemings II, who was not even an idea that Christmas Day, and contemplate offering her my name and my fortune. I felt suddenly as if I were perched backwards on a galloping horse going backwards, far back. The anger at what I was doing drifted away into vague anxiety. I faced the splendid girl with eyes of bottle glass.

I could not interrupt her solitude; I seemed to have lived this before: It was in this damned lilac phaeton again after all these years.

The passports with the king's signature had been delivered. Thomas Jefferson, his two daughters, and his two servants were going home. I had packed up this phaeton myself for the trip back to Virginia. It had stood in solitary splendor in the bustling courtyard of the Hôtel de Langeac while I tried to cope with eighty-two crates of Jefferson's baggage and a slave boy's grief. I shrugged as I had that day, dreading the next image, which I knew would be of James Hemings in his shirtsleeves. He had been busily supervising the closing of the wine crates, making sure that no bottles found their way out of the crates and into the workmen's smocks. There were dark sweat spots on his back and under his arms. His hair was plastered to his forehead as he struggled with the crates and trunks piling up in the courtyard. We were not the only ones in a paroxysm of flight. The fall of the Bastille had been the signal for the first great exodus of aristocrats toward England, Belgium, and America. And James and Sally Hemings, now pregnant, were returning with their master to Virginia and slavery.

I wonder if I was right to have blurted out so much of the past and private life of Thomas Jefferson to his Daughter on that long trip to Philadelphia. A lot of what I said must have shocked or hurt her, yet I forged ahead, determined to justify my role in her parents' secret life. All through it she remained silent, determined, unfathomable.

I rambled on and on, and despair in the guise of Harriet continued to sit facing me, dressed in a yellow plaid redingote surrounded by green velvet, the basket with her ironic black-and-white spotted Dalmatian puppy at her feet. She reminded me so much of my beloved James. There was the same defiance, the same vulnerability, the same prodigious courage in the face of annihilation. Yes. *Annihilation* is a good word. A better one I can't find.

Had I simply assumed that, being an ex-slave, she had more resilience than a white girl of the same age? Did I think Harriet was stronger or wiser being black? Did her one-eighth of Negro blood count for everything and her seven-eighths of white blood count for nothing? Could blackness be that potent, or had the President simply made it all up in that letter to Mr. Gray?

I the undersigned, Hugues Petit, my real name, alias Adrian Petit, my "historical" name of Reims, age fifty-eight, caterer and ex-majordomo of His Excellency, President Thomas Jefferson in Paris, France, ex-overseer of his plantation Monticello from 1794 to 1796, ex-butler to the President at the White House, Washington, from 1800 to 1802, did escort his natural daughter Harriet Hemings from Monticello to Philadelphia, where she disappeared into the white population. Adrian Petit de Reims, in the carriage to Philadelphia, May 19th, 1822.

HUGHES PETIT

5

We have the wolf by the ears, and we can neither hold him, nor safely let him go. Justice is on one scale, and self-preservation in the other.

Thomas Jefferson

Philadelphia! I laughed as I stepped from the phaeton onto Market Street Square and was drawn into the hurly-burly of people of more colors than I had ever seen in my life. These were to be the people that I, Harriet Hemings, the dancer and the ballet master, would have to conquer. Around me swirled a host of horse-drawn vehicles, farmers' wagons, vegetable carts, live animals, and mounted police. When I looked around at the busy, hard-faced crowd, I realized that no one had noticed my arrival.

I looked up at Burwell and Fossett, still seated in the driver's seat of the phaeton. They had been to Philadelphia countless times, and I imagined that countless times they had had the chance to slip away and disappear into the throngs of people that surged back and forth across the red brick square. Why hadn't they done it? Why hadn't my mother escaped when she had disembarked in London, a far greater city than Philadelphia? Then I realized that Burwell and Fossett were as much prisoners in Philadelphia as if they had had chains on their hands and a padlock on their boots. Their whole family was held hostage at Monticello. Burwell had left his wife, my aunt Betty, and his children; Fossett was married to Edy, and their children Simpson, Martin, Beth, and Robert belonged to my father. Fossett could no more leave them than leave his eyes or his legs. Our eyes met in silent comprehension as Fossett's arms swept me into an embrace that lasted only a second, but was long enough for me to breathe in his dusty smell and feel the power of his accelerated heart.

"You free now, gal. Never lower that head. Look everyone in the eye. There's no need to be afraid. There's no slave catchers looking for you 'cause I would know if they were. Besides, you're sent here by your father, as a white girl. If you ever see me on the street, you don't have to speak. People in Philadelphia will think it strange for a white girl to speak to a Negro unless he works for her."

"I saw you come into a world of slavery, Harriet," added Burwell, "and now I've taken you out of that world. Rejoice and be reborn; that's what God had in mind for you."

I understood that it was not fear nor search for freedom that had driven me out of the Negro race. I knew it was shame, unbearable shame. Shame at being part of a race of people that could with impunity be treated worse than animals.

"Is that what he really had in mind for me, a lie?" I whispered.

"A white lie," Burwell answered with a grin and a thunderous explosion of laughter that made people stop and turn their heads. That was the moment I saw an unforgettable lady of color come toward me as if she knew me. I stood petrified. Of course she recognized me! How could she not? I was as black as she was, wasn't I? She had on a wide straw hat trimmed with pink King George roses and green ribbons and lace. She was dressed all in deep bottle green striped with black, and her wide skirts were pulled back into a gigantic bustle, which fell in a train and gave her the look of the gentry. She held a matching umbrella over her head, and she navigated the busy square like a superb and stately ship that slipped past me in serene magnificence, so close I could have touched her but I didn't dare. The crowd around her faded and the noise ceased and the lady of color and I were alone in the square. She smiled in recognition and then shook her head in regret, her eyes inspecting me from head to toe, first in friendly curiosity and then with frigid horror. I tried to speak but found that as in a dream I could not. I reached out, hoping to touch her, but the world reappeared and the lady sailed by me with no hint of recognition. In confusion I turned toward Petit. He took my arm and led me across the huge mall toward the big green-and-gold letters of a tall, imposing building.

I gathered my courage and walked the gauntlet straight across the square to Brown's Hotel, my step elastic, my chin high, a slight smile on my face. Didn't I look like a young girl just out of school or a convent, hardly rich, but gently reared? Hadn't the waiter held the door as we entered, just as my knees gave way and Petit squeezed my arm? The image of the colored lady would haunt me for the rest of my life.

It was at Brown's Hotel on Market Street Square that I consumed my first meal as a free woman. Spring vegetable soup, radishes and butter and fresh sardines, deep-fried hake, lamb chops and new potatoes sautéed in butter, poached eggs in puree of collard greens, shrimps in batter, dried fruit, sugared fruit and pineapple spring strawberries, and champagne Moët. I memorized the menu like music. The savory words danced to the sound of Petit's running commentary. Did I know, Petit asked, benign larceny had assured the fate of the humble potato? In order for potatoes to be accepted as a vegetable, King Louis XVI had a potato field planted in the center of Paris, then surrounded it with his republican guards as a ploy to get Parisians to steal them. Or did I realize that pineapples came from Peru? Or how truffle was loved for its taste and its characteristic as an aphrodisiac? What? Didn't I know Aphrodite was the goddess of love? Or that a meal without cheese was like a beautiful woman missing an eye . . .

I glanced at my own reflection in the restaurant mirrors. Even sitting I was tall, taller than many men. My bright green eyes and my auburn braid reflected back: I saw a dreamy, remote girl, somewhat countrified against this opulent crowd. Nevertheless, I could hold my own. I tilted my head, turned my gaze on Petit, and laughed at his story.

During that long carriage ride, he had told me so much about his life in Paris with Mama and Uncle James that I felt I was his confidante.

My uncle James refused to acknowledge the destiny of concubine for his sister, Sally Hemings. He had decided she was not going to enter that strange circle of complicity between the Wayleses, the Jeffersons, and the Hemingses. But dark forces in the guise of family ties, and crimes, entered and wreaked havoc. From the very morning of his sister's seduction, in the winter of '88, James suffered from nightmares: Bloody sheets like tentacles would reach out to engulf and strangle him. They would bind him and cause him to be thrown bodily into brimstone and fire. That was my uncle's recurring dream. He was convinced that my mother's freedom was his own salvation and that without it, he was a doomed man. Day after day, he led her through the intricacies of life in France, in the embassy, in the grand house, in the great city. Around them swirled the rumblings of the French Revolution, and it gave a poignant counterpart to their struggle against Thomas Jefferson's will.

When he broke his wrist while riding with Maria Cosway and it began to heal badly, my mother took over the care and bathing of her master's injured hand, and through these simple ministrations an intimacy grew up—innocent at first, then more complicated and darker, incestuously linking destinies. Martha the jealous daughter and Martha the dead wife, Maria the adored arrival and Maria the absent lover. And my mother herself: half sister and stepdaughter, sister-in-law and slave.

I could tell Adrian Petit mourned James even now, twenty years after his death. And I suppose that's why he felt compelled to talk about him so much, especially to me. For me, James Hemings was only a legendary and eccentric uncle who had lived abroad for most of his life and had died a suicide in Philadelphia. Adrian wanted me to know the rich comic sound of his laughter, the yeasty smell of his body, the aching loneliness in his eyes. Adrian told me James had lived the life of a monk and had been chaste all his life.

" 'I will never spill my seed as a slave to breed more slaves,' " Adrian had said with James's voice. " 'I have never known a woman, Petit, and won't until the day I'm free.' "

But James, explained Petit, added such a mischievous and freewheeling style to this priestly avowal that it was impossible to reconcile the two. It was as if he had two identities: one which existed in the shadow of slavery, invisible, menacing, and ultimately cruel; and the other, its twin of sunniness and amiability, laughter, and, above all, youth. He was the youngest twenty-year-old Petit had ever met, and the provincialism of old Virginia had not yet worn off him or my father in those days. James and Petit had made lots of plans, too. James was going to finish his apprenticeship in the kitchen of Monsieur du Tott, and then he was going to demand his freedom from my father on the basis of living on French soil, where slavery had been abolished. And then the two of them were going to start their own catering business right there under the arcades of the Palais Royale, sure that they would find both backers and clients. "Of course, neither James nor I ever realized that dream!" exclaimed Petit.

"Your mother was carrying your brother Thomas, and your uncle James had become a first-rate chef when they left Paris in eighty-nine," Petit continued. "I remember thinking how easy it would have been for them to have remained in France. James could have commanded a first-rate position and salary as a cook, even with the exodus. I was sure he would never see the shores of France again. From one of the upper windows overlooking the courtyard, I saw Martha Jefferson calling to James and waving him into the house. He was her uncle as well as yours, and I remember that day how shocked I was, for after your mother had run away, James had told me the whole Byzantine story of your family. I, who was quite inured to the bizarre ways of the French aristocrats, had no idea of the genealogy that could exist between Virginia aristocrats and their servants—into the second and third generation. One day James had tried to extricate himself from the demands of your father, but he had been humiliated and outmaneuvered. Your father, as both master and diplomat, was unconventional, imaginative, resourceful, and tough. Poor James didn't have a chance against him. Neither did your mother. At the end of his 'explanation' with his master, James found himself facing seven more years of servitude: in return for his French education, he would be freed as soon as he had trained another cook at Monticello to take his place. It was the 'least' he could do to avoid being a traitor, 'a serpent at my breast.' "

" 'I'll never steal myself,' " Petit said James had told him one day. " 'He has no right to force me to do so . . . to make a criminal and an outlaw out of one who served him so long and loyally. He must free me legally and openly.' That day the disappointment was too much for James. I found him weeping behind a stack of half-packed trunks," Petit concluded. "Only two people saw him, me and your half sister Martha."

"That's what I'm doing, isn't it?" I said. "Stealing myself. Making myself into a criminal and an outlaw because Father can't face a little unpleasantness with the Virginia legislature."

"It's more complicated than that, Harriet. . . ."

"Not for me."

"Even for you. Especially for you. You mustn't hate your parents for what they did or didn't do."

"You say 'they.' When have they ever been 'they.' My father commanded and my mother obeyed. Something she's still doing."

Suddenly Petit fell silent and then spoke in a tone of voice I had not heard before.

"You should change your name, Harriet . . . Harriet Petit, perhaps."

Petit flushed at saying out loud what he obviously held dear in his heart. I looked at him in surprise. Why? I thought. But then, why not? He had guided me safely out of slavery. It was little enough to ask. The name Hemings only bound me to generations I had this day renounced.

"Yes," I said, "Harriet Petit, orphan."

I took Adrian Petit's surname mostly to make him happy. He was an old bachelor, he said, who would leave nothing behind when he returned to France. The Hemings name was notorious, he said, so why risk someone's remembering? "I would be honored to offer you my name as well as my protection."

That first night in Brown's Hotel, I carried to my pillow feelings I had never experienced before. I truly believed myself to be free. I didn't care if it was because of my color—or my father. I was free because I was white. What was the feeling of whiteness? Did it simply mean I could lay my head on my pillow without the fear of its being snatched up and sold the next day? Or bashed in by a jealous mistress, an irate overseer, a petulant son or daughter of the house? Did it mean that I would not be dragged hair-first out of bed to accommodate the lust of some white passerby or a member of the big house? Did it mean my mind could finally be used for something more than counting biscuits or bales of cotton? Or did it simply mean that my head was a valuable, unique appendix to a valuable, unique human being, with all the dreams and wishes and hopes and fears of the human condition?

At daylight I heard women crying their wares: fresh fish, berries, radishes, and all kinds of vegetables. I rose, dressed, and sat at the window to watch life go by. Philadelphia seemed a wonderful place.

I soon moved in with Monsieur Latouche, a famous caterer in Philadelphia and a friend of Petit's. He had worked for the Prince d'Ecmuhl and the Duc de Rovigo in Paris. Before settling in Philadelphia, he had served in the Russian ministry in Washington, where he and Petit had become friends. They had started their catering businesses at about the same time, and had known the same success. Monsieur Latouche was married to a Philadelphia lady named Margaritte, who took me to her fulsome bosom like a daughter and the orphan that I pretended to be. It was Mrs. Latouche who was responsible for my being accepted at Bryn Mawr Seminary for Women, a Unitarian two-year girls' college, founded just sixteen years before by a French Huguenot family.

Monsieur Latouche, who was more restaurateur than caterer, often complained of the monopoly the Negro caterers had of the ball and party business in Philadelphia: ". . . The blacks rule the catering business in Philadelphia with Henry Jones, Thomas Dorsay, and Henry Minton cutting up the pie in three slices. But that black Robert Bogle at Eighth and Sansom makes more money than all of them put together!"

I felt lost, sick at heart before such unmasked hatred. I knew it didn't threaten me, but it showed humans in such an inhuman light. I saw a kind of insanity, something so obscure its very obscurity terrified me.

He and Petit seemed to have a lot of friends and a lot of memories in common. As two immigrants, they had vastly different views of the United States. And many times Mrs. Latouche (who never called herself Madame Latouche—too French), Petit, and I found ourselves on one side of a discussion concerning American idiosyncrasies, with him on the other, especially about race.

These discussions upset me, for they nearly always ended with contemptuous, inhuman remarks about the Negroes, whom he would refer to by names I had never heard before: coons, apes, monkeys, gorillas, animals, jigs . . .

The first weeks, I continued to awake at dawn, sitting bolt upright in bed, my heart pounding, frightened by the noise of a passing carriage or the toll of a bell. I got into the habit of leaving the boardinghouse before anyone was awake and wandering alone through the narrow, red brick streets to the wharf. There I would stroll amongst the stalls of merchandise being laid out under the big canvas umbrellas, lingering in front of the huge painted signs of the waterfront stores and workhouses. There was energy and enterprise in everyone's bearing, an arrogance born of being free agents. Soon, to my delight, I became a recognized part of the scene as I lingered amongst the stalls of dry goods straight off the ships from Birmingham, or purchased bread and milk for breakfast. I began to receive smiles and nods of recognition from the hawkers and vendors and became one with the throngs of housewives with their baskets, shopping early. At first the smiles were timid, reserved, and I would smile back shyly as I was handed my purchase. But soon I was greeted as "Miss," then as "Miss Harriet." I noticed white people's eyes no longer slid off me as if I were invisible at worst, a bale of cotton at best. They neither focused their eyes over my shoulder nor glazed them over in nonrecognition of my humanity. They now looked me square in the eye, curious, friendly, appraising, teasing. Miss Harriet, a young lady. Little Miss. And my heart almost burst with gratitude for these unthinking banalities, then shame for being grateful would engulf me.

Hands that would have recoiled from touching the Negro Harriet Hemings, grasped mine. Women who would have snatched their skirts back in horror if the Negro Harriet Hemings had brushed against them, smiled warmly and excused themselves. Vendors who would have snatched a bonnet out of the hand of the Negro Harriet Hemings, forbidding her to touch it with her black hands, placed it upon my head themselves, commenting on its shape, price, and becomingness.

I began to look forward to my morning stroll, my eyes no longer avoiding those of white passersby, but frank and friendly, my step light and springy, my smile spontaneous and wide. I was no longer afraid of the world.

I began to watch white faces and think about them for the first time. I had studied, thought about, and welcomed only one white face in my life up until now: my father's. I had memorized every facet, shadow, and expression in silent, secret, jealous love. But I would have had a hard time describing my white cousins precisely, since my eyes had always slid off their likeness. My memory, even for my own color, was bad. But I began viewing the features and expressions of black faces just as I did with white ones. I waded into those northern faces as into the sea, looking slowly and carefully at each one.

First I discovered that each face was amazingly different, and so when I actually began to look at people, there was no more familiarity in my world.

I wondered if this were true for everyone in hiding. I felt so strange and so lonely that the most profound, the most moving sight in my mind became strange people's white faces. Eyes and mouths concealed I knew not what and secretly asked for other things: the rapturous smile of the old man who sold peanuts by the church gate, or the young newspaper boy, whose face was as blank as an unprinted page of the broadsides he flourished over his head, but whose yellow eyes and long black lashes reminded me of my mother.

Even Petit's face came under my new scrutiny: its contours and blue-tinted lower portion, its thin, almost black mouth, its foreigner's cast, were things I had never noticed before.

To my surprise, I realized that white skin was not white at all, but gray and lavender, peach and rose, blue and green, nut and cantaloupe, the color of my pineapple dessert and the color of new potatoes. There were high complexions and sallow ones, deathly white and deep brown. My father, I realized, had a truly fair complexion with its undertones of rose and green which I had in turn inherited. I recalled the tiny blue veins at his temple and the orange-colored mole at the corner of his mouth and the delicate blue of his eyelids. The world became a kaleidoscope, revealing colors hidden under other colors.

The colored people I saw stood out like sentinels in this mass of strangers, signposts of familiarity and humanity, although their northern accents astounded me. Their colors, too, took on new, mysterious tones of bronze and copper, ebony and mahogany, lemon wood and midnight blue, the black of Virginia coal and red of Virginia clay. Some were high yellow and I couldn't separate them from whites and couldn't tell if they were black, or blacks pretending they were white, or whites with a touch of the tar brush. I was convinced that every black face recognized me for what I was and simply looked the other way. Yet despite that, looking people in the eye was the revelation of my life. The things I saw there were so monumental, so fierce and mysterious, yet so familiar, so exhilarating that I wondered why I had never tried it before. From being unable to fathom the slightest meaning in a face, I came to read them like the pages of a book. From believing it was impossible to know what people thought, I became a mind-reader of extraordinary talent. I was on intimate terms with the whole world, and with every strange face that crossed my path never to return. I was a companion to strangers, black and white. And it was purely for that vision of my father's youthful face that I examined the secret, mysterious, unique faces of the white people I met in the streets of Philadelphia.

Philadelphia was a pretty seaport, the most populous, extensive, and handsome city in America, according to Mrs. Latouche. For someone who had never even been to Charlottesville, it was indeed a busy metropolis in the shape of a chessboard, with each street part of a grid, attached at right angles to the others. Its founder, a Quaker named William Penn, had laid out his "city of brotherly love" in strict geometry. The formula had been copied by other cities from the Mississippi to the Great Lakes. Philadelphia's ships and seamen were famous; its riches depended upon the fertile soil of its hinterland and its seaport. The city's coat of arms was a plough and sheaves of wheat over a ship under full sail. The best families, Mrs. Latouche never tired of saying, were merchants and landholders, and the great estates in Lemon Hill and Germantown were as extensive as southern plantations.

In the mornings, Mrs. Latouche and I would venture out on the red brick streets, which, according to Mrs. Latouche, were cleaner than those of any city in Europe except Holland. London was the only capital better lighted at night, and none had so many tree-shaded lanes. The Quaker city had good hotels, theaters, restaurants, circuses, bookshops, libraries, and famous publishing houses. It had once been the capital of the United States, and my father had been sworn in as Vice President here. It was where he had written his Declaration of Independence. Even my mother had paid a visit to Philadelphia.

Shoulder to shoulder, Mrs. Latouche and I would sail by the narrow red brick row houses with their white wood trim and their white granite stoops on our way to the wharves to watch the sailors unload the cargo boats which had sailed from the Pearl River in China to the Delaware harbor, carrying silk and curry powder, window blinds, umbrellas, porcelain, bamboo, fireworks, and tea—tons and tons of tea, Lepchong, Pouchong, Souchong. I quickly became addicted to this fragrant, delicious drink, and Mrs. Latouche began to take me to the China, India, and Orient Emporium for afternoon tea.

Philadelphians taught me my first real perception of race hatred—an all-consuming ignorance and contempt for black people that literally took my breath away. For unlike the South, where the races mixed indiscriminately, in Philadelphia whites and black were strictly separated and segregated. Mrs. Latouche had never even met a black man or woman, nor had one set foot in her house except me.

In the weeks before I left for school, I searched the streets of Philadelphia for signs of my father's passing, or my mother's, or my uncle James's. According to Petit, my uncle James had spent his last days in Philadelphia in a boarding-house from which one could see the forest of masts of the clipper ships that sailed into the harbor. Sometimes I would wander down to the docks alone, inventing some kind of errand to be done amongst the markets. I would stand leaning into the wind, much as I had seen my mother do, and scrutinize the horizon as if I, too, expected my ship to come in. And it would, I vowed. It would. But of course I first had to learn how to navigate in this new world. And I vowed never to turn back, despite the dawning hostility and loneliness. I would complete this journey into whiteness.

One day, I felt happy and safe enough to write home. Home? Was Monticello my home? Had Monticello ever been my home?

JULY 3, 1822

Master,

As you know from Burwell, I am safely arrived. Adrian Petit has presented your letters of introduction, and your acquaintances (not knowing who I am) have given me a cordial welcome. I have been enrolled in a Unitarian school for women in Bryn Mawr, a village not far from Philadelphia. It is not a convent like Martha's Abbaye de Panthémont in Paris, but a religious institution of high moral teachings which believes that slavery is wrong and contrary to the teachings of Christianity. My teachers are, without exception, abolitionists—how fine a word and how well it sits on my lips—and to them I am an orphan from Virginia whose little schooling was accomplished at home and whose family, except for her uncle Adrian, has been wiped out by yellow fever.

I am much older than the other girls. In the past month, I have visited all the places in Philadelphia you told me about. Mama says you fell and hurt yourself just after I left—that you slipped on a rotten step and rebroke your wrist. My prayers are that it is healed and you are recovered. Which doctor came? Again I thank you for the fifty dollars, which Petit has deposited in the First Bank of Philadelphia. I shed many tears for us all.

Your former servant and daughter,
Harriet

SEPTEMBER 3RD, 1822

Dear Harriet,

We received your letter by the usual means Saturday last and are happy for your safety and anxious for your future. The reproach—nay, the bitterness—in the necessary description of yourself as an orphan is well deserved, but believe me, there is no other way. Do not judge your loneliness too harshly. I recollect that at fourteen years of age, the whole weight and direction of myself was thrown on myself entirely, without a relation or friend qualified to guide me. You are twenty-one. Solitude forms character and invokes independence, for, in the end, one can depend only upon oneself. That, and what one can lay up as treasures of the mind. Therefore, honor and obey your tutors and teachers, for they hold the key to the inner life that no misfortune, no loss, no grief can snatch away from you: a trained mind is real freedom. Depend only upon yourself until you find that other half for which you will forsake all others. Then depend upon him. Where you have passed, I can neither hurt nor help you, I can only remain,

He who loves you—
Th.J.

P.S.: My wrist is healing passably well but with age the process is intolerably slow.

Roaming the red brick streets, looking at myself in anything that reflected my image: the large plate-glass windows of the shops or market streets, the windows of public coaches, the eyes of passersby, I began to smile, first to myself, then at others. And surprisingly, people smiled back. Men doffed their hats. Women nodded. Children stopped to stare. And I thought: If you knew who I really was, would you still be smiling?

6

Everything in this world is a matter of calculation. Advance then with caution, the balance in your hand. Put into one scale the pleasures which any object may offer; but put fairly into the other the pains which are to follow. . . . The art of life is the act of avoiding pain. . . . Those which depend on ourselves, are the only pleasures a wise man will count on: for nothing is ours which another may deprive us of.

Thomas Jefferson

Once at school, I began to learn how far from Virginia I really was.

The first and the best friend I made was Charlotte Waverly. Music and speed had brought us together. Or vice versa. We were the two tallest girls in the entire college, and Charlotte was the fastest. But I could run, too. I had been racing my brothers through corn and tobacco fields for a decade.

One day we came face-to-face on the school grounds. After eyeing one another for a moment without exchanging a single word, we picked up our skirts and shot off, neck and neck, in a sprint down the knoll which rolled gently away from the main building and ended at a stone wall along the highway. Our hoops were around our waists, our drawers showing, our pigtails flying, and the entire school was cheering us on. I was winning as we approached the gateway which marked the boundaries of the school grounds, when I realized that something more was at stake than a footrace. I had one second to decide whether to win or lose against Charlotte. I chose as a Virginian slave would have chosen. Charlotte won by a hairbreadth, and we fell into each other's arms on the clover-speckled lawn, panting like puppies.

"I'm Charlotte Waverly," said the tall, strong blonde who had me pinned to the ground.

"I know who you are. I'm Harriet Petit, the new girl."

"I know you're new and I know you're the oldest girl in the school. A pleasure to meet someone who can give me a run for my money."

"The pleasure is mine."

"Your southern accent is not half as terrible as I've been told."

"You have something against Virginia accents?"

"We've just had a footrace, you don't want to have a fistfight as well, do you?"

"You sound like you grew up with boys."

"I did. And so did you, otherwise you would never be able to run so fast."

"True."

"How many brothers?"

"Four. Thomas, Beverly, Madison, and Eston. And you?"

"Four. Amos, Charles, Zachariah, and Dennis." She paused, then added, "We've got a lot in common."

That day I not only secured my place as the second fastest girl in school, but, more important, I initiated a friendship with the most popular and socially powerful girl at Bryn Mawr. The girls who had ignored me as "Aunt Harriet," because I was so much older than they, now vied for my company. I found them more or less equivalent to the white cousins I had played with since childhood. They held no particular mystery and gave no particular worry since, unlike my Virginian masters, they could not, arbitrarily and at the drop of a hat, turn into violent masters with dangerous tantrums and obstinate demands.

To say I was never homesick would be a lie. How, I asked myself, could I regret slavery? Slavery had been my only family and my only home until now. I yearned for the familiar and evil alike. I disliked this northern climate with its harsh accents, its stiff, strange people. I craved my aunt's warm bosom and the smell of smoked bacon and cornpone on hickory embers, the pinch of chilled springwater on parched lips, the practical jokes of Daniel and Maynard, the extravagant ghost stories of Uncle Poke, the scent of new-mown hay and of honeysuckle, of fresh-scythed wheat and tobacco blossoms.

I dreamed at night of soft Virginia slave accents echoing along Mulberry Row, the deep bass of a lonely soloist in a potato field, the rumbling laughter of fathers at rest, the soprano cries of mothers commanding children to bed, the feel of smooth-spun cotton as it flowed from the rough raw fibers, the sound of Eston's violin, Matthew's trumpet, Harold's harmonica, and Feller's flute, of Sister's tambourine and Mama's spinet, of the calls of whippoorwills and wild wolves, the mating song of mountain elk and the thrust of the Blue Ridge against the smoky streaks of twilight sky. How we made happiness out of nothing. How we snatched life out of doom.

~

A year passed and I gave up letting Charlotte win all the time. At least once a week we tied our skirts up around our waists and raced up the knoll, knees pumping, hair loose, arms flailing pell-mell. We ran like boys, knees up, elbows bent, head down. The fact that we did this in heavy skirts, under which was a layer of petticoats instead of britches, hadn't perturbed any of our male siblings. One of Charlotte's brothers had explained that it was no more unfair than the fact that girls had to learn to dance backwards.

"It's your destiny . . . like having babies," Amos had told her. "If you ever have to run from a man, at least you'll have a fighting chance . . . and you'll have to run in your clothes."

I reached the top of the knoll first, gulping in air by bending over at the waist, to ease the stitch in my side. As I straightened, Charlotte tackled me from behind, throwing us both onto the cool grass. Charlotte's face was pressed close to mine, and her breath fanned the tendrils of my hair. She flung her arms over mine and, still panting, rested her head on my chest. I had never had a friend like Charlotte, and I experienced a wave of tenderness for her.

Yet how would I forever keep up the careless facade of happiness necessary to retain Charlotte's attention? Even those girls at school who did not like Charlotte had to admit that she was possessed of unlimited charm, which lay not only in her conventional—blond and blue-eyed—appearance, but in her outlook on life, which was as cheerfully shadowless as her face. In fact, she was so fond of the sunny side of things, she was inclined to regard gloominess or introspection as an illness akin to insanity, and she would avoid the company of anyone she felt fell into that category. She believed a witty answer turned away the wrath of teacher and parent, and that the oil of reason should always be poured on trouble or misery. I was always afraid of vexing her and kept my problems and unhappiness from her. I only learned much later that it was this resistance and ferocious mystery that drew her to me. She found me profoundly different from anyone she had ever known, and she often told me this, her wide eyes clouding for a second because she didn't know how to name it.

Charlotte sat up first, and before I could draw up my knees, she noticed my bare ankles. She touched the right one, gingerly tracing its contours. "What's that?" she asked innocently.

It was a sisterly gesture, but I drew back sharply from her touch. Every gesture, every moment which corresponded to her safe, happy life had a double meaning for me, a kind of elongated shadow of my former life. She had learned to run to beat the males in her own world. I had learned to run to escape a beating or more from those in mine. I realized she could never understand, and any attempt to explain a life in such contrast to her own would be impossible, like impossible love. . . .

"When you were a child . . ." she would begin. *I was never a child, Charlotte; I was a slave child.*

"What did your brothers want to be when they grew up?" *Grown-up male slaves, to survive until the age of twenty-one . . . Charlotte, oh Lordy.*

"Why do you jump so when I put my arms around you?" *Because I'm afraid. Afraid you'll turn into Ellen or Cornelia. Afraid you'll turn into a white mistress. . . .*

"When are you ever going to come home with me?" *When I'm sure I won't be asked to use the back door. . . .*

"Why are you so sad, Harriet?" *Because I'm beginning to love, and I can't let myself love anyone I'm bound to lose.*

"I was hunting with my father one day, you see, and I caught my ankle in a squirrel trap," I replied. Somehow the pathos of my answer brought unbidden tears to my eyes.

Everything that pointed to happiness seemed to come at once, at the end of 1823. First, there was Petit's offer of Thursday-afternoon piano lessons at the Philadelphia Conservatory. Music, which had been my refuge for so long, became the only truthful thing in my life.

The music I had discovered as a child at Monticello had always nurtured in me an ideal universe, a universe pure, perfect, and free of prejudice. Music was so just and fair in its application (everyone, after all, played the same notes, from the same page, with the same instrument, and it was only their individual talent which delineated a good performance from a bad one) that it seemed a parable. Facing a sheet of music, I felt myself free, on equal terms with anyone to extract its essence, unravel its mystery, and conquer its difficulties. Music was its own master and belonged only to itself.

One day, I had accompanied my mother to Bermuda Hundred, my grandfather's plantation. While playing in the barn there, I discovered, in an old crate, a whole book of sheet music. When I asked my mother what it was, for it was clear it was not a real book, she said, "Why, that's music written down." From the moment I realized that one could read music and reproduce it from notes printed on a page, my world changed. My father later explained to me the singular integrity and inviolability of a written score. "You can equivocate and interpret the written word," he had said, "but a note on a page means one thing and one thing only, just as a number represents only its own unique measurement. A two can never be a four and a six is not a nine turned upside down. There is no second chance in music, Harriet. And there is no forgiveness."

From that moment I knew what I wanted! No forgiveness. I already knew I would never have a second chance.

It was the discovery that one could read and write music as one could read and write books that changed my way of thinking. I discovered my mother had been taught to read music, and she taught me. It was my first notion that my mother was more than she appeared to be, that she had had a different life in the past than she had at Monticello. Even though Eston had learned to play by ear—a flute, then a guitar—and surpassed me in virtuosity and finesse, my ability to read, assimilate, and memorize music was far superior. I was soon able to transcribe a simple melody and play it back on whatever instrument was at hand. I drew score music and began to reproduce the music in my head. Eston repaired my mother's cordless spinet, which had been shipped from Paris by mistake. It opened the door into a world of fixed, mathematical perfection where nothing, nothing could touch me.

The Latouche house, where I stayed when I came home from school, was only a few doors away from Fourth and Vine streets, where the conservatory stood on the corner with the University of Pennsylvania's Anatomy Hall, the leading medical center of the United States, which took up the rest of the city block. The Latouche family had a music room in which resided a harp and a Thomas Loud piano. The floors were painted black, and there were gold-painted chairs along the walls, and potted ferns and palm trees. I thought it the most elegant and beautiful room I had ever seen. There was a glorious Persian carpet in the center of the room, and a Waterford crystal chandelier hung from the high ceiling. Venetian blinds and yellow satin curtains trimmed in green silk hung at the windows, and painted garlands of flowers decorated the upper walls and ceilings, which were tapestried in yellow-and-white-striped silk. Mrs. Latouche played neither of the instruments. The room had been the decorator's idea, and Mrs. Latouche had simply acquiesced because she liked the idea.

The first time I saw the Loud piano, I burst into tears.

"Why, child," she asked me, "do you play?"

I was too excited to answer. I walked over to the gleaming instrument in my slow, dreamy orphan's gait and sat down. Sat carefully and flung my skirts behind me with a double swimming motion. Still without a word, I started to play by memory. I played firmly, smoothly, my face at rest, now more forcibly, but never loudly. The piano was an excellent one, rich and round in tone, like my breathing. Trancelike, I played everything I knew until I had been playing for several hours. Mrs. Latouche had gone out to get her husband, and the housekeeper had come in to listen. Then Petit had come in and remained perched on one of the gilded chairs like a little monkey, transfixed.

He had said little that day, and it wasn't until the end of the year that he announced that he had acquired an audition for me at the conservatory next door. My lessons and instruments and sheet music would be paid for by him. The conservatory was the only one in America that accepted women musicians, he said.

For the next year, Charlotte and I would take the public diligence into the city on Thursday mornings, when I would have my weekly lunch with Petit and Charlotte would visit her family on Waverly Place. Afterwards we would meet in front of the white stone Palladian building, surrounded by its tall, gilded iron fence, our music sheets under our arms, and walk through the gates into what I considered heaven. Here I could forget everything, even the lie. I became as anonymous as the black notes dancing across the scored paper. I had been accepted in piano and piano scoring, and had been asked to choose another instrument. Rather than the fiddle, which I knew I would never play with any finesse, I had chosen the violoncello, a somber, ponderous, and supremely beautiful instrument. The weight, the bulk, and the size made one feel as if one were lugging a dead body around, but I loved even this. I was a strong girl who had hauled more than a few cotton bales. I named it Alexia, and often spoke to it in the same tone of voice I used for Charlotte.

At the conservatory, only sound existed, not color. Life itself was made up of it. Discipline came so easy to me that I could never understand Charlotte's complaints over music practice or her chronic lack of attention.

In the year I had been at school with Charlotte, we had forged a passionate friendship like those one acquires in early adolescence. We fell in love without ever unraveling the mystery that had attracted us to each other. We spent so much time together, we were like a single person in two bodies who guessed each other's thoughts and anticipated what the other would say. We had overcome the petty jealousies and reciprocal cattiness that characterized feminine friendships. Charlotte was the anchor in my vastly changed and troubling world. Without blackness to set me apart or whiteness to persecute me, I began to experience the natural rhythm of my mind and body. I began to breathe differently, to hold my head at a different angle, to look outside the small antediluvian world that had been mine.

But secretly I was obsessed with notions of concealment. I became, in fact, attached to a dual life as observer and dreamer. I existed in perpetual alertness, ever fearing the untoward to happen. Only with Charlotte did I let my guard down, and, in doing so, induced a series of events that were as unpredictable as they were unpremeditated.

"Solitary pleasure," said Charlotte, in her usual abrupt way of beginning a discussion.

"Solitary pleasure," I repeated, putting a period at the end so as not to laugh.

"There's nothing like it, Harriet. You'll never have to depend on your husband for satisfaction."

"And what do you know, Charlotte Waverly, about solitary pleasure?"

"I want to know if you think it is a sin."

"In the eyes of our professors and the pastor, it is."

"Oh, well, I know that. But boys do it all the time—my brothers do it until their tongues hang out like puppies'. I've seen them."

"I . . . had brothers, too. I know what they do."

"Females," began Charlotte importantly, "are capable of giving each other extreme pleasure independently of the male sex. . . ."

"Hum . . ." I said, wondering just how far Charlotte was going to go. I knew she loved me. I loved her, and I knew how easy it was to confuse the senses and substitute one yearning for another.

We were lying on the banks of a shallow brook that ran through the woods in back of the college. The water shone like steel, so motionless that one could see one's image in it as if it were a mirror. The feathery curl of a flying wasp cut across its surface and then was gone. I felt listless and reckless and almost annoyed that Charlotte's infatuation was to become a ritual of passing from girlish friendship to a new stage of whatever was in store for us as grown white women.

"I love you," she said.

"I love you, too, Charlotte."

Lazily, she placed her hand on my cheek. I closed my eyes and let the tepid breeze off the cool water sweep over my face and neck. We were shoeless and stockingless and had pulled our petticoats up so that the weak April sun could warm our legs. One of Charlotte's limbs had entwined in mine, and lazily I turned my head to follow her caress. I lay there opening and closing my eyes. The brilliance and then the blackness were like the world as I saw it: divided into halves, one of light and one of darkness. The half where she was, was all of joy, hope, and light; the half where she was not was of gloom and darkness.

The world I knew also was divided into those who had a choice and those who had none.

Charlotte began to kiss me with sweet, simple kisses.

"Do you know what to do?" I asked.

"Yes."

I turned my head away from her lips for a moment, as a swimmer taking in air would do. I had no intentions of resisting Charlotte; on the contrary, there had always been a deep sensuality in our sisterly affection, and as her lips and hands moved over me, untying, loosing, stroking, pulling, releasing, I tried to fathom my true feelings for Charlotte. I realized it was as it had been at Monticello: my will against her power. I was determined that my will would overcome her whiteness. Our lovemaking became a sedate combat to see which of us would emerge as the winner. We were, surprisingly, as equally matched in this as in footraces. In the end, as we waded out into the silent sheen of the brook, our skirts bunched around our waists, neither of us had achieved the upper hand.

"Look down, Harriet. You are so beautiful."

And indeed, in the mirror of the creek, I made out the wavering burgundy triangle trembling on the surface of the darkness. Charlotte was so blond, one could hardly tell where her belly ended and her sex began. We began to laugh then, long, sumptuous laughter that floated on the water like skimming butterflies and echoed out into the tepid spring air. It was the kind of raucous laughter that females indulge in only between themselves, adagios of breathless sounds that come from the throat, the bosom and belly, the sex. Laughter we never showed men.

Our complicity lasted, with gaps of years in between, well into our middle age. We confided in no one. We feigned indifference to the point where we earned the reputation of coldness and prudery. We read forbidden novels, collected methods of avoiding pregnancy, studied medical journals. We formed our own secret erotic society of two from that day. We were to grow old together, marry, survive our children, lapse quietly into that transcendent peace of matched couples, through three marriages.

⌒

My goal up until now had been an individual one, a promise, a special dispensation, a private purgatory. When I learned that my desire was the foundation of a whole movement to set every member of my race free, I felt as if I had fallen from another planet. I had never read an antislavery tract or witnessed a slave whipping. I had heard that two white cousins in Kentucky had murdered a slave by amputating his limbs and then burning the torso in the fire he hadn't made just right, but Kentucky seemed far away, and the story more like legend than reality. I didn't know what black laws were, nor could I find Mississippi on a map. Of the danger of my father's double life or the sorrow of my mother's broken dreams, I had but an inkling. As for the white cousins I was now impersonating, I knew them best for their ignorance, careless cruelty, and greedy need for affection.

Then I met Robert Purvis. I was in the hall of the conservatory, and he was on his way to a rehearsal of the gentlemen's choir. He was a pale, light-haired young man who greeted Charlotte by name, being a friend of her brother Dennis. He was accompanied by a very tall man in the somber medical clothes of an apothecary, named William John Thadius Wellington. The two friends were in great contrast to each other. Purvis was blond, loquacious, and self-assured. Wellington was dark, with the awkward aloofness of a scientist and dreamer. Both were handsome. Purvis, assuming I was white, quickly proceeded in the merriest way to explain to me that he was not. It seemed to be a standing joke with his friend, whom he called Thance.

"I am not, nor ever have been, a white man," he drawled, his mouth quirking with suppressed laughter at my surprise. His blue eyes were full of sharp light, which seemed to narrow his face into one concentrated beam. He was the son of a slave and a repentant Louisiana plantation owner who had freed him and his mother and sent them north, where he had attended Oberlin College in Ohio. The fortune left him by his father Purvis had dedicated to the cause of antislavery. He now attended the University of Pennsylvania despite, he said, its prohibition of Negroes, women, and Jews. There was no recognition of my own duplicity in the clear, candid eyes, only friendly curiosity and the mild look of contempt from a man who has decided never to give his heart or his fortune to a woman.

"What actually is the use of being a powerful, rich white man when there are so many of them? A powerful, rich Negro, however, is another story. He can move a whole race toward emancipation. I can move my own mother's brothers and sisters and my own grandmother's brothers and sisters out of bondage. That's real power. I have a great deal of money and I intend to use all of it to agitate for the end of slavery in the United States of America.

"May I invite you ladies to a meeting of the Philadelphia Anti-Slavery Society next Thursday, for I am sure you must get your families' permission," he continued. "It will be held at the Benjamin Franklin Library on South Street, and there will be foreign as well as Negro speakers. The ladies' auxiliary sits in a cordoned-off section totally segregated from the men."

I blushed deeply. We were two white women speaking on equal terms and quite freely to a Negro. I saw Charlotte out of the corner of my eye, trying to signal to Purvis. What was she trying to tell him? That I was a Virginian, daughter of a slaveholder? Orphan of a Tidewater first family? I stood there staring not at Purvis but at his friend, whose eyes had drawn mine into his.

He wore his dark, lustrous hair combed straight back and tied with a ribbon. The eyes that focused on mine were extraordinarily long and narrow and so dark they could have been midnight blue. I found myself staring into a gaze of singular intensity, which, despite its fathomless depths, transmitted some far distant felicity like that of a happy childhood.

"Miss . . . Miss Waverly, help me out, please." He smiled.

"I'd like to introduce you to Miss Petit, of Virginia," Charlotte emphasized.

"Miss Petit, Mr. Wellington, a friend of my brothers," she concluded.

"Delighted, Miss Petit." Wellington smiled, his eyes melting. "You'll have to forgive us. We're late for practice," he said as he took Purvis's arm a little too roughly to be entirely innocent.

"Listen; they've started without us," he said as he hurried Purvis, who was looking over his shoulder at me in admiration.

The music wafted out into the corridor, and Charlotte and I, not daring to enter the hall, stood outside listening. Suddenly a single, beautiful voice, taking the solo part in an oratorio I was not familiar with, raised itself above the rest. It was the voice of a tenor baritone, of such depth and tenderness that the sound rushed over me like water, bathing my eyes and lips, running down my throat and over my shoulders and down my back to the base of my spine.

"That's old Wellington," laughed Charlotte as she noticed the expression on my face. "The voice of an archangel and the reputation of an atheist."

But at that moment he could have been Satan himself. I had never heard such a glorious voice.

7

Would the world be more beautiful were all our faces alike? Were our tempers and talents, our tastes, our forms, our wishes, aversions, and pursuits cast exactly in the same mold? If no varieties existed in the animal, vegetable, or mineral creation, but all more strictly uniform, catholic, and orthodox, what a world of physical and moral monotony it would be.

Thomas Jefferson

"I strenuously contend," Purvis told us at the next meeting of the Anti-Slavery Society, "for the immediate emancipation of our slave population. I will be as harsh with the truth and as uncompromising as justice itself. I am in earnest. I will not equivocate. I will not excuse. I will not retreat a single inch, and I will be heard. I take it for granted slavery is a crime—a damning crime. I am a crime. Therefore, my efforts shall be directed to the exposure of those who practice it."

I stared in horror at Robert Purvis. No one had ever told me in so many words that slavery was a crime.

"And," he added, "if anyone objects that the Constitution—the beloved Constitution—stands in the way of such a program, I can only reply that if the Constitution sanctions slavery, then the Constitution is wrong. The Constitution is in league with death and in covenant with hell."

I looked around in alarm. Father's Constitution. It was like damning the Bible. It was like predicting the end of the world. Slavery was God's will. Slavery was eternal!

"And," he continued, "I regard all slaveowners, including my own father, as guilty of that crime and therefore as vile, despicable men."

Purvis had not recognized a fellow traveler in color, if I could be so called. I had nothing to fear from him, even if he knew the truth. A man without guile and incorruptible, his life was laid out in a grid as straightforward as William Penn's city.

"Generally speaking," he said, "men must make great and unceasing efforts before permanent evils are created, but there is one calamity which penetrated furtively into the world. At first scarcely distinguishable amid the ordinary abuse of power, it originated with an individual whose name history has not preserved, then wafted like an accursed germ and spread within the society. This calamity is slavery.

"Christians of the sixteenth century reestablished it as an exception, indeed, to the social system, and restricted it to the race of mankind; but the wounds thus inflicted upon humanity, though less extensive, are far more difficult to cure. This arises from the circumstance that among the moderns, slavery is fatally united with color. No African has ever voluntarily immigrated to the New World, whence it follows that all blacks who are now here are either slaves or freedmen. Thus the Negro transmits the eternal mark of his ignominy to all his descendants, even though the law will abolish slavery. Wherever the Negroes have been strongest, they have destroyed the white; this has been the only balance that has taken place between the two races. I see that in a certain portion of the United States, the legal barrier separating the two races is falling away, but not that barrier existing in the manners of the country: slavery recedes, but the prejudice to which it has given birth is immovable. In those parts of the Union where Negroes are no longer slaves, they have in no wise drawn closer to the whites. On the contrary, the prejudice of race appears to be stronger in the states that have abolished slavery than in those where it exists; and no states are so intolerant as those where servitude has never been known."

⁓

I began to study abolitionist literature and the narratives of escaped slaves. I read memoirs of reformed slave traders and ship captains like my great-grandfather. Mesmerized, I stared at posters of slave auctions, rewards for fugitives, and maps upon which were traced the contours of the continent called Africa. I realized how small the world of Monticello was, and how enormous the wound that poisoned the wholeness of my country. I learned of slave revolts in Cuba, Santo Domingo, and Jamaica. For the first time, I contemplated my father's double life, as dangerous in its own way as my own.

I plundered books, newspapers, and pamphlets for news of him. I memorized his public life, looking for clues to myself. I read about him as ambassador, as Secretary of State, as President, trying to assimilate the image of the stranger who had written the Declaration of Independence, bought half of the United States, and never freed my mother.

One day, Mrs. Latouche took me to task over attending so many meetings.

"My dear, as much as I partake of the progressive ideas of abolitionism and antislavery, I must, in the name of your guardian who is not here at the moment, point out to you that these meetings are no place for young girls. You and Charlotte should think seriously about how you compromise your reputation as serious and sheltered young ladies by attending them.

"The conservatory is one thing, and bad enough, I might add. But that Library Company! It is a hotbed of abolitionism and radicalism. I know you follow Charlotte in everything, but being a member of one of Philadelphia's first families, the equal of the Biddles, the Ingersolls, the Girards, the Wartons, and the Rittenhouses, Charlotte can do what she well pleases and get away with it. You, an orphan with no fortune, must be a lot more careful. You have only your beauty, your health, and your respectability. Your talent as a musician is simply nice icing on the cake. There's no question of your getting mixed up in any radical movements with . . . mixed public meetings."

"You mean interracial meetings, Mrs. Latouche." My voice took on its most lush and seductive sweetness.

"I mean meetings where the two sexes are represented promiscuously in the same hall."

"I see."

In spite of my boldness in attending the abolitionist meetings, fear was never far from me. One day I turned into Hamilton Alley having slipped out of the house early for a walk along the quay, my only moment of the freedom of movement I had enjoyed as a slave, for now I had to be chaperoned everywhere. I sensed a tall man following me. Sykes! I tried not to hurry, so as not to provoke him into a pursuit. His footsteps echoed along the long, painted brick corridor with high, shuttered windows and hitching posts of white marble. It was broad daylight: I knew I would soon hit the wharf with its milling crowds and merchandise stocked stories-high to be loaded into the waiting clippers. My heels clicked on the fired-brick pavement, my hand went deep into my pocket, my fingers clutched the knife as I stopped short, took a deep breath, and turned around. The man stopped ten paces in front of me. I was almost faint with fright.

"Mr. Wellington!"

"Miss Petit. I didn't mean to frighten you."

"Well, I don't know who has frightened whom," I said, my heart pounding.

"I've seen you many times in this neighborhood."

"Well, I live around here. What are you doing in this . . . neck of the woods?" I said, trying to control the tremor in my voice.

"The pharmacy school of the University of Pennsylvania is just at the corner there"—he pointed behind him. "I'm a teaching assistant there, and that's where I have my laboratory. Our . . . our warehouse and apothecary is down on Front Street, about a five-minute walk. My father founded our company in 1789 . . . if you walk by you'll see the sign, 'Wellington Druggist and Apothecary Supplies.' Isn't it fortunate we met that day of the rehearsal? Otherwise I wouldn't have been able to address you on the street. God bless Charlotte Waverly."

He said this with such fervor and such sincerity that I laughed in relief.

"I thought you were about to attack me."

"Oh, my God. Oh, my God—so I did frighten you. How stupid. How cowardly of me. I just couldn't get up the nerve to speak to you. Let me walk you home . . . but first let me restore your good spirits with a . . . water ice? Tea? Chocolate?"

"Tea, please. I love tea."

"There's a place near the depot called the China, India, and Orient Emporium, which has a tearoom where they serve their own teas, hot or iced or in sherbet."

"I know it," I said, delighted to go to a favorite place.

"You do forgive me?"

"Yes," I replied, almost bursting with joy.

Arm in arm, we turned into Chestnut Street at Sixth and started toward Dock Street, walking beneath the canopied stalls of the booksellers and publishers that were concentrated along those six blocks. We passed Independence Hall and the United States Post Office to arrive at the Wharf and Walter Street, where excursion boats sailed for New York and Cape May. Mansions, warehouses, and tradesmen's shops were all crowded into the block running south along Front Street. There we found Beck's China, India, and Orient Emporium along the waterfront overlooking the harbor, bearing on its top story the iron plates advertising the Insurance of Houses from Loss of Fire Company. Under the awnings, which stretched out to the thoroughfare, sat ladies and gentlemen, sampling Mr. Beck's teas from around the world.

The harbor, in the early-morning light, was a forest of masts and furled sails. The sailcloth awnings cast a golden hue over the crowd, the rough board tables and chairs. The tables were covered with white tablecloths, and on them sat huge blue-and-white porcelain samovars which were filled with the customers' special order. The heavy traffic of merchants, insurers, dockers, hawkers, strollers, gentlemen, ladies, washerwomen, and sailors glided on foot between the bales, crates, and cargoes of the world: rice and cotton and tobacco from Virginia, spermaceti oil from New Bedford, horsehides from Montevideo, coffee from Brazil, dollhouses from Cologne, linen from Finland, rum from St. Croix, brandy from France, and opium from Turkey. Bales of tea were stacked about everywhere in front of the Emporium— Hyson and Indian, Gunpowder, Imperial, and Souchong.

Seated, we too took on the amber color of the awnings. I was happy I had taken, for no particular reason, great pains with my toilet. I wore a Scottish plaid taffeta of green, black, and gray, trimmed in black grosgrain, and a porcupine hat trimmed with green ribbon and a whale green swallow which curved around my ear. The dress had a white Irish lace cravat and white ruffles at the sleeves. I had bought some music from Can's Publishing House and now put it down on the extra seat beside me. Its bright yellow cover turned ochre in the light.

"The pharmacy school is just down there," repeated Mr. Wellington, pointing northward toward Swanson Street. "The school's only ten years old and the first in the United States. Pharmacy is just now being recognized as part of the medical profession, thanks in part to my father. Before, we were just druggists selling tea like Mr. Beck."

"At home, we had quite an apothecary."

"You southern girls are so well versed in herbal medicine. I always listen to home remedies. You learn a lot."

"My grandmother was the expert in our family." Stick as close as you can to the truth, I thought. Then I thought: Oh Lord. One day I'm going to have to tell him.

"Country medicine holds a great many surprises for us."

Thance Wellington was wearing a top hat and his heart on his sleeve. He looked baffled yet happy as he set his hat down on top of my sheet music. His strong, handsome face held an expression not far from that of Independence, that same puppy-dog warmth to his grin. A single black lock of hair strayed over his forehead, and I noticed how brown his face, hands, and wrists appeared, set off and surrounded by his white linen. Even seated, his long, rangy body seemed to spring from the ground with a force of its own. Nothing in my life had prepared me for the effect this somber, innocent-eyed northerner had upon me.

"Please don't laugh at me, Miss Petit."

"I'm not laughing, Mr. Wellington."

"There's something so final about this," he said mysteriously. His magnificent voice was low and tentative, as if he were transmitting a precious secret.

"I know," I replied just as mysteriously, although I was thinking, with utter tenderness, this was a final resting place. "How long have you been following me?" I asked.

"Oh, months—ever since that day at the conservatory."

"I see."

"No, you don't. This, this kind of thing . . . is not an ordinary occurrence . . . at least not for me. It blasts one's soul. The piece of membrane and gristle we call the brain. The organ which separates us from other primates because it recognizes death, this"—he tapped his head—"has gone as charred as coal because of you." Mr. Wellington looked around the teahouse dramatically.

"Of course, I wouldn't change anything," he said, smiling. A magnificent row of even white teeth appeared in the brown face.

Ah, my dearest, I thought, but I would. I would. But not you. Not you, Mr. Wellington.

"I know this is most irregular, but I hope you'll allow me to call upon you, now that I've frightened you half to death. I've got tickets for the last concert of the season at the Music Fund Hall. I've seen the program. I know you'll like it. Leon Bukovsky is conducting for the first time in Philadelphia. I know your tastes in music . . . please say you'll go with me. . . ." His hand trembled. It was a beautiful hand, long and squarish, with veins that stood on the surface and inspired a well of tenderness in me.

"I'll have to ask my guardian."

"Of course. I would like permission to write to you formally."

"Yes. I should show it to Uncle Adrian."

"Of course."

A shadow passed. Whether it was overhead in the sky or in the interior of my soul, I don't know.

"You won't change your mind, Miss Petit?"

"I won't change my mind, Mr. Wellington."

An hour passed. As we sat amongst the other couples, sipping our tea, I was grateful for Charlotte's coaching in the ways and formalities of the Philadelphia gentry. School had taught me manners, comportment, and polite conversation. Reading and being with Charlotte these last two years had polished my pretensions into something resembling the white girl I was impersonating. There would be, I knew, no major mistake, no untoward behavior. Harriet Hemings of Monticello was only a fleeting image that I caught in the mirror from time to time in a gesture or a thought, but firmly relegated to the past. Not only had I forgotten myself, I had forgotten my mother, my father; I played the orphan perfectly. I realized everyone was pretending about one thing or another. And everyone had secrets. Not necessarily something to hide, as I did, but thoughts, events, and disappointments that they would just as soon not tell the world. The simplicity of Virginian life now held a bemused charm as I realized how intricate, dangerous, and full of subterfuge the North was.

Moreover, being the first city north of the Mason-Dixon line, Philadelphia had its southern sympathies. Many southern families vacationed and shopped here. And as merchants and shipbuilders, Philadelphians did a great deal of their business with the southern states. I fretted over the slight chance that a Tidewater family with sharp eyes and a good memory might unmask me. Or was I being melodramatic? Whom could I possibly meet? And where?

"You're a cousin of Charlotte's, Mr. Wellington?" I asked him.

"Yes indeed."

"She's my best friend. I have no relatives."

"No family at all?"

"No family since a yellow fever epidemic in the Tidewater several years ago. My entire family was wiped out. My uncle Adrian is not really my uncle, but he's the closest kin I have left. In this world there are few so alone as I," I said with sincere feeling.

"Oh, my dear . . . Miss Harriet."

Words were no longer needed. A lassitude took hold of me as if I had swum a great distance or climbed a huge mountain, or drunk a great deal of Madeira. Perhaps it was only the intoxicating smell of Beck's China, India, and Orient Emporium, with its thousands of spices and hundreds of teas, amalgamated with an overwhelming, worldless odor of mystery, distance, and dreams. Perhaps it was Thance Wellington.

⌐

After that first invitation, the Music Fund Hall became one of the few places Thance and I were allowed to go alone. Petit and Mrs. Latouche considered it cultured enough and public enough not to create a problem of propriety for a modern couple, for that is what we had quickly formed. If older men, Charlotte's brother Amos, colleagues from the conservatory had harbored ideas about Harriet Petit, Thance Wellington quickly put them straight. Miss Petit was his girl.

After the last concert of the season, which ended on July 4, most families moved from the sweltering confines of the city to the outlying counties, Germantown, Cape May, Lemon Hill, Anamacora. I had been invited to Charlotte's family's house in Cape May for the summer. On the way to the concert, Charlotte had warned me, with some amusement on her part, what to expect.

"My mother thinks she ought to have a heart-to-heart talk with you at the Cape, since you are practically engaged. Since you have no womenfolk of your own, she's elected to explain . . . sex to you."

"But Mrs. Latouche has decided to explain sex to me."

"She doesn't like Mrs. Latouche, the caterer's wife."

Charlotte turned in her seat and left me to contemplate the idea of Mrs. Rupert Waverly telling me anything about the opposite sex. My lips twitched. I had my hands full trying to control Thance's passion and my more stubborn doubts. Charlotte scrutinized my face and screwed hers up prettily.

"To tell you the truth, I believe I shall never be seriously in love. I always discover something comical in a man, and then it is all over. If he doesn't seem ridiculous, he is awkward, or stupid, or tiresome. In short, there is always something that discovers the ass beneath the lion's skin . . . I shall not let myself be caught by any charm. Thank heaven the mania I have of finding out people's faults will prevent my falling in love with one and all of the Adonises on earth."

At the concert a certain abstracted calm took hold of me as I sat as close to Thance as I dared. I reveled in the voluptuous knowledge that I held him in such thrall that he would never renounce me, never substitute another for me, and never leave me. I thought less of my own yearning than of the torture I could inflict.

"You've never told me you love me," he whispered, as the orchestra began.

I felt Thance's panic as I withdrew myself, as I always did when he mentioned love. It was not a physical withdrawal, but a mental one, a sudden, slavish renegation of hope. It would come on me suddenly and without warning and could blind me like a bursting shell and cut my breath like a blizzard wind. I stared at the flickering stage lights. Tonight was one of those nights. Love with the joy drawn out of it: loneliness.

I turned away and concentrated on the stage. My middle finger touched every hairpin on my head as if each were a note of music. The gaslights lit the edges of my hair and made the fine edges burn like a bush. I looked at the score in my lap. The pristine notes on the white-ruled paper stared back mockingly. How could I love him and keep lying to him? Why was his suffering my joy and my shame?

The stage lights intensified and ghostly shadows spread like Chinese lacquer onto the singers, who floated on the music, pale as milk. I put my hand out and touched his knee gently.

"Don't be angry with me."

"I'm not angry with you; I'm in love with you."

"So you say."

Thance grasped my arm, encompassing it in his one hand, leaning forward.

"Damn you," he said, holding me prisoner.

I shook my head and glanced at the silhouettes of Charlotte, Daniel, and Luivicia that stirred with the flickering light. Then I studied Thance's profile outlined by the stage lights. I knew at least one of his secrets. Thance suffered badly. He had injured his twin in a terrible accident as a child and felt himself apart, marked like Cain.

"Kiss me before the lights come up." His voice came softly out of the shadow by my left shoulder, as if he had moved away from me.

"Why?" I exclaimed in surprise.

"Why?" he echoed sardonically.

I turned and looked at him fixedly, despairingly, for some moments. Then I leaned sideways and kissed him slowly. He pulled back, shocked, while I sat transfixed by the fire he had ignited in my joints. We couldn't touch, but my voice caressed him.

"Now what's wrong?" I drawled.

"There's a space between us," he said in a low, unconscious voice, as if he were speaking despite himself.

"But I'm very near," I whispered, gaily raising the tonality of my voice to pure chromatic sweetness, like a singer. For once, I felt really happy. I smoothed the score on my lap.

"You're distant. Always distant," he said, sulking.

"Well, we can't very well change that now," I said triumphantly, having him completely at my mercy. I could discern his face in the darkness as he leaned back in his chair. I found him beautiful in his stillness. His masculinity surrounded him like perfume, emanating from the dense, molded contours of his evening clothes, and I loved looking at him. I imagined the music circulating through his veins like blood. My hands slumbered on my open score.

The notes fell like soft raindrops, mingling with the slight rustling of my skirts. I deliberately suppressed the formidable attentiveness and unyielding concentration of Thance's presence and submerged myself in the music. I felt myself drifting into a profound sleep, the first great sleep of my life.

"It's fine for you," Thance whispered resentfully. "You aren't in love. But this wound, this infinite opening of my soul, Harriet, this unfolding of my own self, leaving me unfinished, homeless, dissected like a piece of flesh under my own microscope, is the cruelest of events. I can't analyze it or slice it or study it. I will have to take hold of myself. I will have to keep the unfinished business of this yearning through everything you can inflict upon me, but I will never give up. I will not leave you alone, whatever you say or do. When I contemplate you, Harriet, I feel the same as when I look into my microscope and find the quenching knowledge of life's possibilities, the magic of every molecule of matter there, squirming under my eyes. You hold the key to the riddle of my own existence. You may just think I'm tearing at your heart like a little boy who pulls off flies' wings or tears open flower pods just to see what's inside."

I looked up, barely aware of Thance's words. Why, I wondered, was an icy wind blowing through my heart?

In the close dimness that smelled faintly of whale oil and perfume, the music swelled to its climax. I read the notes off my score, my face flushed and burning, immobile in the velvet plush armchair of Charlotte's mother's box.

"It's beautiful . . . beautiful," I sang in a strange, rhapsodic voice. "There's something so final about it," I whispered. "Like the end of myself. The final resting place. My home. Do you see what I mean, Thance? The music seems so fragile, golden, soft, heavy, yet like gossamer made only of warmth, its brightness burns the pith of my mind . . . blasts my soul. Oh, Thance. You're left helpless, sightless, mindless. You don't want to be free—for anything to be different. Utterly enslaved, you suffer. Do you know what it's like to suffer when you are a woman? A silk whip tears you, and every stroke cutting into your flesh."

"Oh God," groaned Thance. "You sound like a victim of some magical rite, torn apart and given to the heavens!"

But I wasn't talking about the music.

"Other men have fallen in love, Wellington; you're not the first. Nor the last. Beware of southern girls, my friend." I laughed.

The lights rose and applause broke out as if for my last line. I looked around, fingering my gloves, searching the face I so adored, proud and afraid at the same time. Perhaps I could exasperate him to death, I thought. But he simply smiled weakly, shaking his head, his tranquil, dark eyes shining with love.

I wasn't always so cruel. Thance and I had wonderful times that year. We walked Independence past Philadelphia Hall, took boat rides together at the Fairmount Waterworks, or returned to sip tea at Beck's Emporium. Charlotte, Daniel, Amos, Thance, Cornelius, Robert, Frederick, Susy, and Clyde and I ran in a pack that spring. A few weeks before graduation from Bryn Mawr in June, Thance invited me to visit his laboratory at the university.

"I've been researching something fantastic. I must show you."

"How shall I get in?" I said. "They won't let a woman in."

"Why don't you dress up like a boy?" Thance said without thinking. "You'd make a pretty apothecary's assistant. Haven't you ever wanted to be a boy?"

"Always. There's not a woman alive who hasn't wanted to be a man at some point in her life," I replied without smiling.

Apothecaries and their assistants wore long, saffron-colored smocks, cut like double-breasted butchers' smocks, with huge buttons and tiny pillbox hats of the same heavy sailcloth cotton. Often they wore them over street clothes; unbuttoned, they billowed like yellow fins. They sometimes wore white cuffs on the bottoms of their sleeves to protect their wrists from various compounds and minerals, like the corrosive acids and, above all, mercury. I was entitled, as an assistant, to an indigo smock only, with a matching hat. This was how Thance and I were dressed as we raced up the steps of the Pharmacy School building at First and Sansom streets. A nonchalant concierge waved us both in, and I tried to keep a straight face as we marched down the corridor to his office, our hands clasped behind our backs, my feet pinched in Petit's two-sizes-too-small boots. Thance's reading spectacles hung around his neck, and as the light from the overhead skylights struck them from time to time, they flashed like a coded message.

"Har . . . Harry!" he said, laughing. "Come," he continued as he seized me by the arm. "I've been reading some incredible articles on a new criminal science called digital fingerprinting. You take an imprint in ink of the fingertips of each hand of any person. Each individual can be identified precisely and scientifically in one hundred percent of cases, for no two people's fingerprints are the same . . . isn't that incredible? The lines of your fingertips have never been duplicated in another human being in a million years—not once, and they never will! They are more personal, more exact than . . . your intimate soul . . . and they are scientific."

"You mean," I said slowly, wrapped in my own dilemma, "that no one can ever really change the identity they were born with?"

"Identity is not a matter of change or chance. It is a fixed particularity given at birth to every human being. And it is inimitable. Let me show you."

Thance led me toward a pile of books and papers on a desk illuminated even in broad daylight by a beaconlike gas lamp. Gently he took my index finger and brought it down upon an ink pad and then pressed it upon a piece of white paper. The minuscule swirls and lines of the tip of my finger were reproduced on the paper. I stared in astonishment. Then he did the same with the remaining fingers of my left hand.

"The ancient Chinese and Egyptians both knew about fingerprints as a means of identification, but they never connected it with differentiating each man from all the rest of the human species, never saw it extended far beyond anything human imagination had invented up until then. Now I have just received a copy of the thesis of the scientist Johannes Purkinje, a professor of physiology at Breslau University in Austria who has just published a fantastic paper on this incredible phenomenon of nature. He has demonstrated that fingerprints can establish the identity of a person at different stages of his life from babyhood to old age and for some time after his death.

"Look, Harriet. These are my fingerprints, and I asked my brother Thor to send me his. They are not identical even though we are twins! We can be different morally, intellectually, and biologically. By nature of our fingerprints, we are as distinct as if one of us was black and the other one white."

"You mean you and your brother are identical in every way, except for your fingerprints?"

"Fingerprints have the unique merit of retaining all their particularities throughout life, and so afford a more infallible criterion of identity than any other bodily feature. My twin could try to impersonate me, and he could in many ways, but his fingerprints would betray him.

"These," he said, holding up my hand, "are your fixed human personality, given to you at birth, an individuality that can be depended upon with *absolute* certainty. You can only be you! Lasting, unchangeable, always recognizable, and easily proven. This autograph cannot be counterfeited or disguised or hidden away; it never fades, becomes illegible, or changes shape or form by the passage of time—incredible."

Thance pressed my hand against his cheek, perhaps in affection, perhaps forgetting the ink remaining on my fingers, resulting in my leaving five black marks on his cheek. I looked up in horror, and Thance, realizing what he had done but never dreaming of what he had really done, began to laugh. Then he raised my hand to my own face and left upon it the same black marks.

"There," he said, "now we are truly and scientifically one—even after death—for we carry the same fingerprints."

A chill ran up my spine as I turned and looked into the laboratory mirror. Could those marks prove I was a black fugitive slave instead of a free white

Virginian? Almost reading my thoughts, Thance went on, "Great expectations were raised and then dashed, namely that fingerprints could indicate race and temperament."

"You mean Nature invented this inviolable differentiation, but not according to race?"

"Exactly." Thance looked surprised.

"You can't tell if a man is black or white . . . or Chinese?"

"No."

"And yet it is the only true identity fixed by God?"

"Nature," said Thance, confused yet moved.

"God has created us separate, with a separate, unique destiny, and then given us proof of it—given us proof of our own uniqueness of soul, our own God-given peculiarity, right here in our hands."

"Why, Harriet, that's beautiful."

"It's proof of God's infinite variety—of the infinite possibilities given to man for discovery . . . like music . . . like mathematics."

I turned away as fear stole my breath and turned my forehead dewy.

And I had thought I could hide. . . .

＿)

Slowly I took out my handkerchief and methodically, without rushing, removed the black spots from Thance's face, then from my own, and lastly from my fingers. As I replaced my handkerchief, my hand touched my dagger. No man on earth would ever know I was the President's daughter.

"Marry me, Harriet."

I looked full at him. He had not sensed my terrible panic.

"Thance, no." I looked at my smudged fingerprints. They were proof—proof of my dishonesty and fraud. They couldn't prove I was black, but they proved I was a bastard for all times. . . . an uncontrollable desire to scream or to laugh engulfed me.

"Please don't laugh at me."

"It is I who doesn't want to be laughed at," I whispered.

"Do you love me?"

Defiantly I lifted my mouth. Thance's lips were soft, deep, and delicate. He waited a few minutes, lost in the kiss. Then I felt a shade of sadness come over him.

"I shouldn't even be with you in public without a chaperon, let alone kissing you in the middle of the University of Pennsylvania," he said. "My God! I've just kissed a man!"

We both began to laugh.

At the same moment, a grimace of mocking irony at my own charade tore at my mouth.

Which disguise, I wondered, was the funniest? White or male? I smiled enigmatically. Thance grinned happily, filling me with contagious delight because that was how a baby smiled.

"Thance, oh, Thance," I laughed helplessly.

I pulled his head down and kissed him into bewilderment. Dressed like a man, free from encompassing corsets and heavy skirts, my body molded itself along the length of his, and I felt his own contours blend into mine. I was more like some powerful, fitful sigh than a woman, my muscles elastic, my body mindless, my spirit soulless, fitting into Thance in one perfect forceful line. How strange, I thought, this breathless awful freedom. Not far away somebody was singing in a voice that resembled his.

> And so, being young and dipt in folly
> I fell in love with melancholy.
> My heart to joy at the same tone.
> And all I loved—I lov'd alone

⌒

"He is asking you! He's bought the ring! A magnificent ruby!"

I bit my lip. "Charlotte, it's not true."

"Oh, but it is. There's nothing like Philadelphia Unitarians to keep a secret. Of course, you'll be the last to know. But if you don't choose me as your best maid, I'll kill you."

"Charlotte!"

"My mother says that of course everything must be discussed, the marriage contract, the engagement. But the widow Wellington was most comprehensive and most generous. She realizes these are modern times and one can no longer choose one's children's spouses."

"But she hardly knows me."

"It seems you made a great impression on her, and she thinks you are a fine musician and very beautiful. But she's frankly weary of what she calls southern belles, spoiled, indolent, useless creatures that they are." Charlotte giggled at this, and I let out a snort that rocked her back on her heels.

"A southern belle . . ."

"A poor southern belle—it seems they are the worst . . ."

"*Who has died*, I thought, *who has married, who has hanged himself because they cannot marry . . .*"

"Well, his mother is under the impression he did ask and that you have said yes—that day in the laboratory."

"Charlotte, I said no." I turned away from her to try to get my bearings.

"Well, if you did, nobody heard you. And you're not serious! You wouldn't turn down Thance. A boy like that—"

"Charlotte, I can't . . ."

"Oh, it's so exciting!" she rattled on. "The only missing element is what the mysterious, reclusive Thor will think."

"I understand he is abroad."

"In Africa. He joined an expedition to the Natal to gather medicinal plants. It seems there are more specimens in the Natal than anywhere else in the world. The Sutos and the Zulus are famous for their pharmacopoeia."

"Africa . . ."

"He's been gone for almost three years."

"Is he really Thance's double?"

"Oh yes, although he's older by twenty minutes."

"What's he like? Thance never speaks of him."

Charlotte lowered her voice.

"Thance blames himself, but it wasn't his fault."

"What wasn't his fault?"

"The accident."

"What accident?"

"We were adolescents of fourteen or fifteen. Thance and Thor had been playing in the barn of the family farm at Anamacora, and their play had turned a little rough. Half quarreling, Thance pushed Thor off the hayloft and he fell quite a distance. Under normal circumstances it would have been a harmless fall for a strong boy, but hidden under the hay was a pitchfork that had been forgotten or abandoned by someone. Thor fell on it—it punctured one of his testicles. It was a terrible wound. He almost bled to death. According to the doctors, it has rendered him sterile. Thance feels he castrated his twin and murdered his progeny. It has tormented him. The accident came not more than a year after their father had died of typhoid while treating American sailors in the naval squadron patrolling the Barbary Coast."

I stared at Charlotte and thought how much the accident sounded like some sorrowful tale of slavery.

I asked Charlotte how she had found out such details, which should have been kept hidden from a young girl of her age and station.

"Thance talked to me as a sister when he was trying to come to grips with his own remorse."

"And Thor?"

"We know Thor is a survivor. In many ways he prevailed. He finished school and signed on for his first scientific expedition. He's been gone more or less ever since. He recognized Thance as the head of the family. No one really knows what he's like. I do remember that the twins had telepathy between them. They could communicate with each other without uttering a word. I know Thor will like you, but never let him know that you know, or that I told you, about the accident. He hates to be pitied."

So do I, I thought.

"Of course not. I thank you for telling me. It . . . it explains many things about Thance," I said, but what I thought was that Thor's wound was one of those unyielding, incomprehensible sorrows that only a slave woman had the power and the knowledge and the will to assuage—one of those slavery-like mutilations that never healed, never ceased, to throb unendingly in unfathomable grief.

I gazed at Charlotte with new respect.

"You're right," I said, "about being sheltered and spoiled, of thinking the world owes you happiness."

I took Charlotte's hand and drew it against my breast. I listened to my own heart and the stillness around us.

~

The parlor of the Wellingtons' house, which stood on the waterfront near Bainbridge Street, was ostentatiously simple. Every object in the large, airy rooms had its place and enough space to set it off. The Wellingtons were people of good circumstances. The druggist Wellington had left his widow a large, flourishing pharmacy and laboratory and several pharmaceutical patents and licenses. His twin sons had followed in their father's footsteps. He had two daughters—one married, one unmarried—and his youngest son had entered the medical profession. The widow Wellington resembled no one if not my father. It was as if I were staring at a female Thomas Jefferson. Her hair was dead-white flax, and she wore it crimped into a pompadour in front and swept back into a net behind. She had sea blue eyes like him, except they bordered on violet instead of aquamarine, and she had a low, melodious voice shorn of the familiar harshness I had come to recognize as upper-class Philadelphian. She sat in a large, cherry-colored, covered armchair, and the reflections from the harbor stroked her face with gold and green. She was not old, perhaps fifty-three or -four, but her body must have settled early into stoutness and middle age. She had rosy cheeks and was dressed all in black, with a cameo pinned at her throat. As I remembered her, she had none of the energy or vibrancy of my mother, or even my grandmother. Why I thought of Elizabeth Hemings at that moment I will never know, but my grand-mother's face came back to me and her voice resounded in the quiet room.

Get that freedom for your children.

Of course, I had not for one moment thought about my children—never considered their status in this deception. The one-sixteenth of black blood which constituted the one drop that condemned them to the condition of their mother.

"You are not a Catholic."

It was not a question but a statement.

"No, Mrs. Wellington, I grew up without a formal religion."

"I don't believe in mixed marriages."

"I beg your pardon?"

"In marriages between Roman Catholics and Protestants or Jews. I thought because of your Creole blood you might be Catholic."

"Thance told me that as a scientist, he was attached to no religion."

"Exactly, Harriet. I may call you Harriet? His father believed the same. They are both deists."

"So was mine. But I am not opposed to converting if this would make you happy. The Unitarian faith is, I feel, the religion of the future."

My coldblooded appraisal of Mrs. Wellington told me that candor in all things would be appreciated. My visit had been orchestrated to the last degree. Petit had left me at the door and I had entered the front room alone, hesitant yet assured, shy yet serene. I had worn a green tartan dress with a plaited bodice, white collar and cuffs, and large mutton sleeves. My pillbox hat was green, and it had a green veil dotted in red. The outfit complemented my hair and accentuated my fairness. I had prayed I wouldn't like Mrs. Wellington, thus making it easier to deceive her. But I did like her. There was frankness in her smile and attentiveness in her face. There was warmth and welcome. I wouldn't have to lie. She would see what she wanted to see—a strange, countrified, Virginian orphan, as poor as peas and potatoes but fairly well-read, with "possibilities," a fake pedi-gree, and southern sensibilities.

I had curtsied, European-style, when I entered—a long, low, graceful swoop which had pleased her—and at Petit's suggestion, I had kissed her hand as young women did with older women in Europe. She had flushed with embarrassment and pleasure and had left her small plump hand in mine.

"Come, my dear, tell me about yourself, Miss Petit. Thance has bent my ears back about you, but that isn't the same thing. I understand you and Thance would like to be married at Christmas."

"That's Thance's wish."

"Would it be possible for you to set a date when we know when Thor can arrive?

"Of course, we want him here for the wedding."

Mrs. Wellington smiled proudly. "You had four brothers, I understand?"

"Yes . . . all dead."

"Oh, you poor, poor child. Life is sometimes so pitiless." She paused then, looking me over from head to toe. "I want to be frank with you, Harriet. I have no interest in thwarting my son's desire. I admit I would have preferred a girl from Scranton to a Virginian. Not that I have a prejudice against southern women, but I have found that in general, they learn from the cradle that southern belle's Machiavellian talent for manipulation. The southern climate encourages indolence, and the proliferation of Negro servants a certain . . . shall we say, helplessness. These defects do not diminish with marriage, but are reinforced by the pampering and indulgent possessiveness of their menfolk. The climate also encourages sensuality, and owning other people and having the power of life and death over them induces a kind of reckless fatalism. I'm afraid the work ethic we instill in northern girls is greatly lacking in southern women. . . ."

"Madam, where did you learn such erroneous information concerning southern ladies? I assure you, most of them lead the lives of pioneer women, sharing the work of running farms and plantations with their men. They rise at dawn, organize large houses, have heavy social engagements, are nurses, doctors, midwives, cooks, and farmhands as well as southern belles. There are more log cabins in the South than mansions. Since most live on isolated farms and plantations where everything must be handmade and the farm self-sufficient, they must be seamstresses and weavers, candlemakers, soapmakers, honey-gatherers. When they have slaves, they must train and supervise them, rising at dawn and retiring long after their men and servants. They must give birth to their children in the wilderness, often without the assurance of even a midwife, and as always, Nature in the guise of storms, floods, bugs, drought, epidemics. . . . All must be dealt with on God's terms. I do believe, Mrs. Wellington, that you do us an injustice."

"And your family, Harriet?" she continued smoothly without thinking, while despite myself, my blood boiled in indignation.

"When I *had* a family, it was large and slaveholding, but it no longer exists, except in memory. I am a girl alone in the world who has no past and is uncertain of her future."

Mrs. Wellington softened visibly. "Oh, I know that to keep such people as half-civilized Negroes in line takes a lot of courage. Living in such close proximity to such savages can only be accomplished by strict discipline and segregation and violent punishment. White women who must live in constant fear of rape and revolt from Negroes must use gratuitous cruelty as a method of self-defense.

"My poor Harriet. I am here to remedy your past. My son loves you very much."

"And I love him," I replied defiantly.

"I do not believe you mentioned what church you attend."

Again, I thought, this question of religion.

"Why, that of Charlotte," I replied.

"Why, that is my church. Have I passed my future daughter-in-law without realizing it?"

"I imagine you have your pew, while I sit in the gallery."

"It's true. I usually leave before the gallery descends."

Imagine my gratification that Mrs. Wellington had supplied me with my excuse for never having been to church at all.

"I would like you to have a talk with Reverend Crocket soon. You must get Charlotte to sponsor your membership as soon as possible."

As the afternoon wore on, in the safe, comfortable room furnished with solid English furniture, polished brass, and colorful throw rugs, bits and pieces of music came back to me. Not music I was practicing, nor music that was in the popular repertoire of the day; the melodies I heard that long afternoon were old slave-working songs, crying songs, half-remembered nursery rhymes and children's rounds, gospels, and even old Gabriel Prosser's stomping rhyme to which white people danced without knowing the words. The notes swelled through my mind like the sunbeams that danced through the tall white curtains. Suddenly I wanted to go home. I wanted my mother. . . .

"*Maman,*" I whispered, and then blushed scarlet when I realized I had said it out loud and that Mrs. Wellington had heard me and had risen and taken me by the shoulders.

"My dear," she said, "come meet your future sisters."

She rang, and her daughters Tabitha and Lividia entered. They were tall, dark, and good looking, with clear complexions and raven black hair. I was far fairer than either of them. Tabitha was married to Janson Ellsworth, a regimental doctor, and Lividia was only fifteen, yet as tall as I and as mature as her sister. I tried to sort my feelings. These Wellington women would constitute my new family. They would, as time passed, supersede my real family at Monticello: Critta and Dolly, Ursula and Bette, Peter and John, Dolly and Wormley. Eston, Beverly, Madison, and Mama. There were the whites as well—Martha and Thomas Mann, Ellen and Cornelia, Meriwether and Francis, Virginia and the President. All of a sudden, they all seemed to crowd into the room along with Tabitha, Lividia, and Mrs. Wellington until they, and my lie, had taken up all the space, milling around the quiet room, each with indelible sets of fingerprints, touching each and any object that came under their gaze, sliding around the mantelpiece, the fireplace, the piano, the silk curtains, the waxed breakfront, the library table, the bookcase, the Chinese vases, the lacquer boxes, the Queen Anne wing chairs, the silver teapot. Gingerly I touched the metronome on the piano. My blackened fingerprints would be left on this new family as well as the old.

I sat down at the pianoforte without speaking, and played simple pieces, skimming over the ivory and ebony in time with the ticktocking metronome and with my coldblooded lie. My fingers flew over the keys as lightly as they could for I feared they would leave black stains on the clean surface. But nothing happened.

8

There are absurdities into which those of us run who usurp the theme
of God and dictate to Him what He should have done.

Thomas Jefferson

The law library at the University of Pennsylvania had been built in 1797, as a replica of Louis XIV's Bibliothèque Nationale in Paris. It had a cast-iron-and-glass dome which gave it natural light, a balcony around its four sides, and a collection of forty thousand volumes. Thance had once told me that the vaulted crystal palace which now surrounded me had cost almost seven million dollars.

I was dressed in a short jacket and trousers, my braid hidden under the high collar of the wide-shouldered jacket and a wide-brimmed blue felt hat, a pair of round, steel-rimmed spectacles perched on my nose, a short lock of clipped hair falling over one eye. I looked very much like any of the other young clerks doing research for one of the many lawyers in the area, disguised as a boy as I had been that day at Thance's laboratory.

The custodian hardly looked up as I walked by, and the bored librarian simply indicated to me where to sign in. As I penned Thance's initials, my hands trembled inside leather gloves, which I wore to conceal the fact that my hands weren't those of a man. Even if women, Negroes, Jews, and dogs were prohibited, what could they do, I thought, except ask me politely to leave?

I quickly wrote out my request and silently handed it to the clerk. My heart accelerated as I slipped into the nearest stall at the end of a long row of desks screwed to the hardwood floor. Whale-oil lamps with green glass shades were poised at each stall. I must have closed my eyes, because suddenly I heard a loud *thump* as three oversized leather volumes punched in gold slammed down beside me.

"Please sign here, sir."

Again, I forged Thance's signature. Slowly I pulled off my gloves and pulled on the white clerk's cuffs and gloves used to protect the book pages and my jacket sleeves. I stared at the title before I lifted the cover of the first volume. *The Black Laws of the State of Pennsylvania—Status Regulating the Comportment of Free Blacks in the State of Pennsylvania.*

> *A free black convicted of committing fornication or adultery with a white shall be sold into servitude for seven years. The white party punished as the law directs in cases of adultery or fornication to one year in prison and payment of a hundred-dollar fine. Whites who shall cohabit or dwell with any Negroes under pretense of being married shall also receive such punishment.*
>
> *In cases of interracial marriage, the free black is to be sold into slavery, and children from such a marriage are to be put out to service until they reach the age of twenty-one. The minister who performs such a ceremony shall be fined one hundred dollars.*
>
> *Any free black or mulatto harboring or entertaining any Negro, Indian, or mulatto slave or fugitive will be condemned to twenty-one lashes and a payment of restitution. If unable to pay the fine, he will be sold into slavery to pay his debt.*

A grimace of mocking irony at my own naiveté tore at my mouth, which hung open in surprise. So this was the North, was it? This was where I was to be married in a church, before God and society by an ordained minister. This was where I was to walk down the aisle, amidst music and flowers, to my bridegroom.

The book-lined walls seemed to explode into endless space. There was no escape. Wherever I went, the eternal hell of negrophobia went with me. Whatever limits there were to this planet, I would never be safe. My crime would follow me to death, and if I persisted I would carry everything and everyone I loved with me. For these pages spoke not of slaves but of freedmen. Black freedmen. There could not be, as Adrian Petit had pointed out, a white slave, just as there could not be a black American. It was a contradiction in terms—an aberration in a white man's country.

The words danced across the page like notes of music, and a persistent tune droned on and on in my head. Stupidly, I was humming Yankee Doodle! Then I realized it was the buzz of a muffled scream against each affront on the life of a free person of color in Pennsylvania: forbidden to vote, forbidden to run for office, to bear arms, to pilot riverboats, to serve in the militia, to meet in groups, to carry a weapon, to be found on the streets after eleven P.M., to loiter, to be drunk in public, to be more than ten minutes from his or her residence without being accompanied by a white person, to practice medicine, to practice law, to practice usury on a white person, to own a private carriage. Free colored people had separate courts, separate schools, separate churches, separate cemeteries. They were dealt the death penalty for rape, buggery, or burglary inflicted on a white person. They were publicly whipped for robbing, stealing, perpetrating fraud, or carrying a pistol, sword, or other arm. Free Negroes were required to pay a poll tax of five hundred dollars to the state to guarantee their good behavior.

I read on, my face flushed, my chest burning, my braid slipping out of my high collar. Humiliation and foulness flooded me as if the ink on the pages flowed like poison into my blood. We, the Hemingses . . . I felt naked. This was far worse than rape, this violation of one's most intimate and cherished illusions. I heard the voices of all of those I loved, of the family I missed, of those like me who loved their country despite what had been done to them. Even this secondhand knowledge of my father's country was not really mine because I didn't belong to the country of which he had been President.

The custodian threw a casual glance my way. I didn't seem to be taking any notes.

A lone tear fell. Then another, so hot, so caustic that I wondered that it didn't burn straight through the page. I had found what I had been looking for. My place.

I looked up in alarm as the library clerk approached. He was coming to get me. I half rose, then sank again into the leather armchair, almost knocking over the oil lamp.

"Here you are, sir, the bound copies of the *Richmond Recorder* for the year 1802. Would you sign this, please?"

The volume was as heavy as a child in my arms. Mechanically I opened the book, riffling the pages until the article dated September 1, 1802, emerged as if from an underground well. It was called "The President Again," and it began:

It was well known that this man, whom it delighteth the people to honor, keeps and, for many years, has kept, as his concubine, one of his slaves. Her name is Sally. The name of her eldest son is Tom, who bears a striking resemblance to the President. The boy is ten or twelve. His mother went to France with Mr. Jefferson and his two daughters. The delicacy of this arrangement must strike every portion of common sensibility. What a sublime pattern for an American ambassador to place before the eyes of two young ladies. . . . By this wench Sally, our President has had several children. . . .

So this was what my mother and grandmother had meant all these years when they referred to the "troubles with Callender" and "James's tragic end." They had been like litanies to me for so long that they had actually run together and become "TroubleswithCallender" and "James'stragicend." I traced my fingers along the black letters. This was the real world. My father had been defamed and my mother trampled in the dust. Now an old, sick, and forgotten man, shunned by his own country, very nearly bankrupt, he was still writhing in the trap of his crime of miscegenation.

There is not an individual in the neighborhood of Charlottesville who does not believe the story; and not a few know it. . . . Behold the favorite, the firstborn of republicanism! The pinnacle of all that is good and great! In open consummation of an act which tends to subvert the policy, the happiness, and even the existence of this country.

Why was my mother, I wondered, such a dangerous and overwhelming subversion of the happiness of the United States of America, which my father had invented?

The noise of the sea roared in my ears. I looked around to see who else had heard, but there was only the sordid green penumbra of recorded history prohibited to women, Jews, Negroes, and dogs.

Mute! Mute! Mute! Yes, very mute! will all these republican
printers of political biographical information be upon this point.
Whether they stir or not, they must feel themselves like a horse in
quick-sands.

But it was I who was standing on quicksand. I had no breath left in me.
I was sinking. The words and letters blurred on the page until they forced
a groan like that of a woman giving birth. My hand rose to the throat which
had emitted the sound. I looked around, but not one of the scattered clerks
or students bent over their notes and books had heard.

"They will plunge deeper," I read, "until no assistance can save them."

My eyes went to the end of the article, seeking escape, seeking relief, but
finding none.

We should be glad to hear of its refutation.

We give it to the world under the firmest belief that a refutation
never can be made. The African Venus is said to officiate as
house-keeper at Monticello. When Mr. Jefferson has read this
article, he will find leisure to estimate how much has been lost or
gained by so many unprovoked attacks upon

J. T. CALLENDER

"James T. Callender." I repeated the familiar name, then rose unsteadily,
leaning my weight against the open book.

I don't remember leaving the library, but my departure must have been
quite ordinary, for no hand came to rest on my arm, no word restrained me,
no gesture of mockery or derision followed me out of the halls. Once outside,
I leaned against a tree and was violently ill.

∽

"Don't hate your father," Petit said.

We were sitting in the restaurant of Brown's Hotel while my guardian tried
to explain.

"I think at this moment I hate everyone in the whole world."

"Not Thance, surely."

"Yes. Even him."

"I know you think something like what happened to your parents can happen to you and Thance."

"Of course I don't. We are, after all, only ordinary mortals, not the President of the United States and the famous Dusky Sally."

"Don't hate your mother, either," said Petit.

"I hate myself. For being afraid and lying all the same, for listening to insults hurled at my race when white people think they are amongst themselves. I hate Thance for loving me and obliging me to lie for his sake—in order to keep him. And then I'm ashamed of hating him because I truly love him and I will not lie to someone I love."

Petit's thick eyebrows drew together in one uninterrupted line shadowing his eyes.

"You should never have read that article."

"There was no way to avoid it. I was *born* to that article," I said in disgust.

"But to dress up like a boy!"

"I had to get into the library, Adrian! They don't allow women or dogs or Jews, or *Negroes* inside. They don't even bother *mentioning* Negroes; it's too absurd—like a monkey talking. When I exited from that bastion of hypocrisy, I threw up all over my disguise."

"Oh, Harriet."

"Don't you understand, Petit? Thance is just another one of them. I'm in love with the enemy . . . just like my mother. I vowed *never* to be like my mother!"

I stared defiantly at Petit, challenging him to contradict me. By this time, I had spent enough time with white people to see the side that they reveal when they were among their own color. And it was as demeaning as the side southern masters showed their slaves. They might conceal their hatred in public, but I, a fly on the wall, an alien, a black woman, had learned what white people really thought about blacks, and knew that their anger at me for having tricked them into believing I was one of them would be immutable. Hadn't this trickery been the real source of Sykes's anger all those years ago? Around us the lunchtime diners swirled in multicolor, resembling the cashmere shawl I wore. Everything fit into place. Each gesture, sound, and movement: well-fed, happy, white northerners. Only I was out of place.

"I realize the language must have shocked you."

"Oh, it wasn't the crudeness of the language, but the intensity of the hatred . . . murderous hatred. My mother was one of the most hated women in the United States! That's what made me sick to my stomach."

"You've grown up in one afternoon."

"I want to go home."

"You impersonate a white girl and then don't know how to act like one," Petit said cruelly. "Do you really think happiness and adoration will pass this close to you again?"

"It's against the law," I whispered.

"What's against the law?"

"Miscegenation."

"What's that?"

"Mixed marriage. Amalgamation. The marriage of a white man to a black woman, or vice-versa, is a *crime* punishable by fine and imprisonment. A man from South Carolina invented the word. It's not in Webster's dictionary. It's not a real word at all. . . .

"One-thirty-second of black blood brands you a Negro and thus ineligible to marry a white. It's called the one-drop law."

Petit laughed out loud, and the waiter near us turned obligingly.

"Oh, Harriet"—he lowered his voice—"there are also laws against fornication and adultery, but the world is full of prostitutes and cuckolded husbands."

"And illegitimate children," I added, "like me."

"Many very great men have had illegitimate children—most princes of the blood and even some popes! It is as old as the world, Harriet."

"I always believed that somehow, in the end, he would recognize us children. Now I know he never will."

Petit said nothing, for he knew what I said was true.

꙳

Petit took me to an address on Vine Street not far from Brown's Hotel. "This is where your uncle James died. I have always believed his death was connected with that newspaper article Callender wrote. I have always believed that it was James who alerted Callender to the story. The story was so well protected from the outside world by everybody, white and black, in Albemarle County that it must have been a family member. Callender was a dangerous, ambitious journalist who earned his living and certain other rewards by exposing scandals concerning political figures. That's what your father hired him for in the first place.

"James had been trying to get your mother to run away for years. He was obsessed by her freedom. Twice he came back for her from Europe. He blamed himself for what happened in Paris, though he surely couldn't have prevented your father and mother from falling in love. He was determined to extricate your mother from your father's grasp. James was in Richmond a few months before the scandal broke, and so was Callender—in jail. I believe James informed on your father to Callender in the hope that the scandal would force him to send your mother and you children away, which meant in effect freeing them. Thus James would have rescued his sister—at least in his eyes. He told me himself that his manhood was at stake and that he would never be free himself until your mother was free.

"When James realized this last strategy had failed, and that he had only succeeded in endangering your mother and contaminating the only reality of her life, he was filled with remorse. Either your father's political friends caught up with him and he didn't put up a fight, or he, in fact, took his own life before they could do it for him. James was found hung in his boarding-house room. Callender was found drowned in the Potomac in three feet of water, and *that* was no suicide. Both deaths were blamed on drunkenness. But no one has ever figured out how James could have hung himself from the rafters with no chair, or how a grown man could drown himself in a puddle.

"It was an election year for your father. The scandal spread to London and Paris. In America, the stories made front-page news, a medley of pornography, absurdity, and political satire. You were the child of that scandal, Harriet. You had just been born."

I looked up at the blank facade of the narrow, three-story, red brick house with its long, narrow windows in white trim and its three white marble steps. The dark, mysterious windows seemed impenetrable. All my questions hurled themselves against that implacable silence, the tall lilac door, the polished brass knocker. If there were voices from the past, they didn't speak to me.

"And my father didn't do anything about it, Petit? Reply or challenge Callender to a duel? He didn't lie about it? Or get others to lie for him?"

"No."

"Where were you?"

"In Washington, the eye of the storm! Such an avalanche of calumny. Your mother was the talk of the United States, and your father had no choice except to barricade himself behind silence in the President's House and wait for the wind to change. Your grandmother sent Martha to Washington to preside over the presidential table and dampen the gossip. James thought your father would exile your mother. But the President did no such thing. And so here you are. Here we are, twenty years later."

"And you think someone found out it was James who had informed on my father to Callender?"

"Well . . . it was hardly a secret in Richmond, all this. Nor in Charlottesville. Someone of the gentry broke the protective wall of silence around Monticello."

"But you think it was James?"

"It's indeed strange that both James and Callender died violent deaths."

"And what was he like, this Callender, when he was alive? You knew him?"

"Callender called himself the best political writer in America—a great journalist who was unjustly maligned and persecuted. He was called a drunkard even in an epoch of heroic drinkers, a coward, and a hired jour- nalistic assassin, but, strangely enough, never an outright liar by any of his victims. He had a nose for dirt and human folly. A lust for the weaknesses of the powerful and the vulnerability of men in the throes of passionate, illicit attachment. He also had his own set of perverted rules justified by a lot of hogwash about freedom of the press and the people's right to know. He thought James Thompson Callender deserved better than what was his lot in life.

"He was a huge man physically, with blondish hair prematurely white and a handsome pugilist's face. Lord knows how many times he had been beaten up. He had the high color of a native Scotsman and of a heavy drinker. And though he was a young man, he affected a beard and spectacles and a queue of gray hair to make himself seem older. He stooped because of his height, limped because of a gunshot wound, and staggered because he was usually drunk. Most gentlemen would not pay him the compliment of challenging him to a duel. It was said he had a fine political mind, yet it is impossible to say whether he ever considered any event rationally or without prejudice. He was therefore a very dangerous man—arrogant, too—and as a specimen of white trash, he knew the American people loved reading scandal much better than dull truth.

"Callender was a kind of magnet of calumny and misfortune, a man on the outside of respectable society trying to get in, and knowing he never would. He was a classic scapegoat, yet one who could make the rich and powerful tremble. I suppose this is what appealed to James, so blinded by his own obsession and hatred of a former master who was also his half brother-in-law. At any rate, I know James and Callender knew each other in Philadelphia. James made the fatal mistake of taking him into his confidence.

"I've often noticed that the more liberal and democratic one's thinking is, the less tolerant of political attack one is. Dictators are a lot more philosophi- cal about being dragged through the mud—at least until they decide to chop your head off. Callender's attacks threw your father into a fury. He became even more rigid and secretive, retreating into his ivory tower and letting his subordinates take the heat. Your father was too proud ever to admit loving your mother. A man who has always had his way, as your father has, seldom finds happiness. His luck, or power, breeds unrealistic desires which can never be fully satisfied. He is progressively worn down by impatience, indignation, a sense of betrayal and injustice. During those scandal years, your father's heart was worn down minute after minute, like water wearing down a stone. And Callender could never bring himself to offer him mercy because . . . because your father . . . had had his way . . . for so long. Do you understand? Of course, your father and his key men considered Callender a common blackmailer. I never forgot the terrible scene I was inadvertently witness to. 'The money is mine, not as your high-flown charity,' Callender shouted, 'but as my due as hush money.'

" 'You are a damned rascal and a damned eternal mendicant—a base ingrate!' the President had retorted.

" 'You are the one who employed me as a writer. You have it in your power with a single word to extinguish the volcanoes of reproach! Yet with that frigid indifference, which forms the pride of your character, you stand neutral. I thought you loved me!' "

" 'Not anymore. Any money you get from me from now on will be charity.'

" 'Charity, my foot! You ordered me to expose Hamilton's love intrigue, to defame Washington and Adams, favoring me with gifts of money and praise. I have your letters, remember?'

" 'Damn my letters! I want them back.'

" 'Over my dead body.'

"Your father gave the order for the Republican party newspapers to cut Callender to pieces. They dredged up his old life in Scotland and accused him of blackmailing his old patron, Lord Gladstone. And soon a tornado of abuse was unleashed—the squallor and horror of the death of Callender's wife, his writing as filth, blasphemy, and pollution. The Republican newspaper editor Meriwether Jones realized that to hurl insults would not stop the spread of the Sally Hemings story, so he began by blaming you children on somebody else. 'Is it strange,' Jones wrote, 'therefore that a servant of Mr. Jefferson's, at a house where so many strangers resort, who is daily engaged in the ordinary vocations of the family, like thousands of others, should have a mulatto child? Certainly not. . . .' Certainly not since Jones himself had a black mistress whom he had moved into his house. This had so offended Callender that he moved out, refusing Jones's hospitality, which he had enjoyed for months. Then Jones accused Callender with the murder of his,

Callender's, own wife in an unspeakable way. This was all Callender needed. He printed what he knew about your mother. "If Thomas Jefferson had not violated the sanctuary of the grave (Callender's dead wife), Sally and her son Tom would still, perhaps, have slumbered in the tomb of oblivion," he wrote.

"There was no stopping the scandal: articles, poems, insults, dirty jokes. Callender was threatened with tar and feathers, horsewhipping, and murder. Your father's Republican friends were warned that if they did not cast Jefferson overboard, like the prophet Jonah, the party would be gone forever. Many Federalist editors reprinted Callender's material, and many begged your father for evidence of his innocence. They waited in vain. His silence was seen, of course, as evidence of his guilt. When no denial came from your father, the newspapers made their own inquiries and printed the proofs of what they found. They admonished him again and again for 'not having married some worthy woman of your own complexion,' as they put it."

"Poor Papa," I whispered.

"Poor Sally Hemings. And if it was James and not one of the Virginia gentry who gave Callender his information, may God have pity on his soul."

"The ballads and the riddles were the cruelest. And my mother saw them."

"Some of them, surely. Meriwether Jones wished Callender in hell via the James River . . . 'Oh!' he wrote, 'for a dose of the James River,' and that is where he ended," sighed Petit. "Callender's body was buried in haste; the same day he drowned, without any official inquiry and without ceremony."

Like a veil being torn away, I remembered my mother describing how this same Meriwether Jones danced a jig on the front lawn of Monticello when he heard that James Callender was dead. And I remembered the howls of grief and weeping of my mother and grandmother when news of James's death was brought by Burwell.

"Ah, Harriet," Petit said, "don't try to understand everything at once. Especially not your mother and your father. Meanwhile, take a good look, Harriet, then forget this house where James died. This building is no longer a part of your biography."

"I've changed my color, Petit, not my soul. . . ."

"Why do you young people always assume you are the only ones with delicate feelings, noble sentiments, and an inviolable soul? Souls are bought and sold every day, and not all of them in slavery. And there are all kinds of slavery—the slow erosion of the heart, of the mind, of the body. This you will learn as you grow old!"

But that day, I never intended to grow old. I wasn't going to be the fugitive, the criminal, the thief, and the orphan that my uncle, my father, and my mother had made me. I was going to marry Thance.

I gazed up once more at the tall, narrow, three-storied red brick house. The green-gabled roof with its twelve chimneys and the white woodwork and sashes and white marble steps suddenly seemed ominous. The bland, curtain-less windows and the lilac lacquered door seemed to hold some sinister message. MASSON'S BOARDING HOUSE. BED AND BREAKFAST FOR SINGLE GEN-TLEMEN. Or those ready to commit suicide, I thought. I recalled the description of my uncle's cynical laughter and his favorite saying. According to Adrian: "Have you ever met one white man who did not ask you for something or take something away from you?"

I shivered and clutched Petit's arm even tighter.

"God stand up for bastards," I whispered.

9

The Almighty has never made known to anybody at what time he
created it, nor will he tell anybody when he will put an end to it, if
he ever means to do it. As to preparations for that event, the best way
is for you always to be prepared for it. Our Maker has given us all
this faithful internal monitor, and if you always obey it, you will
always be prepared for the end of the world; as for a much more
certain event, which is death. This must happen to all; it puts an end
to the world as to us.

Thomas Jefferson

Charlotte had been right about the ring—it was a magnificent sapphire set in antique gold. I willed myself not to think as Thance slipped it on my finger.

"It is rather exceptional," I said, "that your best friend tells you about your engagement instead of the other way around."

Thance threw back his head and laughed. The black cowlick rose, then fell in place across his forehead.

"Your lips said no that day, but those beautiful emerald eyes of yours said yes."

"Did they really?"

"Oh, yes."

Thance drew me in and bent to kiss me. His eyes were calm and happy. His hands slipped under my armpits and along the curve of my bosom. This evoked a strange sensation. My breath came sharply and my eyes narrowed. He stepped back.

"Harriet, Harriet," he whispered hoarsely.

"I got a second invitation from your mother today. This time with my guardian," I said, pulling us both back from desire's edge.

"You don't mind?"

"No. I realize it's a scary thing for her—another woman in her son's life."

"Then . . . you have no more doubts? No reticence? You will marry me?"

I smiled without answering, my heart accelerating. What was I going to do?

"Thor will be returning in time for the wedding. I've written to him. I couldn't get married without him. You do want a wedding, don't you, Harriet?"

My eyes turned as dark and hard as flint.

"I want to be married in a church. I want to walk down the aisle. . . ." My throat felt dry and raspy.

"Then it's settled?" Thance insisted.

"I don't know. I don't . . . it's much harder than you think."

"I don't understand you, Harriet."

"Thance, you don't have to. Just love me, and forgive me." Suddenly I knew I must escape from this lie.

⌒)

From the beginning, I had tried not to fabricate myself for Thance. The childhood I recounted was the one I had eavesdropped on, lurking in the shadows of the big house, watching Ellen, Cornelia, and Jeff bask in the affection of Thomas Jefferson. For Thance's benefit I grafted the life of my white cousins onto my own.

"My father went away the year I was born," I told Thance, "and I hardly saw anything of him except in summer until he returned home in retirement. I was eight years old by then.

"On the winter evenings, when it grew too dark to read, in the half hour which passed before candles came in, we all sat round the fire as he played with us, teaching us childish games. I remember 'cross-question' and 'I love my love with an *A.*' "

"I love my love with an *A,*" Thance whispered, fingering a fold in my skirt.

"When the candles arrived we became quiet. He would take up his book to read, and we would not speak above a whisper lest we disturb him. Generally we too took a book. Often I watched him raise his eyes from his own book and gaze around the little circle of readers and smile. . . ."

I faltered as I told Thance, for even now I felt the burning pain of the jealousy I had felt so often. "And when the snow fell, we would go out with shovels as soon as it stopped, to clear it off the terraces so that he might have his usual walk without treading snow. You see, he was quite old. He was fifty-eight when I was born.

"I remember his giving us the novel *Tristram Shandy*. He who drew the longest straw could read the book first; the next longest straw entitled the reader to the second reading; the shortest straw was the last who got to read the book."

I turned away from Thance, deep in memory.

How Beverly and Eston had lusted after those books, I thought. The books rarely came down to us except in tattered fragments. During the building of the university, wagonloads of books would arrive and Beverly would go down to the storage depot and hang around them as if they were Saturday-night prostitutes.

Thance waited expectantly.

"Often," I continued, "my father discovered, we knew not how, some cherished object of our desires, and the first intimation we had of his knowing the wish would be its unexpected gratification. I had, for the longest time, a great desire to have a guitar. One morning, on serving—I mean, being served —breakfast, I saw the guitar, which belonged to a lady in the neighborhood who was moving west, but she had asked such a high price for it that I never, in my dreams, aspired to its possession. My father told me if I promised to learn to play it, it was mine. I shall never forget my ecstasies. I was sixteen. I had had a terrible accident."

"The time Charlotte said you caught your foot in the squirrel trap?" said Thance gently.

"Yes. And as a consolation I got a guitar—not a new one, of course, but mine," I lied.

"Oh, my darling Harriet, how I wish to be that old guitar, to be the first wish of your heart."

Sadly, I turned his long, square hand over in mine.

Throughout the winter, I continued my tales about my imaginary life with my father at Monticello, inventing solitary walks and intimate conversations, birthday presents and Christmas celebrations. I invented wild horseback rides across Monticellian fields and excursions to Richmond for shopping. Everything seemed to flow so easily from the observations and dreams of the first twenty-one years of my life. I so forgot the lie that it was summer when the recognition of what I was doing began to consume my courage.

I was staying with Charlotte's family on Cape Cod, and Thance, Amos, and Dennis would come up to visit us.

The days were full of pale liquid sunshine. The whole summer had been the most serene, the happiest I had ever known. Life itself, which had always seemed so precarious to me, had taken on the sheen of safety and contentment. I felt myself loved, and at last I loved in return. I wanted to marry Thance Wellington and for a brief time, I saw nothing to hinder me. I looked back at Thance, riding slightly behind, lazily, his dark head flashing like jet in the soft coastal lights of August.

Even from a distance, his silhouette as we rode together was as familiar as it was dear: the smallish head with its thatch of black hair, the thick neck and shoulders of a rower, the straight back and long, muscular legs encased in dark green riding britches and boots. Moreover, if I closed my eyes, I could imagine the long, square hands, the flecks of yellow deep in the black eyes, the perfect white teeth in the beautiful mouth, the clipped chin, the pale shadow of beard, the perfect shells of his ears, the eyebrows, in their shape of the "fs" of a violin, that almost grew together over the bridge of his nose. I had seen him working bare-chested in the Waverly potato field one day with Dennis and Amos, and so I knew there was soft, dark down on his chest and lower arms and the amazingly smooth muscles of a strong field hand.

I urged my mount to a trot, throwing Thance a conspiratorial wave, and he saw it and followed me into the stand of woodlands just beyond. We drew together, and the two horses were so close they rubbed flanks as we moved forward and kissed like two passionate equestrian statues thrown together off their respective pedestals, unable to touch anywhere except on the lips. The woods closed in on us, forming a cocoon of green shell shot through with dappled light that made a low canopy over our heads and caught us and held us in a dream beyond the world's touch.

I was shocked when he drew away from me and the walls of my cloister dissolved and I found myself once again prey to the touch of air, to sound and color, to the rustlings of Charlotte's mount approaching. In those brief moments before brother and sister crashed through the woods, I had time to savor my victory: I had achieved the impossible dream I had pursued ever since I could remember.

"If you were nothing more than the sound of your voice, I would love you," said Thance.

A vagrant beam of light fell across the clearing and lay briefly on the glistening, papery birchbark, illuminating the peeling strips as if the trees were on fire. I forgot the secret between us. I forgot everything except the happiness that was mine and the twin ardors of love and ambition Thance stood for. The world seemed filled with plenty and as much promise as the season itself.

"Meet me tonight. My room. Midnight . . ."

Charlotte and Amos broke into our sanctuary, laughing. We rode back together along the coast, the sea to our right, passing the scythed meadows edged with sloping hills and the sepia of fields. They exuded the stale sunburned sweetness of wheat stubble, the salt of low tide and marshes, the faint smell of surf. Summer and happiness had reached their apogee. Charlotte's back receded in the hail and glitter of rolling surf, following her unbelievably raucous laughter. Once I had captured a future by speaking on one hand and holding my tongue on the other.

Now, I thought, was the time to put my future in Thance's hands.

That night I slipped through the half-open door like a shadow, and I stood in the middle of his room and listened to the low rustle of delight in Thance's voice, its cadence and inflections, its hard northern accent and open vowels, and bright timbre as he spoke. The voice seemed to be drawing itself together in strange, violent pangs. He kept talking, begging me to listen to the love in his voice.

"There's a light in you I want to keep burning." He said this as if he had been thinking of it for a long time.

"What kind of light?"

But he didn't answer. The silence hung still as the moon. I had to break it, break out, free myself.

"My life," I began, "is a lie. I feel as if nobody could ever really love me." I said this with half-closed eyes and a luminous pause between each word, utilizing the slow, languid Virginian drawl like a musical instrument: a high, clear clarinet note drawn out like a prelude to a dirge.

"That's ridiculous, Harriet. You only want to torture me."

"You know that's not true!"

"Ah, well, words don't matter anyway, Harriet. You came."

"Yes. I came . . . I came to tell you . . ."

"Then how can anything else really matter?" He was touching my hand, talking disconnectedly. "If ever you go away, I have no other home," he said in a voice so low and soft it seemed unspoken.

The moonbeams gathered in bunches on the polished floor and then separated, dispersing over the surface until another random movement of the curtains re-collected them.

Standing there, I thought of my mother's secret room filled with furtive presents, guilty bribes, melancholy mementos. Rag piles. I recalled a succession of Christmases when my mother would distribute the presents to the slaves—the pitiful molasses drops and cheap lengths of wool and calico, the cast-off finery of the white family, secondhand boots, mended undergarments, but never paper for my music scores, or pen and ink.

Was I going to trade myself for a new enslavement, that of love?

"So much can be said without words when we love," Thance said.

"Yes, no words are necessary between us," I replied, and suddenly I felt like a person saved from the gallows by an act of God—not absolutely terrified, but stunned and bewildered in the face of a miracle. What was the use of a confession? Thance would have his own way, just as all men did. And deep down I was seduced by that idea. I stared at him with all the envious intensity of a person slowly awakening from a drugged sleep.

Sometimes I felt I was acting out a fictional scene in a novel. Did I really love him, or was this too an affair of the imagination—a blind, willful reconstitution of my childhood vow?

"Yes, I love you," I said, not coming any closer to him. He said nothing; perhaps he didn't understand what importance was attached to my words. Perhaps he considered them natural since I was standing in the middle of his room in the middle of the night in my dressing gown. My heart had ceased beating. Let him see what he was getting, I thought. Let him see me without words. I let my wrapper fall from my shoulders to the floor in a heap of light, and stepped out of it. It was a delicious moment, for he remained as motionless as I did, without uttering a syllable.

Indeed, the woman who stood before Thance was really two persons. What in the flesh were all of Harriet Hemings's dilemmas to *me*? I tabulated, analyzed, copied, and wept over the future privileged life of Harriet *Petit*, but to *me*, to myself, my bones, my hair, my teeth, my flesh, all that was quite immaterial. It was my pride, my self-love, my selfishness which suffered or wept or rejoiced; but *I myself* was there only to love Thance and to watch, to relate, to reason over those great mysteries of white privilege, just as Gulliver must have looked at the Lilliputians.

I knew in some ways Thance was unreal. He was a supposition of what a romantic hero should be: good, refined, artistic, scientific, intuitive. He cut a handsome figure with his handsome silences and his handsome solitude. He caught my playful thoughts in flight, followed the ingenious idea, laughed and cried at the right moments. He had beautiful eyes and a caressing hand. His white teeth shone in his handsome mouth. He loved nature and trips and the countryside. Music and books. And he adored me. When described this way, he was banal, very banal, a scion of romance for girls. But he had a trait that made him unequaled: he recognized my true worth. And he was mine. Thus he was me. And for me, he was love.

"For God's sake . . ." came his husky voice finally, "please leave."

I wandered through the darkened house. It seemed that the blackness was touching me, kissing, caressing me. I felt blessed. My flesh sang. My skin tingled. I touched myself. Everything was dark, soft, and beautiful like Thance's eyes. Outside the windows, little lights shone on the water and laughed from its surface. And I laughed back. I was free and alive. I ran outside. I was filled with inner sunlight and a breeze stirred like the one that had ruffled my mother's skirts the day I left home. The moonlight, which lay heavy on the branches and on the deep silence, intoxicated me. And into this silence I walked, the gravel spitting under my bare feet with a gentle crisp sound, and then peace and quiet. I listened. Was this happiness? What was I? Nothing. I who had been crying since the world began. What did I want to be? Everything. Why hadn't I told Thance who I was while I stood there? If anyone had seen me go into Thance's room, near midnight, not even the Almighty Himself would have been able to convince anybody that I was still innocent . . . of everything.

"Do I understand that you have ferreted out something comic in the personage of Thance Wellington?" said Charlotte, as we walked arm-in-arm toward the beach, late in the summer.

"Comic? What makes you say that?"

"You laugh a lot these days," said Charlotte.

"People laugh at absurdities that are very far from comic," I replied.

"We laugh from a sense of superiority. We laugh at love because it often puts us into cruel or ridiculous situations," said Charlotte, "which, for those of us who are fairly free from that delicacy of the heart, makes us feel pleasantly superior."

"Do you always have an explanation for everything, Charlotte? I'm not feeling superior, or heartless, or triumphant," I said.

"He's afraid of you," said Charlotte darkly.

"Thance, afraid? Of me?"

"Well, Harriet, you are a formidable girl . . . to lots of men. You have this . . . this mysterious, untouchable air of . . . of fatality about you. I've surprised you, staring off into space like a doomed heroine, waiting to be rescued. Then all at once, you'll just simply . . . extinguish yourself."

"Extinguish myself?"

"Well, sort of like a dying star, millions of miles away. One moment you're there, shining and beautiful in a distant kind of way, and the next, you've simply vanished, as if someone had snuffed you out."

I laughed nervously. This *was* comic and somewhat frightening, but fascinating.

"A young girl, you know, is something like a temple," continued Charlotte. "You pass by and wonder what mysterious rites are going on in there, what prayers and what illusions. The privileged man—the lover, the father, the husband—who is given the key to the sanctuary hardly ever knows how to use it. At times, by chance, I've looked into your eyes, Harriet, and seen the saddest desecration—something I don't understand—as if some shadow had kept your childhood out of the sun." I glanced sidelong into Charlotte's eyes. She was coming close, too close.

Her hand touched our interlaced arms.

"Some gratuitous cruelty you have suffered has left you reckless, or even more, ruthless . . . given you a kind of mournful callousness. Perhaps it is only the loss of your family. But if I were not afraid of wounding you, I would say you had a cynical vision of reality."

"Does that mean you believe I could marry Thance without loving him?"

"Well, why not? Most women don't marry only for love. You are a person who has had everything snatched from you quite brutally."

"Charlotte, spare me your magnanimity! I don't have to thank him for having fallen in love with me. If he loves me, what business is that of mine?"

.   ⌒

Adrian Petit greeted me by tossing his hat and gloves onto a chair.

"You were right. My interview with the widow Wellington resembled an interview with Thomas Jefferson himself! She even smells like him," said Petit.

"She likes horses, I believe." I laughed. "She doesn't resemble Thance at all."

"God knows that's true. However, she got down to business in her no-nonsense way. 'I cannot, dear sir,' she said, 'hope to, nor do I wish to, thwart our children in their hearts' desire. I will admit that I would have preferred a northern girl to a Virginian. Southern women, I find, have a *peculiar* outlook on life. Perhaps my prejudice against them is only that—I would hate to think I was so closed minded.'

"As a Frenchman who has lived in the South," I told her, "I can assure you that my Harriet is of an entirely different breed."

" 'You're French, Mr. Petit?' she asked. 'Why, yes,' I answered as she looked at me suspiciously. 'What did you think I was?' 'German,' she answered. At that, I knew we were in the soup.

" 'We're a scientific family, Mr. Petit, not a rich one, although my husband left us in comfortable circumstances. But we do not make a criterion of anyone's worth in terms of money. I do understand that your young orphan is penniless; nevertheless, my son is adamant. So I thought we should meet to discuss our young couple's future. My son is adamant,' she repeated. 'He loves Harriet and will have no other. Money aside,' she continued, 'we know nothing about her family,' and I thought, oh God, why couldn't they have eloped?

"Moreover," continued Petit, "I didn't know what exactly, if anything, you had told Thance, and what Thance had told his mother. Anyway, I tried to be as honest with the widow Wellington as I could. 'Some of the best blood in Virginia flows in her veins,' I said. 'Unfortunately the epicurean tastes and lack of business sense of her menfolk bankrupted the family even before the yellow fever eliminated them all. There is no estate. No dowry. No inheritance. There are no other male family members, or women for that matter—only a few slaves too old to have any value. Her mother was educated in France and spoke the language well, as does Harriet. Harriet was gently reared. She's a good musician, but I'm afraid still quite countrified—' "

"Countrified!" I interrupted, but Petit went on talking.

"I told her I would provide the wedding. I remembered you said you wanted one, and a mount and carriage for you, and I would, of course, hand over the small amount I invested for you. 'I'm afraid,' I said, 'you must accept Harriet at face value, without justifications or third-party qualifications.'

" 'I know that, Mr. Petit,' the widow answered. 'My son has already done that.'

" 'And she him,' I replied.

" 'I much enjoyed my interview with her. She is a charming individual and a very beautiful girl. Thance, of course, worships the ground she walks upon.' "

" 'I believe one of your daughters was a schoolmate of hers.'

" 'Yes, last year and the year before. Little did Lividia guess that she would become Harriet's sister-in-law. Lividia's opinion of Harriet is quite high, and she too holds her in great affection. In this we are fortunate.'

" 'So she has conquered the entire family?'

" 'Except for Thor, who will soon be home from Africa.'

" 'I wish I could do more out of loyalty to her father, but my means are somewhat limited. Once Harriet is married, I intend to return to France and to my mother, who is almost ninety. I have great debts and financial responsibilities. At my death, however—'

" 'I'm not concerned so much about finance, Mr. Petit. Thance will be a practicing pharmacist with his own apothecary, and is a stockholder in the

Wellington Drug Company. They will be quite comfortable.'

" 'And happy,' I added.

" 'We can't change history, can we?' said Mrs. Wellington.

"I thought that was a strange but apt way to put things, and replied, 'Or the human heart.'

" 'Do you believe in fate, Mr. Petit?'

" 'In chance, Mrs. Wellington.' "

10

Of one thing I am certain, that as the passage of slaves from one State to another, would not make a slave of a single human being who would not be so without it, so their diffusion over a greater surface would make them individually happier, and proportionately facilitate the accomplishment of their emancipation. . . .

Thomas Jefferson

The monthly meeting of the Anti-Slavery Society had just started when Robert Purvis entered the dim, cramped hall and sat down beside Thance and me. He took my hand, raised it to his lips, then issued a low whistle and wriggled my hand to make the sapphire sparkle.

"The stone, Harriet, is exquisite!"

"Thanks, Purvis. Now if you'll just let go of my fiancée's hand before you unscrew it." Thance laughed.

"Something fantastic has happened in Richmond," he said, barely able to suppress his excitement. "The Virginia legislature has passed an official resolution requesting the governor to ask President Monroe to obtain a territory on the African coast, or some other place not within any of the states or territories, as a colony for such persons of color, now free or who may be emancipated within Virginia, to which they may be transported. It's called the American Society of Colonizing the Free People of Color of the United States. Or getting rid of them."

"You mean deport all Negroes who are not slaves out of the United States?" I asked incredulously.

"The society's attention is to be directed exclusively toward the colonization of free persons of color and contains no allusion to slavery. Denunciation of slavery is unconstitutional, but the society is permitted to represent colonization as an antidote to slavery and as tending to effect its abolition at some future date."

"Anything the legislature of Virginia approves must be bad," interjected Thance.

"One of the framers of the resolution was none other than Thomas Mann Randolph. Thomas Jefferson's son-in-law!" exclaimed Purvis. "Sometimes I wonder if the solution is *not* another country," he added.

"Robert, that's ridiculous," I almost shouted. "Negroes are Americans. They are born in America. It's their country. Why should they be deported? The first slave ship arrived in Jamestown at the same time the *Mayflower* arrived in Plymouth!"

"Bravo, Miss Virginia—"

"Black soldiers fought under General Jackson at New Orleans. Even *that* slaveholding general admitted they had partaken of the perils and glory of their fellow white citizens. Jackson even told the President how valiant these soldiers were, and promised that the government would reward their exploits as they deserved. And what do they get? Colonization!" interjected Thance.

"Not from Monroe, at any rate," I said, remembering him riled at my father's dinner table, pleading against both compensation and colonization.

Purvis turned and studied me quite carefully. His eyes had iridescent irises which turned over images like a magic lantern. The plaintive expression of his face gave him the allure of someone who was always about to say something, then had thought better of it. I realized I had made a great mistake in mentioning the man who had been my father's private secretary and was now President. It was too specific. Too close to the truth.

"Well, that's really funny, coming from you," joked Purvis.

"Oh, that . . . that's just Virginia," I replied.

"This kind of thing doesn't only happen in Virginia," he answered.

"You know, Robert," I blurted out, "you could be white. I never would have known."

"I know. I thought you white southerners could spot us a mile away, Miss Virginia," he laughed. An interesting aspect of the American caste system is the phenomenon called "passing" . . . passing, that is, for white. No one knows how many light-skinned slaves pass into the white population, and whose descendants stay there. The effect of passing, whatever its extent, is to neutralize the effect of miscegenation, race mixing, which is a crime punishable by fine and imprisonment in America."

"Fancy that . . . ," I replied.

"All slaves in Louisiana should have left with the British," continued Purvis slowly, still peering at me. "At least, upon setting foot on British soil, they would have automatically been free."

"You mean simply by arriving on British territory one is emancipated?"

"Why, yes," he replied, astonished at my naiveté. "One can't be a slave—or a fugitive slave—in a country which no longer recognizes slavery."

Purvis and Thance excused themselves to take their seats in the men's section. Charlotte took the seat on my right, but I hardly noticed; my mind was on Purvis's last words.

My blood quickened. Simply by arriving in London, I could change my status from fugitive slave to freedwoman. I could escape two moral dilemmas at once: the one imposed by my father and the one imposed by Thance's proposal. I could be free of both "crimes" at the same time.

My attention turned toward the stage, where a speaker was describing his escape to the North. He had escaped dogs and armed slave patrols, had almost drowned, had suffered frostbite and eaten raw rattlesnake. He had pried a bullet out of his forearm with his teeth and had drunk his own blood to keep warm, and he had pulled out half his hair to keep his sanity. His wife had died under the lash, and his epileptic son had been fed arsenic by his master. I thought of my luxurious ride to Philadelphia and my first meal at Brown's Hotel. I thought of my deception of every friend I had. Was there a creature more despicable than I? Halfway through the narrative, Charlotte grasped my hand with trepidation. I looked down at the two clasped hands. They could have belonged to the same person.

"There is no dawn for the slave," the narrator ended. "It is forever night."

There was a hush in the hall. Charlotte disengaged her hand. I rose, wishing solitude, my eyes brimming with tears, but the woman next to me, sensing my anguish, took both my hands in hers.

"Oh, my dear girl. Don't despair. This battle for emancipation of the black man shall be *won*, I promise you. Now, you may differ with me as to the mode of operation, as to the best means of obtaining a common objective. You might think that first the chains that bind the Negro slave ought to be *lightened*, whereas I think the chains should be thrust *asunder*. You might think, for plausible reasons that we ought to *mitigate* the rigors of slavery and *alleviate* the condition of the Negro, while I think that the first thing to be done is to resort to the eternal principle of *justice*. But, although we might *differ* as to the means of attaining the ultimate object, I'm sure we differ not at all as to the *object* of the common aim—the utter extinction of slavery."

"Oh, I do believe in the utter extinction of slavery . . . even if it means the extinction of my own family."

"You're a southerner, aren't you?"

"Yes," I replied.

"Well, God bless you, my dear. God bless you. Oh, pardon me, my name is Mrs. Lucretia Mott."

"Harriet. Harriet Petit of Virginia."

"While there is one slave, can any American woman say she's *free*? Can any American woman say she has nothing to do with *slavery*?"

I nodded my head in agreement.

"*Truth* is the same for all humankind. There are not truths for the *rich* and truths for the *poor*, truths for *white* and truths for *blacks*, truths for *men* and truths for *women*; there are simply truths."

I had never heard a woman speak as she did. I listened intently as she continued.

"Nowhere but by my investigations of the rights of slaves could I have acquired a better understanding of my own rights as a woman. The antislavery cause is the school in which human rights are more fully investigated and better understood than any other. Is this country a *republic*, when but one drop of colored blood shall stamp a fellow creature for a slave? Is this a *republic* while one half of the whole population is left in civil bondage and sentenced to mental imbecility? Can you truthfully say, as an American woman today, in 1825, that you are *free*?"

"No."

"Come, after the meeting, you must meet a friend of mine who is to be a delegate to the Anti-Slavery Convention in London this summer, where in this very year, five thousand four hundred and eighty-four petitions have been presented in the name of abolition. Her name is Dorcas Willowpole."

"Is this some kind of slave auction?" I murmured angrily to Adrian Petit over our weekly lunch at Brown's Hotel. "Thance has already spoken to his mother. His mother has already spoken to you. You've already replied. Charlotte's mother has already told Charlotte. Thance has written his brother. Charlotte's told me about my own engagement. I suppose you've written Monticello? Don't you think I might be consulted?"

"Harriet, you are wearing Thance's ring."

"That his mother picked out—"

"That belonged to his mother and his grandmother. That's quite different. Why are you in such a panic?"

"I thought the North would be different! I thought I would find freedom! Equality! Instead, I've found how white people really feel about the Negro!

They believe my brothers, my mother, my uncles, my family are beneath contempt—a race so steeped in immorality, sloth, insensibility, and lack of intelligence that nothing they say either in front of them or behind their backs can offend them! They hardly know that we have seen the backsides of white people too long to be shocked. How can I marry one of them? They who are supposed to be so strong, so superior, yet are so frail the least opposition sends them scurrying for cover."

"Oh, Harriet. How can you say such a thing—"

"How?" I interrupted. "The United States government wants to deport the whole free black population of America back to Africa whence they came. But not the slaves—oh, no, they don't belong to themselves, nor back in Africa. They are to stay because they are too valuable, but free people of color are expendable."

"Where did you hear this?"

"At the Anti-Slavery Society meeting last night."

"Harriet. Let's put things in perspective. Our small dream has little to do with the politics of slavery!"

"And why not? I'm a fugitive slave. As much so as the poor man whose tale I heard last night. Am I not considered just as much a criminal as he? And as black?"

"Harriet, what can I say to you? This is all beyond my competence. I'm only your guardian, not your conscience. Why don't you write to your father and mother? Unburden yourself to them and abide by their judgment. Surely your father must have known you'd be faced with this predicament if you passed for white. He must have some philosophy."

"Yes," I replied bitterly. "You told me his philosophy. 'Since she is white enough to pass for white, let her be white'—that's his philosophy! Be white and keep quiet. Endure the insults, the contempt!"

"And what about your mother? Surely she can help you."

"Oh, I know her philosophy: 'Get that freedom for your children.' That was my grandmother's litany to the day she willed herself to die . . . freedom at any price. At any price, even this one."

"No one promised you it would be easy, Harriet."

"No," I said wearily. "Nobody promised me anything. . . . I'm not going to marry Thance, Petit."

He looked up to see if I was joking.

"And pray why not, Harriet? You have everyone's blessing."

"It's against the law," I whispered.

"What! Not this again?"

"But imagine if he found out from a third party!"

"From whom, Harriet? Me? Who knows, and who would tell?"

"Everybody at Monticello knows. Everybody in Charlottesville knows. Everybody in Richmond knows. Three presidents know! Callender let the whole damn world know!"

"What they know is that a Harriet Hemings exists, perhaps. They don't know that Harriet Petit exists. Or Harriet Wellington."

"My children won't know who they are."

After a long silence, Petit said, "Harriet, Thance loves you."

"I know. That's why I'm leaving Philadelphia."

"Leaving?"

"At the library company's meeting of the Philadelphia Anti-Slavery Society, I met Lucretia Mott. She introduced me to Dorcas Willowpole, a delegate to the Anti-Slavery Convention in London this September. She was looking for a travel companion. She offered me the job, and I accepted."

"You did what?"

"I accepted."

"Thance will never allow you to go."

"Thance is not my master."

"Why so far away, Harriet?"

"Automatic emancipation. Setting my foot on British soil makes me legally free. Just as it did my mother, forty years ago. A multitude of fugitive slaves have done the same, have tasted freedom there. Don't you see, Petit, if I go I will no longer be an escaped slave, but a free woman in reality, not in deception. And I'll set Thance free. He will no longer be committing a crime for which he could be imprisoned or fined, just as my father could have gone to jail over my mother."

"Harriet, don't be crazy!"

"I'm perfectly sane. Mrs. Willowpole and I have decided to go to France after the convention. Paris has always haunted me, Petit."

"You're running from happiness just like your mother when she *left* Paris. Your mother gave up freedom for love, and now you're giving up love for freedom."

I knew Petit was using his most potent argument to hurt me. He was desperate.

"For truth, Petit. I must free my heart. Perhaps there is a . . . different kind of happiness . . . without Thance."

"You might also invent another algebraic equation for yourself. One part slave, one part criminal, one part victim, one part lover, one part opportunist, one part coward, one part thief, one part tragic heroine. Why make Thance unhappy over something neither he nor you can change? Can't you just postpone the wedding? Perhaps make Thance understand? Tell him the truth!

"Harriet, give Wellington a chance; tell him."

"I *tried* to tell him. He didn't *let me* continue. And I'll never marry a man I can't tell! I'm going, Petit."

Petit rose and came toward me. I backed away.

"Why are you looking at me like that?"

"Because I'm thinking how much you resemble your uncle James."

"No one forced him to return home."

"Oh, yes. Your mother. He was not going to let her return to Virginia and slavery alone. He was not going to let her throw away her freedom. . . ."

"As I'm doing?"

"I don't know what you're doing, Harriet. Or think you're doing."

"Don't be angry with me."

"I'm not angry, Harriet. I love you. I only want you to be happy."

"Then you can see I can't lie to Thance about who I am."

"I see you have a genius for making yourself unhappy. Just like James."

"I'm proud to be like him."

"He was dead at thirty-seven."

"That gives me fourteen years."

"You'll break Thance's heart."

"He'll survive."

"And you, Harriet?"

Calm, I thought. Calm. When was I going to have some calm?

"At least when I set my foot on the docks of London, I'll be an emancipated woman. Not just a fugitive white Negro impersonating my masters. The transient fact of slavery is fatally united with the permanent fact of color. If I'm no longer a slave, I'm no longer black either."

"You are taking a colossal risk. Perhaps Thance won't wait for you."

"I can't expect him to, especially since I'm not going to tell him the real truth," I said. "Will you come with me, Uncle?"

"No. Someone has to stay to look after your future interests, because, by God's will, you may change your mind. When I cross the Atlantic again, it will be forever, and that won't be until I've accomplished my last service to your father—your happiness and safety."

"I doubt I'm ever coming back, Petit."

For the first time, Petit looked frightened. His little monkey face screwed up in pain as if I had really been his daughter. But I was escaping my dilemma by the same route my father had always taken—flight.

"How cruel you are, Harriet."

"I came from a high school of cruelty," I answered. "I'm the President's daughter, remember."

～

St. Paul's Unitarian Congregation Church was situated on the southeast corner of Washington Square in the center of the city. I entered the vestry by the side door. My religious instructions were almost over, and I was to be received into the church at the same time as the marriage banns were to be posted. Neither of these things would now occur. I sat down in the choir, totally abandoned. My father had advised flight. My mother, silence. My white lie had become red, then purple, then black. I wouldn't tell either of them that I was leaving the United States. I worried Thance's ring off my finger and wrapped it in my handkerchief and shoved it into my skirt pocket next to the dagger. In the walk from here to the Wellingtons' I would leave behind all the happiness I would probably ever encounter in life. My hands held out before me were steady and my heart beat slowly, subdued and unaltered. Harriet Hemings of Monticello had learned sacrifice and destitution at her mother's knee.

Reverend Crocket entered to light the candles.

"Why, Miss Petit. What are you doing here? Thance wouldn't like to see you abroad so late in the evening."

"I just stopped by to pray. I'm on my way to the Wellingtons' now."

"Perhaps you would allow me to accompany you. I have almost half an hour before the service."

I hesitated. Should I tell this kindly man I was about to break a sacred promise? No. He was just another white person, and I was sick to death of them.

"Thank you. That's very kind of you."

"Is there something troubling you, Miss Petit?"

"I understand you baptized Thance . . ."

"Oh yes, my dear. Thance and Thor—both of them."

"So you've known them all their lives."

"Yes indeed. Fine boys."

"I understand there was an accident when they were children, and Thance hurt Thor. He's never told me how."

"Is this what's brought you here, Miss Harriet . . . may I call you Harriet?"

"I just wondered . . ."

"In Thance's mind he blames himself, but really it was a simple accident," he began, "or God's will. I think that is all you need to know. Are you having doubts about marrying Thance?"

"Yes."

"Ah, but that's the most normal thing in the world, my dear. The sacred sacraments of marriage and conjugal love are the most serious and honorable of all men's promises. They should never be taken lightly. You love Thance?"

"Yes."

"Are you afraid of the . . . conjugal duties of marriage?"

"No, Reverend."

"You are orphaned, I believe."

"Yes."

"Ah, what a sad thing for a young girl, not to have her mother to talk to on the eve of her marriage, or her father to give her away."

My father, I thought. Even if he is no longer my master, he is still my father. The father I had left on his knees, his foot caught in the rottenness of his own rotten kingdom. And my mother. I had left her as though she were half-drugged in a field of tobacco with the moths and the butterflies. Despite myself, tears started down my cheeks. Did I dare admit that I was homesick? My father's house was a two-day diligence ride from here. Why couldn't I bring myself to return to see them?

"I want my mother," I sobbed softly.

"I know, my dear girl. I know. But God in His wisdom has made that impossible. I am sure she is looking down upon you this moment in love and compassion. You must rely only upon yourself."

The Reverend Crocket walked me the short distance to the Wellington House. The *Montezuma* left for England on September 24, and I had already told Mrs. Willowpole I would be on it. Today was the twelfth. Too soon, perhaps. Or too late? I pulled the bellpull and waited. The vicar stayed until the maid opened the door; then he tipped his hat and bowed.

~

Thance was not home.

He had left word that he was staying late at the laboratory and having dinner with a friend at his club. My ex–future mother-in-law was also not at home. Baffled, I sat down in the entranceway without taking off my hat or gloves. But a maid came and conducted me to the front parlor. To pass the time, I began to play Mrs. Wellington's Loud piano, softly, with my gloves still on.

Just as I heard a key turn in the lock, the clock in the hall struck ten
o'clock. I hoped it wasn't Mrs. Wellington, for how could I explain such a
night visit? To my relief, Thance's voice echoed from the entranceway.

"Here? Did she say why?"

I stood as Thance entered, poised for flight or fight. I still had my hat and
gloves on, and one hand reached into my skirt pocket, wanting to fold itself
around the ring, but touching the dagger instead. It gave me courage.

"Harriet, you're not ill?"

"No, I'm . . . well. I came from a visit to Reverend Crocket at church. He
told me he had baptized you."

"He told you about Thor, didn't he?"

"No."

He stood there, pale and trembling.

"No. He's never mentioned Thor to me."

"I would have told you, in time."

"I came to tell you I can't marry you," I blurted out.

"I *knew* this would happen. I *knew* something would spoil everything.
Spoil the only happiness I've ever achieved. I knew I was cursed—cursed
from birth."

"You can't believe in curses, Thance. There's something in my past I can't
reveal to you, and since I can't reveal it, I won't marry you with it hanging
between us. My decision is irrevocable." I held out the ring.

He began to pace up and down, darting a furtive, tragic glance my way.

"Harriet, you must not make this decision lightly. If you would like more
time, I should be happy to wait. I was wrong in rushing you. I'll give you
more time; we'll postpone the wedding."

"Thance, it's not that. I'm leaving for London on the *Montezuma* in twelve
days. I'm accompanying Mrs. Willowpole to the Anti-Slavery Society Convention."

"Without discussing it with me? When did she make you this offer?"

"At the last antislavery meeting."

"And you've kept it to yourself all this time?"

"Thance, you don't understand. I must go to London. I'm sorry I've
deceived you. I've come to give you back your ring. I have no right to the
happiness you offer me."

"It's my happiness I'm thinking of."

Thance had turned deathly pale. He tried to speak several times, but could
not. Beads of perspiration stood on his forehead. He went to the sideboard
and poured himself a brandy.

"Please don't write or try to follow me, because I won't have the strength to go through with it otherwise."

"Harriet, I don't know . . . for Christ's sake . . . leave me . . . leave me some hope. Don't close the door."

"I must."

"There's someone you're going to join in London? There's someone else?"

"Oh, Thance. Of course not. I'm going as Mrs. Willowpole's companion. There's no one else. How could there be? I accepted your proposal!"

Thance had turned and taken several steps toward me. He was close enough to seize me, or to strike me. Our eyes locked.

"Please," I said. My heart was a lump of coal.

"I'll take you home, of course."

Just as we were leaving, Mrs. Wellington entered in a cloud of scent and silk, shocked to find us alone in the house at such a late hour. It was obvious she suspected the worst, until she saw our faces.

"My God—children, what's happened?"

"We've broken our engagement, Mother."

"But—"

"Harriet is leaving for London on the twenty-fourth."

"But, my child . . ."

"Please, Mrs. Wellington, don't ask me to explain my behavior. Believe me that I accepted Thance's offer of marriage in good faith . . . and . . . gratefully."

"Harriet, you're making a terrible mistake. You love my son; I know you do. Marriages like this one don't grow on trees for—"

"Poor orphans," I interjected.

"Mother. Please!"

"Harriet, I warn you. If you walk out of this door now, you'll never enter it again while I'm alive."

Thance's mother literally blocked the door. In her caped evening dress, turban, and ostrich-feathered fan, she resembled some outraged Turkish sultan whose harem had been defiled. How she reminded me of Thomas Jefferson as she converted our pain into her principles.

I curtsied so low my shawl brushed the floor, and at the same time, I grasped her hand in supplication.

"Don't make me regret that I'll never marry."

"Harriet! You . . . you're not entering a religious order, a papist? Not after your profession of Unitarianism!"

"Mother!"

"I still strive to unite religion with . . . perfect liberty," I replied. I rose as I did. I towered over Thance's mother, and her bulk seemed to wither before my fury at being made into an equation once again. She stepped aside. She was afraid of me. Thance's hand at my elbow steadied me as we descended the brownstone steps. I slipped and would have fallen if it had not been for his grasp. I knew he could feel me shaking.

"We'll take Mother's carriage; it's late," he said almost dully.

We were silent, side by side, all the way to Fourth Street. Suddenly, Thance began to cry silently, abandoned. I was annoyed that he had acquiesced so easily. Perhaps, like me, he believed he didn't deserve happiness.

I slipped the ring into his coat pocket without his knowing it.

PHILADELPHIA
SEPTEMBER 24TH, 1825

Maman

By the time this reaches you, I will have set sail for London, England, on the *Montezuma*, as traveling companion to Mrs. Dorcas Willowpole, a delegate to the Tenth Anti-Slavery Society Convention.

Although it is a magnificent sloop, I feel as though I am to be cast adrift in a tiny rowboat onto the expanse of the Atlantic Ocean. I read and reread your letter of the fifth, trying to take courage in the fact that you were much younger than I when you crossed the Atlantic with Maria. Moreover, you did not know you were heading toward possible freedom. But I know that this voyage is my passport to true rather than false emancipation. Setting my foot on English soil makes me forever free as a matter of law, and gives me the moral right to call myself so.

I returned Thance's ring and his offer of happiness because it was tendered and accepted under deception. It is sad that I must add to his suffering after the tragedy of his twin, which is indeed a story worthy of the cruelest tales of slavery. I take his heartache with mine on this voyage.

Remember me.

Your loving daughter

To my utter surprise, Charlotte spoke not one word of reproach to me. When I asked her why she didn't demand an explanation, she said, "Did Thance demand an explanation?"

"No."

"Then why should I? If you want to tell me, you will."

"I'm terrified that Thance will jump out of the shadows at every turn. The doorbell, the sound of a carriage wheel, a footstep, makes me faint."

"Thance is . . . devastated."

"You've seen him?"

"Yes."

"Did he ask what you knew?"

"Yes."

"And . . ."

"I said nothing, which is the Lord's truth, Harriet." She caressed my hair. "Remember I told you once that young women were like cathedrals—great, anonymous mysteries. I've always felt that about you, Harriet."

"You'll come to see me off tomorrow?"

"Yes."

In spite of myself, I said, "Do you think Thance will come?"

"My God, Harriet!" Charlotte exploded. "You kill a man and then you expect him to tip his hat. The man's in bed," she continued, "being taken care of by his sister and his twin."

"Thor? Thor is back?"

"For the wedding, remember? Imagine his despair—"

"Oh, my God," I gasped. "Oh, my God."

"You're coming back?"

"Oh, Char! I don't know . . . whatever happens, it's chance. . . ."

"I believe you're destined for one of the twins, but I don't know which—"

"What a bizarre thing to say."

"And I don't suppose there's any use in asking you one last time to reconsider, or at least to explain, *your* bizarre . . . your suicidal behavior?"

"I can't, Charlotte."

"Well, I'll say it this once. Don't go, Harriet. I beg you."

"I must."

"Why break everyone's heart who's come to love you?"

"Perhaps because of that love, Charlotte."

We looked deeply one into the eyes of the other. Our friendship was intact, as was the mystery.

"I've got you some books for the voyage. *The Poems of Phillis Wheatley;* John Burke's *On Hero Worship;* John Fitzgerald's *The Slave Trade;* and Laclos's *Liaisons Dangereuses* in French. Remember, you read my copy this summer. I've made a list of the books to send me from London."

"You'll come to see me off tomorrow?"

"I wouldn't miss the adventures of Aunt Harriet as she ruins her life and throws away her chance of avoiding old maidhood, while welcoming the chance to drown at sea, with open arms."

"Oh, Charlotte, I do love you."

"With you as a friend, who needs heartbreak?"

"Take care of Independence for me."

"I thought Mrs. Latouche was taking her."

"I prefer you."

"You're afraid that she'll spay her, and you know I won't! When you come back, we can make her a proud mother."

On the day of my departure, Petit was still trotting after me with instructions.

"You're sure Charlotte will take good care of Independence?"

"Of course—she likes dogs."

"Did I give you the address of the American embassy in London? It's in Grosvenor Square, exactly where it was when your mother arrived."

"Petit, I know. I've heard the story a thousand times. I know the address—"

"I don't imagine you will run into her in London," he said, "except by reputation, but Maria Cosway has many paintings hanging in London galleries even now, and her miniatures are famous. I believe your father and she still correspond—imagine the Abbess of Lodi and the President!"

Petit, the old gossip, was incorrigible. Cosway had never come to America, and my father had never returned to Europe. They could not have seen each other in forty years. Even the warmest memories paled, I imagined, after so long a time. Or perhaps not. It was quite possible I would never see Thance again. Would his memory fade with time, evaporate with the years?

A dull pain struck my midsection.

"You didn't tell my father?"

"Harriet, I was obliged to. But if he has received the letter, he has not, as yet, responded. So I assume he doesn't know. He has no power to prevent you from leaving, Harriet; you are twenty-three years old."

"It's not that I need their permission . . . it's just that . . . a white slave arriving in London, just like my mother . . ."

"I'm sure your fiancé, even now, would prefer that you did not—"

"You understood James, Uncle. Why not me? I refuse to live my life as a cipher, an outlaw. But then, don't most bastards feel this?"

"The master loves you, Harriet. I know he does. Do not underestimate him."

"I'm still dreaming that he'll call me daughter, one of these days."

Petit shook his head, as he often did when confronted with the snarled family history of the Hemingses and the Jeffersons, but to me, it was quite clear my father had not freed me. He had merely acquiesced in my stealing myself.

1825

11

In fine, I repeat, you must lay aside all prejudice on both sides, and neither believe nor reject anything, because any other persons, or descriptions of persons, have rejected or believed it. Your own reason is the only oracle given you by heaven, and you are answerable not for the rightness, but uprightness of the decision.

Thomas Jefferson

My trunks had been sent aboard the *Montezuma,* and Petit and I decided to walk the few blocks to the docks through the early-morning crowds for the last time. Perhaps it was my own emotion, but the quay, the wharf, the harbor all seemed more chaotic, anarchic, and brilliant than ever. As we descended the white marble steps of the Latouche's, we heard the sounds of Front Street before we saw them. The sighs and groans of the hawkers and the piercing cries of the auctioneers rose like a miasma over the low two-storied row houses, set together like red-coated soldiers, one after the other, identical, white-trimmed, green- or black-shuttered. Then we heard the roar of the traffic—carts and mounted horses, carriage horses and diligences, stage-coaches, mules, donkeys, two-wheeled carts laden with fresh country vegeta-bles; smelled the itinerant pushcarts full of spices, Philadelphia scrapple, German sausages, gumbo soup and sauerkraut, baked pretzels and pickled herring, all mingling with the aromas of whale oil and peanuts, petroleum and Oriental spices, tea and grain, perfumes and incense, hay and horse manure.

Oh, the London docks could not be more exciting than this, I thought, as we finally burst into Front Street and saw the great hulks of the sloops and frigates and their stately, heaven-piercing masts, heard the caterwauling of seagulls overhead and smelled the brackish water that lapped the freshly painted hulls of every color man could invent—yellow, black, green, and navy blue. They shimmered and were reflected in the water of the Delaware River, while above them rose a horde of painted figureheads: stern, majestic, comic, frivolous, they came in every possible style from Black Sambos to gilded gargoyles, from golden-haired mermaids to salt-smeared death's heads. And the flags . . . flags of silk which swept the whitening sky. Merchant flags and banking flags, ships' flags and nations' flags. Coats of arms, bands, stripes, eagles, stars, sunbursts, circles, squares, checks, and rings. They fluttered, dropped, wept, were taken up again by the wind, then floated, waved, flounced, oscillated, curtsied, swaggered, and furled.

Somber, black-frocked bankers and merchants strode the quay from ship to ship, a rigorous contrast to the ships' gaudy rigs. The sailors, too, were decked out in a score of different uniforms, or a riot of civilian finery, with duffel bags and shoes thrown over their shoulders and on their heads wide-brimmed straw hats or elaborate plumed caps, swaggers, sombreros, panamas, and fezzes.

My heart began to beat faster. Music from the ship's orchestra floated on the air, which was already burdened with sound and smell. I would miss my lessons, but the musical world of London would be mine, I thought. Could it be that I was happy?

At the gangplank of the *Montezuma*, we saw Charlotte and Amos drive up in a public hack. Independence on a leash came bounding out of the door first, attached to a straw-hatted Charlotte, who was followed by Amos in uniform. It was not until years later that Charlotte told me that Thance and Thor had both been in the carriage. If this was so, Thance's last sight of me was of my turned back of white muslin and gray silk moiré and a wide green train. My hair was hidden under a wide panama hat, and I snapped my black lacquered fan to heel Independence, who still trailed behind me. If Thance had seen my face, would he have seen my grief, or only the flushed excitement of a young woman facing a journey into the unknown? I climbed up the rough plank steps, stumbling a bit and holding onto Petit and Charlotte.

The rest of our party was already on deck. Robert Purvis and several delegates to the convention and officers of the Philadelphia Religious Committee lounged under canvas canopies. Mrs. Willowpole was with her married niece, Esther, and her dog, Sylvester, who immediately took up with Independence. To my surprise, several schoolmates had shown up. The same girls I would have asked to be bridesmaids at my wedding.

After all the introductions, hugs, and tears were over, and the excellent wine Petit had brought in our hamper was finished, I knelt down to embrace

Independence again. Charlotte knelt beside me, her arm around my shoulders. Her last words to me were, "How can you be this cruel, this selfish, and this stupid?"

"The luck of the Irish, I guess," I shot back, as she pressed a small package into my hands.

"This is from me . . . and Thance. Remember us."

She rose and started down the gangplank.

Now it was Petit's turn to offer a farewell gift. He handed me a packet of letters.

"Most of these are copies of James's letters to me, but you'll find a few other surprises as well."

I put my arm around the little man with whom I had spent a fateful night in a lilac phaeton, my mentor and my Moses, whom I had come to love.

"This is the continuation of our journey, Uncle," I whispered gently. "It had to be this way. I know that a new destiny is waiting for me in London."

"Harriet, for heaven's sake, don't go to Paris. There's too much unrest there since the Revolution of twenty-two. Since the last Bourbon, Charles the Tenth, ascended the throne, there's been nothing except political discontent, social unrest, and workers' revolt. The city is a hotbed of radicalism, crawling with Austrian and English spies and talk of a new revolution and a president-king."

"Why, Petit, other travelers have come back with stories of a fabulous city of light; rich, elegant, and cultivated, fitted with Napoleonic monuments and having wide boulevards—there are theaters, good restaurants, and a happy, fun-loving populace. Why, it's the safest city in the world, with the best police force!"

"A *secret* police, inherited from the Emperor Napoléon, that has almost total power over the population."

"Petit, I'll only be a tourist, not a military attaché! Why should I have anything to do with the political situation in France?"

"You don't understand the French, Harriet. They'll take to the streets and riot at the drop of a hat! There were pitched battles and barricades in twenty-one."

"Just like in eighty-nine?" I murmured softly.

"You would just love that, wouldn't you?"

"I can't promise I won't go to Paris, but if I do, I'll be very careful and I'll write to you before . . . so you'll have time to worry. And I love you."

"Promise."

"Promise."

The ship's bell rang for visitors to quit the ship. It rang once; it rang twice.

It rang three times; the sound, like large tears, descended slowly, floated on the surface of all the other sounds, then on the oily water itself, and finally sank into the harbor's depths. I thought of Thance's beautiful voice, hollow with grief, yet still clinging to its burnished copper tone. Did I imagine I heard my name?

Our ship had more than a hundred passengers in steerage, thirty in first class, and a crew of forty-six, not including the orchestra. She was a luxury ship built not only for transport and cargo, but tourism and the comfort of her passengers. Mrs. Willowpole and I stayed on deck, as if indeed we were waiting in a darkened theater for the curtains to open on a long-anticipated play we knew nothing of: the plot, the playwright, the actors, whether it was a comedy or a tragedy. The sun outlined our hands on the railings, our profiles, the contours of the brims of our hats, and the fringe of our cashmere-patterned shawls. The moon had won its balancing act with the sun and it stood full and luminous in the sky, outlining the shore, the horizon, and the waves as we pulled out into the Atlantic.

That first evening, Mrs. Willowpole set out our schedule. We had separate cabins, but would meet for breakfast on the bridge. Mrs. Willowpole cherished her privacy, she explained, and ever since her husband had died, she could not bear the thought of sleeping in the same room with another person, not even her own children. She had discovered the enjoyment of waking up alone, and was loath to relinquish what she considered a luxury.

"You'll forgive me, my dear," she pointed out, "but I'm beginning to enjoy the riches of solitude after thirty years of conjugal bliss. I no longer have to wake up and say good morning to anyone before I've had my coffee."

After breakfast, she would dictate her correspondence (which was handed over to ships that crossed our course at certain specific rendezvous). We would read together until eleven-thirty, when a prayer meeting was conducted by the ship's captain. I was free to join her in her daily stroll around the decks before lunch or to retire. My afternoons were free and I was to meet the widow at five for afternoon tea, which for first-class passengers was served in the captain's dining room. After tea, I was to read to her until seven, when we would dress for dinner. As she retired early, I looked forward to long evenings by myself, reading until late into the night.

Tears came later. Every night they reigned, hopeless, longing, and bottomless. It didn't seem possible that there were so many tears in one human body. If we were born with a ration, I thought, I surely had used up my allotment for this earth. But every day I rose and bathed my eyes in chamomile, thankful for Mrs. Willowpole's passion for privacy.

⁓

I grew very fond of the widow. I had never, except for a few teachers at Bryn Mawr, come in contact with any woman of a comparable intellectual level. Although Mrs. Willowpole had not been educated formally, as her brothers had, her father had spared no expense or effort to bring her up to their level at home. She had read everything, and her long life with her minister husband had put her in contact with the best minds of America and the Continent. She had been allowed to listen to anyone who came to her father's table, and she had presided over that of her famous husband. She had written essays and articles and published them under her own name. She had even studied medicine during a brief period when the newly founded Jefferson Medical College had admitted women. This had lasted only two years, after which it, like every other medical school in America, became exclusively male.

She was a Unitarian and a native Philadelphian, daughter of a rich farmer and herself a teacher. Since her husband's death, she had devoted her considerable energy and fortune to the abolition of slavery, in the face of ridicule, physical threats, and social ostracism. She was a wiry, stern, soft-spoken woman of fifty-two, with a round, pretty face flanked by two bands of tidy sausage curls held in nets on either side of her cheeks, which were rosy and highly colored without the help of a rouge pot. Her eyes were robin's egg blue, with yellow retinas, and their enormous size gave them a permanent expression of ingenuousness which belied the sharp intellect behind them. She shared that intellect and the range of her knowledge with me during that crossing, making me feel that my real education had begun. For the moment, no woman had dared, or been allowed even if she had dared, to speak in public. But I had no doubt that when that time came, Mrs. Willowpole would be one of the most brilliant and impassioned speakers in the United States.

This small, determined, somberly clad lady would pace the deck, sometimes with a book in hand, often extemporizing and speaking into the wind, as if indeed she were in training for public speaking. And I listened, enthralled and appalled.

I blamed my father that my mother's intelligence had been unmastered and unhoned, growing uncultivated and melancholy in the wilds of Monticello, unharvested, squandered on the petty woes and intrigues of plantation life. This would have been my fate, I repeated over and over to myself, except for Petit and Mrs. Willowpole. Day after day she became more and more precious to me. My schoolgirl mind and manners were slowly subjugated to a metamorphosis of Mrs. Willowpole's making.

⌒

Every night I cried, and every morning on deck, I listened to Mrs. Willowpole expose her views on love, sensuality, charity, sex, and the state of degradation to which women were reduced: objects of pity or victims of madness. I began to wonder if I had been duped into believing I could overcome love.

"Only children should be innocent, Harriet," she once admonished me, "but when the epithet is applied to men or women, it is but a civil term for weakness. Consequently, the most perfect education, in my opinion, is an exercise to strengthen the body and form the heart. In other words," she repeated over and over again, "we must enable a woman to attain such habits of virtue as will render her independent. It is a farce to call any being virtuous whose virtues do not result from the exercise of its own reason. Do you understand, my dear? This was Rousseau's opinion respecting men: I extend it to women. The illegitimate power which we obtain by degrading ourselves is a curse. Love in our bosoms takes the place of noble passions, and our sole ambition becomes inspiring emotion rather than respect and this . . . this *ignoble* drive destroys all strength of character! If women are, by their very constitution, *slaves* and are never allowed to breathe the sharp, invigorating air of *freedom*, they must languish forever like exotics and beautiful flowers relegated to nature."

Mrs. Willowpole's soliloquies thrust and parried, retreated and advanced, crossed swords of wisdom and struck home with amazing precision. Often her words were sharper than the dagger in my pocket. I despaired of ever being the strong young female she was determined to make me into. I had too many secrets. I was, by her very definition, the opposite of all she stood for: a coward.

And as in a good novel, there was on board a true southerner, who expounded his ideas on the southern way of life and slavery. His name was James Henry Hammond, of South Carolina. He addressed himself mostly to a young Englishman, Lorenzo Fitzgerald, until he found out Dorcas Willowpole's opinions. There were three gentlemen besides Mr. Fitzgerald and Mr. Hammond at our dining table: Mr. Elijah Stuckey, an Englishman, and two Americans, Mr. Desmond Charles of New Hampshire and the Reverend Moatley of New Orleans.

"I endorse," said Mr. Hammond unexpectedly, "without reserve the much-abused sentiment that slavery is the cornerstone of our republican edifice. At the same time, I repudiate as ridiculously absurd that much-lauded but nowhere accredited dogma of Mr. Jefferson, that all men are born equal."

There it was again, I thought—my father's Declaration, like a touchstone, the monument around which every question in America revolved. And for the second time in my life I was face-to-face with racial hatred as shown to other white people. This was what they really thought about us.

"I agree," said the Reverend. "No society has ever yet existed, and none will ever exist, without a natural variety of classes. The most marked of these must be, in a country like ours, the rich and the poor, the educated and the ignorant, the whites and the darkies."

"What about the Christian and the infidel?" said Lorenzo Fitzgerald, twitting the Reverend.

"Why, yes. That too. I do believe red men have souls," said Reverend Moatley. "I believe black men do as well."

"Let's get back to the question at hand—slavery and property," said Mr. Charles.

"That time does *not* consecrate wrong is a fallacy which all history exposes; the means by which the Africans now in this country have been reduced to slavery cannot affect us, since they are our property, as your land, Mr. Fitzgerald, is yours, by inheritance or purchase and prescriptive right."

I flushed at the word *property*—where had I heard it the first time? *Tampering with my property* . . . my father, that night.

"Man cannot hold *property in human beings.*"

"The answer is that he *can* and actually does hold property in his fellows all over the world, in a variety of forms, and he has always done so," replied Reverend Moatley.

"I firmly believe that not only is American slavery *not* a sin, it is especially commanded by God through Moses and approved by Christ through his apostles," said the florid, dark-haired Mr. Hammond, sitting next to Lorenzo Fitzgerald.

I'd heard speeches against slavery, been taught that it wasn't eternal; now I was going to hear one in favor. This was the first time I had encountered a slaver as a free woman. I didn't know what to do—or what to say. He seemed to be speaking only to me.

"You cannot deny that there were among the Hebrews 'bondsmen forever.' You cannot deny that God especially authorized His chosen people to purchase 'bondsmen forever' from the heathen, as recorded in the twenty-fifth chapter of Leviticus. Nor can you deny that a 'bondsman forever' is a 'slave.' Slavery is condoned in the Bible; that was His meaning, His revelation."

"My plan for getting rid of slavery, that foul stain upon our American character, is to find a country wherein to colonize the blacks," said Reverend Moatley.

"Hear! Hear!" replied Mr. Charles. "Casting an eye over the map of North America, I behold in the West and Southwest a vast extent of country which is occupied by some wandering tribes of Indians and perhaps a few intruding whites. There is a large surplus of land that might be appropriated to the blacks and Indians. My first objective would be to secure that country," said Desmond Charles.

"In other words, take the land for a colony of blacks away from the Indians that you've already exterminated," said Mr. Fitzgerald. Here was the other argument, I thought. Exile and deportation, colonization. No one even considered the possibility of cohabitation. Never acceptance. Never.

"Exactly," cried the Reverend excitedly, Mr. Fitzgerald's irony completely lost upon him. "The major part of the free blacks would immigrate to a country where they would be lords of the soil. Where they could sit down under their vines and fig trees and drink at the pure fountain of Liberty."

"And who would compensate us for their loss? Would the United States pay reparation for our property?" intoned James Hammond. "It is a fallacy to suppose that ours is *unpaid labor*. The slave himself must be paid for, his labor all purchased at once and in advance, and for no trifling sum. Mostly paid, Mr. Fitzgerald, to *your* countrymen, which has certainly assisted in accruing some of those colossal English fortunes and splendid piles of architecture you English are so fond of.

"How unaccountable is that philanthropy which closes its eyes upon the English working class and turns its blurred vision to *our* affairs across the Atlantic. You people preach against decrees promulgated by God!" he concluded.

"We *British* have terminated it in our own colonies, and in England, and I pray for its early extinction in British India, but it is the United States of all the civilized world where irrational *fear* is the key to opposition to emancipation. Americans seem to believe in some kind of mystical super Negro of incredible potency and strength, a para-God whose wrath, if unleashed, would pull down the whole white race and white society. I ask you, if a government has sufficient force to keep a population of slaves of any description in subjugation, can't it *a fortiori* do this with a population of the same persons in a state of freedom?

"Enfranchisement does not increase the physical force of the Negro. It only takes away the chief motive for rebellion. He does not suddenly become a superhuman because he is free—exempt from the influence of legal authority. Accountability simply passes from the arbitrary power of the owner to the equitable authority of the law. Every well-constituted community has the right to punish promotion of disorder or violence—the police have a more powerful influence, both moral and physical, than the slave master and are less likely to provoke acts of insubordination."

"We are told they must be made Christians before they can cease to be slaves. I ask you, is the true way to win them to Christianity to keep them in slavery? And what about those who owe their freedom to being the object or offspring of a licentious intercourse without any preparatory instruction in religion and morals to fit them for freedom, except those of their guilty fathers? Freed by whim, by fantasy, usually with the master at death's door. Let's expose once and for all the hypocrisy of those who, while violating every principle of Christianity, clamor for the necessity of promoting Christian instruction."

I gazed at Lorenzo Fitzgerald in surprise, petrified by his strange discourse.

"Our sole purpose is to apply moral sanction to the slaveholders themselves," said Mrs. Willowpole meekly at last, unable to remain silent any longer.

"Sweet 'moral sanction,' indeed. What slave has it freed? Supposing we were all convinced and thought of slavery precisely as you do. Do you imagine you could prevail on us to give up three billion dollars in the value of our slaves, and three billion more in the depreciation of our lands in consequence? Was any people ever persuaded by any argument, human or divine, to voluntarily surrender six billions of dollars? You see the absurdity of such an idea. Away, then, with your 'moral sanction.' You know it's nonsense," replied Mr. Hammond.

"Negro slavery," said Mrs. Willowpole, rising to her feet, "is contrary to reason, justice, nature, the principle of law and government, and the revealed voice of God!" Her complexion had turned a bright scarlet, her lips trembled with emotion, and tears stood in the wide blue eyes. Her auburn curls seemed to have redressed themselves and stood out like mule ears on either side of her head. She seemed to grow in stature, rising and rising, and practically levitated from the holystoned deck of the ship's dining room.

I myself was quaking. I felt ill and too fearful to say anything. I had fallen into a venomous and bottomless vat of hatred and negrophobia I hadn't dreamed existed.

Mr. Fitzgerald and Mr. Charles were on their feet as well, attempting to calm the dispute which was about to explode.

"Please, Mrs. Willowpole . . ."

"Mr. Hammond . . . I beg you, sir . . ."

"There is no reason . . ."

"Let us pray . . ."

"I'm afraid, Miss Petit, your chaperon is quite beside herself," said Lorenzo Fitzgerald.

"She is perfectly lucid," I replied coldly, staring down his horrified look. "Man-buyers are exactly on the same level with man-stealers. Because you know slaves are not—cannot be—honestly come by, what slave trader is more honest than a pickpocket or a brigand? Perhaps you say, 'I do not buy my Negroes; I only use those left me by my *father*.' So far, so well, but is it *enough* to satisfy your conscience? Had your *father* a right to use another as a slave?" I said in my best, most seductive Virginia accent.

This time I grabbed Mrs. Willowpole's arm as tightly as a vise and steered her toward the door while Hammond sat there glaring, deliberately remaining seated. Then slowly, belligerently, he rose, his hands resting on the table.

"Allow me to say, ladies, that this is *exactly* why the female sex should not be allowed to meddle in public affairs. Your temperaments are not suited either for debate or for the contrariness of differing opinion. Let a man contradict you, and you fall back on your womanly prerogatives, enjoining the male to temper his argument with chivalrous considerations, which a woman *who holds the opinions of a man* is not entitled to. Speaking as a free white man, I assure you that my sentiments are those of every slaveholder in this country," he shouted after us as we fled.

The operative and rotund vowels of Mr. Hammond's South Carolina accent piped us out of the door, along with the ship's rolling sea motion, which slammed it shut behind us.

⌒

We stood on the weather deck, leaning into the sea spray, shawlless and hatless and as breathless from the sharp wind as from Hammond's diatribe. Mrs. Willowpole was visibly shaken. Her placid face had taken on a scarlet tinge, and her breath caught in her windpipe in little hiccoughs like those of a scolded child.

"You see, you see, I am not fit for this fight. A man's anger so unnerves me I cannot think. I babble and bluster, I lose my place in my thought, simply because some man, who resembles my father or my husband or my brother, raises his voice.

"I'm too much a product of my upbringing. Never contradict a man in public, never allow him to leave the room angry, express an opinion only when solicited, never deliberately provoke a male of your own class—all those rules one must forget . . . in public life."

"There are ways to get what one wants without outwardly breaking the

rules, Mrs. Willowpole; for women not so fortunately born as yourself, it is
a matter of survival," I answered her, thinking how convenient it was to have
learned, very early in life, to face down an angry white man.

"Why, Harriet, what would you know about women of that class?"

"Did you not say that they are our sisters?"

～

"Pistols, swords, or fishing rods?" Lorenzo Fitzgerald laughed as he rose at
our arrival at dinner that night. I had had to persuade Mrs. Willowpole to
make an appearance; otherwise we never would have been able to eat in the
dining room again. She had been surprised at my equanimity in facing an
angry white man. But I had learned to do that at Monticello. Instead, it was
Mr. Hammond who had changed tables.

"That was certainly a lively discussion at lunch. I never dreamed that Mr.
Hammond had such conservative views of the slavery question, or your
chaperon such radical ones."

"Mrs. Willowpole is not my chaperon, Mr. Fitzgerald. Rather, I'm her
traveling companion. Much like . . . a lady-in-waiting or a social secretary."

"Well, they are very different, those two things, and I doubt that Mrs.
Willowpole would have a lady-in-waiting if she were English—or for that
matter a social secretary."

"Would 'friend' be suitable?"

"Now, Miss Petit, don't get huffy about your mentor or guardian or
whatever she is to you. The incident at lunch is forgotten, and a jolly good
row it was. Your little speech was . . . admirable . . . and for a Virginian,
absolutely astounding!"

I smiled, despite myself. Lorenzo Fitzgerald reminded me of Charlotte's
brother Dennis, except that he was an Englishman, and an Englishman such
as I imagined them all to be.

He was the youngest son, I'd learned, of a military man whom he had
disappointed by not embracing the same profession. But he had made up for
it by being adopted by a childless uncle, and had been sent to Oxford
University to study law, thus escaping the lot of English younger sons who
were forced to join the army or the clergy, or to immigrate to America. He
had undertaken instead not only the Grand Tour of Europe (two years) but
a Grand Tour of the New World as well. Lorenzo Fitzgerald had traveled
to the United States and Mexico and Brazil, and had stayed more than three
years amongst "cousins," as he called all Americans. He was going to write
a travel book, he told me. In America he had visited the western territories
as far as the Missouri; he had been to Mexico City and the Louisiana

Territories. He had seen New Orleans and Atlanta, Richmond and Charlottesville, Boston and Philadelphia. In Latin America he had been to Cuba and the West Indies, Rio de Janeiro, and Caracas. In the coming days, he would tell me about all of them.

"You don't know much about your own country, Miss Petit. Geography was not, I take it, one of your strong points at school. Or were you educated at home?"

"Most of my life I stayed home, but I've attended Bryn Mawr Seminary for Women for the past two years. But you are right. Geography was not one of my strong points."

"Sometimes it is easier if one can draw the country or the continent one is memorizing. For instance, Virginia is shaped like this," he said, taking a small pad from his pocket and drawing a rough triangle. "It sits more or less here in the continental United States, which looks like this. Here is Boston. Here is Philadelphia, and here is Richmond. The Louisiana Territory is down here, where Florida almost reaches Cuba, which looks like this. Santo Domingo is here. Three thousand miles away is Buenos Aires, Argentina. Here is Caracas, here is Rio de Janeiro, and here is Mexico City, where the king of France tried to mount an invasion of Louisiana and set himself up as emperor of Mexico.

"Now out here is what the entire continent of the Americas looks like from Greenland to Tierra del Fuego. I've been here and here, here and here, here and here. Now this is the Atlantic Ocean, and this is what the British Isles look like. This is Ireland, Scotland, Wales, and this is England. Over here is the Continent, as the English call Europe. This is the Mediterranean Sea. Here is Africa."

"Africa?" The melodious name rolled off my tongue.

"Yes. And tomorrow I'll draw Turkey for you, so at least you'll know where you're not going. What did they teach you in Philadelphia?"

"I begin to wonder."

"Well, my father was a military topographer. By age six, I could draw the outline of any country in the world. By eight, I could place the capitals and major rivers and their longitude and latitude. By eleven, I was up to military fortifications, mountain ranges, and secondary rivers"—he laughed—"and the miles between them. Which is probably why I hate the military and love to travel."

"May I keep all these?" I asked.

"I drew them entirely for you. I'm determined you'll at least know where the Mississippi is before we reach London."

"I know where the Mississippi is."

"Oh, yes—over in Texas."

"And from there we go . . . have you ever seen a map of the moon? Or the constellations? My father is also a visionary, like Leonardo da Vinci. He's convinced that we will travel to the stars in ships in the next century, if not in this one."

"Travel to the stars?"

"I'll start with a map of Jupiter. Do you know that in India, at the observatory in Karnatik, they have drawn a map of the planet Mars? It is said that they even have a map of Paradise."

12

On the one hand, shake off all the fears and servile prejudices, under which weak minds are servilely crouched. Fix reason firmly in her seat, and call to her tribunal every fact, every opinion. Question with boldness even the existence of a God; because if there be one, He must more approve of the homage of reason than that of blindfolded fear.

Thomas Jefferson

We had been at sea two weeks before I opened Petit's letter. With trembling hands, I untied the ribbon and broke the seals one night around midnight when I had already been asleep and had awakened, as if I were myself a burglar and a thief, or as if, at any moment, someone would come bursting into the cabin demanding to know who I was and what I was doing here. My heart had accelerated and pounded in my ears. Perhaps Petit, in a paroxysm of guilt, had confessed my false identity to Thance. Or perhaps in a pique, he was abandoning me to my fate, refusing ever to see me or help me again.

PHILADELPHIA
MIDNIGHT, SEPTEMBER 23, 1825

My dearest Harriet,

These are copies of letters your uncle James wrote to me during his two stays in Paris after his emancipation. They are in turn sad, funny, brilliant, morose, dejected, and full of hope. Very much as you must feel now. Perhaps you will read them before you reach that city. Even if you don't go, they will allow you to know your uncle and his life a little better, and in turn that of your mother and yourself. Enclosed also is the scarf James wore the day of the Bastille. As you can see, it is perfectly preserved. It scaled the ramparts of the Invalides and the moat of the Bastille and rode about his neck all the way to Versailles. Cherish it.

I imagine you have been on the high seas several weeks now before you open this; I don't know why, but I know you well, Harriet. Perhaps you've changed your mind about your decision. If so, do not hesitate to take the next boat home from London. There will be no reproaches, neither from me nor from Thance, poor boy. You are the light of our lives, and leaving you on the *Montezuma* was the hardest thing I've ever had to do. I had imagined you on my arm, walking down the aisle at the St. Paul's Unitarian Congregation Church in a few weeks. I cannot write of it without pain and even tears. It is a good thing Thor Wellington is home to help Thance, who has taken this even harder than I feared, although I don't think that Thor will allow him to harden his heart against you. But beware, Harriet, you are gambling high and wide. Life is not made only for your convenience, although there are those in it who would wish it so for your joy. I am one of those who misses you and prays for your health and happiness every day.

I have made my last will and testament. It is, along with my other papers, at the notary public Sillbourne and Brothers at Front and Arch. If anything should happen to me, I have left you all my worldly goods except the farm in Champagne, France, where my mother still lives. I would expect that you provide for her in the last few years, nay months, of her already long life. I depend upon it. And I remain, your uncle Adrian and your adopted father. Remember your work. Remember Thance. And remember your parents who love you.

Yours in service and tenderness,
Petit

Slowly I threaded the long red silk scarf around my neck, pulling it tight. I turned the letters over and over in my hand. They were the originals. Petit had kept only copies for himself. I brought them close, under my nose. They had a charred, moldy smell like burned leaves after a rainstorm. The signature was huge, bold, and scrawled across the page. Every free space was crowded with small, meticulous writing, even the margins, which James Hemings used after filling the page itself. When he ran completely out of paper, he wrote between the lines.

The first was dated Paris, 1796. It described how he found the city after the Reign of Terror and his search for his old aristocratic masters, destroyed by the Revolution. "I've found work in one of the great houses not far from the Hôtel de Langeac, but everyone is afraid that the government will soon fall into the hands of an obscure Corsican general named Napoléon Buona-parte."

How I lament the passing of the great houses where I had hoped to find work but which have been gutted and burned during the Terror, their occupants either in exile or guillotined like the poor Queen. "Citizens," as Frenchmen now called themselves, are be-ginning to look askance at the servant class as well. Traitors and spies abound. Many cooks' heads have come off along with their masters'. I congratulate you for having had the good sense to escape when you did.

Robespierre is dead, but nothing can bring back the Hermitage to glory and beauty, or the Tuileries or Marly—all destroyed. Maria Cosway has left her husband run away with an Italian castrato by the name of Luigi Marchese ... the big London scandal of this year.

In letter after letter, James followed the chaos and civil war of the Direc-tory and the rise of Napoléon, as his own career progressed from kitchen to restaurant. He was now working in a restaurant on the Quai d'Orsay called the Varaine. His dream was to open a catering establishment of his own. He kept a strict diary of all his ideas, recipes, and culinary-decorative inventions for that future time. Each letter, I realized, had its own particular flavor and atmosphere, from funereal to burlesque; from melancholy shades of purple to bright magenta; in them, he poured out his hopes and dreams to Petit. But there was one letter which struck me like a blow, for in it he spoke of his love for my mother.

It was dated at the end of 1799 and had been written to tell Petit that he was returning to our shores to reclaim his sister.

PARIS
DECEMBER, 1799

Old friend Adrian,

I've finally booked passage on the *Tartaguilla* for home the beginning of the year. I should have written to you before now, for I may already be on the high seas when this reaches you, which means I will see your ugly face sooner than you expect me.

These past years have been hard and I am resolved, at last, to take my destiny and that of Sally into my own hands. In all this time, just as I've never ceased to love her, I've never ceased to writhe with shame at her concubinage and resent her slavery with rancor, as I never did my own.

Between us and in the most profound secrecy, I hope soon to tell her this. I should never have left Monticello without her, for without the twin spirit of my sister, I am less than alone, I am desolate, I think of her continuously. If she dies, I die. If she lives in bondage, I live in bondage. For years now, the very sanctuary of my soul has been on fire. My brotherly love trails behind my relation to God, for it was Sally, not God, who always lavished her love on me as a slave, a love all at once simple, faithful, and material. Our hearts merged in childhood, where as a boy I stood my ground against all the mute, incessant attacks against her beauty, her inner fire, her inner self. She was exceptional, Petit, and her betrayal of our childhood, at the behest of Thomas Jefferson, was my extinction as a man. If the person you love most on this earth and in whom you have placed all your confidence betrays you, it produces in you doubt in any divine justice.

Ever since that night at the Hôtel de Langeac, I've never had a quiet place; where none have access, even though the very thing I search for, solitude, is the very thing that is killing me, like the bloody sheets in my nightmare.

And so, to resuscitate my life, I must take a stand against this kidnapping. To love as I love is difficult. It is difficult because it is the highest testimony of your own self. It is the masterpiece that everything else prepares us for . . . and the only emancipation.

Pray for me, Adrian, as I pray for myself. I would gladly kill Thomas Jefferson if I thought that would assassinate her love for him, which rightly belongs only to me, but alas, a murder might even fix it more strongly in her heart. No, she must see him for what he is and despise him.

If I should fail at this, I am lost. Perhaps I'm lost at any rate, but, oh God, how I love her.

Jimmy

MASSON'S, PHILADELPHIA
1800

Adrian, old friend,

She despises me. *Me!* Not him.

She accused me of making her world a bordello when all I have ever wanted was the opposite. "My whoredom," she said, "is yours and you know it." She is right, and it never leaves me, even in sleep.

What will become of me, who needs her freedom more than I need my own? I am not a man, if I cannot free her.

Have booked passage for Barcelona, on the English ship *Supreme* in three days. I must think. I only despair on American soil.

Jimmy

A series of letters from the capitals of Europe followed. Letters full of descriptions of Madrid and Barcelona, of great houses in Calabria and Avignon. All with the same refrain. How could he free my mother? What could he do to persuade her to leave Monticello? And then . . .

RICHMOND
1801

Adrian,

I'm home for good this time. I've got a plan. Think back to our conversation on the quay. I've decided to go through with it. I'm compelled to. As it is, my life is worth nothing. She'll thank me in the end.

Love me as I love her,

Jimmy

It was dawn before I slipped the letters back into their envelope.

Mr. Fitzgerald ignored a visible pull on his fishing line, which he had cast over the railing amidships. "One day, very soon, your country will spread from the shores of the Atlantic to those of the Pacific Ocean. On the east and west, its limits are those of the continental shelf. On the south it advances to the tropics, and it extends upward to the icy regions of Newfoundland. But Americans do not form so many branches of the same stock as in Europe. The three races of Americans are naturally distinct and, I might add, naturally hostile to each other. Insurmountable barriers have been raised between them by education and law, origin and characteristics, but fortune has placed them on the same continent where they do not amalgamate."

We were sitting side by side. The light danced on the water and, far out at sea, we could see the backs of dolphins.

"I believe that the Indian nations of North America are doomed to perish, and that by the time the Europeans shall be established on the shores of the

Pacific Ocean, that race of men will have ceased to exist. They had only two alternatives, war or civilization—in other words, to destroy the Europeans or become their equals. The Narragansetts, the Mohicans, the Pequots—who formerly inhabited New England—exist now only in memory. The Lenapes, who received William Penn upon the banks of the Delaware only a hundred and fifty years ago, have disappeared. The last of the Iroquois begged alms from me. I penetrated more than a hundred leagues into the interior of the continent without finding a single Indian. They are destroyed.

"But the Negroes' destiny is interwoven with that of the Europeans. These two races are fastened to each other without intermingling; and they are unlikely to separate entirely or combine entirely. The presence of a black population upon its territory is the most formidable of all the ills that threaten the future of the Union."

"How can you say that, Mr. Fitzgerald? It is not a black problem, but a white one. The two races arrived here at the same time. It is plainly not blacks who threaten the Union. And if slavery were *not* black, it would *still* threaten a democracy and a republic. I repeat, it is not the blacks; it is slavery."

"Miss Petit, in the state of Maine," Mr. Fitzgerald continued, "there is one Negro in three hundred inhabitants; but, in South Carolina, Mr. Hammond's home state, fifty-five percent of the inhabitants are black. It is evident that the more southern states of your Union cannot abolish slavery without incurring great dangers which the North had no reason to apprehend when it emancipated its black population. The North managed this feat by keeping the present generation in chains and setting their descendants free. But it would be difficult to apply this method to the South. To declare that all the Negroes born after a certain period shall be free is to introduce the principle of liberty into the heart of slavery; imagine, for one moment, a person maintained in a state of slavery from which his children are delivered! The North had nothing to fear because blacks were few in number there. But if this faint dawn of freedom were to show three million black men of the South their true position, the oppressors would have reason to tremble. After having enfranchised the *children* of their slaves, the South would very shortly have to extend the same benefit to *all* black men."

Imagine, for one moment, a person maintained in a state of slavery from which his children are delivered. . . .

"Little Miss Virginia—why so gloomy? This won't happen in our lifetime, but I believe it will happen with violence and in war. If I were called on to predict the future, I should say that the abolition of slavery in the South, however it comes about, will, in the common course of things, increase the repugnance of the white population for the blacks. I base my opinions upon my observations throughout your country. I have seen that northern whites avoid Negroes with increasing care as the legal barriers of separation are removed by the legislature; and why shouldn't the same result take place in the South? In the North, the whites are deterred from mingling with the blacks by an imaginary danger; in the South, where the danger would be real, I cannot believe the fear would be less."

"And you believe slavery will not last forever?" I whispered.

"It appears probable that in the West Indies islands, the white race is destined to be subdued. Upon the continent, the blacks. Do you believe slavery will persist, Miss Virginia?"

"Yes."

"Ah, your own origins are showing at last!"

"No, Mr. Fitzgerald. I believe slavery will last because it is *black*. If it were *white*, it would have been abolished long ago—like indentured servitude."

"America is all a parody," said Lorenzo, "a mimicry of her parents; it is, however, the mimicry of a child, tetchy and wayward in its infancy, abandoned to bad nurses and educated in low habits. The South considers itself the frontier, the guardians of the cherished ideals of laissez-faire and private property, of small government and fierce independence. They think they can roll back time or stop it, but they can't.

"It is a nation derived from so many fathers that in commingling the thoughtless, the dissolute, and the turbulent of all nations, they neutralize one another, resulting in a people without wit or fantasy. And without fantasy, the race problem will never be solved.

"Whatever may be the efforts of Americans in the South to maintain slavery, Miss Virginia, they will not succeed. Slavery is now confined to a single track of the civilized earth, attacked by Christianity as unjust and by political economy as prejudicial and by the principles of democratic liberty and the intelligence of our age as inhuman and criminal. By the act of the master or the will of the slave, it will cease; and in either case, great calamities will ensue. My indignation does not light upon men of our own times, who are instruments of these outrages, Miss Virginia. I reserve my execution for those who, after a thousand years of freedom, brought slavery back into the world."

We sat, as we always did, Lorenzo with his face toward the sun, mine turned away to protect my complexion, extracting its last feeble warmth as we drew farther north and farther into autumn weather. Our large hats were no longer of straw but of felt. Mine was tied securely with James's scarf, which wound around the crown of the hat and under my chin. Mr. Fitzgerald's was secured by a leather strap attached to his brim. As we watched for seagulls, whales, and shark fins, I felt very close to unburdening myself. I dragged the melancholy weight of my uncle's fate with me everywhere on the ship. My throat closed and I murmured Lorenzo's curse under my breath: "God damn the man who brought slavery back into the world after a thousand years."

The *Montezuma* was in sight of the cliffs of Dover before I found the courage to open Charlotte's package to find a gold locket and a letter from Thance. The packet had lain on my night table next to Uncle James's letters night after night for almost six weeks, forbidding and accusingly silent.

Now that there were, according to Lorenzo Fitzgerald, three thousand miles between me and Thance, perhaps it was safe at last to open his letter. I turned it over slowly in my hand then shoved it deep in my skirt pocket next to my dagger. No, I thought. Not yet. I'll think about it tomorrow. . . .

The locket contained a portrait of Charlotte's pretty face, and opposite hers was the image of Thance, staring up at me forlornly. When had they had time to order expensive miniatures? Surely as a wedding present, I thought, not as a farewell. But even so, Thance didn't look happy, or was I simply reading sorrow into a face retrospectively, as one does when one gazes at a portrait of a someone you loved who has died. It was in his eyes. Death. Abandonment. Pain.

I placed the locket around my neck. I was glad I hadn't worn it until now, the end of the journey. I walked up to the weather deck and there, almost blocking the sky, were the cliffs: a mountain of deathly white stone that sprang out of the sea like towers of salt, their tips lost in the mist, their fogged silhouette like dagger points, piercing the surrounding blue of the Atlantic. Suddenly the whiteness loomed down on me, and I stepped back in terror, my hand on my throat.

"Magnificent, are they not, Miss Petit?" said Lorenzo Fitzgerald, who had joined me on the weather deck.

I wanted to be alone, yet I put my arm through his. "Please. Call me Harriet. We're almost to London."

He said nothing, but I felt a tremor of surprise run through him. It was unfair, I thought. I would never love anyone but Thance Wellington. Nothing would change that. Lorenzo could draw me all the continents in the world. Tonight, my last night aboard, I would read Thance's letter.

An eerie light struck the massive cliffs as the sun disappeared, turning them a navy blue, and we passed between them into the North Sea. We passed so close I smelled their hoary breath. A flaky ash settled upon the boat and melted into the waves from the chalk boulders above me, distributing a fine veil of powder on my ungloved hand, so white, resting on the rail next to the chamois-sheathed one of Lorenzo's.

For now, I had passed through the straits into the singular identity of a white American.

I suppose Lorenzo Fitzgerald felt me shiver, for he put his hand over mine and squeezed it gently. It was a brotherly gesture, intimate only in its human warmth, but I withdrew my hand quietly, hoping not to offend him, but determined to keep my distance from him. I had let down my guard once and fallen in love just as I'd dreamed. The rude awakening was more than I could bear a second time. I loved Thance with an aching, desperate certainty that I could never love anyone else.

PHILADELPHIA
THE LAST NIGHT

Harriet,

It seems that I should not despair. At least that is what Thor tells me. I will leave with him for Cape Town as soon as we can book passage. This will put even more miles between us, which God knows is necessary. Africa, my brother tells me, is God's cradle for pain—especially for white men. He created it so.

And I release you from your promise to marry me. You are free. Because I love you.

                                                            Thance

13

They mistake for happiness the mere absence of pain. Had they ever felt the solid pleasure of one generous spasm of the heart, they would exchange it for all the frigid speculations of their lives.

Thomas Jefferson

We arrived in London in time for a funeral. The last hero of Trafalgar, a famous lord admiral, had died, and his catafalque was being towed up the Thames by a score of harnessed black horses in silver trappings and stiff-plumed headdresses moving in unison like a sea of black wheat. As the *Montezuma* glided toward London Bridge, we passed white stone palace after white stone palace, each draped with black bunting. Flags flew at half-mast and the peals of hundreds of church bells filled the air, as if a thousand silver coins had been flung upward and now rained down.

The ship's orchestra had ceased to play, and the captain had lowered his colors to half-mast. The body, we were told, was being taken to Westminster Abbey, where it would lie in state for three days, near all the other national heroes buried there.

"The only thing he regretted," murmured a fellow passenger beside me, "was that the Napoleonic Wars only cost England forty thousand dead. 'Cheap victory,' he always said."

"I suppose one could call this a bad omen," I said to Lorenzo.

"Not at all. What it means is that Napoléon's ghost has finally been put to rest after ten years, and Europe is for the moment at peace."

The orchestra resumed playing the prelude from *La Traviata*, which they had played on the wharves of Philadelphia, as the gangplank was lowered. I

rushed to join Mrs. Willowpole. As we slowly descended, arm-in-arm, I tried
to imagine my mother at fourteen, leading Maria toward the Adamses waiting
for them on the quay, thirty-eight years ago. Carefully, I placed my foot on
English soil. I brought my gloved hand to my lips and then, pretending to
stumble, dropped to my knee as I placed the kiss on the terra firma of the
London docks. My white gloves came away with the imprint of the sooty,
wet cobblestone. I stared at them. They had hidden my fingerprints. My
movements had been so speedy and disguised that Mrs. Willowpole hadn't
noticed my gesture, and thinking I hadn't been observed, I turned toward her,
only to find Lorenzo at my side. He had seen everything. *What are you
hiding?* his eyes asked.

"Let me escort you ladies to your hotel, if no one is meeting you at the
docks. My man and carriage are here, and it would be a pleasure and an honor.
I can't let you roam the streets of London in all this turmoil."

We let ourselves be led toward an elegant dark green equipage upon which
sat four coachmen in dark green livery. In less than a half hour we had turned
under the soaring arch of London Bridge and were heading up Water Street
toward the city, which was paralyzed by traffic. Shops were closed and it
seemed as if everyone in London was out on the streets. There were hundreds
of Napoleonic War veterans amongst the civilians who had swarmed into the
city for the funeral. Soldiers in every kind of uniform imaginable occupied
every free piece of ground. And around them and the noisy, rowdy population, rose what was surely the greatest city in the world majestically. Paris
couldn't be greater, I thought. First of all, it was a stone-and-brick city. Even
the poorest of habitations were timber, brick, and stucco. And it was a tall
city, many of the buildings being four or five stories high. The mansions of
Richmond were laughable, I thought, as we drove at a snail's pace past
Carlton House, Burlington, St. Paul's Cathedral, and Westminster. It took
us nearly three hours to cross the city.

☙

Our rooms were as comfortable and beautiful as any I had ever seen. The
walls were papered in buff-and-gilt fleur-de-lis-patterned wallpaper, and the
furniture was an odd but pleasant mixture of French Empire and English.
There were bookshelves, a palm tree, and an ottoman. To my delight and
surprise, there was an upright piano with faded red silk fluting across the
front, and in one corner stood a very fine harp. The carpet was red with a
buff pattern over polished wooden floors. The beds in the two small adjoining
rooms were four-posters with damask curtains that matched those at the large

sash windows. There was even a water closet and a real bathroom, which did not, however, have any plumbing.

Relieved and happy, we settled in. The next Monday we set out for the opening of the convention in a hired carriage.

When we arrived at the cavernous Oxborn Hall, which was still and somewhat appropriately draped in black, Mrs. Willowpole was told she could not be seated on the floor as a delegate because she was a woman. Women, the convention manager explained, were relegated to the spectators' gallery, in the very rafters of the hall. They had no right to vote, to speak, or to participate in the debates. Copies of the speeches were not distributed to the gallery. There were no ladies' toilets, and women were not allowed to eat at the men's buffet. There were no reserved or numbered seats for ladies, and they were not allowed to use the front door, but rather one side entrance and the fire staircase. If these rules were not complied with, one would be physically ejected from the hall.

For a few moments we stood there, disarmed.

"We have traveled thirty-five hundred miles," began Mrs. Willowpole. "We have accreditation."

"I can't help that, madam. In our program you are listed as a man." He looked up sternly. "Dorcas," he said, as if he were speaking to a child, "is a man's name. I never heard of any woman named Dorcas. And you didn't put 'Mrs.' or 'Miss' in front of it. Dorcas Willowpole is a *man's* name. You used subterfuge to accomplish your accreditation, madam."

"That's because the organizers of the convention have never read Shakespeare. Dorcas is the name of a *shepherdess* in *The Winter's Tale!*"

"Well, madam, if I had been your father, I would have opposed such a name."

"I demand to see my compatriots on the floor."

"You'll have to wait for them to come out of the hall into the street or use the side entrance, the same as for tradesmen. Can't let you in the front door."

"Now you know," murmured Dorcas Willowpole, "what if feels like to be a Negro."

We reached the spectators' gallery disheveled, winded, and apprehensive. Would we be allowed to remain here at least? Despite everything, we found the cream of female British abolitionists in high good humor. There was Hannah More, the poet, and Amelia Opie, wife of the London portrait painter and a writer of romantic novels. She had written a poem I had read called "The Negro Boy's Tale." Hannah More, a friend of Dr. Wilberforce, moved in the fashionable circles of London, and as she did so, she carried with her a print of Clarkson's drawing of a slave ship and its instruments of torture. She too had written several poems on the subject, the most famous of which had been published in Philadelphia.

Holding court in the cramped gallery was the formidable Elizabeth Heyrick, who had made the biggest stir of all among antislavery people on both sides of the Atlantic. She was a Quaker lady, residing in Leicester, a friend of all the prominent antislavery Friends: the Gurneys, the Buxtons, the Frys, the Hoares. Her pamphlet, entitled *Immediate, Not Gradual, Abolition,* called for emancipating the slaves at once as the shortest, safest, and most effective method.

"Well, Mrs. Willowpole, welcome to the slave deck." She rose to shake hands with us like a man, then laughed good-naturedly as she handed each of us a copy of Thomas Clarkson's latest pamphlet, *Thoughts on the Necessity of Improving the Condition of the Slaves in the British Colonies, with a View to Their Ultimate Emancipation,* one of dozens that had been published on the occasion of the convention and the Parliamentary elections. One of her new arguments embraced the utter futility of trying to appeal to, or compromise with, slaveholders. Gradualism was the masterpiece of satanic policy, and did not materialize in anything. The only method was to take the high ground on the basis of justice, then enforce majority opinion against slaveholders.

"Those same men down there," said Amelia Opie, "are discussing our future as well—whether we shall be allowed to go beyond writing from our homes to public meetings and public speaking. So far we have been allowed to organize ladies' auxiliary societies only; in that, you Americans are ahead of us. I am the president of the Female Anti-Slavery Society of Birmingham."

She smiled and held out her hand. She was young and very beautiful, with clear gray eyes and a wonderful English complexion. She had so many of the attributes of what was considered beautiful in a woman, she seemed almost a cliché. She was blond and small, vivacious, with a radiant smile, perfect teeth, delicate arms, hands, and neck, a generous bosom, and a refined air of distractedness and artlessness that had the same irresistible effect on men, women, and children. If I had not known where I was, I would have imagined I was sitting at a fashionable dressmaker's waiting for a fitting, rather than listening to a denunciation of the most violent brutalities in the world. Moreover, it was Amelia Opie's butler who hauled a picnic lunch up to the gallery for the ladies.

⁖

Down on the floor, the convention was being called to order, and the delegates asked to take their seats. I marveled at how easily I fell into thinking about other people's slaves, as if I were not part and parcel of that multitude.

I had suffered less, it was true, but perhaps I had been more wronged.

We were, after all, not talking about the three million American slaves, who were a minority in all the states except South Carolina; we were talking about the eight hundred thousand West Indian slaves who outnumbered the British planters almost ten to one. As Lorenzo had pointed out, it was inevitable that the blacks would sooner or later eradicate the whites in the West Indies. And it was just as mathematically sure that American slaves would never achieve their emancipation through the force of numbers. In America, with the tacit support of the North, the planter class in America was the ruling political class of the whole country. This stranglehold on power would have to be broken before anything else could be accomplished.

The new antislavery zeal in Britain was at its zenith, and Wilberforce was its pope, I was told by Dorcas Willowpole. The impassioned voice of Dr. Wilberforce rose with great power and seemed to sweep away the very walls of the hall, leaving his audience amidst the sheen and motion of the Atlantic Ocean, which rolled in with a mighty whorl of current and movement. And upon it sailed a slave ship of a hundred and twenty tons, fitted with planks for three hundred blacks, with two feet of headroom and a space six feet by two feet for each man chained between decks. There were ships, it seemed, that held as many as six hundred Negroes, a quarter of whom would die or commit suicide before the rest could be loaded. So smaller, faster boats were more economical. The unnamed slaver glided away from shore into the blank universe evoked by Dr. Wilberforce's hypnotic voice, headed for Africa, its hull filled with Liverpoolian trinkets and iron fetters for two hundred and fifty. It was a voyage for which I had no preparation. It was as if the small, frail man below were pulling me headlong into my own biography. This was no individual slave narrative, set in the familiar confines of a southern plantation. This was the mythic, cosmic legend of the Middle Passage, the triangular crisscrossing of the Atlantic between England, Africa, and America. This was the beginning of the indomitable, overwhelming voyage that had wrenched my great-grandmother from the place where she was born and inflicted on her unimaginable suffering. My throat tightened as the story's slaver dropped anchor at the mouth of the Gambia, ready to pick and choose and load the cargo for which it had made its hazardous journey; an ordinary slaver, on an ordinary errand, navigated by ordinary men.

I sensed a prayer forming within me: *Please don't let me hear this.* My lips pleaded with Dr. Wilberforce's voice. This was no slave tale of old; this was the Book, the Bible, the Passage. But there I sat, under the burning tropical sun, listening to the thunder of the sea, waiting for our cargo from the interior. Suddenly the column burst onto the beach, a long, undulating line of fettered, bleeding, stunned, and stuttering humans, all naked, all wild-eyed with the hardship of the march. First there were ten, their heads forced upright by means of a common yoke; then there were fifty, bowed low, as still as stone, kneeling on the deck of the ship, being examined by the ship's doctor, jumping and dancing in a strange ritual visited upon them by the captain. Then came the bartering: brass kettles, cowrie shells, looking glasses, steel knives, cases of rum and brandy, bolts of vivid cloth, and penny necklaces of colored beads in exchange for men and women.

Dr. Wilberforce's incantation rose with the stench he described of burning flesh, "red-hot branding irons coming down on the shoulders, buttocks, backs of women, children, and warriors alike, writhing in pain, being held down by the sailors, the brazier glowing like the eye of God." His voice had metamorphosed into the single cry of agony that issued from the living men on deck, exploding onto the sea's undulating surface into which I and the hall and London itself had disappeared, leaving only the heads and shoulders of the audience below, as if they bobbed in the surf, their sighs of protest quieting into a pious and awed silence. But Dr. Wilberforce would not be silenced. He continued on, describing the instruments of the trade: the funnels and pliers to wrench open the mouths of those who refused to eat; the shackles and yokes of all kinds for wrists, ankles, necks; instruments to pull teeth, pluck out eyes; alligator-hide whips that tore the skin off in little coils; branding irons; plugs for dysentery that sometimes caused slaves to vomit their own feces; and instruments of pure torture—clamps, thumbscrews, garrotes, spiked collars. These were the methods that served the logic of pure brutality: the rape of women, the forced feedings, the suicides, the revolts, and the jettisoning of living cargo overboard in the wake of pursuit by British slave patrols.

Wild, demented cries rose in a maelstrom around the voice and form of the diminutive Dr. Wilberforce. The slaves, stacked two feet apart, rolled helplessly on the unplaned planks, taking the skin off their backs and sides in the suffocating darkness. The floor of the hull became slippery with blood and mucus, and men went insane and tried to bite off their shackles and irons. Like a sleepwalker I moved through this infernal slaughterhouse, chest-high among the rough planks, my skirts trailing in indescribable muck, through the putrid slave hold where a candle would not burn. Dr. Wilberforce's saintly, intoxicating voice wound through the epidemics of smallpox and malaria and the bloody flux, outbreaks of insanity, and slave revolts. In panic, I glanced at Mrs. Willowpole, my mouth open, gasping for breath, fighting a rising nausea. There were tears standing in her eyes. She reached over and grasped my hand.

"Courage, my dear. I have heard Dr. Wilberforce's litany many times, but no matter how many times, one is always annihilated by the horrors of his narrative," Mrs. Willowpole whispered next to me. I took a deep breath. I was trembling uncontrollably now, in the grip of shock over this inventory of absolute evil. The tiny man below still turned and spun like a weathercock in the turbulence of his own speech.

The ship had reached Cuba now, with one-third of its cargo still alive. I had heard of the Cuban slave markets, the scramble sales, the barter for sugar and rum, and the transfer of illegal slaves with false papers to the New England schooners, which in turn transported them to the Carolinas and Louisiana. This was how my great-grandfather had transported my great-grandmother. In this evil nightmare, my grandmother had been conceived. This was who I was—*what* I was. This Passage was my fingerprints.

I continued to stare into the swirling, impenetrable void surrounding the doctor's voice, from which issued the cries and screams of children being sold away from their mothers, men being manhandled in the scramble sale, women being raped on barn floors until the cries subsided into the faint, distant washing of waves on a beach, which I realized was applause from the spellbound audience. It was over.

I shifted away from the women seated in the gallery, repulsed and strangely remote from them, as if I had descended from another galaxy. The crash of the sea was still in my ears, and I felt intensely aware of my physical being, my lungs still breathing in the insupportable stench of the ships, my hands, my eyes, my shackled ankles. I drew myself back into consciousness from the depthless ocean, from the vast horror upon which I had been blown and tossed.

My own petty, indulgent occupations, my vain ambitions and longings, my selfish and egotistical strivings had disappeared in the void of Dr. Wilberforce. What did the humiliation of my own domestic slavery in the tiny confines of Monticello have to do with this immense, this cacophonous manifestation of pure evil? Even as my mind tried and tried to encompass the meaning of what I had heard, and to filter out a tiny foothold in it where my mind could rest and gather its wits, it dawned on me that comprehension was impossible. There was no way under it or over it or around it. I had to plunge into its heart like a swimmer, not knowing if I would ever rise to the surface.

I shied away from my employer's touch as we rose. Below, people were stirring. Dr. Wilberforce had received a standing ovation, and now the men were moving about, talking to one another, greeting acquaintances, coming alive . . . relieved and happy that they were on dry land. But for me, there were only the murmurings and explosive sounds of my own dry, fervent lips praying and the click of my own tongue against the roof of my mouth and the bitter taste of God's malevolence.

↶

One day when Mrs. Willowpole was busy with her committee meetings and Lorenzo Fitzgerald had gone to Manchester on business, Amelia Opie took me to visit the new picture gallery at Piccadilly Square. As we walked through the large central gallery, filled with Italian pictures and Dutch still lifes, I stopped before a large framed engraving, staring at the engraved copper plate beneath. It read: THE PROGRESS OF FEMALE DISSIPATION AND THE PROGRESS OF FEMALE VIRTUE. INSPIRED BY HOGARTH—MARIA COSWAY. It was dated 1802. Suddenly there was proof that this companion of my father's Petit had told me so much about had really existed. Everything he had said came back to me: the letters which the painter Trumbull had delivered back and forth between them; the strange, erratic wandering life for which she was notorious; and the seclusion in a convent in Lodi, Italy. Hanging next to her painting was her engraved self-portrait. It showed a beautiful and fragile lady of fashion in the elaborate hairdo of the day. Her arms were folded across her décolletage, staring out of the frame. There was much to remind me of my aunt, Maria Jefferson Eppes, and I was not being fanciful in seeing a resemblance to my mother.

"A fine if wasted talent, Maria," Amelia said.

"You know her?"

"When I was very young. I think I saw her once or twice at balls or musicals, always exquisitely dressed. She used to affect Oriental turbans and lavish Ottoman shawls. She had a monster for a husband, but he was an extraordinary artist, a painter of miniatures. No one took Mrs. Cosway's talent seriously. How could they, in the face of her husband's genius? He was very close to the Prince of Wales before he became king, and kept a splendid residence at Schomberg House. They were both part of the prince's entourage until he became regent. They had one daughter, whom Maria abandoned at six months to travel on the Continent. Six years later, the child died and Cosway fell into a deep melancholy. Maria returned, but he became more and more eccentric. Richard Cosway was dropped from the king's society, and that's when Maria Cosway fled abroad again. She traveled more and more frequently and finally ran away with an Italian castrato, Luigi Marchese. Richard Cosway finally died in 1821 and Maria, who was raised a Catholic (devout or not I cannot say), then removed herself permanently to Lodi, Italy, near where she was born, and returned to the religion of her childhood. She had founded a convent in 1812 called College della Grazie, part of an order known as the Dames Inglesi, and she became its abbess. Why did you stop in front of this particular painting, Harriet?"

"Nothing . . . the title, I think. It is very well drawn, don't you think, for a copy? And the portrait. It has a haunting quality, don't you think? Such sad eyes . . ."

"Maria *is* sad, I think. At least her life is. She was famous for being headstrong and eccentric—a true artist. It was said that it was her father who pampered her into believing she had great talent. But her husband balked at her painting for money. She could never attract any important patrons—or if she did, she was accused of artistic improprieties rather than artistic talent, as if a woman could not attract interest except through her sex. She couldn't have loved her husband, curious monster that he was—a dwarf: deformed, capricious, and degenerate. It seems that when they lived in Schomberg House, he had a private entrance to the king's chambers through a tunnel built from there to Carlton House. But come, I want to show you the Van Dyck, which is truly a wonder."

But I lingered before the melancholy portrait. My mother, buried alive at Monticello, and Maria Cosway at Lodi were both women detached from the real world. As mothers, both had abandoned their rights to their children, Maman by remaining a slave, Maria by running away. Stillborn mothers. What would Amelia Opie think, as a writer of novels, if I told her all I knew about Maria Cosway?

Slowly I turned and followed Amelia without looking back. I began to dream not only of Paris, but of Lodi.

Our work was almost done. Our reports on the conference were completed. The letters and manuscripts for publication in Philadelphia were ready. Mrs. Willowpole continued her frantic traveling and visiting, sometimes depositing twenty cards in a single day. I spent my time transposing lectures, copying letters, and writing reports. When I had a free moment, I raced out to the music shops in the Burlington Arcade in Piccadilly and browsed hungrily through all the newly published sheet music. Everything was to be completed and sent by December so that we could avail ourselves of Amelia's invitation to spend a month in the country at Christmas.

Life had settled down to a routine. Every day, Mrs. Willowpole would do her accounts, invitations, and thank-yous at her little davenport table, writing with her new steel pen made in Birmingham, which she had bought in Woburn Walk in Bloomsbury. It was a beautiful writing instrument, decorated with a polished bone handle and necessary if one was to keep up with the times and not be thought old-fashioned. She bought one for me, and I sent two home to Monticello for Christmas, one for my mother and the other for him, although I couldn't imagine that my father would ever write with anything except a quill pen.

We were more and more attached to our "little home," as Dorcas Willowpole called our furnished lodgings. Lorenzo, Brice, Mrs. Willowpole's nephew, and his friend, Sydney Locke, another young lawyer from the city, had fallen into the comfortable routine of dining with us or inviting us to dine as often as three times a week. Or the gentlemen would pass by for sherry, or for high tea or a game of backgammon. I had continued the backgammon lessons Lorenzo Fitzgerald had begun on board the *Montezuma*. I had learned quickly and easily because the game was so similar to music. One had to have rhythm, be able to count and memorize, and have at least a musical notion of mathematics. Even the noise of the dice pleased me. My fingers now flew around the board as if it were piano keys. The combination of talent tempered by pure chance appealed to my double life, in which gambling was necessarily a part. More than often I beat my employer and even began to hold my own with Lorenzo. What I did not realize until my employer teasingly pointed it out to me was that I was now surrounded by three eligible young men!

LONDON
THANKSGIVING DAY

My dearest Charlotte,

Rec'd. yours of the 15th. The weather isn't half as bad as I expected it to be at this time of the year. It is gray, of course, and night falls close after five, because we are so much to the north, but no race knows more how to live cozily in a cold climate than the English. They have invented a million comforts, not the least of them excellent chocolates, high tea, hot scones, golf, a devotion to cats and dogs, chintz material, country houses, wool tweed, umbrellas, bagpipes, cathedrals, King Edward roses, forty-branch candelabras, the men's club, and, since inactivity is considered reprehensible, not to say immoral, a host of games even the most serious adult can indulge in. Much reading is done—novels, religious and historical works, and magazines. Travel books are also in vogue, especially those about the Grand Tour. And everyone reads the London *Times*—ironed. You may draw or paint, do fancywork, rolled rapper work or embroidery, make models in wax or pictures with shells, press flowers in books, paint trays, decorate bellpulls, paste postcards in albums or magazine pictures on screens, sew dresses from paper patterns cut out of *The Englishwomen's Domestic Magazine*. There are kaleidoscopes to play with, and stereoscopes and zoetropes, which make pictures of animals run and jump. There are magic lanterns and folios of prints and watercolors of birds to look at. There is butterfly and beetle collecting, jigsaw puzzles, cards, board games, paper and pencil games, whist, and loo, piquet, and Pope Joan, bridge and backgammon, chess and faro. Above all, dear girl, there is music. All other games are played to running conversation and small talk, at which the English excel as no other race, except that in Italy, it seems, men actually talk to women. Anyway, every spare moment I have I devote to music. Our work here is finished, and we have several months before we leave for Europe. So I plan to profit all I can from the music, great and small, that's in the city: concerts at St. Paul's Cathedral, Opera at the Royal Opera House in Covent Garden, chamber music at a dozen associations and societies. Oh, Charlotte, everything is here, Mario and Tosca, Norma, Lucia and Rigoletto. I heard a concert by a great continental musician, George Bridgetown, a mulatto of African and Polish descent who executed divinely a violin concerto by Giornowich, another by Viotti, and a rondo by Grosse. Music is everywhere, in private homes, especially in the country, but also in the gardens and amusement parks. I attend any and all: operas, operettas, chamber music, quartets, piano concerts, musical solos . . . everything.

We have an invitation from Amelia Opie. A month in the country, with all my time for music. Sydney, Lorenzo, and Brice will be there, and God knows how many tons of people! Surely worse than any Virginian plantation. And they have as many servants as a South Carolina slaveowner, not, of course, counting agricultural workers. As many as seventy servants may sit down to dinner every day downstairs, while fifty sit down to dinner upstairs. Amelia herself employs a valet, a coachman, a postilion, a gardener, a boy, a housekeeper, a housemaid, a laundrymaid, a dairymaid, and a general maid in London. In the country she has double that number, and between the loftiest of the upper servants and the humblest of the lower, there are as many grades and ranks as in the aristocracy itself. She says more people work as domestic servants than at any other occupation, except agricultural workers: almost a million of them. And are the working-class poor worse off than the American slave? No, no, and no. Although a revolution of the poor is inevitable. Will the British arrive at abolition before we do? Yes, I would guess in less than ten years. There is a fervor here that has not reached our shores yet, but ours will surely come.

Dorcas says there are two kinds of time, real time and intellectual time; that is, the time it takes an idea to arrive to the consciousness of mankind. Immediate and worldwide emancipation's time has come, and we will both live to see it. That first day, at the convention, when, for the first time, I heard Dr. Wilberforce speak and stared absolute evil in the face, even as my soul shriveled, Charlotte, I knew as Lorenzo had assured me on the boat: slavery was not forever. I have vowed to live to see this cancer wiped from the face of the earth. It justifies everything I've done.

My sisterly love, I wear your locket over my heart.

Harriet

P.S. Did you get the last packet of books? And the music? I know I forbade you to speak of him, but have you heard if they've arrived safely?

That winter, as cold rain and mist settled over London and we burned oil lamps in the middle of the day, merino lambs like those on my father's plantation grazed in Hyde Park, and people sold coal and wood in Liechester Square and hay in Haymarket. London was so filthy with coal soot that blackness rained down with the famous fog, and armies of laundresses labored to keep the upper class clean. The filth of London made a cult of whiteness. The gentry changed clothes several times a day in a struggle that determined social standing and made whiteness a symbol of social order and beauty. Young women flaunted white muslin dresses; young men exhibited dazzling white linen that they sometimes shipped to Holland to have starched. Veils, gloves, overshoes, hats, raincoats, fog glasses, every protection was needed in the desperate fight to keep clean. A speck of dirt was considered ungodly, and its confrontation a war on evil, anarchy, and the forces of darkness. Desperately the Englishman fought the demon soot. Pale complexions, like white dresses, were considered the Holy Grail. I was much complimented on mine.

⁓

Lorenzo had told me Amelia Opie's country house, called Roxborough, was in Richmond, Surrey, one of the loveliest and most comfortable seats in all of southern England. We drove through the wrought-iron gates and up the mile-long drive past the clipped green velvet sward toward the white-stone and red brick manor, built in the manner of the architect Palladio, and arriving at the north entrance where an army of stewards, butlers, and housemaids was lined up at attention. I discovered for myself how vain were the pretensions of Tidewater gentry to architectural splendor.

The house was surrounded by fine pastures, splendid flocks of sheep, orchards, fields of hops and corn, dairy farms, and herds of cattle. Richmond was upriver from London, along the Thames estuary. Thousands made their living from the sea, and there were lead and coal mines in the Mendip Hills, forges in Sussex, tin mines in Cornwall, and ironworks in Birmingham. I marveled at how, on its surface, England was so rich, happy, comfortable, placid, and pleased with its lot in life and its place among nations. It was very far from what I had learned at the convention about England and its cities like Liverpool, where the very stones smelled of slaves' blood.

Happily, country living was much simpler than life in London, and although Mrs. Willowpole and I knew that we would be obliged to change our clothes four times a day, the meagerness of our respective wardrobes would be less apparent, since the ladies would all affect "country" simplicity. But we had each brought the one article of clothing absolutely essential to country living—a red cloak in which to walk to church. They were famous in Buckinghamshire and Bedfordshire, and were great, ample capes of crimson or scarlet of finest wool, double-milled and of such an intense dye that they threw a phosphorescent glimmer whenever they moved. They could be seen from miles away on the heaths, and on Sundays, it was beautiful to behold the women in them, assembled for church in the yard, reflecting every ray of the sun and glimmering like a stand of poincianas. In a few years they would disappear from fashion, but in 1825 they were worn over the calicos, velvets, and silks of both the aristocracy and the gentry classes. As Americans, we were considered exotic nobility, the highest rank possible, and treated with the deference reserved for visiting sultanas.

Mrs. Willowpole and I had time to speak to each other in low voices before Amelia Opie, in a magnificent tea gown, arrived to greet us. We had been talking of what all the world might hear, but it was the common effect of such a room as we were in to oblige us to speak low, as if a loud voice would distort the painted murals on the ceiling, or shatter the excellent chandeliers hanging amongst them, or make one of the meticulous leatherbound books that lined the walls and the circular library tables to fall over on their sides.

"Children," cried Amelia Opie, "what a lovely time we're going to have!" This was not the antislavery, political-pamphlet Amelia Opie, but another, up until now unknown to us, creature called the English chatelaine. And we were about to embark on a ronde called the English country-house party. I use *ronde,* but I could have used *etude, mazurka, waltz,* or even *variations on a theme, concerto,* or *symphony,* for a country-house party resembled nothing if not the changing rhythm, tempos, rigorous beat, and flogging execution of a piece of music. In fact, the English country-house party was opera, sometimes more comic than anything else. As when the sandwiches left outside a countess's door as a signal to her lover that the way was clear were eaten by another houseguest who had gotten hungry on the long road to his room. But sometimes the country house erupted in tragic little pieces of reality.

On our last day in the country, Lorenzo and I sat at the edge of the artificial lake and watched the swans sail back and forth, eyes alert for food, predatory beaks ready to strike any land creatures that moved within range. Amongst them was one magnificent black male who moved amid the others with remote and ironic dignity.

"You make fun of me. I love that, you know," said Lorenzo.

A carefully arranged perspective fanned out behind the black swan like a tapestry, arranged in the current fashion of meticulously imitating the chaos of nature by having a slew of gardeners torture the landscape back into a vision of a primitive Eden. The ideal garden was now considered to be irregular, comprising sloping, undulating expanses of grass, sinuous walks and streams, classical temples and follies, and, if possible, at least one genuine ruin. Artificial brooks and lakes like this one abounded, spanned by romantic stone bridges and moats. Amelia Opie's husband had spent a fortune making his park resemble the best landscape paintings.

"A swan's bite can break the arm of a grown man," said Lorenzo.

"Hum," I said, staring instead at the imitation lake, in the fake landscape, surrounded by artificial ruins, all placed on a man-made knoll which then dipped into a forged wood, while swans swam about under a counterfeit Roman arch.

"I could almost wish, Harriet—" He stopped suddenly and hesitated. It was so unusual for Lorenzo to falter that I looked up at him in surprise. At that instant, something about him, although I couldn't say what, made me wish I was back with my mother, or my father, anywhere but where I was, for I was sure he was going to ask a question to which I did not know, and would never know, the answer.

I remained calm, as if I had been condemned and was merely awaiting execution, my prayers and confessions already hanging in the air along with the noose. It was despicable of me to shrink from hearing any speech of Lorenzo's, for I had the power to put an end to it. I would simply tell him who I was and what I was and count on his surprise and humiliation to guarantee his silence. It would be more a war cry than a confession—more a retaliation than an answer. After all, I couldn't keep running away every time a man asked me to marry him. I pulled my red cloak around me closer, despising myself. Hadn't I deliberately led Lorenzo into admiring me? Hadn't I practiced on Lorenzo, on Sydney—even on Brice? I wondered idly if he had written out his proposal of marriage, or if he was going to ask me now, in person, in this fake Eden.

"Harriet, do you love anyone else?"

"Lorenzo, before you go any further, let me say this: I am not what you think I am or what I *appear* to be. When you find out, you'll regret this moment as I do now. I did not know you cared for me in that way." But of course I knew; how could I not know? "I have always thought of you as a friend, and would rather go on thinking of you as that."

"Ah, Harriet. Forgive me . . . I've been too abrupt with such a subject. Only . . . let me hope that one day you might accept a declaration. Give me the poor comfort of telling me you have never seen anyone else whom you could—"

"Oh, Lorenzo, if only you had not gotten this fancy into your head!"

I was shocked by my cold, calculated decision to use Lorenzo's love as a test for confessing my secret to Thance. They were enough alike. And in my callous naiveté, I really believed I would be doing them both a favor. They were both white, weren't they? Then their reactions would be the reactions of *all* white men. . . .

"I am not what you think I am," I repeated. "I cannot listen to what you want to say without forewarning you. I am the illegitimate daughter of the third President of the United States, Thomas Jefferson, and a slave, Sally Hemings. I am therefore, as you must realize from your travels in America, not only a bastard, but a Negro . . . an African, if you like. Is there . . . anything, now, that you wish to tell me?"

It was a much more brutal revelation than even I had intended. Lorenzo's total disbelief turned it into the punchline of a joke. I almost laughed myself.

Instead, contempt mingled with pain at my having astonished him in this way, and my lip curled in slight disdain.

With an imperious air, he said, "You, a colored woman? You're about as black as I am." I hung my head. "Good God, look at me. You can't be serious, Harriet!" he exploded. "Why not King George's bastard, while you're at it? Is this some kind of American-style humor?"

But he knew I wasn't joking. I had discovered a submerged streak of rage and cruelty I hadn't known I possessed. It now blew around poor Lorenzo, someone who had become a friend and the person who understood me almost as well as Thance. Yet I wasn't sad.

"Harriet," he groaned, his voice a reservoir of pain. "You should make allowances for the mortification of a lover."

"The fact of my birth is not your mortification, nor mine. I don't feel sorry for either of us."

And then he said something so human, so pathetic, and so pitiful, I almost loved him.

"You must love me a bit to have told me something so prejudicial."

"To my happiness?"

"To everything. To your future . . . to your very survival!" he sputtered, loosing his cool intonation.

"Do you think that all Negroes are unhappy because they are not white?" I said.

"But you *are* white!"

"If I'm white, then why do I see pity in your eyes?"

It was like the story of the Eastern potentate who dipped his head into a basin of water at the magician's command, and ere he took it out, saw his whole life pass before his eyes.

"Because of your illegitimate birth," he whispered. "That's not to be forgiven."

My eyes widened.

"There is an injury where reparation is impossible," murmured Lorenzo. "Neither wealth nor education can repair the wrong of dishonored birth. It's a matter of geography . . . illegal aliens crossing an inviolable frontier."

This time I did laugh, because he was perfectly sincere. It was not my drop of black blood, nor even my role as an impostor; it was my rank as a bastard from which he recoiled. It was so English. And so absurd.

Illegal alien, I thought, burning with shame. What a perfect name. What a perfect name for what I was in my own country. It had been self-deception to believe I could escape. I could be as fair as a lily, as beautiful as a houri, and as chaste as ice, and I would never be anything more than black contraband.

"He . . . your father sent you away . . . here?"

"No."

"There is another man. Someone you love, whom you are protecting as you haven't protected me."

Suddenly I sensed that he was as anxious to leave me as I was for him to do so. We swayed over the abyss of my revelation like two drunks.

Almost as one, like automates, we turned at the sound of the dinner gong, the silvery sound reminding me of the funeral bells that had tolled my arrival in London.

"Come," he said, not unkindly, his voice rough with unspoken grief.

"No," I whispered. "I'll follow in a moment. I want a few moments alone . . . please."

He bowed, and as he straightened, our eyes met unaccountably. There was no recrimination in his, and no recollection in mine. Only sadness. Had I, despite everything, been a little bit in love with Lorenzo? As soon as he was out of sight, I turned and leaned weakly against a juniper tree that must have been a thousand years old. Once, long ago at Montpelier, I had prayed that the bark of a juniper tree would scrape my white skin from my bones. No tears came. I felt my first streak of defiance. I was young. The world was open. There would be others.

8 P.M.
Roxborough

My dear Lorenzo,

I have never thought of you but as a friend. Nor will I ever. Please, let us both forget this afternoon ever took place. If you think my deception has tormented you heartlessly and without reason, think a bit of my dilemma and forgive me. You are grieved, but not irreparably. You are wronged, but not indelibly. I release you from the promise *you made to yourself,* not to me, in a moment that will never fade from my memory. What are we anyway, at this moment? A brother and sister. For you know me better now than any person on earth!

I don't have to ask you never, never to speak of me again. Your pride will do that, and you will probably have no more opportunity. In a few weeks, I leave for Paris with Mrs. Willowpole and Brice (who are as innocent of my lie as you were). Even though I wrong them, leave me this possibility. I have trusted you with the power to ruin my life in exchange for the unhappiness I've caused you. I beg you only for silence. Remember I am a fugitive.

Good-bye.

H.

14

We are not immortal ourselves, my friend, how can we expect our enjoyments to be so? We have no rose without its thorn; no pleasure without alloy. It is the law of our existence: and we must acquiesce.

Thomas Jefferson

Our little group, Dorcas, Brice, Sydney, and I, spent the rest of the winter in London. The absence of Lorenzo, which no one dared question, added to my melancholy. It was as if I had been living in a coma up until now, sleeping in the dust of Monticello, while a cosmic struggle of life and death, blood and commerce, had been raging right over my head for three hundred years. I now copied with familiarity the great names of antislavery: Wilberforce, Clarkson, Benez and John Wesley, Abbé Raynal, Nathaniel Peabody, and Granville Sharp. Places that had only been shapes Lorenzo had drawn for me were now as real as my trembling hand as I copied Cuba, Antigua, Santo Domingo, Haiti, Jamaica, Brazil, Sierra Leone, Guinea, Tobago.

I had read the latest tracts, knew the titles of the famous associations: Society for the Abolition of Slavery, Society for Mitigating and Gradually Abolishing the State of Slavery, Society for Promoting the Emigration of Free Persons of Color, Society for the Civilization of Africa, Society for the Suppression of the Slave Trade. I knew all about the king's plans for compensated emancipation, the Seamen's Act, the Emancipation Act, the Fugitive Slave Act, the crusade against slave-trade piracy and for immediate abolition. In five months I had become a walking encyclopedia of suits and countersuits, court cases, and hundreds of petitions, evasions, imprisonments, alliances, parliamentary censures, manumission laws, and the internal slave trade in the United States.

Slavery was not eternal.

The pain of Lorenzo faded, and I almost forgot the possibility of his denunciation or even his blackmail. I was surprised by the number of rich English Quakers leading the antislavery organizations in Britain: the Gurneys and the Buxtons, the Forsters, Sturgeses, Allens, Braithwaites. They urged Dorcas Willowpole to consolidate her efforts with abolitionists in England and France. Almost as if to make up for her lack of official acceptance, we were lavishly entertained and squired about on sightseeing trips to view hospitals, working-class neighborhoods, and the shocking, fetid slums of London. Distinguished Britons called at our boardinghouse. Even the famous debonair Thomas Clarkson visited us with his daughter-in-law and bestowed on Mrs. Willowpole a lock of his hair, which she was to preserve carefully and take back to the States, where she distributed it strand by strand.

By March, all our reports were in, our letters written or answered, our good-byes said. We left for Paris, taking a coach from Hatchett's New White Cellar. Just before we left, Lorenzo answered the letter I had written to him at Roxborough House.

Harriet,

Don't despise me. I have a heart, notwithstanding my silence. As proof of it, I believe I love you more now than ever—if I do not hate you for the disdain with which you have treated the truth. As for your secret, upon my honor, it is safe with me, for I will carry it to my grave where it shall rest beside my *hacret lateri lethalis arundo.*

Enzo

There are two routes from London to Paris, one by Dover and Calais and the other by Brighton and Dieppe. Since I made the arrangements, I chose the route Adrian Petit had taken with Maman and Maria. With us in that carriage sat a shadowy presence: my mother. Her voice was only one of a quartet of voices that accompanied me throughout my stay in France. Maman, languid, sweet, melancholy, and mournful, was first violin; Father, an octave lower, had a voice I had never heard before, amorous, secretive, lightheaded, and resonant. Adrian Petit, tender and earthy, cynical and funny, was the cello; and James, passionate, ominous, bitter, contagious, joined in an incessant bass. The voices wove through my consciousness, each with a line or a laugh, a cry, or a reproach, a description or an invitation, a lie or a sultry denunciation.

We slept at Dover and crossed the channel by day. The next morning we departed from Calais and crossed the marshy valley of the river Somme to Amiens, then sped through rolling fields to the splendors of Chantilly. We stayed overnight and reached Saint-Denis at noon. The spires of its cathedral pierced the custard-colored sky, and the edifice itself lifted from the surrounding golden cloth of wheat. We reached the Hotel Meurice on the rue de Saint-Honoré the following afternoon. After leaving our luggage and Mrs. Willowpole at the hotel, Brice and I stepped onto the cobblestone street, which was within walking distance of the Louvre. I listened to a voice that seemed to be my father's speaking to me from the many shadows, the sparkling fountains, the white buildings.

FATHER: *Tell me everything. Who has died and who has married, who has hanged himself because he cannot marry.*

Cannot marry. The words seemed a prophecy and an injunction until James's voice interceded.

JAMES: *Slavery is outlawed in France. We are on French soil. That means you are emancipated. Free.*

MAMAN: *I don't believe you. You make so many jokes, James, tell so many farfetched stories.*

JAMES: *I slapped your mother's face more in my own rage than at her disbelief. She didn't believe me! Her own brother. Freedom to Sally Hemings was a vague, glimmering place from which no one ever returned to prove it actually existed.*

From the hotel I could see the Place de la Concorde and the Champs-Elysées stretching beyond the invisible mansion where my father had lived. Then James's voice returned.

JAMES: *I hadn't seen my sister for three years. She had been eleven and I nineteen when I'd left Monticello as valet to Thomas Jefferson. She would bring the sweet breath of Monticello and family news—but she would also bring the reminder of slavehood I had never forgotten. Never mind that. I was free on French soil and, thinking myself free, could even look on my master with a certain affection.*

FATHER: *I told Sally I was going away to Amsterdam. Suddenly the words "Promise me" burst from her, more a sob than anything else. I looked at her*

in amazement, then drew her head up and looked deep into her eyes. Deep in
their golden centers was a dark pinprick. My own reflection.

And my mother's voice, almost unrecognizable, described the anguish and
ecstasy of first love.

MAMAN: *One day, six months after I'd arrived, I passed a gilded mirror in the*
entrance of the hotel and was pleased with what I saw. I had recovered from
my smallpox, was learning French and new and independent ways of thinking,
and my eyes no longer slid off the inspection of whites. I could even look them
in the eye. What joy I felt when I picked up my skirts and raced as fast as
I could from the Champs-Elysées, across the fields as far as the bridge of
Neuilly. I would run until I had a stitch in my side and then pause, listening
to the pumping of my heart, the whistling of my breath.

FATHER: *I did not consider myself a vain man, but I was quite pleased with the*
likeness the sculptor Houdon had begun of me. I had just seen the plaster for
the first time a few days before Maria and Sally were to arrive with Petit. I
had become something of a dandy in my manner of dressing, favoring creamy
dun and sapphire worsted and red patent-leather high-heeled shoes.

It was Petit now who took up the theme, reminding me that I had
promised to go to Paris not only to learn something about my parents but
to learn something about myself. My guardian continued.

PETIT: *When we arrived, Maria Jefferson burst into tears at the sight of her*
father, and Sally at the sight of her brother. James finally took Sally into his
arms. I do believe Jefferson was intimidated by his own daughter, mostly
because, as he later told me, he would not have known her if he had met her
on the street.

"Aren't you tired?" said Brice. "We've been walking for an hour—
perhaps we should go back to the hotel. After all, we have all spring in
France."

But we continued along the banks of the Seine, crossing the river at the
first bridge we came to and finding ourselves facing the stone mountain of
Notre Dame, its twin towers gleaming in the sunlight, its slate roof catching
the golden tint of sunlight which had just broken through the low-lying haze
that often covered the entire valley in which the city of Paris found itself. And
there, the voice of my mother caught up with me again.

MAMAN: *Perhaps I had always known that he would claim me. Hadn't the same thing happened to my mother and my sisters before me? I watched him secretly to see if he knew, but I realized he would know only when the moment arrived. I could hasten or delay that moment, but I was powerless to prevent it.*

⁓

I said to Brice, "Let's go to the seven-o'clock mass before we go home."

Notre Dame was immense. At the end of the longer nave glowed the famous stained-glass rose window, a disk of flame and color that seemed to hover like an apparition over the congregation at prayer and the crowds strolling amongst the endless arches and pillars. The darkness accentuated the luminosity of the windows behind us. The chords of the great organ filled the space, grandiose and transcendent.

It was a requiem I didn't recognize. I stood transfixed by its beauty and power, ravished by the music that had reduced the worshipers and tourists alike to tiny points on a nappe of sound surrounded by stone pillars and molten glass. Petit's voice wove itself insidiously among the notes.

PETIT: *I saw this affection between the ambassador and his slave develop. They seemed drawn to each other by mysterious threads I did not completely understand, until James explained to me that they were literally the same family, related by blood and by marriage to each other. The ambassador's wife had been her half sister. I would never understand, perfect servant that I was, discreet in my service, correct in my silence, loyal in my protection of the ruling class and their privileges, this particular American family.*

I knelt then in the somber, soaring music and wondered if by the time I left Paris I'd have solved the pulsations of my own heart toward my kin any better, or understood the lineage that made me idolize and despise both the blood that made me a Hemings and that which marked me a Jefferson.

⁓

It was dark by the time we got back to the hotel, and the hotel guests in the lobby brushed past us on their way to dinner. Mrs. Willowpole was already dressed and downstairs.

"Well, where have you been, children?" she scolded. "We'll be late for dinner if you don't hurry."

That night I lay in my bed and listened to the night sounds: carriages grinding the cobblestones, gaslights hissing, church bells striking the hours, and at sunrise the cries of the nearby market of Saint-Honoré. My voices were at rest, but they would return.

I would have loved to share those voices with Brice or even Dorcas Willowpole, but they were too close to the truth and Lorenzo's words too livid and fresh. Each night, in the seclusion of my room, I would interrogate my voices—first Petit, always the perfect guide and valet; then James, the angry young man; then my father, the bemused patrician, the American in Paris; and last my mother, the slave girl. Their chorus lulled me. Complex, contradictory, self-serving, or brutally honest, each presented its version of those two winters in Paris in which my father had seduced my mother and my own biography had begun.

Brice and I spent many hours with his guidebook for English tourists. Every sinew in my body was straining toward the Champs-Elysées and my father's mansion, which stood at the wrought-iron gates of the Chaillot, until one day as we started up the rue de Saint-Honoré, I said, "My father lived in Paris for a time when he was very young. He . . . he had a minor diplomatic post as a secretary to the American ambassador to King Louis, just before the Revolution."

"Who was that?"

"The ambassador?"

"Yes."

"Thomas Jefferson."

"Really? I'd forgotten he'd been minister before being President. Was that before Benjamin Franklin?"

"No, after. From 1784 to 1790. The embassy was just up the Champs-Elysées at the Chaillot gates."

"Well, we'll have to see if it's still there, some thirty years later. A lot of great houses were destroyed during the Revolution, and more have been torn down by Haussmann to make his grand boulevards and roundabouts. It's a wonder Napoléon could steal enough statuary to fill them. But is not the Egyptian obelisk an awesome sight?"

We turned up the promenade of the Champs-Elysées, which bristled with multicolored flowered borders: tulips and hyacinths, lilies of the valley and crocuses spread like Oriental carpets, escorting the strolling couples and the prancing horses of the Paris gentry. We passed the Tuileries gardens, filled with children who darted about amongst the stone facades like butterflies. The elaborate lacquered carriages, equipages, calèches, and cabriolets moved down the famous chestnut-shaded promenade behind trotting pairs. I wondered how many secrets like mine were buried under the surface of this luxurious city. There were no secrets like mine.

I stood looking up at the imposing white stone facade of the Hôtel de Langeac, which had served as the embassy. Behind the high, gilded-iron fence, the well-kept gardens spread out in a triangular form of clipped box hedges and miniature cypresses. I thought I saw a figure move fleetingly behind a window, but it could have been my imagination. Could it have been James? I wondered. This time the voices chanted a libretto.

MAMAN: *Thomas Jefferson was occupied with the mysterious Maria Cosway and rarely saw us except for Sunday dinner. I was jealous—her exquisite manners, her magnificent gowns, her radiant smile, her blondness, her haughty condescension and proprietary airs, which made James mimic her behind her back and Petit raise his eyebrows.*

JAMES: *My bad nature was considered melancholy, even romantic, by the French, and they indulged me in it. Everyone thought I was so handsome, even noble, and I could disperse my latent anger with one delicious smile.*

MAMAN: *Fear overwhelmed me a thousand times a day. Blood would rush to my head so that I clutched a velvet hanging on the back of an armchair. At night I fell asleep sitting upright on the side of the bed. My body would be turned away from the door, but my head and shoulders would be turned toward it. There was no lock, but I would not have dared turn a key even had there been one. Lord keep me from falling down.*

FATHER: *I possessed something I had created from beginning to end without interference or objections or compromises. In a way I had birthed her. As much as I had my daughter. I had created her in my own image of womanly perfection, this speck of dust, this handful of clay from Monticello.*

I had no idea how long I had been standing there. My presence seemed to be a command for her. I surveyed her like a man who, afraid of heights, scans a valley from the ledge of a tower. I rushed toward her with all my will and loneliness, with no words passing between us except those most potent of words, ruler of the mighty as well as the helpless. "Je t'aime," I said, and she had answered, "Merci, monsieur."

MAMAN: *I was seized with a terrible yearning. Nothing would ever be the same again. Nothing would ever free me of him. Nothing would erase those strange words of love which in my weakness, I had to believe. I felt around me an exploding flower, not just of passion, but of long deprivation, a hunger for things forbidden, a darkness and unreason, of rage against the death of the other I so resembled. I became one with her, and it was not my name that sprang from him, but that of my half sister.*

JAMES: *I discovered the concubinage of my sister when I turned back the counter-pane of my master's bed.*

MAMAN: *That day James took part in the fall of the Bastille, he had come back feverish, battered, and dirty, to dazzle the audience of the Hôtel de Langeac with the story of its fall. His eyes seemed to say: "This slave from Virginia's made history today. This slave ran with the Revolution. I am mine. We are going to take ourselves to freedom. If God let me do this, then God will let us have our freedom without stealing it." He smiled and I smiled back.*

JAMES: *Men don't free what they love. I had surprised Thomas Jefferson more than once looking at Sally Hemings as I had often seen him contemplating some rare object he meant to keep. It was the look of a man who both coveted and had the means to possess what he coveted.*

FATHER: *Promise me you will not abandon me again.*

MAMAN: *I promise, Master.*

FATHER: *I swear to cherish you and never desert you.*

MAMAN: *Yes, Master.*

FATHER: *I promise solemnly that your children will be free.*

MAMAN: *As God is your witness?*

FATHER: *As God is my witness.*

FATHER: *Bolt the door.*

The facade of the Hôtel de Langeac swam before my eyes.

"Brice," I said softly, "do you think we could hire a carriage to take us to Marly? We passed it on our way to Paris. It is supposed to be . . . the most beautiful park in France."

The next day we all drove over the handsome stone bridge of Neuilly to Bougival and from there to the famous machine of Marly, a hydraulic wonder built a hundred years earlier to raise water from the Seine to the aqueduct and reservoirs of Versailles and its twin—the royal château of Marly. My voices were all in disharmony. Every object was beautiful to my father. But my mother's voice interrupted. "Your father promised me there would never be a white mistress at Monticello." As I looked down from the heights of the village of Louveciennes onto the great existing park, James's voice reconstructed it in my mind's eye. Then my father's voice joined in: "How beautiful was every object, the pont de Neuilly, the hills along the Seine, the rainbows of the machine of Marly, the terrace of Saint-Germain, the château, the gardens, the statues of Marly . . ."

MAMAN: *It was the summer of my fifteenth year that I saw Marly for the first time. It seemed to float above me, the earth, in its own nature, its own sky, its own sun.*

PETIT: *Imagine a young woman come with her love to Marly, standing beside him.*

MAMAN: *I was beginning to understand this strange, impulsive, melancholy man, full of contradictions and secrets, who owned me, my family, and his unborn child. How did it matter that he was master and I slave? That he took more space in the world than most men did not concern me, neither his fame nor his power. I cherished him. The future, like Marly, stretched out before me, total and shoreless. The surrounding fragrance drugged me and made me careless of what awaited, just beyond my view.*

MAMAN: *The gardens, canals, terraces stretched for miles. On each side of the magnificent palace were six summer pavilions connected by sidewalks bowered with jasmine and honeysuckle. Water fell in cascades from the top of the hill behind the château, forming a reservoir where swans floated. In the main canal, glistening marble horses mounted by bronze men cavorted, and here and there one could see tiny gems which were ladies moving along the path and labyrinths. The only sound was wind and water; all human sound had been reduced by the vast scale to silence. That day convinced me that there was no Virginia. No slavehood. There was no destiny, it seemed, that did not include this place, this hour, this Marly.*

Like a ghostly mirage, the contours of the demolished castle seemed to have engraved themselves into the thin bluish atmosphere, and its foundations traced themselves in the double-hued grasslands below us.

I returned many times to Marly before we left Paris for good. I'd stand there on the heights and try to imagine my mother gazing down at the same panorama. My mother had not come, as I had, from the enlightenment of four years of freedom, but as a slave girl, her only identity, only to hear her brother proclaim slavery a sin. She had stood here and listened to her lover promise there would never be a white mistress at Monticello. She had believed him when he promised her children would all be free. . . . And wasn't I free? Free to detest my mother the slave, or adore her. Free to condemn my father the master, or forgive him. But how could I do either? Paris hadn't given me the answer.

"Lorenzo's coming to Paris."

"What?"

"I've spoken to Aunt Dorcas. I don't think we shall wait for him. Several of my acquaintances have confirmed that the political situation in France is extremely volatile and dangerous. Charles the Tenth is sure to be overthrown, and a new republic formed. There are riots in the provinces, and it is only a matter of time before unrest reaches Paris. Which means revolution . . . barricades, street fighting. It's happened before. I think we should leave now."

I wasn't following Brice's logic, but I asked submissively, "Where?"

"Why, to Italy! We could leave in a few days. Our passports are in order. We just have to get them back from the prefecture. You mentioned once that you yearned to go to Florence."

I studied Brice. Was he protecting me as a brother, helping me flee from Lorenzo out of pity, or abducting me for his own purposes? Whichever it was, I could visit Italy without having to beg or scheme for it.

"It's true," he said, "that the newspaper headlines are alarming. The Estates General is calling for a republican constitutional monarchy, and there are strikers in Lyon and riots in front of the National Assembly. It seems Louis Philippe has returned from exile in America."

America . . . I felt as if I were being pursued by Sykes again. Wouldn't America ever leave me alone? My face must have shown my alarm.

"Then it's settled. We leave for Italy. And Dorcas thinks we should spend a few days in Lausanne . . . where she has some people to see. I'll make the arrangements this time."

We stopped for a week in Lausanne. By the time we arrived in Florence, I had made up my mind to find out if Maria Cosway was living or dead.

105 RUE DU RIVOLI, PARIS
MAY 1ST

My dearest Charlotte,

After the shattering experience of the convention and the new life in London, I survived a tragicomic misadventure in Amelia Opie's country house in Surrey. I didn't know whether to laugh or cry, so I have fled to Paris.

Arriving by coach from Calais, I had the strange feeling I had been here before, in another life. Everything seemed so familiar—landscapes, descriptions, the city itself, with its *magnifique* art and luminosity, its gardens and monuments. I've never seen a people who will erect a monument in bronze or marble to everything and anything at the drop of a hat. There are still traces of the Revolution. In the place where the Bastille used to stand, they have erected a huge column of gilded bronze to the glory of the Revolution and the victories of the infamous, now-destroyed dungeon. The people of Paris can't be ignorant of their history when they have a monument on every corner!

For weeks I have heard voices that accompany me everywhere— cajoling, intimate, loving voices, plaintive, happy, tormented, exuberant, mysterious—you would think Paris was haunted. Perhaps it is, for me. I was happy to leave England. I have had my fill of Englishmen and their bizarre way of looking at life—form is all, content nothing; moreover, it is better not to think at all, but merely follow the rules—remain on one's insular little island and never breach an etiquette or a frontier. And who makes the rules? Men. And they insist it is for our (women's) own good —that if the world's affairs were left to women, there would be only emotion, anarchy, and chaos. I have seen in London what these same men have perpetrated on the world—the myriad sufferings, so great we women couldn't possibly do worse, so great we can't even imagine such depths of cruelty. But being closer to nature and children and common sense, I truly believe, Charlotte, that we can do better. And as I roam Paris with Brice Willowpole and my voices, which have in a way become my family, just as Paris has become a kind of home. I will be loath to leave this place. Perhaps I'll never leave, although Dorcas and Brice insist we should quit Paris for a while to avoid political disturbances here. And where are we going? Italy! I have always wanted to see Italy, and I intend to go to see if an old friend of my father's in Lodi is still alive. I intend to surprise her, and perhaps the riddle wrapped up in a dilemma, as Brice calls me, has a rhyme or reason and Lodi has the answer. At least I pray God it does.

Do you see Thance? Is he in Philadelphia or abroad? Oh, Charlotte, Charlotte! Voices. The opera again tonight, and new voices to go with my old ones. Music is the only safe place for me, the place no one can hurt me. Perhaps, in a way, I have composed an opera of my own here: fatal and tragic and romantic. The voices I hear in my head in this country. But they haven't answered my question, Charlotte. They haven't answered my question.

Your loving and lonely Harriet

15

The wheels of time moved with a rapidity of which those of our carriage gave but a faint idea, and yet, in the evening, when one took a retrospect of the day, what a mass of happiness we traveled over.

Thomas Jefferson

On the fifth of May 1826, at 8:50 A.M., our three figures spread one thick black shadow across the treeless piazza of Lodi. The town lay under the dauntless Italian light, which was what I imagined light in Africa must be like. The square in which we stood was perfectly silent except for a lark's song, and there were no villagers abroad but for a bandy-legged old man trailing four saddled mules behind him. Reigning over the rectangular space to the north was the Church of the Crown of Santa Maria of the Annunciation, a handsome, squat, rectangular edifice with a golden roof of glistening Byzantine mosaics. As if by consensus, we had all dressed in black: Brice in a black frock coat, black trousers, and straw hat; Bruno, our guide, in a black shirt open at the neck and black pantaloons stuck into filthy black boots, his black carbine slung over one shoulder; and myself, in a high-necked, black linen dress trimmed in grosgrain galloons and eyelets. The train of my skirt swept the ground, leaving a trail of corrugated dust which erased my footprints. The black veil attached to my straw hat served to hide my face as well as keep out the dust, which rose in miniature whirlwinds from the parched earth. I held a black parasol over my head, which merged into the long inky outline: flesh, transparent shadow, and black cloth with the shadow of Bruno's gun as unicorn.

Brice and I had left Dorcas Willowpole inspecting the village *fabbrica* for which Lodi was famous and which produced white procelain dishes, pierced with elaborate and delicate cut-out designs called *jourance,* the most expensive and beautifully wrought porcelain in all of Italy. I had explained to Dorcas Willowpole that I had a private and urgent pilgrimage to make to the College della Grazie convent of the *Dames Inglesi,* in Lodi, and she had suggested that all of us go, concluding that the famous cathedral and its even more famous porcelain were well worth the trip. The hotel in Florence had insisted we hire an armed guide and coachman, and had sent us Bruno, as dark as his name. He now stood between Brice and me, a broad-chested, silent giant with the profile of a face on a Roman coin. It was he who insisted on the mules, explaining to us in his halting English that the convent was erected on one of the hills surrounding the village and was a good four-hour climb.

I looked up at the rolling hills. I had traveled to London to find out something about world slavery and had discovered it was not infallible, but doomed. I had traveled to Paris to find out something about my mother's slavery, and had encountered the echoes of impossible love. And now I was in Lodi to find out something about my father's slavery: that fateful crossing of disparate lives called destiny. In Lodi I would find the famous woman painter Maria Cosway, who had briefly been my father's mistress and was known as *la maestra* for her profession and *la madre* for her convent. She educated English ladies of good family, sheltered and trained novices, country girls who were promised to the order, and gave refuge to abandoned or divorced wives, disgraced and pregnant young girls, repudiated mistresses. And illegitimate daughters, I thought. Perhaps this was just the place for me.

The devout Catholicism of Maria Cosway, Dorcas had explained, was the only facet of her reputation that was not dubious. Her piety had been recognized by the emperor of Austria, Francis I, who had made her a baroness for having established a branch of the religious order called the *Dames Inglesi,* which meant "the English ladies." And so this title had been added to the others by the villagers, who referred to their Italianate English benefactress and landlord as *la baronéssa maestra Maria, madre della Dames Inglesi e nobile donna.*

The scent of mule manure that surrounded the old man made me hold my breath as Bruno helped me mount sidesaddle. Brice had insisted on coming along as my chaperone and the two Italians doubled as bodyguards. The Italian states of 1826 were in the throes of popular revolt against Rome, and a wave of republicanism had swept a new general-bandit called Garibaldi into power. I noticed that Bruno wore the black shirt and the red bandanna of the general, while the old man wore a white band across his forehead, which symbolized the aristocracy and the pope. The old man, whose name was

Acromeo, would have found nothing unusual in a lone English lady climbing the Baroness's *monticello,* as he called it, to my astonishment. No one had ever told me that *monticello* meant "little mountain." But Brice had been adamant. No white lady for whom he was responsible was going to go anywhere with two strange Italian bodyguards in the Piedmont hills, which were full of bandits that the ruling family, the Gonzagas, periodically ordered their soldiers to either kill or exile.

It was a quarter to two before we reached the white-and-yellow walls of the abbey and rang the cowbell attached by an iron chain to the heavy, iron-studded wooden doors. They swung open almost immediately, as if we were expected, and before me stood a nun in crimson and white, outlined against a long allée of cypress and oleander trees that seemed to stretch into infinity and then drop suddenly into the sky. She held a basket of food for the guides and was followed by a servant, who carried a pail of water for the mules. When Brice made a move toward the open doors, the Italians re- strained him, explaining that no men were allowed beyond that boundary. At his quizzical look, I only shrugged, remembering Dorcas's remark at the convention: "Now you know what it feels like to be a Negro."

The gardens were laid out Italian-style, alternating fruit, vegetables, and flowers in rigid geometric patterns of colored greenery transversed by long alleys and vistas which ended in statuary or marble fountains. We passed orange and olive groves, lemon trees clipped in topiary, and fruit trees standing in squares of lavender and rosemary. Jasmine and morning glory climbed over stone walls, some crumbling, which divided the gardens from the fields in which I could see workers moving. The scents of basil and magnolia mingled with a dozen other fragrances in a riot of odors that climbed the walls like roses, settling on the sun-baked walls like mist. Through the opening I could see the vineyards in the distance on the surrounding hills, their slopes pierced with serpentine rivers, which flowed amongst the cornfields and rice paddies, dotted with cypress and evergreens.

I stopped for a second and slowly raised my veil and took off my straw hat in order to feel the sun on my bare head. I closed my eyes against the magnificence that existed in the same world with injustice and misery. Could I belong here, I reasoned, rather than in a country that despised me, where a single drop of blood that recalled my origins was enough to raise a barrier of disgust and revulsion that I could never transcend?

I followed the nun, whose name was Sarah, into a rectangular interior court lined with mosaic-encrusted pillars supporting high arched arcades that pro- vided shade and portals for the nuns' cells that gave onto it. Each cell had a window and a wooden hatch for food. The pavement was of thick white stone and slabs of terra-cotta, and terra-cotta pots held flourishing oleander trees in blue, white, and magenta.

We had arrived at the chapel of the Church of Santa Maria della Grazie and the abbess's loggia. Would I care to refresh myself, asked Sarah, before my interview with the baroness? I accepted and was shown to one of the rooms giving onto the court, which proved to be a large, airy, and simple room of red and yellow brick with a white marble floor, furnished with heavy northern Italian furniture. There was a bedstead draped with a white muslin mosquito net, a table with a simple chair, and an armchair. To one side was a high, deep cupboard and a small carved stool. There was an oil lamp, and on the walls hung the white porcelain plates of Lodi and a blue-and-white porcelain crucifix.

I laid my hat on the bed and removed my gloves. I washed my face and hands in the blue porcelain basin beside the bed. I smoothed my hair by rote, as there was no mirror, although I could see my reflection in the washbasin. I looked very severely Philadelphian and extremely American. I heard the door latch lift behind me and another English voice say, "La madre superiore will see you now."

What did I expect to learn from this strange, eccentric courtesan-painter about my father's past? Did I want only to verify that she had actually existed, had seen him, touched him, loved him? What did any of this have to do with my mother's choice of slavery over freedom?

The abbess rose as I entered the room. I did not know what my greeting to her would be; there was no need, for she greeted me first.

"But you are American . . . Patsy! Is that you? . . . but no, you cannot be; you must be her . . . daughter. You are one of Martha Randolph's daughters? Surely you are a member of Thomas's family?"

The abbess stopped, confused, almost angry. She couldn't tell me who I was. Then she smiled at me.

"I'm not Patsy's daughter," I said. "I'm her half sister, Harriet of Monticello. The President's natural daughter . . ."

I flung the words defiantly into the stunned, expectant silence. What could be worse than trying to explain oneself? But the smile remained.

"A natural daughter of Mr. Jefferson? Patsy's half sister?" said Maria Cosway.

"Yes."

"And your father sent you to me?"

I looked down at my hands. I wished it were true. Should I lie?

"No," I replied. "He doesn't know I'm here. Or even that I know of your existence. I don't know why I came, except . . . no, my father has not sent me away in the way you think . . . as a recognized bastard . . . in the English manner. For we are many children at Monticello, in truth slaves since we are our mother's children, but allowed to run away when we are twenty-one and pass for white."

"Pass . . . for white?"

"Yes."

"Aren't you white?"

"A slave can't be white . . . at least in America."

"Ah . . . I see."

"You mistook me for my half sister."

"Indeed. And your mother's still alive?"

"Yes."

"And you are the youngest?"

"No, I have two younger brothers."

"How old are you?"

"Twenty-four."

"Twenty-four—you look much younger," she said pensively. "Imagine, a letter to your father is on my desk. We have corresponded as friends for all these years without our ever having seen each other since Paris. Once, long ago, I had thought to visit him in America, but I never did."

I stared at the abbess. She was everything I hated. I hated her because she was white. I hated her because my father had loved her once. I hated her because perhaps he still loved her. I hated her because she had shared more of my father's life through his letters, living three thousand miles away and absent for over thirty years, than I ever had sleeping twenty-one years in his house.

"Please, sit down, Harriet, before you fall down."

Maria Cosway was as beautiful as my mother, and like my mother, her adventurous life seemed to have left no trace on her face. Her body was so wrapped in white linen that there was little to see of it. Her habit was a medieval one of layers of starched linen caught high under the breast and hanging in a bell to the floor. It was covered by a starched apron in front, and behind by a wide, capelike train attached at the shoulders by two gold pins between which was suspended a heavy gold chain carrying a large, jeweled, magnificent crucifix. Her coif was triangular and hung to her shoulders. The stiff linen was held by a pale blue cotton crown made from galloon ribbon, which formed a cross over her skull and fitted tight across her brow. It was held in place by a chin strap, so that only a small portion of her face was visible. To the ribbon of her crown was attached a monocle which she had pulled down over her left eye, enlarging it to twice the size of the other.

The great blue cyclopean depth swam with unasked questions.

As she leaned forward, the long sleeves of her habit swept forward onto the table that separated us. The lens glinted in the late-afternoon sun and sent a kaleidoscopic pattern of light onto the wall. I noticed she was ample, almost fat. As she rose, an iron rosary and a ring of keys clashed at her waist, reminding me of my grandmother.

"You are incognito, then?"

"It is rather an extravagant name for what I am, but yes—one could say that I am incognito."

"You are not . . . wanted by the police?"

"No."

"You think I am a part of your father's life that's been hidden from you?"

"All of my father's life has been hidden from me."

"You . . . look so much like Thomas Jefferson, one can hardly deny your kinship."

"I came with a delegate to the antislavery conference in London."

"How fitting." She laughed. "Your father had a very bizarre attitude toward freedom. He wanted it for some and slavery for others."

"The attitude of a Virginian."

"So I'm told."

"His letters are about Monticello's beauty and freedom. America is a place I should like to visit . . . to paint."

"You . . . still paint?" I asked despite myself, my eyes following her as she walked from behind the table to my side. I had to turn my head and look up at her, my hands folded in my lap.

"No. I have abandoned art for the glory of God," replied Maria Cosway, turning away from me and beginning to pace. "Do you believe in God, or are you of the persuasion of your father?"

"I'm a Unitarian."

"He wrote to me that he's quite taken with Unitarianism. That it is the religion of the future—a kind of modern deism. Did you know that?"

"No."

She turned toward me, her back to the window, and lifted her monocle.

"You came here for a reason, my child. What is it? You are very beautiful, and obviously your education hasn't been neglected. *Someone* has taken care of you. If not your father, then who? Who has raised you?"

"Adrian Petit," I whispered.

"Adrian! The majordomo of the Hôtel de Langeac! *Plus ça change . . . ,* And he's the one who told you about me, *n'est-ce pas?*"

"Yes."

"And he told you everything, I suppose."

"Everything that he knew."

"Petit knew everything."

"And I believe he thought that you, who also have lived a double life, might have the answer to my own dilemma."

"Ah, so you're in love . . . with a man who doesn't know who you are."

"How did you guess?"

"Hardly difficult for one who has led, as you say, a double—nay, a triple, nay, a quadruple—life, my dear. But why, since you are not *my* daughter, should I care what you do with your life? It is not . . . this habit which makes me infallible. On the contrary—"

"Because you are an artist."

"I thought I was once. But what do you think art has to do with life?"

"An artist invents his life."

"Ah, Harriet, when I was your age, I thought I was doing that. I thought all things were possible." She held out her arms, and the sleeves of her habit caught the slight breeze coming from the open window like sails. The keys at her waistband struck a flat, musical chord. "Now I know there is no such thing as a double life—or a single identity. I have come to believe here in Lodi in a heresy . . . We are only grains of sand in God's hand. It is obnoxious and ostentatious to believe we have a *life*, a free will, a destiny other than that which God has already, in his wisdom, given us—predestined forces, preordained for us. Of all of God's creatures, artists are the most insubordinate, the most infidel, the most pretentious, and therefore the most sinful. Not only do I consider my life a heresy, I consider my painting a sacrilege."

"And music?"

"The same, of course. Why? Are you a musician?"

"I aspire to be."

"As bad as, if not worse than, painting."

"But Bach, Haydn, Schubert! All to God's glory, surely these are not abominations!"

"They are not reality, either."

"Then nothing is real?"

"Nothing." Her mouth turned down in contempt. "So you see, Harriet, since nothing is real, nothing is deception. Or rather, everything is illusion: me, your father, your mother, your color, your sex, your race. Freedom is illusion—so is death. Does this help you? Is this what you wanted to hear?"

"I don't know—"

"Don't lie, Harriet. You want my permission to live a life of illusion, as a nonexistent color, for love. Isn't that it? Your lover—your fiancé, perhaps —is white and you want to be that, too. For him and to spite your father. But as a painter I must tell you that color only exists in relation to another color, that the edges of one color touching another is what produces not only both colors, but a *third* color that lies between the two and which defines the first two. You are that third color, neither the one nor the other, but which invents both. What would your mother be without your father? But what would your father be without your mother? If there were no black people, white people would have to invent them."

"Did you love my father?"

"You mean is your father lovable, don't you? Is it possible for you to love him after everything he's done to you? Your father is a genius, Harriet, and people, especially women, must make great concessions to genius."

Yes, I thought, my mother, frozen in time in the depths of her tobacco fields, had made great concessions. How Maria Cosway, frozen in time in the frame of her convent window, resembled her! Were they different, one from the other? One buried in servitude to my father at Monticello, the other buried in servitude to God at *her* monticello? And my father *being* the God. They were like twins, this abbess and that recluse, bitter and unforgiving sides of the same coin. Yes, this eccentric, bohemian abbess had lived a life of such willful egotism and fantasy and deception that my idea of her being my mother's twin was absurd. Nothing was more different from my father's and mother's life than that of *la maestra*.

Yet, that afternoon, she gave me the courage to invent myself as my mother had not done. I couldn't say I liked Maria Cosway, but I couldn't say I hated her either. She just *was*, like an act of nature, a totally amoral creature —a cat, a tree, a rock. A part of the complicated and mysterious man who had sequestered my mother for thirty years. She urged me to suppress the slave in me, to suppress the fugitive in me, to suppress the daughter in me. To reach out boldly and seize life as well as love. To take what I wanted without totting up the price. And what would be left of Harriet Hemings? I asked. Her answer was, "Names are the purest of all accidents."

～

She had lied in the beginning by claiming she had given up painting for the glory of God. Maria Cosway painted still, and supremely well. She herself had executed the frescoes on the walls of the private apartments in which we now stood. The fireplace was sculpted as a cavern cut out of the rock, and opposite it a sculpted fountain played. The salon walls were painted with views representing the four quarters of the globe.

"This," said Maria Cosway, pointing to one corner, "is the hill where I intended to paint Monticello and your father's university, but your father never got around to sending me a description. Perhaps you could describe them to me so that I may finish my room." She smiled.

My heart stopped. Asking me to describe Monticello was like asking an escaped convict to describe his penitentiary. Yet it all came back to me in a flood of longing, the west lawn, the shade trees, the dome, the winding serpent wall, the sad corridors, the yellow curtains, Mulberry Row . . .

"My father's mansion stands on a little hill as you have drawn it. Its form is based on the Pantheon in Rome, or the Marché des Halles in Paris, which I have seen. There is a facade divided into three sections, left and right wings, a central hallway, and a porch designed in the Greek manner, held by six columns. The roof is domed and rises several feet above the line of the facade. He was very much influenced, as he must have told you, by Palladio. The proportions of the house are small. There is no main staircase. My father hated staircases, so he almost forgot to put even a small one in. The house is built of red brick with white trim. The columns are painted wood, as is the frieze of the facade. The glazed windows are sashes and are not the French doors one would ordinarily expect in a house of this design.

"The university, on the other hand, is much more grandiose. It is built on the plan of an academic village, using diversified architectural forms rather than one massive building. But the main building is again built on the principle of your Pantheon, a rotunda, but of half its diameter and height only. It has a central atrium covered by a dome, and the facade is Palladian Greek revival with a frieze porch of six columns and an exterior stairway leading up to the entranceway. Here too the facade is divided into three, the right and left wings being lower than the central hall. The building is only two stories high, and the dome about three."

"Thank you," said Maria Cosway, all the time sketching as I spoke.

"The university hall is also surrounded by shade trees and gardens, in the Italian manner. In the distance are the Blue Ridge Mountains. I hope this helps you," I said, my voice trembling. "Monticello is one of the most beautiful places in America. My father spent his whole life building it, and with what was left of his fortune, he built his University of Virginia. My uncles did all the ironwork, all the carpentry and nail work; the glazing of the windows was done by my cousin Burwell. The roof and gardens, floors and stairways were all done with my family's labor."

"You must tell me more while we have supper. I cannot let you go back to Florence hungry."

In the unfinished room, strewn with scaffolding and golden light, we sat down to supper opposite one another. There was macaroni soup; frittata of liver, brains, and courgettes; boiled beef; sausage. A fine bouquet of flowers in a china vase was placed on the table. A dish of veal with truffles, *merenda* of peaches, roast turkey, custard pudding, roast veal, and rice patties. There were delicious wines and fruits, cheese, and a fine dish of ice cream as hard as the Alps. Not a meal I would have expected of someone who had given up worldly pleasures.

Afterwards we withdrew to still another room, her *cabinet,* filled with prints and books, drawings and curios. It gave onto a wide balcony which looked out over the landscape and the bridge of Lodi, where a famous battle had been fought. Like my father, the Baroness Cosway had built herself a fortress of beauty and solitude where nothing it seemed in the world could ever touch her—just like my father. Everything was curiously Italianate and spoke of music, beauty, luxury, sensuality. This was not a convent for the poor, but, like Panthémont, for the rich, the well born, and the privileged.

"I would love to draw you, Harriet. Here, let me make a small sketch before you leave." My host's small, blue-veined hand reached out and touched my chin lightly, tilting my head slightly to the left.

I sat in the lengthening shadows as Maria Cosway took up pad and pencil and began to draw. Faintly, in the distance, I heard a girls' choir chant a Te Deum. The music rose and was lifted out of the retreat and into the gardens amongst the alcoves of vines, the fruit and olive trees, the flower gardens and statuary.

"Your father wrote me in 1822, it must have been just after you left Monticello, that he had been here in Lodi in 1786 with the Count del Verme of Milan and passed a whole day here from sunrise to sunset, in a dairy, watching them make Parmesan cheese . . . strange to think of your father actually being here . . . before I chose his place as mine. . . . Do you believe in fate, Harriet?"

"I believe in chance."

"You say you play, Harriet? The choir is rehearsing for our next concert. Perhaps you would care to remain here and play for us."

I closed my eyes and imagined remaining in the convent. Safe, in Lodi.

"Why don't you stay?" Maria Cosway said suddenly, as if the idea had just occurred to her. "I would like you to stay. I think you need a rest from your double life, and you can tell me anything. Any secret. This is, after all, a convent."

I hesitated, surprised. There was touch of genuine concern in her voice, which was also tinged with a loneliness I knew well.

"Sometimes one must rest from inventing oneself," she continued. "It is a great comfort to remain in the company of someone with whom you don't have to pretend. Your father knew this and often said it."

I found myself speaking to Maria Cosway, and she to me, with a fervent intimacy that in one part of my mind astonished me even as I spoke. I revealed feelings long buried within me: my shame at my illegitimacy, the confession about my color, the deceit of my father's silence, the bitterness of my mother's abandonment, my disgust at my betrayal of Thance on the one hand and my contempt for his innocent trust on the other, my loneliness, my inability to see the true meaning of my mother's renunciation, the fear of my double identity, of its being discovered, my repugnance at being forced into the role of an adventuress.

"There are worse things than being an adventuress. Any woman who makes a life of her own will be accused of being one."

"I'll never be like other young ladies," I cried. "How can one pass suddenly from childhood to maidenhood?" I said to her. "How does it happen? Little by little? In a single day? Perhaps it only comes about through misfortune or love. If I were trying to be funny, I should say the two were synonymous, but I won't say it because I think love is the most beautiful thing in this world."

"Then you have the soul of an adventuress," said the abbess.

"No," I said, "I could compare myself to a sheet of water which is frozen below and only agitated on the surface, for nothing interests or amuses me at *bottom*. . . ."

"Well, I'm forty years older than you, and I'm still at an age when there is intoxication even in death itself. It seems to me no one loves everything as I do—I often spoke to your father about it—the fine arts, music, books, society, dress, luxury, excitement, calm, laughter, tears, love, melancholy, humbug, the snow, the sunshine, all the seasons, all atmospheric effects, the silent plains of Russia, the mountains around Naples, the frost in winter, autumn rains, spring with its caprices in Paris, the Bois de Boulogne. I remember Marly before the Revolution . . . quiet summer days, beautiful nights bright with stars. I admire, I adore it all—just as your father did. We are born sensualists. We can get drunk off of thinking, off of books or a scientific treatise as easily as off of champagne or Madeira—even easier. Everything appears to me sublime. I would like to encompass all: God, eternity, love, pleasure. My sin is both pride and gluttony: I always wanted to see, possess, embrace it all, be absorbed in it and die. Since I must in two years or twenty die, let it be in an ecstasy, not of the flesh anymore, but of the mind, of faith—in quest of this final mystery.

"You seem appalled, Harriet. Didn't you know your father was like that, too? Exactly like that?"

⤳

Every evening I felt sore and discouraged, having spent my strength in fury and despair thinking about *what to do?* Go back to London? Go to Rome? Stay here? Return to Philadelphia? Get married? Confess? As a young girl I wasted all this time in excesses of romance and silly eccentricities. If I was destined to be nothing, I thought, then why these dreams of glory ever since I could remember anything? Because of my father?

One evening as we sat in the corner of the world Maria Cosway had painted as Monticello, I finally told her about my fears of Thance—not just my lie, but my submission, even as a white woman.

"How can one ever be too particular in the choice of a husband? Even in your case! I have even felt indignant at the condition of women. I am not so crazy as to claim equality, as you Americans are demanding, which is a utopian idea—besides being very bad form—for there can be no equality between two creatures so different as man and woman. Really, I don't demand anything, for women already possess all that they ought to have, but I grumble at being a woman because there is nothing of the woman about me except the envelope."

"You've renounced being a woman?"

"Let's say I've renounced men, and am a faithful worshiper of celibacy." She continued, "Her service becomes more fascinating the longer I remain in it. An artist has no business to marry anyway. For a man, it may be well enough, but for a woman it is a moral wrong, for she must either neglect her profession or her family, becoming neither a good wife, a good mother, nor a good artist. My ambition to become a good artist made me wage an eternal feud with the consolidating knot . . . to my everlasting grief."

I listened to her, engrossed in my own grief. What was I going to do? Time was running out.

"Are you sorry you ever married Richard Cosway?"

"I was sold to Richard Cosway—by my father. The same father who had raised me, convinced me that I was an artist, as he was. That I was capable of real work. The greatest works of art do not make art greater. Art does not succeed itself, just as one is not able to transmit beautiful sentiments. Art lives and dies in the unique heart of him who carries it, just as feelings only live and expand in the souls of those who feel them. What did Voltaire say? 'There is no history, only fictions of various degrees of plausibility.' There is no history of art, either, Harriet. There is only the history of the artist. Your father was an artist—not of objects, but of ideas."

"My father doesn't love me."

"Never say that, Harriet. Your father loves you as much as he loves anything not written down on paper."

I gazed up at the empty hill of Monticello. Where was he at this moment?

"One must understand, color dissolves form. It is a law of nature only artists remember. A black point appears smaller than a white or a yellow point, even if they are the same size. As soon as calm becomes the principal purpose of observation, the accurate, the real notion of form disappears. One might say that black is a phantom color, anointed by man. It is all colors; it is what you want it to be; it absorbs everything and renders nothing to the surface. Colored planes juxtaposed to each other have mutual influence on their different values. They lack, extend themselves, disappear one into the other, according to the laws of the marriage of colors. To see color with temperament, and to extend it on the forms moderated by logic, is to have two souls—or at least an unbalanced soul."

I stared at the baroness in astonishment. Could her treatise on color be applied to life? At that moment, I believe I loved Maria Cosway.

Before we parted, Maria Cosway reached into her pocket and brought out a fair-sized gold locket. It caught the light as it turned on itself like a lie.

"I have something for you I no longer need."

Inside I saw a masculine reflection of myself, with the cold blue eyes of my father. It was he. Or it was me. I looked up at the abbess, who was smiling. She had given me the portrait of my father that John Trumbull had painted for her in 1789.

"Have it," she said. "It belongs to you. To your biography."

"How do you know I am who I say I am?" I repeated. And this time she answered.

"Because you came here, magnificent girl."

"Pray for me, *madre*."

"Oh, don't worry. I intend to, Harriet."

LODI, ITALY
MAY 19, 1826

Postscriptum:

Thomas, I attach this postscriptum to this, my last letter to you, my friend, in the hope that this news will reach you before the subject herself returns home. Your natural daughter, Harriet, found me and came to see me. I knew she was yours, for she is the spitting image of you in female beauty. For one moment, dear sir, I found myself back with you and Martha and Maria in the Paris of 1787, a part of our lives which now seems more a cautionary tale than reality. When we were surrounded by love, friends, and fame. I invited her to stay with me and she did, for two weeks.

Harriet told me what you never revealed to me: the Negress Sally is *still* by your side, though her children have all disappeared or will do so by your hand one day. What a strange way to treat offspring! There is nothing that so corrodes the soul as the loss *in any way* of a child of your flesh and blood, be it to death or to whiteness or to ill feelings or exile. Make peace with your daughter, friend. Do not die without setting her free. You are the only one who can do this; no piece of paper can. You owe her that.

You once said the sun does not shine on a being whose happiness you wished more than mine, that you wanted to bind his beams together to gild the room in which I lived and the road I traveled. Your daughter, who styles herself the President's, and who cannot dispose of her own existence without committing some kind of fraud, has inspired this affection in me. You said you would not permit yourself to believe that we are to meet no more until we meet where time and distance are nothing. But, my dearest, we *are* at this hour and have dire little time to reconcile ourselves to it.

Harriet told me a strange story about fingerprints. How they are unique and untransferable, embossed forever like a silhouette of one's soul . . . like love, the ultimate identity. Because I am a Catholic, it is easy for me to believe this. And because I am an abbess, Harriet's confession makes me responsible for her salvation, which is in your hands, between father and daughter.

Vespers begins. Too bad you will never see the fourth corner of the world.

Adieu

FLORENCE
MAY 19, 1826

My Thance,

It's my birthday. Whatever hurt I've done you, you may inflict on me tenfold for the rest of our existence.

Great love produces great puddles of discontent.

Whoever told you I was perfection?

I'm coming home to you if you'll have me. I'm coming home, anyway.

Harriet

Harriet Petit could be the daughter I, Maria Cosway, abandoned, then lost to death in my folly to live the life I thought I deserved. This cold-blooded President's daughter also wants to live the life she thinks she deserves, and she has had the tenacity to knock at my door, intrude upon my life, and even demand from me retroactive restitution for being free and white!

Fathers. Daughters. I've worked far into the night sketching my perjurious operatic libretto: my ex-lover's enchanted mountain, the Holy Grail of freedom; exiler of emancipation; the black knight James; the blind prince Thance; the white knight Lorenzo; the charmed dagger; Adrian the magician; Dorcas the fairy godmother; Martha the villainous half sister; Sally the black queen; Harriet the bewitched princess; and King Thomas exorcist of color. And there, just under the patch of sky, is Maria Louisa Cecilia Hatfield Cosway, sixty-five, widow, recluse, and notorious adventuress and prostitute, procuress, abbess, and mother superior, educator *par excellence* of the next female generation. What more can a woman hope, but to love once more?

Tonight I shall pray that Harriet's life be not one all of falseness. There are people destined to live history. She's one of them. I believed once I was, too, but I realize now I'm only one of those noughts, a footnote to the biography of my dead husband, my dying lover, even to the Negress. All of them own the earth I only rent. And I so wanted to walk upon this planet like a heroine of old, to be a player in life's fable.

I the undersigned, Baroness Maria Louisa Cecilia Cosway, née Hatfield, abbess of the Convent of the Dames Inglesi College della Grazie in the duchy of Lodi, Piedmont, Italy, white female, born in Genoa the sixteenth of June 1760, English citizen, widow, age sixty-five, do hereby swear that on Sunday, the nineteenth of May 1826, the bastard child of Thomas Jefferson, Harriet Hemings of Monticello, did leave my convent after a visit of a fortnight, to return to America. That same day, I did add the above postscriptum to a letter I addressed to Thomas Jefferson Esquire, Monticello, Albemarle County, Virginia, United States of America, and did post said letter by packet boat on the twentieth, 1826.

BARONESS MARIA LOUISA CECILIA COSWAY

16

The problem has just enough of the semblance of morality to throw dust into the eyes of the people and to fantasize them; while with the knowing ones, it is simply a question of power . . . real morality is on the other side.

Thomas Jefferson

A squall of seagulls hazed the bright summer sky and circled around the sailors perched on each rail and mast as we sailed into the Delaware estuary just before noon on the twenty-ninth of June 1826. Brice, Mrs. Willowpole, and I stood on deck and watched the low Philadelphia skyline come into view: the two-storied warehouses and clapboard stores, the shipyard with its scores of masts, new red brick factories, and the gray-green hills and farm-lands just beyond the steeple of St. Martin's Episcopalian Church. After the magnificent harbors of London, Calais, and Genoa, this was an unprepossessing landscape in which to begin the second quarter-century of my life. Even in her own comfortable circumstances, Dorcas Willowpole was as I—a lone woman with suspicious motives. My protector squeezed my arm, as delighted to be home as I was apprehensive.

I felt as old as the hills. Thanks to Mrs. Willowpole's generous stipend, I was wearing a pale green-and-white-checkered calico suit trimmed in navy blue piping and bows. Skirts were slowly getting wider and wider; the narrow, petticoatless dresses of a few years earlier had been replaced by lavish, tight-bodiced canisters, below which yards and yards of material fell to below the ankle and spread at least a foot on each side. From now on the skirts would spread like tar on water in ever-greater circles until they were as stiff as sails and measured five feet in diameter. Waistlines, too, had dropped and were now compressed with bone or ivory into a smaller and smaller circumference by the growing width of the crinoline. My hand went to my head, on which perched a wide, pale green Borsalino fedora, named after the most famous hatter in Italy. It was almost as wide as my skirt and lined in a deeper shade of green silk. The floppy brim slanted rakishly over one side of my face, and a long chiffon scarf held it in place, the scarf's ends wrapped around my chin and down my back. I carried a green suede carpetbag and a small purse of white kid which matched the white kid gloves I wore.

As I descended the gangplank of the *Aurora*, I saw the lone figure of Adrian Petit, with Independence, waiting for me on the quay. Thance was not there. Nor was Charlotte. We embraced and he handed me a letter from Monticello. It was from my mother and it was more than three weeks old. My father was dying and wanted to see me for the last time.

"You know about this, Adrian?"

"Yes. Joe Fossett, who delivered the letter, told me. I was afraid to forward it to London in case it crossed you. . . . Harriet, you look magnificent —older and wiser, but such splendor!"

I knelt down to embrace Independence; then Petit lifted me to my feet and beamed, happiness screwing up his face like a withered peach.

"My little girl's come back!"

To trouble, I thought.

"I've a lot to tell you, Uncle. A lot I didn't write."

"I've read between many a line, Harriet. Everything can wait. You must get back to Monticello."

"I've vowed never to return to Monticello."

"Perhaps you can finish what your uncle James tried to do and never succeeded. Rescue your mother. There is nothing more to hold her there with your father gone."

Petit, with his shrewd French mentality, had hit on what he thought would be the only argument that would make me return home.

"You didn't tell Charlotte I was arriving?"

"I told no one. That way your trip home doesn't have to be explained, not even to Mrs. Latouche."

"And Thance?"

"Thance is not here, Harriet. He and Thor are still in Cape Town, though I believe they will be back on these shores before the summer's gone." His eyes seemed to warn me: one thing at a time.

"But I wrote to him . . . from Italy."

"Then his mother has forwarded it to him. Perhaps; or perhaps not . . ."

"I saw Maria Cosway in Lodi. She still lives," I blurted out suddenly. "She gave me this." I took the miniature of my father off the waistband of my skirt, where it hung next to my watch and Thance's portrait.

"Now everybody's got one, thanks to that devilish romantic Trumbull," said Petit mysteriously. He cradled the miniature in his hand tenderly, as if it evoked a thousand memories.

❧

I was able to book passage that same day on a ship to Richmond. Taking only my small carpetbag with me on the steamer that ran between the two cities, I said my good-byes to Brice and Dorcas, who were themselves taking a steamer for New York.

I intended to find my brother Thomas, who had lived in Richmond since I was a little girl. He had a house in the suburbs, far from the center of the city. Upon arriving in Richmond, I went straight to his house. As I entered the front gate, the door of the pale green clapboard facade swung open noiselessly without my knocking and closed just as silently behind me. I had been three years old when Thomas ran away from Monticello, and I had not seen him since. I was greeted by a strange, blond, curly-headed giant of a man with a somber countenance and sour disposition. He was thirty-six years old.

"How do you know I am, who I say I am?" I said, smiling, as he stood there without speaking.

"Who else could you be, Harriet?" he responded. "You're here because he's dying."

"Have you seen him?"

"I haven't seen him in twenty-two years, and I don't expect to see him, living or dead. I've even changed my name to Woodson, the name of the man I work for, so I don't have to acknowledge him as my progenitor. Just like you've changed yours, as you've told me. You're Petit now. Miss White Petit. You didn't have to pass, Harriet."

"What choice did I have, Thomas?"

"Same choice as me. I've stayed on the black side of the color line."

"You wouldn't know it to look at you."

His laugh was harsh and bitter. "Obviously you think you'll be happier in the white community. But that's your idea of happiness—a high social status, a safe home and family that no one can take away from you. Things white people take for granted. What I don't understand is how you would want these things enough to sacrifice your true family for them. If you are willing to repudiate your family, your past, your history, and everyone you love just to be white, I won't cause you any more pain than you have already caused yourself by hating you . . . you're already living in an insane asylum."

"You can't live in dignity as a Negro . . ." I began.

"My salvation from complete despair is in my belief, the belief of our forefathers, that hatred is not directed against me as a man, but against my race, my color, my pigmentation. *I* can live in dignity as an individual, even though as a Negro I cannot."

"Oh, Thomas."

"It's funny about passing. We disapprove of it, yet condone it. It excites our contempt, and yet some admire it. We shy away from it with an odd kind of revulsion, but protect it." He paused. "What you're doing is very dangerous, Harriet. Once Father's dead, your cousins could kidnap you, hold you against your will. Put you in chains."

"They wouldn't dare!"

"What! Martha? Jeff? The Carrs? Who the hell do you think you are, Harriet, with your store-bought clothes and your English accent and finishing-school airs? You're a nigger down here! Movable property. Up north, too! You are being precipitous, Sister."

"I had to come back. I came back for Mama, to take her away from here. Otherwise, what's to become of her?"

Thomas looked at me with such charged pity that a wave of seasickness overtook me.

"You think because he's dying, he's going to set you free, don't you? You think on his deathbed he'll redeem himself and say the words you've dreamed of all these years. 'My little girl, I'm sorry I enslaved you. I apologize for what I did to you. Please forgive me. I love you . . . I hereby free you and your mother because I love you.' Poor dunce! He's not going to do it," Thomas continued softly. "He can't. It's against his principles. It's against the principles of his country."

Silence.

"You realize," he continued dully, "that if anything happens to you, I'm responsible. I'm your oldest brother. And the only free one around. Eston and Madison can't raise a hand against their masters. I'm the one who'll have to come and get you . . . with a shotgun."

Thomas accompanied me as far as the Pantops plantation and then left me abruptly, saying that he hadn't set foot on Monticellian soil for twenty-two years and he had no intention of doing so now. My father's mansion was only a quarter of a mile's ride from there, and I spurred my borrowed horse onward to what I still imagined was home. I reached the ridge that overlooked Monticello just before sundown and caught my breath as I breached its craggy frontier.

Distance and golden light masked the decrepitude of the scaling paint and crumbling brickwork, the still unrepaired planks of the veranda steps, and Robert's rusting ironwork. The house sat in its triangular square of soft green, with its mighty shade trees and the serpentine wall of its gardens. Behind it ran the pale beige line of Mulberry Row, the regular square fields of sassafras, which stretched into the larger fields of not-yet-harvested tobacco. The Rivanna River flowed along the northern frontier in a silvery curved highway and branched off into the tear that was Blair Creek. There were already lights in the windows and smoke from the chimneys. There were merino lambs grazing on the west lawn and a loaded wagon parked there. I could even see shadowy figures behind the sash windows, children playing on the front lawn, people still working in the fields, and horses grazing.

The world that slavery had made lifted itself from the valley below and rose to clutch at my throat. It seemed it wanted the very life I had snatched away from it down there.

With its pretensions, plain masonry, and wooden pillars, the structure seemed so much smaller than in my imagination that I wondered that it hadn't been magically replaced by a smaller replica. The loneliness I had staunchly denied these four years overwhelmed me, not for slavery but for this place, which was the only place to which I belonged, the only place on earth that knew my real name.

"*Maman*," I whispered.

⌒)

"You've turned into a beautiful woman, Harriet."

"Thank you, *Maman*."

It could have been four days rather than four years since I had seen my mother. Not a day of my absence showed on the surface of her face or body.

She was dressed not in her black homespun with her linen apron and her white turban, but in red-and-green plaid taffeta, with a yellow apron and a small bustle or "cushion," as if she had dressed to please me. The yellow background of the plaid picked up the tones of her golden skin and golden eyes, and the ruby earrings from Paris that she always wore gleamed in the torchlight.

"Papa?"

"Weak. We think he's had another stroke, but we can't be sure. Burwell swears he'll last until the Fourth of July."

"Did he really ask me to come, or did you make that up, *Maman*?"

"He asked. He asked, knowing what risk you ran coming here. He thinks he can still protect you from your white family while he's alive."

"Remember, *Maman*, I've set foot on British soil. I'm emancipated."

"As a matter of *your* conscience and for the benefit of your fiancé, but not in the eyes of Virginia, you aren't. You'll soon belong to your half sister Martha."

My mother said this with such malicious relish, a pinprick of anger flared in my breast, despite all my promises to myself. She *liked* saying it, as if the words justified her own slavehood.

"As far as the black laws of Virginia are concerned, to a slave patrol, a sheriff, or a bounty hunter, you're still a fugitive slave. People in Mulberry Row are going to start talking," she continued in her beautiful, honeyed voice.

"Well, let them if they don't have sense enough to keep quiet," I replied angrily, allowing my own drawl to get deeper and more Virginian every moment.

My mother said nothing in response. Instead she reached out timidly and on tiptoes drew me into her arms, trying to enfold me with her tiny body until I squeezed her tightly against me. I felt a wave of pity and tenderness. She was so small, so fragile. My abbess of Monticello.

"After this is over, you're coming with me," I said.

"Don't even think of it, Harriet. I'll never leave Monticello, except in a pine box."

"We'll talk about it when the time comes," I said, all at once feeling the fatigue of the journey, of the sea voyage, of facing my dying father, of everything.

The plantation closed in around me. I could feel the presence of my cousins, my aunts, my nephews, my brothers and half brothers-in-law of both complexions: the Carrs, the Eppeses, the Jeffersons, the Randolphs, and the eternal Hemingses. They were all still fighting and struggling in this little anthill of slavery.

"Who's at Monticello?"

"Everyone. Martha and all the children. Cornelia, Ellen. Jeff has taken over running the plantation. The Eppeses are here. Peter Carr is here to see Jamey and Critta."

"I meant the Hemingses, Mama."

"Peter's still cooking. Critta, Thenia, Robert, they're all here. Joe Fossett. Mary and Martin, Bette and John, and, of course, Wormley and Burwell . . . your brothers . . ."

"No one's escaped?"

"You sound like James, the time he came back from Spain to fetch me . . . begging me to run away from Monticello."

"After Father's death," I said, "there's nothing to keep you here."

We were standing outside on the porch because my mother had not yet invited me into the house. The night sounds of Mulberry Row fell, making concentric musical murmurs escaping from the rows of sheds and wooden cabins. There were the sounds of preparation of the evening meal, mixed with work songs lifting off the fields as they emptied of laborers. The screams of children's games, mothers' commands, and an almost audible fragrance rose from the red clay road like a single note unfolding.

Why had I come home at all? To mourn or to gloat? I glanced at my mother, her elegant profile outlined against the rough wood of the kitchens. What had I expected from her? Revolt? Admiration? Fantasy? She was incapable of surprising me. She had a technique of yielding to the stronger will like a plant or an animal, without reflection. She had done this with my father, and now she was doing it with me. I sighed. There was no getting around her or over her; one had to walk through her.

Tired of standing on the porch, I brushed her aside and entered the kitchen. My mother shook her head as if to say that I had taken on all the airs of the white woman I was impersonating. But in Philadelphia, I had learned to move in a different way. My body pitched forward into space, unselfconscious and fearless, instead of holding back, bent in confusion or diffidence, balancing the pros and cons of bringing attention to oneself. I had come to expect a certain level of respect, a certain degree of attention to my voice and opinions. I had acquired with my northern education certain liberties. I believed I was entitled to them because my voice, my opinion, my person were valuable in themselves. And, of course, my mother noticed. She was very good at noticing things like that.

Inside, the very air of the kitchen, with its familiar aromas, seemed to shrivel my disguise. I became once again Harriet Hemings, errand-runner, spinner in the weaving factory down the road. I stood there for a moment, my heart beating. The kitchen's clutter and meanness seemed poorer and more sordid than ever when I compared it to the roomy, bright kitchens of English country houses, with their silver and polished copper, their porcelain-and-steel stoves and dazzling arrays of neatly displayed utensils. The door of the larder was open, an unthinkable breach of discipline in this house, and I peered at the rows of preserves and smoked meats, country cheeses and salted fish, curds and pickled cherries. From the ceiling hung a dozen smoked hams, round bacons, and links of sausage. Memories of innumerable suppers, dinners, breakfasts, and barbecues lurked in that larder. Visions of lines of carriages arriving, of bouts of cricket on the west lawn, of black and white children romping on the green, barking dogs, snorting horses, pony carts, slave orchestras, banjos, violins, music. I turned back into the room. All that was in the past. Death and poverty had seized the soul of this house and would never relinquish their grip again. My father would leave his white family paupers and his black family with only their bodies to sell. I smelled it. I felt it. I tasted it.

"Sometimes," my mother said, "it's so bad, he doesn't even remember who he is or who I am or any of Martha's children. Only his houses. He remembers the names of his houses. Jeff Randolph has taken over his affairs, but he should have left them in Madison's hands or Eston's, 'cause Jeff, sweet boy that he is, doesn't know anything about running a dying plantation— or saving it. He's been forced to sell off the best slaves after having had to sell all the other plantations."

"But Father promised Martha Wayles we would never be sold! He's letting Jeff sell her own uncles, nieces, nephews, her half sisters and brothers."

"When," replied my mother, "has that ever stopped a desperate master? Jeff wants to clear your father's name of debts, and he must do it by selling and selling."

"What about what he owes us—the Hemingses? You and Uncle Robert, Martin . . . all of us."

"It was always your father's weakness to imagine himself superior to the necessary art of being capable of holding one's own in the world of business. And now, in the wake of disaster after disaster, it is hard to know whether it is more dangerous to stand still or to move. The habits of your father's life, his tastes, his extravagances, his associations, his education, even the trustfulness of his character, his want of business skill, his sanguine temperament— everything that makes him a Virginian made him prey to incompetence and ingenuousness, unhappy speculations and bad loans. And now bankruptcy is staring us in the face.

"Even Eston complained that his father knew nothing of the adroit chicanery of running a property: feigning bankruptcy, fraudulent conveyances, signing over one's assets to a wife or daughter. The President has never even heard of such tricks as sending coffins to the graveyard with Negroes inside, supposedly carried off by some sudden imaginary disease, only to have them be 'resurrected' in due time, grinning, on the banks of the Chattahoochee River. He was completely ignorant of double bookkeeping, unsecured loans from banker friends, using political influence to insure failed crops. And as Eston put it, if as a Virginian he involved himself like a fool, he suffered himself to be sold out like a gentleman. And to combat it, he frantically tried to save at least a part of his dream: the mansion and the university. Thomas had appealed like a beggar to the Virginia legislature for permission to auction off his lands in a lottery to pay his creditors, carefully, humbly enumerating his lifetime of service to the nation. He indulged in a terrifying tantrum when he learned that his old friend General Lafayette had been given more than a hundred thousand dollars in gifts and bonuses from a grateful United States for service rendered during the Revolution on his visit here. And yet my Thomas, the creator, the inventor of the Revolution, stood there with holes in his boots. Even the lottery was a failure. Nobody bought shares.''

I was shocked.

"Don't mention the lottery to your father. He thinks it has saved his house and that he's dying solvent.''

"What does Thomas Mann say to all this?''

"Martha Jefferson's husband still refuses to step his foot over the threshold of this mansion, Harriet. He, more than anyone, has changed since you left.''

"But you haven't, Mother.''

My mother looked up, surprised, as devoid of personal vanity as ever. "Haven't I?''

"As a little girl I remember you just as you are today, *Maman*; it's incredible how little you've changed. Time doesn't seem to touch you.''

"Sorrow does, though.''

"How can you be sorry? You'll soon be free.''

"I'll never be free.''

"Surely he'll free you with his last breath,'' I said, unable to keep the crying out of my voice.

My mother said nothing. Her straight, slim back was turned away from me as she fumbled with her ring of keys and finally found the one to the larder. She pushed the door shut and locked it.

"No.''

"Then run,'' I cried. "Leave with me before it's too late.''

"Oh, Harriet, I'm too old to start running.''

"Don't be silly, *Maman*. Freedom is not running—it's existing for the first time!''

I turned then, hearing someone approaching, and saw Burwell hurrying down the passageway that connected the kitchens to the main house. By now every slave at Monticello would know that Harriet Hemings had returned home.

"Quick, go down to Grandma Elizabeth's cabin until I signal that the coast is clear,'' he admonished.

To my surprise, Burwell was adamant. If I was to stay at Monticello, I would have to hide like the fugitive slave I was. I was truly back in the United

States. And so I found myself in my grandmother's abandoned cabin, which served as a depot for my mother's furniture, peeping out of the boarded-up window at the moon-drenched Mulberry Row. But even distance and darkness could not disguise my brothers Eston and Madison as they hurried toward the cabin. Then I couldn't see them anymore because of the tears in my eyes.

Before I could even turn up the lamp, I was swept into a wild, brotherly embrace. Eston had grown at least three inches. He was the exact height of his father, whom he resembled like a twin. His blue eyes danced in the lamplight, which threw reflections onto his mane of red-gold curls. He smelt of clean sweat, topsoil, and wood chips, and his hard, lean body cleaved to mine as if it had just been rescued from some terrible, accidental danger. Scampering around him, barking like a puppy, was Madison, still gray-eyed and sandy-haired, waving and flailing his arms like a choir conductor. Our shadows threw themselves on the walls, packing cases, and the low ceiling in a macabre dance as we twirled around in a triple embrace, laughing and crying. I had so much to tell them that when I had finished it was dawn.

"So that's what it's like to be free," said Eston.

"Now, what's it like to be white," said Madison.

"Aw, Madison, let up! You're always running off at the mouth! Harriet's not passing, not tonight."

"Same problems, Madison. Same sun. Same moon. Same rain. Same sky," I answered. "Same—"

"Shit," said Eston. "If there's no difference, Sister, why bother?"

"I never said there wasn't a difference. The biggest difference is not *being* white, but the white world, as I've explained to you. What do we know about anything, buried here with slavery in this tomb? We're ruled, owned, sold by people who can barely read and write. Monticello is a speck of dirt on this planet, an insignificant, provincial backwater. There's a . . . a whole world out there. And there's a whole movement—call it antislavery, call it abolition —to free all slaves in this hemisphere. This is what our southern masters hide from us . . . and there's a whole continent that exists which is ours—Africa. I can even draw you a picture of it."

"Exists in what sense, Sister, except as an invention of white folks, a bottomless lake for thieves and abductors?"

"That won't always be so, Eston. When I left home, I believed slavery was meant to last forever. Now I know that was a lie. The slave trade is abolished. Next, slavery will be. The world is moving faster that you can imagine. American slavery is doomed in the modern world with its phenomenal new inventions, new processes and the new mode of living created by these wonders. It's a matter of time, but I truly believe we—you, me, Jeff, Ellen, Cornelia—will live to see it."

"Whites and blacks as equals?"

"Whites and blacks free from backbreaking labor. I've brought you every abolitionist tract I could get my hands on. The writings of Wilberforce and Clarkson and dozens of others. Give them to anyone who can read."

"But you haven't told us what it's like to be white."

"For God's sake, Madison, I've told you. There's no difference between white folks and us. Except . . . perhaps the point of view."

Eston laughed, but I was serious.

"I know there's no difference between white folks and black folks; look at our family. No, what I want to know is what it's like to be white—that has nothing to do with differences," he said.

I stared at Eston. I knew what he meant, but I didn't know how to answer him. White people were still white people. He wanted to know if white people had the same contempt for us from behind our backs that they had in front of our faces.

"We think of white people as human beings, as we all are, but they think of us as somehow different . . . *humanly* different from them. If we pass someone who is suffering, or worse off than ourselves, or in jail, we say to ourselves, 'There but for the grace of God go I.' White people," I said slowly, wanting to make myself understood, "say, 'There, but for the grace of God, *never* go I—because I'm white.' They truly believe there is a superior race and an inferior race. And even the poorest, meanest, most ignorant white man considers himself blessed because he belongs to the superior race. Because we are there on the bottom to prove his superiority. What white people see when they look at you is not visible. What they do see when they do look at you is what they have invested you with—you know, sin, death, and hell. What most white people imagine that they can salvage from the storm of life is really, in sum, their innocence. They think that being black is a fate worse than death."

"And, Lord, ain't it true," Madison laughed.

"Yes. They would rather be dead than be considered like us—not human."

"But they're the ones that invented that lie!"

"They believe the lie they invented."

"Like you, Sister?" asked Madison.

"Yes. I believe the lie I've invented."

"Because you're in love with one of them," said Eston.

"No regrets, Harriet?" said Madison, always the agitator.

"Plenty of remorse, Madison. I want to take *Maman* away from here, with or without papers," I said.

"She'll never go. And we won't go without her."

"Surely we'll all be freed in Papa's will? He promised," added Eston.

"He's got to free *Maman*, too," I answered.

"I have to see it to believe it, Harriet," said Madison.

"We'll know soon enough. But you stay out of the Randolphs' way—stay in Richmond."

"Remember you still ain't got no papers, Harriet." It was Madison speaking.

I pulled out my passport, signed by the President of the United States.

"I've got this, Madison. Signed by John Quincy Adams."

Madison took the folded letter as if it were made of gold.

"It says that I am an American, a citizen of the United States, and that as such I am protected by my government, which demands my safe passage . . . even in Richmond, Virginia."

"Your safe passage," murmured Eston. "That's really something . . ."

"Safe passage demanded or not, Cornelia'll have your precious *President's* passport, if you don't get off Monticello—"

"Will you shut up, Madison? We have no right to tell Harriet what she should or shouldn't do!"

"And why not? We're her brothers!"

"Because," said Eston slowly, gazing wistfully at the passport, "we've been living up our father's rump for too long, that's why," he growled. "Harriet is free, white, and over twenty-one. This passport says so. She can do what the hell she pleases. She's one of President Adams's favored citizens."

"Tell me, Harriet, what do white people talk about amongst themselves?"

"Us," I said without smiling.

17

Thou art the most incorrigible of all the beings that ever sinned. . . .

Thomas Jefferson

In the early morning of the Fourth, my mother burst into the cabin, awakening me.

"Hurry," she said. "Burwell says to come."

He couldn't be dying, I thought. He couldn't be dying because he had not yet called me daughter. It was my passport to life.

"Hurry, Harriet! He's held on until now, but he'll never see the fifth dawn. The whole family's assembling. If you want to say good-bye, you must do it now."

Burwell's turbulent brown face drew close to mine, and his eyes, wild with grief, held mine in a brief, hollow commiseration. Did his terrible grief have to do with my father's death or his fear, like every slave's, of being sold?

"Burwell . . ." I began. But he made a sign of silence.

"Five minutes, Harriet. The white family is on its way. They'll soon be outside his room, waiting for me to change him. He's awake and in great pain."

Quickly we mounted the back stairway to the second floor, and then, just as quickly, I descended the tiny staircase that connected the bedroom with the second-floor hall. My skirts bunched up as I squeezed myself along the steps no wider than a foot. I was alone. My mother had stayed at the top of the stairs. "Remember," she whispered, "even if he's no longer your master, he's still your *father*."

I entered the room and passed by the foot of the bed, then squeezed by his wooden clotheshorse with all his jackets hung on it, each one embroidered

by my mother with the date it had been made. A pallid ghost lay on Thomas
Jefferson's bed, propped up with a dozen pillows, like a stuffed rag doll. The
odors of arsenic, mercury, and opium filled the room along with another, less
definable mixture of smells—mint, camphor, old skin, old breath, old bones.
The eyes were sunken and closed. I set down the lamp, bent forward to kiss
the pale forehead, my temples pounding. At once he opened his eyes, and I
found myself drowning in two pools of foaming blue sea. Cataracts.

"Sally?"

"Master," I whispered, "it's me, Harriet."

"Harriet?"

"Harriet Hemings. Your very own."

He fixed his curdled eyes on me. It was a curious, riveting gaze, as if he
were trying to figure out the solution to a riddle, or a joke he'd forgotten.
Then he smiled, a sweet, fascinating smile—the smile of a young man. The
smile of Maria Cosway's locket.

I came nearer and nearer to the abyss. He tried to push me away, but I
leaned into his withered body, and his head came to rest on my bosom. He
spoke into my chest, too weak to break my embrace.

"Oh, Harriet, Harriet! It cannot be that all men must go through this
horrible thing."

I was kneeling now, and had taken his hand. All my defiant words withered
on my lips. And yet I had to say what I had to say; it was essential to my
life. He seemed forlorn and alone. The great hands resting on the sheets were
so fragile and useless that I felt a scream knock against my windpipe. I didn't
dare break the silence. Finally, he said, his smile blurred with laudanum,
"You've come for your mother?"

"You've got to free her," I whispered tensely. "You promised."

I drew back to look into his eyes. "You've got to free her before you die."

"Only Burwell admits that I'm dying."

"I admit it. That's why I came."

"And you're taking your mother?"

"Yes. If you free her."

"You must know that to free her I would have to banish her from Virginia
or relive the scandal. Don't ask me, Harriet."

"But what does it matter now! You're dying! You're leaving her! You're
leaving her to the mercy of Jeff and the others!"

"I did the best I could for you children."

"Call us by our names! Harriet, Eston, Madison, Beverly, and Thomas!
Call us by our names!"

"Oh, Harriet, Harriet, have pity on your father. I allowed you to run away. I offered you safe passage. I proposed you for whiteness, and of what use was my generosity and good usage? You come back to harp at me on my deathbed. How can you be so cruel?"

"You sent for me. I thought you wanted to free me legally."

"I never sent for you. It's too dangerous. You could be seized as my property."

So, my mother had lied to get me here. . . .

His white hair stood up in tendrils all over his head. His breath smelled of cancer. I felt no tenderness for him at all, yet tears rose and rushed down my cheeks. Where had they come from? All the blood had drained from the top of my body and had collected in a puddle in my loins. I felt as heavy and weighted as if I were in irons. I couldn't stop crying. For him? Because of him? The knife in my pocket weighed like a log. Could I kill my father when he was already dying?

I looked at all white chaos of plump pillows surrounding him. I was strong. It would be over in a second. A peaceful, timely death. Could I be as stupid as I must appear, standing here in this room, weeping, holding a pillow in my arms? In twenty-four hours, or thirty-six or eighty-four, he would be no more. Why was I crying? I had nothing to cry about. I was free, white, and over twenty-one.

"Harriet, don't cry, please."

What did he believe my tears meant, I wondered, since I didn't know myself.

"Have pity on a dying man."

A sound burst in my head and my throat at the same time. No more, I thought, no more.

"Have pity on a dying man! When did you ever have pity on me—on *Maman*? I looked for you so hard . . . without ever finding you. I longed for you, called after you," I cried out. "I'm calling you now, and even with your dying breath you won't *answer* me.

"You imagine you are beyond possession, Father, but you are mine as much as I am yours. You are stuck here in this room with me, and you'll die here in this room with me—a slave to your slave daughter. You can't even pick up a glass of water without me!

"Should I tell you the story of my life, Father? How I have searched for you all over Europe? I wanted to live a double life—my life's self, reflected by myself. The great enigma was you! You! Even your ex-mistress couldn't explain you! She faltered and procrastinated and invented and lied, but she didn't explain to me why you wouldn't love me, or her, or even *Maman*. You are neither good nor charitable. You are only *great*. You are only glory and beauty. You do not know how to love.

"I have struggled to see you apart from myself, apart from everything, from everyone. You, the elusive, the unique truth of my life. And now I'm speaking to you as if my tenderness for you were not an obsession, were not an aberration, for what daughter would love a father who *sold* her?"

He rose up off his pillows then.

"I am not a coward, and I keep my word. I am faithful to myself, impenitent with myself, and indulgent toward others. Even to you, Harriet. That is me, the man. I am the best of comrades, the most honest friend, an artist in the widest sense of this word. I am cruel in my most tender affections. I have disgust for the things that are most dear to me. Nothing sweeps me away because everything is so clear to me. I dream large; I see small; I do not know how to bend. I have not found my equal because someone who would understand me as I understand myself would be too strong a person, like you, Harriet, to need me. Like you, I am pledged to moral solitude. How much akin are those who elicit the mind rather than the heart, because under its influence all my faculties take wings, detach themselves from the daily and seek the ideal. Maria understood this. Your mother, too. Pity will never make me lovable. Not even love will make me lovable. Only to the dispassionate mind . . ."

As I listened, everything fell into place. I was not my father's legitimate *or* illegitimate property. I was only *me*.

What most white people imagine that they can salvage from the storm of life is really, in sum, their innocence.

"Father, I have sat and dreamed and called after you. I have cried tears of deliverance, of passion, and rushed to a bedside where human love has never been seated. I escaped you, yet you still torment me with all the torments in the world: fear of the dark, fear of being left alone, fear of never finding safety . . . fear of being white . . . fear of being black . . . fear of never being loved . . .

"Is it just illusion that ties me to you? All there is is mirage, vision. I tell myself stories; I invent sympathies for myself. And each time that a part of my odd construction falls, I remain wearied because I begin to catch a glimpse of reality!"

"Things that are imaginary, desirable, dreamed, invented, feared are not only your domain, Harriet," he answered. "Much as I believe I have loved you, it was one of those impossible things in the eye of reality."

Perhaps he was too weak to speak further, for there was only silence from the red silk draperies and the tortured sheets. My father sank into their red and whiteness. His cobalt blue eyes pleaded for peace. But I wasn't in the mood for peace, even as one tear started down his cheek.

"I love all things that are not. That could be the motto of my life," he said.

I knelt down and placed the pillow on his chest. Then I laid my head upon the pillow. I could hear the *thump-thump* of his heart, feel it even through the goose feathers, surging into my inner ear.

Feebly he tried to push me away, and his hands caught in my hair. But I was, at last, much stronger than he, and I clutched him to me, holding his bony shoulders in thrall while we wrestled in a kind of silent war, locked in an embrace that was more serpent and prey than father and daughter.

"Leave me alone, Daughter. Let me die in peace."

"No, I'll never leave you. Even death won't separate us. Because I am you. I've got your . . . fingerprints."

I buried my face in the bitter, soiled bedclothes to silence my shrieks. I had done the one unforgivable thing for a slave—I had hoped.

"May your soul burn in hell, Father." And then I pressed my lips to his, sinking into an incestuous kiss as if I could draw from him enough substance to go on living.

Suddenly it was not a sick man's voice, but the familiar patrician voice of old, high, lilting, Virginian, "Whatever my transgressions, I've made my peace with them and your mother. How dare you come here to my deathbed and contradict her own wishes. It is she who will not go."

It was a suave synthesis of both the truth and a lie, something my father was a genius at creating.

"She'll be safe here at Monticello," he pleaded.

I rose then, full of strength. I rose like an outraged goddess. I clutched one of the pillows in front of me. But in my heart I knew *I could never kill Thomas Jefferson.*

"You think Monticello is safe, but it isn't. It's gone. Everything's gone. You are alone and dying. Your haven, your home, your *fortune* are gone."

"Why this pain . . . why this pain? Would that it might cease a moment!" he sobbed.

I turned, defeated, love exploding in my chest.

"Where's your medicine?"

"No, no more, Harriet. No more."

In the shadows by the medicine table, I caught sight of Burwell, who had been standing there all the time.

"You dared speak to the master like that!" he hissed at me.

"He's not my master!" I screamed. "He's my father!"

Burwell was shoving me toward the door as Thomas Jefferson half rose from his bed. I snatched a letter that was lying on his table. It was unopened and bore the return address of Maria Cosway. I tore it into small pieces and scattered them to the wind. *WHITE PEOPLE.*

I walked out of the house by the front door and started down Mulberry Row in the sturdy, dreamy, orphan's stride I recognized as forever my own.

⁀

The last person I wanted to see was my half sister Martha Jefferson Randolph, but she walked into my grandmother's cabin without knocking.

"I want you off the plantation now, or I swear I'll call the patrols out on you."

"Hello, Martha."

I stared at my twin, or rather my twin weighted with thirty years. The same height, the same color, the same hair, bleached, faded by time. The eyes, nose, and mouth were similar, yet fate had turned one into plainness and the other its opposite. She stepped inside the door, her manner that of the proprietor of my body.

"Don't 'hello' me! If you want to know how I found out you were here, one of your fellow slaves betrayed you."

"I don't care. I'm not leaving until he's dead."

"His creditors are waiting for his last breath, too. You risk sale here, Harriet. My father is bankrupt—everything is going to pay his debts. You wait until he's dead, and you may have to run for your life."

"You'd like that, wouldn't you?"

"Yes."

"Why do you hate me so?"

"Because you're an offense to southern white womanhood. Look at you. You don't belong here. You don't belong anywhere—not in this country. You and your kind are what we hate most. You think you can cross the line God has drawn between us."

"It's not God that's drawn the color line. It's people like you, Martha. I only want—"

"I know what you want. You want the same thing your prostitute of a mother wants, and you'll never have it, either of you! You'll never be his, and he'll never love you. Can't you get that through your thick, woolly head? He doesn't care to love you, and even if he did, we, the Randolphs, the Carrs, the Eppeses, the Wayleses, *won't let him!*"

I backed up as Martha approached until my back was against the wall and her pale face was close enough to kiss. I smelled her body and her breath and thought: This is me when I'm old; there is no difference. We are all the same, white on white, blood on blood, and nothing will ever untie us. I did belong to her, just as she belonged to me. Two white women. We circled each other as if we were attached by invisible cords, drawing back only to be jerked forward again by an unyielding bond.

"Go back up north and fool those Yankees who don't know any better with your white face, because down here you don't fool anybody!"

"You think that would change anything!. No matter where I go, I'll still be your half sister!"

Martha clapped her hands over her ears.

"I won't listen to your lies!" she screamed.

At twelve noon he was dead. A long wail rose from the slave quarters and hovered over the plantation like the wings of bats. The President died without any of the Randolphs or the Hemingses beside him. Burwell and two men—his secretary, Alexander Garrett, and a nephew, Samuel Carr, who, many years later when he himself was in his grave, would be accused of fathering us all—had been the only people in the room.

Burwell went about the business of burying the dead. A dry-eyed Martha stomped up the steps of Monticello as if she had been personally wronged. I took refuge in my grandmother's cabin again, along with my mother, which was where Burwell found us.

"I'm freed! Robert and Robert's half brother, Joe Fossett, are freed in his will. Madison and Eston are freed in the care of Robert until they reach twenty-one." He paused. "He didn't free no women."

My mother continued to smile as stupidly as Burwell continued to weep. Even I smiled, along with her, grinning like a magpie as I sat there beside her in my grandmother's house. So everything had been a joke. On me. On *Maman*. On the President.

Then Burwell turned to me and handed me an object.

"The President said you should have this," Burwell said.

I recognized it from Adrian Petit's description. It was a gold box, the *présent du roi*, a departure gift King Louis XVI had given to my father when he left Paris in 1789. On its cover was a portrait of the king and, surrounding the portrait, a constellation of empty holes. The holes, according to Petit, had been set with four hundred twenty-one diamonds. They had been removed on my father's orders because the Constitution of the United States forbade its public servants from accepting any gift from a foreign government or prince. After much procrastination and anguish, Petit had explained, and not wishing to have the matter taken up by Congress, my father had had the diamonds removed and sold instead of returning the present. He had used the proceeds of the sale to buy his reciprocal departure gift for the French minister, expected of diplomats leaving the Court of Versailles. Petit had brought the king's box back to Monticello along with the rest of my father's luggage when he had rejoined him. The king's mutilated *présent du congé* lay in my lap. Instead of freedom, I had just inherited from my departed father a portrait of a famous decapitated man surrounded by empty spaces from which everything of any value had already been secretly and surreptitiously removed.

18

My only comfort and confidence is that I shall not live to see this!

Thomas Jefferson

AUCTION LIST

Barnaby —————— $400	Amy —————— 150
Hannard —————— 450	Joe to be free in July next —— 400
Betty old woman ——— no value	Edy & her child Damie ——— 200
Critta —————— 50	Maria 20 _____
Davy senior (worth nothing) ~~250~~	Patsy 17 or 18 —————— 300
Davy junior —————— 250	Betsy 15 —————— 275
Fanny _____	Peter 10 —————— 200
Ellen —————— 300	
Jenny —————— 200	Isabella between 8 and 9 —— 150
Indridge (the younger) _____	
Bonny Castle _____	William 5 —————— 125
Doll (of no value) ————	Daniel 1½ Lucy's child ————
Gill —————— 375	
Isaac an old man —————— 0	Good John, no value ————
Israel —————— 350	Amy same ————
	Jenny Lewis (of no value) ———
	Mary (Bet's) young woman —— 50
James —————— 500	Davy —————— 500
Jersy —————— 200	Zachariah —————— 350
Jupiter —————— 350	Nace —————— 500

Nance an old woman —— no value	Louisa 12 ——————— 150
Ned ————————— 50	Caroline 10 —————— 125
Jenny (of no value) _____	Critta 8 ——————— 100
Moses ———————— 500	George 5 ——————— 100
Peter Hemmings ———— 100	Robert 2 ———————— 75
Polly (Charles' daughter) —— 300	Infant valued with Ursula
Sally Hemmings ———— 50	its mother ————— 60
Shepherd ——————— 200	I have omitted Aunt Marck's and
Indridge the elder ———— 250	mine, also the 5 freed ones
Thrimston ——————— 250	The ages are set down as near as I
Wormsley ——————— 200	can come at them without the book
Ursula	
and her young child ——— 300	Johnny to be emancipated
Anne & child Esau ———— 350	July next ——————— 300
Dolly 22 19 —————— 300	Madison same ————— 400
Cornelius 18 17 ———— 350	Eston same 400
Thomas 14 —————— 200	11,505

[signed] THOMAS JEFFERSON RANDOLPH

"It's the list for the auction," said Burwell. "It was lying on Jeff Randolph's desk." He held out a sheet of paper. It trembled in his hand.

"Is my wife on there, Harriet? I can't read."

Slowly I studied the list of adjudged Monticellian slaves, at least half of them Hemingses of one color or another. My mother's name was forty-second on the list. She had been estimated as being worth fifty dollars.

Now it was my hand that trembled. My voice was husky and strange to my ears.

"She's on there," I said, but I meant Sally Hemings.

"How much?"

"Fifty dollars."

"Thank God I got enough to buy her." He sighed. I looked up at Burwell, squinting as if I were trying to make out the human shape at the end of a long tunnel.

"Not your wife, Burwell, my mother."

The words hung over themselves like willow branches in a storm. I heard my own cracked, charred voice hoarse and thick with coagulating tears. The world turned on its axis then righted itself, but I still had to cling to the doorframe of my grandmother's cabin to keep from falling. I swayed, rocking back and forth like a cradle. The tears I had not let fall all these years, nea, all these centuries poured out unbidden, unchecked, unwanted, but there was nothing I could do to stem them.

I could no longer see the list, which still quivered birdlike in my hand. My mother, my beauteous, sublime mother, was adjudged worth fifty dollars. Thomas Jefferson's wife was being sold by his grandson for fifty dollars. My mother would be sold to the world for exactly the price they had put on Old Eagle.

"Lordy," whispered Burwell. "A slave never knows, does they?"

Without really knowing how I got there, I stood facing my nephew Jeff in my father's study.

"I've come to buy my mother," I said.

"Harriet? I heard you were in these parts. However, as a friend I suggest you leave."

"Not without my mother!" I raised my voice. It must have been tinged with hysteria, because Jeff rose in alarm to his six-foot-three-inch height. He was almost but not quite the facsimile of Thomas Jefferson that Eston was.

"Now you calm down, Har. There's no need for you to *buy* her. My mother's freed her and has petitioned the Virginia legislature to allow her to stay here in the state. Grandpa wanted it this way. She could do no less than bow to his wishes. And I'm bound by my honor, as a southern gentleman, to respect that. I respect that," he repeated tentatively. Jeff kept the desk between us as if it were a river or a moat neither of us could cross. "On my honor, I'm taking her off the list. There's nothing to buy."

I stared at him in silence. Martha hadn't even bothered to tell me she had freed *Maman*. Did she think that gesture would absolve her? Or that *she* could free my mother after a lifetime of waiting for him to do it?

"If you've *got* fifty dollars, you can buy one of the children . . . Louisa's hundred and fifty dollars, or what about Mary Bet's young girl, Thenia? She's thirteen. She's worth fifty dollars, I guess. Let's see here . . . here's the list and the adjudged prices, she's not on my list. You'll have to stay here long enough to attend the auction or get somebody to do it for you. I can't just sell anybody off the list at the estimation price, 'cause they may go higher . . . you see?"

"You mean I'll have to wait for the auction?"

"Like everybody else. After that I wouldn't hang around here if I were you, Harriet. I'm committing fraud by concealing you. Everybody knows who you are."

I met Jeff's eyes, which had the appraising innocence of his caste. I knew what he was thinking: A Negro wench. A fancy, worth a pile of money. What a waste. Yet he didn't have the guts to do it. I knew that, too. The hatred I felt for my white nephew burned like an iridescent halo around his head. There was the sulfurous scent of it in the room.

"I swear, girl, I can't tell you what hell I've been going through. The lottery was a complete failure. Grandpa died owing more than one hundred twenty-five thousand dollars. To the end he thought the lottery would save Monticello. But nothing's going to save Monticello, you understand? We're selling, ticketing, labeling, and pricing every stick of furniture, every sheet, curtain, dish, every book, rug, painting, sculpture, each vase, clock, table, horse, mule, hog, and slave that was his. All his God damned parts and particles; his choices, his favorites, his guns, his wines, his hands, his eyes. This is the sorrow and pity, I tell you, of my life. To see Grandpa's things ... his people parceled and lotted and priced by old whispering Tom and his auctioneers. Him and his whole life probed, handled, weighed, and inspected, everything animal or human he possessed or loved auctioned off as if it were Old Eagle."

I'd never heard of a horse committing suicide before. But that's what my father's stallion, Old Eagle, did. Not more than twelve hours after the President had breathed his last, Old Eagle ran himself to death in the fields and mountains where his master had ridden him every morning for thirteen years.

I stared at Jeff, watching him pretend I wasn't there. He would be happy to see me go. He was always nervous in my presence. My white ways and airs made him feel, I suppose, cheap. Small. Guilty. He always looked at me with that strange stupid gape of moral confusion, as if he had to decide every single day of his life just who I was and why. And Lord knows I had done nothing to make him feel guilty. I hadn't made this world. I hadn't made slavery. I hadn't made *him*.

The value of the slaves had gone down, he lamented. They were worth nothing. I found myself thinking the only one worth something was me, but Jeff protested that he wasn't a master. He was, he said, only a man with feelings. "It was bad enough being responsible for my grandfather," he said, "without being responsible for the world." He shook his head with some despondency and went back to his accounts. "Lord Almighty, Harriet," Jeff said to my back, "it's all gone . . ."

I the undersigned, Thomas Jefferson Randolph, white male, age thirty-four, eldest son of Thomas Mann and Martha Randolph, grandson of my namesake, Thomas Jefferson, do hereby swear I advertised for the auction sale in the county of Albemarle the whole of the residue of the personal property of Thomas Jefferson, dec., consisting of valuable Negroes, stock, crops, etc., household and kitchen furniture. The Negroes are believed to be the most valuable for their number ever offered in the state of Virginia. The household furniture, many valuable historical paintings, busts of marble and plaster of distinguished individuals, one of marble of Thomas Jefferson by Ceracci with its pedestal and truncated column, a polygraph or copying instrument used by Thomas Jefferson for the past twenty-five years, with a set of steel writing pens made in London. I do declare that the sale being inevitable is a sufficient guarantee to the public that it will take place at the times and places appointed.

THOMAS JEFFERSON RANDOLPH

EXECUTOR OF THE ESTATE OF THOMAS JEFFERSON, DEC'D.

19

I am permitted by the innocence of the scenes around me to learn to practice innocence toward all, hurt to none, and help to as many as I am able.

Thomas Jefferson

"The sale being inevitable," I read, "is a sufficient guarantee that it will take place at the times and places appointed." Veiled and thus disguised, I stood beside my mother in the voracious crowd and watched every other Hemings sold on the block to the highest bidder. Critta's daughter Maria, who had been omitted by Jeff as belonging to Aunt March on the list, so white she was mistaken for me, fetched the highest price and gave birth to the rumor that the President's daughter herself had been sold away from her birthplace to New Orleans. It was a legend that would grow with time and be amplified, causing me to read of it in strange places and at strange moments in my life.

I bought Burwell's wife for him; then I concentrated on saving the little girl I considered my niece, Thenia Hemings, a fragile thirteen-year-old granddaughter of my aunt Bet, whose whole family had just been sold away. I paid seventy-five dollars for her, all that was left of my wages from Dorcas Willowpole. My mother and I could only watch the dispersal of the rest of our family on the pine floorboards of the auction stand erected on the west lawn. As Thenia was led away, my uncle Peter stepped on the block. I rushed from the crowd, gagging. James's ferocious voice followed me.

You think I would spill my seed as a slave? To father other slaves! You think I would enrich some white master by breeding more slaves for him? In Paris I vowed I would never touch a woman. My life has been celibate, Sister. I have never known a woman . . . known a woman . . . known a woman . . .

"Oh, Thance," I moaned, "Thance, answer me."

But it was James's laughter that answered. *Since when do slaves marry?*

⌒

"I'm never coming back here for you again, *Maman!*"

"I know. I've still got Madison and Eston."

"They want to go west, *Maman*. They've got to get out of Virginia by next year or risk being sold back into slavery!"

"No, Martha fixed that. She's petitioned the Virginia legislature to let them and me stay."

"I know," I conceded wearily. "Jeff told me. I tried to buy you, but you weren't for sale. Martha probably got some satisfaction out of keeping it from me."

"She tried . . . she freed me just before the auction. She had manumission papers all made out, waving them around. I told her what she could do with those papers." My mother's face darkened. "She called me a receptacle and a whore. She said you weren't his children. That you'd never be his children."

"So Papa told Martha to do it. What a coward!"

"Don't talk about the dead that way."

"The dead! He's made me a thief of myself!"

"Hush," said my mother. "He always considered you free, even here. All you children. It was me he kept. Only me."

"And now?" I said.

"It's me that's staying. I'm too old to go west with the boys. They'll have to wait until I leave in my little pine box. Monticello won't be sold. Martha has managed to keep a few acres and the empty mansion. I am finally the mistress of Monticello. She's let us keep a cabin down on the south boundary and three acres."

"Is that fair?"

"Fair or not, that's it. You'd better leave here, Harriet. Martha's on the warpath along with Cornelia and Ellen. Your father's freeing of Eston and Madison is an open admission of their birth. Your running here as if you were a free white woman is another. If they find you in Richmond, they'll have you arrested out of spite."

"Don't worry; I told you I'm never coming back here again."

"I know. But I'm glad you came back this last time. Think how you would have felt if your father had died with your curse on him."

"You never heard me curse him."

"Yes. But I did."

I looked at my mother in amazement.

"I visited Maria Cosway when I was in Italy," I said. "She gave me this."

I took out the miniature and showed it to her, and she took out an exact replica and showed it to me. We gazed at them both in silence. Nothing ever seemed to surprise her.

"It's fitting that you and Martha, his only two living daughters, should have his image. The third locket belongs to me. I guess we'll never know how many more John Trumbull made, will we?"

"Don't you want to hear about Maria Cosway?" I wasn't going to tell her about the unopened letter.

My mother turned to me, her eyes pure yellow metal.

"What does Maria Cosway have to do with me?"

The two portraits turned slowly on their chains like twins. The light struck them, bouncing off the delicate filigree of the cases.

I knew that the Father could no more detach himself from the Daughter than the Daughter from the Father. Harriet believed that her father's death meant that she was rid of him. She believed that if she dragged me North, to so-called freedom, she was *rid* of me. But she was mistaken, just as James was mistaken. Like a multiheaded beast, we cannot divorce our destinies one from the other. Whoever sacrifices truth to illusion lives only for the next day. I knew this, for I had lived my whole life this way. Assuming false roles, double identities, duplicate emotions was the vocation of slavery. Everybody led a counterfeit life down here. But in the real world? I'd never asked myself whether Harriet was an imitation white or an imitation Negro. In my fictitious world of dreams and visions, it hardly mattered, because all of it was, frankly and hypocritically, insane.

But where was Harriet to turn, divided as she was to the vein? Her master Thomas Jefferson lies dead. Does he lie buried as an imitation father or a real one? Harriet had to face him alone, her will against his naked power. But is Harriet an imitation slave or a real one?

It seemed to me that this was between Father and Daughter. Between WHITE PEOPLE.

Why are daughters so unforgiving? Oh, Harriet was an armed camp: cautious, secretive, proud. She'd been that way ever since Sykes. She'd carried that grudge against me, Sally Hemings, against her father, against the world since she was knee-high. I do believe my daughter drank in all that bitterness and anger with my milk. She had been conceived the summer when, ballot by ballot, Thomas Jefferson was being elected President of the United States. The scent of fear, power, and machinations had swirled around her infant head. Fear because of James T. Callender. Power because envious men like John Hamilton coveted the highest office in the land. Machinations because of my master's own naiveté and the ambitions of our old enemy, Aaron Burr. Then, too, Harriet had been born in the shadow of death. First Jupiter, her father's body servant of fifty-seven years, then her father's nemesis, Callender, which at least shut him up. And finally James's self-murder.

Her infant ears must have heard my screams when Thomas Mann Randolph announced that James had hanged himself in Philadelphia. She might even have heard Meriwether Jones's hoots of joy as he danced a jig on the front lawn upon hearing that Callender had been silenced forever. Or perhaps her small face had shriveled in the heat of my curses when my eldest son, Thomas, was banished from Monticello to dampen the gossip about his birth.

All these truths Harriet had grown up with, and she had taken them with her in the lilac phaeton on May 19, 1822. But what exactly was the truth? Truth in Virginia had the life of a blossom: it grew from a long-forgotten seed. A fact like assassination or suicide had scarcely happened before the genuine historical kernel of it had disappeared—annihilated by fabrication, rhetoric, imagination, pride, and self-interest. The passions, self-delusions, and fantasies of the South, both black and white, simply flung themselves over poor truth and devoured it. It always happened to truth around here. Virginians tended so much toward virility that skepticism, an essential to clear thinking and, in consequence, a realistic appreciation of life, did not exist. That is to say we were constantly driven back upon our own imagination, and our belief was limited only by our capacity to conjure up the unbelievable.

And so, although everybody knew Harriet was a bastard, knew she was a slave, knew she wasn't by fact or fiction white, knew she would have to annihilate all these facts by *fraud* if she were ever to be free, that little grain of veracity had disappeared into the lilac carriage. A whole race of liars lived down here in Virginia: black, white, and mulatto liars whose only subject of conversation was Truth and Beauty. They were the ones who had set up our greatest pillar of falsehood: that with every gesture and emotion, with every breath we took, with the very pollen we inhaled, we had not entered into white people as deeply as white people had entered into us.

I the undersigned, Sally Hemings of Monticello, colored female,

age fifty-three, born on my father John Wayles's plantation, Ber-

*muda Hundred, in 1773, daughter of Elizabeth Hemings, ward-
robe mistress, slave wife, and sister-in-law to Thomas Jefferson,
mother of Harriet Wayles II, 1801: and six other children by the
President: Thomas Jefferson, 1790; Harriet I, 1796 (deceased);
Beverly, 1798; Thenia, 1799 (deceased); Madison, 1805; and
Eston, 1808; do hereby declare that this affidavit is a true representation of my state of mind the day of the auction, the fifteenth
of January, 1827.*

SALLY HEMINGS

Things were very different this time as I stood on Market Street, which was covered in deep snow, at the public coach depot, clutching Thenia's hand, waiting for Petit and Charlotte to come fetch us. I still wasn't free. Thomas Jefferson's power over me persisted even in death. I still lived on the edge of an abyss, confronted by the same dangerous world in which my identity challenged my dead father in solitary combat. But I was no longer afraid. What I intended to do, I intended to do for love, not in spite of it. It was, I thought, no more despicable than reenslaving oneself. As if in mockery of my brave resolution, I spied the glorious colored lady gliding toward me, her cabbage-rose hat rising and falling amongst the crowd as on the crest of waves. She approached me obliquely, as if she had been perched on my shoulder all the time, or under the crook of my arm. Her derisive laughter carried across the veil of whiteness that hid the red brick square.

I looked down at the voiceless Thenia. She hadn't uttered a word since she had been adjudged for seventy-five dollars. How was I going to drill into this small piece of wreckage from the past that I was passing for white? That I had a false identity, a false name, and a false color? Thenia gazed back at me, her dark brown eyes wide, her hair drawn back neatly, her new wool coat with its tiny lace collar and bell sleeves like shiny, bright armor in the sun. I was determined to keep her with me for as long as I could. She was my anchor, my fetish, my conscience, my witness. She was also my fire bell in the night, my eternal threat of betrayal and exposure. I needed her.

"You must never call me Harriet again. Or Aunt. I've freed you. You are no longer anyone's property."

Thenia shook her head from side to side in silence.

"Not to my face and not behind my back . . . someone may be listening. Not even in your sleep. Who am I?"

Thenia tried to answer. I saw the muscles in her face screw up in two little bunches; her eyes became even wider with the effort, so great that they filled with tears. Still no sound came.

"Who am I?"

She pursed her lips and grimaced, her smooth cheeks filled like apples, her eyes squeezed shut.

"Mmmm-iss Pe-Pe-Petit."

She was breathing heavily with the effort of speaking. There was an unwritten law amongst runaways that a darker-skinned relative could never betray a family member who was passing for white. She was as afraid as I was.

"It's all right, my Thenia," I whispered. "You never have to say another word to white people if you don't want to."

The colored lady swept by, contemptuously, trailing her musical guffaw, which bounded after her like Independence chasing a cherished rat.

Thenia and I had no sooner begun to unpack when Mrs. Latouche knocked at our rooms and announced that Mr. Wellington was downstairs. The color that rose to my cheeks must have confirmed what she had already guessed. I had sailed three thousand miles to find him again. As if I were bound for the auction block, I descended the stairs, Independence at my heels. The parlor door was open, and the shock of seeing Thance's familiar silhouette almost made me recoil. He turned, and as I took several steps toward him, he held up his left hand, as if to ward off a stranger. His eyes held astonishment and surprise, and there was something unfamiliar about them, as if the passage of time had somehow redrawn his features, but only by a fraction.

"No, Harriet," he said suddenly as I advanced, but before he could step beyond my reach, I was in his arms, my mouth covering his. He was here. He had received my letter. He had forgiven me. For one moment, his lips responded, and then I was seized and almost lifted off my feet.

"I'm not Thance, Harriet. I'm Thor . . . Theodore, Thance's twin. Forgive me."

Blindly I stumbled back. The African twin. "Oh, my God," I said, my face on fire. Thor rushed on, stuttering as he explained.

"Thance tried to get here in time, but he won't arrive until next month. His . . . his doctors forbade him to travel before the end of his quarantine, and then he had to await a steamer leaving from Cape Town."

"Quarantine?"

"He's been ill. A few weeks before I left Cape Town, he fell ill with a mysterious fever after treating some sailors off an American slaver that had been towed into the harbor by a British patroller."

"But why Thance? He's not a doctor."

"They couldn't diagnose the fever, which was not malaria or any of the common African ones. So they sent for me."

"For you?"

"Yes. I'm a specialist in tropical medicine."

"For a slaver?"

This was the war, I thought, that was going on between the British patrols and the pirate slave ships.

"The whole ship was decimated. Not more than a dozen sailors survived."

"And the slaves?"

"The cargo?"

"Yes, the cargo."

"Some hundred were saved out of a cargo of over four hundred. We saw none of them. They had been emancipated in absentia directly off the ship and transferred to a British schooner bound for the West Indies."

"And Thance caught their fever?"

"Yes. I blame myself for taking him with me."

"No, it's my fault. If I had been there . . ."

"Harriet. That wouldn't have changed anything. We would have gone anyway. It's our job. I brought back thousands of specimens of African medicinal plants and other medicines. We were cataloguing them. Nothing would have stopped us." He paused. "Harriet?"

I looked up into the eyes of the perfect stranger who was the double of my heart's desire. There was something tougher, more durable in his identical contours. It was in his eyes as well.

"Don't you want to know the message I am to deliver?"

"I think you have already delivered it."

He smiled Thance's smile and drew together the dark eyebrows that made two curves like the *f*-shapes on a violin. "He still loves you. He has never ceased to love you, and he will never love anyone else. He wants you back on any terms you care to impose. It's in the letter he wrote and gave me when he received yours."

He handed me a thick envelope. I recognized the large, sprawling handwriting.

"Do you know why I left for Europe?" I said, turning to him.

"I don't . . ."

"Because I am not what I seem, Mr. Wellington, and I'll never be."

"And why did you come back, Miss Petit?"

"Because I learned in Europe that most people are not what they seem."

"He doesn't care about your . . . your secret, whatever it is."

"And he doesn't want to know?"

"No."

"And what about you?" I said with as much cruelty as I could. "Would you care to know, for I am prepared to tell you."

"Tell me if you must. But I swear before God I'll never tell another living soul, and that includes my brother. You've made him a happy man. I refuse to make him an unhappy one. But you said yourself that nobody is what he seems. You thought I was Thance, but I'm not. Oh, that I were," he whispered softly.

"You are made of the same stuff as Thance. And I would like to trust you."

Thor Wellington sucked in his breath as if he were about to receive a blow, while I stood over the abyss, leaning into it as my mother had leaned into the wind, ruffling the tobacco blossoms. Outside the door stood Thenia, who could prove everything I said. I opened my mouth, but nothing came. There was only silence. *I am the natural daughter of the third President of the United States, Thomas Jefferson, whom I cursed as he lay dying the Fourth of July 1826. I love him and hate him and I have forgotten him.*

Was it fair to Thor, a perfect stranger, to reveal my most intimate secret? Would it be easier than confessing to Thance? Then I remembered my experiment with Lorenzo. What harm would waiting a month more do? I had waited all this time. I had waited all my life.

MBABANE

(UNDATED)

My dear Harriet,

Impossible to sleep. How to begin the most important letter of my life? By thanking God it will be my last to you before we are joined together, never to be separated again except in death.

This dawn, my heart, my spirit are so light I should deem myself feebleminded with happiness. Everything I see is ravishing. I feel before having seen the state of the heavens: an admirable serenity of azure. A moon almost full still reigns in the sky, fading with the dawn. The air has an incomparable suaveness, heady, caressing, light. . . .

I want to be good and I want to be wise. I curse the convalescence which keeps me from rushing to you.

Thor, who will sail in a fortnight, will place this in your hands, which I kiss with all the fervor of a resurrected soul and the ardor of a heart redeemed. I read and reread your letter. I fold and unfold it. Smooth it out. I hold it to the light, perhaps to indulge myself that there is one more word of love. I place it to my heart knowing you have touched it, perhaps even pressed it to your lips. The words I hold in my hand are scentless. How glad I am you didn't coquettishly try to perfume them like a banal billet-doux, for not only is this letter a letter of love, but of war, of peace, a threat, a promise, a cry from the heart, a treaty, a poem. Moreover, no European fragrance could match the perfume of Africa. Any of those scents would seem stupid, insipid, and artificial in this luxuriant nature where, in an instant, one beholds enough beauty to last a lifetime; where the spine of a butterfly can ravish your eyes and your emotions for hours; where the fauna grows as you breathe, metamorphosing from instant to instant with the light, the temperature, the moisture in the air, like magic. In fact, African life—plant, animal, or human—responds to the beguiling force of nature as to a lover's: not condescendingly or halfheartedly, but without reserve, generously, in a rush of squirming humus burrowing into mulatto earth.

How fast time flies! The terrible months when time was interminable, when night never moved and I was awake before every dawn, when even exhaustion was no guarantee of peace or sleep. Then Thor placed your letter in my hand and my headache left, my eyesight cleared, my burning throat emptied. I stood on wobbly legs and roared. And Thor rushed in in alarm and found me weeping with joy on my feet at last. And we walked to the end of the settlement and took the road that rises toward the hills to a ridge that gives way to a great forest, a million years old, as dense as granite. The last rays of the sun lit its top. A great silence first; then, as the shadows grew, the forest filled with strange noises, fighting cries and songs of birds, evocations from unknown animals, the rustling of foliage that bespeaks of heaven knows what animal or what whisper of God. A troop of monkeys chatter nearby, but we don't manage to see them. The butterfly I captured, zebra-striped with a belly of blue and edged in yellow, I press into this letter.

Next day. All along the road, a mixture of tribes, both men and women, hurry toward the town carrying on their heads produce from distant villages—sweet potatoes, cornmeal, etc.—in great baskets covered with palm leaves. When we pass, they all put down what they're carrying and salute military-style and then, before we can return their salute, they burst into hilarious laughter. We must be hilarious. The joke's on us here.

Fifty feet from where I write, the great vaporous curtain of the falls, silvered by the great clarity of the moon, which here seems bigger than ours, insinuates itself amongst the elephant grass. At sunrise, the falls are veneered with a single column of light the width of a building. The falls are really twin falls, because the cascades are divided by a verdant island which separates the waters so that one cannot see the two falls at the same time, and one is amazed that what one is admiring in its majesty and amplitude is only *half* the waters of the *fleuve*.

Africa is a strange continent where heat pierces the body and transforms it back into the dust from which we are all made.

Enough—I cannot write more. My hand still trembles, not from weakness, but from love. I enclose with this my letters to you which were never sent, that had no destination except my grave. There are a hundred, I believe. In chronological order, you will read the day-to-day happenings of our expedition and how many times I thought of you.

The small package contains gems I would like you to have set in a necklace by a fine jeweler in New York or Philadelphia. Workmanship here is not of the greatest order. Mother can help you. It is a wedding present from

Your Thance in happiness

"You can't break a man's heart the way you did and then expect to come back a year later and pick up the pieces. Who do you think you are? *What* do you think Thance is?"

Charlotte's stern Unitarian eyes were lagoons of recrimination.

"Charlotte, how do you know what I've decided?"

"*You've* decided! It took all of Thance's strength, plus ours, to get him on that boat to Cape Town . . . to save his life."

For a moment I imagined that Charlotte was in love with Thance. My heart stopped. No. If Charlotte had wanted Thance, she would never have let him leave for Africa. I remained silent under her recriminations. Each hurtful, defiant word of my adored Charlotte was like a balm to the deep open wound I now carried, for it helped me harden my heart.

"The trouble with you, Harriet, is that you are so engrossed in your own insignificant problems that you don't seem to realize other people suffer because of you."

"Thance was ill and you didn't even write me," I accused her.

"But I *did* write to you—in Paris," Charlotte cried. "My letters were returned, marked 'address unknown.' That was in July."

"But I was—" I stopped.

"Yes, Harriet. Where were you?"

"I was . . ." *the residue of the property of Thomas Jefferson*—pleading for my life.

"He could have died . . . and I wouldn't even have known it," I said out loud.

"Perhaps he has died, and it is Thor who has taken his place," Charlotte said bitterly. "You wouldn't know the difference."

At that moment, I wondered if Charlotte loved *Thor*.

"How can you suddenly be so hard-hearted?" I said.

"Because," insisted Charlotte, "you've always been cruel to people who love you . . . the more they love you, the crueler you are." She burst into tears then, and between sobs, she said, "Where were you, Harriet? What are you hiding? Where did Thenia really come from?" she whispered.

I studied Charlotte. My Charlotte. Her ignorance was the price I had to pay for the friendship I held dearest to me.

Two men walked down the gangplank of the ship called the *Galleon*. Both wore white planter's suits with indigo blue shirts and wide panama hats, but one man was white and the other was black. Thance returned home less than nine weeks after my encounter with his twin. Weeks in which I read and reread the letters he had written me from Africa, and in my heart answered each, one by one. The Africa that Thance described haunted me much more than the map Lorenzo had drawn on the *Montezuma*.

The darker man was handsome, with a wide, square face, shrewd, intelligent eyes, and deep dimples in each cheek, accentuated by what I would learn were tribal marks—his fingerprints—carved into his skin. He had other marks, too—three horizontal slashes on each temple. They flashed like dark signals with his burst of conversation as the two men set foot on the quay. Thance held on to the other man's arm for support, and his suit hung loose on him; he had not yet gained back the flesh he had lost to his illness. They were still too far away from me for me to hear the conversation that held them both in such thrall, but they turned together as Thor raced across the busy wharf toward them.

"Thance!" he called. "Abraham!"

The three joined in an embrace that sent a pang of jealousy through me, although I knew it wasn't fair. Soon Thance would leave the others behind. Soon I would look into his black eyes and rest. The odyssey was over.

The two brothers and the man between them turned. Thance broke loose and raced across the cobbled walkway. He smelled of salt, love, and Africa. He looked so young.

He didn't kiss me. Not even my hand. We were much too shy, too embarrassed, by so many strangers gazing from the deck of the *Galleon*, from the wharves, from the carriages parked pell-mell around the pier.

"Let me look at you," he said softly. "You are more beautiful, not the same, but more beautiful. You're wearing the necklace."

"Your mother helped me. Mr. Duren, at Bailey, Banks, and Biddle, worked day and night to finish it in time," I said shyly. "She's waiting for you at home."

I had been lucky to have gotten off so easily with the widow Wellington. But Thance's narrow escape from death in Africa had made her ready even to renounce her vow never to allow me into her family again.

"I'm so happy, Harriet."

"So am I."

He broke away from me then and turned toward Thor and the smiling brown man, who had approached us.

"This is Abraham Bos'th, who took care of me at the hospice. He is a great apothecary and homeopath whom I'm going to introduce to Philadelphia's pharmaceutical wonders. He's come to work for us at our new laboratory. His tribe is the Ndebele."

I extended my hand, but Abraham Bos'th bowed over it instead.

"Ndebele men never touch white women, except in sickness," said Thance.

I blushed and turned to hide my shock. I hoped that Mr. Bos'th (whose name would soon be Americanized to Boss) liked me, for I admired him on the spot. For all my London campaigning, I had never met an African before.

I had brought Independence with me, and now she crowded around Thance, wagging her tail until she spied a cat, which she went darting after at maximum speed, knocking several empty produce baskets over as she went.

"Independence," cried Thance, "come back here." He laughed. But she had already leaped off the pier in pursuit of her prey, into a barge tied up very near us.

"I have never seen such an animal," said Bos'th. "She must be very rare."

"She's a purebred Dalmatian. Her race comes from Croatia, on the Adriatic Sea. Normally they're bred for hunting, but I've never indulged her in that sport, so she has to satisfy her hunting instincts on rats, water, field, or city . . . or cats. Her name is Independence."

He smiled. "A very good name. A noble name, Independence."

He was grave and shy, but a small smile hovered around his lips.

"I am very happy to be here for your wedding, madam."

"Harriet," I said. "Harriet Petit. Is this your first transatlantic crossing?" I asked, then stopped, confused and embarrassed, confronted by a black man who had come to America from Africa of his own free will.

"Yes. I've sailed the west coast of Africa as far as Freetown. But of course that's not the same as really crossing the ocean."

"And how did you learn to speak English so well?"

Abraham's eyebrows rose quizzically, and his tribal scars at each temple squeezed into two black, raccoonlike holes around his eyes.

"Ah . . . at the mission school in Cape Town," he said. "There I was given my English name. I also have an African name, which means 'chosen,' or 'enigma,' as far as I can make out in your language." Abraham cast his eyes around our small welcoming party and lingered on Thenia, who was holding her hand over her mouth and staring at him in fascination.

I looked around the docks, with their conglomeration of people going about their business, asking me nothing and expecting no answers from me. Indifferent. Indiscriminate. Indistinguishable. What cruelty to inflict on Thance the secret my father had labored so diligently to conceal for forty years. As if my encounter with Thor had disarmed the ticking time bomb of my identity, I decided to think about it by and by, when I was calmer. After all, I had the rest of my life.

20

She seemed pleased.

Thomas Jefferson

I wondered if my mother would have appreciated the irony of my white knight in shining armor having been dipped in the African sun. But my mother was not here.

Thenia was the only member of my family at my wedding. She stood, her heart-shaped face with its noble forehead and oversized eyes, like a package of brown earth from Monticello. She was the stand-in for father and mother, sisters, brothers, aunts, and cousins. She was all I had. My link to the truth.

As I walked down the aisle, dressed in white, on the arm of Petit, I thought that life, which until that moment had caused me so much uncertainty, was nothing more than a long series of contracts, ceremonies, insurance policies, promissory notes, and preordained words with which humanity entertained itself in order not to commit murder. Everyone had the same terror of the unknown. The church, whose colored-glass windows looked out onto the harbor of the largest city in America, closed around me. Beyond was the vast expanse of the Atlantic, and beyond that the old world, where everything had been invented, including slavery. And a simple fact came to me like a vision, the kind of vision explorers have when they set foot on a new continent: the inhabitants were not convulsed with hatred, but paralyzed by fear. Instead of my frightening them even more, I thought, I had only to help them learn to know me as I really was, which was no different from what I wanted to be or what *they* wanted me to be. Nor was this congregation any different from what I expected of them, neither better nor worse than what I would make of them in my heart. After all, they were only white people.

As I proceeded down the aisle, an endless bridal train trailed behind me, attached to a dress of Irish lace trimmed with silk roses and satin bows. In one deep pocket lay the familiar dagger of my youth. The air hung thick with the mingled scent of many flowers, perspiring men in expensive morning coats, and artificially perfumed women, who watched as I advanced serenely into their world.

I peered into each face, and saw only the affection, honest good wishes, and sentimental effervescence that the exchanging of marriage vows inevitably evokes. My in-laws' harsh Philadelphia accent, with its broad *a* and hard *d*, seemed so unmusical to my ears that I vowed to keep my southern accent. I would remain Virginian at least in this. It was the only thing of all my past life that I would preserve. I had been married in church as I had promised myself, before God and society. I had married for love. I had chosen my husband and I had come to him a virgin.

In a stroke of irony or sentiment, Petit had arranged the wedding reception at the hotel where I had eaten my first meal as a white woman. Thance and I would spend our first night as man and wife in a room there before leaving for Saratoga Springs on our honeymoon. The orchestra, in formal dress, filled the restaurant's Palm Court, with its greenery and crystal chandeliers, with the newest waltzes, and several musicians from the conservatory joined them. There were songs and toasts and finally a prayer from the good Reverend Crocket. "May this young and beautiful couple enjoy the fruits of love and devotion, of Christian morality and Christian charity, forever after!" intoned the Reverend. At my request, he added a prayer to remove the scourge of chattel slavery from the annals of the nation by abolition.

It was Thor who gently placed the newly ironed newspaper announcement of my wedding in my lap.

On Saturday, March 1st, 1827, Miss Harriet H. Petit of Al-bemarle County, Virginia, married Mr. William John Thadius Wellington of this city at St. Paul's Unitarian Congregation Church on Washington Square at eleven A.M. in the presence of friends and family of the groom's mother, the eminent Mrs. Nathan Wellington the former Rachel Lysses du Graft of Scranton and Wilmington, member of the board of St. Paul's Church and of the Philadelphia Academy. The bridesmaids were Miss Charlotte Waverly of Waverly Place and Miss Lividia Wellington, sister-

*in-law of the bride. Miss Petit is a member of the Philadelphia
Conservatory Orchestra, a graduate of the Bryn Mawr Seminary
for Women, and a member of the ladies' auxiliary of the Philadelphia Anti-Slavery Society. The groom is a son of the late scientist
and pharmacist Dr. Nathan Wellington, and is a graduate of the
University of Pennsylvania School of Pharmacy. The couple will
honeymoon in Saratoga Springs, after which they will reside at No.
120 Church Street in South Philadelphia.*

Printed on the back page of the notice of my marriage was the following
advertisement:

*Twenty Dollars Reward—Ran away from the subscriber, on the
14th instant, a Negro girl named Molly. She is 16 or 17 years of
age, slim made, lately branded on her left cheek with an R and a
piece is taken off her ear on the same side; the same letter R is
branded on the inside of both her legs.*

ABNER ROSE

FAIRFIELD DISTRICT, S.C.

The stark letters of the slave advertisement gave the event on the reverse
side its finality: a marriage of North and South, of black and white, of fugitive
criminal and pillar of society, of bastardy and white legitimacy.

That advertisement would follow me through life as the shadow of my
wedding. Every time I took out that clipping, the other stared back at me like
a twin.

My wedding gift from the State of Pennsylvania was a new law called the
Personal Liberty Law, which made kidnapping a fugitive slave a felony. I
should have been safe. But interracial marriage was still a felony in Pennsylvania. William John Thadius Wellington was a criminal like my father before
him, liable to fine and imprisonment for miscegenation. I could be fined,
jailed, publicly whipped, and my children sold into slavery for having accepted him.

When I saw my husband standing in our room, outlined in a white haze from the gaslight, he didn't seem like a man to me at all, but like the incarnation of a great phase of my life that had ended. He was the final approximation of it. My whole being seemed sharpened and intensified into a single spear of love. I didn't expect it, nor did I know exactly what it was. It merely took hold of me with exquisite, terrifying force and power. Drawn into this flame of love, which both enhanced me and denied me at the same time, I entirely revoked my previous existence. My husband's unknowing face above me was as pure as a priest's. His beautiful black eyes emitted such a force of will that I touched my forehead to see if I was still alive.

Thance kissed my face slowly, gently, with a kind of childish delicate happiness, surprising me with soft, blind kisses, which were like strange moths—perfectly still and sweet, setting themselves on my soul and my secret. I became uneasy for the first time since the wedding and I drew away for a moment, shame perhaps. Then, to show I was a happy, willing wife, I turned and held him tightly against me. I hadn't told him anything. I wouldn't tell him anything. Yet, in the small center of the flame he had created was the unyielding anguish I had invented by not telling him.

He drew up my chemise slowly, carefully, and buried his face in my sex, kissing my nether lips until I swooned. Far, far away I heard a small lament as he settled into me. The pain cast a new spell, then burst as Thance withdrew and lifted me with his strong arms. My damp chemise wore the small badge of triumph. I closed my eyes as tears of happiness washed away my thoughts and I was anchored by the world where he was, which was light and joy and happiness, and where he wasn't, which was gloom and fear and emptiness.

My thoughts drifted into unconsciousness. And then came back. They disappeared again and returned like ghosts, each time more faint. The colored lady with the cabbage rose drifted in and out of my line of vision. Her tinkling laughter and her mockery surrounded me. Then the image burst into a mimosa tree, and I was back at Monticello, in the little vegetable garden behind my grandmother's cabin. My mother was leading me by the hand. Fragile and delicate, cloudlike, the mimosa tree rose on its pale trunk and spread its long, level arms. My mother pointed to it. Among the trembling leaves, the feathery puffs of sweet blossoms shivered as if thousands of tropical birds were perched there. The tree seemed to light the garden, my grandmother's cabin, and all of Mulberry Row. Its heightened fragrance wafted over everything. My mother (or was it my grandmother?) pointed again, and the scent swayed like a serpent.

I had a sensation of pain; the ends of my fingers and between my legs were stinging. Now was the time, I thought, to relinquish my soul and resist no more. My body had yielded; why not my mind? But then I knew that love was just another kind of command: a new master's voice.

"Harriet, my darling," he whispered. "Don't be afraid . . . it's only the first time this happens. I'll never hurt you again in this way. My adored wife . . ."

Moonlight ate into the drops of tepid water, turning them to fiery diamonds that fell from the sponge I held like an offering in both hands. I held the sponge higher, letting rivulets of light flow over my neck and chest and down into the pitch blackness of the water beneath me. In the darkness, the droplets flashed and clustered, secretly dancing, dispersing and then reuniting in configurations, rocking, moving forward, then falling back as if in panic. They worked their way back again persistently, making a semblance of fleeing as they advanced, always flickering nearer to the rim of white porcelain. The cluster grew larger and brighter as gleam after gleam fell until it became the ragged cabbage rose on the colored lady's hat. The frayed moon shook down upon the basin, and I heard Thance's voice faintly calling me back to bed.

My husband never understood how a proven virgin with no past to speak of could be so wise in the ways of pleasing men, or use her body so convincingly under the imperatives of conjugal love. But conjugal love was what I had dreamed of, lived and fought for since the age of seven. Perhaps it was because I had learned so young that my body was not my own that I was now able to bestow it lavishly and freely, as if bondage had shown me whatever new thing I needed to learn. I had grown wisdom in my fingers, for I knew now with what gentleness or violence I should touch or hold, kiss or press Thance's flesh. With gravity I received the furious hunger of my husband's desire. If it was against all scientific reason for me to guess what would please him or show myself adept at physical passion, it was also against all scientific reason for two people who hardly knew each other, with no ties between them at all, with different characters, different upbringings, even different sexes, to find themselves suddenly committed to living together forever, to sleeping in the same bed, performing the most intimate of attentions, and sharing two destinies that perhaps were fated one day to run in opposite directions.

1836

21

That a change in the relations in which a man is placed should change his ideas of moral right and wrong, is neither new, nor particular to the color of the blacks. Homer tells us it was so 2,600 years ago. But the slaves of which Homer speaks were white.

Thomas Jefferson

Nine years had passed. At the point where I take this story up again, six children had been born to me and were alive. There were my newborn, golden-haired twins, William John Madison and William John James, their weight like a hush in my arms; Jane Elizabeth, three; Beverly, five; Ellen Wayles, seven; and Sinclair, my eldest, nine. I had lost no child to illness or accident. My labors had all been easy, even with the twins, and my children were without blemish or handicap. None of them knew they had inherited the condition of their mother and were legally American slaves.

My worldly identity had been established as the younger Mrs. Wellington, Philadelphia matron, mother of six, wife, sister-in-law, daughter-in-law, abolitionist, and musician. I owed much of my success to my mother-in-law, who had stepped aside to allow me my own social circle, and the rest to Charlotte Waverly Nevell of Nevellstown, who had remained my closest friend. My impersonation suited me well, my family was in good circumstances, and my children adored me for myself, not my color. I considered myself a happy woman. I believed myself safe. The turning point in my double life arrived in 1836 when two things happened. One was the result of the inevitable ax of time; the other, so unexpected and so incredible that even today I wonder if I dreamed it.

We had moved from our house on Church Street to a large house in West Philadelphia. The Wellington Drug Company had its establishment at Front and Arch streets. Thance had his laboratory next to the Wellington warehouse, where the new pharmaceuticals and the medicines he developed with Thor were manufactured. Patents had made my mother-in-law and the company rich, and Thor returned regularly from his African expeditions with new ideas, plants, and formulas.

I had continued my antislavery work, and Thance never objected to our involvement in the illegal activities of the Underground Railroad. After that first fateful meeting with Emily and Gustav Gluck, a German couple we met on our honeymoon, they remained our friends and an important part of our lives. Emily Gluck had begun by asking me if my maid was slave or free, since she recognized me by my accent as a Virginian. "Oh, Mrs. Wellington," she had said, "please don't be offended. My object is to speak to you about the great and heroic role the southern woman has in this titanic struggle for the soul of the United States of America."

I had sat shocked and speechless. Here was a white woman, pleading with me to consider the wrongs of chattel slavery. The potential slave catcher had turned into a shining Joan of Arc, ready to lead white women and their slaves to freedom and mutual recognition. Dumbfounded, I listened to Mrs. Gluck, her voice trembling with conviction, her eyes shining with indignation, as she pleaded the cause of immediate emancipation for the southern Negro.

"We must denounce not only those who are guilty of the positive acts of oppression, but also those who connive at its continuance. I am truly uneasy at my having suffered so much time to pass away without having done anything for relaxing the yoke of the most degrading and bitter bondage that ever ground down the human species."

I had flushed deeply. I had been free for almost three years. Yet all my efforts had been directed toward my own egotistic security and comfort and worries about my crime of miscegenation, my father's guilt, my husband's trust. I had crossed the color line to escape the fate of slavery and I had left everyone I loved on the other side to face the consequences, without much thought. Here had been my conscience speaking to me across the starched white tablecloth of a luxurious spa in the Adirondacks foothills on a pale September morning. I learned that the Glucks were members of a German pacifist group called the Druids, very similar to the Pennsylvania Quakers. They abhorred violence against either humans or nature, weapons of destruction like guns and cannons, and armed warfare for whatever reason. They condemned organized religion as the perpetrator of more violence than any other institution and believed that only the natural sciences, not philosophy, would save the world. The Glucks, in a way, saved me. For they were the ones who set my feet squarely on the path of active abolitionism. Dorcas Willowpole had prepared my mind, and Emily Gluck would prepare my actions.

Thanks to Emily, I was more involved in the abolition movement as it grew and expanded into a world movement, fighting the gangrene of American slavery, which marred the surface of a prosperous North, an intransigent South, and a booming West. After the Nat Turner rebellion in 1831, when hundreds of hunted slaves had to flee Virginia for their lives, Emily and Gustav established an Underground Railroad station on their farm in Pottstown. The station signal was a lighted oil lamp held in the painted hand of a wooden black groom that stood outside their barn. There was a hiding place in the cellar under their house which connected to the barn and from which a tunnel ran to a deserted barge on the Schuylkill River. From there the fugitives escaped by river or canal to the northwest and Canada, aided by sympathetic barge and steamer captains who plied the waterways between Philadelphia and the Erie Canal.

One Indian summer day in September, a manumitted slave couple presented themselves for an interview at Emily's Philadelphia Committee for the Protection of Freedmen and Fugitive Slaves. The committee had established an office close by Thance's apothecary, and I worked there as a volunteer twice a week. The couple's name was Marks. But when I looked up, I gazed into the eyes of Eugenia, whom I hadn't seen in fourteen years. Eugenia had been born at Monticello in 1801, the same year as I, a slave of Thomas Jefferson.

Strangely, I felt no alarm or panic; I waited calmly for a sign of recognition. Eugenia couldn't be standing before me without realizing who I was! She was my birth twin! Yet not a flicker of acknowledgment passed between us. I was a white woman, and she and her husband were manumitted slaves in danger of recapture. His name was Peter Marks, and he had been born in Charlottesville in 1793, a slave of James Monroe, my father's friend and the fifth President of the United States. He had been freed in 1831 by the Monroes' daughter, in accordance with her father's deathbed wish. Peter Marks had then entered into the employ of an army officer, Alfred Mordecai. This same Captain Mordecai had bought Eugenia for two hundred fifty dollars from my cousin Cornelia in 1833. Under the captain's roof, Peter and Eugenia had fallen in love and married. The captain had formally freed

Eugenia, but was obsessed with the idea that at his death, or while he was called to active duty, Eugenia or Peter or both would somehow fall into the hands of bounty hunters and be reenslaved.

"Mr. Monroe's daughter never petitioned the Virginia legislature for permission for me to stay in Virginia, as Mr. Jefferson's daughter did for the Hemingses. And neither did the captain when he freed me," said Peter Marks. "By law, after a year we could no longer stay in Virginia as freedmen. That's why we left. Rumor was, that's what killed the most notorious slave in Virginia, Sally Hemings. It was said they had tried to run her and her sons out of Albemarle County. But that isn't so. She died of heart failure when word got to her that Monticello had been sold out from under her to a Hebrew druggist in Charlottesville, and that he had cut down all of Thomas Jefferson's shade trees."

"Died?"

To them this is only another slave story, I told myself over and over, as the room whirled like a tornado.

"And when did this happen, Mr. Marks?"

"About two weeks ago," said Eugenia Jefferson, speaking for the first time.

"She dropped dead on the west lawn of Monticello after the new owners cut down all the shade trees. Census-taker named Nathan Langdon found her. You would have thought it was his mother, the way he carried on. I just hope those new tradespeople who own the mansion now won't decide to dig up the cemetery as well.

"We've been here since Saturday. That happened Thursday a week. We hightailed it out of Charlottesville. It seemed like a sign to me—my being born at Monticello and all, like the Hemingses . . ."

It was only, I repeated to myself, a slave story of old to them. *I didn't have a mother. I was an orphan. But I had renounced my mother just as I had renounced everything black, brown, or beige. If she no longer existed, how could she be dead?*

I trained my eyes on Eugenia, concentrating on her yellow-and-black-checkered dress, the wooden buttons, the poor quality of the homespun. It was slave-woven—probably in the weaving cottage on Mulberry Row where my nonexistent mother had sent me every morning for sixteen years. Maman. I felt the nauseating rising of a howl like a wolf cub. *You died without ever seeing any of your grandchildren.*

I sat there in a daze, continuing to write as Eugenia and Peter took their leave, their precious freedman's papers in order, thanks to me.

Then the nascent sense of desolation I must have carried within me all these years, but denied with every fiber of my body, engulfed me with loneliness, and dislocation. Thomas had already said it. So much denying. So much severing. My happiness dissolved before my startled eyes. This was a bad dream. Stand up, Sally Hemings. Stand up! You couldn't have died while I laughed, fed the twins, listened to music, played my piano, sorted laundry, arranged bouquets, set the table with white linen and silver and wine. My heart was a pilot light of rage and shame. I had abandoned my mother to her fate at Monticello, *without ever thinking about her again.* In my greed for my own life, I had been crueler than any slave master, crueler than my father. I heard the distant flapping of wings and a faraway *tap-tap,* which sounded like my metronome but was my foot under the table, beating wildly, trying to run. I realized I had the same frozen smile on my face that my mother had the day my father died. Had I believed she would live forever? I had believed slavery would last forever. The ballad they used to sing about Sally Hemings was a far, far away refrain.

> *Her spirit haunts that place all cover'd with wool*
> *And patiently waits for Thomas to pull*
> *The tongue by its roots from her head . . .*
> *Behold me, false Ethiopi, behold me, he cried,*
> *Learn the cause and effect of the evil.*
> *God grant that to punish your falsehood and pride*
> *My ghost, with a message from hell cut and dried,*
> *Should come at this moment, stand close by your side.*

Passing had given me a worse burden than any slave's because theirs could be lifted, but mine never would. I had left her for what I considered a more important life, and now she had left me—alone in this white, white world. I had struggled all my life against everything that was hostile to me. Now I gave way—surrendered. But no tears came for my mother, just as she had not wept for my father. We were tearless women. But still the rhythmic *tick-tock, tick-tock* of my feet running in place, running, running . . . drumming on the sides of the huge partner's desk at which I sat, replaced them.

～

"How could you have waited so long to get word to me?" I screamed at Eston, who showed up at my door a few days later in a covered wagon, posing as a traveling Bible salesman.

"Sister, there was nobody to send. There aren't any Burwells or Fossetts to send flying up the East Coast with messages. We've been on the road for a week, and we're dead tired. Before that, we were too busy packing the wagons to head west. We *did* make the long detour for you. We could have crossed the Appalachians at Knoxville instead of coming all this way to Pennsylvania and having to cross at Ferryville. Everything happened so fast. One day she was there, in perfect health, talking, cooking, gardening, and the next morning she was gone."

"Nevertheless—" I protested.

"If you had stayed in touch, Harriet . . . but then, there was no warning. Believe me, she wasn't sick, Harriet. Not a day."

"Does Beverly know?"

"Couldn't find Beverly. Not yet. But we'll find him. You don't happen to know where he is?"

"No."

"And Thomas?"

"Thomas refused to attend his father's funeral and he refused to attend his mother's funeral. Said he didn't belong either to the Hemingses or the Jeffersons."

"She wasn't sick a day," Eston insisted. "She had been uneasy and suffering from melancholy, ever since I took her to Jerusalem for Nat Turner's trial."

"You were there?"

"*She* was there. There like I've never seen her before. Her decline started then. She would compose these long soliloquies on how she had loved the enemy, how her life had been wasted. She began visiting the cemetery every day, alternating between Grandma's grave and our father's. The word got to her about the straits the Randolphs were in, living like poor white trash at Edgehill, with all that brood of children, without a cent."

"Cornelia sold Eugenia," I said, "for two hundred and fifty dollars."

"No wonder."

"Eugenia and her husband, who had belonged to James Monroe, showed up at the Freedman's Protection Committee office while I was on duty. Eugenia didn't recognize me. She told me about Mother's death as a part of the story of their escape. Like an old slave story."

"What do you mean, Eugenia didn't recognize you?" said Eston.

"What I said. People see what they want to see."

"And what do you see before you?"

"My brother," I said.

"A white man," said Eston. "I'm going to pass for white out west, Harriet.

Madison has decided to remain on the black side of the color line. We'll part ways at the Missouri. He's going to buy land in northern Wisconsin. I'm moving on to points west. You were right, Harriet. It's easy to reinvent yourself once you've made up your mind. And what does it change, really? You're still you."

I said nothing. It was Eston's decision. But I wasn't all that sure about still being myself.

"Moreover, we've seen the last of Monticello. It is in ruins. Robert's ironwork is falling off its hinges; Joe Fossett's paint is peeling; the whole house has sunk to one side and leans; the dome is cracked; the rooms are empty, glass panes in the sash windows broken. The wind howls through the grand hall. And the rain. And the snow. If houses have souls, this one's dead and gone to hell and damnation. And now this wreck's been sold out of the family forever. It will never be a Jefferson's again."

Eston paused and looked down at his prop, a copy of the King James version of the Bible. "I have built my mansion on sand—"

"Eugenia didn't recognize me!"

"And what if she did, Sister? You know there's an unspoken rule amongst black folks. She never would have given you away—especially in public."

"But she really *didn't* know, Eston. There was no recognition in her eyes."

"Harriet, she saw a powerful white lady who was going to protect her and her husband from slave catchers. How could she imagine you were the fugitive slave Harriet Hemings? Don't you see that? Once you cross the color line, you *are* an invention. How could you not be? The color line itself is an invention! You are not perceived as the same person—not because inside you aren't, but because people see you differently. You are their creation, not your own. I know that. And I know what I'm doing about it. I'm going to be rich one day, Harriet. Not like Thomas Jefferson, land-poor, hobbled with mortgages and credit, dependent on crops and weather, and prices set in London and New York. No. I'm going to be a man who sets prices, for a whole industry. The power industry—steamboats, steam engines, and steam locomotives. I'm not changing my race to be a farmer.

"I'm going to marry a girl as white as I am, but *colored*. Didn't know it at the time; she's a runaway out of Virginia. Fell in love with her on sight. Haven't a clue to where she is now. But I'm going to find her. I've got the rest of my life to look for her."

In the past nine years, Eston had changed from a gawky eighteen-year-old boy to a powerfully built, finished man. His hands were huge. His feet, planted on the floorboards of my kitchen, seemed to be rooted like trees. The broad shoulders on the six-foot-three-inch frame seemed to take up all the space. He was dressed in homespun and leather, farming clothes, and he was armed. He had on soft kid Indian boots and buckskin trousers, with a black-and-white-checkered shirt that reminded me of my father's red frock coat, and a red bandanna was tied around the thick column of his neck. The freckled face so resembled the miniature it was uncanny.

"How do you like seeing the portrait of yourself in the locket?" I asked him.

"What portrait?"

"Why, the one you just handed me. The portrait of Papa in Mother's locket."

"I've never opened the locket."

"Weren't you ever curious to know what was in it?"

"No. As far as I was concerned, it belonged to you."

"There's a lock of Father's hair, and a miniature of him painted by John Trumbull in Paris in 'eighty-nine."

I handed him back the locket. Slowly he opened it and stared at his image. He whistled low and then shut it.

"Take it," I said. "I already have one. There are three; Martha has the last." Eston's huge hand closed around the gleaming object.

"Isn't Madison coming to see me?" I asked.

"He's still at sixes and sevens with you, Sister."

"At least tell me if he's all right."

"He's married—married to a freedwoman named Mary McCoy. They're in the wagon. They have a daughter, Sarah. Mama's first grandchild . . ."

He looked away, embarrassed, remembering my children.

"If Madison won't come, perhaps Mary and Sarah will."

"I'll get the baby," said Eston. "Mama loved that baby."

When Eston returned, he was holding a fat, brown, beautiful three-year-old, my niece, Sarah, the only grandchild my mother had ever held in her arms. As I took Sarah in mine, all the weight and contradictions of my life swept down upon me. I began to sob, deep, hollow, helpless, wracking sobs. My hand shaded Sarah's skull so that my tears would not scald her.

My brothers left at dawn, with their overflowing wagons. Eston had left me the objects my mother had willed to me: the letters, the pendulum clock, the Louis XIV writing table, the bronze clock, the French flag, and the ruby earrings, which I gave to Sarah. I kept the box of letters, the pendulum clock, and the writing table. I put the bronze clock aside for Thenia, should she marry.

I knew the journey west was long, hard, and, once across the Missouri, dangerous. They would cross the Susquehanna and pass the Appalachians at Youngstown, where their route would take them to Zanesville and Columbus, Ohio, then to the frontier town of Terre Haute, Indiana. From there Madison would head north to Vandalia, Illinois, and Eston would ford the Ohio at Wheeling and continue south to Missouri. There he intended to change his name from Eston Hemings to Eston Jefferson.

As if the Missouri itself were the color line, my brothers parted there and lost track of each other for thirty years. From that moment, each of our lives, black or white, unfolded according to its own criteria, and our parents' graves were left untended for a quarter of a century.

⟅

While my brothers roamed the West, my brother-in-law roamed the southern tip of Africa. Almost as soon as Thance and I were married, Thor left on a scientific expedition. During the years that followed, he made expedition after expedition, restlessly collecting his specimens, verifying his work, cataloguing, and writing. He wrote back letters as handsome as he was.

Thor wrote letters from the ends of the world—Cape Town or Durban or as far north as St. Paul de Luanda—letters of such beauty and descriptive power that each was read aloud dozens of times. He described the flora and fauna, the landscape, the people, the weather, the animals, the expeditions, all the human comedy of life lived as if on a different planet, sequestered, enveloped, hermetic, yet open to vast vistas, momentous discoveries, and wild adventures.

Each time Thor returned to Africa, he took Abraham with him, and each successive journey resulted in a more and more pensive Thenia. That she was in love with Abraham was evident.

Abraham was everything that was admirable in a man. The work he and Thor accomplished under dangerous but exultant circumstances had attached them in a bond of friendship that was as strong as that between the twins. Abraham had finally been allowed to study at the new Jefferson University pharmacy school in Philadelphia, and though he would never receive a diploma as a pharmacist, it was a personal triumph for him and Thor and also Thenia, who loved the idea of Abraham attending the school named after her former master. Brilliant, determined, and tough, Abraham planned to return to his native land one day for good.

In Africa, Thor and Abraham had no contact with the slave piracy that went on much farther north, along the coasts of Guinea and Sierra Leone, but they had heard of Captain Denmore and his British patrols, the freeing of the

slave barracoons at Lumbata, and they rejoiced, as I did, when the warring
kings who supplied the slave cargo signed a peace treaty in 1833.

IN CAMP NEAR THE VILLAGE OF KOKAULUOME

My dear Ones,

You have never seen a sunset until you have seen one here, with great
rafts of fire smoldering among the dark loaves of clouds and into this circle
of orange, the noble, stupendous gray elephant lifting his mammoth head
and trumpeting his happiness. His mighty silhouette wades through the
coarse grass, which reaches his belly but is over the head of the average
man, beckoning his family (two females and their calves) to follow. . . .
The world turns red in his wake and the sun disappears below the horizon
as if a lantern had been blown out. Night descends like a curtain of lead.
The Africans themselves bless sundown as they curse the sunrise, which
brings the volcanic heat, so fierce it fries one's soul. But in the highlands
the climate is almost temperate, tolerable at least for a white man, heaven
for the Zulus, who immigrated to these parts from the southern desert
plains a hundred years ago.

Abraham and I, Kelly, Tournewell, and the others have joined forces
with Drs. Swin and Carrington, a Scottish botanist and a naturalist, to plan
an excursion into the bush around Ladysmith. As one group, we are safer
and more efficient. There is a Welsh anthropologist named Kenneth Sum-
mers who is studying the Hottentot tribe, looking for what he claims is the
birthplace of humankind. He holds long conversations about it with Abraham, whose tribe also believes this land was the birthplace of man. When
Abraham's work in Philadelphia is completed, he intends to return home
for good. Strange, the bearers and assistants treat Abraham as a European
rather than as an African. Strange, too, how quickly the transformation
takes place. He still translates for us, of course, but his relations with the
people of the various villages where we go to collect specimens and
remedies are more deferential than when he was merely a "mission doctor."
The fact that he has been across the sea, they feel, has irrevocably changed
him and his relations with his—I was going to say *former* tribe. They find
him contaminated with western ideas. Strange to think of xenophobia
here . . . but the fact that despite his riches and position, he will not buy
nor accept as a gift a wife, is an inexplicable lapse of good manners. But
now I know the reason for his chaste behavior.

There was an eclipse of the moon in the early hours of this morning, and
I watched it with him. The shade entered its perimeter a little before 3:00
A.M., and by 5:30 it was wholly darkened. Then it was lost in the haze of
early morning. I had only seen the moon eclipsed once before, and never

in such a majestic landscape; this momentous, mystical experience we shared. Abraham told me the Bantus believe an eclipse is the Lord of the Sky walking past his harem, which is lit exclusively by the moon, to choose a bride whose face must not be seen by any man. So he darkens the sky to prevent voyeurs. It was so beautifully told that at that moment I knew that Abe loved Thenia, has loved her from the first time he set eyes on her —is not destiny strange! And he has been waiting for her to grow up to make his declaration, which he intends to do when we return. His exposition of this love he's carried so long was one of the most elegant and touching I have ever heard. And since we *all* know Thenia has been hopelessly in love with Abe ever since he walked down the gangplank of the *Galleon*, I do believe we are in for a wedding very soon. He says he thanks the gods that she is not an *African*, for he would have to pay a hell of a bride-price for her. . . .

Abe Boss is invaluable to me. I could never begin to gather and catalogue the specimens we've collected in the past months without him, nor the remedies and prescriptions he's gathered on his own from the priests and medicine men of his acquaintance. The Wellington Company profits from all of this, and since he has been refused his diploma in pharmacy, perhaps we could offer to set Abe up as an apothecary—in his own shop—a Wellington subsidiary. I might speak to Mother about it when we get back.

Since the dry season, we have built our camp out of sight of the sea, on the high ground between the Lummocks and the lagoons. It affords some defense against marauders. We have set up a real laboratory here, where I store and label my specimens. My distilleries are bubbling, my alcohol jars are full . . . I did make some banana brandy the other night. . . . It is almost cozy with our camp beds and chairs, our rush matting underfoot and dyed indigo cloths hanging on the walls.

I feel I have somehow earned the right not only to live and work in this place, but to love it.

Yours,
T. Wellington

There was dead silence; then the whole family stood up and cheered. That was how Thenia Hemings got engaged to Abraham Boss.

⤳

"Help!"

I heard the cry before I saw a young brown-skinned woman, her skirts hiked up, her feet flying, racing down Front Street, passing as she did in front of the Wellington apothecary just as Charlotte and I emerged. The girl passed close enough to us for me to smell the faunlike scent of unadulterated terror. She was pursued by a warden, a policeman, and two men who looked like slave catchers. Charlotte and I flattened ourselves against the doorway of the warehouse. The men caught up with her and tried to place fetters on her wrists as she struggled to escape. The cornered girl made grunting noises like a trapped animal, and her eyes began to roll back in her head. Sykes, I thought. Sykes. Sykes. Sykes. The world turned red. Not blood red, but dark burgundy, like wine or the color of closed eyelids against the sun. Before I knew it, a patrician southern drawl likened to the absolute authority of my father, its timbre like the pure notes of a clarinet, ejaculated onto the spring air.

"What does this mean, Officer? Why are you arresting this woman?" The regal solidity of my voice made the men draw back as I approached.

"Fugitive, miss. Got a warrant and a reward out for her."

"Impossible," I heard myself say. "She works for me. She works in this warehouse here. Let her go!"

"No, ma'am. She's an escaped slave. She corresponds to this here description—right here!"

"But, Warden, you know this advertisement is *void* in Pennsylvania! We have a personal liberty bill here. Kidnapping a fugitive slave is a felony! You are helping a criminal, sir!"

"I'm just making *sure* she has her pass, ma'am, and is no more than ten blocks from her place of residence. I was arresting her under the black laws of Pennsylvania for vagrancy and street walking, when this gentleman claimed her too!"

The warden handed me a slave advertisement, which I read slowly, my mind racing.

"Can't you see she isn't the one? Can't you see she isn't light brown complexioned at all? She's high yellow, which is not the same thing. Her eyes are not gray, but chestnut. She isn't eleven stone, and where is the dog-bite scar on her left wrist?"

I took a chance that the bounty hunters couldn't read or couldn't read much. I held up the girl's left forearm.

"Besides, I just explained to you that she's my employee. Her name is Thenia Hemings. I will vouch for her. I know these people all look alike to you, but surely as a trained policeman you can tell the difference between light brown and high yellow, between gray eyes and chestnut ones, between a round face and an oval one, between a flat nose and a sharp one, between kinky hair and straight hair. Look! She can't be more than sixteen years old.

Yet it says here you are looking for a woman of twenty-five! Does she look twenty-five to you?"

"Well, then, why did she bolt, if she wasn't guilty? Why didn't she say she worked for you? Just took off, hightailed it out of the tavern."

"Tavern! Gentlemen! Because she didn't have her papers with her! Because she was running home. I have her papers. You would have arrested her for prostitution. She is terrified of jail—with good reason! Isn't that true, Thenia?" I said, praying.

The brown face had cracked in despair. Now a faint glimmer of hope illuminated it.

"Yes, mistress."

"You have papers to prove who she is?"

"At home. If you like, I'll have them sent over to the station house at once. You'll release her in my custody."

It was not a question but a command.

"Officers, I'm Mrs. Thance Wellington. There's my name, in huge green letters above my head. I apologize for my . . . servant. She shouldn't have been abroad without identity papers, and I do apologize. It is my fault and I take full responsibility."

I modulated the tone now to a deep resonant one that bespoke "responsibility," and then filled it with soothing Virginian sweetness.

"Oh, dear. If my husband finds out . . ."

My voice trailed off, my eyes flashing green wells of contriteness.

Charlotte was speechless. She had no more seen this girl in her lifetime than I. She opened her mouth several times to speak, but found she was unable to do so.

"And Mrs. Waverly Nevell of Nevelltown is a witness. Aren't you? You know, of course, who Mrs. Nevell is, Warden?"

"Of course, ma'am."

The poor mute Mrs. Nevell nodded in agreement. The two bounty hunters glared at us but didn't dare dispute my word—a white woman's word. They moved away, and the small crowd that had gathered dispersed. Inwardly I was trembling and laughing at the same time.

"Why, Harriet, you told a barefaced lie to that policeman," whispered Charlotte, more in awe than reproach. "You . . . you cowed them with your voice . . . and that impossible southern accent! You are absolutely crazy! What's got into you?"

The vision of Sykes and his whip floated in the heavy, humid air. I had had no choice.

"I guess I don't like big men with whips chasing small Negro girls. I don't like slave catchers and bounty hunters. I don't like the idea that some southerner can come up here and stalk the streets of Philadelphia and kidnap Negroes. The South can't dictate to us with its fugitive slave laws."

Could I tell Charlotte, I wondered, of the abject horror of seeing myself in that girl?"

"Do you think I'm wicked?"

"No. I think you're brave. But what will you tell Thance?"

"We won't tell Thance anything. Perhaps we'll send her to Robert Purvis; he'll know what to do. We saved the girl." I looked around at the forlorn figure cowering against the red brick wall.

"What are you going to do with her now?" murmured Charlotte.

"I'm going to take her back to the laboratory. Nobody's there. I can't take her home. We must send her to Emily Gluck, but how?"

"Your maid?"

"Thenia? *Both* without papers? Too dangerous."

"Don't worry. I'll take her," Charlotte replied. "You'd better get someone to take . . . your maid's papers over to the police station."

"Oh, God. They're in Thance's safe. I'll have to ask the accountant, Mr. Perry, to open it for me."

"Well, for God's sake, don't send Abe with them. Send a white man."

As soon as we were inside the empty laboratory, the girl fell to her knees and grasped my hand, kissing it.

"Get up off your knees," I said softly. "You don't have to kneel to me. I apologize for the entire white race."

Those words of kindness shattered the last of her defiance. She collapsed, sobbing, and her whole story poured out. For a moment I considered sending Charlotte away. This was not a story, I decided, for her ears. Then I thought, looking around at the endless shelves of labeled brown bottles, the flacons of acids and mysterious powders, the test tubes and distilleries which exuded a bitter, acrid, medicinal smell, *I can't protect my friend forever.*

The bondswoman's name was Mary Ferguson, and she was indeed the girl in the advertisement. She had escaped from a rice plantation in North Carolina and was completely alone in the world. As her story unfolded, scenes of Mulberry Row danced before my eyes. When the real reason she had run exploded from her soul, it was too late to protect Charlotte.

"My master tried to conquer my will. Not for any real reason—I never gave him any reason for displeasure—but because it was his will against mine. It was a . . . game. One day he called me in and got a rope and tied my hands behind me and tore the dress from my back and beat me with a cowhide whip. For pleasure. When I asked him what I had done, he took up a chair and broke it over my head. The next day he sent for me again. He hit me with a stick until I was dizzy. In the fight with him, I bit his finger. I fought and scratched him. The next time, he decided to use another weapon —his sex. He told me to undress. He tied me to the bedstead and beat the backs of my legs until I was forced to kneel to him."

As I knew they would, quiet sobs had begun.

"When I couldn't move, he forced his . . . sex into my mouth. After that, I had no more strength to defend myself. He took me any and every which way, but kneeling before him was his favorite. For three years. Every day I suffered in my spirit. I lowed like an animal when he came after me. He used me until I got with child, and when it came, the baby, white as snow, my mistress took it away from me and sold it to a passing slave trader who had a nursing slave—just like a bundle of rags. Then she used my milk for her own baby. And even before it was dry, he came after me again. I thought, If I don't run, I'm going to kill him. So I ran. She might have been glad to get rid of me, but he sent patrols out after me."

"What about the dog bite?"

"Oh, that. Got that when I was eight years old. Set the dogs on me and my mama. That's ancient history."

I sat dry-eyed, but Charlotte was sobbing uncontrollably.

"Char," I said softly, taking her cold hands in mine to comfort her. "We've got to send her to Emily. She'll know what to do. We can't hide her."

"What if the police come back looking for her?"

"They'll find Thenia, and they won't know the difference."

"Thenia . . . Thenia has a story like this one, too . . . doesn't she?" murmured Charlotte.

"Yes," I replied without elaboration.

"And you?" said Charlotte.

"What do you mean?"

"Is the reason you love Thenia so because your family did something terrible to her once?"

"Why do you ask that, Charlotte?"

"Because sometimes you seem to carry within yourself a terrible secret— a guilt like a terrible weight . . . I've seen it in your eyes. . . ."

"Yes," I said. "My family did something terrible to Thenia."

"Is that why you love her more than you love me?"

"I don't love Thenia more than I love you, Charlotte. I love you both. I've loved you longer."

"How long is ten generations, Harriet?"

"Well, if you count from Plymouth Rock, I'd say we have until 1860."

"I don't care what you or your family did . . . it doesn't change how I feel . . ."

"I know. I know, Charlotte. Sometimes I think you'll love me to death."

"And you lied to a constable officer! For someone you've never seen before! And made me lie with you!"

I grinned wickedly, showing all my spectacular teeth, and rolled my eyes.

"Oh, Charlotte, it was only a white lie."

Suddenly, I realized I could have gotten both Thenia and myself jailed. But Thenia was free and could prove it—she had her papers. I was the one who was neither white nor free; and had commited along with my husband the felony of miscegenation. I was the one who shouldn't have been more then ten city blocks from my place of residence without a pass. I was the craziest Negro I knew. An odor like burnt cork hovered in the air around me—or emanated from my own person. It wasn't fear, I knew, yet I couldn't put my finger on what it was. I felt more alive than ever before in my life. I almost danced a jig to the reckless, intoxicating exhilaration of mortal danger. I dissolved into helpless, hysterical laughter. Innocently, Charlotte joined in. We laughed until we cried.

I hid the story of Mary Ferguson from Thenia. I had tried to make Thenia's life until now as safe and secure as I could. She had never gotten over the sale of her family, and even now any announcement concerning slavery in the newspaper or the mention of a runaway could throw her into a stuttering fit, drench her in cold perspiration and such violent trembling that she had to take to her bed. I had taught Thenia to read and write; she was a skilled midwife and a teacher at the First African Methodist Church Sunday school—the only available school for black children. She was now twenty-three years old and she had been deeply in love with Abraham Boss from the first day she had laid eyes upon him.

I had promised Thenia a wedding someday, and now that Abraham had proposed by proxy, so to speak, they were to be married. She would at last have her own family and home. I would lose the witness of my former life to Abraham, who had become a registered apothecary and the general director of our supply depot. Over the years, Thenia had grown into a beautiful woman, whose looks were the talk of the First African Methodist Church and whose body was the dream of every man that prayed there. Her dark hair was worn pulled back in a bun, accentuating her high mahogany forehead, and so tightly held that her enormous, black-fringed eyes turned upward at the corners from the tension. She favored ruffled, high-necked blouses that accentuated the length of her magnificent neck and the amplitude of her splendiferous bosom. Abraham adored her, though the black community, according to Thenia, thought Thenia should have married an American.

Nevertheless, on a cold Sunday in December, with snow on the ground and hoar in the air, Abe and Thenia rode in our carriage to the church where they were wed. She wore a long, beautiful, white velvet dress with a train, my wedding veil, and the pearl earrings her future husband had given her for their engagement. The Bishop Richard Allen, who presided over the ceremony, would probably have had apoplexy if he had heard what Abe whispered in my ear before the ceremony: "I'm doing this for Thenia, but someday it will have to be repeated all over again when we go back to Africa. I'm a Muslim."

Abraham gazed at me from beneath lowered eyelids and smiled.

"I hope this doesn't shock you, Mrs. Wellington," he said, his round liquid eyes holding mine. "I was born into the religion of my ancestors and my tribe, a nation that has no family names. I was captured and sold to Protestant missionaries in Durban at the age of six and forcibly baptized as a Anglican. At twenty-one, I converted to Islam, and for the love of Thenia, I have become a Methodist so that she can be married in the church. To me, one religious ceremony is worth another. When I return to Africa, I revert to the natural religion of that continent: Islam. When I go into the bush seeking specimens, I revert to the religion of my ancestors. You may believe it to be immoral to crisscross the lines of belief like that, but I find it more immoral to fight a religious war. Since there is only one God, religion is like opening and closing a door. The light beyond remains eternal and immutable. Your husband, as a scientist, agrees with me that to be born into a certain religion, as to be born into a certain race, is the purest of accidents. Of course," he continued, "I have never told my little Methodist."

"Your secret is safe with me."

We exchanged spectacular smiles. Secrets. Was there anyone who didn't have them?

"Why, after all these years, won't you call me Harriet, Abraham?"

And so, in this same year of 1836, Thenia and Abraham Boss set up their apothecary in the Moyamensing district of Philadelphia. Abraham continued to work in the afternoons for Thance, who supplied him with merchandise. Thenia minded their little wooden-front store and served as midwife, pharmacist, nurse, and, in many cases, pediatrician, to her neighbors.

The death notice of my half sister, Martha, appeared at the end of that year in the *Richmond Times*. It had been sent, unsigned and without comment, by my silent, sullen brother Thomas, whose handwriting I recognized on the envelope. She had survived my mother by only nine months. Her body had been laid to rest across the head of the three graves in which lay buried my father, my other half sister Maria Eppes, and my mother's half sister, Martha Wayles. Martha was not mourned by me. I felt no pity or sympathy for any of my white family, or for the plight of Cornelia, Ellen, or any of the others. I had always detested Martha Randolph and everything about her, perhaps because I resembled her in many ways. But her airs, her synthetic gentility, her cruelty to my mother had made her my enemy. And now that my enemy's corpse floated by me, vanquished, I tried to find some better memory of her, even if only the fact that she had freed my mother at her father's request. As for her eleven living children and seven grandchildren, from what I had learned of the world they had built, they could rot in hell, all of them. I wished them the same suffering they had imposed on their slave family.

The deaths of Sally Hemings and Martha Randolph, the last Monticellians, convinced Adrian Petit that he should return to France. Old and fragile at seventy-six, he would do what he had been threatening to do for eleven years —retire to his village in Champagne and his now-legendary ninety-two-year-old mother. He even came to ask my permission to go, as if he were still employed by Thomas Jefferson. Still the perfect valet—loyal, discreet, cynical, an exceptional liar, a genius of subterfuge and everybody's friend.

I sometimes wondered if Petit's notorious sideburns weren't actually the wings of Mercury, so much of his life had been spent as a go-between for others. He had no wife, no children (except me), and no home. He neither smoked nor drank, played neither cards nor horses, and if he had ever been in love, no one that I knew had ever discovered with whom. His only sin had been that of gluttony, and old age had taken care of that.

"Look what I have for you, Petit." I opened the specially made box. Inside was James's newly cleaned and polished stiletto. The dull steel gleamed and the modest silver-worked handle did nothing to relieve its lethalness. I had wanted to surprise him with a going-away gift. To do it, I had disarmed myself.

"I want you to have this," I said. "It's your *present du congé*. I've carried it with me every day since the age of sixteen. It belonged to James. I don't need it anymore. Take it to France with you. Take him back to where he was free."

Adrian's eyes widened. "How did you get it? I recognize it, my dear. I gave it to James myself."

"It was one of the few possessions Thomas Mann sent back with Burwell when he found James's body. When I . . . at sixteen, my mother gave it to me. I have carried it as a weapon ever since."

Adrian looked sharply at me. "And you think that now you don't need it —will never need it again?"

"For what?" I smiled. "I'm protected by law, by society, by Thance. And by my white children. Why should I need it?"

Petit caressed the dagger lovingly. "I would never relieve you of it. It was James's banner, his declaration of independence, his cry, his chic, his grief, his warning, and his protection. A talisman, if you like. It should stay on this side of the ocean—with you, where it belongs. It is James's proclamation that he defends you, that his claim to familyhood is legitimate, that he's your uncle. Your protector. I had no idea it had fallen into your hands. How strange life is. It was my present to him at Christmas in 1796."

He closed the box and handed it back to me.

"So long as slave power exists in this country, so long as this land is divided into free and slave, you, my dearest Harriet, can no more lay down James's arm than you can come out of hiding, confess to Thance, recross the color line, go back to the beginning, emancipate your children who are not, in justice, even yours. As long as slave power exists, there is no resting place for the fugitive, no end of the journey. I pray that day will come, Harriet, but for the moment it is not on the horizon. Instead, there is a rather bleak dawn with new travails, I fear, new confrontations, and if I understand anything about the slave oligarchy I once served, it will *take* arms—and a second revolution—to resolve it."

"The famous southern duel with pistols?" I smiled.

"Yes." And he did not smile. "James knew this. And so," he continued, "I leave James's warning in your keeping. Of mementos of him, I have quite enough." He paused. "I often wonder what my life would have been if I hadn't answered your father's summons . . . twice."

"You, not answer a bell, Adrian?"

He laughed. "Ah, well, you're right. At least you are safe, as I promised your father. And my will is in order."

"Don't worry about me, Petit. I'm rich."

"Yes. Isn't that incredible? Something neither of us planned on, did we?" He laid a gnarled hand on mine. I smiled and took it in my own and laid it on my cheek.

"You saved my life."

"I did it . . . for Sally Hemings."

"I thought you did it for him."

"I . . ."

"It's all right, Petit. They're all dead now. All the Monticellians."

"You forget yourself and your brothers and the Hemingses who are still in slavery, scattered all over the South," he said that day.

"I don't forget, Petit," I replied with passionate coolness. "I'll never forget. Slavery won't last forever. I'll find every one of our kin. And together we'll find all the ones we've lost—even those lost to whiteness."

After all, we're all Monticellians . . . aren't we?

The whole damned country.

22

We have the wolf by the ears . . . and we can neither subdue him nor turn him loose.

Thomas Jefferson

I'd been a "white" member of the Philadelphia Anti-Slavery Society for three years, under the presidency of Lucretia Mott, the same Lucretia Mott who had arranged my voyage to London with Dorcas Willowpole. There were black members—Sarah, Harriet, and Marguerite Forten, Hetty Burr, and Lydia White—but none of them suspected me of passing. The society sponsored antislavery fairs and were an auxiliary of the Vigilance Committee of Philadelphia, which had been organized by Robert Purvis to aid destitute fugitives, providing room and board, clothing and medicines, informing them of their legal rights, and giving them protection, both moral and legal, from kidnappers. By acting as if I were a fly on the wall, I had found out what white people really thought of us.

All of them were so open about how they felt about black people. That they were beneath contempt; a race so low in morality, sensibility, and intelligence that nothing said to them or behind their backs could offend them. As my white acquaintances vented all their secret fears, anxious sexual fantasies, and unconscious hatreds, oblivious of my true identity, I felt an indulgent superiority. This evidence of white frailty thrilled me, because I could send them scurrying for cover. I became famous for my wicked and upbraiding tongue in defense of the colored man. I spoke out from my invincible armor of whiteness, and I spoke for every black man, woman, and child that had ever been born. For every injustice they suffered, every death they witnessed.

It was a dangerous, reckless game. Misplaced respect offered to an impostor of the white race, I had learned from Sykes, could elicit murderous anger in a deceived white man. Sykes had decided to kill me over that affront.

But neither death nor punishment frightened me anymore. I had become impervious to my mixed blood—indifferent to it. I no longer fought or defied it. I was simply the composite of the two races which had made me.

Thor was coming home after an absence of two years. I decided I would plead for a new and dangerous enterprise as soon as his ship dropped anchor. Thance and I had been thinking of moving both the laboratories and ourselves out of the city to Anamacora, giving up the house in West Philadelphia, which, with the twins, had become too small for our family. The seclusion of the country would allow me to organize an underground station for fugitives escaping from Virginia and Maryland over the Blue Ridge Mountains and by canal and the Susquehanna River.

I believed myself invincible.

"The risks involved," I began, "are minimal in relation to the great cause we would be serving." We were in the library, just the three of us, having coffee.

"You know I've never opposed you, Harriet, in your devotion to the antislavery cause. I've respected your wishes ever since you came back from London a convinced abolitionist. But this, this is going too far! An underground station at Anamacora, under Mother's nose, is out of the question! Think of *her*. Think of the children. Think of me. What if something happened to you? There's been more than one shootout at these stations, and informers and spies are everywhere. I imagine there's a file on us down at City Hall anyway, between your memberships in subversive organizations and Thor's mysterious operations in Africa. Remember you had a bad scare last year with Passmore Williamson. He could have implicated you in the Johnson scandal, and you would have been sitting in the Old Moyamensing Prison! And what about your friend Lucretia Mott? When she left that antislavery meeting in Norristown arm-in-arm with William Lloyd Garrison, she could have been killed by that crowd. No, Harriet. For the sake of your children, you cannot go any further in this . . . Underground Railroad than you already have!"

Thor was strangely quiet as he lit his pipe and studied me curiously.

"Anamacora is already surrounded by stations," I said. "The slaves are sent from Reading Pine Forge and Whitebar to Philadelphia. From Philadelphia through the towns of Bristol, Bensalem, Newtown, Quakertown, Doylestown, Buckingham, and New Hope, our backyard."

"Harriet, I don't want you repeating those names. Suppose one of the children were to wander in."

"Harriet," said Thor slowly, "just how involved are you in this clandestine operation? How much do you know? Or can you even tell us that?"

Thor stood leaning against the fireplace, his long body curled around it as if seeking a memory of the tropical heat he had abandoned nine weeks earlier. His long supple hands were in continual motion, as if he gathered medicinal herbs even in his sleep. There was no hostility in his voice, only concern for his nephews and nieces and mother. Surely he who had experienced the slave trade firsthand would understand, I thought, so I plunged ahead.

"For your own sake and the children's, I can't tell you everything. I can say this, however. New Jersey is closely allied with Pennsylvania and New York as a center in the fugitive slave network. The main route leads across the Delaware River to Camden, through Mount Holly, Broadtown, Pennington, Hopewell, Princeton, and New Brunswick. I cannot name the conductors of these stations. Slave hunters in search of runaways operate headquarters there. At the Raritan River Bridge, east of New Brunswick, they sometimes stop the trains to search for runaways. To prevent this, local train conductors (real ones, that is) serve as lookouts, warning their coworkers when to transport the slaves in boats to Perth Amboy. Some sea captains take the risk of hiding fugitives, and hire them to pump water from their canal boats. Others transport runaways to safe ports in New England or New York. A small but steady stream have thus entered New York. Five thousand of the twenty thousand blacks in this city are fugitives. One of the best-known conductors is the Quaker Isaac T. Hopper, who is backed by Arthur and Lewis Tappan's fortune. Some of these men and women have been in hiding since Gabriel Prosser's conspiracy in Virginia, the Denmark Vesey uprising of 1822 in South Carolina, and Nat Turner's rebellion in Virginia."

I took a deep breath and tried to control the tremor in my voice.

"The railroad's underground routes center in cities like Philadelphia, New York, and Boston. In each of these three cities, for example, exist vigilance committees, sometimes composed of Negroes alone, sometimes of both Negroes and whites, to aid the fugitives. The vigilance committees work with underground conductors in Maryland and Delaware, who carry more than a hundred fugitives a year and who are in constant fear of being betrayed. The committee also has ties with two or three sea captains who, for a fee, bring passengers hidden in their ships from more southerly parts to Wilmington or here. The various committees hide fugitives usually in the Negro sections of the city, provide them with clothes, and if they wish to seek more security farther north, pay their expenses to move on by carriage, wagon, train, or ship. The vigilance committees try to keep track of the arrival of slave catchers from the South and if possible warn their intended victims. When Negroes are seized without adequate proof that they are slaves, the committees try to obtain court orders to free them.

"Many who get as far as New York resume their journey toward Canada, and they pass through the shore towns to New Haven; from there, two routes extend northward, one to Southampton, Southwick, and Westfield, Massachusetts, the other through North Guilford, Meriden, and Hartford, Connecticut, to Springfield, Massachusetts. The two routes join at Northampton, Massachusetts. In every one of these towns, there are people or organizations of pronounced pro-slavery ideas, people glad to see the slaves sent back to the masters they are fleeing and not adverse to putting hunters and dogs on their tracks. Shall I go on and lead you all the way to New Brunswick and across the border to Canada?"

I stopped and took another deep breath. I had a stitch in my side, as if I had just run a marathon race.

"God Almighty, Harriet!" Thor whistled low and shifted position. "Now tell me what you know about Captain Denmore and Shaka Zulu, and Lord Brunswick, and the Cape Town Riders."

I was trembling.

Thance walked over to me then, and wiped away a tear, which had slipped unheeded down my cheek. But Thor just stood there, his eyes riveted, as if he could see straight through me. Was he wondering what or who had gotten into his family?

"My God, Harriet, you are up to your neck in this," exclaimed Thance. "You are not Dorcas Willowpole, who has no responsibilities except for herself, or Emily Gluck, who has been fanaticized by her husband's guilty conscience, or Thenia, who was a slave herself—you are a white woman with the responsibility of six children, plus, if you'll be so kind, a husband and your in-laws."

"As a white woman," I continued, "I can do a lot that, for instance, Harriet or Sarah Forten, or Lydia White, cannot do. I can go anywhere, do anything, within sane reason—"

There was a great snort from Thor.

"Remember Prudence Crandell? She's white, too, and reasonably sane. She tried to start a school for little colored girls in Massachusetts. They burned her down, sent her to jail, and nigh lynched her!"

"I'm not a heroine, Thor. I only want to do my duty as I see it. I realize my first duty is to Thance and the children. But I do feel at least a willing mind to encounter reproach and suffering, almost to any extent, to advance this cause. If Anamacora is out, it's out. If you will let me one barn, let me one. But nothing I've said leaves this room, I must insist."

The twins stood transfixed. They seemed to be having a conversation between themselves by reading each other's mind. I knew the twins could communicate without speaking, and I watched the expression on their faces change from awe to consternation.

As for me, I flushed with shame. I had broken one of the rules of our organization: giving out secret information to nonmembers. But I had named no names, except those truly in the public domain. I had cited no real conductor or collaborator. But perhaps I had gone too far. And now I had no one to turn to for advice. I couldn't very well tell Robert Purvis or Emily Gluck that I had informed on their network to my husband and my brother-in-law in exchange for a barn.

"The mayor claims that ninety-nine percent of Philadelphia's white citizens are opposed to abolition!" said Thor.

"Nevertheless, this city has always maintained its ascendancy in the movement, thanks to the Quakers," I replied.

"The American Anti-Slavery Society has less than three hundred members," responded Thor, "and even if a dreamy poet liberal like John Greenleaf Whittier has taken over the editorship of the *Pennsylvania Freedman* and has greatly improved its literary style, his political efforts at propaganda have brought disaster upon disaster to the Negro community.

"Harriet," he continued, "antislavery is considered so subversive that any action taken against its proponents is considered legal, and that includes firebombing their houses, running them out of town, tarring and feathering them, beatings, burnings, and murder. Mobs see themselves as patriots, and the whole movement is seen as a conspiracy against the nation formented by British agents."

"The alternative to slavery," said Thance, "is either race war or miscegenation, and this last accusation can always be counted upon to stir up the brutality of the mob."

"Do you expect me to do nothing and watch racial violence become a feature of American life?"

"It *is* a feature of American life, Harriet," said Thor. "Houses are burned, people are injured, and attacks on Negroes are frequent and go unpunished. Look what happened to Boss when he was set upon by that Irish gang."

"You're telling me, Theodore Wellington? I was the one who was awakened by Abraham's cries."

"And don't forget how those fools who decided to reenact the Boston Tea

Party raided your offices, seized a warehouse full of antislavery pamphlets, and threw them into the river. Thank God the offices were closed. What if they hadn't been?"

"I . . ."

"And what happened to Pennsylvania Hall after the Anti-Slavery Convention of America met there, and blacks and whites paraded arm-in-arm? I'll tell you what happened. An out-of-control crowd burned the building to the ground!"

"Thor, I know all this. I'm neither a child nor an idiot."

"I wonder just *what* you are, Harriet. This desire for . . . danger. This playing with your life and the lives of those you love," said Thance.

"The burning of Pennsylvania Hall strengthened our cause," I whispered. But I knew that ever since Mary Ferguson, I was intoxicated by danger . . . by playing with fire.

"Yes, and so would a mob pulling Mother out of her bed at three in the morning, looking for a way station," he replied.

To her credit, my mother-in-law always held her tongue in connection with my abolitionism, remarking only once that since I had a house full of children to take up my time, she wondered if my early orphanhood was not the cause of my morbid interest in the welfare of black people.

Was I fighting a losing cause? I had counted on Thor's support, but he was even more terrified of my putting myself in danger than Thance was. How could they know that I had been in danger all my life? I tried a last ploy.

"How about here in the city? How about a hiding place under the laboratories, with a tunnel that would connect it to the barge depot on the Schuylkill Canal? It's been discussed. We have boat captains ready to take escapees from there. Abraham and Thenia could act as agents instead of me."

"Harriet!"

"It's settled, Harriet. No station. Not now or ever. Not here or in Anamacora. Why, even Purvis would be against it."

"Purvis's farm in Byberry *is* a station," I said. "He and his brother have been carrying out their work for over fourteen years."

"Harriet, Robert Purvis's devotion to this cause is, as we all know, almost suicidal, and I think we understand why. I also think he deems you worthy enough of his friendship not to have your own involvement go beyond the ladies' auxiliary."

"Harriet, my dear," said Thor, seconding his brother, "don't try to be a hero."

My blood was boiling. It wasn't fair. Not only had I to convince Thance, but Thor, too. It was double indemnity, and that was unconstitutional. Only cold-blooded logic would save me now. I remembered what Thor had said about verifying his scientific experiments: as proof of reaction, conduct the experiment in reverse.

"You speak," I said, "only of the danger, the social stigma, the futility of it. What about justice? You know the Fugitive Slave Act is still being carried out in Pennsylvania despite the law. You know it's wrong to allow slave catchers on northern soil. What," I said, suddenly inspired, "if it were Thance and not I who was convinced of the absolute necessity of this action? Enough to risk *his* reputation, his fortune, his good name? What if it were Thance whose honor had been converted to the cause, and I were the one who opposed him on the grounds of danger, indifference, unacceptability? Wouldn't you very soon find me and Mother Rachel standing outside *your* cellar door with lanterns in our hands?"

The twins almost spoke as one, so astonished were they. Because in all scientific logic, that's exactly what would have happened.

"Harriet," said Thor, "you have a devious mind."

"More like a steel trap," said Thance.

"Where did you learn to argue like that?" The question hung in the air.

"In politics," I said. I wasn't the President's daughter for nothing.

Before the year was out, I had my station. Not in Anamacora but on Front Street. Abraham dug a tunnel from an empty vat in the supply room of the laboratory to our cellar. From there to a barge on the Schuylkill was a few meters. A pilot sailed the fugitives to Terrytown, and then another conductor led them to the Purvises' farm at Byberry, where Jean Pierre Burr, the illegitimate mulatto son of Aaron Burr, dispatched his charges to Albany and the borders of Canada.

Thenia now lived in a separate world from me, divided by the color line. Philadelphia's blacks had developed a community life of their own, centered around their own needs. They supported nineteen churches, one hundred and six beneficial societies. They maintained their own insurance companies, cemetery association, undertakers, building and loan association, labor unions, and fraternal organizations such as the Masons, the Odd Fellows, and the Elks. They operated their own libraries, organized their own lectures and debates, a Philadelphia Library Company for Colored Persons, a Debating Society, and for women, the Edgeworth Literary Association. They were outlawed from voting, and of the 302 black families living in Moyamensing, where Thenia and Abraham lived, half of them owned personal wealth of only four dollars and forty-three cents per family. The rest owned nothing.

But the daily violence in Moyamensing turned it into a seething medieval ghetto. Philadelphia, it seemed, was a metropolis of such odious prejudice that there was probably no other city in the world which hated the Negro more.

"Colorphobia is more triumphant here than in pro-slavery, Negro-hunting New York," retorted Robert Purvis when I told him of Thenia's complaint. "Complaint!" he continued. "There is not perhaps anywhere to be found a city in which prejudice against color is more rampant than in Philadelphia. It meets you at every step outside your home and not infrequently follows even there. The city has its white schools and its colored schools, its white churches and its colored churches, its white Christianity and its colored Christianity, its white concerts and its colored concerts, its white literary institutions and its colored literary institutions. The line is everywhere, tightly drawn between them. Colored persons, no matter how well dressed or how well behaved, ladies or gentlemen, rich or poor, are not even permitted to ride on the horse-drawn streetcars through our Christian city. Halls are rented with the express understanding that no person of color shall be allowed to enter, either to attend a concert or listen to a lecture. The whole aspect of this city's segregation at this point is mean, contemptible, and barbarous. Every black Philadelphian is considered by a white Philadelphian as a slave, an ex-slave, a potential slave, or a designated slave under God, and treated accordingly."

What was it, I wondered, that made them fear and hate us so? It couldn't just be color—look at Purvis; look at me. It must have been something we *did* to them. Or, I thought suddenly, that they did to us. Our skin was merely the mirror of their own crime. If a man wrongs you, he also hates you because he's wronged you. We never forgive those whom we have wronged.

⁓

And despite my hatred of Martha, her death, coupled with that of my mother, made me feel even more alone and vulnerable. I was tormented with grief and tortured with guilt. I believed my mother had wanted to tell me something she would only have revealed at the moment of her death. She, like my grandmother before her, like all slave women since the beginning of time, had this secret they had to convey to their daughters, and I hadn't been there to hear. I hadn't even stood over her grave to grieve. Naked fear invaded me. With my mother and Martha dead, there was nothing to prevent my cousins from claiming me or blackmailing me. What if they had had Eston's wagon train followed to find me? Ellen, Cornelia, Samuel, and Peter had made no promises to my father to free me.

"Your wife's a fugitive slave. Our property . . . financial difficulties . . . a draft on your bank for . . . for . . . how much would Thance be willing to pay to save his wife? Or better still, to buy her back? Do I hear ten, fifty, do I hear a hundred thousand dollars? Do I hear all? Everything? A fortune? Financial ruin like my father? Or nothing? Everything I'd ever achieved, ever possessed in life, lost. Or worse, how much would my mother-in-law be willing to pay to protect her precious white grandchildren—slaves, all of them? I began to imagine I was being followed. I began to have my old nightmares about Sykes. Then, one day, I saw him on the streets of Philadelphia. At Sixteenth and Pine, almost in front of the conservatory. He wore a Stetson, a white collar, and a pistol with cartridges. After nineteen years, he was one of the few people I was sure would still recognize me anywhere. It *was* Sykes.

Deliberately, I turned my back and spoke to Mr. Perry, our warehouse accountant.

"Mr. Perry, you see that man over there? I want you to find out who he is."

"Yes, ma'am."

Mr. Perry reported back. "Name's Horton. He's a bloody slave catcher from Virginia."

But I knew it was Sykes. I was sure. I would never forget. Never. He was no Horton. He had changed his name, just as I had changed mine.

Soon after that, illogical and unfounded fears startled me awake in my bed. I took to getting up in the middle of the night to check on the children. Methodically, I would go from room to room, like a sleepwalker, counting them. Sinclair, Ellen, Jane, Beverly, Madison, James. Each night they were there, safe, white, asleep in their beds, fists closed, their breathing soft, scented. Regular, legitimate, legal, my heart would pound.

Once Thance caught me at four o'clock in the morning in the twins' room.

"You frightened me," he whispered, so as not to wake them. "I woke up and you weren't there," he complained.

"I thought I heard something or someone, a burglar . . ."

I had communicated my unspeakable fears to Thance. I gazed up at his smooth, handsome face, sleep-glazed and incredibly blank, like an oversized room, pale, immense, beloved, filling my life, monumental and all-encompassing, blocking out the shadows. I began to tremble. I had *seen* him, Sykes. He was right here in this city, stalking me. *Where are your papers, Snow White?* He was coming to get me. I felt a tremor of frigid cold as Thance took me in his arms.

"Harriet, what's the matter with you? You've been dreaming . . . a nightmare. There's no one here but me . . . us . . . you've ruined your nerves with this slave smuggling. Jesus Christ, you've got a knife in your hand!"

I stood there, my soul shriveled with terror, cold and unfeeling, clutching my dagger as if a veil of ice separated us. As if Sykes himself were standing between us.

23

But what is chance? Nothing happens in the world without a cause. If we know the cause, we do not call it chance; but if we do not know it, we say it was produced by chance. If we see a loaded die turn its lightest side up, we know the cause, and that is not an effect of chance, but whatever side an unloaded die turns up, not knowing the cause, we say it is the effect of chance.

Thomas Jefferson

Dr. Wilberforce's dream came true on August 1, 1838, the day slavery was abolished in the British West Indies. From that time on, all eyes were turned toward the United States. Eight hundred thousand slaves had achieved freedom. The day, and the date of this victory, became an annual celebration for the free black population in the northern states of America.

British abolitionists arrived in numbers to agitate in America. George Thomson, whom I had met in London with Dorcas Willowpole, came with his plan for gradual emancipation: first free the children, then the old, then the grateful slaves, and last of all the revengeful residue. Charles Stuart, whom I had met in Birmingham, also came. Both were superb orators and preachers, both had run afoul of the law, and both were attacked by the antiabolitionist mobs that had become the hallmark of the 1830s. The same year, Harriet Martineau attended the Boston Female Anti-Slavery Society's convention and spoke from the platform. It was the most daring feat any woman had achieved, to address a mixed audience in public. She railed against the Protestant and Catholic churches' failure to take a stand against slavery:

all men were guilty—Baptist, Methodist, Episcopal, Presbyterian. She stormed about the reluctance of the American Friends to cooperate in racially mixed antislavery societies. She denounced everything and everybody, then wrote about it. But she wasn't the only one.

A flood of British anti-American, antislavery travel books were printed or republished. Edward S. Abdy's *Journal of a Resident and Tour in the United States* took to task the hypocritical North as well as the slave-owning South. He took my father to task for being guilty of miscegenation. The rumors of my father's slave children were commonly reported, and I found myself more than once reading of myself as the President's daughter. I read *Men and Manners in America*, by Thomas Hamilton. He accused my father of railing about liberty and equality and the degrading curse of slavery, yet bringing his own children to the hammer. My father's epitaph, he concluded, should read: "He who dreamt of freedom in a slave's embrace. . . ."

I stared at the ugly words and then closed the book softly. I looked over at eleven-year-old Sinclair, who was reading, slouched over his lessons at my writing table under which Madison and James were playing. The girls and Beverly were in the nursery from which the widow Wellington had just descended. As she entered the room, I looked up with real pleasure: it was one of her many visits from Anamacora, usually at the beginning or end of her monthly business meetings in Philadelphia. Thor was home. This meant a lot of activity at the laboratory, the depot, and the apothecary. We now had our own warehouse from which issued new railroad tracks. And we owned a clipper ship that sailed between the Cape and the city, bringing home tons of medicinal plants, cocoa, and coffee. But again my personal world seemed to be closing in on me. Petit wrote to me that he had read in the *Royal Gazette* that Maria Cosway had died in Lodi the fifth of January 1838 and was buried beneath the nun's chapel in her convent.

Then, at the end of the winter, Rachel Wellington sat down on the bed beside me, her eyes red from weeping. We had lived peacefully together as mother and daughter for twelve years. Now we struggled with the eternal question of mortality. The odor of morphine and the indescribable advance of mortal illness now hung about her still robust and undiminished body.

"I'm dying," was all she said that day, as she buried her face on my shoulder and clung to me, her tears soaking into the collar of my dress, revealing what she had known for some months.

"Don't tell the twins," she said. "Not yet, because it's going to take a long time."

Like my grandmother, Elizabeth, my mother-in-law died hard. But instead of a rough slave cabin, suffocating under a Virginia August sun, my mother-in-law died in a white canopied featherbed, her children and grandchildren gathered around. Her suffering no longer dulled by morphine or opium, she complained, just as my grandmother had done, that her heart wouldn't stop beating. And like my mother before me, I pressed hard on the emaciated chest, willing her release as my mother had willed that of Elizabeth Hemings. But Rachel Wellington refused to give up the ghost. It took cholera to kill her, and on the morning of August 1, 1839, she finally expired, in the midst of a full-scale epidemic, which had broken out in the working-class slums of Philadelphia.

Like dominoes, all the women who had dominated my life had fallen one after the other, all at the same age, as if each, like a badge of honor, had been allotted the same number of breaths. Rachel Wellington left the flourishing Wellington Drug Company and a personal fortune, which she divided equally into five parts, willing the fifth to me as if I had been her natural daughter.

I had become a woman of independent means, as well as the only Mrs. Wellington.

The year that had begun in ice and ended in cholera drew to an end. Winter had commenced the fifteenth of November and continued until the fifteenth of May. Sleighs went dashing up and down the streets, their bells clear and sweet; ladies, looking rosy and warm, and gentlemen, carefully wrapped, skated on the Delaware where ice stretched out over the waves. The children learned hockey and made ice palaces, and the poor begged wood and food in the streets. Then the weather changed and a great thaw broke up the masses of ice on the Delaware. The river shuddered and was lifted from its bed, causing great flooding of its tributaries and inundating the western part of the city with water. Then suddenly it was summer without any spring, and the fetid back alleys of pristine Philadelphia began to throw off the effluent that caused sudden and horrible death: cholera. Whoever had brought it to Anamacora, and we believed it to be the iceman, had done my mother-in-law a favor.

Several of our laboratory workers who had been in the city came down with the sickness but were saved. In other parts of Philadelphia, the wide gap between the fragrant green city of the well-to-do and the slums of the poor was unbreachable. Extremes of filth and misery and loathsome disease met the eye everywhere: horrid heaps of manure from hog and cow pens; putrefying garbage; carcasses in decomposition; filthy rooms and children; damp, dirty cellars and tenements; full and foul privies in ill-ventilated, crowded alleys, which gave off noxious gases. Many of the localities where the epidemic raged were jammed one upon another, filthy and poor, without ventilation or drainage, plumbing or a water supply.

When the epidemic began, Thor's brilliance and Thance's labor had made the Wellington Drug Company one of the most prosperous drug companies on the East Coast, famous for its research and patent medicines. While I held my breath and gathered the children around me at Anamacora, Thor and Thance begged, pleaded, and cajoled the city administration for sanitary measures rather than prayer to fight the epidemic—to no avail.

Philadelphia had long been the center of medical education in the United States, and every year a thousand medical students, many from the South and particularly Virginia, flooded the city. Yet for over fifty years, medical science had been at a standstill in meeting the needs of a rising population, impoverished immigrants, and the poor sanitary conditions and rising mortality rate of the working class. This was the Jacksonian era of democracy, public education, and respect for the common man, but public health care, as well as the great pharmaceutical inventions, were still several decades away. Yet the twins strove to overcome all these things; Abraham Boss and Thenia, too, worked ceaselessly in their own neighborhood. And when at last the tide turned at two thousand three hundred cholera cases, both Thor and Thance were recognized by the City Council for their work and were awarded, along with thirteen physicians who had been in charge of the hospitals, a silver pitcher in gratitude for their services. It was the first time pharmacists had been so honored.

Philadelphia now was probably the cleanest city in America. The sidewalks were washed constantly, the marble steps were spotlessly clean, the population stood at one hundred thousand, and the center of the city had moved west to Seventh Street, since half the population now lived west of that line. An omnibus service had started hourly runs between the Merchant Coffee House on Second Street and the Schuylkill. And another mode of conveyance appeared—the cab, abbreviated from the French *cabriolet*. The cab carried two passengers inside and a driver outside on a box to the rear.

Row upon row of handsome brick houses, three or four stories high, with baths and water closets, were being built. Spectacular public buildings like the Merchant's Exchange, the United States Bank, and the United States Mint rose. Streets were now lit by gaslight, which everyone agreed was the most dazzling, clean light that they had ever seen and which made Philadelphia, expanding in three different directions, the best lit city in the world, with the exception of Paris.

Charlotte and I were sitting in a cab on our way to lunch at Brown's Hotel, as had been our habit for years. She had picked me up at home, and when I got in, three-quarters of the space was already taken up by her considerable girth. Charlotte, like Philadelphia, had expanded with time, wealth, and promiscuity. Even the displacement of her firm but corpulent body created a small turbulence of air, beautifully perfumed by Guerlain. Within this whirlwind of scent, she was perpetually short-winded.

"I think my husband is having me followed," she announced when I'd closed the door.

"What! Don't be foolish, Charlotte. Why would he do that? You're the one who put a detective agency on *his* tail."

"I'm no woman's-rights female, but I am against women being *forever anathema masanatha* in society for the *same offense* which a man gets away with *every* time. *This* is a *very, very* great injustice."

Charlotte's husband Andrew had turned out to be a petty reprobate who, little by little, had become a notorious philanderer, for which, one day, Charlotte had decided to give him a taste of his own medicine. She had taken a lover, a charming southern gentleman named Nash Courtney, who visited Philadelphia and the Drake Hotel once a month. Charlotte's husband had found out and had threatened to call the Virginian out in a duel—even though dueling had been against the law for decades in Pennsylvania. Being a southerner, Charlotte's paramour had readily accepted. "Dueling is still tolerated in New Jersey. Let's go."

Charlotte was now afraid she'd be a rather young widow with three very beautiful children, rather than the emancipated free-love advocate she had planned. She was terrified.

"Harriet, I know I've done some foolish things, and this is probably the *most* foolish, but I really can't take this whole thing seriously," she had told me. "Two grown men! But they're dead set on going ahead. Who do you think could . . . intervene?"

"Your father?" I asked.

"He isn't speaking to me."

"Robert Purvis?"

"Oh, Andrew would never accept a nigger as an intermediary," said Charlotte.

"I thought Robert was your friend," I said.

"He *is* my friend! That's what he *told* me when I asked him to intervene!"

"Oh, Charlotte, this is not Russia! Andrew is not Alexander Pushkin!"

"I think they're going to do it," she repeated dreamily.

The duel took place at 5:00 A.M. on a dusty spring morning in a potato field on the farm of a certain Harry McMillian. Nash Courtney was seconded by a relative from Jefferson Medical College and Charlotte's husband by, ironically, the natural son of Aaron Burr, Jean Pierre Burr. Charlotte's lover was slightly wounded but died of blood poisoning several days later, thus enabling Charlotte to avoid the scandal of having her husband accused of murder.

During that year of genuine mourning, Charlotte and I were again drawn together as we had been through the years at certain difficult times in our lives. When this happened, we fell into the tender erotic bonds of our school days. Our luxurious society was intact, and our retreat into the sensuality and carnal voluptuousness of our adolescence was more a reaction to fear and the passage of time than to the deaths of Nash and Rachel Wellington. Charlotte was sure she was going to die and go to hell for what she had done. I was sure I was going to die and go to hell for other reasons. Sometimes I walked past a mirror and saw no one reflected. That frightened me more than anything. And so I indulged Charlotte's carnality. In her adoring eyes I saw the old self-deceiving Harriet, reckless, obdurate, selfish, still youthfully beautiful. The gulf between the true Harriet and the fiction I had created for all others had grown into an abyss of self-delusion. I felt I could let down my guard with no one except Thenia. So there was only Charlotte.

Sexual love between women of our class was one of our best-kept secrets. Sequestered and idle, in need of company and kept out of active business, arts, and politics, as well as our husbands' clubs, sports, and intellectual life, we turned to each other, fell in love, wrote passionate love letters, established intense friendships, and indulged in pleasures which were no longer solitary. I pleased Charlotte and kept her desirous of me even as I felt the shame of an inadvertent impostor. I imagined, as our lips touched, telling her who I was. I couldn't be sure I wouldn't be ridiculed and accused, disowned and ostracized, not for having done anything wrong but for *being* wrong.

I felt bogus according to Charlotte's criterion of worth. False according to her criterion of authenticity. Our commingling of flesh had something perverse about it. Like the kiss I had placed on my father's dying lips. I always took the male role because I had to keep her in my power. I didn't want to see Charlotte turn from intimate friend and comrade into Lorenzo Fitzgerald. I didn't want her eyes to widen in disbelief, then narrow in contempt as Lorenzo's had done. I was too afraid to test her. I loved her too much. I needed her. So I played the adoring mentor to her chagrin and her trust. I made her lose thirty pounds and renew her wardrobe twice with glorious dresses from Perrot, Lanvin, and the new department store, Wana-maker and Company. She decided that black and indigo blue were "her" colors, as they accentuated her fair skin and blondness. She looked twenty years younger, which caused her husband to fall in love with her all over again, and he stopped womanizing and became devoted to her. They spent the next two years on an extended second honeymoon, traveling in France, Italy, and Germany. There was as much ironic justice in Charlotte's bid for female emancipation as there had been in mine.

As for Thance, the dread of losing him took possession of me each time I sought to speak, and rendered it impossible for me to do so. The belief that moral courage requires more than physical courage is not poetic fancy. I would have found it easier to face a lynch mob than tell my husband and children who I really was.

24

I hope in God no circumstance may ever make either seek an asylum
from grief . . . I would pour my tears into their wounds; and if a drop
of balm could be found at the top of the Cordilleras or at the remotest
sources of the Missouri, I would go there myself to seek and bring it.

Thomas Jefferson

SOMEWHERE NEAR THE MOZAMBIQUE BORDER, TRANSVAAL

My Loved Ones,

There has been incredible change here since the Zulu forces were defeated by the English, and the Boers have fled toward the north into the provinces of Orange, Transvaal, and Lesotho. This is a three-sided war which is both a civil and a national war. The Boers against the English, the English against the Zulus, and the Zulus against all. The English commander has his hands full, and if he doesn't receive the reinforcements he's asked the Queen for, there is no way he will be able to reoccupy all the provinces where the Boers are threatening to secede, to the great surprise of the Zulu princes, especially the Ndebele tribe, whose ancestral territory it is.

In a country ten times more underpopulated than the West of the United States and twice as large in territory, one would think that some kind of territorial treaty could be worked out. The Zulus, of course, are being treated like our American Indians, although the former immigrated from the north a bit more than a hundred years ago — with malice, arrogance, and mendacity. The confederacy built by Emperor Shaka Zulu twenty years ago, and which gave even Britain's Foreign Office a fit of apoplexy, has fallen into disarray, with the various tribes fighting and warring amongst themselves, dissipating their fighting strength in petty quarrels between princes and chiefs.

The British, of course, are masters in taking political advantage of ambiguous situations and have managed to persuade the Zulus to attack the Boer wagon trains reaching Orange. The princes and ministers don't seem to realize it is the English who are ultimately their enemy, not the Boers. The Boers, like our western settlers, have no place else to go, and they will stand and fight off every attack the Zulu nation will mount against them, while the English in the Cape and the Portuguese in Mozambique rub their hands in glee at the full killing fields.

Meanwhile, our expedition has wrapped up its latest work and we are on our way back down the coast to Durban: a hundred bearers, cooks, and guns, six medical wagons and mobile laboratories, a herd of oxen, a menagerie of walking food supplies, sixteen field tents—in other words, an army. We have to keep on good terms with everyone in order for our work to go on. We can't afford to anger either the Boers, the English, or the Zulus. There is a French-German team here at the same time, and we have decided to paint yellow crosses on all our tents and wagons, and paint our crates and bearers' loads with the same cross. It may not save us from a Zulu attack, but we hope it works with our Christian brothers.

We are nearing the rainy season, and although there is no rain yet, it is a misty morning, the sky is cloudy, and everything is gray. Abraham says there is nothing any sadder than Philadelphia, but in Philly, this kind of weather tends to inspire meditation, reading, study, listening to music. Here it tends toward memories, and I find that a phenomenon occurs here which is so very extraordinary that I have spoken to several of the French scientists about it. It is this: my memory of this country—that is, how I think of it when I am in the States, for example—is so vivid, that is to say, I have imagined it in my thoughts of it so strongly, that my recollection of it fights with the reality before my eyes.

I look out on a splendid plain of elephant grass edged in gray mist, receding into the distance of gray hills, where a pair of sea eagles whose wings are wider than an elephant's head fly over. In the center of this landscape, a baobab tree which can shade twenty people stands outlined in the mist, its one-thousand-year-old branches sweeping out like a maestro conducting a symphony orchestra. But is what is before my eyes real, or is this the memory I've carried of this scene superimposed on the reality before me? It seems that in many cases, we are so enamored of our false images that even reality itself cannot transform the imprint in one's mind's eye. One sees what one wants to see. . . .

In five days we will leave Durban and start home. It's been two years. Either I've turned into a Flying Dutchman or a blasted Zulu, I'm not sure which. Or rather, take your pick.

Kiss your children for their uncle. And yourselves. This letter is for Lividia and Tabitha, as well as you two dears. I think much of Mother. May God bless you and keep you.

Th. Wellington

Thor's research into herbal medicine and homeopathy had made him famous. And no sooner had he arrived home than invitations poured in for conferences and lectures. Thor's time was taken up almost entirely, and his work at the laboratory with Abraham was carried on at night, while a stray fugitive or so climbed in and out of the laboratory vats that covered our secret passageway.

Thor seemed oblivious of these nocturnal goings-on, and we never spoke of them or even mentioned the words *runaway, bounty hunter, police, sheriff, slave.* Thor's connection with Africa and Africans was such a pastoral and nonviolent one that it seemed wrong to impose a different kind of allegiance on this dreamy passionate scientist until it was absolutely necessary.

Thor lived with us because it was the only home he had except the expeditionary camp in Africa. When he wasn't out working, he was home with the children, playing or writing letters. I often played the piano for him. If only there were some way, he said, that music could be carried with you, without the services of an entire orchestra. I had had a letter-copying machine like my father's made for him as a coming-home present.

Often when I walked by the laboratory on my way to the warehouse or the wharf, I would peek in and see Thor and Thance busily sorting their thousands of specimens. Bent over their worktable, they were difficult to tell apart.

"Why don't you put labels on your own smocks so people can tell you apart?" I said.

"*You* can tell us apart," laughed Thor.

⌒

I remember it was raining and it was very late at night. The drops made a rapid hissing sound on the skylight windows. I walked past the window of the laboratory, my cloak drawn over my shoulders. I intended to return to the warehouse offices, and as I walked by I thought I saw Thance. He was to leave for the Cape to join a new scientific expedition, and he was taking Abraham, who had not been back to South Africa in more than seven years, with him. Once again, Thenia had refused to sail with Abe, postponing their "country wedding." She was afraid of ships, afraid of large bodies of water, afraid of Africa. I had tried everything to convince her that a sea voyage was as safe as riding the Pennsylvania Railroad. Thance seemed to be searching for something. Beauty, Independence's granddaughter, followed at my heels as I opened the door of the laboratory.

"Thance?" I said as I walked in, my wet skirts dragging. I pulled my cloak off my shoulders just as the dog, shaking the rain from her back, spied something moving behind one of the storage vats and made a run for it, brushing by me. The motion wheeled me around. I was caught off balance, and I felt myself slipping. To break my fall, I grabbed the nearest shelf. A voice behind me cried out in alarm.

"Harriet! Don't touch those shelves!"

Dreamily I recognized Thor's voice, as the folds of my cape caught on a fragile wooden shelf and it came tumbling down, bringing with it dark glass bottles, cascading one onto the other like dominoes. I stepped back to avoid the breaking glass, but my foot caught in the hem of my dress, already snagged on the shelf, and I was pitched forward onto my hands and knees, the steaming liquids making a pool around them. The noise of the cascading bottles made a sound like a cannon, drowning out Beauty's frantic barking. The broken bottles all had carefully written labels: silver nitrate, vitriol, sulfuric acid, carbolic acid, formaldehyde, oxalic lye . . .

The liquids and their gases spread out from my cloak, which protected the rest of me, but my hands were on fire. A searing pain shot up my wrists and forearms, so fierce it stopped my heart. Almost at once, two strong hands gathered up my wrists and, amidst my terrible screams, dragged me forward toward the water pumps. The water gushed over my wrists as I struggled against the pain, which was pulling me under. The room spun and I lapsed into unconsciousness.

When I awoke, I was propped on the Chesterfield sofa in Thor's office. My hands were on fire. I looked down at them. They were tightly bound in muslin mittens. I began to cry.

"Harriet," said Thor gently, "drink this, please. You had an accident. Your hands have been burned, but only superficially. They will begin to heal in a few days. I've dressed them with a pomade I made of hickory tree moss and coconut butter, used for burns in Africa. Can you move your fingers?"

Slowly I tried to move my thumb; although only with great pain, I could move the fingers of both hands.

"Yes," I said, looking down on the white bundles.

"You stopped your fall with your hands, thank God."

I groaned.

"Oh, my God, Harriet. If something had happened to you . . . your face . . ."

"I was careless."

"I was so frightened, seeing you . . . Harriet . . . my God, Harriet, I was so scared."

I closed my eyes. When I opened them again, Thor was staring down at me; his face held the same expression as his twin, his eyes the same helpless love.

"I blame myself entirely," Thor was saying. "Those bottles should be locked away."

"Beauty had no business in here. I was distracted, an inexcusable fault in a laboratory. I'm sorry."

"*You're* sorry! It was entirely my fault!"

"Oh, Thor, that's not true. I'm not a child. I'm not your responsibility."

"But you *are* my responsibility. From the first day I saw you, I knew you would always be the only woman I would ever feel responsible for."

There it was. He was shaking, his eyes bright with unshed tears. The blood had drained from his face. He hadn't wanted to say any of this. I hadn't wanted it.

"Your brother's wife," I said, warning him.

"Yes, my brother's wife. My beloved brother's beloved wife. As beloved by her brother-in-law as by her husband."

His words hung in the air like a silk banner, fluttering with unspoken yearnings and pain. How much more bizarre and convoluted could my family life become, I thought, almost laughing. Imposture, miscegenation, a double life which was now a triple or quadruple life. Perhaps I should have been sold in New Orleans after all. That would have been one of the more banal occurrences in my life. Now I had seduced my brother-in-law.

"I love you both," I said truthfully. "I can hardly tell you apart."

This last was a lie, like so many of my lies. I knew very well who Thor was and who Thance was, and I had no trouble at all telling them apart.

In two weeks, because of Thor's medicines and the fact that he had so quickly washed them with water and alkali (I still heard the gushing pump, its iron wheeze, Thor's calm voice), my hands began to heal. Healthy skin had begun to grow on the burned palms. The dead flesh peeled off. The pain diminished. I could once more hold an object.

Thor took off my bandages and left only gauze mittens tied loosely around my wrists. Then one day, when no one was around, I took off the mittens and inspected the insides of my hands.

In shocked disbelief, I realized that I no longer had fingerprints! The tips of my fingers were as smooth and white as marble. As smooth and white as the backs of my hands, which had been untouched. In the center of my palm, where my life line ran, there remained scar tissue, crisscrossing its center as if laid on by a whip. I had seen such scars on runaways. But even these scars would soon fade, leaving only tracks of white, like fine lace against a palm even paler than before.

My blank fingertips were the only lasting souvenir of the accident. My identity was erased. I felt both sad and jubilant. My heart beat faster. It was a sign, I thought, as I stared at my mutilated hands. My oblivion was complete. The injury of my birth eradicated. But was this retribution or deliverance? Tears of confusion welled in my eyes. Did this make me my father's daughter or the contrary?

In the weeks that followed my accident, Thenia visited me almost every day, her six-year-old Raphael in tow. During the first visit, we stared at each other in silence. Thenia had not wanted to burden me with her problems, and I couldn't begin to explain the importance of fingerprints to her. But eventually I learned Thenia had been keeping a lot of things from me. Abe wanted to return home to Africa. He saw no point in accepting the indignities of life as a northern black and was disheartened by the hatred and rejection he found everywhere. Abe wanted his sons to live in his own country, and although he had come to learn Western methodology and had been admitted to the Jefferson College of Pharmacy, he had been refused admittance to the Apothecary Guild. He had even been refused a peddler's license for patient medicines. He could learn more on an expeditionary field trip of six months than he could here, labeling Thor's samples, running Thance's warehouse. Abe was going back to the field.

Thenia was afraid of Africa, and she didn't want Raphael to go. Abe was allowing her to stay until he returned from this expedition, but it was the last reprieve. He was going back to Africa, and he wanted Thenia with him.

"If I leave, I'll never return, and I'll never find my family. I'll never se-se-see them aga-ga-gain," she wept. "As long as I am here, there's hope that I can find them: Mama, Daddy, Doll, Ellen. But if I'm *there*, I'll never find them. And I'm pregnant again," she continued. "If I tell Abe, he'll think it's because I don't want him to go. But if he doesn't return in eight months, this baby'll be born without its fa-fa-father."

"They'll be back before the birth of the baby, Thenia. And I may be pregnant myself. Or maybe it's because of the accident that I haven't had my migraine this month."

I was forty-three years old. My grandmother's last child had been born when she was forty-three.

⁓

Thance said little to me about the accident, as if evoking it would evoke another long-ago accident. He and Abraham left for the Cape on our own ship, the *Rachel*, the end of January. Although Thance had little experience of Africa, Thor was on the verge of discovering a vaccine and had acquiesced to his twin going.

The *Rachel* carried a cargo of whale oil and would return with a shipment of raw materials for medicines, plus Zanzibar spices and red pepper. The *Rachel* reached Cape Town in the spring of 1843.

25

Yet the morality of a thing cannot depend on our knowledge or ignorance of its cause. Not knowing why a particular side of an unloaded die turns up cannot make the act of throwing it, or of betting on it, immoral. If we consider games of chance immoral, then every pursuit of human industry is immoral.

Thomas Jefferson

It was the twenty-first of March 1843, in the bush near Bulawayo, South Africa, twenty days after Abe's and my arrival.

I had always sensed a strange loneliness in my wife, Harriet, from the very beginning. Even though I and the other Wellingtons surrounded her with love, there existed an inner furnace of solitude in Harriet which consumed her day and night, fueled by God knows what terrors. I once found a dagger in her skirt pocket and discovered she went abroad armed.

My mother put it down to Harriet's sudden loss of her entire family in the yellow-fever epidemic, but my mother blamed that tragedy for everything she didn't understand about Harriet. I felt it to be more a sense of displacement than of loss, as if Harriet, having been thrust out of her native South into the world, with no other protection than a distantly related guardian who himself was a foreigner, had become a displaced person herself: a domestic immigrant in her own country.

During the long voyage on the *Rachel*, Abe and I spent our time working in our makeshift laboratory or speaking of our respective wives. Through Abe's evocation of Thenia, I thought to discover some clue to Harriet's secretiveness. I suspected that Thenia knew my wife much better than I. I also suspected some southern family secret between them, and I wondered if Abe was privy to this information. If he was, he didn't let on. He seemed to know as little about Thenia as I knew about Harriet, except that they were both Virginia orphans: one black and one white. I knew my wife had rescued Thenia from slavery, had educated and protected her, and in turn Thenia had lavished fierce love, loyalty, and silence upon her.

I wondered about many things that were mysterious to me. Harriet loved me, I was certain. But that love seemed to bring her no serenity. She seemed to live in perpetual contradiction with something inside herself. Sometimes I found her staring at Sinclair or me or one of the twins in the strangest way. Her children seemed to have some other, supplemental meaning for her. God knows she was a perfect mother, protective as a lioness, just, patient, and infinitely adoring. Yet a bonfire of rage seemed to burn inside her, and there existed a well of loneliness so deep, so sad, that even the force of my love was inadequate. I could not free her from her internal enigma and the flame of its everlasting sadness and eternal silence, try as I might to quell that belligerent flame, it burned like a nightlight in her soul, even in our most intimate moments—moments so fragile, so passionate, so superb that to speak of them makes my heart stop in remembered happiness. I never understood *the origin* of her distress, and not understanding it induced in me a corresponding loneliness. To combat the feeling, I threw myself into my work and drew away from her mysteries, which seemed to me altogether too southern, too perverse, especially since she had all that might be deemed happiness for her sex: a spouse, a home, her friends, an adoring family, devoted children, and a talent for music.

But Harriet was afraid, and her fear, I believe, expressed itself in a certain detachment from her children, as if they were not to be loved too much for they might be snatched away at any moment. As if they were not *hers*, but only *in her keeping*.

She also possessed a fanatic abhorrence to any kind of oppression or inhumanity to man, an almost irrational rile which manifested itself in an exaggerated enthusiasm for all kinds of causes: abolition, world peace, temperance, transcendentalism, women's rights, protection of animals, protection of Indians. She espoused them all with a fervor and dedication hardly matched in her own domestic life. I do not exaggerate. After Thenia's marriage, she refused to employ Irish nannies for the twins because Irish thugs had beaten up Abraham Boss. She railed against the fact that Philadelphia's blacks were not allowed to ride in the new horse-drawn streetcars. She risked her social standing and that of our entire family by hiding fugitives. She petitioned Congress on behalf of mulattoes suing for their freedom, on behalf of the antislavery cause, on behalf of immediate emancipation. Her excuse was always the magnanimous one: she had so much—so much love, luck, money, health—that it was criminal not to share her good fortune with the unfortunate, the disinherited of this earth.

Music made her cry. Pictures made her cry. Novels made her cry. Orphans, babies, old people, even Negroes made her cry. Melancholy became the *fleur de peau* of her character, yet her glowing high spirits, her beauty, which she considered a burden, gave it lie. She had not aged one single instant in sixteen years. I had taken on a few gray hairs, I tired more quickly, and the spectacles I had once used as a conceit were now a real necessity. Yet my wife's skin was as smooth, her complexion as fresh, her body as firm, slim, and strong, her hands as fine and unblemished as the day I met her.

Charlotte used to tease me by saying Harriet must sleep in the embalming fluid I used for my specimens. Even Thor, returning home after long absences in Africa, would comment on the remarkable preservation of Harriet's beauty. Sometimes we would speak of it far into the night. We praised her looks, her southernness, her courage, her will, her sweetness, her intelligence, her devotion. Often I would gaze at her while she slept and, with wonder and gratefulness, thank the generous God who had placed such a woman in my keeping. At times I had the distinct feeling that Harriet felt *she* protected *me*, and that, too, pleased me. A warrior woman like my mother (God rest her soul) had always had a particular attraction for me, but Harriet seemed to aspire to more than this. She searched for roles which placed her in the center of tragedy, comedy, or farce, it didn't really matter which, as long as she deemed it Life.

Thor always brought that sense of life back with him: that crowded nuance and musk of the unknown and unknowable Africa, with its exuberance, its mystery, its violence and brutality, its danger, its fatality. He would blow in with Africa's smells and hazards and elucidations, and Harriet would smile and burn and glow and present him a new niece or nephew. Then he was off again, returning years later to a new niece or nephew and to our laboratory, where his foliage and bark, roots and leaves and spores, were dissected and analyzed, distilled into science, knowledge, pharmacy.

The mysteries of alchemy linked Thor and me together as brothers night after night, in experiment after experiment, repeating the same gestures, distilling the same substances. In a way, this was what I had wanted to do with Harriet. Distill the essence of the woman, hammer her into a powder, bottle her, put her on a shelf, study her, adore her, admire her color, her taste, her viscosity, and believe that what was on the label was in the vial. Because I didn't believe in chance. I didn't believe I would ever commit another mistake after that first and fatal one with Thor. He believed that that mistake, which had separated him from me forever, which had made him worth half of himself, like a slave, would carry me safely through the rest of my life.

Harriet believed this, too: that the one overwhelming tragedy of her life would carry her through, pay for her passage through the rest of time. How could she have known that other, egregious rules were at play? In trying to eliminate the accidental from my life, I brought about its fatality ten times over. Chance. What the scientific mind excludes.

A slip of the lip. In the intimacy of a warpped starry night on the *Rachel,* Abe referred to Thenia as Harriet's niece. In all innocence, I didn't even ask him what he meant or to repeat what he said. Each star had burst with revelation. My mouth fell open and I swallowed the closest one—a burning, brilliant coal which raced through my entrails and rose a hot clump in the back of my brain. Harriet's mother had had to be a colored woman. A slave. God. Damned. Virginian. He had made Harriet lie to her children.

I listed like the *Rachel,* sinking, moving forward, drawn by the pluck of some great force from within, for home, for country, for my sons, for Harriet . . . and the deck went by slowly, inexorably, like the great, slow blade of the Schuylkill.

Wait! I feel a draft behind me—like the small tornadoes we suffer on the Transvaal plains. There is the whistle of steel. A thud. A kind of blindness filled with extraordinary pain. There is nothing wrong with my eyes, but a veil of darkness has descended over them like pitch. Except it's red. It's my own blood. Help! Help! Abraham. Abraham is near me. I hear him. He's screaming something—what? I can't make out what it is. Suddenly, I see his arm hacked off. He looks surprised. He swoons; his arm flies off in space, its finger still pointing. Or is it I who have sunk further down into blood? Another blow, this time sharpened steel, not wood. Oh God. It makes a different sound. Harriet. My wife. My love. This is death. A shroud of memory engulfs me. My mother's hand on my brow, how my father's dark green tartan overcoat smelled in the rain, the night Thor fell, Harriet's wedding dress and her scent of roses, Sinclair's freshly washed hair. The twins. Oh, Harriet, my chest is open to the sky. My heart is beating outside its cavity. So beautiful to see. There's Abraham and Mother. Stop the drums. This is death. This is death. This is death. Harriet . . .

BY DIPLOMATIC POUCH VIA THE AFRICAN PATROL VESSEL, *WANDERER,* WITH A COPY TO BE DELIVERED BY HAND BY CAPTAIN LEWIS OF THE *RACHEL.* MARCH 23, 1843

Dear Madam,

As Brigadier General, Division Commander of the Third Regiment of Her Majesty Victoria's Royal Scouts and Lancers, I have the sad and tragic duty to inform you that the expeditionary camp of Dr. William John

Thadius Wellington was attacked Sunday night, March 21, near Bulawayo, by a raiding party of Zulu warriors in revolt against the authority of the Royal forces of Her Majesty's Third Regiment near Durban in the Province of Natal and in retaliation for an unprovoked attack by Boers against the Zulu village of Bulawayo, which caused the death of the Ngwane Prince, Ngoza. A military rescue mission which arrived in the early hours of Thursday, the 22nd of March, 1843, found the camp devastated and all its occupants massacred. The raiders were not apprehended. Wellington's body was found and buried with full military honors on the spot to await your instructions. His assistant, Abraham Boss, himself a Ndebele, was found nearby badly wounded, and when he subsequently died of his injuries, his body was buried next to your husband's.

Please believe me, Madam, that you elicit my highest respects and deepest condolences and sympathy. Our Foreign Office will forward to you the complete official report on your husband's death.

May God have mercy on Dr. Wellington's soul.

Respectfully,
Brig. Gen. Banastre Tarleton II

26

I was born to lose everything I love. Others may lose of their abun-

dance, but I of my want, have lost even the half of all I had.

Thomas Jefferson

The shape of the world. The line of the Equator. The Tropic of Cancer. How many times had Thance explained to me how the world turned?

Brigadier General Tarleton's letter was already posted, and the world turned on its axis. Oblivious, I continued living, as yet deprived of knowledge, as half my life disappeared. The children and I waited for news from the Cape via the clippers, the barques, the schooners, the packets, the brigs, and the sloops that crisscrossed the oceans, the world, the line that divided it into northern and southern hemispheres.

Perfectly happy, I wrote out my inventories in the warehouse, bathed my children, listened to the woes of the twins and the joys of Ellen Wayles and Jane Elizabeth, ran my house, grew my vegetables, invented my menus, laid out clothes, counted linen, paid bills, played music, and rescued runaways. I polished the prosperous surface of my false life until it glistened like a pane of glass.

And I believed life continued in harmony with this circular, diametrical motion of the seasons, the tides, the constellations, and a woman's cycle. I was four months pregnant and so was Thenia. We planned this unexpected gift as a homecoming present for Thance and Abraham. I stored this knowledge up inside myself, surrounded first by my womb, then the armor of my body, and beyond that, my house, my city, and my comfortable place in American society as Mrs. Thadius Wellington.

The *Rachel* arrived April thirty-first, four months ahead of schedule. Even before she docked, she dispatched a longboat to the wharf, where the captain found Thor and me at the warehouse. There was no need for words. The early, unexpected, and unannounced arrival of the empty *Rachel* spelled disaster. The captain's face, his helpless gestures told us the rest. And suddenly my world stopped turning on its axis.

"I should never have let Thance go alone . . . even with Abe." Thor's cry of despair and anguish froze my own grief into a diamond-hard compassion for him.

Word was already out that the *Rachel* had returned empty when Thenia burst into the warehouse. But, like all of us, so enamored with our own pumping hearts and circulating blood, she could stare death in the face and still disbelieve. She ignored the captain and addressed me directly.

"Our ship is in, but where's Abraham?"

"Abe's in Africa," I said, "with Thance." But she must have seen death written at my temples like Abe's tribal scars. She stopped in her tracks. I saw her feet do a little hop, then a shuffle, as if she danced on hot coals.

"Aw, God. They're not coming back. They ain't ever coming back!"

"Thenia, there's been . . . an accident . . . a raid on the field camp near Durban. They were killed. Both of them."

I braced myself for her howl as I heard Thenia's sharp intake of breath.

"We don't know why it happened . . . a retaliation for a raid by the Kaffirs . . . to steal sugar or the medicines or take the guns . . . it could have been anything. There are English raiders, Kaffir raiders, Zulu raiders, Noumie raiders. . . . There's a civil war beginning in South Africa," the captain continued pointlessly.

Thenia's open mouth never uttered her scream. Instead she turned to Thor.

"Then why did you let them go?"

In one fatal second, the mantle of guilt Thance had worn since the accident with his brother was transferred to the shoulders of Thor. Cain's mark had changed twins.

Thenia reverted to the same silence as after the slave auction. I wondered how much a woman was supposed to bear in this world. She had lost her family somewhere in the South, and she had lost Abraham somewhere in Africa. The only black man we had ever met who had come voluntarily to America would never return again.

"If you're going back to the Cape, I'm going with you," I told Thor. "I can't leave Thance in Africa. He doesn't belong there."

"The *Rachel* must recover her cargo—and honor the Wellington Company's obligations," Thor explained. "I will bring Thance's body back."

"I must go, Thor. Thenia wants to go, too. She feels guilty about not allowing Abraham to return to Africa years ago. Now he's returned for good —without her. Sinclair should come, too."

"He's too young."

"He needs to see his father's grave in order to accept what has happened. He has a right to stand over it and mourn." I sat down and looked at my blank fingertips.

Our voyage was a pilgrimage, not so much to recover Thance's body as to seek our reason for being alive, and for our unborn being alive, although I hid the fact from Thor that both Thenia and I were with child. He would have forbidden us to make the journey.

When all hands were assembled, we would make sail on our three-masted, six hundred-ton tea clipper carrying a crew of twenty-eight men. The *Rachel*, like her namesake, was stout-hearted, sure, and quick. She would deliver us to the Cape of Good Hope colony in only forty-five days. As preparations went forward for the departure, news of Thance's death spread throughout the medical corps of Philadelphia. We received the condolences of the entire pharmaceutical world. Then, just as we were to set sail, word came from Rheims that my beloved Petit, my guardian angel, my mentor, my Moses, my last link to the past and to my father, was dead. The last person I saw before we left was the indomitable and tender Charlotte.

"I hope to God you're strong enough for the trip," she said.

"I have to be, Charlotte, or face becoming a cipher for the rest of my life."

"Oh, Harriet, did we think when we were in school that our lives would cause men's deaths!"

"That's a strange thing to say, Charlotte."

"Is it? I'm sorry."

"What is it, Charlotte? I know you well enough to know you have something on your mind."

"You won't be offended?"

"Well, Charlotte, we have been friends for twenty-three years and we've had our ups and downs, but they have never shaken our love for each other."

"I'm going to say one more thing, and then I'm never going to raise this subject again."

"What is that?"

"That perhaps it was Thor, not Thance, that you should have married in the first place."

I gazed solidly into Charlotte's eyes.

The next day, Thenia, Thor, Sinclair, and I boarded the *Rachel*, each wrapped in our own private grief. But I had found a reason for living in the new life in my womb. This child was the key to my future, as well as a gift of reparation from Thance to his brother, Thor. Perhaps it would allow Thor to accept Thance's death as the will of God.

Once we arrived in Cape Town, Thor threw himself into the unfinished work of his twin, as if to avenge his brother's every second. He retraced his steps, redid his experiments, regathered his specimens, and completed his expedition. We had more than a hundred bearers, gunmen, cooks, guides, interpreters, and African apothecaries. The expedition moved slowly and ponderously through a landscape of such variety, beauty, and power that I began to wish I could draw or paint. Sinclair, on the other hand, took to sketching plants and specimens, as well as landscapes and even portraits of various members of the crew. Thenia kept her Bible with her at all times; sometimes she held it almost as a shield. Her Western clothes and manner were a puzzle for many of the men in the expedition, and they finally relegated her to the status reserved for white women, whether nuns, female missionaries, or Queen Victoria—sexless. But Thenia was a handsome woman at thirty-two, and Thor received quite a few marriage offers for her, the most extravagant being a dozen white shorthorn cattle and a rifle. He had also received several offers for me, but not in the class of those for Thenia, he laughingly told us. Nevertheless, he teased, he was considering several of them.

Chalk was the color of mourning in eastern South Africa, so I shed my black Philadelphia mourning for white. Every morning I'd watch Sinclair draw for a while, then listen to Thenia read aloud from the Bible. I'd then follow Thor on his rounds. I seemed to be the only person on the expedition who had no work, no passion, only grief. I didn't capture the myriad butterflies or pluck flower specimens. Yet the land spoke to me and the landscape gripped me in a powerful embrace, and all the lament of the voyage could not dislodge my feeling of expectation.

For two weeks we traveled under armed escort, a patrol of British soldiers leading the way. When we arrived at the place where Thance and Abraham had been ambushed, the luxuriant vegetation had already begun to erase every trace of the two lonely graves, marked with rough crosses. We watched silently while the two bodies, wrapped in canvas and oilcloth, were dug up by the soldiers and placed in the palanquin that would take Abraham to his village and Thance to the English cemetery at Ladysmith. After much discussion, Thor and I decided we would not take Thance back to Philadelphia after all, but leave him in Africa with Abraham.

Abraham had a consecrated grave in his village of Nobamba, facing Mecca. The ceremony performed by the elders was simple and brief. I drew back at the burial, unable to propel myself any closer. The small swelling of earth and the rounded clay headstone imprinted with verses from the Koran reminded me that I had never seen my mother's grave. I watched as Thenia knelt and gathered a fistful of yellow earth in her hand and transferred it gently into her handkerchief. Then she took small pieces of all the offerings that had been laid at the head of the grave.

"I'm satisfied," she said as she returned to my side. "I'm leaving him here, and I'm never coming back. I'm glad you're leaving Thance here, too. He does belong in Africa."

Ladysmith was only a day's travel from where we were, and the white cemetery was on a small knoll outside the city gates, which faced westward, toward home. The Lutheran minister improvised a simple ceremony, but Thor's eulogy was stupendous. Brigadier General Tarleton bestowed full military honors, and to my surprise, Thenia lifted her voice and sang a cappella. The rich tones drifted over the valley into the hills and vanished like the mist that rose from them. Like Thenia, I gathered a handful of the same earth to which I had committed my beloved husband, buried it in my handkerchief, and placed it deep in my pocket next to James's dagger.

There are landscapes and there is one landscape. Sinclair sketched the knoll for me and then executed a watercolor of it from his sketches. He didn't draw in his father's grave or the others, but left the knoll smooth and empty. I thought of Maria Cosway's empty corner of the world at Lodi. And I knew this African knoll would always occupy a corner of my heart, peopled as it was with Thance's body and Thance's soul and Thance's ghost.

I knelt finally in a gesture I hardly understood myself, and whispered *my* name into the sown earth. How many absolutions did I need, after all?

⌒

I was happier for Sinclair than for any of us, knowing it meant everything to an eighteen-year-old heart to kneel at his father's grave. We ordered a new headstone but left the old cross at the foot and bade Thance good-bye. He would be apart from us, but not from the earth that bore him and the sky that covered him.

As Thor and I stood at the foot of Thance's grave, I thought of our first meeting, when I had mistaken the mysterious African twin for my future husband.

"I always think of this landscape," Thor said tentatively, "as being biblical somehow ... I know it's unreasonable, but I've always felt a kind of closeness to creation in its serenity and vastness; its purity, its mystery . . . as well as its violence, its unmercifulness. The pristine dawns, rains, and storms, the foliage and Edenlike vegetation, the feeling that the whole universe is in one leaf here, although I'm not a religious man, as you know. The Bible is sublime literature, not gospel for me, and I'm even less of a Unitarian than Thance. Yet, as a scientist, I cannot collect, study, and behold all that exists in nature and therefore in creation, without a sense of awe. To gaze into the African constellations and deny that a Creator intended those distances, that infinity is impossible. Sometimes at night, instead of stargazing, I'll take out the Bible and read a chapter or two to calm myself, to . . . situate myself . . . in the midst of all this frightful and indifferent wilderness. And the other night I read a tale in the Old Testament of Tobias, the son of Tobit, who asks to marry his kinswoman, Sarah, and her father Raquel agrees because it is the precept of Moses." He paused and looked at me.

"According to Moses," Thor continued, "a Hebrew is commanded by God to marry his brother's widow as her nearest kin so that her children shall not be fatherless and so she shall not pass out of her husband's clan into the hands of strangers. In the Bible story, Raquel sends for Sarah, takes her hand, and gives her to Tobias, saying, 'Take her to be your wedded wife in accordance with the law and the ordinance written in the book of Moses.' "

There was only the silence of the forest and the light flutter of butterfly wings. The sheet of paper Thor was holding in his hand was trembling violently.

"And you think," I said, "that this is what we should do? Adopt the law of Moses?"

"That's a question that I wouldn't dare answer, Harriet."

"Then it's I who should answer?"

"Perhaps you should consider it in the light of where we are standing and for whom we are grieving . . . and the love I have always borne you . . . in time . . ."

"The biblical tale is a lovely story, but it's only a story," I said. *An old slave story*, I thought, *a way to keep the scattered, enslaved tribes of Israel together.*

Sinclair and his brothers and sisters were now fatherless, just as I had been in name fatherless, and my mother before me. It was even against the law for my mother, or my mother's mother, to reveal the identity of their children's father. How ironic to have run away from fatherlessness only to have my children returned to that bitter prison.

"I already love you." Thor continued, "as much as I loved my twin."

"I don't know if I would love you the way I loved your twin," I said.

"It will never be the same, I know. It would be wrong if it were the same, or if we tried to imitate another's love. But I do love you, Harriet."

"And this is sufficient for you?"

"More than sufficient, Sister."

We looked down at Thance's grave. A giant eucalyptus tree shaded him, and a shallow brook ran through the landscape nearby. The English had a knack for choosing cemeteries, as well as gardens. And so, with the African midwinter, which was like our Spring, we began the long march home. We were not particularly aware of danger, but it was all around us. Drums had announced our coming and drums would announce our going. The white man, too, had his drums—the first telegraph line had been established between the colony military command and Fort Monroe, more than fifty miles away.

We sailed from Durban around the horn of Africa in a Dutch frigate to the Cape colony, where our own ship, loaded with Thance's specimens, his whole movable laboratory, awaited us.

As we left Africa, I could not find the words to express the complexity of my feelings. But in my dreams, over which I had no power, my feelings burst upon me in all their starkness. I dreamed I was the wife of both twins and loved them both, and that both men visited me and lavished their caresses upon me and divided me between themselves. One kissed my blank fingers while the other embraced my deceitful lips, identical sexes pressed upon me and into me, the twins' bodies moved like a double-edged dagger, entering from opposite sides as I was lifted by hands, mouths, identical chests, downy flanks, foreheads, double ears and collarbones, tiny folds along identical necks, noses, eyes. Tenaciously, I clung to them both in ecstasy and happiness, contorting my contraband body against them both in exultation because there was no other way. I always awoke from this erotic fantasy as from a nightmare, devoured by heartsickness and fire.

Seven weeks after the *Rachel* dropped anchor in the Philadelphia harbor, seven months after her father's death, and a year before I married Thor, the baby girl I carried, and whom I called Maria, was born. Thenia's baby came a week later, and she named him Willy. From the first, I considered Maria

Thor's child. The circle was closed, and on the rock of Maria, Thor and I built our house and our happiness. A new happiness. Not the same happiness as with Thance, or its shadow or imitation. From Africa, there would be new fingerprints.

I had vowed never to resemble my mother, Sally Hemings. Yet like her not only was I still a slave, I was a slave who had taken my brother-in-law as my husband. This time my wedding gift from the State of Pennsylvania was a Supreme Court decision, which revoked Pennsylvania's Personal Liberty law which had made Fugitive Slave Kidnapping a felony and restored the Fugitive Slave Act. I was once again a runaway after all these years.

27

Falsehood will travel a thousand miles while Truth is still putting on its boots.

Thomas Jefferson

That day on the knoll, I stared down at the quaking sheet of paper I still clutched in my hand. There is a kind of amazement that forgets to ask questions. I felt Harriet was almost angry with me, and I rejoiced. I loved Harriet as shamelessly as one loved existence. It was a deathless, stoic, and indecipherable kind of love. It reawakened every morning in every limit of my body, as well as my soul. It seemed unbelievable that I, Thor Wellington, had lived so long with the idea of suicide. The maimed twin. The crippled half man watching as my brother, Thance, produced child after child. As I stood besides his grave, I was just as bewildered as before, but now, despite my grief, I was joyfully bewildered.

In those last weeks, I had begun somehow to believe in God, but without thinking of Him. I took on that metaphoric state of mind in which the world always seemed different to me from the way it apparently was, and for perhaps the first time since the accident, I no longer felt shut out, but lived in a radiance of utter conviction; what we were doing was right. It had become for me an interior metamorphosis. I imagined a God who opens His world like a hiding place.

"It can only do harm to imagine more than one can experience," said the liquid, southern voice of Harriet.

"It is for you to decide such a thing . . . "

When she looked up, I was disconcerted, and as her glance, still dark from emotion, crossed mine, the only thing I wanted out of life was to inspire her confidence, her womanly rather than her sisterly love. Even as I attempted to stamp them out like a campfire, new feelings took hold of me and connected me with certain thoughts: duty to Thance, honor to his wife, protection, continuity, tranquillity, joy. The infinite cold stupor in which I had been steeped until now gave way to the warmth of blood vitally streaming back into my limbs, my sinews, my heart, and my head. I was right in my stubborn adoration, right in my divination of my twin's desire in this. I had stood over his grave and asked him what he wanted me to do, and then had proceeded to read his mind and answer my own heart.

From the corner of my eye, I could see Harriet's slightly upturned nose, the curve of her jaw, the lobe of her ear with its earring, her soft lips, and the strands of gray that mingled in the fair copper hair. There was a severity in the face that seemed not carved out of a hard material like ivory or sandstone but made out of something much softer, something which had hardened under the impact of some great secret. It was as if this supremely feminine, self-possessed face had been remolded into hard, ascetic details by an indefatigable and incommunicable will exerting itself on a softer, more internal primary material. I had spent many long hours in Africa contemplating Harriet. I was amazed that this interior sculpting had taken place over the years without my knowledge. I had long ago forbidden myself to contemplate Harriet, annihilating even the intelligence of whether she was beautiful or not. Harriet had been my brother's wife, my own sister, whose beauty I couldn't even acknowledge except as a corollary to my brother's good luck. Now I wondered how much more I didn't know about my twin's wife.

"One must never flee from chance," I said in my confusion, polishing my spectacles, which had misted over, unaware that for Harriet, my words rose out of an interior conversation with myself, one to which she had not been privy. She was so startled by my declaration that the slits of her eyes opened and her gaze held something indefinable and feminine which was unguarded and probably not intended for my eyes.

A beautiful woman is a dangerous thing, I thought. Her person exudes as much power as a prince, a pope, or a president. Obsessions, fascinations with such a woman had brought down emperors and princes.

And their power was fickle, arbitrary, and absurd. It had no strategy and in many cases, no *raison d'être* except its own end, I thought as Harriet began speaking slowly and carefully, sometimes glancing up at me as we began to walk along side by side.

We moved away from the grave, in each other's company, out from the trees into the open space at the edge of the hills, without either of us deciding whether we would now follow one of the paths into the valley, and if so, which. Instead, we walked along the promontory for a fair distance, talking, then turned back and passed over the same ground for the third time, as if neither of us knew where the other was going and each was trying not to interfere with the other's plans.

"Naturally, I do not imagine one can show anyone else what to do," I said. "But life is never simple. It becomes unmanageably confused only when we think of ourselves. The moment one doesn't think of oneself, but asks how one can help someone else, it becomes very simple. And there is the child to think of." Harriet was silent and I rambled on, afraid.

Could it be that Harriet acquiesced only to protect Thance's unborn child? Harriet was rich. She didn't need my fraternal or paternal protection. It was I who needed her.

Her arm seemed to twitch, but then something stiffened in her; one army of thoughts seemed to engage another in battle.

I continued, looking away from her, "We attach so much importance to whatever is personal. We speak of living our lives to the fullest . . . accepting life on its own terms, seizing destiny. For what is it that is supposed to be accepted or seized? How can we know the reason we were born, or the way we will die? Is everything acceptable in every way, in whatever confusion?"

At last she asked, "The mind or the instincts, Thor? Morality or character? Selfishness or love, Thor? I have lived selfishly, immorally, and by instinct all my life."

"If our higher nature is to be lived to the fullest, our lower instincts must learn remuneration and obedience," I answered, recalling a confession she tried to make so long ago.

"It's always simpler to look after others than after oneself," she said, turning her lighthouse gaze upon me.

"Harriet, I believe you to be one of those far from egotistical people who, though they may believe they are always thinking about themselves, do not look after their own interests at all. And this is what I want to do for you —what I've always wanted, since I first laid eyes on you. And this is far removed from ordinary selfishness, which is always looking out for its own advantage."

"You've formed a picture of me which is not necessarily true." Harriet smiled. "Don't confuse what I am with what you want, Thor. I'm a free woman"—she sighed—"but I do love you." Her head bowed in submission, yet I wasn't duped. There was nothing subdued or submissive about Harriet.

"Believe me, Harriet, what makes one truly free and what deprives one of his freedom, what gives us true bliss and what destroys it is something that every honest human being knows in his heart of hearts, if only he will listen to it!"

"I'm listening," she said quietly.

"To Thance or to me?" I replied just as quietly.

"To you. I know the difference between you and Thance. You look at me with Thance's eyes, you speak to me with Thance's voice, but I know the difference." She gave me a look full of curiosity. "The question is, do you know the difference between me . . . and me? Can you tell the difference between black and white?"

We were walking along the knoll which gave us a vast view of the deep valley hollowed out below and the sweeping grasslands, with their flocks of flamingos like encrustations of coral under the majestic African light. Harriet stopped and, with the straw hat, which she had been swinging in her hand, drew a line through our conversation.

But my mind had already been put to rest. She had accepted. My head burst with an intensity of feeling that nearly knocked me over.

Though I stood there solidly planted on the ridge, overlooking the African steppes and badlands fringed with dark forests and hazy mountains, I felt myself being drawn out of myself and through her, as though I had been given a second body.

"Why are you so different, Harriet?" I said, pausing as an eagle swept the sky above us like a bullwhip. And like a flick of that whip, she turned, her face ghostly white.

"Because I am the best dancer and the ballet master," she said, her sad eyes the transparent reflection of the verdant African landscape that framed her. Then she held out her palms to me. "This is what I am."

I seized the pale fingertips, enclosing them in my own, not daring to do more than kiss each. I knew it would be a long time before we would embrace.

I, William John Theodore Wellington, aged forty-six, born the tenth of March 1800, white American male, chemist and apothecary, did on the third of November 1844, in the city of Philadelphia, marry the widow Harriet Petit Wellington, my sister-in-law, in the presence of her family and mine, her sons, Sinclair, Beverly, Madison, and James Wellington, and their sisters, Jane and Ellen, and my sisters Lividia and Tabitha. I did at this time also legally adopt my brother's last child, Maria Elizabeth Wayles Wellington, born after his death, the third of October 1843, as my legal heir and daughter.

WILLIAM JOHN THEODORE WELLINGTON

1856

28

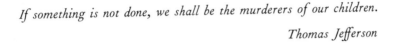

If something is not done, we shall be the murderers of our children.

Thomas Jefferson

It was the coldest winter in memory. The whole city groaned under a yoke of cruel Arctic frost that swept down from Canada, freezing the lakes, rivers, and even the harbor in ice so thick that even hundreds of skaters and Dutch sleighs propelled by blown sails couldn't crack the surface. The new suspension bridge which spanned the Schuylkill River was covered with gargoyles of icicles and ghostly veils of frost, under which it groaned, shuddered, and glistened like Carborundum in the bluish northern light above the thirty-sixth parallel, the line which divided the United States into North and South, slave and free. The *Rachel* was prisoner in Philadelphia harbor, a chilled, immobile hulk, covered with crystal, her gold letters dripping with icy needles, her rails, planks, and ropes sculpted in congealed salt scum.

I sat facing the black panes of glass that separated me from the darkening world beyond, filled, it seemed, with scurrying, moving forces, like tiny pieces of metal sucked up onto the U of a magnet. Blindly they crossed onto its arms, breaking and re-forming like a marching army. The windows, on which I hadn't pulled the drapes, were frosted in delicate swirling designs, and the kerosene lamps sent a lighthouse beacon which filtered onto the courtyard. The beam bounced skyward, piercing the wall of evil coldness like a lance. The conservatory, which had been built onto the back of the house, was warm and cozy, heated by a Swedish coal-fired stove of painted blue-and-white porcelain. The delicate tiles gave off a radiance that duped the ferns and rubber plants and palms into believing they lived not in ten-degree-below-zero weather, but that they had regained the Equator and were somewhere loose on the thirtieth parallel in the wild, solitary landscape where we had left Thance and Abraham thirteen years ago.

I spread out my sheets of music, a transcription by Franz Liszt of Bellini's Italian opera *Norma,* and my blank fingertips came down on the smooth ivory keys of the Pleyel pianoforte, my most cherished possession. The notes exploded through the room as the bars of music echoed and elevated Norma's conflict between her duties as a high priestess and her emotions as a woman in the opera's closing scales. My fingers flew over the keys, the discriminate, painful strains of *Pui lènto* in B sharp leapt out, precise and unbending, swallowing the plaintive top of the oscillating melodic grains which threaded in and out of the sober base of *Padre tu piagi,* "Father, you are crying," then resurfaced in the plaintive cry of *Guerra, guerra.* I spoke and sang to the piano, cajoling it, tempting and seducing it, trailing Liszt's magnificent virtuoso notations, humming the notes or singing them, speaking under my breath, following the black soldiers that marched across the score page in formation, discriminate, uncompromising, inalienable. I closed my eyes for a moment, my hand moving now lightly and softly over the reprise of the fantasy's climax, *Padre tu piagi.* "Father, you're crying," I sang under my breath as the last notes of the closing sequence drew to an end, the tendons and muscles of my neck and shoulders loosening, shifting, and flowing. The roots of my hair curled; my eyes gleamed behind my gold-rimmed spectacles. It was too hot in the room; the sheen on my nose and forehead became liquid. My hands on the keyboard were no longer those of a young girl, but were freckled with age marks and blue-veined, the skin rough despite all my creams and ointments. But the strength was still there, the fingers still long and straight. On my left hand, my two wedding bands gleamed in the warm gassy illumination.

Beauty's daughter, Independence IV, stirred by my feet as I leaned away from the piano, then let the final *presto con fùria* chords come crashing down. I let my hands rest on the surface of the ebbing music, trying to gather in the last strands of happiness the music offered me. It was a brilliant virtuoso piece of fifteen minutes, which I would never dare play in front of any public except my family, but whose B-flat *Pui lènto* was the most sublime piano passage I knew of. *Guerra.* War.

Beyond the panes of glass, forces were gathering that would make even the word *war* a newly minted one. Even the heavens were holding their breath and rationing the clouds of white, lazy flakes that would soon swish out of the sky and cover everything. I suppose it was because I had been fighting the private war of my own double identity for so long that I smelled war long before it came.

Behind me, as on a stage, the semicircle of my white family made a crescent of blurry, familiar shadows against the light. Christmas had passed and New Year's Day was approaching, but the tree still stood weighted down with garlands of trinkets and pretty decorations kept from one year to the next. Like life, I thought, a chain of insignificant, glittering decorations strung together and draped in a way one could describe as "beautiful." Suddenly I spun myself around on my stool, alarming the dog and eliciting a big smile from Maria.

"Mama, that was fantastic. To think we have Norma in our living room, thanks to Mr. Liszt."

"He dedicated it to Marie Pleyel."

I smiled at my middle daughter, Jane Elizabeth, who was as beautiful as the aunt after whom she was named. She was a good musician and a loving if conventional daughter. With her hair piled up and in black velvet, she looked older than her twenty-three years. Quiet, intense, obedient, she had a nascent charm; her dark good looks gave her an aura of drama that was far from her natural disposition. She had learned to enhance this effect with burgundy, black, dark purple, and somber forest green dresses. In a few months she would be married to an army lieutenant surgeon on tour in Wyoming. My son Beverly was twenty-five. Old enough, I repeated like a litany, to run. Beverly, too, reminded me of the brother he was named after: goodness itself, with a kind of diamond-hard ambition and will that belied his graceful, almost southern demeanor. He was a strawberry blond, with gray eyes and freckled skin. The only really fair person in the family except for me. Beverly looked a lot like me, but most of all, he looked a lot like his grandfather. His voice had remained high and girlish, and he had a laugh just like his. Ever since he was a child he had spent his time fixing things, growing things, taking things apart, and putting them together again. At eight he invented a miniature distillery; by ten he had already collected and named most of the flora and fauna at his grandmother's country house. He would be a good doctor. He had graduated from the University of Pennsylvania as an M.D. in 1855. One day he brought home from college a classmate, John Hill Callender. Fate would have it that he was the grandson of my parents' nemesis, James T. Callender. I gazed at the two young men, innocent of everything.

We never forgive those whom we have wronged. . . .

As John Hill bent low over my hand, I wondered which of the three of them was twirling fastest in his grave . . . John Hill Callender was even engaged to marry a great-grandniece of Thomas Jefferson . . . my grandniece.

I wouldn't think about that now; I would think about it when I was calmer.

The twenty-year-old twins sat near their sister. Madison and James were ready to enter college. William John Madison and William John James were equally tall, lanky, loose-jointed, and athletic. They were self-possessed beyond their years, and their bright cheerfulness seemed to be a hallmark of placid, rational, contained characters. In fact, they looked a great deal like their father and his twin, Thor. They had the same swarthy smoothness and black eyes with flecks of gold. They had grown several inches in the past year and had not yet learned what to do with their bodies, which made them seem suspended somewhere between the quiet competence of young men and the rollicking antics of childhood.

Sinclair, my eldest, no longer lived at home. He had married three years ago and lived several blocks away, but he often stopped by in the evenings. He was the first medical doctor in the family, and Thor was uncommonly proud of him. It was Thor, after all, who had nurtured him into brilliance and diligence, a rare combination of intellectual rigor and poetic intuition. As a matter of fact, everyone agreed Sinclair was the family poet and intellectual, as well as a scientist. Grave and somber almost to a fault, he was more like my brother Thomas Woodston than any of his nearer relations or his own brothers and sisters, who deemed him boring. But he had a quiet seductiveness and a wicked humor all his own, which, under his disguise of conventionality, was as incisive as his surgeon's scalpel.

Maria, sat on the floor next to Thor. At twelve she was still full of promise and baby fat. Her round, undefined face held the promise of great beauty, and her mind had, even now, a radical, phantasmagoric, burlesque quality that spoke of unquestioned brilliance if not real genius. She was being watched carefully by Thor, who saw in her an exceptional mind combined with the gift of synthesis and poetic conjuncture which was the mark of a true scientist and intellectual.

I had been lucky with my children. Maria and Madison seemed especially marked for exceptional achievement. My eldest daughter, Ellen, had married also and now lived with her husband and two children near Terrytown in Bucks County. I was a grandmother as well.

My skirts made circles on the carpet as my knees swung the piano stool back and forth. I took off my spectacles and drew my handkerchief out of my sleeve. I cleaned my glasses, and as I swung, the weight of James's dagger pressed on my knee. I smiled. Would I never feel free enough to lay down my sword? Would I never make peace with . . . I looked over the several feet at my adored and adoring family. My white people. I adjusted my spectacles.

"Would you like to play, Maria?" I asked.

"No, Mother. I think your concert is not to be surpassed."

"You don't have to surpass me, Maria."

"It would only be boring."

"It would not," said Thor. "I hear your teachers are more than happy with your performances. They think a career as a musician is not out of the question."

"It wouldn't be, Papa, if women were allowed to play in symphony orchestras. But they're not."

"But this is not true in Europe," I said. "Only the United States is so backward about such things."

"Nevertheless, I'll never regret my training," Maria continued, "even if I never use it for more than giving music lessons to snooty children."

"James, will you stop that horrible habit of smoking your father's cigars? It's unhealthy!"

"Yes, Mother."

"And come give me a kiss."

"Yes, Mother," he repeated reluctantly.

As I held my twin son tightly, my brightest, my favorite, and inhaled the young male sweetness, my eyes were drawn in complicity to Thor, my love, my husband, my anchor, the father of my fatherless children, the one thing that kept me sane in the world in which I lived.

Thor looked up and smiled. He was still a handsome man. The slight thickening of his jaw and the new mustache streaked with gray surrounded the same chiseled features, the same black eyes under their thick eyebrows in the *f*-shapes of a violin, the same wide high cheekbones, the same high complexion, now permanently bronzed by the sun. I had never returned to Cape Town after that one trip to see Thance's grave. But Thor had continued to conduct his expeditions, refusing to bow to my pleas, but he had curtailed the length of his trips in deference to his responsibility for his brother's children. Sometimes Sinclair went with him. And every time they went, they visited Ladysmith. Sinclair would always write to me from that grassy knoll and send me dozens of delicate watercolors of the landscape.

Thor now had years of research behind him. The material he had gathered was sufficient for hundreds of studies without ever making another trip to the Cape. There were thousands of specimens in the laboratory, and scores of experiments going on. He had even published posthumously in London all of Thance's papers and research on fingerprints. The thin volume was on the shelves of the library next to Francis Galton's definitive monograph published the same year. He often kissed my blank fingertips without mentioning the accident. I wondered if it had crossed his mind these past fourteen years. Everyone else who would remember, except Thenia, was dead.

There was now a railroad car that passed through the warehouse, taking the Wellington Drug Company's merchandise by steam engine west to Illinois and southwest as far as Arkansas. Arkansas had been added as a slave state in 1836, while Iowa had been added as a free state in 1846. Fifteen free states and fifteen slave states made up the Union. A bitter battle had raged on over the admission of Missouri, Oklahoma, and Nebraska, which had resulted in the Missouri Compromise. Now the admission of Kansas would tilt the delicate balance between slave and free states. That's what we talked about, like everyone else in America, a country of twenty-three million people, four million of whom were slaves. In South Carolina and Mississippi, slaves outnumbered whites, and in Louisiana they equaled them. In Alabama they were roughly three-sevenths of the population. Just north of Charleston, they were eighty-eight percent, and on the Georgia seacoast, eighty. In central Alabama they were seventy percent, and along the Mississippi belt they outnumbered whites nine to one. Out of a southern white population of six million, only five percent owned slaves and three or four thousand families owned most of them, lived on the best lands, enjoyed three-fourths of the income, and wielded the political and intellectual power that was concentrated in that aristocratic group to which my father had belonged.

The old issue of slavery in the territories had been torn open again by Kansas and Nebraska. By the terms of the Missouri Compromise, all this rich, fertile, empty land beyond the Missouri River was closed to slavery above the thirty-sixth parallel. The frontiers of Kansas and Nebraska touched Missouri, which would probably become a free state as well. A new bill had been introduced in Congress that enraged Free Soil men and superseded the Missouri Compromise. It left Kansas and Nebraska open to settlers bringing slaves with them, and would allow the inhabitants to decide whether they would enter the Union slave or free. The Utah and New Mexico territories were free to decide on slavery, despite New Mexico being below the thirty-sixth parallel. To open these westerly, virgin prairies to slavery struck millions of us in the North as unforgivable.

And then, a strange and obscure Supreme Court case exploded into the national conscience: *Scott v. Sandford*. The court's scandalous decision on the side of slaveholding had drawn a tighter and tighter knot around bondsmen and bestowed on slave masters new powers to recapture, pursue, and control their troublesome "property." It had curtailed the liberties not only of free blacks in both the North and the South, but of white citizens in the North who wanted nothing to do with owning slaves.

Dred Scott had spent most of his sixty-odd years as the slave of an army surgeon, John Emerson, who had taken him into the free territory of Illinois and to Fort Snelling, above the thirty-sixth parallel. At Fort Snelling he married a female slave of Emerson's, and had a child born free by the provisions of the Missouri Compromise. When his owner died and his widow inherited them, friends of Scott advised him to sue for freedom on the grounds of prolonged residence in a free state. Eleven years later, his simple suit for freedom had become a rallying cry of slavery and was appealed before the Supreme Court.

In 1857 the court ruled that Dred Scott was separated from the Constitution and all the rights it bestowed, and that he was not a citizen. Negroes were not included in the "all men" of my father's Declaration, men whom God had created "equal." For that matter, claimed the court, at the time of the Constitution, Negroes were regarded as beings of an inferior order—so far inferior that they had no rights that a white man was bound to respect. The court ruled that Dred Scott's sojourn in free territory did not make him free, because a ban on slavery was unconstitutional. The justices had decided that the Constitution protected slavery and the property of slaveowners in all the states and territories. It was hereafter a slaveowner's Constitution, not a free man's. And the North cried never, never, never.

The name of Dred Scott was on all our lips that night.

"I cannot prove that the Dred Scott decision is part of a conspiracy to expand slavery, but when I see a lot of framed timbers, which I know have been gotten out at different times and places by different workmen—Stephen Douglas, Franklin Pierce, Roger Taney, and President Buchanan, for instance—and when I see these timbers joined together and see they exactly make the frame of a house, I, like Abraham Lincoln, find it impossible not to believe that those inspired carpenters all worked upon a common plan, trying to push slavery forward till it shall become lawful in *all* the states, north as well as south."

Thor was glancing through the newspapers Sinclair had brought him.

"Slave power," said Sinclair, "controls the President and fills all the offices. Not only do they count three-fourths of their slaves as electorate in order to augment their representation in the Senate and the House, which allows them to control the electoral college, I do believe they intend to extend slavery by Supreme Court decree into all the states in the Union. They're going to do it by chipping away at the Missouri Compromise and all other laws that protect the free territories."

"No court would dare such a folly!" I cried.

"No court? What about the past steps leading to the hangman's court of Dred Scott? The silencing of the presidency, the loading of the Supreme Court with southerners, the Fugitive Slave Act, and finally the Kansas-

Nebraska Act? And what will follow?" I looked up expectantly for his response. "I'll tell you, Mother," continued Sinclair. "The South wants the addition of Cuba and Haiti as slave territories, and the revival of the slave trade on the world market. The Dred Scott decision is an alarming prediction of things to come. If a slave is movable property in the territories, why not in the free states as well?"

"That would mean that a slave master could bring his 'movable' property into any state in the North against our will," I said.

"The Scott decision, my dear, has already put slavery in all the territories. I'm afraid the next step *is* to establish it in all the northern states," retorted Thor. "In the name of social concord, we are asked to swallow the idea that whoever wants slavery has the right to have it—that the Negro has no share, humble or not, in the Declaration of Independence," continued Thor. "This notion is blowing out the moral lights around us and preparing us for making the institution of slavery perpetual and national."

"It is never treated as a wrong," I added petulantly. "What other thing that you consider as a wrong do you deal with like that? Perhaps you *say* it is wrong, *but* President Buchanan never does. You quarrel with anybody who says it is wrong. One must say nothing about slavery *here*, because it is not *here*. You must say nothing about it *there* because it *is* there. I personally cannot live that way."

"What, then," said Thor in anguish, "becomes of the Union?"

"The Union splits," I said.

"Let the division come with violence if necessary, rather than submit to slave power," Thor added with such vibrato that his voice hung suspended in the air.

"Who made you a Black Republican?" I asked, laughing.

"You," he said tenderly.

That's why I always count the beginning of the war with Dred Scott. It was Dred Scott who forced white people to admit they considered all Negroes, free or unfree, a fugitive population. A population without a country and without rights. The very definition of black in America was "fugitive." All blacks in America were fugitive. They themselves made up a fugitive population, ready for oblivion, for invisibility, always running away, crossing borders, frontiers, color bars: a race who couldn't fix themselves anywhere that wasn't a place where they were apt to be gotten rid of, hunted, maltreated, hidden; to be ignored, refused, and unrecognized. And perhaps because I lived in enemy territory, I saw it clearer than darker Negroes—than Thenia or Raphael—or white Americans like Thor or my children.

The dichotomy of my life made clear to me what my white family couldn't see —we were a nation of fugitives: Irish, Germans, Italians, and Swedes. All in flight from one thing or another, all in quest of my father's idea. Yet only fugitive blacks were considered aliens in their own country. These fugitive Europeans became true-blue Americans in one generation, yet two hundred years of residence had not produced one true-blue American black, as far as they were concerned.

But then the event that truly galvanized the country occurred: John Brown's raid on Harpers Ferry. John Brown was a white radical and Free Soiler, a dedicated abolitionist who heard "voices" and followed them. He had already waged a notorious guerrilla war in Kansas in the cause of Free Soil. And his plan had been to seize government property and incite the slaves in the area to insurrection and the establishment of a stronghold in the southern mountains of Kansas.

On the night of October 14, 1859, with his sons and a small group of followers, he went ahead with his plan and occupied the town. The insurgent army of slaves never appeared simply because he had given them no previous notice—no plan of battle, no provisions, no escape routes. Brown was attacked and defeated by a colonel named Robert E. Lee, who killed ten of the band including three of Brown's sons, but John Brown was taken alive and hanged on December 2, 1859. When I reached my bed, entered, and pulled the covers up over my head, I turned my back to Thor, who slept the sleep of the just. In moments his hand slipped around my waist and pulled me into his embrace. He sighed contentedly, his head nestled in the nape of my neck and my long braid. His gesture was tender, possessive, trusting, and innocent. All the things I felt none of, that night.

⌒

Civil war was almost upon us. One could feel it in the tense, suffocating atmosphere of the country. One could hear it in the hysterical shouts and cries of the crowds at political rallies. The war was like a tidal wave held back by a wall of crystal; so much as a whisper would shatter everything. Something bigger, greater, more momentous would take its place.

Lincoln's election convinced the South that it would have to remove the authority of the federal government from its soil by force. Less than three months after the inauguration, the Confederate States of America organized itself, drafted a constitution, and established itself in Montgomery, Alabama. First South Carolina, Georgia, Florida, Alabama, Mississippi, Louisiana, and Texas, then Virginia, North Carolina, Tennessee, and Arkansas seceded from the Union.

Through the long, weary months while Lincoln vacillated over the border states, the northern pro-slavery press and the merchant and industrial class tried to buy peace for the North by granting concession after concession to the South. The South confined its war efforts to threats and declarations, wearing cockades, and displaying palmettos and rattlesnake flags and their thousands of cannon. Until one day, President Lincoln decided to resupply Major Anderson and his beleaguered garrison at Fort Sumter and the rebel states used their firepower against the flag. That day everything and everyone changed.

Madison and James had come bursting into the Freedman's Protection Committee's office like cannons themselves with the news. "The Rebs have fired on Fort Sumter! Lincoln's declared war! It's in all the papers!" It was April 12, 1861.

Thank God, I thought. The slaveholders themselves had finally saved the cause of abolition from ruin. Our greatest danger had been the monstrous concessions Lincoln had accorded the slave states and the border states in exchange for peace. He had practically begged them upon bended knee to return. He promised not to touch slavery in the Confederate states; to leave it be as it was. He promised the border states to keep the Union as it was, that he would protect the institution of slavery as set forth by the Constitution.

"I have no tears to shed over the fall of Fort Sumter," I said. "They have spiked their own guns. They have shot off the legs of the compromisers and compelled everybody to choose between patriotic loyalty and pro-slavery treason. God be praised," I told Emily Gluck that day outside the Freedman's Committee offices. "Lincoln cannot sacrifice the slaves to the Union and thus save it, because there is no longer any hope of saving the Union."

I turned to Emily. "The South wasn't forced to do this," I continued. "The government stood waiting, praying to be gracious. Kind. It treated the South's treason as some sort of eccentricity that a few months' patience would probably cure. But all that's changed now." Thank God.

"Oh, Harriet, our national sin has found us out! No foreign power is about to chastise us, no king, offended by our prosperity, has plotted our destruction: slavery has done it all. Our enemies are of our own household. It is civil war, the worst of all wars."

⋑

"Emily is right," said Thor that night. "The South has lifted its hand against the government of the United States itself and defied its power. For twenty years we did everything we could to conciliate, gain the favor, and secure the loyalty of the slaveholding class. We've persecuted the Negro, swallowed the

Dred Scott decision, hanged John Brown. We've enacted harder Black Codes, let slave hunters hunt humans like beasts all over the North, repealed the laws designed to prevent the spread of slavery, and in a thousand ways given over our strength, our moral and political influence, to increase the power and ascendancy of slave power. And now, this is our reward—the Confederacy comes with sword, musket, and cannon to overthrow the government. The power we used to crush the Negro has overtaken the white man. The republic has put one end of the chain on the ankle of the slave and the other end around its own neck."

"How long you think it'll take us to whip the Rebs?" said Madison eagerly. But Thor went on as if he were speaking to himself.

"The American people and the government may refuse to recognize it for a time, but the inexorable logic of events will force upon them in the end the fact that the war that has now befallen us is a war for or against slavery, and that it can never be put down until one or the other of these forces is completely destroyed."

"Well, Ma," said James, "you got your wish. We're freeing the slaves."

"We've bound up the fate of the republic and that of the slave in the same bundle, and the one and the other must survive or perish together. To separate the freedom of the slave from the victory of the government, to attempt a peace for the whites while leaving the blacks in chains, will be labor lost."

"Goddamn the Confederacy!" interjected Madison.

But the tone of Thor's voice frightened me. It was the voice of a doctor who had just diagnosed a death by cancer. It was firm, slow, full of compassion, but inexorable, precise, weary, even cruel. This was the longest speech he had ever made about slavery. It was the only one he had ever made in the presence of my sons. The twins were twenty-five years old. Old enough to run. Old enough to fight. Old enough to die.

⤳

Outside, people were dancing in the streets. The long agony of waiting and indecision was finally over. Homes, stores, and streetcars were bedecked with banners in the wake of Fort Sumter, and Philadelphia would soon turn into a war city. The President's call for troops set men drilling everywhere. Philadelphia's quota was six regiments. There was no way I could keep Madison, James, Beverly, and Sinclair from volunteering. Sinclair joined the navy and Madison, James, and Beverly joined the Twenty-fourth Pennsylvania Cavalry Regiment, which was soon incorporated into the Army of the Potomac. Raphael Boss was not allowed to enlist in the army, but the navy readily accepted him on the schooner *S. J. Waring*. Soon, regiments in dark blue and light gray were drilling in the streets of Philadelphia. Recruiting centers, hospitals, and the Union Volunteer Refreshment Saloon of Philadelphia were doing a booming business. The war would be short. Ninety days. The war would be sweet. The South would return to the Union as it was after having been taught a good lesson in Yankee soldiering.

"Let me tell you something, Mrs. Wellington," Thenia said. "We are going to beat our slaveholding Virginia cousins. Raphael and Sinclair and the twins and Beverly are going to whip those lily-white asses till they cry 'Uncle.' "

And then she threw back her head and laughed till she cried. She laughed and her laughter was so much like the breezy colored lady in Market Street Square that two pink cabbage roses grew right out of Thenia's topknot.

The booming wartime city of Philadelphia was soon ungovernable, with its welter of tiny jurisdictions that impeded police work and encouraged the reign of hoodlums like the Moyamensing Killers. Fifty-one other known street gangs of adolescents and young men battled each other for territorial rights on streetcorners, terrorized passersby, and covered walls and fences with scrawled slogans. Pitched battles routinely broke out between the fire department and the gangs. Anti-black, anti-Catholic, anti-Irish, anti-German, anti-southern riots broke out throughout the city. Several lynchings and near lynchings were reported in Moyamensing; one was that of a Negro married to a white woman. The mayor reorganized the police department to give him maximum control over the city, and he began to enforce the Sunday "blue laws" against liquor sales, newspapers, and amusement parks in accordance with the Quaker principle of the sanctity of the Christian Sabbath. The growth of population as the city girded itself for war was so great that the real-estate market was not old enough to have acquired a reservoir of deteriorating older houses into which the poor might move as the better-off departed. The rich still occupied the center of the city between Chestnut, Walnut, Spruce, and Pine streets, and the poor had to build houses for themselves in the slums of Kingsensing or Richmond just next to them. Bad streets and the absence of transport obliged workers to live as close as they could to the mills and factories that began to turn out Union uniforms. Domestics and menial workers gathered in the alleys and side streets behind the town houses of their employers. Philadelphia became a teeming anthill of small, low, single-family houses as the city's gridiron expanded into the suburbs and even the countryside to infinity.

At first Philadelphians could scarcely believe that the slavery controversy had embroiled the country in civil war. Everything southern was still exalted and worshiped. Philadelphians had never imagined the North agitating the slavery question to the extremity of war, because they themselves did not like Negroes. Nothing really changed this attitude, even when armed and uniformed colored troops paraded in the streets.

The war brought Thenia and me closer than we had been since Abraham's death. She had continued running the apothecary and working as a midwife. Her only dream was that somehow she would get to Richmond during the war and be able to search for her family. Already runaway slaves were streaming into Union barracks and forts; most of them were promptly returned to their masters under direct orders from President Lincoln. Only General Frémont in Missouri and General Butler in Maryland had attempted any solution to the problem of fugitives crossing military lines. Frémont simply emancipated them and then conscripted them into the army as laborers, and Butler confiscated them as contraband and set them to work as well.

"If they're property," said Thenia, "then if they fall into the hands of the enemy, they are the booty of war."

"Except," I said, "that this is the only booty that can *walk* into the hands of the enemy."

The President was furious that his generals had taken the issue into their own hands. He, Lincoln, had no intentions of interfering with slavery in the South. He ordered Frémont to revoke his emancipation decree and Butler to return all the contraband he had confiscated. But the name *contraband* stuck.

"I just know there're some Hemingses crossing over those lines, taking their contraband asses to freedom. I just know it," said Thenia.

"There's an old Chinese curse Thor told me the other day—'May you be granted your fondest desire.' "

I had my "fondest desire." Thomas Jefferson's precious Old South was torn to shreds. It lay there in the streets of Philadelphia, while the Irish and the Swedes and the Poles and the Germans danced all over it. We were being led into war by a backwoods lawyer of dubious pedigree on the basis of my father's own Declaration. My proud Virginia cousins had taken the final step to their own annihilation. I should have felt exhilarated, but instead a strange lethargy hung about my soul and a cold loneliness invaded my heart. My husband, my sons, my friends, my employees, even Thenia were all shut out of this . . . this despair, which was also happiness. I couldn't explain it to myself and I couldn't explain it to Thenia, who was filled with pure joy at the possibility of killing southerners, nor to Thor, who was tortured by visions of carnage and destruction beyond any conceivable measure and any previous war.

People at the warehouse and the laboratory sometimes stopped speaking about the war when I entered. I knew why. Despite my reputation as a Black Republican, a Free Soiler, a Unitarian, and an abolitionist, I was in their eyes a Virginian. It was assumed my secret sympathies were with the Confederacy. I was completely alone.

29

The Almighty has no attributes which can take sides with us in such
a contest.

Thomas Jefferson

New red-white-and-blue bunting had been draped over the cast-iron colon-
nade of the Philadelphia, Wilmington, and Baltimore railroad station in
August 1862. Steam from the black, snout-nosed engines hovered under the
cast-iron-and-glass cupola, which filtered the sunlight through its tight grid
of sandblasted panes into a torrid yellow mist. It swirled in clouds around the
shouting, striving crowds, or rose in tiers from the great engine wheels and
smokestacks. The tinted glass, the thick smoke turned everyone sepia, leaving
only the stark blackness of the locomotives, heavy and puffing in their
exertion like sacrificial bulls.

The station was like the city: transient, noisy, dangerous. Newly recruited
soldiers from New England, New York, and New Jersey thronged into troop
transports that would carry them south.

Sinclair and Raphael were already gone. The twins were about to join their
cavalry regiment in Baltimore, and would soon be incorporated into the
Army of the Potomac. They hadn't consulted me on their enlistment, but
after the disastrous campaigns waged by Generals McClellan and Pope in the
first year of the war, the President had requested three hundred thousand
more volunteers—over the initial million recruits. Madison and James had
answered the President's call to defend the cause of the Union.

Beverly and Thor were all that were left of my men, and they too were
due to leave. Beverly had already volunteered and was waiting for his
commission as an army M.D., and Thor was assigned to Washington as a

liaison officer between the army medical corps and the United States Sanitary Commission. Soon I would run the Wellington Drug Company alone.

In the far corner of the shed, an army band played "John Brown's Body," which had been transformed by a woman named Julia Ward Howe into the "Battle Hymn of the Republic." In one night, according to legend, Mrs. Howe had turned a folk hero's music into a Republican hymn because God had whispered the words in her ear. It had swept the North like wildfire, catching the temper of the time, the awesomeness of the moment. It had become a marching song, a dirge, a ballad, an aria, a barcarolle, a serenade. Men and women sang it as a spiritual, an oratorio, a berceuse, a lullaby, a prayer.

Soldiers adapted it in the field, women crooned it to orphans, and bands and orchestras, harmonicas and bugles trumpeted it as the soul music of the Union. Everyone now knew the words by heart as they wafted over the hissing and coughing of the black engines.

Mine eyes have seen the glory of the coming of the Lord,

He is trampling out the vintage where the grapes of wrath are stored,

He has loosed the fateful lightning of his terrible swift sword,

His truth is marching on. . . .

No one spoke of the ninety-day war anymore. Lincoln's army was riddled with jealousies and indecisions amongst its commanders, and fear of the superiority of the Confederate forces. The indisputable numerical, industrial, and logistical strength of the North had not produced a decisive victory. People spoke of lack of leadership, of unpreparedness in the ranks, of confusion and mismanagement in the command, but everyone knew the real reason: the confusion over slavery.

To entice the secessionist states back and to keep the border states in the Union, the President claimed the war had nothing to do with slavery. That to save the Union he would free all of the slaves, some of the slaves, or none of the slaves. But slavery wouldn't stay out of the war. From the first moment the first slave emancipated himself by escaping over the lines to the Union to become enemy contraband, the war had become a war about us.

From a distance, I watched my twins saying good-bye to their sweethearts in the presence of the girls' mothers. The boys were dark-haired and dark-eyed, with long legs and wide shoulders that looked dashing in their new, Philadelphia-made, blue-and-gray uniforms. Even though they were joining their company by train, they wore both the spurs and sabers of their cavalry regiment, the Twenty-fourth. Yet they were awkward with their weapons of war, like children playing games. But this was no game. Their voices drifted over to where I stood, despite all the noise of a thousand other leave-takings. The train hissed and pawed the ground like an impatient war-horse, and the girls tied homemade sashes around the boys' waists and stuck hand-embroidered handkerchiefs in their pockets as if indeed this were just a game. But the game had already claimed fifty thousand lives.

"Did you know that the French general Lafayette once said that had he known at the time that he had come to the aid of slavery, he would never have drawn his sword in defense of the United States?"

The precise, French-accented voice of Maurice Meillasoux always took me back decades. At the beginning of the war, a strange envoy from my past had shown up and become part of our household: Maurice, the grandnephew of Adrian Petit, had arrived in Philadelphia, much as Lafayette had almost a hundred years ago, to join the Union army, take on its fight, and live to brag about it. Maurice had traveled in the West and in the South before his arrival in Philadelphia. After reading Sinclair's letters about how boring the navy was, he had decided to join one of General Frémont's regiments—many of which were composed of free-thinking Germans, passionate antislavers, in Missouri—and was waiting for his orders to move out.

"At least, dear Maurice, you know for whom you're fighting." I smiled.

"What amazes me is that anyone can believe that this war can be fought as if slavery were a detail. A rebellion sustained by slavery in defense of slavery can only be suppressed by moving against slavery."

"I cannot agree more," said Thor, resplendent in his new brigadier general's dress uniform, which he had donned in homage to the twins' departure. "To fight slaveholders without fighting slavery is worse than a halfhearted business."

"And what about not allowing black men to enlist?" replied Maurice. "Let the black man get the brass letters of the U.S. on his chest: let him get an eagle on his button and a musket on his shoulder and a bullet in his pocket, and there is no power on earth which can deny that he has earned the right to citizenship. They would probably fight harder than the white northerner!"

"That's just the point, my dear. Lincoln cannot ask white men to fight for the Negro, or there'd be insurrection in the ranks—total anarchy. They just won't do it." I shook my head sadly.

"I don't believe that," said Maurice. "First of all, I believe it is a military necessity both in the North and the South to use black men to fight, and second, if leadership comes from the White House, the man in the street will see the justice of it and follow."

"Cabinet members Cameron, Chase, and Blair agree with you," Thor added. "They're branded radicals."

"They see what is necessary," continued Maurice. "It is one thing to drive the Rebels from the south bank of the Potomac or even to occupy Richmond. It is another to secure and hold in permanent subjugation a tract of country nearly as large as Russia, seven-hundred-fifty thousand miles square and twice the size of the original United States. Napoléon couldn't do it any more than King George the Third could!"

"An argument of military necessity must be developed. Southerners boast that slavery is a pillar of strength to the Confederacy since it allowed her to place in the field a force so much greater in proportion to her population. Slaves constitute more than half the labor force; they raise the food for the army; they build its fortifications; they haul the supplies; they repair the railroad lines; they work in mines and munitions—the South drafted slaves into service before they began drafting white men as soldiers."

"The very stomach of said rebellion is the Negro in the form of a slave. Believe me, arrest that hoe in the hands of the Negro, and you kill the rebellion in the very seat of its life."

"While in theory this is a domestic insurrection, in practice this is war—Lincoln has already admitted it by proclaiming a blockade and treating rebel soldiers as prisoners of war. Confiscating enemy property is a military action. Slaves are property? Fine. Ben Butler did it back in May 1861 at Fortress Morse—he refused to return three escaped slaves to a Confederate colonel who cited the Fugitive Slave Law because, since Virginia was no longer in the Union, the Fugitive Slave Law no longer applied," reasoned Maurice.

"What about the border states?" continued Thor.

"Damn the border states. A thousand Lincolns cannot stop the people from fighting slavery," said Maurice as he flashed a smile. "Secretary of the Treasury Chase wants us not only to free the contrabands but to arm them. And Secretary of War Cameron backs him up."

"Take their damn property. That, dear Harriet, is abolition in action. Emancipation is a means to victory, not an end in itself. I have no hobby of my own with regard to the Negro, either to effect his freedom or to continue his slavery . . . but war is on their side."

The two men smiled and glanced over at the twins, who were free, white, and twenty-one and didn't care about anything except fighting.

A lifetime of change had been compressed into the past year. The slaves themselves continued to convert themselves into contraband. I glanced at Thor, who was still in deep conversation with Maurice. Contraband was a good name for what I was—Father's unidentified, "lost" merchandise, fallen off the wagon in Philadelphia. Contraband.

A train whistle blew, and the troops and officers milling around the platform began to board the trains. The band began to play "The Star-Spangled Banner." Madison and James moved toward me, their fiancées and the girls' mothers trailing behind them in balloons of white lace, white silk. Skirts had become so wide that almost six feet surrounded each female, and we all resembled galleons or watermelons, depending on one's point of view. We were impossible to transport, impossible to set at a table, impossible to undress. The women, like a flock of multicolored swans, approached. There was only small talk now, and the dreaded last minutes before the good-byes had to be said. There was no more talk about slavery or military necessity; there was only women's fear, badly concealed, and the irrational war fever of the young. Why did young men find war so beautiful?

"Mother," whispered Madison, at the very last moment, "your blessing?"

"God bless you, my darling. And God keep you. Come home to me."

"But of course," he laughed. "We'll have those Rebs licked before June."

"June! Why, there's no Mississippi Valley left, and McClellan's army of one hundred thousand can hear Richmond's churchbells. With us coming, there are one hundred thirty-five thousand men closing in on Jeff Davis's Richmond. Why, Richmond's doomed by the first of May!"

"That is where you're from, is it not, Mrs. Wellington?" The cool northern voice fell like new-blown snow on my shoulder.

"Yes, it is," I said, praying I'd have to say no more.

"It must be a terrible conflict for you . . . as a southerner."

"There's no conflict between one's country on one hand and traitors on the other," I replied coolly. "When the South frees its slaves and returns to the Union, then I'll consider myself a southerner."

But what cold agony and fury invaded my soul as I watched James and Madison swing their long, graceful bodies into the passenger wagon and watched my future daughters-in-laws' handkerchiefs flutter, my husband's breath catch in his throat at their leaving, and Maurice's light laughter ring after the last good-byes.

"Leave a few Rebs for the French," he shouted, "before the British recognize the whole lot of them and try to take back their colony."

For the first time since the war began, Charlotte, Emily, and I agreed on something. We joined the United States Sanitary Commission as nurses. Charlotte had dreams of us becoming the North's Florence Nightingales; Emily and I agreed that our work with fugitive slaves was futile, as they only had to cross over the Union lines and be "confiscated." And although Thenia, as a midwife and apothecary, was the most qualified nurse of us all, she was accepted by the Sanitary Commission's recruiter only as a laundress.

"But she's an apothecary and a midwife," I protested.

"I'm sorry, ma'am, but I've got my orders. Cleaning and laundry's all nigger women are allowed to do. No nursing."

"Well, what if she's my . . . assistant? What if I cannot carry on my work without her? She carries my nursing bag. She rolls my bandages. She prepares my medicines," I lied.

"If she's your *servant*, well, that's another thing, Mrs. Wellington. I'll put her down as your mammy, all right?"

I flushed with anger and despair. I couldn't meet Thenia's gaze. This was all the protection I could offer my own niece.

"What's her name?"

"Mrs. T. H. Boss," said Thenia.

"Yes. But what's her first name?"

"I don't have a first name," interjected Thenia.

The recruiter looked at me. "She telling the truth?"

"Of course."

"If you vouch for her, she can stay."

"And nurse?"

"Mrs. Wellington, I've already told you, colored women can *only* cook, clean, and launder—no nursing."

"Is winning this war of any avail?"

"No, ma'am, not for niggers."

"Thank you."

"Why wouldn't you give your name?" I asked Thenia as soon as we were outside.

"Because if a white person knows your first name, they'll call you by it. I don't take to no total strangers calling me Thenia. I don't answer to 'auntie' or 'mammy,' either. If they don't know your name, they can't humiliate you with it. I'm Mrs. T. H. Boss to everybody who doesn't have the right to call me mother or wife . . . or sweetheart, Mrs. Wellington."

The recruiter approached, just as Thenia and I were leaving.

"I must say, madam, this war has accomplished several social miracles if you count black soldiers and women nurses," whispered the recruiter as she took me aside. "An ancient tradition has died," she said. "It has always been supposed that army nursing was strictly a job for enlisted men or for trollops. But Nightingale and the Crimean War changed all that. Here we are a corps precisely like the wives, sisters, and mothers our soldiers have left behind. A female nurse may be the only woman in a camp of seven hundred men, but she is treated with all the respect, protection, and kindness which is any white woman's right."

"But many colored ladies are highly skilled nurses by habit and training, yet you refuse them," I interjected.

"The corps, dear lady, is lily-white for a good reason—we cannot have even the *suspicion* of the lax morals or prostitution so insidiously associated with colored women. Our reputation must never be brought under the least question by military or church authorities. Matron Dix bans young girls and beautiful women also, Mrs. Wellington. I wonder indeed how you got in yourself." She smiled.

"There is no woman in America who has more moral rectitude than Mrs. Boss, and that includes Matron Dix."

"Well, I'm sorry, but one wouldn't know it by her color, madam."

"I've joined, too," interjected poor Charlotte ingenuously, "but then my weight puts me out of the young girls' competition," she said, and laughed.

⁓

The war made a lot of marriages. Beverly married his sweetheart, Lucinda Markus, days before leaving for the front, his commission as a medical doctor in hand. He had been posted to the Fifty-eighth Pennsylvania Regiment as an M.D.

"I feel so helpless," he said, "like a blind man in a room with an elephant. I know that filth and primitive sanitary conditions breed disease and infection, but why? I know how blood poisoning invades the circulatory system, causing death, but how to control it? I know there's a connection between bad water and cholera, between filth and epidemics, between infected water and typhus . . . I *know* bleeding, cupping, and leeching patients is barbaric and wrong, certainly for infectious diseases. I know mercury is a disinfectant agent when administered in the correct dosage—but what is the correct dosage? Oh, Mother, we are on the brink of momentous discoveries . . . in Europe, Pasteur, Lister, Parmentier . . . all too late for this war. God help us, twice as many soldiers die of disease as are killed in battle. A soldier is more likely to die of blood poisoning than from a shell dropped on his hospital. Country boys die like flies of smallpox, erysipelas, and diarrhea. Dysentery cuts through regiments like a scythe. Pneumonia kills more soldiers in every war than sabers. I know there's a link between mosquitoes and malaria, just as I know that the distilled bark from the African yar tree can cure certain lung infections. I know there is a way to prevent gangrene from spreading without amputation."

Beverly studied Thor, who sat with his head in his hands.

"I'm only a pharmacist. An apothecary, Beverly. Great doctors and surgeons are working on all these problems and more! I can only give you an apothecary's explanation for any of your worries. And even so, I have no way of imposing these ideas on the medical corps."

"Beverly will, one day," I said, smiling.

"Perhaps," replied Thor. "I hear you've canceled several orders we should honor by contract, Harriet. Why?"

"I refuse to honor orders for medicine and drugs destined for below the Mason-Dixon line."

"Ma, if they have a contract—" Beverly began.

"I don't *care* if they have a contract. There's a blockade on, and a rebellion."

"Yes, but the government has said that we are entitled to honor contracts already signed."

"Perhaps. But not I. Not one barrel of Wellington chloroform, not one vial of Wellington iodine, not one ounce of Wellington morphine gets sent south by me. Not one Wellington drug is going to assuage the sufferings of the South's sick or wounded. Let them bleed and let them die, let every drop of blood drawn by the lash be paid for in kind and in suffering—I don't care."

"But these orders have been paid for, Harriet."

"I've returned whatever payments we have received. I've refused certain British orders because they are transshipped to the Confederacy."

"My God, Harriet."

"I will fight you on this, Theodore Wellington. Not one drop of medicine from Wellington Drugs will ever, ever help the Confederacy."

I suppressed a flicker of regret, but not remorse. I saw my father's aquamarine eyes, smelled the odor of laudanum and morphine that had hung over his deathbed. Were there cousins who would die because of what I was doing? My heart closed in childish logic. They could have changed all this once. They started this war, and now it was too late. Why hadn't they done something before it was too late?

"You're a hard woman, my dear, and not an honest one. We've promised these supplies; we've given our word."

"Since when was one's word expected to be honored in relations with traitors to the United States? The South has no rights or privileges a northerner is bound to honor . . . does that sound familiar?

"This is total war, Thor," I continued. "War against the army. War against civilians. War against women and children. Why? Because *slavery* is war; against civilians, women, children. And what Lincoln will eventually do to destroy the South will make my little war efforts look like a game of dominoes. And I rejoice in it."

"My God," said Thor softly. "There is nothing so ferocious as a reformed southerner."

"It's true," I said. "My family sinned. And now they have to pay. Even the innocent."

Thor left to take up his new post in Washington, and Beverly left for the front.

Harriet Tubman looked like an ordinary, tiny specimen of humanity. Like Frederick Douglass, she had also refused to follow John Brown to Harpers Ferry, to Brown's surprise and bitter disappointment. And now, with John Brown in his grave, she continued alone in the steps of his martyrdom, which seemed to shadow every word she said. For her courage and shrewd audacity, she was known as General Tubman. For bravado in securing her own family's freedom, she had no equal. I sat next to Emily in the large auditorium as her words pierced me.

"I had crossed the line of which I had so long been dreaming. I was free, but there was no one to welcome me to the land of freedom."

Where, I wondered, were my half brothers and sisters? Where were Thenia's mother and aunts? Where were Critta, Dolly, Bette, Edy, and the souls of my sisters Thenia and Harriet I? Where, in fact, were Eston and Madison? Was Thomas dead or alive? Was my brother Beverly on this continent or in South America? Where had all the runaways gone? How far? How long? How many oceans, rivers, lakes had my own flesh and blood crossed? How many were in their graves or grieving?

It was Emily who slipped her arm around me, guilty, perhaps, that she had involved me so deeply in this struggle, which had taken its toll in nervous exhaustion, but not for the reasons she supposed. It was because every face I saw could have been one of my kin, every face held a question to which I had no answer—why? when? and how long? I was sobbing now, and Emily led me from the hall. I stood with a glass of water in my hand, not drinking, furious at myself for my own weakness. I had almost succumbed to sentimentality and compromised my disguise for a speck of womankind who had reminded me of what I had forgotten, that I was not, would never be, alone.

I saw in Emily's eyes the question I had caught in Charlotte's eyes that day on the quay. They asked me the same eternal and unanswerable question: "Who are you, Harriet?"

When we reentered the hall, a new speaker held the crowd spellbound. It was the emblematic slave woman Isabella Van Wagener, better known as Sojourner Truth.

"Wait until you hear her," whispered Emily. "I couldn't let you leave without this. Try not to get too excited, Harriet, and try to control your emotions, for she plays upon them like no one I know. Of all the women preachers, she's the best—better than Silpha Elow, better than Jarema See, better than all of them."

"I know," I whispered, "she's a protegée of my old London friend, George Thomson."

"You'll be glad you stayed."

Isabella Van Wagener was a coal black giant of a woman, rawboned, broad faced, with a husky masculine voice famous for expressing truths her fellow abolitionists and feminists dared not utter in public. Tonight was no exception. She had never learned to read or write, and so could not generate the books, letters, and poems that were necessary to fame, as Tubman and Wheatley had. Yet her ability as an unintimidated and articulate speaker powerfully reminded the world, and white feminists in particular, that black women were women too. She was about to begin her famous tirade. The first time she had roused an audience with it, she had bared her breasts to an auditorium of thousands because someone in the crowd had accused her of being a man. Her rough country voice, as full of deep thunder and as commanding as Frederick Douglass's, filled the hall.

"Men," she began, "say that women need to be helped into carriages and lifted over ditches and to have the best seat, but nobody ever helped me into a carriage or over a mud puddle or gave me the best spot. And ain't I a woman?" The hall roared back the answer.

"Look at my arms. I have ploughed and planted and gathered into barns and no man could head me, and ain't I a woman?"

Now there was stomping and shouting, whistles and clapping as she worked the crowd.

"I can work and eat as much as a man and bear the lash as well, and ain't I a woman? I have borne thirteen children and seen most of them sold off to slavery and no one heard me grieve 'cept Jesus, and ain't I a woman?"

This was not exactly true, Emily whispered to me. Isabella Van Wagener had five children, none of whom had ever been sold. But, Emily added, it certainly sounded better. And what, I thought, was wrong with adding a slave story of old, true a thousand times over, to one's own?

It was about this time that Charlotte introduced me to Sarah Hale, who had come to Philadelphia from Boston to edit *Godey's Lady's Book,* the most popular women's magazine in America. My first encounter with Sarah Josepha, as Charlotte called her, reminded me somehow of my meeting with Maria Cosway, except that Mrs. Hale was about twice the size of the late abbess. Yet, in a way, they were in the same business, educating and cultivating domestic manners in the wives and daughters of the middle class. They both had the wild aristocratic imaginations of adventuresses, which they also recognized in me. Their beauty was defined by this aura of double or triple lives with *rebondissements* and changes of routes and directions, new strategies, and new men which gave them, whether they were actually beautiful or not, a projected power, grace, and worldliness.

Sarah Hale wasn't beautiful, but the sensuality and magnetism she exuded attracted both men and women. Tall, with a large, leonine head set on wide shoulders, a high forehead, a full nose, she had a thin, determined mouth that turned up at the corners but promised a stubborn nature. Her temper was unladylike and her thirst for power translated itself into a hilarious sense of irony in private. Offsetting this were heartbreakingly beautiful violet eyes that shone with both radiant intelligence and provocative seduction. They were eyes that could start a war, it was said, and they disguised a ferocious ambition to be the best magazine editor in the business. And she was. She had set about her task by offering the most for her subscribers' money and outdistancing her rivals in number of pages, color engravings, and inserts, which included, to my delight, a piece of music separately printed. She paid the highest prices in America, which got her the best writers: Edgar Allan Poe, Washington Irving, Nathaniel Hawthorne, and Oliver Wendell Holmes. She paid one cent a word, or twelve dollars for a thousand-word page, and up to fifty dollars for a poem. A ten-page story by Edgar Allan Poe had been bought for the unheard-of price of $250. Sarah Hale also published more fiction by women writers (whom Hawthorne called "a damned mob of scribbling women") than any other magazine, including the *Atlantic,* and she paid them at the same rate as men.

"Women are going in for novel-writing with a vengeance. I think there is a great future for the new generation in that: all those husbandless *bachelieres* taking up their pens," she often said.

Charlotte loved her because Sarah had set herself up as an editorial voice for women's rights, while Charlotte had only flirted with the idea. Sarah wrote a monthly column called "Editor's Table," where she gave advice and crusaded for a better world for women and children. No topic was too controversial for her to take on, including political candidates (even though women couldn't vote), the federal government, slavery and abolition, women's suffrage, child care and nutrition, child labor and factory conditions, and hospices for the poor and elderly.

Sarah was a huge success. She had an opinion on everything, and *Godey's* had become the American woman's bible, with one hundred thousand subscribers. Charlotte and I took to the habit of dropping into Sarah's publishing offices in the late afternoon once a week to take her to tea at Brown's Hotel, which was just across the square. In Brown's, we would discuss everything and anything, from the cut of a Parisian sleeve to the progress of the Indian Wars in Wyoming to the opera news from Europe to President Lincoln's new disaster in Washington. Sarah had ideas on equality, temperance, unwed mothers, social security, unions and the labor movement, treasury bonds, slum landlords, and even my father.

The book Sarah handed me across our table at Brown's was bound in white paper and had the illustration of a young girl tottering on the railing of a bridge with angry, frothy waters below waiting for her leap. I looked at the title. It was called *Clotel, or the President's Daughter*.

"It's the newest antislavery romance from London," said Sarah. "The publisher sent it to me to serialize, but the story seems too farfetched for me. It's about Thomas Jefferson's slave children. It was written by a fugitive slave, William Wells Brown, and has been very highly received in London. If you like slave narratives, you'll love this one," she added. Her lilac eyes held mine, but I could read nothing in them except what I had always read. She didn't know; she wouldn't know. She couldn't have guessed.

"I wrote Mr. Wells that I thought some editorial changes ought to be made for the American readers—after all, this is a rumor that has been around for some time. The American version, since we already know the story, doesn't need so much explanation, just action. Let me know what you think of it."

I took the book home with me and read it straight through, separating the folded, uncut pages into which European books were bound, I thought, in great poetic justice, with James's stiletto.

But God by His Providence had otherwise determined. He had determined that an appalling tragedy should be enacted that night within plain sight of the President's house. But as the pursuers crossed the high drain for the passage of sloops, they beheld three men slowly approaching from the Virginia side. They called on

them to arrest the fugitive, whom they proclaimed a runaway slave.
As she came near, they formed a line across the narrow bridge, and
prepared to seize her. For a moment she looked wildly and anx-
iously around. On either hand, far below, rolled the deep foaming
waters of the Potomac, and before and behind the rapidly ap-
proaching step and noisy voices of pursuers, showing how vain
would be any further effort for freedom. Her resolution was taken.
She clasped her hands convulsively and raised them, as she at the
same time raised her eyes towards heaven, and then, with a single
bound, she vaulted over the railings of the bridge and sank forever
beneath the waves of the river!

Thus died Clotel, the daughter of Thomas Jefferson, a president
of the United States. The body of Clotel was picked up from the
bank of the river where it had been washed by the strong current,
a hole dug in the sand, and there deposited. Such was the life and
death of a woman whose virtues and goodness of heart would have
done honor to one in a higher station of life, who, if she had been
born in any other land but that of slavery, would have been honored
and loved.

I sat reading my "biography" with an eerie feeling of jubilation, turning the pages with my blank fingers. How dead was I? I shivered. I felt cold, as if I really had jumped into the ice-clad Potomac and drowned. Hadn't I drowned? Wasn't I dead? Hadn't I chosen oblivion rather than slavery? The fictitious life of Harriet Hemings, written by a fugitive slave, had been read by millions of Englishmen and Sarah might now serialize it as antislavery propaganda. *Clotel, or the President's Daughter.* What else could I wish for? It was even better than my station on the railroad, and that made me laugh.

"Mother, what are you reading? Another antislavery tract from London?" It was Maria who stuck her head over my shoulder.

"No, *Uncle Tom's Cabin.*"

"Then why are you laughing?"

"I always laugh when I read *Uncle Tom's Cabin.*"

For weeks I left *Clotel* lying around ostentatiously on tables, shelves, mantelpieces. Sometimes I left it open, sometimes closed. But no one picked it up or even glanced at it. Finally I gave it to Thenia, and she never returned it.

Sarah decided against publishing *Clotel*. Having found a new American romance about slavery written by a free black doctor, Martin Delany, who had graduated from Harvard in 1852, she published that instead.

⁂

The red, white, and blue bunting of the spring of 1861 faded and fell in shreds. The ninety days came and went, as did the musical chairs of generals in Washington. The war's summer campaign wilted.

On the Fourth of July of that second year, the President affirmed yet again that he had no intention of interfering with slavery in the states where it existed and that since the Constitution protected slavery, he would vow to preserve the Constitution and the Union. Even those who hoped the war would destroy slavery held their peace.

"Give him time," said none other than Robert Purvis. "Let us stand still and see the salvation of God rather than add anything to the general commotion." Purvis was sitting in my office at the warehouse, having not found me at the Protection Bureau. The hot, humid Philadelphia summer was upon us, and Robert sat fanning himself with his straw hat.

" 'The general commotion,' " I said. "This is lethal war, Robert. Lincoln has crossed the Rubicon. Total victory is his only chance now."

"Not yet, my dear Harriet, he hasn't yet touched slavery. The South can still come back."

"You mean back down? Never. Their honor is at stake. I know them."

"Congress has authorized another million men, Harriet, for a three-year tour of duty or the duration of the war. A million men, Harriet. Lincoln isn't joking. A million men are all the South's got."

"They have their slaves, Robert. They can send every able-bodied white man in Robert E. Lee's Army of North Virginia against McClellan's Army of the Potomac. While their slaves reap and sow, harvest, dig, build, march, cook, and fortify." To my fury and despair, Jeb Stuart's cavalry had captured five thousand cases of Wellington ether off a steamship cargo at Harrison's Landing, Virginia.

That August, the Union fought and lost the Second Battle of Bull Run, thirteen months after the first. Confederate troops were not twenty miles from Washington. The Rebel lines were advancing in Missouri and Kentucky. Cincinnati was in danger. Stonewall Jackson was about to invade Maryland with forty thousand men. Disgust with Lincoln was universal.

"This is not a war," fumed Emily, "this is a rout."

"God damn them, stealing my ether."

"How can Lee fight?" said Sarah. "He has an army of fifty-five thousand sick, hungry, exhausted men, subsisting on green corn, marching on bare feet, with stragglers falling by the wayside in the thousands."

"They have to come," I said. "They have to take the war north while they have the momentum of their victory at Bull Run."

"No one understands why McClellan, having created a powerful northern army, has never committed it to all-out battle," said Charlotte.

But I knew why. He didn't think he could beat the Virginians. This was our low-water mark and Robert E. Lee knew it. We held our breath to see if Lee's crossing the Mason-Dixon line into Maryland could force the despised, desperate Lincoln government to sue for peace.

The South would call the battle Sharpsburg after the small town there, and the North would call it Antietam after the creek that ran through the battlefield. But whatever it was named by either side, it was called war.

ANTIETAM, MARYLAND
SEPTEMBER 17TH, 1862

Mother,

I have already heard what is known as the rebel's yell enough times so that it barely bothers me anymore. This unearthly wail travels with the Rebs wherever they go and strikes fear in the hearts of those who hear it for the first time and possibly every time thereafter, for there is nothing like it this side of the Infernal, and the peculiar cockcrow sensation it sends down your backbone at such a time can never be explained. You have to feel it.

How such men as the Rebel troops can fight on as they do, filthy, sick, hungry, and miserable as they are, and that they should prove such heroes in combat is past explanation. But watching men in battle, dressing them, caring for them, and sometimes fighting myself, I realize that war transforms and transcends men in ways beyond rational thought. We on the Union side are bound to expunge the dishonor of all our terrible defeats. The shame of still another whipping is not to be borne. I had heard all through the war that the army was eager to do battle with the enemy (a sentiment confirmed by the *New York Times*'s editorial page). But when you come to hunt for this sentiment among soldiers, it is always some other regiment that has it. The truth is, when bullets are whacking against tree trunks and solid shot is cracking skulls like eggshells, the consuming passion in the breast of the average man is to get out of the way. Between the physical fear of going forward and the moral fear of turning tail, there occurs a predicament of exceptional awkwardness. I am honored to report that our regiment didn't falter as we marched slowly forward, in formation, our rifles held at firing position. In a second the air was full of the kiss of bullets and the hurtle of grapeshot. The mental strain was so great that I saw at that moment the singular effect mentioned, I think, in the autobiography of Goethe on a similar occasion—the whole landscape turned red. I will never forget that moment; men were loading and firing with demoniacal fury, and shouting and laughing hysterically. Fightin' Joe Hooker's Union First Corps led the attack, sweeping down the Hagerstown Pike from the north. The Rebs were waiting for him in the cornfield. From five o'clock in the morning until now (5:00 P.M.), the dreadful slaughter raged. At the end of it, twelve thousand of our men are lying dead and wounded. Nothing since the battle of Pittsburgh Landing can compare with this day's fight, either in its colossal proportions or its bloody character.

This is, sadly, the bloodiest day of the war. Two hundred thousand men have taken to the field, and a battle greater than Waterloo raged from 5:00 A.M. to dusk, yet night closes on an uncertain field.

I don't know, Mother, if you can imagine anything like twenty-five thousand dead and dying men, divided equally between North and South. As I write this, my ears are still filled with agonizing cries from thousands left on the field. And my eyes, Mother, saw an appalling, ghastly spectacle upon the slopes of the cornfield as far as the woodlands a mile away. Over twelve thousand bodies were on the ground and enough were alive and moving to give to the field a singular crawling effect from which emerged a single whitewashed church of the Dunker sect, set in the middle of it all. At midday, ten divisions—five Union, five Confederate—were so cut up that we backed off by mutual consent and did no more fighting that day. The Confederates had gone down as the wheat falls before the scythe. At that moment, I believed, for I saw it with my own eyes, that not one body of Confederate infantry could have resisted a serious advance. Lee's army was ruined and the end of the Confederacy was in sight.

No one understands why McClellan didn't send in reinforcements to Burnside, who had driven the Rebels back to Sharpsburg and cut the road to the ford over the Potomac. He let them escape—to say more is to speak treason.

I am safe and well, but our losses have been fearful. Poor Abbott is dead, Mumfried has a slight wound in the leg, Bond is shot in the jaw, Walcott in the shoulders. General Rodman was shot through the chest, the ball passing through his lung. General Monsfield was instantly killed. General Hartsuff of Rickett's Division was wounded in the right ileal region—a serious wound. Colonel Richard Oakford of Scranton, Pennsylvania

(132nd Penn. Volunteers), was killed. Lieutenant Sawyer, 7th Maine, killed, and about one hundred privates of the same regiment wounded. We now find that only six officers of the 20th are alive (not including Surgeon Hayward and myself) out of twenty. I have been promoted on the field. Your dutiful son is now a captain, detailed to run the division hospital with Dr. Diveneel.

Only God knows what we were forced to contemplate this day, and may He have mercy on us, Union and Confederate alike. For there is no more ground to soak up the blood, and so men lie in a burgundy lake of it, commingling northern blood with southern . . .

Oh God, Mother, how I miss you and love you and want to get home to you when this cruel war is over.

Your loving son,
Beverly Wellington

CAMP RAPIDAN
SEPTEMBER 1862

My Wife and Love,

The epidemics in the camp are growing—Asiatic cholera, smallpox, yellow fever—without taking into account typhus, which has caused 265 deaths in Camp Rapidan. Reports from Virginia list 427 smallpox cases, but 433 have died of scarlet fever and 558 of dysentery and 1,204 of tuberculosis. Some of the recruits should never have been accepted, as they were already sick. And the system of substitution whereby a rich man may pay a poor one to take his place in the draft and ultimately on the battlefield is an onerous one, as well as an impractical one, for these substitutes are often in poor and degraded health and die within a few months of entering camp life. No one, of course, knew what it would mean when a million men would be thrown together in regiments and divisions in camps, forced marches, military fortifications, hospitals, and on the road. Sanitary conditions and overcrowding have already taken more lives than bullets, sabers, or shells.

As much as I converse with sages and heroes, they have very little of my love or admiration. Lincoln's appointments and military concessions include too large a number of Democrats: Benjamin Butler, Daniel Sickles, Franz Sigel, Thomas Meagher. He also has to satisfy the aspirations for military glory of politicians—McClellan, who wants to be President; Butler, who wants to be President; Grant, who wants to be President; Hooker, who wants to be President; and Sherman, who wants to be President; etc., etc. Of the whole lot, General Grant is probably the best. But it is worse than murder to give such high commands to Banks, Sigel, and McClellan.

Burnside is as timid as a grandmother; McClellan is almost criminally pro-South, arrogant, disrespectful of the President, although he loves his men and his men adore him. Two-eyed Meade is of two minds: backward and forward; Hooker is insubordinate; Frémont is too isolated from everyone; Pemberton and Hayes are no better than mediocre as probable heroes of the war.

Oh, my Harriet, I begin to suspect that I have not much of the warrior in my composition. The pride and pomp of war, the continual sound of drums and bugles, as well played as any in the world, the prancing and trampling of the light horse platoons, which are paraded in the streets every day, hold no charms for me. I long for domestic scenes, for your playing, for Beverly's new twins. Do you think I am somewhat jaded this morning for one of my years and considering the gravity and insipidity of my employment?

Good night. It is so dark that I cannot see to add more than that. I am, with the utmost tenderness,

> Yours, ever yours,
> Thor

P.S.: Imagine!—it is practically our eighteenth wedding anniversary and not one moment of it has been out of tune with adoration.

FORT WENTWORTH, MISSOURI
SEPTEMBER 17TH, 1862

Ma Tante,

I have not seen any fighting, but much hard riding and marching and much friendly contact with troops mostly from the border states: Kentucky and Tennessee. Ours is only one humble voice, but what I have seen and heard reinforces our conversations about the policy of Lincoln in this war. He wants to put down the slaveholding rebellion and at the same time protect and preserve slavery. That is why he is losing the war both in the East and the West. This policy hangs like a millstone around his neck. Weakness, faintheartedness, and inefficiency are the natural result. The mental and moral machinery of mankind cannot long withstand such disorder. It offends reason, wounds the sensibilities, and shocks the moral sentiments of man. Can you give me one good reason why this should not be an abolition war? Is not abolition plainly forced upon the United States as a necessity of national existence? And is not an abolition war on Lincoln's part the natural and logical answer to be made to the Rebels? Granted, he does this to keep the loyalty of the border states, but is it worth it? It arms the enemy while it disarms its friends, our own northern army. Cut off the connection between the fighting master and the working slave, and you at once feel an end to this rebellion because you destroy that which feeds it. Moreover, I personally feel, from what I have seen, that doing this would not offend the border states.

The Union men in the border states are intelligently so. If they are men who set a higher value upon the Union than upon slavery, many recognize slavery as the thing of all others which is the most degrading to labor and free men. They dare not say so now, but let the government say the word and I am convinced they would unite to send this vile thing to the grave and rejoice in it. What good thing has slavery done that it should be allowed to survive a rebellion of its own creation? Why should your country pour out its blood and treasure in order to protect and preserve the guilty cause of all its troubles?

Moreover, the evil of this policy exerts a chill upon the moral sentiment of mankind. It gives the Rebels the advantage of seeming merely to be fighting for the right to govern themselves. Thus you divest the war on Lincoln's part of all those grand elements of progress and philanthropy that naturally win the hearts and command the reverence of all men, and allow it to assume the form of a meaningless display of brute force, more likely to attract some Lafayette with twenty thousand men to help the Rebels and their four million slaves, than a Garibaldi ready to aid and defend the Union.

Lincoln's slaveholding, slave-catching, slave-insurrection policy gives the South the sympathy that would naturally flow toward the North and which would be mightier than lightning, whirlwind, or earthquake in extinguishing the flames of this momentous slaveholding war. At least that is how I see it, Aunt Harriet.

Perhaps this war should never have taken place, but having taken place, it should at least be for the right reason.

Affectionately,
Maurice

"I'm going to South Carolina."

Willy Boss and I looked up in surprise as Thenia strode into the warehouse, hat, coat, and carpetbag in hand, as if she were already on her way to the railroad station. I straightened up, my bright yellow smock worn over my crinoline skirts making an identical but larger conical shape to my pyramid-shaped apothecary cap. I could have been a pumpkin. I pulled off my gloves.

"Thenia, you can't find anybody there now, in the middle of a war!"

"Mrs. Wellington's right, Ma. What are you going to do once you get there?"

"The government's called for volunteers to help teach the contrabands coming over to the Union side from Virginia. Thousands of slaves are freeing themselves and crossing over to the Union lines. The military is using them to construct earthworks and trenches, and as laborers on bridges and dikes, and for cooks and laundresses, but who's going to *teach* them? Especially the children? A lot of white women, abolitionists, have already volunteered. It beats washing dirty linen for the Sanitary Commission. These people need nursing, too. They're war refugees and victims like any other. Our navy, of which my son is a proud member, has captured the entire coastline of South Carolina and the islands: Hilton Head, Port Royal, and Beaufort are all incorporated into the government's military department of the South. The thousands of ex-slaves there need help. Will you keep Willy for me?"

It was the longest speech I had ever heard Thenia make without stuttering. "Of course I will. But why not wait at least until Richmond is taken?"

"Because Richmond may take years to fall. Because Lincoln may make peace before it falls. People are so fed up with this war, they're saying it's impossible to conquer the South."

"What about Raphael's wife and child?"

"I asked Suzanne to come with me and bring Aaron, but she's afraid of the South. She's a northerner, never been beyond the Mason-Dixon line. 'What if the Confederates overrun Fort Monroe and sell me into slavery?' she says. I say nobody's going to overrun Fort Monroe with my son guarding it."

"Where will you go?"

"To Hilton Head, South Carolina. The relief program has been approved by President Lincoln and Secretary Chase. It's called the Port Royal Experiment. We've been told that all volunteers will sail from New York to Hilton Head on the steamer *United States* in a fortnight. I'll be on it. It will almost be like sailing to the Cape colony to see Abe again."

I stood there in my yellow dunce cap and my yellow apothecary's smock, holding my white gloves and gazing at Thenia with awe and affection. Suddenly, Thenia enfolded me in her arms and I buried my face in her shoulder. With a shock I realized she was a tall, broad, strong woman. Strong. She was the same height as I. When would I stop thinking of her as a thirteen-year-old child? She was forty-nine years old, a grandmother. And she was leaving me and going in harm's way.

"I'll take care of Willy for you, and look out for Suzanne and Aaron."

"Good-bye, Mrs. Wellington."

"Good-bye . . . Mrs. T. H. Boss. And God keep and bless you."

"Well, President Lincoln has a 'great' victory," said Sarah. "Let's see if Salmon P. Chase is right."

"What do you mean?" I asked Sarah outside her office, where I had gone to tell her the news about Thenia.

"Lincoln's supposed to use Lee's defeat at Antietam to issue an Emancipation Proclamation. If the South doesn't come back into the Union by January first, 1863, all the slaves in the Confederacy are free! It was one hell of a cabinet meeting! I understand the Secretary of the Navy, Gideon Welles, stood up with tears streaming down his face two days ago after the battle, crying, 'Nothing from the army! Nothing from the army! Instead of following up the victory and attacking and capturing the Rebels, McClellan has let Lee escape across the river . . . oh dear, oh dear. Your orders, Mr. President, were for him to *destroy* Lee's army. . . .'" Then Chase said, 'If McClellan thinks he is going to get around the President and avoid annihilating Lee, he's wrong unless Lee intends to surrender of his own accord!' General McClellan's told the President that he's achieved a 'great victory,' that Maryland is free from enemy occupation and that Pennsylvania is safe. He'd damned well better be telling the truth, because we're acting on that statement! '

"Then Halleck, general-in-chief of the armies, stood up and said that the character of the war had changed within the last year, and that there was now no longer any possibility of reconciliation. 'We must conquer the Rebels or be conquered by them,' he said. 'Every slave withdrawn from the enemy is the equivalent of a white man put *hors de combat*. It is now a question of subjugation.' The old South is to be destroyed and replaced by new propositions and new ideas. That's what Halleck told the cabinet and the President. Stanton, Chase, Stewart, and Bates agreed. Smith and Blair acquiesced. As did the President. He's to give the South a hundred days to come round.

"Then the President said, 'The people in the rebellious states must understand they cannot experiment for ten years trying to destroy the government, and if they fail, come back into the Union unhurt. If they expect to have the Union as it was, then now is the time, before the Constitution is amended to abolish slavery forever.' At which Caleb Smith said, 'Th-th-there goes Indiana.' And Chase declared, 'Blacks should be armed.' '"

At this, Sarah stopped breathless on the steps of the Godey Publishing House and turned to me, grabbing my hand as if she were shoving a rifle in it. I stared at her without really seeing her. The reality of what she was saying stopped my heart.

Around us thronged a war city: soldiers, sailors, merchants, cabs, carriages, ambulances, couriers, covered wagons, munitions carts, army nurses, elegant cavalrymen on horseback, foot soldiers shouldering muskets, mules, oxen, stray dogs. A large cannon was being pulled down Market Street on a railway flatcar; omnibuses clattered across russet bricks; to the east the masts and chimneys of ships in the navy yard stuck into the sky, children played, street urchins raced between traffic, an organ-grinder's plaintive song could be heard, while buckboards of army uniforms, tied in thick bundles that resembled corpses, rattled along Market Street on their way to the quartermaster's.

And above all this din and life and striving, just above our heads, hovered the letters of that word, *emancipation*, with which I had cursed my father on his deathbed. There it hovered over Sarah and me, two white ladies discussing a secret meeting of Abraham Lincoln's cabinet. Didn't I consider myself free without this proclamation of Lincoln's? If I did, then why was my heart beating like a troop of thundering bulls, and why was the firmament of my men's faces orbiting around my head like missiles?

If Abraham Lincoln's proclamation went through on the first of January, my husband and sons would be, by force of arms, emancipating their own wife and mother. Thomas Jefferson's grandsons would be doing what he hadn't had the courage to do. I had suddenly become the posterity of two presidents—the one who enslaved me and the one who would set me free. I felt the puzzled, loving eyes of my men all turned toward me. I wouldn't think about that now, I decided. I would think about that by and by—when I was calmer. And I turned my eyes toward Abraham Lincoln.

30

We hold these truths to be self-evident, that all men are created
equal and that they are endowed by their Creator with certain inalienable rights: that among these are Life, Liberty, and the pursuit
of Happiness.

Thomas Jefferson

Sitting here, in the Oval Office at the White House, waiting for the delegation of free black citizens I have to persuade to leave the United States of
their own free will, I can't help thinking that if there hadn't been a Thomas
Jefferson, there wouldn't be an Abraham Lincoln. Oh, not that I'm com-
paring myself to the great Jefferson, the inventor of our national identity.
No, I'm a journeyman President, the Tycoon, unloved, unreelectable, who
has Jefferson's wolf slavery by the ears and is being very seriously manhandled by it—shaken like a brown bear shakes the last piece of meat from a
coyote bone.

President Jefferson must have felt at times as lonely as I do, sitting here
in this rocking chair. What? Oh, I've heard the stories about his secret slave
family. I've snickered with the rest in cabinet meetings about the great
revolutionary and his black Aphrodite. But quite frankly, I feel as another
President did, the only one perhaps who knew the story firsthand and at the
time it happened: John Adams. He said (and he said it as a President, a
Yankee, and a gentleman) that he believed the story was true, and that it was
the tragic, irrevocable consequence of chattel slavery. I believe that too, and
moreover, here I sit, the other tragic, irrevocable consequence of chattel
slavery. The convoluted relationships of southerners with their slaves, who

are often their blood kin, their ancestral twins, their dark shadows, are nobody's business unless . . . unless these relations touch the body politic of the United States.

The whole love story got turned into political claptrap by Jefferson's enemies. The private lives of public men are always more vulnerable, as I have learned, but it is unfair to confuse the political man with the private one. And the fact is, I love Jefferson.

I adore him because he was then, and is now and forever, the most illuminated intellect in our history. He may (or may not) have begat some dark-skinned descendants, but in the process he begat (if you'll pardon the comparison) all of us. All honor to him, I say, who, in the pressure of a war for natural independence, had the nerve, the coolness, the foresight, to take what was merely a revolutionary document and turn it into the vehicle of abstract Truth, applicable to all men and all times. And he knew what he was doing. He knew we were struggling for something more than independence, just as I know now we are struggling for something more than the Union. I remember thinking even as a young boy that Thomas Jefferson and his signers had consummated the greatest promise to all the people of the world with that Declaration. And I am anxious, guilt-ridden, tormented that this Union should continue in accordance with his original idea. I have made war for his idea. I have killed seventy-nine thousand American boys for his idea. I will free slaves for it—even his own. And I will destroy the South for it, even Virginia, because he is the begetter, the progenitor of our national ideal. Americans have no pedigree without it.

There are some, and necessarily some black, who are blood descendants of those original ancestors, the signers, but most of us, in this year of 1864, are common immigrants: Swedes, Germans, Irish, Italian, Polish, who can't look back and trace our connection with the idea by any blood—except what we spill. We can't even speak English, half of us; we are a fugitive, alien, imported population. Only the *idea* makes us feel American—only when we look back at that old Declaration and discover the old man Jefferson saying, "We hold these truths"—then, only then, can we feel our connection to the father of all moral principle in us, and by this, blood of his blood, flesh of his flesh, children of his Declaration. That is the electric cord that links us all together.

Now, this was what I tried to explain to the delegation of black leaders on that Saturday, September 16th, 1862, at 4:00 P.M., in a secret meeting in the Oval Office, when I laid out my plan for transporting all Negroes out of the country (with their permission) and back to Africa or some country in South America where I felt they would be happier.

I was frank, mind you, to the point of brutality. I said I was not, nor had been, in favor of bringing about in any way the social and political equality of the white and black races. I had said the same thing in the debates, and had been repeating it for as long as I have been President. I was not, nor ever had been, in favor of making them voters or justices, of gratifying them to hold office nor (getting back to Jefferson) of allowing them to intermarry with white people.

There were half a dozen of them in the Oval Office. Big, impressive, many-hued men of substance — one, as black as my retriever Lucy; another, whiter than me. I told them that I believed there was a physical difference between the two races which would forever forbid us living together on terms of political and social equality in the same place. And insomuch as we couldn't live together, we must separate.

"Whether it is right or wrong," I said, "I need not discuss, but your race suffers very greatly, many of you, by living amongst us, while ours suffers from your presence. There is an unwillingness on the part of our people, harsh as it may be, to let you free colored people remain with us. I do not propose to discuss this, but to propose it as one fact with which we have to deal. I cannot alter it."

The reaction to this "interview" was summed up in the following manner by my black co-citizens themselves.

"In physical composition, you, Mr. President, may differ somewhat from the Negro," he said (he was the blackest), "and also from the majority of white men; you may even, as you indicate, feel the difference on your part to be *very disadvantageous* to you; but does it follow that therefore that you should be removed to a foreign country?"

"Pray is our right to a home in this country less than your own, Mr. Lincoln?" said another, rather brown-skinned man. "Are you an American? So are we. Was your father one? And your father's father? Are you a patriot? So are we. Then wouldn't you spurn as absurd, meddlesome, and misguided propositions for your colonization in a foreign country? Give me one good reason why we, why anybody, should swelter digging coal in Central America—if there be any. Coal land is the best you know of to begin an enterprise?"

"Moreover, Mr. President," said another, who was distinctly yellow, "when we wish to leave the United States we can find and pay for that territory which suits us best. And when we are ready to leave, we shall be able to pay our own expenses of travel. And when we are ready to leave, we shall let you know. The fact is, we don't want to go now, and if anybody else wants us to go, they must compel us."

"I know that we are inferior to you in some things, President Lincoln," said a most distinguished and elegant clergyman, "virtually inferior. We walk about among you like dwarfs among giants. [Laughter.] Our heads are scarcely seen above the great sea of humanity. The Germans are superior to us; the French are superior to us; the Yankees are superior to us. [Laughter.] This thought of inferiority is an old dodge. If you read the history of the Norman Conquest, the Anglo-Saxon himself was looked upon as inferior by his Norman master and might be found in the highways and byways of Old England laboring in a field with a brass collar on his neck and the name of the master marked on it. *You* were down then! [Laughter.] We are down now. I'm glad you are up, Mister President. I only want to be up also!"

"This nation has wronged us, Mister President, sir," said the fifth, the whitest of them all, "and for *this* reason many hate us. The Spanish proverb is '*O esde que te erre nunca bien te guise*'—'Since I have wronged you, I can never like you.' . . . When a man wrongs another, he not only hates the other man himself, but tries to make all others hate him.

"We rejoice that we are colored Americans, but deny that we are a 'different race of people,' as God has made of one blood all nations that dwell on the face of the earth, and has hence no respect of men in regard to color. . . .

This is our country by birth. . . . This is our native country; we have as strong attachment naturally to our native hills, valleys, plains, luxuriant forests, flowing streams, mighty rivers, and lofty mountains, as any other people. . . . This is the country of our choice, being our fathers' country. We love this land, and have contributed our share to its prosperity and wealth. . . .

We have the right to have applied to ourselves those rights named in the Declaration of Independence. . . . When our country is struggling for life, and one million freemen are believed to be scarcely sufficient to meet the foe, we are called upon by the President of the United States to leave this land. . . . But at this crisis, we feel disposed to refuse the offers of the President since the call of our suffering country is too loud and imperative to be unheeded. . . .

In conclusion, we would say that, in our belief, the speech of the President has only served the cause of our enemies, who wish to insult and mob us, as we have, since its publication, been repeatedly insulted, and told that we must leave the country. Hence we conclude that the policy of the President toward the colored people of this country *is a mistaken policy*."

They wouldn't accept colonization. I didn't tell them my motives for deportation were simple: I would not endanger the perpetuity of this Union.

I would not blot out the great, inalienable rights of white men for all the Negroes that ever existed.

But what I finally said to these black men in the Oval Office, that afternoon, was the following: "Gentlemen, let us discard all this quibbling about this man and the other man—this race and that race and the other race —as being inferior. Let us unite as one people throughout this land until we shall once more stand up declaring that all men are created equal. Whether or not the black man is equal to the white man in mental or moral endowments, in the right to eat bread, without leave of anybody else, which his own hand earns, he is my equal and the equal of every living man in another country. That is the issue that will continue in this country when everyone in this room is dead, gone, and silent."

That was the only thing we agreed upon. No matter that my Secretary of the Navy insisted that any deportation of the Negro population would take forty years and the entire treasury of the United States. Deportation was a dead issue anyway. We had neither the ships nor the guns to compel these men before me to move. And obviously they weren't going to move unless they were compelled. I realize, as my hero Jefferson never did, that these men—who were never going to pass for white—considered their birth in the United States as an American passport. Moreover, they would tolerate no transition between emancipation and citizenship. If slaves weren't citizens, then freedmen were.

Secretary of the Navy Welles and Postmaster Blair finally came to my rescue and ushered them out. I sat there for a long time, alone. Despite the best efforts of the worst men in America, I was stuck, God help me, with Jefferson's idea, and a struggle between right and wrong. I realized that whatever Jefferson had done to make it impossible for me to think of myself as anything except American, he had done it to them too. I thereby conceived the embryo of my Proclamation, on which I didn't consult any Negroes at all. And knowing mankind as I did, I was not optimistic about the outcome. I had always been poorly endowed with the faculty of hope. I had always felt some hindrance or deficiency in that theater; my sentiments had always lacked the sun, even in the height of summer . . . and my sentiments now were those of singular sadness and depression.

If I could save the Union without freeing any slaves, I would do it; and if I could save the Union by freeing all the slaves, I would do that; and if I could save it by freeing some and leaving others alone, I would do that also. But first I needed a victory. Any victory. I made a covenant with God. I would emancipate every God damned slave in the United States of America for victory in Maryland.

I the undersigned, Abraham Lincoln, sixteenth President of the United States, age fifty-four, six feet, four inches tall, born in a log cabin in the backwoods of Kentucky, lawyer, politician, Black Republican, husband to Mary Todd Lincoln, of South Carolina, father of four sons (one deceased), leader and temporary (I hope) dictator of the people of the United States, in the greatest crisis and most tragic interlude in their history, do hereby acknowledge and describe my state of mind on the date of my proclamation the 23rd of September 1862 A.D. to be effective in one hundred days, if the Confederate South doesn't come round, by the first of January 1863.

When I issued the Proclamation of Emancipation which transformed the war in a way I had vowed I would never permit, by turning it from a military response to insurrection to an armed revolutionary struggle, sanctioned by none other than Karl Marx, according to a German journalist who told me he said, "The revolution of 1776 freed the bourgeoisie and the revolution of 1861 freed the working class," I was miraculously serene for a man committing political suicide. But I knew I had to be free, to be my own man, unencumbered from all the political forces closing in on me because it was my name and my name only on that Proclamation. It was my place in history, my belief that the majority of the people of the United States would never tolerate slavery after this war, that was at stake. People were disgusted by slavery. The army would fight with a fierceness and dedication that would resist all pressures for a settlement only for its suppression. I had only to carve out the groundwork and invoke the considerate judgment of mankind. This illegal seizure of property called emancipation would also give the right to the black man of self defense even though I begged them to abjure violence. But, if race war came, it came. I had no more compunction about using black men as U.S. soldiers either. The paper I held before me had taken on a life of its own. The power that seemed to emanate from it almost frightened me. It was only a piece of paper, and unenforceable in most of the country, and probably unconstitutional to boot, yet it glimmered back a holy writ, a moral justification for the terrible bloodletting I had unleashed on my country, a power greater than any I could find in the Constitution, a power equal to Jefferson's idea. I would, with a stroke of a steel pen, free four million human beings. I tried to get my mind around that. With one stroke now, I thought, with no compunction, in theory today, in actuality tomorrow . . . I would drop the word "forever" before "free," because who could promise anything, let alone freedom, forever? That might stump even the Almighty. One thing was sure: I would have to fight this war to the bitter end for what I was doing. These were not the cool compromises of the Constitution, but the passion and fervor of the Declaration. Around me was silence, an awed silence so great that I heard even the scratch of the pen. I looked around at my war cabinet, Chase, Stanton, Blair, all good men. My eyes teared—one fell in the margin. A comma, a footnote, nobody saw it. . . . God Almighty, I begged, stand by me. Then I exhaled.

ABRAHAM LINCOLN

31

The motion of my blood no longer keeps time with the tumult of the world.

Thomas Jefferson

"Now, everybody. Don't move. Please."

The disembodied hand removed the cover from the camera lens. The magnesium lamp flashed in our faces like a shellburst, and the room filled with an acrid smell that mingled with the sweet scent of the fir tree we had put up at Christmas. We had decided to have our picture taken in celebration not only of the day, the first of January 1863, but of the fact that all my men, even Raphael and Maurice, were home from the war, and after one hundred days Abraham Lincoln's Emancipation Proclamation had become the law of the land.

Earlier, the conservatory had shaken with the booming of cannons from the armory, and all of Philadelphia's church bells had retaliated in a frenzy of dissonance as I read aloud the words of the Proclamation of September twenty-third from the headlines of the *Philadelphia Inquirer*.

" 'I do order and declare that all persons held as slaves within said designated States, and parts of States, are, and henceforward shall be, free.'

" 'And I further declare and make known, that such persons of suitable condition will be received into the armed service of the United States. . . .'

" 'And upon this act, sincerely believed to be an act of justice, warranted by the Constitution . . . I invoke the considerate judgment of mankind, and the gracious favor of Almighty God . . .'

" 'Done this first day of January, in the year of our Lord one thousand eight hundred and sixty-three and of the Independence of the United States of America, the eighty-seventh.' "

I had paused after that, my eyes filling with tears, thinking of my father's Declaration, always that reference: my father. He was like a presence in the room, in the nation—as if the whole turmoil of the war revolved around him.

"People—*colored* people—were dancing in the streets this morning," said Maria in her precise and lilting enunciation.

"They're calling it the day of Jubilee."

"Lincoln must think we're losing this war."

"Lincoln doesn't say anything about the slaveowners who stayed loyal to the Union. They get to keep their property, it seems. He's exempted all of Tennessee and West Virginia," remarked Maurice.

"He doesn't say anything about colonization, either."

"Well, he can't very well ask black folks to join the army," said Raphael, "and leave the country at the same time."

"And what about the four billion dollars they're worth? Is the United States going to compensate the slaveowners for their property?" said Maurice.

"Emancipation with compensation! Emancipation with reparation! Emancipation and deportation! That's all I hear!" I replied, my voice rising. "What about emancipation with reparation *for the slave*? Reparation for the crime of kidnapping, baby-snatching, unlawful imprisonment, cruel and unusual punishment? How about compensation for stealing a mother's child from her arms?"

Thor looked at me strangely. "I've often thought of that," he said slowly, "but I never had the nerve to articulate it."

"No, you were busy deporting the entire race."

"No, that's not fair, Mother."

"Why should I cry over the bankrupt South?"

"Why, 'cause you're a Virginian, Ma. Even if you hate the South, they're still your people," said James.

James was right. They were still my people, my Blue Ridge Mountains, my Beaver Creek, my sunrise and my sunset, my field of tobacco blossoms, I thought. But he's your grandfather, I mused. Listen to you all. You own him. You recite him. You memorize him. He belongs to you. You imbibed him with your mother's milk. . . .

"Let the South," I said slowly, "spend every single penny of their treasure, which colored people have earned for them. Let them spill a drop of their own blood for every drop of colored people's blood they've spilled or contaminated. I have no pity and contemplate no mercy for the so-called bleeding Confederacy."

"Is that a prayer, Mother?" asked Maria.

"I think we should pray, Maria," I said.

The Proclamation had made me a woman who was no longer viable. An Underground Railroad conductor who no longer had passengers. An abolitionist whose function had been abolished. I skimmed on the brink of extinction—outdistanced, surpassed, and annihilated by my own biography. People who passed for white in order to be free were redundant. I had been born Jefferson's bastard; I was now Lincoln's child.

A terrible loneliness pierced me, more terrible than any I had known before. My husband and sons would emancipate their own mother and wife. *Without ever knowing it.* It was the *ever knowing it* that snapped my head forward.

The prayer wouldn't come. Outside I could hear the faint sounds of Jubilee like a musical accompaniment. The crack of fireworks had begun, and also the distant rumble of thousands of bodies in motion. The ships in the harbor added their guns to the ones at the armory, and they alternated, keeping time like bass drums in an orchestra with the cymbals of fifty church bells. The sound lifted me off my knees and to my piano, where I sat, my head bowed.

"Play something, Mother," said James.

But I didn't know what to play. I reached down and caressed Independence's great-great-great granddaughter, Liberty. I left marks on her as I left marks on the keys of the piano, because they were stained black with newsprint. I began softly, the first strains of Stephen Foster's new song: "We are coming, Father Abraham, three hundred thousand strong."

Events that spring succeeded one another with kaleidoscopic rapidity. Successive disasters for the Union army and triumphs for the Confederacy emboldened General Robert E. Lee to march his army north across the Mason-Dixon line into Pennsylvania to threaten Harrisburg.

In June, the Philadelphia division of the U.S. Sanitary Commission held its huge central fair testimonial in Logan Square for the benefit of the army and Abraham Lincoln. To our surprise, the President agreed to appear. All of Philadelphia turned out to hear him.

Lincoln's speech was directed against Philadelphia Peace Democrats.

"There are those who are dissatisfied with me," he began. "To such I would say: You decry peace, and you blame me that we do not have it. But how can we attain it? There are but three conceivable ways. First to suppress the rebellion by force of arms. This, I am trying to do. Are you for it?"

At this point, there was much applause and cheering and stamping of feet.

"If you are, so far we are agreed. If you are not for it, a second way is to give up the Union. I am against this. Are you for it?"

A storm of booing and stamping and whistling and cries of "No! No!" filled the tent.

"If you are, you should say so plainly. If you are not for force, nor yet for dissolution, then there remains only compromise. I do not believe any compromise embracing the maintenance of the Union is now possible. The strength of the rebellion is its army. No compromise can be used to keep Lee's army out of Pennsylvania! Only Hooker's army can keep Lee's army out of Pennsylvania; and I think can ultimately drive it out of existence. . . ."

More cheers and cries of "Hear! Hear!" and hurrahs filled the air. The President was a mesmerizing speaker, looming on stage like a black hawk, his dark hair standing straight up on his head, his gunmetal eyes intense and gleaming, the lines of his face and forehead seemingly traced in black crayon on a complexion darker than a Negro's.

"But, to be plain, you are dissatisfied with me about the Negro. You dislike the Emancipation Proclamation; you say it is unconstitutional—I think differently. The Constitution invests its commander-in-chief with martial law in time of war. Is there—has there ever been—any question that by the law of war, property, both of enemies and friends, may be taken when needed? The Emancipation Proclamation and the use of colored troops constitute the heaviest blow yet dealt to the rebellion. You say you will not fight to free Negroes. Some of them seem willing to fight for *you* . . ." Over the cheers of the colored people in the auditorium, he continued, ". . . to save the Union. Whenever we have conquered all resistance to the Union, if I shall urge you to keep fighting, it will be apt time, *then*, for you to declare you will not fight to free Negroes. . . ."

I stared at the figure onstage. Had I lived a white life so long that I no longer put myself in the category of the people he was talking about? What was I? If I was as white as I pretended, why did my blood boil at the word *Negro* in the President's mouth? He considered it little more than a category, as my father had, or my husband did. When, I wondered, would *Negro* equate with *American* in the President's mind? Which algebraic equation of sacrifice and suffering would he use? One-half? One-third? One-sixteenth? As if in answer to my question, the President continued.

"I think that whenever Negroes can be got to act like soldiers, it leaves just so much less for white soldiers to do in saving the Union. . . ."

Anything the white man left him to do, couldn't do himself, was too dirty or dangerous for him to do . . . so that was to be the President's equation.

"Does it appear otherwise to you? But Negroes, like other people, act upon motives. Why should they do anything for us if we will do nothing for them? If they stake their lives for us, they must be prompted by the strongest motive—even the promise of freedom. And the promise, being made, must be kept."

The auditorium was getting restless. A scuffle broke out in the back. Thor and Charlotte's husband left a group of men in uniform to join us.

"Lee is in Pennsylvania. Hooker is to turn his army around and march north to meet him, except that Hooker don't know where he is," a voice roared from the back of the tent. But the President continued serenely, defending his actions.

"It will then have been proved that, among free men, there can be no successful appeal from the ballot to the bullet. . . . And then there will be some black men who can remember that, with silent tongue, and clenched teeth, and steady eye, and well-poised bayonet, they have helped mankind on to this great consummation. While I fear there will be some white ones unable to forget that with malignant heart, and deceitful speech, they have striven to hinder it."

The applause, boos, whistles, cheers all began before the President was finished.

"Let's find Robert E. Lee first!"

"Fire General Hooker!"

Over the din of noise and movement, I heard Thor's voice raised in argument with Andrew Nevell.

"There can be no army without men," he said. "Men can be had only voluntarily or involuntarily. We have ceased to obtain them voluntarily, and to obtain them involuntarily is the draft, Andrew, the conscription."

"We can't find the numbers," Andrew Nevell was saying.

"I know much complaint is made of the provision which allows a drafted man to substitute three hundred dollars for himself; yet none is made of that provision which allows him to substitute another man for himself!" interjected Gustav Gluck.

"The substitution of one man for another is the provision which really favors the rich over the poor, but this being an old and well-known practice in raising armies, nobody objects to it," replied Andrew.

"Isn't that what we're doing by allowing colored men to volunteer? Substituting a black man for a white one? After all, the overriding principle of the draft is simply involuntary servitude," said Gustav.

"Lincoln's right about that—let the darkies, or at least some of them, do it," Nevell replied.

"What's the particular hardship now?" exclaimed Thor. "Shall we shrink from the necessary means to maintain our free government, which our grandfathers employed to establish, and our own fathers have maintained? Are we degenerate? Has the manhood of our race run out? Do we need Negroes to fight for us?"

"There is something too mean," said Thor, "in us Americans looking upon the Negro as a citizen when we are in trouble and as an alien when we are free from trouble. When our country was in trouble in its early struggles, it looked upon the Negro as a citizen. In 1776 he was a citizen. At the time of Jefferson's Constitution, the Negro had the right to vote in eleven states out of the old thirteen. In 1812, General Jackson addressed them as fellow citizens. He wanted them to fight! And now, when conscription time has come upon us, the Negro is a citizen again. Join the army! Dig ditches, trenches, earthworks! He has been a citizen just three times in the history of our country, and every time it has always been in order to get killed."

Emily, Charlotte, and I left the tent and our menfolk behind, arguing. They were, as always, defending their manhood and their country with *our* sons. I smiled ironically. As a mother, I would gladly have paid three hundred dollars as a substitution for any of my sons. By slave-auction standards, that price was a true bargain.

Robert E. Lee could bring this war to a triumphant end for the South over the divided, confused Union if he succeeded in winning one more victory on northern soil. I knew southern pride and southern character well enough to know the general was gambling everything on the next battle. And the next battle would be here, in Pennsylvania.

1863

32

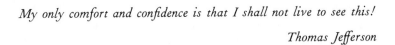

My only comfort and confidence is that I shall not live to see this!
Thomas Jefferson

Robert E. Lee invaded the North, marching into Pennsylvania. From that day on, my twins' lives became one swift succession of forced marches, becoming ever longer and harder as they rushed to find the Army of Northern Virginia. Night and day blended together over the miles: through dust and through muck they marched, in the broiling sun, in flooding rain, over prairies, through defiles, across rivers, over last year's battlefields where skeletons of dead soldiers still lay exposed and bleaching; weary, without sleep, tormented by newspaper rumor that their enemy was in Philadelphia, in Baltimore, every place where he was not, until they found out where he was: at Gettysburg, a small village not thirty miles from their grandmother's country house in Anamacora.

As expected, Emily and I were assigned by the Sanitary Commission to the field hospital they established near the site of the anticipated battle. I left Maria in Anamacora, chose a saddle horse named Virginius, packed my bags, and set off to Emily's place to fetch her. We could reach the Commission's advance pavilion at Taneytown, about thirteen miles from Gettysburg, in a day's ride. I took only a few things with me: white gloves and extra under-clothes, Thance's telescope, Thor's pistol, a compass, a watch, and the photograph we had all had taken on January 1, and a Bible. There was no one to spare either at Anamacora or the Gluck's farm to ride with us, so Emily and I escorted each other, armed and on our own swift horses.

Near Gettysburg we passed a white rectangular stone-and-stucco building sitting on a small ridge surrounded by vineyards and peach orchards. It was

St. Joseph's Convent, and surrounding it we could see stacks of arms and wisps of smoke from the fires of the army camp. The square belfry rose like a Tuscan tower over the soft hills, and one had a bird's-eye view of the entire valley with its rivers and woods, a small cemetery, and the village itself. It seemed the safest place in the world.

Many of the nurses at Taneytown came from honored families, some bearing the names of universities and hospitals, factories and mills. I was Mrs. Wellington to everyone I encountered, and that was the name I would carry into this battle. But secretly I bore another name as famous and illustrious as any. I had carved H.H.J. on my leather nursing kit to remind me I was also the President's daughter. I had come here not only to nurse, but to bear witness. Before long, I was sure, I'd be reunited with Thor, who was on his way from Camp Rapidan, and Madison and James, who were somewhere on the road to this place. It had taken them three weeks and me forty years to arrive at this rendezvous.

Emily, Dorothea Dix, and I spent the rest of the evening taking inventory of the supply tents: jelly pots and bottles of syrup, blackberry and blackcurrant; shirts, drawers, dusting gowns, socks, slippers. Rags and bandages were folded in their crates. Barrels of coffee, tea, and soft crackers. Tamarinds, piled in sacks. I personally went through all the medical supplies of alcohol, creosote, nitric acid, bromide, iodine, permanganate of potassium, morphine, codeine, camphor, laudanum, syringes, tin cups, wood splints and crutches, buckets, stretchers, bed sacks, and blankets. There were earthenware containers stamped WELLINGTON, as well as our barrels of chloroform and ether.

On July first, the accidents of time and place were established for all. It was then that we began to hear the dull booming of the guns, as the empty surgery room stared out at us in mute expectation.

"There's a rumor," said Emily, "that Lincoln has replaced Hooker with Meade. Pray God it is so."

The Third, First, and Second Divisions of the Army of the Potomac were all massed near the southeastern base of Round Top on the Taneytown road —nearly one hundred thousand Union men facing the same number of Rebels. The two armies had finally found one another.

Matron Dix recognized Generals Meade and Gibbson as they rode by. We checked and rechecked our supplies and inventory. The rows upon rows of empty hospital beds seemed a white scream in the deepening darkness, floating, diaphanous exclamation points of death and disfigurement.

We hardly spoke. The surgeons and doctors arrived. The ambulance carts drove up in the moonlight and lined up. The black work gangs dug and spaded through the night, in silence. It would be expected, I supposed, on the eve of such an event, that one would have peculiar feelings, something extraordinary, some great arousing and exciting of the faculties commensurate with the event itself; this would be very poetical and transcending, but there was nothing of the kind at the Sanitary Pavilion. The Army of the Potomac were old soldiers who had suffered many defeats and too much death and destruction in their ranks to lose any sleep over it now. No, I believe the army slept soundly that night.

In the moonlight, I sat down on a railroad tie with the thought of writing Thor, knowing my letter would never reach him on the road, but I found that my hand shook uncontrollably.

On the morning of the second, the weather was thick and sultry; the sky was overcast, with low, vapory clouds and drizzle. I took out Thance's telescope and observed all the movement on the crest near the cemetery I had passed yesterday. Men looked like giants there in the mist, and the guns of the frowning batteries appeared so big that I was relieved to know they were ours.

"Matron Dix has asked me to take a supply of morphine over to the nurses at the convent," I told Emily as I saddled my horse. "I'm taking my telescope. I'll be able to climb to the top of the bell tower to see what I can see from there."

As I rode away from the depot, the first rumblings of cannon and what seemed like the roar of the sea, but must have been the marching of thousands upon thousands of soldiers' feet, rose, like a faint echo from the earth. When I arrived at the convent, I tethered Virginius and reported to the mother superior. I left the supplies with her and entered the bell tower, climbing to the very top, hoping to see what I had just heard.

As I lifted the telescope, I could see that the troops had been drawn up into ranks in the form of the letter U, the troops facing outward, and the cemetery within the sharpest curvature of the line, due south of the town of Gettysburg, which lay deceptively peaceful under the July haze. Three roads converged on the town, forming a sixty-degree angle. The easterly one was the Baltimore Pike, which passed by the cemetery; the farthest west was the Emmettsburg road; between these, the Taneytown Road ran north and south and united with the Emmettsburg road between the cemetery and the town. The high ground between them was known as Seminary Ridge, and spread out upon it were eighty thousand blue-clad soldiers and their guns, and upon their flanks was the cavalry. This was the battle formation of the Army of the Potomac.

But I could see nothing of the Confederates at first, so cleverly were they concealed in the woods north of the town. At last they began to reveal themselves to the west and northwest of the town, as they moved in masses of gray through the woods of Seminary Ridge. I lowered the telescope, my whole body trembling. I had to get back to Emily and the hospital. Suddenly the entire landscape before me turned into a great, heaving, blue ship of state; the vaulted clouds above had blown themselves into the shapes of sails, the earth moved as if it were a rolling sea. Before my eyes, thousands of blue-clad men and some squadrons of cavalry began moving down the slope and across the narrow valley that divided North from South. This was the first wave of the battle formation of the Army of the Potomac.

I might have heard the rattle of ten thousand ramrods as they drove home ten thousand cones of lead. The earth moved sickeningly, the bell tower trembled, and a deafening roar like the end of the earth rolled over the universe. To my surprise, I found myself sitting on the floor as if I had been knocked down by the sound. I got to my feet, but instead of fleeing down the bell-tower steps, I lifted the glass for another look as specks of Rebel gray flowed out of the woods to meet the blue wave.

Then there began to appear countless flashes and the long, fiery shouts of the muskets, the rattle of volleys mingled with the thunder of the guns. The long gray lines swept down upon the blue and mixed with them and the battle smoke, and now the same color emerged from the bushes and orchards on the right. Oh, the din and the roar and—suddenly, for the first time, I heard in the distance the rebel yell, thirty thousand strong. The hair on my head and the back of my neck lifted, and I squinted against the sky, now darkening with smoke. I was all alone in this world, watching this spectacle. I would die here, I thought. There was no escape.

Mesmerized, I watched the world become one sheet of fire. From Round Top to the cemetery stretched an uninterrupted field of battle. To watch the fight in the valley below me was terrible, but what must it be like when one was in it? All my senses were dead, except that of sight. The roar of cannon and the yells of the Rebels all passed me unheeded, for my soul was all eyes and saw all things that the smoke did not hide.

To say it was like a summer storm with the crash of thunder, the glare of lightning, the shriek of wind, and the whistle of hailstones would have beggared the symphony of sound of two hundred and fifty cannon spitting upon the smoke-darkened sky: incessant, pervasive, heating the air above my head, shaking the ground, remote, nearer, deafening, earsplitting, astounding. One could not compare it to a storm, which is an act of God. This was a human procession of hurrying, falling, crawling, running, crouching men.

The guns, however, were not of this earth, nor interested in humans. These guns were great, infuriate demons whose mouths blazed with smoky tongues of living fire and whose sullied breath milled around the miniature figures and along the ground like the sulfur-laden smoke of hell. Those pitiful, tiny, grimy men, rushing, shouting, their souls in frenzy, plying the dusky globes and igniting sparks, were in league with these demons of war and obeyed them like willing, happy slaves.

I found myself shouting, then whispering, as the Rebels hurtled forward and the long, blue-coated lines of infantry delivered their fire down the slope. Men were dropping on all sides, by scores and by hundreds: poor, mutilated creatures, some with an arm dangling, some with a leg broken by a bullet, were limping and crawling toward the rear. They seemed to make no sound. It was now the Union men whose growls and yells overturned those of the Rebels as they advanced. A blue wave rolled up upon the gray rock and smashed them. I began to shout as the Rebel line broke and began to flow backward like tears.

Covered with smoke and soot, I groped my way down the bell-tower steps, tripping, my drawers wet with urine, my face black. At the bottom I stumbled out among the first wave of wounded. They were lying in lines and heaps outside the chapel door, and had begun to pile up against the sides of the belfry. Many had made it back from the front walking or dragging themselves and, now exhausted, could not go any farther. Some were tearing at their clothes, trying to see their wounds, for they knew that a stomach or chest wound was mortal. A long, pathetic row of semiconscious men lay on the ground moaning and twitching fitfully, completely unattended—men who had been shot through the head or whose wounds, upon hasty inspection, had been pronounced hopeless and who had been put aside to die as quickly as they might. Not far away, outside one of the hospital tents, there was a long table where doctors were amputating arms and legs, with an army wagon standing by to carry off the severed limbs and return for a new load. A new world had been born while I was in the belfry.

In the chapel, planks had been laid across the tops of the pews so that the entire auditorium was one vast, hard bed jammed with wounded men lying elbow to elbow and head to foot. There I stood, aghast and awestruck, chest-high in an endless, undulating sea of suffering anguish.

I started up the center aisle, fording the two breast-high banks of wounded men who cried out for me, reached for me. Blood had seeped through the spaces between the planks, and my skirts dragged in it, mixed with water that swirled in the trough made by the chapel's broken pavement. The white-coifed heads and shoulders of the nuns floated by, disembodied, as I struggled toward the crucifix, which hovered over the assembly of hurt men from its altar. I reached it finally and then, in a stupor, not knowing what to do next, turned back.

Like a sleepwalker, I moved through this infernal slaughter-house, chest-high among the rough planks, my skirts trailing in indescribable muck, through the putrid slave hole where a candle would not burn.

There was no time to pray. There was no time to think. A surgeon grabbed me by the arm and turned me toward the hospital tent outside. "No! Don't stay here. You're needed outside." My eyes met those of the surgeon, and I allowed him to lead me out of the chapel and into the sunlight toward the surgery and a pile of arms and legs and waiting, wounded men, standing as if they were in a ticket line.

Hours later I found Virginius, unleashed and calmly grazing just outside the bell tower. I collapsed against his vibrant, warm flank, sobbing. When I had enough strength, I slowly pulled myself up onto his back and made my way back to the Sanitary Commission depot.

My mount shied away from the corpses, unwilling to tread on dead men or beasts; the animals appealed with an almost human gaze, and the humans stared back like beasts surprised in death. They were all so quiet, lying beside each other; South and North, Virginia and Massachusetts, some with composed upturned faces, some in tormented positions of pain and fear, but as darkness dimmed the carnage, they all seemed only wrapped in sleep.

The doctors and medical corpsmen were working with torches now, trying to separate the dead from the living. Many who still lived would have to wait until daylight for attention. I could no longer see. Then, in the lurid crepuscule, I did see something—a gray shadow, a raised arm, a prone Union soldier who cried out an appeal. Was the shadow trying to rob him or kill him? I was the only witness. Around me slept only dead men. The circling torches were far, far away. Before I realized it, a flash of light had pierced the twilight. I heard a shot ring out, and the scent of exploded gunpowder burned my throat. The Union boy who had lifted his arms in supplication was safe. The Rebel deserter fell dead beside him at my feet. I had killed a man. The ache from the recoil of Thance's pistol made me lower my arm.

The wounded boy half-crawled and I half-dragged him to Virginius. With our last strength, I hoisted him onto the horse's rump. There was no way my exhausted mount could carry us both, so I walked him back to the hospital. When I got there, the boy in blue had died. I looked for someplace to cry and, finding none, pulled Virginius's blanket over my head and cried once again into his flank.

"Harriet, I thought you'd been killed!" Emily looked up at me reproachfully as I entered the hospital tent, as if I had taken fright and run off to safety. "Where were you?"

"At the convent."

"You missed everything. They've announced that the field is ours . . . according to the generals. God in His mercy has given the victory of today to the arms of the Union."

"This field will never be ours," I said. "This *day* will never be ours! I abhor the slaughter of this bloody day," I said, finally weeping. Then I remembered why this day was bloody. The Confederates were making war for the freedom to own me. And mine.

"You must wash a bit, Harriet," said Emily.

But I refused. My face was as black as my real color, and I intended it to stay that way—tonight.

Emily and I looked at each other. If we had hoped that what we had lived through the day before was a dream, we were deceived. Our blouses were stiff with dried blood; our muscles ached; we stank to high heaven. Matron Dix convened her civilian nurses, and whoever they had been the day before, they were no longer that person. Yet none of us had deserted. No one had fallen ill. No one was weeping. I looked around at these dry-eyed, exhausted white women, and my esteem for them moved and surprised me.

Ain't I a woman?

We washed, put on clean white aprons, and started to work, as dawn broke.

At twelve noon, July third, Emily said, "What sound was that?"

There was no mistaking it. The distinct, sharp sound of the enemy's guns, once more. Everyone turned in the direction of the sound. Directly above the crest was the smoke and then the noise of cannons. In an instant, before anyone could exchange a word, as if that were the signal for a race, began a series of startling loud boomings.

The nurses of my watch were stifling their cries; the cries of the wounded for water and help rose and fell like a musical accompaniment, the projectiles shrieked long and sharp, men cursed, hissed, screamed, growled, sputtered with sounds of life and rage, and each had a different note that I could almost write.

I imagined the silent gray line advancing with the Union guns bellowing in their faces. The blue line approaching to within footprints of the gray line and firing point-blank. A great, magnificent passion came upon me. Not one that overpowered and confounded, but one that blanched the face and sublimated every sense and faculty. The armies did not cheer or shout. It was exactly as Beverly had described it to me; they growled. It resounded even behind the lines, the sound of that uneasy sea mixed with the roar of musketry; the muttering thunder of a storm of sounds. Later, I would know what had happened, but now the line sprang: the crest of the solid ground, with a great noise, heaved forward—they swept by, men, arms, smoke, fire, followed by a universal shout, that of the charge of Pickett's Division. The battle of Gettysburg had ended.

None of us had any notion how long a time passed from the moment of the first guns until they ceased, and all was quiet. Suffice it to say that on the night of the third of July, the Confederacy withdrew, and on the morning of the fourth of July—the day of my father's Declaration, the day of my father's death, the day, thirty years ago, that I cursed him in fury over my bondage —that day, the Union forces again occupied the village of Gettysburg. The victory had cost sixty thousand dead, wounded, and missing. I looked about me. Where the long line of the enemy's thousands had advanced, silent men in gray were scattered and strewn amongst the trampled grass, as were other thousands of silent men in blue, all intermingled and amalgamated for eternity. Rain fell as I rode back to the convent, unable to resist the vision I had found there.

33

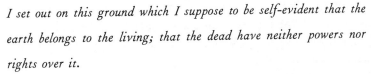

I set out on this ground which I suppose to be self-evident that the earth belongs to the living; that the dead have neither powers nor rights over it.

Thomas Jefferson

Watching the battle of Gettysburg from the relative quiet of an anonymous pauper's grave outside Philadelphia, I felt more like God than James Hemings of Monticello. I was pulled back almost a full century to the hour of my birth. A hundred-year-old man *is* history, and perhaps the instinctual knowledge of the Last Judgment is universal, because a life that leads to death is a perfect emblem for a history that has led to this sprawling, spanking-new killing field being consecrated as a national metaphor to insanity. Yes, this is James Hemings you're listening to. I'm contemplating my niece Harriet, who has lived her double — nay, triple — life so that she can stand there with her fake identity, sobbing for the fake sacrifice of this fake moment of (I admit) indisputable greatness of this fake nation. But why must these moments always occur on battlefields, in cathedrals, or in graveyards, and in this case, a battlefield and a graveyard? Because history favors the mass effect: plenty of action and a cast of thousands, bit players that enter and exit by the millions, the dead filling in the background so that there in the sky, the phosphorescent chariots of the great, surrounded by clouds, thunder, and lightning, can appear as drums rumble and clarinets spike. Just like now. The mist rises, the sky smells of heat and rain, the clouds part, and there it is: the terrible armada, the great surge of the mob across the moat of the Bastille, the grand Army of the Potomac. I guess historical illumination is always like that, spotlighted from the left, with lots of chiaroscuro.

My white namesake, James, has died on Seminary Ridge to free the mother he didn't even know was a slave *and* black. Like most white people, he didn't know the words of the song he had been dancing to, and I don't really have an opinion about that except that *she's* just like the mother she never wanted to be. I've followed my niece's adventures for fifty years, hopping, skipping, jumping the color line, mistrusting her father, despising her mother, lovingly deceiving her husbands; not adultery or even incest, but—woe is me—a question of color. A question which supremely irritates all black men, dead or alive.

I still have my red, white, and blue cockade from Bastille Day, Paris, 1789. Did you know that? I've just stuck my hand in my pocket and found it. I wonder, did they bury it with me (a gunnysack, some lime, and a hole in the ground) in not, I insist, a common grave? Never let it be said that I racially integrated a mass burial pit. No, the white poor and the black poor are duly separated in Philadelphia.

And you're thinking, Well, really, what really happened to him? Are we ever going to find out? I mean, was he murdered or did he commit suicide that day Thomas Mann Randolph found him, or claims to have done so? Do you really think everything should be historically redeemed from oblivion, reader? I mean, couldn't my fate just stay in the somnolent shadows? As those boys over there know, dead is dead.

Why am I carrying on this conversation, appearing on the scene, interrupting the narrative? Rage, I guess. At my own dry bones, my wormy eyes, my faded cockade, when all I wanted to be in life was one of Abraham Lincoln's three hundred thousand. One thing about being dead, you don't get any older. And at thirty-seven, I am a fine fighting man, and if they didn't let me fight as a black, well, I would have done what Harriet, Eston, and Beverly did. Pass for white, since white people don't even know what white is except it is not Negro and they are fighting for the right to be called non-Negro. I'm simply lying here itching for a gun. I've long ago forgiven my murderer. And Callender as well. Forgiven my father. Forgiven my brother-in-law. Forgiven the world. It was only politics as usual. How can I speak of assassination with fifty-nine thousand assassinated boys staring up at me. Forget it. Forget me. I feel a great tenderness for my grandnephew James down there. And I know, like all the dead, that it's not over. Only half the price is paid as of now. Only half the grief. Only half the pain. Only half the shame. Harriet's going to lose another son. The South is going to fight to the last. And the North is going to blunder on and finally grind them into the earth because America is indivisible. Forgiveness? I don't think Harriet is ever going to find it. I don't know if she wants to anymore. She has all these other problems—being emancipated by her own white sons and all—and their being in the dark about it. But most of all, the great American nightmare of waking up one morning with a drop of black blood in their veins hangs over them.

Blood. Harriet waded in it right here without ever taking into account that her whole life has revolved around a single black drop of it for fifty years, just as mine revolved around a single drop of white sperm for one hundred. And a hundred years from now it will still matter. It makes even me, a man who is supposed to be at rest, angry every time I think that a woman would rather be a slave than miss out on almighty love.

I, James Wayles Hemings, a suicide, second son of John Wayles and Elizabeth Hemings and brother to Sally Hemings, brother-in-law and manumitted slave of Thomas Jefferson, do hereby swear that I was at Gettysburg when its ground was consecrated by my namesake James Wellington, dead for the Union without ever knowing he was black, without ever knowing he was emancipating his own mother, this day God made, the Fourth of July, in the year A.D. 1863.

Why are colored people's triumphs always in graves?

JAMES WAYLES HEMINGS

34

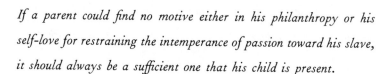

If a parent could find no motive either in his philanthropy or his self-love for restraining the intemperance of passion toward his slave, it should always be a sufficient one that his child is present.

Thomas Jefferson

I would ride up to the cemetery on Seminary Ridge. I liked to look at the forlorn and pockmarked sign that forbade by ordinance the use of firearms within its perimeters. I wondered what all those quiet sleepers must have thought when twenty-pound Parrott shells thundered over them and solid shot crushed their headstones. Virginius shied away from a dead horse as I dismounted beside the broken pieces of a statue of a lamb that had guarded some child's grave. I tied the reins to the wheel of an abandoned gun carriage.

Surreptitiously, I took from my nurse's bag a piece of broken mirror I used to tell if unconscious men were dead or alive.

I could hardly believe what I saw. My hair had turned half-white, my eyes had faded to watery jade, my cheeks were sunken and hollow, and there were dark rings under my eyes. My fair skin was burned by the sun, and there were small lines of worry pulling at my mouth. I could hardly tell whether I was a man or a woman, since not a mite of my sex's magnetism shone out. My joints ached and my chest harbored the weight of closing scores of dead men's eyes—a load as heavy as a confession and as impossible to lift. Because of it, my heart fluttered, sometimes in a steady beat, sometimes as jerky as a flea.

As I looked over the wasteland, I saw Thor from very far striding up the ridge toward me. I recognized him from his walk, the set of his shoulders, the silhouette of his twin. My heart leapt, first in delight and then in dread.

How had he managed a furlough? I started toward him, my arms open, my eyes shining until I was close enough to see his face. It was the face of an old man. The thick thatch of dark hair still fell over one eye, but it now had an inch-wide streak of white in it, as if he had dipped it in whitewash. His step was slow and his broad shoulders stooped in the blue serge of his uniform. I noted dully that he had been promoted. There was a major general's bar on his sleeve and shoulder. Then I waited patiently like a dray horse for him to take me by the shoulders; to look at me with love and pity; and to tell me which one was dead.

Instead of a greeting, he uttered one word, "James."

The flash of grief was like a spinning bullet. It corkscrewed through me effortlessly, trailing ingots of pain.

"There's almost nothing left of his regiment. The Twenty-fourth was on Seminary Ridge, facing Pickett's Division. Madison is alive. He was with him to the end."

"You mean it was *here*?"

"Harriet, I'm sorry. I loved him as much as you did. Forgive me. I would gladly be dead in his place. Forgive me."

Forgive me. That's what all white people said. Forgive me. Forgive me. Forgive me. I couldn't forgive them anymore.

"A work gang of colored freedmen buried James near their camp," continued Thor. "They were army laborers working on repairing the railroad. Madison and I went to their prayer meeting that night and listened while they sang. They had collected themselves under the fly of a tent and had installed a table where their leader sat—about thirty of them, so black it was as if they had brought in the darkness from outside . . . or the African night all the way from the Cape. I felt . . . at home. Madison knew the words to all the songs. They seemed to be under no one's orders. They set up their meeting and prayed as only black people can for James, who had died so young. I don't know why, but I went over to the quartermaster's and hunted up some army-issue yellow bandannas and took them back. We laid them on the table, and one by one the men came up and took one. I told them that the Union bandanna was proof that they were fighting for the United States and was a symbol of victory . . . and that they had prevailed over the Confederacy and that they should wear their bandannas with as much pride as a full Union army uniform.

"They tied the bandannas around their necks, or their heads, or their sleeves. They were very proud. They sang one more song, 'Sweet Religion.' "

"And Madison?" I stuttered over his name in fear.

"I left him at the field hospital. They took a bullet out of his thigh which missed, thank God, the bone. The surgeon said if he could walk he could try to reach the depot here tomorrow and get himself evacuated to Philadelphia by train."

"But I have my horse here. I can go and fetch him, and he can stay with me."

"He sent me to you first because he dreads seeing you without his twin, since he thinks James was your favorite."

"Oh, Thor! How could I love one more than the other. They're two sides of the same coin, just as you and Thance . . ."

Thor's eyes met mine in silent communication. Did history really repeat itself? Or only family history? Thor's face was drawn and haggard, his eyes hollow and pained and red-rimmed, with a growing network of lines around them. The beautiful mouth was one single line of fury. His voice, like mine, was hoarse and raspy from the pall of smoke, the sting of gunpowder, and the stench of rotting bodies that rode the winds out of the valley. I had suffered in my flesh and spirit from what I had witnessed. I was unwashed, my hair streaked with white. My breath was heavy. My uniform was filthy, permeated with the liquids and gangrene of death. I fumbled for a comb, wishing for some rouge; then the immensity of what had happened dawned on me.

We were in each other's arms. Thor's rank smell and my own mingled in a maelstrom of battlefield sweat and blood. His tears dropped on my bound head, and mine made one more stain on his filthy uniform.

"Oh, Harriet, what a brave woman you are. I would salute you if I did not already worship the ground you walk on."

"I love you, Thor."

"There's no time."

"There'll be time."

"I'm leaving you alone again. Saying good-bye again."

"People as old as we are should say good-bye to each other each night before they lie down to sleep, since each night might be their last," I said.

"People as old as we are should also say 'I love you' each day. Each day is a gift."

"James was cheated."

"Madison will be here soon."

"And you'll be gone."

"I believe a new battle will be fought in the days ahead. That's why we're sending the surgeons south. Lee is trapped on this side of the Potomac, which is unbridged and flood-swollen. Meade must destroy him there."

"Then it's not over?"

"No, Harriet, it's far from over."

"I must stay here until every wounded soldier is evacuated or buried."

"Charlotte is coming with the next contingent of Sanitary Commission volunteers," said Thor.

"Charlotte?"

"Your best friend."

Didn't Thor know I had no best friend to whom I hadn't lied?

When Charlotte arrived, as fresh-faced and energetic as always, unmarked by tragedy, she and Emily buried their jealous animosity and we made a trio known to the men as the Auburn-haired Angels, although we had all turned gray.

It seemed impossible that one soldier amongst so many could find his mother amongst so many, but Madison Wellington stepped into my hospital ward a day later.

"Nurse."

His voice was light and plaintive. I was glad I was washed and dressed in fresh white and navy, my hair clean and braided, my scissors and probe and smelling salts on a ribbon around my neck. He stumbled toward me, limping but alive, stronger, taller, and heavier than I remembered him. I saw James's eyes, James's hair, his nose, mouth, ears, bearing. James's shoulders, James's hands. Oh, Lord God, his voice, his mouth, his form, his life, his half.

"Thank God."

"Oh, Lordy, Mama. Mama, I love you."

It had been a long time since Madison had called me that.

"You're alive, Mad; that's all that matters now."

"Mama, how can you say that, with James dead? I should never have let him . . . he wouldn't have joined up if I hadn't talked him into it. It's my fault he's dead."

"Shush, darling. You were spared—for whatever reason, God took James. Nothing can change that. Grieve for James, but never blame yourself. God bless you for being alive."

"Do you believe in fate, Mama?"

"I believe in chance."

I let him cry. I could hold him as I had when he was small. We rode up Seminary Ridge and roamed the makeshift graves marked with wooden crosses, dug by black men, looking for James's. We finally found the pitiful splintered wood. I vowed to carry him back to his grandmother's house in

Anamacora when this war was over. I told Madison how I had accidentally eavesdropped on the battle from my bell tower, had witnessed the horror and might of it, but he didn't want to talk about the war; he wanted only to talk about his brother and their childhood—the belongings James had collected, his love letters from his girl, all the accoutrements of a young man's life. There was so much I hadn't known about my son; so much of his life—as any young man's—had been a secret to me, secrets he had taken to his grave. We left behind the foul, overpowering stench of the unburied dead, which robbed the battlefield of its glory and the survivors of their victory.

By the time we came back to the Sanitary Commission Pavilion, the railway cars were ready to leave and men were boarding them. I put Madison on the train to Philadelphia and safety in the care of his sister at Anamacora.

My labors and those of Emily and Charlotte continued for another four months.

"Why is it that the southern boys, dying, never speak of slavery or their cause? How can it be that they have fought so bravely and well and died so nobly for such an ignoble cause? They call it their states 'rights,' but it comes out 'stat-rats.' "

"I don't know, Charlotte . . . I don't know . . . ," I replied. In the heat of the battle and the fight against death, I had forgotten about southern "rats" and the "cause."

On the fourth of July, five thousand horses and eight thousand humans had lain dead, scattered and sweltering in the heat. The horses and mules were burned, trading the smell of burning flesh for that of rancid decay under the driving rain. White-masked and retching, groups of soldiers, black teamsters, Confederate prisoners, and local civilians covered the bodies with a layer of earth as fast as they could, but even after the corpses were hidden, the scene was repellent with the soft rise and swell of bodies. The whole town of Gettysburg was one makeshift cemetery, fetid and steaming as the summer wore on and relatives arrived to rifle these troubled graves, looking for their dead.

To our despair, General Meade did not attack Lee's army at Williamsport as Thor had announced. When he finally got his army in place on the nineteenth, he found nothing but rear guard. Robert E. Lee's slippery Rebels had vanished across a patched-together bridge during the night. Lee had been allowed to escape again. The war would go on. The South would go on because it had to go on. It was no longer "the cause," but pride. Southern pride.

The last railway car of mutilated men departed for Pittsburgh on the seventeenth of November. I could rest at last; I could go home to Maria and Madison at last. I could grieve at last. There was only one more duty.

35

He has waged cruel war against human nature itself, violating its
most sacred rights of life and liberty in the persons of a distant people
who never offended him. He is now exciting those very people to rise
in arms among us, thus paying off former crimes committed against
the liberties of one people with crimes which he urges them to commit
against the lives of another.

Thomas Jefferson

The thicket of feathery crosses above which aerial ghosts still fought under round suns of Indian summer bled in pinpoints, like shafts of broken wheat that flowed to the horizon. Abraham Lincoln arrived at Gettysburg to dedicate the cemetery, laid out in the shape of a huge amphitheater, where eight thousand men lay buried under neat wooden crosses.

As I surveyed the wide, gently rolling valley almost a mile wide, I thought that the broad highway of white crosses could just as well have been that of those bell-shaped, purple-hearted white flowers I had waded through to reach Sally Hemings the day I changed my race. Like bouquets of them, the graves spread as far as one could see. They carpeted the valley like white thistle planted in rows, as if they would grow and be harvested, fertilized by the fresh bones of a whole generation. Silent cannon rested on grassy embankments like sleepy brown cows, sentinels of census takers, keeping watch on the dead, thirty thousand strong.

I had never found my uncle James Hemings's grave, and I decided then and there that this cemetery, where James, my son, his namesake, lay, was his final resting place as well. I don't know why I thought of him that day; I hadn't thought of my uncle James in years. Yet there he was, as Adrian Petit had described him to me, his spirit, at my left elbow as I closed my eyes against the glare of the sun and the speechless memory of the battle I had lived through.

≈

Up on Seminary Ridge, a sound gathered that I recognized from the third of July. It was a sound no one who had ever heard it would ever forget, the immense, woeful spectral groan coming from thousands and thousands of human throats: cursing, grunting, roaring, howling, and weeping their way through a fight to the utmost limit of primal endurance and savagery. There had never been and never would be another sound like that one, and my ears pricked up with it like those of an animal who scents his valetudinarian killer. Up my spine it rose, as my heart accelerated and my throat closed and Emily's awful words came back to me: "This cannot be borne by men born of women or women who have borne men." But it had been, the proof being that we were here, in this place, to commemorate its being borne.

The speaker's platform, hung in red, white, and blue bunting, seemed terribly far away, as if it were a child's cardboard playhouse painted onto the blue sky. On it ruminated a lot of black-clad men in black top hats, one taller, thinner, and uglier than all the rest. The black-hatted, black-coated, black-trousered, black-bearded men had stood back and parted for one of their kind, the granite-faced, half-shaven, beautyless, hollow-eyed man who had sent my son to his death. I stared down at the rushing armies now asleep. Behind me stood Madison and Sinclair, Emily and Charlotte, Raphael and Willy and Thor. It was not a time for pride but for pity, but I felt pride lifting Madison and Sinclair out of their grief as the President prepared to speak.

Far away, over the field, I saw him stoop, a piece of paper flutter, the Union flag snap in the wind then straighten, lift his hat and settle into slated immobility.

The tall, gaunt scarecrow's voice shot back like a burst of thunder.

"Fourscore and seven years ago our fathers brought forth on this continent a new nation, conceived in liberty and dedicated to the proposition that all men are created equal.

"Now we are engaged in a great civil war, testing whether that nation, or any nation so conceived and so dedicated, can long endure," the high-pitched voice intoned, and to my surprise, the equally harsh and high-pitched voice of my father, but with a Virginia rather than a Kentucky accent, answered him:

When in the course of human events it becomes necessary for one
people to dissolve the political bands which have connected them
with another . . .

"We are met on a great battlefield of that war. We have come to dedicate a portion of that field as a final resting place for those who here gave
their lives that that nation might live. It is altogether fitting and proper that
we do this."

and to assume among the powers of the earth, the separate and
equal station to which the laws of Nature and of Nature's God
entitle them . . .

"But, in a larger sense, we cannot dedicate, we cannot consecrate, we
cannot hallow—this ground. The brave men, living and dead, who struggled
here, have consecrated it, far above our poor power to add or detract,"
intoned the thin, tall man on the platform.

A decent respect to the opinions of mankind requires that they
should declare the causes which impel them to the separation.

"The world will little note, nor long remember, what we say here, but it
can never forget what they did here."

We hold these truths to be self-evident, that all men are created
equal, that they are endowed by their Creator with certain inaliena-
ble rights, that among these are Life, Liberty, and the pursuit of
Happiness. . . .

"It is for us the living, rather, to be dedicated here to the unfinished work
which they who fought here have thus far so nobly advanced. It is rather for
us to be here dedicated to the great task remaining before us . . ." continued
Lincoln, his voice flailing the stiff breeze.

That to secure these rights, Governments are instituted among
Men, deriving their just powers from the consent of the governed . . .

". . . that from these honored dead we take increased devotion to that cause for which they gave the last full measure of devotion . . ."

That whenever any Form of Government becomes destructive of

these ends, it is the right of the people to alter or abolish it . . .

". . . that we here highly resolve that the dead shall not have died in vain, that this nation, under God, shall have a new birth of freedom."

And to institute new Government, laying its foundation on such

principles and organizing its powers in such form, as to them shall

seem most likely to effect their Safety and Happiness.

". . . and that government of the people, by the people, for the people, shall not perish from the earth."

The two recitals merged in aria, one in my head, one on the platform below me, the voices counterpointing each other in a melodious fugue that wove in and out of the crisp afternoon as if two incomparable musical instruments, different yet in harmony, played a duet of lyric splendor.

"Father . . ." My voice carried because there was little applause. The sound was as sharp as a rifle shot. But it was too late to stifle that cry. I was transfixed, as if for the first time I had heard him speak. Why had those long-forgotten words come back to me, and why had they echoed in the words of that distant black figure, now turning woodenly toward his seat. People were startled, yet they behaved with a strange subjection, as if the words still rested on the surface of the air, and, like water on parched earth, had not yet penetrated the roots of the crowd's consciousness.

I remember, I couldn't have been more than four years old. My father suddenly swung down from his horse and swept me up into his arms, then lifted me high above his head, his huge hands propelling me upward into the sky, which raced by my floating body in such a pandemonium of happiness that I shrieked with delight while my mother screamed with fright.

"This one," he exclaimed, "will live!" I tumbled downward like a joyous angel fallen into his laughing chest.

"Mother?" said Sinclair. His tall body leaned protectively toward mine; his brave, innocent eyes held only the beginning of knowledge. He hadn't been at Gettysburg. His superb uniform caught the sunlight and turned golden, the copper buttons gleaming, his dress sword like a stab of sunlight, his silhouette cut out against the field of crosses. I turned away from my white son as I had turned away from my slave mother that day she stood etched against a field of flowers, a blinding pain bursting at the nape of my neck. Tears came then, as I wept.

1864

36

Indeed, considering numbers, nature, and natural means, only a revolution of the wheel of fortune, an exchange of situation, is among possible events.

Thomas Jefferson

It was the third year of the war. At Washington's Birthday Ball, we danced on the graves of the South, while across the river, the Confederacy danced on ours. The celebration at the Union Army headquarters on the banks of the Rapidan River, began promptly at 9:30 P.M. Railroad cars full of officers' wives and daughters had come from as far away as Philadelphia to join those wives who attended the ranking and influential military in their winter quarters. And across the river, like a twin image, were Robert E. Lee and the Confederate encampment, who were celebrating the President's birthday with *their* ball. Blithe notes of music wafted across the frozen Rapidan, which served as the line of demarcation between enemies. The visiting womenfolk, like Maria and me, were housed in wall tents, and since a woman in the monumentally wide hoop skirts of this year's fashion could neither ride a horse nor walk on the muddy planks of an army camp, we were transported in white-topped army ambulances. The mood was deliberately gay, as if the music, the stylized embrace of the waltz, might pull us all out of the tendrils of a gloomy winter and the terrors of still another campaign in the spring of a war which had gone on for almost forty months. Nevertheless, the officers in their dress uniforms wore spurs to the dance floor, and the women who swirled in their wide crinolines wanted only one thing: to create an illusion for a moment of an era which was dead, in both North and South, forever.

It was wartime, and our private grief merged with the larger collective grief of thousands of fathers who had lost sons, mothers who wept for one, or even two or three, wives who would never sleep in their husbands' arms again. Maria wore a yellow ribbon over her white-gloved wrist in homage to her brother.

Beverly, stationed at the hospital at Rapidan for the winter and resplendent in his close-fitting blue serge and yellow silk sash, wore his mourning on his sleeve, as did scores of his comrades; on February 15, 1864, black bands were fixed on the sleeves of thousands of uniforms. One hundred ten thousand men were dead, wounded, or missing in the past year. Condolences were as common as good morning.

Standing beside Beverly was his wife Lucinda, who had come to stay with him for the rest of the winter with the twins, Roxanne and Perez, now safely asleep with their nurse in the village. It had been a long time since I had seen this handsome couple together. Beverly had the look of forty instead of the thirty-three he was. But he was happy. He was cramming twenty years of medical experience into two. I glanced over at Maria.

It was not her first ball, but the novelty was enough for her to be flushed with excitement, which only enhanced her complexion, turning it a deep peach rose, which in turn was flattered by the burgundy velvet ball gown trimmed in white roses. Maria's sleek, dark hair was held back in a swath of crocheted ribbons trimmed with the same white roses as her dress, and tendrils fell along her face, out of which peeked my best pearl-and-emerald earrings. She was radiant, and the pack of young officers on the opposite side of the ballroom had already recognized both her youth and her beauty and the fact that she was not engaged. I dreaded the idea of another war marriage, but I realized that the glamour, tragedy, and emotion of war heightened even the most banal attraction to the level of deathless love.

The dancers were acting the parts for which high drama called. The extravagant dresses of silk and lace, velvets, and grosgrain trimmed with everything from silk roses to glittering rhinestones and jet mingled with the colors of the Union military. There were dresses of crushed silk and sheared velvet, embroidered satin and spangled lace; there were gowns of violet and pale green, buttercup yellow and spectacular white, blues of every hue interspersed with mourning blacks and gray. The dress uniforms in white, navy, or Prussian blue glittered with gold braid, brass buttons, shoulder straps, red, gray, or yellow sashes, and short, elaborate dress swords. Broad chests sparkled with combat ribbons, war crosses, and medals. Flowing shoulder-length hair and swashbuckling mustaches graced the handsome faces of young men old before their time. There were colonels who were twenty and brigadier generals who were twenty-five. The orchestra played gallops and polkas, mazurkas and polonaises, quadrilles and waltzes, keeping reality at bay so that the boys and girls could maintain their defiant attitude of lighthearted gaiety.

"*Ma tante,* I think as a kissing cousin, I should at least have the first polka with Maria."

"Maurice," cried Maria, and she threw her arms around him.

"Maurice, don't tell me Grant gave you a furlough for this party?"

"No, *chère tante,* I am here on official business for the general. Of which I cannot speak." He looked around. "Some party, isn't it? It could be the ball the Duchess of Richmond gave on the eve of Waterloo."

"Maurice, don't be facetious."

"Well, it's certainly hot and crowded enough! I hear they built the ballroom from scratch—how American!"

"It's true," said Maria, dropping her dance program, "the army engineers spent a fortnight building it."

"Well . . . my, then, it's almost a bagatelle, isn't it?"

The army engineers had built a cedar and pine shingle building of more than a hundred feet long, and the scent of new wood, beeswax, and varnish mingled with the women's perfume, the candles, the food, the tobacco smoke, and the cinnamon used to flavor the punch. The hall was triple height, and from the ceiling hung all the regimental and headquarters flags the Second Army Corps possessed: some two hundred and thirty. The multicolored silk, shot with greens and blues and whites, stars and stripes, eagles, serpents, cocks and doves, clouds and suns, swords and arrows, halberds and sabers covered the ceiling. The names, numbers, and letters swayed and shifted in the draft of the dancing couples as they whirled by the Chinese lanterns that illuminated the entire assembly with deft golden light. At one end of the ballroom was a raised platform on which there was a theatrical and idyllic reconstruction of a typical army bivouac: clean, new shelter tents, pulled smooth and tight, piles of drums and bugles, tripods of stacked muskets, a fake campfire with a working kettle hung over it, and two magnificent, gleaming, and polished brass Napoléon cannons, as deceptively festive as any instruments of pain and death could be. In the light emanating from the tall, rectangular windows of the ballroom, I could see an assembly of orderlies, adjutants, regulars, cooks, ambulance drivers, couriers, and contrabands standing outside looking in. They reminded me of the assembly of maids, carriage boys, outriders, drivers, valets, body servants, lackeys, and footmen that would gather outside the ballroom windows of Virginia's plantations, watching. I had stood amongst them at Montpelier the night before I fled

Monticello. My foot tapped to the music, if only for a moment; then the strains of Gabriel Prosser's song took over whatever the orchestra was playing.

> *There was musket shot and musket balls*
> *Between his neckbone and his knee,*
> *The best dancer amongst them all*
> *Was Gabriel Prosser who was just set free!*

Wasn't I the best dancer and the best ballet master?

> *"Je t'écrirai, Maman."*
> *"Oui, écris-moi."*
> *"Tu ne viens pas?"*
> *"Non, je ne viens pas.* I'm not coming. . . ."

"We haven't conquered a piece of Virginia soil except what we're standing on."

It was Charlotte, extremely attractive and abundant in pale blue shot silk which matched her eyes. The gown was expensive, elaborate, and unsuitable for her age, yet she looked divine. Her blond hair was piled high, real and fake, into a diamond and moonstone tiara. She wore a *parure* of the same, and carried a huge ostrich fan, dyed to match her ball gown.

"This ball has the selfsame aura as our war," she said. "Stagey, overdone, and overripe with melodrama—not even the nobility of Greek drama. No, this is more Paris, Second Empire, Napoléon III: profit, corruption, collaboration, treachery, treason, villainies, incompetence, cowardice, slaughter . . ."

"Charlotte, such—"

"Ambiguity? Disloyalty?"

Charlotte had never gotten over the needless slaughter at Gettysburg, or the colossal blunder of General Meade, who had let Robert E. Lee get away. Meade was making his way toward us on the arm of Charlotte's husband.

"That assassin. Don't let me say anything, Harriet!" I squeezed her hand.

"All right. Are your boys all right?"

"Yes, and yours?"

"All right. Sinclair is still attached to the *Monitor*, patrolling the Mississippi. Madison has returned to active duty in western Tennessee."

"Too bad Sarah isn't here; she loves this kind of Washington hurrah."

"Ah, but she *is* here. You must know she can get herself invited anywhere in or *near* Washington."

"Well, where is she?"

"Probably eavesdropping on Lincoln's impromptu cabinet meeting!"

"Humph," breathed Charlotte. I squeezed her hand again.

Thor and the general didn't linger long. George Meade laughed and made small talk, tried a joke, and played the role of the victorious major general with nothing particular on his mind. When he and Thor had left, Charlotte said, "It's General Grant we need. We'll never win this war without him."

"Sarah says Lincoln is thinking about it."

"*Thinking*! You mean Abraham Lincoln actually *ponders*? Or maybe he looks into Mrs. Lincoln's crystal ball. If he does, he'll see that he's going to be a one-term President."

"A mother's grief is not to be ridiculed," I replied.

"It's not her grief that's ridiculous; it's her spiritualist and her husband."

I looked across the room first at the ever-twirling Maria Wellington, then at Sarah Hale and her husband, who were heading for us. I didn't want to argue with Charlotte over Mary Todd Lincoln—she was a southerner caught in both personal and national tragedy. She had three brothers who were dead to her because they had chosen to fight for the Confederacy, and she had one dead son. There was nothing like a dead son to drive one crazy, I thought. If I thought I could talk to James through a medium or anything else, I concluded, I would.

"Secretary Chase is going to be our next President," said Charlotte.

"No, my dear. McClellan," said Sarah Hale, and she leaned over and kissed me. She was wearing a Prussian blue dress with extravagant hoops of at least six feet. It was trimmed in silver braid and silver buttons, and it suited her very well. I told her so. She also wore a silver lace mantilla over a gigantic fake chignon.

"My daughter's going to dance herself into permanent exhaustion," Thor said fondly. "Have you ever seen so many boys around one single girl in your life?"

But the memory of Prestonville would not leave me. It was not a bitter memory, but as the happy, heedless granddaughter of the President danced on, I watched the orderlies and regulars outside, a quiet reminder that balls and brilliant officers and everything else rested on those that stood outside, just as it had at Prestonville. These were the men in the ranks who went to no parties and got up at five to parade their strength for the admiration of the officers' ladies. These were the same who left their life's blood on the battlefields, becoming names and numbers on casualty lists in newspapers and pins on a map to their generals. They had a name for themselves now: they called themselves "cannon fodder."

The U-shaped tables were laden with every war-embargoed luxury food. There were French cheeses, foie gras and truffles, and four kinds of pâté, three different soufflés, and a baba-au-rhum. The English had donated bottles of malt and Irish whiskey, punch spiked with cinnamon, plum pudding and fruitcakes, sturgeon, roast beef, and baked goose with mint jelly. There were Italian wines, macaroni and cheese, Italian grapes, and more cheeses. From the Germans came strudel, herrings and potato salad, venison, and wild boar. All contraband from the blockade. The official menu printed by the United States Mint consisted of twenty-five different hors d'oeuvres and sixteen entrees. The buffet was like the war: profligate, incoherent, excessive, indulgent, and slowly spoiling.

No one had left. It was as if everyone sensed that something extraordinary would happen this night. At twelve midnight a sepulchral figure, impossibly tall, dark-skinned, hollow-eyed, with a thick head of hair that had been black three years ago but was now streaked with gray, as was his short, full beard and even his eyebrows, appeared. A melancholy gaze took in the laughing assembly and suddenly a lot of us felt foolish. Beside him was Mary Todd Lincoln, the First Lady, in bright, expensive red velvet.

The band struck up "Hail to the Chief." Business, everyone wondered, or malice? Had the President come in person to fire Meade? The couple strode slowly into the room as the dancers parted as if for royalty, the starkness and somberness of the President contrasting with the almost hysterical colorfulness of the ball and of Mrs. Lincoln's dress. He stopped and greeted one person after another, chatting, even smiling occasionally. It was the first time I had ever had a chance to see the Tycoon, as they called him, up close.

"The sly fox," said Sarah. "Look how polite and cheerful he's being to Meade. I wager in two weeks Meade will be out and Grant will be general-in-chief of the armies. Actually, the Tycoon has no choice. The Confederacy has produced half a dozen first-rate generals, while the Union has only Grant. A million-man army and no commander. No wonder we're still losing this war."

"We're winning it, Sarah," said someone on her left.

"Yes, but at what cost?" interrupted Beverly. Beverly had changed greatly. It wasn't just the aging, or the deep circles under his eyes or his thick blond hair, which was already thinning. There was, even in the walk, a deep, resentful exhaustion, as if his fight against death and destruction, having been so in vain, were now also despicable.

"Perhaps you're right, Mother. What is the use of patching up a man only to send him back to the lines where the *next* time, I'll have less work to do because he'll be dead."

I looked at Beverly in surprise. There was so much bitterness in his voice.

"Mother, even you, with what you have seen, cannot imagine the reality of this war. It has changed, I believe, the American character. We used to think that individual life was sacred . . ."

"Well, Mr. President," said General Meade, his voice carrying to us from the next group of people, "we can't do these little tricks without losses."

I stared into Beverly's light gray eyes, and a shiver of anticipation ran down my spine. The President passed close enough to me for me to touch him.

"Rather than preserve the Union by surrendering the principles of the Declaration, I'd prefer to be assassinated on the spot." The light twang of Lincoln's Kentucky accent left the color of tall sun-bronzed grass as he passed.

And, as if illuminated by a burst of light, I suddenly knew why this celebration of Washington's birthday reminded me of the Montpelier ball, why all evening I had had the impression that I was standing outside with the orderlies, looking in. Inside was lily-white. Even the servants were white. There was no black leg in a shiny boot; there were no double stars on a black shoulder, no glistening sword around a black waist. There were no black officers in the army of the United States. Outside, black orderlies waited patiently for their captains and lieutenants, their majors and colonels, just as I, Harriet, had waited outside with the other slaves for our masters back home. Nothing had changed. No black hand helped steer the destiny of the Union, no black hand was asked—yet how could one deny that a black hand had commenced this second American Revolution as surely as a black hand had rocked the cradle of Thomas Jefferson's children.

All of them, I realized, even Lincoln, danced to a tune they didn't know the words of. So typical of WHITE PEOPLE.

≈

"Nothing in the world is the same now as it used to be—not the war, or the army, or us . . . or, or that matter, this colored man himself we're fighting for," rose Beverly's voice above the music.

A wave of anguish and love swept over me as I reached up and embraced Beverly. My white sons were in harm's way, facing all God's dangers, freeing the mother they had never known. The war had rendered Sinclair, Beverly, and Madison as vulnerable as any slave. They were no safer any more than if they trod Mulberry Row. The war had thrust my whole life's creation, my white family, back into the same dangerous, uncertain world of slavery I had fought so hard to escape. The war had murdered Thomas Jefferson's grand-

son, who had been free and white. What would I do if the war took another?
Or all?

I wondered if God was finished with Thomas Jefferson. Or his daughter.
I swore on the heads of my surviving children that if God took another
grandson, I would go back to Monticello with the victorious Union Army
and dance on Thomas Jefferson's grave and curse the day I was born. I would
never forgive him or Him, so help me. I swore by God, who had denied me
justice, and by the Almighty, who had filled me with bitterness, so long as
there was any life in me and God's breath in my nostrils, I would not abandon
my claim to him, I would never give up: so long as I lived, I would not
change.

Dawn broke through the dark snow clouds, and pink washed the high
vaulted sky, as the last gang of women piled into the last ambulances, their
cashmere shawls pulled over their heads, their hoop skirts making half moons
as crinolines smashed against the sides of the carts. And light flurries began
to fall both north and south of the Rapidan.

CAMP RAPIDAN
MAY 4, 1864

Dear Mother,

We are breaking camp. The dogwood blossoms flutter in the breeze like
flocks of white butterflies, alight on the trees lining the road south. The
regiments are falling into line, cannon-topped wagons creak along the road,
a colored regiment is singing "We Are Coming, Father Lincoln, Three
Hundred Thousand More." In effect, we are a hundred thousand marching
to meet our opposite number on the other side of the river.

I thank God President Lincoln has finally named Ulysses S. Grant
commander of the Union armies. At last, a leader to fight and die for.

God bless you. And God bless General Grant.

Beverly Wellington

On June tenth, Lincoln once again addressed the Sanitary Commission in
Philadelphia: "We accepted this war for the worthy object of restoring the
national authority over the national domain, and the war will end when that
object is attained. General Grant has said that he is going to smash Rebel lines
if it takes all summer." (Cheers and flag-waving.) "I say we are going to
smash Rebel lines if it takes three years more."

"Lincoln had better reiterate his war objects," whispered Sarah, "before
people begin to think he is stubbornly carrying on this war not to reestablish

the Union, but for black abolition. The North wants peace and many want peace, with 'the Union as it was' and amnesty for the South."

"Of those who were slaves at the beginning of the rebellion," continued the President, "a full one hundred thousand have crossed our line as contraband and are now in the United States military service, about one-half of which actually bear arms in the ranks, thus giving the double advantage of taking so much labor from the insurgent cause and supplying the places which otherwise must be filled with so many white men. So far as tested, it is difficult to say they are not as good or better soldiers as any. No servile insurrection or tendency to violence or cruelty has marked the measures of emancipation and arming the blacks."

"The story of Greeley's meeting with the Rebels at Niagara Falls has gotten out," whispered Sarah, "and though Jeff Davis's condition for ending the war of dis-union and independence is as irreducible as Lincoln's for union, the newspapers have caught on to Lincoln's second condition, emancipation, as the real stumbling block to peace. They are saying that tens of thousands of white men must yet bite the dust to allay the negromania and negrophilia of the President: public sentiment is only reacting to our want of military success and the impression that we *can* have peace with union if we would, but that the President is fighting not for union but the abolition of slavery."

The President's voice rose and fell as if in answer to Sarah's complaint: "I deny I am now carrying on this war for the sole purpose of abolition. It is and will be carried on so long as I am President for the sole purpose of restoring the Union. But human power cannot subdue this rebellion without using the emancipation, as I have done. Some 130,000 black sailors and soldiers are fighting for the Union. If they stake their lives for us, they must be prompted by the strongest motive—as I have said before, even the promise of freedom. And the promise, being made, must be kept."

The same day, I received two letters from Beverly.

IN CAMP, BERMUDA HUNDRED, VIRGINIA
MAY 26, 1864

Dear Mother,

Fitzhugh Lee's famous chivalry, as well as his cavalry division, were badly worsted last Tuesday against Negro troops from the garrison at Wilson's Landing. The battle began at 12:30 P.M. and ended at six o'clock when chivalry retired, disgusted and defeated. Lee's men dismounted far in the rear and fought as infantry. They drove in the pickets and skirmishes to the entrenchments, and several times made valiant and foolhardy charges upon our works. To make an assault, it was necessary to traverse an "open" in front of our position, up to the very edge of a deep and impassable ravine. The Rebels with deafening yells made furious onsets, but the Negroes did not flinch, and the mad assailants, discomforted, turned and took to cover with their shrunken ranks. The Rebel fighting was very wicked; it showed that Lee's heart was bent on annihilating Negroes at any cost. Assaults on the center having failed, the Rebels tried first the left and then the right flank, with no greater success . . . the Negro lines held.

We all acknowledge here the solid qualities which the colored men engaged in this fight have exhibited. Even officers who have hitherto felt no confidence in them are compelled to express themselves mistaken. I thought you would like to know this, since you were such a defender of their right to fight.

Your most tender and obedient son,
Bev'ly

JUNE 2, 1864

Mother,

I have not had a moment to write for nearly a week. It has been fight, fight, fight. Every day there is combat and every day the hospital is again filled. For four days now, we have been operating upon men wounded in one battle which lasted only about two hours; but the wounds were more serious than those from former engagements. I am heartsick over it all. If the Confederates lost in each fight the same number as we, there would be more chance for us; but their loss is about one man to our five, from the fact that they never leave their earthworks, whereas our men are obliged to charge even when there is not the slightest chance of taking them. Several times after capturing their works, our troops were not reinforced and had to evacuate immediately, with great loss. These men are becoming discouraged, but there is plenty of fight in them yet.

Your faithful son,
B.W.

COLD HARBOR
JUNE 4

Dearest Mother, mine,

Hundreds of soldiers are pinning slips of paper with their names and addresses on their uniforms so that their bodies can be identified after the battle. The Rebels fight from trenches which are intricate, zigzagged lines within lines, lines protecting flanks of lines, lines built to enfilade opposing lines—works within works, and works without works. The Union was driven out by the Seceshes at the cost of eight colonels and 2,500 other casualties. In all, we Yankees suffered 7,000 casualties. Lee has lost 20 of 57 infantry corps commanders of his divisions and brigades. The men feel at present a great horror and dread of attacking earthworks again.

As I told you at the ball, we are no longer the same men, this is no longer the same army. This seven-week campaign has been another way to fight a war: brutal and intense guerrilla warfare, wanton destruction of civilian property, brutalized women and children, 65,000 northern boys killed, wounded, or missing since May 4.

For thirty days it has been but one funeral procession past me, and it has been too much, Mother! Too much!

Ever remember, with the tenderest of sentiments, he who knows no earthly happiness equal to that of being your beloved son,

Beverly Wellington

HOSPITAL NEAR PETERSBURG
JUNE 20, 1864

Mother,

Our division is relieved from duty in the front line, where it has fought ever since the campaign commenced. Toward noon yesterday, weary, I suppose, of the inaction, a Confederate sharpshooter challenged one of our men to single combat. Lieutenant Jefferson, a fine fellow, standing at least six feet two in his stockings, accepted the challenge, and they commenced what to both of them was sport. Jefferson's great size was so unusual that his opponent had the advantage, and how our men tried to make him give way to a smaller man. But no! He would not listen and became very excited as his successes multiplied, and when darkness stopped the dueling, he remained unscathed while every opponent had fallen victim to his aim.

The lieutenant was so exhilarated that he claimed, with much bluster, to have a charmed life, and said nothing would kill him, and he would prove it in the morning. We officers used every argument to convince him of the foolhardiness of such a course, and assured him of the certainty of his death. But the man seemed crazed with faith in his nine lives. When we left him, he was simply waiting, as best he could, for daylight to begin dueling again.

To our surprise and happiness, the same performance as the day before occurred until a young Confederate lieutenant, who was already aiming at our man, yelled across the redoubt, "What's your name, Yankee? I want to know who I'm shootin' at." And our man said, "Jefferson, John Wayles." And the duelist said, "Darn! My name's Jefferson, Peter Field.

We're probably gawd damned triple first kissin' cousins." And they both lowered their guns, laughing. Then came a tremendous cheer from the Confederate and the Union lines and praises for the Jeffersons' pluck and skill and common sense.

Beverly

FIELD HOSPITAL NEAR PETERSBURG
JULY 4, 1864

Mother,

War! War! War! I often think that in the future, when human character shall have deepened, there will be a better way of settling human affairs than this perfect maelstrom of horror. The question of my going home with the regiment still absorbs me. At one hour I am told there will be no difficulty in being mustered out with the others, and then a rescinding order comes from the War Department and I am left high and dry. For two weeks now this has continued and it worries me. The medical director of the corps says he cannot spare me but what with Lucinda, Perez, and Zerahia, I am sorely needed at home. Lucinda is very depressed at her coming confinement in November.

Beverly

CAMP ON THE BANKS OF THE JAMES
AUGUST 1, 1864
COLONEL THOMAS JEFFERSON RANDOLPH
EDGEHILL PLANTATION
ALBEMARLE COUNTY, VIRGINIA

Pa,

Exhaustion and confusion, worse confounded. Although perfectly well, I am tired and hot, having slept only a couple of hours out of the last forty. We are still in the Wilderness, fighting our way in retreat inch by inch. The Eighth Brigade has been in no important action since I last wrote: our loss was then so terrible that they have spared us a little. Colonel McAfee is now in command as major general. Ransom was shot in the head. The Yankees fight determinedly, and our forces facing them are almost equal, but they drive us each day. We are both on a race for Richmond, and I wonder which will get the inside track. If we do, our journey will be forty miles shorter than theirs. Feeling as I do now, the thought of a forty-mile march makes me weep. Robert E. Lee is determined to keep fighting, and either win or lose, this thing can't last much longer, for one side or the other must yield from sheer exhaustion.

I'm sitting on the ground in the woods, leaning against a log and writing on my knee. Soldiers, bonfires, and kicking horses are everywhere. Dust is sweeping over me like smoke; my face is black with dirt and sweat, my clothes soiled, torn almost to pieces, and filthy with lice and vermin. I am desperately hungry. I am too tired to sleep, too tired to stand, and should dislike to have Ma or the girls see me. If it weren't for General Robert E. Lee, I would lay down my arms and walk home. Seven men deserted to the enemy from Ransom's brigade last night; also four from Wise's and two from Gracie's.

Have the Yankees damaged Edgehill, Pa? I hear Bermuda Hundred burned to the ground. Thank God you got leave from the Militia to get home to see to Ma and the girls. The sun is just setting. But whether we shall march all night, go out on a picket, or lie down to sleep—the thought of sleep makes me silly—I don't know. We never know what we may be doing in the next five minutes except dying. By God, we cannot, cannot withstand another siege.

Kiss Ma, Virginia, Lane, Ellen, and Tabethia. I've heard that my brother Meriwether has made captain and has been cited for bravery. God bless him. God save the Confederacy and Jeff Davis. God bless Robert E. Lee.

Your loving son,
Major Thomas Jefferson Randolph Jr., adjutant quartermaster
Headquarters, Artillery Corps,
Army of Northern Virginia
Petersburg, Confederate States

HANOVER JUNCTION
AUGUST 1, 1864

Mama,

I can scratch only a few lines, being up to my elbows in blood. Oh, the fatigue and endless work we have! About one night in three to sleep and so nervous and played out that sleep is impossible. The hospital is fast filling up with poor fellows who last night charged the enemy's works on the other side of the river.

We are some fifteen miles nearer Richmond than when I last wrote, and the strongest works of the Confederacy are at this point and at the South Anna River. Wherever we stop, we quickly build elaborate networks of trenches, breastworks, artillery emplacements, traverses, a rear line trench, and a cleared field of fire in front with the branches of felled trees placed at point-blank range to entangle attackers.

This is a new kind of relentless, ceaseless warfare, Mother. Since the beginning of the campaign, the armies have never been out of contact, one with the other. Some kind of fighting, along with marching and digging, has taken place every single night. Mental and physical exhaustion has begun to take its toll. Many a man has gone crazy since the campaign began from the terrible pressure on mind and body.

We have had a deal of forced marching lately, and the heat has been almost intolerable. At times it has seemed as if the sun's grasp would lay us out, yet we march all day and through volumes upon volumes of insufferable heat.

It seems to me I am quite callous to death now, and that I could see my dearest friend die without much feeling. That I could see *you* die, or Dad, without feeling anything. During these last three weeks, I have seen probably no less than two thousand deaths—among them, those of many dear friends. I have witnessed hundreds of men shot dead, have walked and slept among them, and surely feel it possible to die myself as calmly as any —but enough, Mother. The Rebs are now pretty near their last ditch, and the fight is fearful. Ambulances are coming in. . . .

Bev. Wellington

LIEUTENANT COLONEL ESTON H. JEFFERSON
HEADQUARTERS, THIRTEENTH REGT.
OHIO VOLUNTEER CAVALRY (DISMOUNTED) COMMISSARY
FORT GREAT FALLS, MISSOURI
AUGUST 1, 1864

Dad,

Received yours of the 20th. We are now fourteen miles from Richmond, having marched pretty steadily southward ever since I last wrote. Oh, why will the Confederacy not burst up? How can they continue to fight so desperately for such a despicable cause? True, we are drawing very near to Richmond, but the tug-of-war will come at the Chickahominy River. Although the Confederates had the shortest road, we stole a march upon them before they could reach and stop us. By making a hard forced march, my captain, Peter Kirkland, saved many lives. The morale of the enemy is injured by their having to fall back in retreat so far while that of the Union Army is correspondingly improved. They are now pretty near their last ditch, and the fight here will be fierce and stormy. I've had no word from Beverly in weeks. Have you? As for my health and well-being and morale, they are all intact despite so many mistakes, heartless attacks, and the senseless slaughter. That's because of the men's extraordinary endurance and courage. The Seceshes are drowning in their own blood, and we the U.S. manage only to keep our own heads above it. Pray for me as I pray for you, Mother, Beverly, and Anne.

Your obedient son,
Lieutenant John Wayles Jefferson,
Second Ohio Volunteer Regiment

HEADQUARTERS, THIRTEENTH REGT.
OHIO VOLUNTEER CAVALRY (DISMOUNTED)
REPORT OF LIEUTENANT COLONEL AND COMMISSARY OF SUBSISTENCE
    ESTON H. JEFFERSON
U.S. ARMY OF OPERATIONS, MISSOURI DIVISION
AUGUST 1, 1864
FORT GREAT FALLS, MISSOURI

ULYSSES S. GRANT
LIEUTENANT GENERAL
WASHINGTON, D.C.

General,

Five minutes ago an ordnance boat exploded, carrying lumbers, grape, canister, and all kinds of shot over the point. Every part of the yard used as my headquarters is filled with splinters and fragments of shell. Colonel Babcock is slightly wounded in the hand, and one mounted orderly is killed. At the wharf, killed: 12 enlisted men, 2 citizen employees, 28 colored laborers. Wounded: 3 officers, 15 citizen employees, 86 colored laborers, as well as your obedient servant.

Eston H. Jefferson

CAMP ON THE BANKS OF THE JAMES
AUGUST 20, 1864

Mother,

I am retained. General Hancock says I must remain. Yesterday, a small —no, a large—miracle occurred. By the invitation of their commander, I boarded one of the gunboats to watch the firing of one of their hundred-pound Parrott shells into the enemy earthworks, which were two miles distant. And having had that pleasure, I felt upon my shoulder a heavy yet familiar hand and the sound of laughter I would recognize anywhere.

"Brother," said the voice, "you sure as hell look like hell." Sinclair! It was Sinclair in the flesh. Unbeknownst to me, I was on the *Monitor*! We fell into each other's arms with more tears than females would let flow on such an occasion. But it seemed to me that my brother had been sent by preternatural forces to lift me out of my doldrums, to soothe my scarred and weary soul. I stayed on board and we dined together. We spoke of everything: you, Dad, Lucinda, Maria, Perez and Roxanne, my Lucinda, our twins, the new baby, everything except the war. We wept and laughed a great deal and were so loathe to quit each other, Sinclair asked for leave and we came ashore together. He slept with me in my shelter tent which, he said, confirmed his conviction that anyone who volunteered for the army infantry was a candidate for an insane asylum.

Your adoring son,
Bev. W.

August 25, 1864
PETERSBURG, VIRGINIA

Mother,

Sinclair is gone. It is very quiet here at the field hospital, in front of Petersburg, but oh, so hot! And the combined efforts of ticks, fleas, and black flies make life almost hell. At four o'clock in the morning, which means dawn, I am awakened by the buzzing and humming of these busy insects at their pestering task, and this labor doesn't cease till we poor mortals are again lost to them in the darkness of the night.

How war changes one's character, Mother. This accumulation of experience changes careless boys into sober and thoughtful men—men who trust and who feel that whatever happens, in the end it will somehow be for the best; men who val—

37

~

If Pride of character be of worth at any time, it is when it disarms the efforts of malice.

Thomas Jefferson

"Atlanta is taken at last!" Charlotte beamed as she opened the door of her town house to me herself on September 3, 1864. "Lincoln's reelection is assured. The Confederates evacuated Atlanta after burning and destroying everything of military value in it. The following day, the bluecoats marched in with bands blaring 'The Battle Hymn of the Republic.' Sherman has announced to the President that Atlanta is his and fairly won!

"Sherman and Farragut have knocked the bottom out of the Chicago platform and saved the party of Lincoln from irretrievable ruin," exulted Charlotte. "They are going to be wiped off the face of the earth." Charlotte's voice stopped as she noticed the thin strip of a War Department telegram in my hand. I held it up, unable to speak.

There was the dull boom of cannonfire coming from the celebrations downtown at the docks as I stood there, holding in my hand the telegram which had been addressed to Thor.

HQ, ARMY OF THE POTOMAC,
PETERSBURG, AUGUST 1864
BY TELEGRAM TO THE SURGEON GENERAL'S
OFFICE, SANITARY COMMISSION WASHINGTON, D.C.
TO THE ATTENTION OF MAJOR GENERAL WILLIAM JOHN THEODORE
WELLINGTON

Major General:

I have the sad duty to inform you that on August 25, your son, Major Beverly Wellington, was tragically felled on the field of honor by loose artillery fire — as one hundred men of the 148th Pennsylvania, under the command of Colonel J. Z. Brown, went over our works in front of Fort Morton near the Crater and the enemy's picket line opposite Fort Sedgewick. The line for about two hundred yards was carried and eight prisoners taken. The casualties in these operations were: 4 officers and 63 men killed, wounded, or missing. Major Wellington, who was close to the Second Corps hospital tent, was killed by a round of Union artillery that mistakenly fell short onto the field hospital. This gallant young surgeon was conspicuous for his spirit and brave conduct, his Herculean efforts in securing the wounded and dying and rescuing them from the field. He was a remarkable surgeon and a fine officer.

I have the honor to be, Major, very sadly and most respectfully, your obedient servant,

T.H.S.A. McParlin, Surgeon and Medical Director, Army of the Potomac for General Ulysses S. Grant, General-in-chief of the Armies of the United States.

P.S.: General Grant did not want you or Mrs. Wellington to learn of Major Wellington's death from the published casualty lists.

Charlotte gazed up at me through her thick spectacles like an owl, then down at me as I sank to my knees, the telegram fluttering to the floor.

"It's not some kind of mistake?"

"No more than anything is a mistake."

"He was scheduled to be mustered out in time for Lucinda's confinement." I looked up at Charlotte. "Must I lose them all? Is this the price?"

"Oh, my darling, darling, you must not give in to despondency. The President has authorized Horace Greeley to bring to Washington any proposition of Jefferson Davis's in writing for peace that embraces the restoration of the Union and the abandonment of slavery," she said gently. "This cruel war will be over soon, and with a victory for the Union. Beverly gave his life for it."

Without ever knowing . . . I sobbed, as I collapsed against Charlotte's knees. *Without ever knowing he was freeing his mother.*

We clung to each other, entwined on the wide canopied bed. Charlotte kissed my face and hair and hands and tried to stop the tears that wouldn't stop, not even for victory itself. We embraced as we had that day by the river so long ago, when our lives had been unwritten books, unbound, pageless, imprinted only with the passionate will to live and to love. Now it seemed we waded in the River Jordan, a river of grief and suffering beyond human understanding. Beverly had suffered it and had finally refused it. Had let it kill him . . . his own people . . . his own mother.

Charlotte and I lay quietly, listening to the noises of the celebration which reached us from Market Square.

"This stupendous, this outrageous, cruel war will surely be over one day, but I may not live to see it. . . . Perhaps I'll see Beverly before you do, and will give him your love."

"Charlotte . . . what do you mean? What is this insanity? Of course you'll live to see the end of this war!"

"If God so chooses, I suppose. I, who have always been so fastidious in life, hate the idea of rotting inside with a tumor. No. Don't say it, Harriet. The doctors have given me six months to a year. I haven't told Andrew— my devoted Andrew. I haven't told the children. I've told only you, Harriet. And you must keep my secret. Promise me. I've told you because you know I tell you everything; I could never lie to you or conceal anything from you. We are sisters."

Secrets. My own cancerous lie closed my throat as I gathered Charlotte into my arms. My friend. My sister. My mentor.

"The love we bear one another will outlast my death and this war. I hope only that our grandchildren will grow up to marry," said Charlotte.

Tell me who has died, who has married, who has hanged himself because he cannot marry. . . .

And outside, the guns would not stop. Nor would my lips unseal, except to pray for Charlotte's survival.

Victory was just a matter of time, everyone proclaimed. But the Confederacy remained as erect and defiant in defeat and deprivation as ever, and it was to break their spirit that Sherman set out on his march from Atlanta that September. He had expelled the civilian population from Atlanta in retaliation for the Confederate Army having burned the city down in their retreat rather than have it fall into his hands intact. Then he unleashed sixty-two thousand hardened Union veterans to march from Atlanta to the sea, living off the land, cutting a swath through the heart of Georgia, slicing the Confederacy in two, to advance on the rear of Robert E. Lee's army. He would, insisted Sherman, demonstrate to the world that Jefferson Davis could not resist the over-whelming power of the North.

"I can make the march and I can make Georgia howl," he had said. "War is cruelty and you cannot refine it. We cannot change the hearts of these people of the South, but we can make war so terrible and make them so sick of war that generations will pass away before they will appeal to it again."

And I reveled in this vow of Sherman's. I wanted the pain of Beverly's assassination to be engraved in every southern woman's heart, as it was in mine. And since I was a southern woman, I knew how to do it: with a cruelty equivalent to that which had been perpetuated on their slave population. They had made war on black people—men, women, and children—and now we would make the same kind of war on them; young and old, rich and poor, men and women, civilian and soldier—all would feel the hard hand of war just as we had felt the hard hand of slavery.

I stood in the middle of Charlotte's Prussian blue bedroom and lavished my personal blessings on Sherman's vengeance and thought how the women of the South would hate us, hate us with the same burning blood that flowed in my own veins—the best in Virginia.

IN THE FIELD NEAR NEW MARKET HEIGHTS, VIRGINIA
SEPTEMBER 30, 1864

My dearest wife Mary McCoy,

You can be proud that in the flash of dawn, your husband was in the column of three thousand colored soldiers in close column by divisions, right in front, with guns at right-shoulder arms, that charged New Market Heights. Seems damned strange to be toting a gun so close to home, Mary, but hadn't I told myself that maybe I could kill for my freedom in this war?

We had to take New Market Heights, which faces Richmond. It is the key to the Seceshes' right flank on the north side of the James River. It is a redoubt built on the top of a hill of some considerable elevation, then running down into a marsh. In that marsh was a brook. Then rising again to a plain, which gently rolled away toward the river.

General Butler told us "that work must be taken by the weight of your column: no shot must be fired." And to prevent us from firing, he had the caps taken from the nipples of our guns. He then said, "Your cry when you charge must be 'Remember Fort Pillow!'" How could anyone forget, I asked myself. Three hundred black soldiers had been murdered by the Confeds after Fort Pillow had surrendered, just like the Confeds had promised: a felon's death for slave insurrection. If taken alive, we would be shot. Our white officers were to be put to death as well, for inciting Negroes and mulattoes to rebellion. Never mind that *they* were the Rebs and traitors, and *we* were United States soldiers. And the Seceshes murdered the black women and children of the fort as well, executed the wounded, and buried some Negroes alive. Just like the good old slavery days, I tell you.

And so, with all that in the minds of the men, knowing no quarter was to be given us, that capture meant death, the order was given to march forward. We marched forward steadily, as if on parade, went down the hill across the marsh. And as we waded into the brook, we came within range of the enemy, who opened fire upon us. We broke a little then, and our column wavered. Oh, it was a moment of most intense anxiety, but we re-formed when we reached firm ground, marched steadily on in closed ranks under the enemy's fire until the head of the column reached the first line of abatis, some one hundred and fifty yards from the Seceshes' works. Then the axmen ran forward to cut away at the wooden defenses while a thousand Rebel soldiers concentrated their artillery and poured heavy canister fire from the redoubt down upon the head of the column, hardly wider than a clerk's desk. All the axmen went down under murderous fire. Other strong hands grasped the axes in their stead and cut away at the abatis. Again at double-quick, we moved forward to within fifty yards of the fort, there to meet still another line of abatis. The column halted and there was the very fire of hell pouring down upon us. The abatis resisted, and the head of the column seemed literally to melt away under the rain of shot and shell. The flags of the leading regiment went down, but a brave black boy seized the colors. They were up again and waved over the storm of the battle. Again the axmen fell; with our bare hands we seized the heavy sharpened trees one by one and dragged them away, and the column rushed forward, and with a shout which still rings in my ear, we went over the redoubt like a flash and the Rebs never stopped running for four miles. They knew what any black soldier would do to any Reb prisoner after Fort Pillow. In the track of that charging column, in a space not wider than six feet and three hundred feet long, lay the bodies of 543 colored men. Old General Butler came up from the rear on horseback and rode amongst them, guiding his horse this way and that way lest he profane with his mount's hoofs what seemed, to everyone still alive, the sacred dead.

But I'm alive, Mary McCoy. I refuse to die in this war. And I pray only that God spares our sons in their battles.

Brigadier General Butler's Brigade
Forty-fifth U.S. Colored Troops
Army of the James
Your loving husband,
Madison Hemings

SAVANNAH, GEORGIA
DECEMBER 23, 1864

Dear Mother,

This is probably the last letter you will receive from me before the end of the war. Beverly's death has ignited in me a terrible lust for revenge. Our orders are to "destroy all we cannot eat, steal their niggers, burn their cotton and gins, spill their sorghum, melt their railroad rails, and generally raise hell." If we didn't have a reason before, just before Thanksgiving several prisoners who had escaped from Andersonville arrived within our midst. They had nothing but rags on their backs. Emaciated and starving, these prisoners of war wept at the sight of food and the American flag. Oh, Mother, the men howled with rage at the thought of tens of thousands of their comrades perishing in that pigsty in the midst of barns busting with grain and food; our goal now is to liberate that prison camp by Easter.

It is a terrible thing to destroy the sustenance of thousands of people, and I am sorely pressed to see it; however, nothing can end this war but some demonstration of the Confederacy's helplessness. This Union must be sustained at any cost, and to do this we must war upon and destroy the Rebels—cut off their supplies, destroy their communications, and produce among the people of Georgia a thorough conviction of the personal misery which attends war. If the terror and grief of Sherman's march shall help to paralyze the husbands and fathers who are fighting us, it is mercy in the end. It seems that some Georgians said to General Sherman, "Why don't you go over to South Carolina and serve them this way? They started it." But General Sherman had intended to do that all along. So now we are marching sixty thousand strong through South Carolina to crush Lee's army, but also to wreak God's vengeance on South Carolina. We wreck their farms and factories. We burn their plantations and kill their cattle. The people's very will to resist must be devastated. We're making something called "Sherman's neckties" out of what's left of their railroads. We heat the rails over a bonfire of wooden ties and twist the iron around the nearest tree. I almost tremble at their fate, Mother. But this is where treason began, and, by God, this is where it shall end! Our purpose is to whip them, humble them, stalk them to their innermost recesses and put perfect fear and dread in them. And in sorrow and pity we will do that.

Your obedient and loving son,
Madison Wellington

Christmas 1864. Lucinda brought Beverly's twins and her new babe in arms to Anamacora permanently. I had insisted that Perez, Roxanne, and John William would be safer (although there was no danger in her staying in Philadelphia) and more comfortable there. Beverly's death weighed heavily on everyone's spirits, but Sinclair, who had been the last to see him alive, was the most despondent. Beverly's death seemed to have triggered a latent melancholy in Sinclair that alarmed both Lucinda, his wife, and me. It seemed to us even more morbid than the long, never-ending, ever-inconclusive war. Everyone was sick of the war, and many were saying so. There was defeatist talk and talk of peace without the abolition of slavery, an idea so perverse and so obscene after the loss of so many lives that even the President was obliged to declare, "I hope this mighty scourge of war may pass away. Yet, if God wills that it continue until all the wealth piled up by the bondsman's two hundred and fifty years of unrequited toil shall be sunk and until every drop of blood drawn with the lash shall be paid by another drawn with the sword, so it must be said, 'The Judgments of the Lord are true and righteous altogether.' "

It was another cold winter like 1856, and the conservatory windows were opaque with hoar and ice. On the Delaware, dark figures skirted the thick ice, and frosty laughter added to the mist that had enshrouded all of Philadelphia's waterways and canals. Spidery snowflakes had begun to fall, and clung like lace mittens to the windowpanes. The air was so frozen it resonated like chimes, and against the whiteness surrounding us, we could only embrace once more the glittering green fir tree and the crackling fire which cast us all in bronze. Despite everything, we tried to make a joyful Christmas for the children. Maurice was back from Missouri, where he had fought against General Price and his "allies," the Quantrill gang, at Pilot Knob. Thor was home from Camp Rapidan, and Madison was about to return with Maurice to active duty in Georgia under General Sheridan. We had a war marriage to celebrate as well, for Maria had fallen in love with one of her professors at the medical college, Zachariah Battle. Zachariah had served on the western front, had been wounded at Battle Creek, and was mustered out of the army in September. He had begun teaching at the Jefferson Medical School Hospital, which Maria attended for courses in biology. They had met in the hallway, and it had been love at first sight. Zachariah, brilliant and somber, soon joined the husbands of Lividia and Tabitha in running the now-sprawling Wellington enterprises, which included petroleum and railroads, shipping and coal mines, as well as drugs, medicines, and medical research.

At the beginning of the war petroleum had been discovered in western Pennsylvania. During the war it was soon recognized that it could serve as a substitute for the ever scarce whale oil used in lamps and street lights. Through the railroads we became the principal carriers of the black gold to its markets. Philadelphia also became a storage and refining center. Wellington Drugs benefited from the petroleum boom as a refiner and manufacturer of petroleum products, including a famous patent medicine, and as a storage center and transporter.

The Wellingtons had grown very rich, but the war had made hundreds of millionaires. The demands of war had boosted the northern economy to new heights of productivity.

Lincoln's annual address to Congress had only confirmed what every prosperous merchant farmer and businessman already knew. The people's purpose in maintaining the integrity of the Union was never more firm nor more unanimous. Our resources were unexhausted, and we believed them to be inexhaustible. With 671 warships, our navy was the largest in the world. With a million men in uniform, our army was the largest and best equipped that had ever existed. And despite the deaths of three hundred thousand soldiers, immigration and natural increase continually made up the loss. We had more men now than when the war began. We were gaining strength every day. We could maintain this contest indefinitely.

I thought of the deep waters closing over my white family in the South. There was no money in the Confederate treasury, there was no food to feed the army, and there were no troops to oppose General Sherman as he closed in on Savannah. Sherman's latest telegram to Lincoln had read: "I beg to present you, as a Christmas gift, the city of Savannah, with 150 heavy guns and about 25,000 bales of cotton." To which Lincoln had responded: "Many thanks to you for your great success. Taking into account the work of General Thomas, those who sat in darkness, see a great light."

Indeed, as I gazed at my Christmas candles, I realized the defeat of the South and very old enemies was a matter of months if not weeks. General Thomas's Army of the Cumberland, including an entire Negro division, had annihilated the Army of Tennessee at Nashville and was now chasing the remnants of the Rebel army back to Mississippi. The war had killed one-quarter of all the Confederacy's white men of military age. It had killed two-fifths of southern livestock, ruined ten thousand miles of railroads, and destroyed forever the labor system on which southern riches depended. Two-thirds of southern wealth had vanished in the war—it had simply strolled away, as I had done forty years ago.

"Play something, Grandma!" I looked down at three-year-old Roxanne. Her eyes danced in the reflected light of the lighted tree. I picked her up in my arms, a warm, living bundle of my flesh, and carried her over to the piano. There would be no romping mazurkas, or lilting waltzes or polonaises tonight. No Wagner or Beethoven, or Verdi transcriptions. I played "Tenting on the Old Campgrounds" as a dirge and "When This Cruel War Is Over" as a lullaby. I played "Bear This Gently to My Mother" for Beverly and "I Would the War Were Over" for James and "Tell Me, Is My Father Coming Back?" for myself.

＊

Because I knew she was dying, and because I had never told anyone I loved who I was, I told Charlotte. My Christmas gift to her was the trust I had denied her all these years. What else could I give her except the gift of my black soul?

"I know." Charlotte gently interrupted the end of my recital.

"You *know*?"

"Thance wrote to me from Africa; his letter arrived after his death. Thance's secrets have always been my province, ever since Thor's accident. On the voyage of the *Rachel,* Abe Boss inadvertently let it be known that Thenia was your niece. Of course, Thance didn't know who your father was."

"And you do?"

"Yes. I met your cousin Ellen Wayles Coolidge in Boston through Sarah Hale. She and her husband fled the South when Virginia joined the Confederacy."

"Don't tell me Ellen is opposed to slavery!"

"No. She's opposed secession from the Union. She loves the South. The stories she told me about her childhood at Monticello were the same stories you told me about *yours.* Was not her grandfather your father? She told me there were 'yellow children' at Monticello who were allowed to run away. It was common knowledge. Their name was Hemings. She confessed that when she was a child, she often envied you your freedom to run wild and do what you wanted while she was forced to act out a role and comply with all the conditions and expectations of her sex and her class. She always believed you went to Washington City. You know her son Sidney was killed in '63 fighting for the Union at Chattanooga. And his brother Algernon is a Union surgeon . . . like Beverly."

I squinted hard against the light, which seemed to be streaming into the room from all directions. Like a white miasma, it surrounded me. Even my soul squinted. My arm rose as if I were drowning in the undertow of a thousand unspoken years. Too late.

By this wench Sally, our President has had several children. There is not an individual in the neighborhood of Charlottesville who does not believe this story, and not a few who know it.

"And Thor knows?" My overtaxed heart accelerated.

"If he does," Charlotte said firmly, "I didn't tell him."

"Forgive me," I begged.

"There's nothing to forgive." She turned her head away then. "I understand the color line doesn't stop even at the grave. Still, I've waited for the grave to hear you tell me. All these years."

I cried out then. I had broken her heart with my secrecy and lies, my mistrust and cruelty. And mine broke in return. I had no safe harbor now, not even my children. I was a stranger to them.

Charlotte died shortly after that, her hand in mine, of an overdose of morphine. She begged me to help her, and I raided my own storeroom for the lethal dose.

I was as mute in life as she was in death. No sound of the human voice could express the pain I felt. My grief for Charlotte was as boundless, immense, and inconsolable as hunger, anguish, and the sea. My lack of trust in her solely because of her color haunted me, and stung me, because she died believing she had never understood me, and that was a lie.

I bathed Charlotte's body and draped the furniture in white silk, then filled the room with hothouse flowers. Even though their life insulted her death, I filled every vase with them and stood them on every surface I could find. Only then did I open the door for Andrew and her children.

I, Charlotte Waverly Nevell, white American matron, age sixty, wife of Andrew Nevell of Nevellville, mother of four children (none deceased), member of the Sanitary Commission Nursing Corps which served at Gettysburg, do swear I always knew Harriet's real name and never saw in her anything but what she was, and I loved her for what I saw. I detest Lorenzo Fitzgerald's idea that the accident of birth is irrevocable—an uncrossable frontier. No frontier for an American is uncrossable, including the so-called color line, and no person in the United States is an alien because of his color. I made Harriet's fears my fears, her loves my loves, her desires my desires, because I choose, of my own free will, to love Harriet as my own kind—womankind—humankind. I waited almost fifty years for Harriet to tell me her secret—to trust me and love me as much as I trusted and loved her. I know Harriet considered me unfit for revolutionary love. In her mind, I was too weak, too sheltered as a white woman to assume her identity. By protecting me, by sheltering me with her own body from a fact of life she considered too dangerous for me, she, too, practiced a kind of racism against my color. I should have been Thenia. I wished many times that I had been Thenia. You say perhaps it is I who should have taken the first step and told her what I knew, but what if I had lost her over this? What if the despicable and insignificant fact of my whiteness had been enough to drive her away, separate her from me forever, if she had known that I knew? What strange people we are . . . willing to live sequestered from a person who might be our heart's desire, because of a label, a taboo, a stigma, a fear we ourselves invented. Since I have wronged you, I can never like you. *What Harriet and I had together, no one can destroy. I refuse dying as I refused living, to segregate myself from her, from my better half, simply for the sake of my country. Love is stronger than race, passion is stronger than race, esteem is stronger than race, even Race is stronger than race. Nothing can do all for us that we expect race to do. Love songs are scarce and fall into two categories; the frivolous and light and the sad. Of deep successful love, there is only silence. My soul is rested. May God rest Harriet's. Amen.*

I died this day of December thirty-first, 1864, in the arms of Harriet Hemings

CHARLOTTE WAVERLY NEVELL

On the last day of January of the last year of the war, the House of
Representatives passed the Thirteenth Amendment, abolishing slavery by a
vote of 119 to 56.

"The rebellion is not over yet, although slavery is," reported Robert
Purvis, sitting in my office at the Wellington Drug Company, drinking
Wellington imported tea and holding little Roxanne on his knee. He was
accompanied by Jean Pierre Burr. I studied Mr. Burr, the natural son of
Aaron Burr and a Haitian freedwoman called Eugenia Bearharni. Jean Pierre
was a founder of the Moral Reform Society, a member of the Banneker
Institute, a conductor on the Underground Railroad, and the fair spitting
image of his famous father.

Purvis himself was now the son-in-law of a rich Philadelphia sailmaker,
James Felton, mulatto half brother of the famous abolitionists, the Grimké
sisters.

Not long ago, Purvis had confided in me that for the past twenty years
many natural children of mixed blood had been sent from the South, and in
a few cases their parents had followed and had been legally married here.
Descendants of such children, he said, in many instances forsook their
mother's race; one had become principal of a city school, one a prominent
sister in a Catholic church, one a bishop, and two, officers in the Confederate Army.

"There exists," said Robert, "a penal law, deeply written in the *minds* of
the whole white population; which subjects their colored fellow citizens to
unconditional, unwarranted, and never-ceasing insult. No respectability,
however unquestionable; no property, however large; no character, however
unblemished will gain a man whose body is cursed with even a thirty-second
portion of the blood of his African ancestry admission into their society.

"Why, Harriet? Why this ever-present obscene obsession with the color
of a human being's skin? Why this *irrational fear* of color? This unsubstan-
tiated horror of blackness? Is this repugnance learned or innate? Based on
philosophy, science, or morals? On the Bible and scriptures? On ancient
knowledge or ancient ignorance? Edmund Burke, in *On the Sublime and
Beautiful,* says that, though the effects of Black be painful originally, we must
not think they always continue so. Custom, he says, reconciles us to everything. After we have been used to seeing black objects, the terror abates, and
the smoothness, the beauty, or some agreeable accident of bodies so colored
softens the sterness of their original nature. Black has been with us from the
very beginning, but fanaticism against it has never abated one iota, never.
Burke ends by saying black will always have something melancholy about it,
but is this metaphysic or literary in our country? Why is it that the worst

thing that can happen to an American is to be born *not* white? Because it means to be thrust out of all identity and recognition, to become a negation of everything America has appropriated as her banner—purity, power, whiteness. And so everything she does—rape, exploit, commit violence and war —she transfers to those dark subjects she so abhors. Yet this war proves that we are the center, the very center, of her soul, her history, her dream, her nightmare, her fantasies, her past, and her future. This war, Harriet, is the very watershed of American identity, and black people, we domestic aliens, are its very incunabula—the black, black soul of the United States. I marvel at how you cannot see it. You white people with all your knowledge, logic, money, morals, and enlightenment cannot see it."

"I see it, Robert. Perhaps our very negation is a kind of recognition."

"And you want to hear something else funny?" he continued. "Robert E. Lee has asked Jefferson Davis to draft two hundred thousand Negroes into the Confederate Army! We, who are manifestly and confessedly the cause of the war, are now the hope of both Union and the Seceshes!"

The war finally came to an end with the surrender of Richmond. There, amid the confusion and consternation, the disorder, the panic, and the flames, only the colored population stood still, waiting, as Lincoln entered the conquered city escorted by units from the Twenty-fifth Corps and with ten Negro sailors as bodyguards, only forty hours after Jefferson Davis had evacuated his White House. Thor, on behalf of the Sanitary Commission, went with him. The tall, silk-hatted emancipator found himself surrounded by a cordon of black people shouting and crying, "Glory, Glory to God. Father Abraham. The day of Jubilee is arrived!" Overwhelmed, the President pleaded with his fellow citizens not to prostrate themselves: "Don't kneel to me," he said. "That is not right. One must only kneel to God and thank Him for the liberty you will hereafter enjoy." The air burned blue with the nine-hundred-gun salute the Union Army gave to celebrate its victory.

Thor had written for me to join him, and in Richmond, I felt an obsessive longing to see Monticello, even in smoldering ruins. Perhaps I could find my brother Thomas. Perhaps I wanted to crow over my prostrate white family huddled together at Edgehill. I felt as an old war veteran might feel—I wanted to go home even if it wasn't there anymore. I wanted to end my incessant war with myself and my life. Peace was something I could achieve only by going back to the beginning, even if it meant deceiving Thor once more.

With the excuse of joining Thenia, I left Thor with the President and set out on the road to Monticello on the fourteenth of April, Good Friday, five days after the Confederacy surrendered at Appomattox Courthouse the day after my father's birthday. My buckboard and driver fought the clogged roads leading out of Richmond, which were filled with refugees, black and white, all desperately searching for someone or something lost. Until at last, I stood arm-in-arm with Thenia at the top of the knoll on which stood the log cabin of my mother. I had been compelled by all I lived for to return to Albemarle County and the past, a displaced southerner, a domestic alien, a white Negro come home, the fourteenth of April 1865.

38

For if a slave can have a country in this world, it must be any other in preference to that in which he is born to live and labor for another: lock up the faculties of his nature . . . contribute to the evanishment of the human race. . . .

Thomas Jefferson

April fourteenth, 1865. Everybody remembered where they were that Good Friday, for the rest of their lives.

I had traveled up from Fort Monroe, where I was still teaching contrabands to read, to join Harriet at Monticello. Standing beside her, I stared at the empty, decaying gray facade. Burwell's paint had peeled off, Joe Fossett's iron balconies were rusted and crumbling. John Hemings's shingles were warped or missing. It no longer belonged to Thomas Jefferson or any of his heirs. I couldn't believe that I, Thenia Boss, a free woman, was standing before the crumbling, decaying ruins of my former prison, Monticello. Evil rose around it like a miasma. My entrails cramped and the old forgotten terror of the sale drew over me, as if all this time it had lain dormant in my soul without ever diminishing in size or sound or grief.

I was thirteen, skinny, bandy-legged, spidery-eyed, and up till then not yet a woman, having budding breasts and narrow hips and a high behind. I can see that red block now. My cousin Doll, daughter of Critta Hemings, was a pretty girl, really good looking. Her father was Peter Carr. The day they sold her, they stripped her to be bid off and looked over. She cried bitterly. Howled, really. A sound I'll never forget as she tried in vain to cover herself. People complained about how the slave prices had fallen. Well, she fetched a huge amount of money and was sold to a man from New Orleans.

Our family was all kind of huddled up together in a corner of the yard away from the rest. Old Whispering Joe Taylor, the trader, came along. He was the crier. He was huge and seemed even bigger to someone so small. They said you could hear him knock down a slave five miles away. He was carrying a bullwhip and a pepperbox pistol and he was with another man. He made my sister stand up, and said to the man, "Here's just the girl you want." Mama begged Mr. Taylor not to separate us folks, and hugged Mary and Jane and me to her. The traders and the man talked for a while and then came back and pulled Mary away from Mama and he and the man took her off. Mama started screaming, and just then they knocked my daddy down and dragged him off to another corner of the yard.

Man, man—folks that didn't go through slavery ain't got no idea what it was. There must have been a hundred colored folks in that yard, and the dust and smell of fear was terrible, terrible. It's like it happened yesterday—husbands sold away from wives, children from mothers. A trader didn't think no more of pulling a baby away from its mother than taking a calf away from a cow. A stockyard. The same smell of blood in the air. They came and got my other sister, then my mother. When she was taken away, I clung to her and got dragged a few feet before I got kicked. It was like a shellburst in my head; a terrible pain ripped through my groin, with her screams still in my ears. I remember suddenly feeling the trickle of blood—my menses, though I didn't know what it was. One of my aunts, the last to be sold, hiked up my dress into a ball between my legs and tied her shawl around my hips. She wiped away the blood on my legs, but why had she bothered to wipe away the blood? Why must this particular wound be hidden or held more shameful? It had come, after all, from the entrails of my soul, which had just been murdered. They took my aunt away and then my little brother. Then Whispering Joe came back for me.

"Get your bundle together," he said, then looked at me queerly. "No one told me this heifer was pregnant," he said. "I advertised her for a virgin."

He pulled my dress down around my waist and sold me.

That's why I stutter like a lamb. For a while I couldn't talk at all. Even when I was safe with Harriet.

Harriet's imposture never really bothered me, in point of man's law or God's law, but I never envied her, either. As a practical matter, it gave me many sleepless nights. I loved Mrs. Wellington, but I found her reckless and selfish. I admired her as an Underground Railroad conductor, as a wife, as a mother, as a musician, but her obsession with her master, whom she insisted upon calling Father, and the way she treated her mother stuck in my craw.

I could never have left my mother the way she left hers. And Harriet was so lonely—she was truly an orphan. Imagine being free and white and having brothers one hadn't seen or heard from in twenty years!

Harriet was smart, too. And hard and ambitious and dangerous. At Gettysburg she killed a man. Emily told me. I'll never forget that. Without blinking an eye. She said, "Huh. She didn't tell you about that, did she?" Well, nobody can go around armed for fifty years without once using a deadly weapon, can they? He was a Reb deserter about to rob and slaughter a wounded and helpless Union soldier boy, out of fury or vengence or blood thirst or just plain craziness, who knows. Harriet sent him to hell. And she could have, I do believe, done it in cold blood instead of the heat of battle. In a way, I guess she killed the Reb that killed James, and in another she killed the Rebel in herself that was her father and the Old South. She had one of those old-time constitutions nothing could destroy, like him. Nothing was going to kill Harriet Wellington. Not even a bath in acid.

Which brings me to Abe. I loved the soul out of that man. Whatever I am today, I owe to him or Harriet. If Harriet taught me nerve, he taught me pride. We had a good sex life, too. Times we would lie in bed all day making love. Times I would lie beside him and just watch him sleep—trace the contours of his body with my fingertips, kiss him all over, suck the little soft folds behind his ears or the tendons in back of his knees. He knew how to please a woman, too. Oh, Abe, resting under your grassy knoll so far away. Twenty years now. I never ever really wanted another husband. Abe gave me Raphael and Willy, and Raphael has given me Aaron. I can't complain.

I've always been grateful to Harriet for what she did for me. Like Harriet Tubman, she crossed the line and went back down south to save one of her kin. She gave me what she could of a new life, or what she could spare of her double one.

I gave my services willingly for two years and four months to the United States government without receiving a dollar. I taught the First South Carolina Volunteers, the first regiment of ex-slaves to read and write. And when I got a chance to work for Mr. Pinkerton and the government as a Union spy behind Confederate lines, well, I did that, too. It was General Folksin at the fort who recruited me. He said the government needed black spies who were literate and who could pass as slaves. He warned me that capture meant instant death. I made three forays into General Johnson's camp. I posed, of course, as a laundress. My favorite profession. I worked for General Bragg and, in my shirts and underwear, smuggled coded messages from Union spies who had infiltrated the army. I learned to handle a gun. I shot straight. I could take a gun apart, clean it, and put it together again and reload it in eighteen minutes. I could also read handwriting upside down. And God knows blackness is the best disguise the Almighty ever invented, and not just at night. Even my Union informant never learned to recognize me. Had to tell the bugger every time who I was. Why, another black woman, working for the Confederacy, could have walked in and taken my place without his ever knowing it. I was proud anyway and called myself the black Rose Greensboro.

I never told Harriet about my activities. During the war, I wasn't allowed to, and afterward we didn't see each other for a long time. Anyway, spying is very personal. Something that belongs only to yourself. Of course there was that one thing she never told *me* about her war, either.

Only the auction haunts me. Harriet had sworn to God to curse the day she was born standing on her father's grave if God took another son. Well, God took Beverly. The army surrenders at Appomattox and quick as a flash she's in Albermarle County. No baggage, no notice. Alone.

I was there, looking for my family. My grandson Aaron and I left Fort Monroe and took the road from there to here: the road everybody who was looking for somebody took, William Tecumseh Sherman's army's road.

So there, always by chance or destiny or whatever you choose to call it, I met Harriet. It was as if a silent call had gone out from her to me to gather. The roads were clogged with refugees looking for ex-slaves, and ex-slaves looking for other refugees.

Harriet and I decided to return to the cemetery of Monticello together. We found Betty Hemings's grave. We never did find Sally Hemings's grave. It must have been an uneasy grave, for when we got to the slave cemetery, we found no tomb, no headstone, nothing.

Sally Hemings's cabin was still standing, a lopsided lean-to near the south boundary. As Harriet and I approached, we saw that it was inhabited. Smoke was coming from the chimney. We drew closer, making our way on foot up the slope to the porch steps, and a woman holding a child took fright and ran inside. We followed her and stood smack in the middle of Sally Hemings's poor, mean, ramshackled house. The cabin was made of square-hewn logs, chinked with small rocks and daubed with white clay, then covered with cypress clapboards.

The walls were bare, and the roof had been repaired with old newspapers. There were several children inside, sitting on two benches hewn out of logs padded with gray moss and corn husks. There were three or four rolled-up pallets in one corner, and beyond the front room I could see a bedroom with a four-poster bed and a cradle. There was a table behind which the woman was standing for protection. They were squatters, a family who had moved in during the war.

"This is my mother's house," said Harriet stupidly, not addressing the woman but advancing toward her. The woman backed away, clutching the baby. Another, older woman entered the room from the back.

"Aw, mist'ess," she said. "Please don't evict us from here. We've been here for almost two years wait'en for the white people to show up or something. We can pay you all rent, mist'ess. You the old master's daughter?"

"I'm not going to evict you, and I'm not your mistress," said Harriet. "It's just that this . . . this was my mother's house and I've never seen it."

They looked at each other, then at me uncomprehendingly. The older woman fell to her knees and pleaded, "Aw God, have mercy, mist'ess. We got sick children in the back there. We can't move 'em. They can't sleep in the fields."

"Get up off your knees," screamed Harriet. "Get up. Get up. You don't have to kneel to me anymore."

But one had grabbed the Confederate money from the mantelpiece. It was mixed with the Union scrip that the government issued to ex-slaves.

"You don't understand," Harriet began, realizing that the woman had taken her to be what she appeared to be, by dress and manner. Suddenly there was a scraping on the roof. A kind of *tap, tap,* and then a hoarse screech like a trapped cat.

"*Maman?*" Harriet cried, cocking her head to one side. My hands flew to my breast. The two women fled the house. One squeezed by me to rescue the baby in the back room; the other hightailed it with the one she had in her arms.

"*Maman,* is that you?" said Harriet cooly. My eyes popped with fright. The more courageous of the two women sneaked back to the doorway minus the baby.

"Sally Hemings, is that you?" insisted Harriet. "It's me, Harriet. Harriet! I'm me, *Maman.* Harriet. I'm Harriet. Me. Harriet. Harriet. See?" She held up her palms to the ceiling.

"I'm me," Harriet screamed to the south. "I'm me, Harriet Hemings of Monticello," she shrieked to the east. And to the west she bellowed, "*Est-ce que tu viens?* I'm never coming back here for you again."

Her hair was undone; her green eyes blazed; her voice was an animal growl.

"I'm me, Harriet Hemings of Monticello. I'm me!"

"Oh, Lord, that white lady crazy as a loon," I heard a voice behind me say. To which another voice answered, "That ain't no white lady, Ethel. You don't have to *be* black to be black."

Harriet Hemings of Monticello bellowed as if she had been given the voice of a bullfrog. Her cheeks swelled up and turned as scarlet as Philadelphia brick. The noise on the roof increased, rattling the shingles like a hurricane. Even the floor moved. Then everything was still.

"I'm not coming back here for you again, *Maman*," she whispered, and slowly Harriet turned and with a kind of wave, a kind of small, royal movement of her blank and naked fingertips, she took leave of everything.

"My family is from Philadelphia, you know," she sighed into the uncomprehending faces before her.

That was the last time I saw Harriet Wellington alive. That was the day they assassinated Abraham Lincoln.

I, Thenia Hemings Boss of Monticello, colored female, age fifty-two, daughter of Ursula and granddaughter of Mary Elizabeth Hemings, born the third of June 1813, midwife and apothecary, did on the night of the fourteenth of April 1865 start out again for South Carolina with my grandson Aaron Boss. I followed the path carved out by the victorious Union Army marching to war under Sherman. Hordes of slave refugees clogged the roads, all searching for lost loved ones. Lord God, it seemed like everyone was on the road and nobody had found anyone they loved. It seemed as if the entire race were in motion and in search of that one thing that would make it whole again. But that was never to be. On the twenty-second of August 1865, I found my mother and sister on the Mount Crawford road, just outside of Waynesboro, North Carolina. It did not seem to me as if I were living in the same country in which I was born.

THENIA HEMINGS BOSS

39

I am persuaded; were she to lose you, it would cost her oceans of blood, and years of confusion and anarchy.

Thomas Jefferson

I fled my mother's ghost and ran to the white cemetery and my father's grave. From where I knelt, the naked, windswept, ruined facade of Monticello rose up in the distance through the haze like his shoulder blades: pink, emaciated, inflamed with death's agonies. The President who had enslaved me and the President who had freed me were both history now. The country that had always despised me, be it North or South, had just shorn itself of its double life and was to be "reconstructed." Why not I?

It seemed to me that the world, as on the night of the military ball, was once again divided into dark halves and light halves. The dead President's eyes, melancholy Dalmatian eyes, liquid, long, and narrow; Mongol eyes, Negro eyes that had alighted on mine only once and only for a split second, looked out at me from my father's obelisk. Perhaps it hadn't been my mother's ghost I had run away from, but my father's. For had I not come here to this grave *not* as a daughter but as part of the occupying army? Hadn't I sworn that night that if God took another grandson, I would come back and haunt this grave? Well, God took Beverly and so I'm back, Father. Grandma had a name for it; she called it *sow the wind and reap the whirlwind*. But I hear the music as a dog hears, as all underdogs hear, only the inaudible high notes. I hear wolves crying, their curses melding in the air. Yes, this is my return. There can be a homecoming without a home.

"Father," I whispered, "I have built my life on the edge of an abyss, always confronting a dangerous world in which my identity challenged yours in terrible solitary combat. Now all I want is peace. Peace. Peace. Peace. Come. Come, Papa, let me hold your head in my lap, my arms across your chest, your brow on my breast as I rock you, the vanquished. Peter has made you coffee as in the old days, with molasses, hot and sweet the way you liked. Close your eyes, beloved; let's say our prayers and reminisce about the years we spent together yet apart, equal but separate. You and I merged only in our love for Monticello, its dense forests, blooded horses, and music. We intercoursed only in our ambitious authorship of our own lives. You've lived yours rich and powerful, full of daring and truth. I've invented mine, by the fiction created by myself, which has grown into self-deception and become an abyss. I've been imitation slave and imitation master. I've married twins and borne twins and have lost double sons to death to defeat you. I've borne in silence all my secret doublage: double identity, double indemnity, double allegiances, double color. It was you, Father, *your* fiction that made impostors and confidence men of us all—Eston and Beverly, who doubled for white; Adrian Petit, who doubled for fictitious aristocracy; Thomas, who doubled as Woodston, then tripled as a Union spy, then quadrupled as a loyal white Confederate; Thenia, who doubled as my slave; Mama, who doubled as your wife; Thor, who doubled as Thance; sisters who doubled as wives; wives as slaves; slaves as mistresses; daughters as aunts; sisters-in-law as lovers; sons as lackeys. Lincoln, as the Great Emancipator, planned to deport his Negro citizens; you, as the great democrat, subsisted on the wages of slavery; Sally Hemings, as the great slave captive, sold herself for love, and Uncle James, the watchdog, played the role of a helpless mackerel. Oh, Papa, your great and dying world spawned magnificent impersonators! WHITE PEOPLE

"All *I* ever wanted to be was the best dancer and the best ballet master. And to dance to please myself. I used to sit on the back porch of the mansion and listen to the shrieking laughter on Mulberry Row and not recognize it as despair. I sat there longing for what I thought were permanent things: dignity and respect, marriage, loyalty, a bedroom where only duty lay, because I didn't want to be a slave to love. But when I grew up to be a woman, I found respect doubled by hypocrisy, marriage by death, loyalty by geography, safety by skin color, love by twin passions. Oh. All my cannibal hearts, each doubling back on the other, gobbling up space. Life itself has been doubled by oblivion.

"Imagine, it's the day after your birthday and both my Presidents—you who gave me life and the other who gave me freedom—are dead. Imagine. You know, I've ordered my own tombstone? But what to write on it? HERE LIES TOM JEFFERSON'S MISSING LINK, WHO DIDN'T HAVE ANY FINGERPRINTS? I see my white grandfather's face and hear my grandmother's voice. One says,

'No sale, Captain Hemings, I want to see how amalgamation comes out!' The other says, 'Push down, my heart won't stop beating, and don't forget to get that freedom for your children.' I am as tired of your father-in-law's whining as I am of my grandmother's groans.

"I have survived the horror of offering my flesh and blood to war. I have been rich and poor, slave and free, black and white, daughter and orphan, a white Virginian and black fugitive; a pillar of white Philadelphia society and a no-name bastard, guilty of miscegenation, fraud, counterfeiting, and imposture. What mask have I not worn? When would a hand lift that mask and expose me for what I was?

"But from now to the azimuth, I surrender and lay down my sword, a weeping child, a new American woman."

I, Harriet Hemings, white female American, black female American, age sixty-four, born at Monticello the year my father began his first term as President, mother of seven white children (two deceased), hid in the North as a fugitive slave by passing for white for forty-three years until my unknowing sons, husband, and President emancipated me. I, Harriet Wellington, who could not exist without committing fraud, a Virginia aristocrat by birth who is also a bastard who despised her father and abandoned her mother, who found salvation for her crime as an abolitionist, widow of my husband's brother, musician, a walking, limping panoply of contradictions, did on the day Lincoln died leave my beloved Thenia in the middle of the road to South Carolina and pass once again into the oblivion which I had built myself with nary a tremor in my soul. And it seemed to me I was not living in the same country into which I was born.

HARRIET HEMINGS

40

I think, with you, that life is a fair matter of account and the balance often, nay, generally, is in its favor. It is to apply a common measure, or to fix the par between pleasure and pain, yet it exists, and is measurable.

Thomas Jefferson

Eighteen sixty-nine. Eston Hemings Jefferson here. Chicago millionaire who has thrice crossed and recrossed the color line, changing like a chameleon, negating the fact and fiction of his race with one blink of his baby blue eyes. I should use the initials of my pedigree behind my name: Eston Hemings Jefferson, F.F.V., P.F.W. (First Families of Virginia, Passed for White). I was born on the twenty-first of May 1808, while my father was President of the United States. Like Harriet Wellington, I made a fortune during the war.

I'm sixty-one now; I was seventeen when I was freed by my F.F.V. bastard of a father, and then only in his will. But before I exercised my freedom, which I postponed because of my mother's refusal to leave Virginia, I helped a lot of others get theirs. Perhaps as many as ten or twelve score.

Because of my color I often posed as a white man transporting or escorting his own slaves. All this came after I was a grown man—grown enough to know a pretty girl when I saw one and go chasing after her, too. I hid what I was doing from my mother, not because of any distrust but because it was dangerous work. It was funny the way it got started, too. I didn't have any idea of getting mixed up in the Underground Railroad until one special night. I had gone to another plantation courting, and the housekeeper there told me she had a really pretty girl who wanted to escape over the state line and asked if I would take her. I was about to refuse when I saw the girl. She was as beautiful as Harriet, and it wasn't long before I was listening to the old woman, who was telling me when to take her and where to leave her. For days back home the image of that scared girl with eyes like Harriet, pleading with me to row her across the Potomac, haunted me. And so I did it. I don't know how I ever rowed that boat across the river. The current was so strong, I was shaking. I couldn't see a thing, there in the dark, but I felt that girl's eyes. Finally, I saw a faint light and rowed toward it. When I got there, two men reached down and grabbed the girl. They looked me up and down, astonished at my appearance, but they said only, "We'll take her to Ohio. Thanks."

It was that word of thanks, I suppose, that changed me. It was the first time anyone had ever thanked me for doing anything. I soon found myself rowing boats, driving buckboards, riding saddle, sometimes with one, sometimes with a whole gang of fugitives. I used to take three or four trips a season. Madison found out and joined me.

I didn't hear from Harriet after she strolled until practically the day Father died, in 1826. Thomas Jefferson died of all kinds of complications: a fall from his horse, Old Eagle, a pleurisy attack, heart disease, and just plain old age, but the straw that really broke the camel's back was money. I'd never known my father not strapped for money. He had outspent his official salaries in every appointment he had held from ambassador in Paris to President of the United States. He left debts of $107,000, which the Hemingses—dark, mulatto, and white—repaid with their bodies at public auction. As a businessman who pays his debts and balances his expenditures, I have always found this reprehensible and unforgivable.

When old General Lafayette visited Monticello, in 1824, showered with gifts from the government of the United States, well, Thomas Jefferson just right threw himself a tantrum, smashing a chair, going on about all his "services" to the nation that had not bestowed one gesture of thanks or recognition on him. The United States had not given him one cent in land or cash that would have kept him out of the poorhouse. I suppose you could say he died cursing the country he'd invented.

After I had been transporting slaves for almost four years, my mother died. I carried about twelve to safety on that same night. As soon as she was buried, Madison and I left for the West, and took another dozen with us, posing as our own slaves as far as the Mason-Dixon line. That was the year 1836. We passed through Philadelphia with Mary and Sarah to announce our mother's death to Harriet.

I left Monticello a white man according to the 1836 census, but arrived in

Chillicothe, Ohio, a black one. I searched high and low for that girl whose name I didn't know, who was as beautiful as Harriet. I finally found her. Her name was Julia Anne. I married her.

We had three children: John Wayles, Beverly, and Anne. We moved to Madison, Wisconsin, in 1850, where I changed my race to white and added Jefferson to my name. There I founded the Continental Cotton Company, which made me a rich man. Later we bought the Standard Screw Company of Chicago, which made us even richer. Then, at the outbreak of the war in 1861, I changed my race back to black in order to fight as a Negro. When I realized they were not going to allow blacks to bear arms, even in the North, I passed for white in order to fight. So did my sons. I lost one son, Beverly; my eldest, John Wayles, was a lieutenant in the Second Ohio and was wounded at Vicksburg, but he left the army a lieutenant colonel.

Our eldest brother, Thomas, who had left Monticello for Richmond in his teens, changed his name to Woodson, left Albemarle County when we did, and settled in Jackson County, Ohio. He too got rich in the forties, by discovering coal on his land, and he used the money to found his own town, an all-black community he called Woodson, Ohio. He published an abolitionist newspaper called the *Palladium of Liberty*. His lone son, Lewis Frederick, who never married, moved on to Pittsburgh where he wrote antislavery editorials for *The Colored American* under the pseudonym Augustine. Since the tumult of the war, I have lost track of him and don't know if he is living or dead.

We were an angry set of children, strangers and enemies to our father, stomping all over the color line, back and forth, from Richmond to Chicago to San Francisco. What a ragtag, mongrel presidential family we were: an invisible mother, an unnameable father, decimated by a war we fought over ourselves. Thomas, the utopian colonist, dreaming of a Negro homeland in Woodson, Ohio, or Liberia or some mythical and still-to-be-invented country in South America. Beverly, the white soldier of fortune, who went from striking gold in California to dreaming of his son-in-law as President. Madison, the quiet farmer filled with rectitude and self-righteousness, who has put the fear of God into us all for passing for white. Me, the white capitalist from Chicago with his faith in the American Dream. And finally, Harriet, the great "Duchess of Anamacora," believer in romantic love and race oblivion, who, having achieved one, is now terrified of the other.

Blackness. What is the reward or the justification for this unarmed challenge which brings one nothing but grief? I have voted the fifteen-sixteenths of me a white majority over the one-sixteenth of me that makes me in fact and fiction something the republic invented. The republic couldn't really think that blackness was as potent as all that. The republic simply wanted to place me beyond the pale of my father's own Constitution, to make me invisible to maintain the romance of racial purity in the face of so much argument to the contrary, to deny me the inestimable advantages of being a white American.

This was true of my own children as well, I thought. Did I really love my children less for having no idea of whom they really were? Or did I merely love Julia more for knowing and having shared the danger? I wondered if it was the same for Harriet. Had she loved her twin husbands less or more for their not knowing? Had she felt that same strange combination of contempt and compassion I still felt at times for WHITE PEOPLE?

I often wondered: were we imitation Negroes or imitation whites or bad imitations of both? I suppose we were imitation whites, because as imitation Negroes, we didn't amount to anything.

I stood by and watched all kinds of atrocities against us every day: lynchings and beatings, segregation and discrimination, burning crosses, the Ku Klux Klan. And like a ghost, the thought occurred to me that if my brother Madison were there, he would be a victim, which struck me differently, somehow, from the thought that if I were there, and if I were not white, I would be the victim.

Perhaps, I thought, this was why I reserved my most passionate affection for my grandchildren, who were one generation removed. Did she feel this way about her own children? Would any of them ever be capable of imagining the malignant labyrinth of fear and lies and contradictions, the immeasurable cruelty and suffering that made up the slave dynasty to which we were heirs?

What we shared with one another, but would never share with our children and grandchildren, was not the insult or the suffering, but the badge of insult and suffering. And the badge without the suffering was simply skin, hair, and bone.

The truth was that there was nothing in the world that could do all that we asked race to do for us.

I, Eston Hemings Jefferson, white American male, age sixty-one, born in Virginia, married with three children (one deceased), president of the Jefferson Continental Cotton & Standard Screw Co., assets of one million dollars, did crisscross the color line several times whenever it seemed to my advantage, finally settling permanently on the white side from which I achieved all the benefits and accruements of white citizenship in the United States of America: freedom from fear, oppression, humiliation, dehumanization, and the life-threatening hatred my fellow Americans heap on their nonwhite compatriots. I did this of my own free will, ready to pay the price of oblivion, of loneliness, of fraud, of fear, but also of safety, of esteem, of rewards for my efforts, the corollary being fame and fortune as a white man: a purebred example of the American Dream.

ESTON HEMINGS JEFFERSON

41

Their eyes are forever turned back to the object they have lost, and its recollection poisons the residue of their lives.

Thomas Jefferson

In 1873, a white man came down my road as if God had ordained it and as if he owned the road. That was how white men arrived in Pee Wee, even now, eight years after the war. Hadn't the Albemarle County census taker arrived at Mama's door in 1836 in just the same way, turning her white for posterity to erase my father's crime of miscegenation? Well, reader, it turned out there was another census taker in my life, the Pike County census taker of 1873 this time, and I don't know why I did it, but I told him who I was, Madison Hemings of Monticello, son of the President. I could have gotten myself lynched or torched out over that—damned near thirty lynchings this year alone in Ohio. But I just had to do it. For me it was the coda to the whole God-damned war. I told the census taker in order to give myself a father after sixty-eight years. To set the record straight. It was my own private individual emancipation, my proclamation of identity, and he believed me, just as the earlier census taker had believed Mama. "This man is the natural son of Thomas Jefferson," he wrote beside my name without the flicker of an eyelash. The census taker must have been as shaken by those words as I, but, good functionary that he was, he had obediently written them down. But not without staring in amazement (or amusement) at me. There was a strong family resemblance: pale lashes, sandy hair, light gray eyes, the forehead and chin of my father. However, since I was a taxpayer and a property owner, it was not for him to contradict the man who paid his salary.

I slid sideways from my bay, Double Eagle, to pluck a wild eucalyptus plant growing by the side of the road. I put it in a small linen bag at my waist. It was the best remedy for my cough. I straightened and pulled my hat farther down on my head. I had been riding the parameters of my sixty-six acres since early this morning. The heat shimmered up from the scalp of my fields. It had rained during the night, and the stalks were matted with dew. I breathed in the aroma of the wet wheat warming to the sun, drawing out pulsations of perfume the color of amber which warmed my sick lungs and reminded me of my mother's eyes.

What I liked most was to contemplate my farmhouse from afar. Some houses have expressions, just like people, and mine was like that. It sat in solitary splendor on a flat, stark prairie, like a man on a camel in the desert. The steep gabled roof sat upon the white clapboard walls like a shelter tent, and the white steps of the veranda grinned from the deep shade. Over the door hung a pair of buffalo horns like a waxed mustache, and the second-floor windows gleamed in the light like rectangular spectacles. It was not a friendly-looking house despite the two magnificent juniper trees that flanked it like General Burnside's sidewhiskers. A flagpole stood close to the rear of the house, and the American flag fluttered upon it, lifting lazily with the movement of the tall grass. I had raised the colors every morning since the death of William Beverly Hemings, thirteen years ago. And if an eye could weep, would it believe in such a poor flag as an empty sleeve?

The house stood about three hundred yards back from the road leading into the town of Pee Wee. In this eighth year of Reconstruction there were always people on the road—farmers with their produce, Chinese railroad laborers, journeymen with the tools of their trade slung over their backs, immigrant laborers, fresh off ships which had deposited them at the mouth of the Ohio. But more than any of these, there were the black domestic immigrants, born in the United States yet displaced in their own country and constantly on the move in search of the forty acres and a mule they had been promised.

Many a one I have hired for a day or a year. I always favored the war veterans, the handicapped, and the very young. How many times have I stared at or stared away from the braille of an ancient scar: shell, saber, bayonet, bullet, gunpowder, dynamite, buckshot, mortar, cannon, Bowie knife, hatchet, tomahawk, or whip. A new race of American men, perhaps the first truly American men baptized in the cauldron of the Civil War, had streamed across the western plains for the past decade like one thick ribbon of scar tissue. Then there were the wounds that were invisible: shell shock, amnesia, malnutrition, insanity, depression. Some men couldn't stay put. Had to keep roaming. Some scars were shorn of all meaning. They came hooked up to the strangest faces: docile or rebellious. The only common denominator amongst them was that they belonged to colored people, people of color, black folks, Negroes, niggers, coons, darkies, contrabands, freedmen, ex-slaves, gorillas, jigaboos, African tarbabies. I hired one Georgia boy like that who stayed for almost six months. Ted didn't have much to say to anyone, and when asked about his scars, he'd say they belonged to another life. Well, that was true because there was a before-the-war and an after-the-war for everybody. It just wasn't the same country we were born in. You might say we were a nation of double lives. Just like Harriet.

It was a bitter irony that the country had been reconstructed, but that perpetual darkness had settled over us. Reconstruction, first a hope, had become a hope betrayed. A decade after we had captured Jacksonville and had led the way through the charred streets of Charleston and Richmond, the Union Army providentially becoming an army of liberation, we were once again crushed, terrorized, disenfranchised, and practically re-enslaved. The ex-slaves had settled back almost to their antebellum situation, and our dreams of forty acres and a mule, promised at the end of the war by the Freedman's Bureau, had been stamped into a bitter disillusion by new and terrifying oppression in the Old South. Southern whites resisted our enfranchisement, despite their own state constitutions and the Fourteenth Amendment. New Black Codes to regulate Negroes had risen along with vigilante groups like the Ku Klux Klan. The South had been reduced once more to military rule, and the Freedman's Bureau had become one of the most efficient and corrupt political machines ever known. The Knights of the White Camelia rode riot in sixteen states, burning, torturing, and lynching. America was the only civilized nation in the world that still burned men alive for a crime or an alleged crime.

My cousin Thenia Hemings Boss and her grandson Aaron got caught in that spiral of violence. They were attacked by the Knights of the White Camelia, Thenia for teaching ex-slaves to read, Aaron for registering them to vote in Waynesboro, North Carolina. It happened in 1870. Thenia perished in the flames, a shotgun in her hand. Aaron was pulled out of the house and then lynched. As I said, America is the only civilized country that still burns men at the stake.

I guess you want to know about the war. The old war, not this new one. I fought as a black man while Eston, it seems, changed his race to white to fight. Well, I wouldn't go through all that. I waited. And sure enough, when things got bad enough and dangerous enough, they conceded to the black fighting man. I joined the colored division attached to the Army of the James under General Butler. So did my sons, James Madison, Thomas

Eston, and William Beverly. I was a little long in the tooth, but nobody could prove my age, and I fought in the battle of New Market Heights in the campaign of 1864.

That's not where I got this empty sleeve. I got that in the Crater in '64, trying to save William Beverly. Anyway, on Palm Sunday in '65, when Lee surrendered at Appomattox and the "rebel yell" was heard for the last time and black Union soldiers fired their guns into the ground, the only real American present was General Grant's military secretary, a Seneca Indian. When General Lee remarked that he was glad to see one native American there, Sergeant Parker (that was his name) said, "We are all Americans." Ain't that the truth, as I see it. Grant let the Rebs go home, not to be disturbed by U.S. authority so long as they observed their paroles and pledged allegiance to the United States. The fact that the Secesh soldiers would not be prosecuted for treason didn't bother us none. Artillery- and cavalrymen with horses were allowed to keep them to start planting, which was what we all did next. Six hundred and twenty thousand soldiers were dead for those goddamn stars on that goddamn flag, one death for every four slaves freed.

I imagined a commanding statue dedicated to those men, made of Maryland granite, surmounted by an enlisted soldier in a greatcoat, equipment, fixed bayonet, gun at parade rest, looking toward the Capitol. Beside him would be an artilleryman in full dress uniform standing by a field piece; a cavalryman in full dress with spurs and gloves and a saber unhooked at his side; a sailor in uniform standing by an anchor or mortar. The sides of the monument would be inscribed. On the first side: "A grateful nation consecrates this monument to the 37,300 Negro soldiers who died in the service of their country." On the second side: "They earned the right to be free by deeds of desperate valor; and in the 449 engagements in which they participated, they proved themselves worthy to be entrusted with a nation's flag and honor." On the third side: "During the American Civil War, from 1861 to 1865, there were 178,985 black soldiers enrolled in the United States Voluntary Army. Of this number, 99,337 were enlisted by the authority of the government, and 79,648 were enlisted by the several states and territories. Of these 37,300 lost their lives while serving. They fought in 449 battles, of which thirty-nine were major battles. Therefore, on the fourth side, I would name the most famous battles in which black soldiers fought: Port Hudson, Fort Wagner, Homey Hill, New Market Heights, Poison Shrimp, Deep Bottom, Fort Pillow, Milliken's Bend, Olustee, Fair Oaks, Petersburg, Nashville, Fort Fisher, Fort Blakely, The Crater, Hatcher's Run.

I returned home safe and alive to my Mary McCoy. But she was the one who left—God rest her soul. Her soul had been how I like my coffee: bitter and hot.

When we left Virginia in 1836, we brought our three-year-old daughter, Sarah, with us, leaving the dust of a son in the soil near Monticello. We've had born to us here, in this state where I homesteaded, nine children. Three are dead. The names of the living are Sarah, Harriet, Mary Ann, Catherine, Jane, Thomas Eston, and Ellen Wayles. The dead are James Madison, William Beverly, and Julia. William and Ellen are unmarried and live at home. All the others are married and raising families. My sons all fought in the war: James Madison and Thomas Eston with me, under Butler. William Beverly died outside Petersburg in the famous Crater I couldn't save him from.

Well, it happened in August 1864 at Petersburg. Imagine a regiment of Pennsylvania coal miners who had the idea to build a mine shaft under the enemy lines almost five hundred feet long. General Burnside liked the idea and wouldn't let go of it. He convinced General Grant to agree. They built the tunnel, mined it, and General Grant ordered Burnside to send in a fresh division to lead the assault. The only fresh division was a black division. Our morale was high. We wanted to show the white boys what we could do. Only hours before the operation, General Meade remanded the order and told Burnside to send in a *white* division first. The explosion blew a hole as big as a warship, some one hundred and seventy feet long, sixty feet wide, and thirty feet deep, burying an entire Secesh regiment and an artillery battery under the rubble. The white soldiers, tired, scared, and disorderly, began their assault, led by a drunken commander. But instead of attacking the redoubt, they stopped to gawk at the awesome spectacle of the crater, which looked mighty like hell itself. Then they started climbing down into the crater by the hundreds, milling around down there while the Rebs regrouped and started shooting at them like sitting ducks. The men tried to take cover, but they couldn't climb up out of the hole. The walls were too steep: Crying, screaming, and clawing, they fell like maggots. The black division finally fought their way through the panic-stricken, retreating mob of soldiers and caught the brunt of the Confederate attack. The Seceshes were enraged to see black men in United States uniforms and even those who tried to surrender were executed in cold blood. The greatest dynamite explosion of the war and all we—the Ninth Corps—had to show for it was four thousand dead men. Yep. Four thousand. A lot of black boys. General Grant himself pronounced the epitaph: "The saddest affair I have witnessed in the war." That was my opinion too.

After the war, my son Thomas Eston moved to Colorado and passed for white. His daughter, Ellen Wayles, my granddaughter, married a black man, a graduate of Oberlin College, and now they live in California. Ellen Wayles's husband was the first man of color to be elected to the California State Assembly. What my granddaughter doesn't know is that one of the *white* senators who serves in the State Assembly along with her husband is none other than her cousin Thomas Wayles, Beverly's son, who doesn't even know he's black. His wife is white and he has no reason to believe he is otherwise. It seems that Thomas Wayles is his grandfather's child: brilliant, temperamental, ambiguous, ambitious, and self-centered. Beverly made a fortune during the Gold Rush of 1848. "Nothing," he claimed, "purified the blood like gold," and it also financed his son-in-law's electoral campaign.

One talks about blood—bad blood, tainted blood, the blood of our fathers —but this magical substance waters more than flesh; it waters spirit and mind as well. I lifted myself out of orphanhood because I could. But I did it for Harriet as well, since she felt her bastardy the deepest and the hardest. If she is still alive, perhaps she has reconciled herself to her fatherless state, but I doubt it. God knows, last time I saw her she was happy and ignorant in the same way white people are happy and ignorant. I marveled at that. How had she managed to feel white?

I looked down at my grandson Frederick, who had caught hold of Double Eagle's reins. He was dark like his grandmother Mary, dead eight years now, a casualty of that fratricidal war as surely as if she had fallen on the redoubt of New Market Heights.

"Grandpa, ain't it a bit early for you to be riding abroad? Mornin' mist ain't cleared yet—that dampness'll get into your chest."

"I was just gathering some herbs for Ellen to steam."

"Well, Mama's got your breakfast ready, so ride on in before you catch your death."

"Lord, Frederick, my death has already been caught."

There are two things I have always regretted—that my path never crossed that of my white cousins during the war so I could have killed one, and that I never got to shake the hand of Abraham Lincoln.

I the undersigned, Madison Hemings, colored male, American citizen, born in Virginia in 1805, the last year of my father's first term, widowed father of ten (three deceased) with the occupation of farmer in the town of Pee Wee, Pike County, Ohio, do affirm that I am the President's son and this is an accurate account of my birth and the evil, historic, pathetic, amazing, passionate, and silent relationship between the Hemingses, the Wayleses, the Jeffersons, and the Randolphs. God will take care of the Wellingtons.

MADISON HEMINGS

1876

42

I am of a sect by myself.

Thomas Jefferson

On the morning of the Centennial celebration, May 19, 1876, I stood at the top of the stairs of my mansion at Anamacora fingering a newspaper article deep in my skirt. Every old fear I had cast away in all these years had returned. I was being blackmailed. There was a Callender who had betrayed me. There was a Sykes who stalked me once again. Except this time I didn't know who.

"Grandmother!" Roxanne's silvery voice spirited up the stairs. "The least you can do is come down and read your telegrams before we leave for the fair! They have been arriving all morning. You haven't even glanced at all your presents. You would think today wasn't your birthday. Why, there's even a bouquet of roses from the President!"

The dancing sunlight on the river's surface streaming through the bull's-eye window on the landing hurt my eyes. Time glared at me as I started stiffly down the stairs. The giant calendar upon which I wrote my agenda every day now that my eyesight had faded had a large cross over today, the nineteenth of May 1876. My seventy-fifth birthday had coincided with the Philadelphia Centennial celebrations.

I had taken a great deal of care with my toilet this day. The great mass of red and white hair was pulled back into a halo with a fine crocheted net. My ears were adorned with a pair of splendid, square-cut diamond earrings. My tall, heavy-boned body was encased from neck to ankle in royal blue taffeta. It fell over my voluminous skirts, was drawn back into an old-fashioned bustle, and hung over tempered steel and crinoline, forming a train that dragged behind me like my years. The article in my pocket was already brown from my folding and unfolding it, and as I clutched it once more, my hand came into contact for a moment with the steel blade of James's stiletto. It had become a joke with my grandchildren. "Grandma's dagger, Grandma's dagger," they would chant. And I would reply, "No—*poignard*," and then they would repeat, "Grandma's *poignard*, Grandma's *poignard*." Only little Roxanne had once had the audacity to ask me why I carried a weapon, and I told her it was to cut my flowers. She then wanted to know why her grandmother did not carry garden shears like everybody else. I told her that I was not like everybody else and had never been.

My head swam with dates that spanned three-quarters of a century and all that had happened even before I was born: 1776, 1779, 1800, 1808, 1861, 1865. Everything was present. And now this whole carefully enunciated life, as intricate as a Bach fugue, was in jeopardy. I fingered the newspaper clipping, which someone had sent anonymously and which had arrived this morning amongst my birthday greetings. In it a black man had revealed both his identity and mine: "I never knew of but one white man who bore the name of Thomas Jefferson. He was my father and President of the United States."

Furtively I glanced at myself in the tall gilt mirror in the stairwell. The pale, slightly freckled skin was now as transparent as foolscap. The raging vermilion of my thick wavy hair was halved with white flax. The emerald eyes had dimmed. I no longer had the graceful gait of my youth, but I tried not to favor my aching hip by limping. For years I had fought against the dawning awareness of the uncertainty of my step, my mood changes, the gaps in my memory, and my new habit of waking myself up with my own sobs. I refused to consider the evidences of senility. On the contrary, I ignored them in the most pugilistic way, running upstairs, staying up late, eating whatever I chose, smoking cigars, and drinking wine. I had long ago rejected the refuge of the laudanum, cocaine, and other narcotics that my women friends—those who were not dead—took comfort in. I was old enough to fear pity more than apoplexy.

I smiled to myself. Hypocrisy, ignorance, and blind self-satisfaction had always been on my side, just as they were today. That and silence. Silence had kept me alive and in this world, just as it had my mother. Slaves had always revealed as little as possible about their origins to their children. It was an old trick. Not to speak was not to put into words the hopelessness of having no future and no past. I slipped the article from the *Pike County Gazette* out of my pocket. I didn't have to read it; I had memorized it.

My mother was enciente when she returned from Paris. He always treated us children well . . .

Harriet married a man in good standing in Philadelphia, whose name I could give but will not, for prudential reasons. She raised a family of children, and so far as I know, they were never suspected of being tainted with African blood in the community where she lived, or lives. I have not heard from her for ten years, and do not know if she is dead or alive. She thought it in her interest, on leaving Virginia, to assume the role of a white woman, and by her dress and conduct as such, I am not aware that her identity as Harriet Hemings of Monticello has ever been discovered.

The article had been written by Madison Hemings.

He had broken his silence and someone knew. I racked my brain trying to guess who in my entourage knew that the Harriet Hemings of the article and Harriet Wellington were the same. Lorenzo, the mapmaker who had turned up on Sinclair's gunboat eleven years ago? Sarah Hale? I had never forgotten the look on her face when she handed me *Clotel, or the President's Daughter.* My white cousin Ellen Randolph Coolidge, who had sat out the war in Boston and knew Sarah? Maurice Meillasoux, who might have been told by Adrian years ago? It could be Madison himself, although from the article Madison believed both Eston and I were dead. Or could it be my "biographer" himself, William Wells Brown, whom I had met face-to-face several times at Emily's receptions, once with Frederick Douglass himself. My children? Had someone sent them the article and they had passed it on to me? Then there was Thor. Had Adrian betrayed me to Thance, who had then confided in his brother? The names and faces, both dead and alive, turned themselves over in my mind like a threshing machine. It was as if every character, every personage in my individual history were arraigned before a stern tribunal to explain themselves and be acquitted or condemned according to whether they intercoursed with progress or reaction. Perhaps my silent enemy would be under my roof in a few hours. Was I to have an accusing finger pointed at me—after all these years—in front of my grandchildren?

I looked back into the mirror. What was the meaning of this white face?

I took hold of the banister, ignoring the ache in my hip, the pain in my head, and the *Pike County Gazette* article in my pocket. I drew my breath in, like someone plunging into the ocean, as I descended, leaving a trail of personal dread and the breath of disaster behind me.

Deception takes on a life of its own, I mused. It is independent of your will or actions. It can make every other fact of life, even love, disappear. And now, according to someone, we all had to pay the price. Every single penny of it. And you Roxanne will pay the biggest price: learning that you can't take your whiteness for granted, that you are living the Great American Nightmare: a drop of black blood in your veins, the one drop that, by law and usage, pollutes you and your whole life. Rosanne existed in a reality I was no longer sure of. Was she really mine?

I had vowed I would never be like my mother, but was I so far from her? I saw her in my mind's eye, even now, existing on the frontiers between Monticello and a slave cabin, between power and obscurity, between history and oblivion: the distance between the race that ruled and the other that obeyed. I had always refused to obey. I had always refused to choose between my selfhood and my race. It is the same thin line I've walked all my life. I walked it as I walk down these stairs, having crossed it fifty-four years ago with the blessings of the woman I vowed never to imitate.

My doctors tell me I am dying. Either I will die without letting anyone I've ever loved know who I am, or I will honor my father and my mother and risk my family's everlasting damnation.

Roxanne, in a final irony, was the image of her unknown great-grandmother: she had her build, she had her matte skin and she had her famous amber eyes. She too wore her dark hair pulled back into a long braid, which hung down her back like a bell cord. And sometimes I noticed that her eyelids would slide like shades over her yellow eyes in exactly the same way my mother's had, flattening her pale oval face into a mask of polished ivory. Roxanne had the same deep dimples on each side of her mouth, the same round column of neck, the same heavy bosom. Roxanne's eyes even had that same question in them that Sally Hemings had carried in hers.

"Grandmother!" she cried again. "We're ready for the photograph!" The photographer had already set up his camera. My family was assembled in the foyer under the bust of Thomas Jefferson and my mother's pendulum clock.

Long, long ago I had dreamed of this birthday, surrounded by my descendants. And hadn't it come true? Around my neck hung my brother's portrait; in my left pocket was James's dagger, in my right, Madison's memoirs. At the foot of the stairs assembled my white people. I studied the handsome, placid faces around me.

I wondered how they would feel if they knew that their grandmother was not what she seemed—not the serene Philadelphia matriarch, the "Duchess of Anamacora," but an ex-slave, legally emancipated only eleven years ago by her duped sons and husband. Would any of them accept the idea that they were the President's grandchildren at the price of admitting that they had that one drop of blood that made them black, in law and fiction?

Thor had not changed at all since the war. His hair was still as dark as it was gray, as if each strand of white had been carefully weighed and balanced with a dark one to produce a perfect blend of salt and pepper. He wore his thick hair Western-style, old-fashioned, long and tied in a queue instead of cropped short with sideburns. His face was not so much lined as reshaped with deep ravines and crevices and high plains and summits that had turned his classical features into modified American Indian. But the dark, liquid eyes with their heavy black lashes and the violin *f*-shaped eyebrows which almost grew together had remained the same. Only I knew that Thor had come back from the war addicted to opium. I had hid this from everyone. He had spent a hellish ten and a half years battling his habit, which he had confessed to me only a year ago. The butchery, the horrors, and the unrelenting exhaustion of the war that had provoked his plunge into narcotics haunted him even now. I knew that the easy access to morphine that he enjoyed as a pharmacist had done nothing to deter his monthly visits to opium dens in Philadelphia's Chinatown. His habit had damaged neither his career, his reputation, which was at its zenith, nor his home life, but the secret hung heavily between us.

My grandmother's pendulum clock struck the sixth chime of 9:00 A.M. I took a deep breath. My dream's fabric was tearproof, and nowhere could the finespun be rent unless I chose to do it myself. Madison's memoirs ticked like a time bomb deep in my skirt pocket. How could I find a way of reconciling Mrs. Harriet Wellington of Anamacora with an obscure memoir that ended, "We all became free agreeably to the treaty entered into by our parents before we were born."

I imagined today's grandstands. On the podium, along with the local Philadelphia dignitaries, my husband amongst them, would be the President of the United States and Mrs. Grant, the Generals Sherman, Sheridan, and Butler, Senators Gale and Biddle, and Don Pedro II, emperor of Brazil, the only civilized country in the world that still tolerated chattel slavery. As a member of the ladies' auxiliary committee of the Centennial, I had worked for more than a year with my society friends on the Women's Pavilion. I had seen on the list of exhibitors the name of a certain Eston H. Jefferson of Ohio, president of the Jefferson Screw and Piston Company. How many could there be in the world? He had applied to exhibit the steam engines and the steam pistons that had made him a fortune during the war. I wondered if he had received the ambiguous invitation to my party that I had addressed to "Mr. Jefferson."

I imagined the wide, unpaved concourse leading toward the cast-iron-and-glass building which rose from its carpet of green, reflecting the landscape like a kaleidoscope. Its ten thousand panes of cut glass shimmering like a lagoon of diamonds, two thousand feet in length and five hundred in width. Machinery Hall rose over seventy feet, all iron ribs and transparency. In it I had seen the immense Corliss Engine, the wonder of the exhibition. Vying with the Corliss Engine was Alexander Graham Bell's new telephone. Thomas Alva Edison exhibited the Quadruplex telegraph; George Westinghouse exhibited his air brake; George Pullman showed off the Pullman Palace Car.

In my mind's eye, I saw the colossal, beaten-copper wrist of Bartholdi's Statue of Liberty. The dismembered, gargantuan forearm of the statue holding her torch had been sent to the fair by its French sculptor to raise subscriptions for its completion. I had seen it being erected at the fairgrounds by hundreds of workers, a dreamlike and immense promise of what it would one day be, rising on Bedloe's Island in the New York harbor, one hundred sixty feet high, if they ever got the money to finish it. People would pay at the fair to clamber up the catwalk that circled her wrist like a bracelet. It stood on the concourse, which wound through the four hundred fifty acres of the exhibition park with its two hundred pavilions and monuments, memorials, sculptures, obelisks, and stands. I realized that not one was devoted to, or even mentioned, those dark citizens who had been the cause of the second American Revolution. There was no monument to Butler's or Ferrero's black troops, no mention of the inventions of Eli Whitney or George Washington Carver. No monument to those poor departed souls lost in the Atlantic middle passage, no pavilion dedicated to our history, our heroes, our lives. My life.

The vision of the complicated engine I had seen at the Centennial faded into the sound of the clattering weaving looms at which I had once spun with the other slave girls at Monticello.

My father's voice rose out of the recesses of a half-century: "Beverly says we could build a nail factory run on waterpower right here on Mulberry Row with free labor instead of this pitiful barn filled with seven-year-old slaves. . . ."

Suddenly, as if all the telepathy of childhood had returned, I knew that I had to stay at Anamacora.

"Grandma, are you feeling all right?"

"I'm not coming."

"But, Grandma! Grandpa is waiting for you at the grandstands! What about the reception in the Pennsylvania Pavilion? You're supposed to meet there with Mayor Sweet William Stokley and the emperor of Brazil!"

"Grandma doesn't want to see Mr. Political Scandal, Mr. Spoils Man, Mr. Dirty Streets High Taxes Stokley, or that bloody Brazilian slave trader!" I declared to my grandchild's astonishment. "Let Grandpa do it."

Revolt had finally stirred my soul.

"Tu viens, Maman? Non, je ne viens pas. *I'm not coming.*" "*You asked me in conversation, what constituted a mulatto.*" "*Worse than an auction—selling yourself for whiteness.*" "*Since she's white enough to pass for white, then let her be white.*" "*Look down, Harriet. You are so beautiful.*" "*Of course I wouldn't change anything.*" "*I've changed my color, Petit, not my soul.*" "*Have you ever met one white man who did not ask you for something or take something away from you?*" "*Thance loves you.*" "*My children won't know who they are.*" "*Harriet, give Wellington a chance; tell him.*" "*Well, Mrs. Willowpole, welcome to the slave deck.*" "*There is an injury where reparation is impossible . . . dishonored birth.*" "*Never say that, Harriet. Your father loves you as much as he loves anything not written down on paper.*" "*I love all things that are not. That could be the motto of my life.*" "*I'm not Thance, Harriet. I'm Thor.*" "*Because she didn't have her papers with her!*" "*Aw, God. They're not coming back. They ain't ever coming back.*" "*I'm never coming back here for you again, Maman!*" "*Daughter . . .*" "*Push down hard, my heart won't stop beating.*" "*I've waited for the grave for you to tell me, tell me, tell me . . .*"

I felt the laughter and tears boil up within me and scald over like a cauldron of hot milk. The hundredth birthday of my country, of my father's Declaration of Independence. With a pedigree like mine, what ironic God had placed me on the podium of the celebration of a hundred years of silence? When would they recognize me? When would I belong to them? When? When would I be able to tell this magnificent family of mine who and what I was —that I was theirs with all the love and passion of my soul—without also having to beg them for their forgiveness?

The old yearning returned tenfold, something as infinitesimal as the dust motes dancing in the sunlight striking the marble bust of my father, or the ominous pile of birthday telegrams on the table by the door, or the mocking metronome of my pendulum clock keeping time . . . making time . . . destroying time . . . time that was running out for me, ticktock time, or was that only the sound of my own heart beating—holding me back? Helplessly I kicked against time's walls, thicker than my skirts which twitched under my blow. I dared not limp forward, either as Harriet Hemings of Monticello or Harriet Wellington of Anamacora.

"No, I'm not coming, Roxanne."

My astonished family exploded with protestations and pleas, but I ignored them. I surveyed my granddaughter with the abstract detachment elderly people often affect.

The sun streaming through the bull's-eye window played on Roxanne's sleek dark hair parted in the middle and drawn into two ropes of twisted hair coiled over each ear. She wore a small sultana, the tiny Turkish pillbox hat which was so in fashion these days. On one side was attached a length of fine lace which was pulled under the chin and attached by a brooch. Her dress was blue-and-white-striped, the bodice pleated and tucked into a hundred ruffles that were drawn back into a high bustle. All this and her crinolines jutted out around her in peaks and valleys of silk. With her pagoda sleeves festooned with black ribbons and bows, she looked as if she could at any moment overflow the confines of the world. Her hand rested lightly on the handle of her parasol, which was pinpointed firmly to the floor.

Roxanne returned my gaze with frank affection, then shook her head. She knew better than to argue with an old dying Virginian. Hadn't I tried it once and failed?

"Well, if you're not going, Grandma, I'm not going. I'm staying here with you."

Even as the coach rolled down the driveway of Anamacora without me and away with all my family and I stepped down in the midst of my romping Dalmatians, I knew the past was already on its way. Its calling card lay with all my telegrams on the console inside the doorway. It read:

> *Eston Hemings Jefferson, President*
> *The Jefferson Continental Cotton & Standard Screw Co.*
> *300 Eastern Shore Drive*
> *Chicago, Illinois*

I turned it over as if it were a tarot card. I heard the voice of my murdered Thenia over my shoulder. WHITE PEOPLE.

At 4:00 P.M., slowly, laboriously, I began my toilette: talcum and drawers, stays and corsets, wire hoop, crinoline, underpetticoat, six petticoats, black silk, green taffeta apron, green ribbons, jewels, locket, earrings, lace mittens, mantilla, tiara, more talcum, a bit of rouge, a strand of pearls, Guerlain's "Jacky," and I was ready. What used to be pure joy, for I loved clothes, now took longer and much more effort and produced only the mediocre results an old woman could expect. Beauty was no longer hoped for. Which of my friends had accused me of the coquetry of an actress? I was certainly an actress, I thought.

My house was built of white clapboard and yellow brick, commodious, wide-columned and handsome. It stood like a sentinel on the banks of the Schuylkill River, whose tributaries had run red with the blood of the battle of Gettysburg in '63 but now it had returned to its natural, neutral color: a streak of gunmetal drawn across the jade green sward of Pennsylvania Dutch country.

The conservatory was now a ballroom, and dinner tables had been set up in the other rooms and outside in the veranda. The floors had been stripped of their rugs; bouquets of flowers had been set everywhere; the Dalmatians had been locked in the stables; the torches outside had been lit; the oil lamps inside had been turned down; the candles burned; the crystal chandeliers glowed; the hired waiters and maître d'hôtel stood at attention with their backs to the wall. I inspected the buffets for the last time, gliding by the stacks of plates and banks of crystal and gleaming silverware, the mountain of stiff lace, napkins, the cold platters already set out: waxy *chaud-froids* of veal, glazed cold turkey, Virginia hams, boned woodcock, quails and guinea hens, iridescent obelisks of Maine oysters, tureens of cold asparagus soup, and trout in hollandaise sauce. I felt my fingers trail along the table, the lace of my sleeves mingling with the lace of the napkins. I had hired the best caterer in Philadelphia.

"Congratulations, Mr. Fullom. All this is quite wonderful."

"Thank you, Mrs. Wellington. I hear the President is coming."

"He is indeed so honoring us, Mr. Fullom. I believe we are first on his list of parties for tonight." I gave him a smile of complicity. I listened to the orchestra tune up. My color rose as it always did at the sound of music. I felt free. And safe.

"Excuse me, madam, there's a colored woman who insists on speaking to you. I told her to go around to the back door. She's waiting for you there."

Absently, I took another look at the banquet. As I passed through the kitchen, I stopped to peak under the huge white napkins covering trays of baked bread and homemade cake. Through the filigree of the screened door I could make out only the silhouette of a tall female figure. It was only when I opened the door that I realized, with the dread of a secret murderer, that the colored lady who had crossed my path in Market Street Square over fifty years ago was standing on my back porch. She was the same height, the same color, and she had on the same style of hat, trimmed with huge pink cabbage roses and pink ribbons. But it couldn't be the lady in Market Street Square! She would be an old woman! This woman was vigorous and in the prime of life. She was brown skinned, in her early forties, giving an impression of quiet strength and femininity.

"Good evening. I'm Sarah Hemings, Madison's daughter. They call me Sally at home."

I stared at her.

"You *are* Harriet Wellington?"

I recognized my mother's ruby earrings, which swung with her emphasis and sparkled in the sunlight. Sarah. The three-year-old I had held in my arms and had wept over the day Eston had delivered my mother's possessions.

"Yes," I answered helplessly.

"Well"—she smiled her colored-lady-in-Market-Street-Square smile— "I'm Sarah," she repeated triumphantly.

We stood on either side of the doorstep, but it was more than a doorstep that separated us. We tottered as if on the edge of a precipice. The color line separating us stretched from the Atlantic to the Pacific, from one end of America to the other. I knew that if I stepped over the threshold of my doorway, I would never return to my mansion. And if, on the other hand, Sarah stepped over it into my life, my family would never have another tranquil moment. Sarah's eyes held questions: Who do you think you are? What do you think you are? How long can you pretend you *are* at all?

"I'm afraid you are mistaken. You have come to the wrong house."

"Impossible! I know you. You *are* Harriet of Monticello. How could you not be! You are his spitting image."

"I beg your pardon?"

"Of my grandfather, of Thomas Jefferson."

I laughed out loud then, so true and terrible was this obnoxious farce being played out between us.

"No," I repeated. "I am not Harriet . . . of Monticello. No Harriet of Monticello lives here."

"But, didn't you get Daddy's memoirs? They were published in the *Pike County Gazette*. I'm the one who sent you the article."

So here was my blackmailer. My nemesis. My Callender. Sarah.

"You're really going to stand there and deny me?"

"My dear lady, there's nothing to deny. I cannot be who you think I am. That's all."

Sarah threw back her head and let loose a gale of laughter, laughter that turned my bones to ice. "And *this* is why we fought the Civil War—I'll be damned, Aunt."

"I can't let you in," I whispered.

"And you can't let yourself out, I suppose . . . but who would know unless you told them?"

"God would know."

"God already knows, Aunt."

"Thor!" I cried out as if he could save me, forgetting that I was the liar and he was the lied-to.

Sarah stood there in a smoldering rage, leaning on her parasol, the flowers on her hat trembling. She had beautiful gray eyes. Madison's eyes.

"You know how I found you, Aunt? The family that lives in Grandma's shack told me a white lady came to see them ten years ago. A scalawag who maybe wasn't even white and tried to evict them, but then she changed her mind when she heard 'haunts.' They said I found out her name was Wellington."

I'll never sell myself for whiteness.

"I suppose it's just as well my father wasn't sure whether you were alive or dead. I'm certainly not going to tell him otherwise, because I don't know if you *are* alive or dead. I still remember your tears that day, Aunt. They were so hot they scalded me. I have dreamed of finding you—not to harm you, to love you."

She smiled and shook her head at the futility and childishness of that dream. Her eyes inspected me from head to toe in friendly curiosity. I tried to speak, but, as in a dream, found I could not. I reached out, hoping to touch her, but she turned on herself in that familiar way, like a stately ship heeling, and glided past me. Would she believe her aunt's heart was beating faster because she so resembled her great-grandmother? And because I loved her? How could I really love this beautiful woman dappled in the velvet shadows, leaning on her parasol, radiating innocence and indignation, without telling her that I was as much a part of her as her eyelashes? There was a courage about Sarah, standing there in her self-righteousness that inspired in me the heart-wrenching affection a veteran feels for an officer who has not yet been seen battle.

Carefully, Sarah guided herself, still laughing, through the orchard. Peach trees laden with flesh-colored blossoms genuflected to her, laying down their branches before her as if she were Jesus entering Jerusalem. I gave up trying to shake the peculiar feeling that I *knew* Sarah Hemings. It wasn't fair, I thought, that I knew so much more about Sarah than she would ever know about me. But the kind of ignorance I read in her face proscribed the quality of love I would have liked to have offered her.

"Sarah!" I cried.

At Sarah's retreat, a wild, uncontrollable desolation bore down upon me. A howl like that of a wild animal caught in my throat at this farce and this tragedy. As Sarah's laughter spirited through my head, I felt as if I had lifted the dagger in my skirt pocket against myself and plunged it into my heart.

I heard Roxanne's voice behind me, but I wanted to watch Sarah as she wove through my orchards, appearing, then disappearing amongst the blossoms, her raucous laughter floating backward like a silk banner. The peals of laughter faded until they mingled with the chimes that struck the hour. The orchestra was rehearsing the first crashing chords of Richard Wagner's *Centennial March* for the President's arrival.

"Grandma?"

There was no time left. Or so little. I took Roxanne's hand as one takes the hand of a small child.

"Come," I said to her.

43

Considering history as a moral exercise, her lessons would be too infrequent if confined to real life. Of those recorded by historians, few incidents have been attended with such circumstances as to excite in any high degree this sympathetic emotion of virtue. We are therefore framed to be as warmly interested for a fictitious as for a real personage. The spacious field of imagination is thus laid open to our use, and lessons may be formed to illustrate and carry home to the mind, every moral rule of life. . . .

Thomas Jefferson

I contemplated Roxanne, whose voluptuous, well-made body radiated a kind of pure, untested sensuality of which she seemed unaware, but that would someday be as awesome as my mother's. Yet unlike Sally Hemings, Roxanne was the freest person I had ever known. She was the modern, the new American woman, ready to take responsibility for her own life, ready to reinvent the past. I released my granddaughter's hand while the silent appraisal I had just made of her hovered in the air between us.

The years of my life seemed to flutter away like the lace panels that stirred at the tall windows of my bedroom. Roxanne. It hadn't been blackmail. There would never be another anonymous letter. Only Sarah knew. Why, then, did I have to tell Roxanne? *I had never told anyone I loved who I was.* All of them would be downstairs in a little while. My public. WHITE PEOPLE.

I put all hope in Roxanne, with all the desperate, sheltering love of a fading, dying woman. In the next word from me, she would encompass all the incomprehension, contradiction, and pain of the great American taboo: tainted, impure blood. That one drop of blackness which evoked the disdain, contempt, and ambivalence of a whole country. Her own.

"Grandma?" It was Roxanne's voice, tremulous and expectant.

I began with no preamble, and my story unraveled like silk cords, chapter by chapter, love by love, terror by terror, deception by deception. "Deceptions intended solely for others gradually grew into self-deception as well; the counterfeit rift between imitation slave and imitation master widened and widened and became an abyss," I ended. I implored her to transmit this knowledge only to her own grandchildren, those distant twentieth-century descendants who would probably be more bemused than devastated.

"Promise me that if you ever reveal your true identity to your future family, never tell your own children. Choose a female of your second generation, a granddaughter. Grandchildren are easier to talk to than your own children, and any secret is safer with our own sex."

"Why is that, Maman?"

"Women carry their secrets in their wombs, hidden and nourished by their vital fluids and blood, while men carry their secrets like they carry their genitals, attached by a thin morsel of mortal flesh unable to resist either a caress or a good kick."

No sound came from the shadowed recess as Roxanne struggled to find a way of addressing a woman she no longer recognized; a creature who did not exist, who was the negation of everything she had been taught to believe. There were no white slaves. There could be no white ex-slaves. There were no women like me who had been sired by a great man who had never freed or recognized her. I couldn't exist because miscegenation didn't exist. It was a crime punishable by fine and imprisonment. A crime against America.

It was Roxanne's country, not I, who insisted that one drop of black blood made one a slave and an alien. And that this was necessary in order to perpetuate the myth of racial purity that was the cornerstone of its identity —that her country was, indeed, a white man's country.

"You mean you are . . . were . . ." She struggled with the words.

"The President's daughter." I bowed my head. I so pitied her. I stared at my fingertips.

But Roxanne's eyes had widened in astonishment, then narrowed in, of all things, laughter. She didn't believe a word of what I had just told her. She lifted up her head in a cascade of ladylike giggles that turned raucous, filling every corner of the room. She exhaled.

"Now, Grandma, isn't this some old slave narrative you've heard?"

The one thing my mother hadn't warned me against was disbelief. My granddaughter thought I was lying, but who in America would lie about being black? Who, having been born with the inestimable advantage of being white, would cast herself in the defamatory hell of being black, *here?*

Slowly she circled me, stalking me as one would a wild animal.

"Now, Grandma," she said, her voice caressing me, "you know you're not colored! You're not colored, and neither am I. Nobody in this family is colored! I'm white. Let me . . . let me get Grandpa."

But I held her. "No," I cried. "I've never told him. I've never told anyone I loved," I lied. "I always said to myself that I'd think about it later, when I was calmer, but that day never came. It's like the secrets that slave women must transmit to their daughters of the next generation so that they will survive. I couldn't die without someone I loved knowing and remaining on this earth with that knowledge. It wouldn't be fair to Sally Hemings . . . to him . . . to them. . . . Look," I cried out. "Look at my hands! I have no fingerprints. See? Look!"

"How can you love me," my granddaughter cried, "and repeat such a lie?"

I started toward her, but Roxanne backed away in fear.

"I'm going to get a doctor," she whispered.

"But no, darling, really, I don't need a doctor. I feel fine . . . look!"

I knelt down beside the hearth and stuck my hands into the ashes. They came up black.

"Look, no fingerprints." I pressed my fingers onto the white marble surface of the mantelpiece. "See?" I started toward her, but she drew her arms around herself for protection from me. Her splendid eyes had become a muddy, confused brown in horror or despair, I couldn't tell which. I found myself smiling stupidly. The same smile I had had on my face the day my father died. She didn't believe me. She would never believe me. I had fifty-two diaries, and she still didn't believe me. Nothing on this entire earth would make her recognize me. She'd rather die. Just like him. I thought I heard Sarah's laughter, but it was Roxanne's, and it was plainly, insanely hysterical.

"Is this still some kind of game? Some kind of birthday game?" she said in the voice of a child.

"This—" But before I could answer, Roxanne had fled the room, slamming the door. From behind it I heard her insufferable Philadelphia voice.

"I'm going to get some laudanum."

Where is your medicine, Father?

Then I began to laugh. She must have heard me behind the door. The joke of my life was on me. I was what people perceived me to be, and there was nothing I could do about it. Who would believe me? Who in the ballroom tonight would believe me? It meant, I thought suddenly, redefining the United States of America. It meant moving the furniture around, opening the doors, looking under the bed; it meant rewriting the law of the land; it meant fighting a war; it meant changing their ways. Who was going to do all that for a mere woman—a Negro one, at that?

I would quit this earth a white woman, whether I wanted to or not. I would die with my skin on. That was my predicament, and this was my punishment: the sentence of oblivion. Roxanne would never tell any of her descendants. I was invisible. Forever.

I lifted my head, accepting heaven's verdict. However I found myself "reconstructed," the result was the same. Quite simply, a woman like me couldn't exist. I was, on all levels, simply unbelievable.

My blackened hands raked the walls and sullied the delicate silk draperies, the pale ethereal canopied bed, the enameled woodwork. I left my mark on everything I could touch.

I had autographed my life by telling my most precious grandchild who I was. I now made upon the walls of my room the fingerprints that hung me, claiming it as my own: claiming the life I had lived within. I rewrote history. Black or white be damned, I was Harriet. Hemings. Wellington. A kind of frenzy of exaltation smote me, and tears of liberation from a woman who never cried flowed down my cheeks. My solitary heart contained all the world's colors: all. I refused to be "created" black or white. Whatever I was, my life, my freedom, my loves, were downstairs, waiting. My sin of omission no longer burned at the center of confusion and obsession; instead it burned with the steady carbon of humanity that refused to be extinguished, smothered, or asphyxiated: my mother's, my grandmother's, the African's, my grandfather's, my father's, my husbands', my children's. I was matriarch of a mighty clan, seven times seven; every color, every shade, every nuance, struggling through lives filled with the identical terrors and sublimities of the human condition. I'd be damned, damned, if I would be less.

Hadn't a famous man once told my father that history was merely fictions of various degrees of plausibility? If I was fiction, I breathed, then this country was fiction. Was I plausible? You tell me.

I stared at the mirror over the mantelpiece, but there was no reflection of anyone in it. I pressed my eyelids red-gold, as if by force of will I could engrave my image on its silvered surface. I opened them again, but there was nobody. Then I called out of my whiteness and the edges of eternal darkness.

When I came to myself, I washed my hands carefully and languidly in the yellow-and-blue basin, turning the water inky. I dried them, and slowly they disappeared into my white lace mittens. The orchestra broke into Richard Wagner's march. The President's coach had arrived. I had just enough time to descend the stairway to its music, just as I had planned. Roxanne had failed to lock me in. Her crazy grandmother. I opened the door.

1942

• Epilogue •

• Roxanne Wellington's Affidavit •

Epilogue

⌒

When I was young, I was fond of speculations which seemed to promise some insight into that hidden country . . .

Thomas Jefferson

This is Roxanne Wayles Wellington speaking. I'm the only one left to explain that my grandmother went a little bit dotty on her seventy-fifth birthday, the day of the Centennial. First, that morning she refused to go to the celebrations, so I stayed home with her. She looked and acted absolutely normal. It wasn't until late afternoon, barely hours before the first guest arrived for the reception, that I found her in the orchard. I noticed the ample figure of a lady as she walked away, who wore a large, spectacular hat. I could hear her laughing as my grandmother called out, "Sarah!" Then Grandma, with her back to me, without any preamble and without taking her eyes off the figure in the orchard, took me by the hand and led me to her room, where, to my stupefaction, she declared that she had passed for white all her life in order to escape slavery, and that her father, who was also her master, was the third President of the United States, Thomas Jefferson. She said that she could bear the silence no longer, that she could no longer survive without telling someone she loved who she was.

So she told me.

It was such an extraordinary statement that, of course, I couldn't take it seriously. "Now Grandma," I said, "this is not one of your slave narratives of old, is it?" But throughout her whole birthday party, Grandma persisted with this stupendous story, never leaving my side, pointing out people at the reception who either knew she was the President's daughter or, worse, who were themselves the President's progeny. First she began by declaring that the sitting President, Ulysses S. Grant, was not fit to be in the same room with the daughter of Thomas Jefferson. Then the lady in the orchard, who turned out to be colored, circled the house and walked through the front door as cool as you please, without anyone stopping her. She, my grandmother proclaimed, was Thomas Jefferson's great-granddaughter, just as I was. Then, weaving through her guests, ignoring our sitting President and his wife, she pointed out the mysterious Mr. Jefferson. He, she swore, was her brother, my great-uncle, and the President's son. He was accompanied by his grandson, who was, she explained, Jefferson's great-grandson. A great many people, Grandma claimed, knew who she was, including her oldest friend, Charlotte Nevell, now dead. Charlotte, Grandma explained, had suspected her of hiding a false identity ever since she'd returned from her father's funeral in Virginia in 1826, but they had never so much as exchanged one word on the subject until she had whispered it in her dying friend's ear. Again, I tried to make light of these declarations, laughingly accusing my grandmother of telling me all this because I was engaged to Peter Kirkland and not to David Nevell, her friend Charlotte's grandson, and she wanted to scare me out of marrying him.

But Grandma's whispered accusations became more and more bizarre and delirious. The most famous mulatto abolitionist in the world, Robert Purvis, knew she was the President's daughter; Purvis had told Frederick Douglass! Five Presidents of the United States knew she was the President's daughter, the last being John Quincy Adams. Even poor saintly Aunt Dorcas, as white as snow, didn't escape. How she must be churning in her grave! Dorcas Willowpole knew because Lorenzo Fitzgerald, an Englishman who had begged Grandma to marry him in London in the twenties, had told her after she had confessed to him in anticipation of a proposal of marriage. Grandma stopped before the orchestra, which had just started to play a polonaise, and flung the last accusation over her shoulder: It had been Sarah. Sarah, her own niece. Sarah, to whom she had given Sally Hemings's ruby earrings. Didn't Sarah know that her duty was to protect a relative who passed for white? How was it, I finally asked her, that everybody knew about her past except Grandpa himself, who had been married to her for the past thirty years? But all Grandma said was that she had always thought to tell the twins by and by; when she found a calm moment, but she never had.

But when I asked the colored lady, who was drinking a glass of champagne under the offended eyes of the black waiter, if she was a relative of my grandmother, she answered a surprised no. My grandmother had helped her escape to the North with the Underground Railway in 1836, and had given her a present. She had vowed to return one day to thank her. So how could she be Grandma's niece? She wore a pair of magnificent earrings that caught the light and threw off red sparks in the gaslight. I couldn't very well walk up to Mr. Jefferson and ask him if he was the illegitimate son of the third President of the United States. But I did ask him if he was related to the Virginia Jeffersons, to which he admitted "a passing connection." Moreover, I was certainly not going to discuss Grandma's grotesque confession and dangerous behavior with, Lord Almighty, my future husband, so I abandoned the investigation for the night, thinking I might ask Sarah Hale one of these days when I was calmer.

For, to tell you the truth, I was shaken as only a sane person is shaken when face-to-face with lunacy. For there is a hard, unyielding core of *conviction* in insanity that has a logic all its own and that disconcerts and unnerves normal people. It is like climbing a wall of smooth granite on which there are no footholds, no pick marks of reality to clutch on its surface, upon which one's mind slips and slides helplessly off the edges of its lunatic logic. At her party, my grandmother had been beautiful, so luminous, so elegant. Never had she shone more brilliantly in the configuration of society and her class. Never had Grandpa surveyed her so adoringly, or been so indomitably proud. Yet never had my grandmother been so utterly crazy.

Grandma had promised her mother, she said, to reveal her secret only to a second-generation female of her own family. That was why I, Roxanne, must hear her confession. Secrets were not to be exposed to men, who would wear them the way they wore their sex, so spoke Sally Hemings. And so, the next day, I read her diaries, fifty years of them. They revealed an astonishing secret life of the imagination, with numerous references to Negroes and slavery and emancipation, which proved to me that she was obsessed with race and color and was a staunch negrophile, at least in her imagination. She claimed to have numerous Negro relatives, to have conducted scores of fugitive slaves to freedom. She had even returned to the South herself, she claimed, to rescue her mother. She had letters, she claimed, from Sally Hemings and Thomas Jefferson, but alas, none of them was signed except one. The provocative signature "Th. J." might have been Thomas, but also might have been Theodore, Thadius, Tabitha, Thenia. . . .

There was a fantastic aura to her writing that convinced me that this life Grandma had created for herself was indeed totally imaginary. No. It was impossible that any of this had anything to do with me. She even claimed that she was the only person in the world who had no fingerprints, and indeed she showed me the tips of her fingers, which were as smooth and blank as ivory. And yet, what of the relics? How to explain the locket she gave me, or the exquisite box with the portrait of a French king? From whence had they come, and how had they gotten into her quiet bedroom? They were not ethereal words to be explained away, but objects of substance and weight: gold and enamel and diamonds. And what about the eerie blue-eyed gaze of the man in the locket portrait, which mimicked that of my grandmother? It didn't resemble at all the bust of President Jefferson downstairs. Then there were the names, the dates, the coincidences. It was impossible to prove or disprove. It was simply unbelievable.

Grandma had an accident shortly after that. She took Tamar instead of her own mount one morning, and while Grandma was riding along the riverbank, something or someone frightened the speckled bay. She bolted, reared, and fell into the shallows. Grandma's wrists got tangled in the reins and she couldn't get free. Tamar rolled over on her, and she drowned in less than three feet of water.

In a way, Grandmother's death saved her own grandchildren, for the bay had been bought as a docile, safe mount for them, but after Grandma's accident we learned that Tamar had thrown and killed her previous owner, and had been sold to us without her owner revealing this incident. We shot her the same day, although it pained us to do it, as her pedigree could be traced back to an aristocratic Virginia thoroughbred named Old Eagle.

I will never forget the open-eyed, surprised, even pleased look on Grandma's face, as if this accident had solved all her unfinished business. She was dead without having had time to repent of anything or ask forgiveness or say good-bye. To be sure, death had finally put an end to her life as an imaginary Negro! Grandpa thought that it came from her childhood exposure to them as the daughter of a rich southern planter, and that she had substituted this fantasy family of blacks for the white family she had lost in an epidemic at a young age. And what better father could she have chosen than Thomas Jefferson himself, the father of our national identity.

Grandpa thought Grandma was really afraid of Negroes, as she had been afraid of death, of loneliness, of being abandoned, and this negrophobia was transformed in Grandma's fantasy into abnormal love for them.

He believed Sally Hemings was probably some beloved nurse my grandmother had at a very early age, when she had already been deprived of her own, real mother.

I thought Grandma's diaries, with their obsessive mentioning of colored people, pure-white Negroes, and their neurotic negrophilia, should be destroyed for the sake of our posterity. Grandpa agreed. And before he died, we did it. But Grandpa cried as he did it, as if, he said, he were taking Grandma's life a second time. That was when I began to have my doubts.

I often wonder, even now, if there was a kernel of truth in her ravings. And

I brood sometimes over the miniature of my great-grandfather, whoever he was, which I've always kept. Had this mysterious great-grandfather played a colossal joke on his descendants, on his country, on history, on human nature and the nature of love? Was he laughing at us? I brood too with the fear and dread of a secret murderer, over the obscure and dangerous maggot of black babies.

I, Roxanne Wayles Wellington, white spinster, American citizen, age eighty, born the eighteenth of January 1862, do swear this is the true and concise accounting of the last days of my maternal grandmother, Harriet Wellington, alias Petit, alias Hemmings [sic], alias Jefferson, who with her dying breath claimed with all the vigor, contradictions, and exuberance of her soul to be the President's daughter.

ROXANNE WAYLES WELLINGTON

PHILADELPHIA, MAY 19, 1942

Afterword

As was the title character in my historical novel, *Sally Hemings*, published in 1979, in the present work, Harriet Hemings, her daughter, is a nonfictional personage with a "fictional" biography. Harriet Hemings spent her whole life after age twenty-one as a white woman, hiding under another identity. She was, according to both state and federal law, a "black" fugitive slave, subject to arrest, sale, and re-enslavement, and after January 1, 1863, she was an emancipated "contraband." Such were the contradictions of life in America in the nineteenth century in matters of color.

The poetical, political, metaphysical, historical, and technical complexities of rendering such a situation are, understandably, daunting. As in the case of *Sally Hemings*, a novel historical enough to have been quoted, discussed, and attacked and defended as history, at least forty years of Harriet's life is a mystery: how she felt, what she did and said, how she resolved the crushing contradictions of her secret life. I have tried to project a life that, on the one hand, might have happened and, on the other, is larger than life and encompasses all the themes of filial love, power, enslavement, and legitimacy, both familial and national—in all their implications. Harriet Hemings was not at Gettysburg—or was she?—or could she have been?—or would she have been?—or should she have been?

Harriet Hemings, like Sally Hemings, is one of those minor historical figures caught up in the major flow and major themes of our myths, dreams, and history: censored, scorned, ignored, contested, yet who is also an archetype as much as Jefferson, adored and revered, is. To speak of American myths and the House of Monticello, as one would speak of the House of

Atreus in Greek mythic drama, is not too strong a way to put it. I have, as Harriet Hemings would say, had to move around the furniture of our preconceived notions and precepts of acceptable and standard history in order to accommodate her story, but the story itself is as real as any of the other myths that make up our identity and history, and to which we cling so tenaciously.

Anyone who writes historical fiction knows that life often imitates art. Some of the things that happen to people and that people do to one another are simply too incredible and amazing to be encompassed by fiction, i.e., by someone's imagination. That's what I thought when, just as I was handing in this book, I received word from Monticello that a new child of Sally Hemings had been identified through a letter from Thomas Jefferson to his son-in-law Jack Eppes, in which he announces obliquely and pointedly this birth. This brought the number of Hemings children to seven. I hardly blinked. Somehow the search for the truth is always more absorbing and dangerous than the truth itself. But even my hair stood on end when I asked the name of the newly discovered Hemings daughter, born the seventh of December 1799, nine months after Jefferson returned from Philadelphia. I was told the daughter had been named Thenia. But Thenia already existed! In the pages of the manuscript I had just sent! I had invented her from whole cloth, as a major character, because I needed her as a kind of twin, an alterego to Harriet's false whiteness. My choice of her name had been the purest of accidents. Thenia, the real Thenia, died before she was two years old. If she hadn't existed, I would have had to invent her, or, conversely, if she hadn't been invented, she would have had to exist.

A novel is a legitimate illumination of the ambiguities of historical reality. Written history is *always* interpreted through a writer's sensibility and therefore inevitably fictionalized. One has only to read a biography of Napoléon written by a Frenchman, an Englishman, and a Russian to recognize that with the same acts, and the same facts, a personage can differ so dramatically from one book to the other as to be practically unrecognizable. A fact can be white in one book and black in another. Oral history is closer to truth and to reality, but depends on the fragility of humankind's collective memory. We can only hope to find a grain of truth in the ocean of desert sand which is humanity's written memorial. As Voltaire noted and Harriet reminds us: "There is no history, only fictions of various degrees of plausibility."

Author's Note on
Historical Sources

⤳

Harriet (Wayles?) Hemings was born at Monticello, Albemarle County, Virginia, in May of 1801, the fifth child and third daughter of a quadroon slave, Sally Hemings (1773–1836), and the alleged eleventh child of Sally Hemings's master and brother-in-law, Thomas Jefferson. Sally Hemings herself was the daughter of John Wayles, Thomas Jefferson's father-in-law, by Elizabeth Hemings, a slave who bore him six children after the death of his second wife, and Elizabeth was the daughter of a whaling captain named Hemings and an African. Of the seven children Sally Hemings bore between 1790 and 1808, Harriet was the only daughter to survive to adulthood and fulfill the promise made to all the Hemings children that they would be allowed to run away at twenty-one.

Harriet Hemings grew up on Thomas Jefferson's plantation as a slave, and between 1821 and 1822, she fled Monticello and went north, according to records, to Philadelphia and passed for white.

In 1802, one year after Harriet Hemings's birth, Jefferson was publicly accused of fathering Sally Hemings's children in a scandal that reached national proportions. Although the original article was written by a former employee and protegé, of Jefferson's, a muckraking Federalist journalist named James T. Callender, other Republican newspaper editors, especially in the South, investigated the story, found it to be true and common knowledge in the Richmond-Charlottesville area, and published Callender's allegations, to which Jefferson never replied. For example, the editor of the Maryland *Frederick-town Herald* wrote:

> *Other information assures us, that Mr. Jefferson's Sally and their children are real persons, that the woman has a room to herself at Monticello in the character of seamstress to the family, if not as housekeeper; that she is an industrious and orderly creature in her behaviour, but that her intimacy with her master is well known, and that on this account, she is treated by the rest of the house as one much above the level of his other servants. Her son, whom Callender calls president Tom, we are also assured, bears a strong likeness to Mr. Jefferson.*

Sally Hemings and her children, however, remained at Monticello (her eldest son, Thomas, disappeared at this time) and Beverly, her second son, born in '98, was four years old, and she had two more sons, in 1805 and 1808.

In 1826, Jefferson freed these last two sons, Eston and Madison, in his will along with their uncles John and Robert. These were the only slaves Jefferson ever freed. The other Hemingses descended from his father-in-law went on the block to pay his bankruptcy debts.

In 1836 the Albemarle County census taker listed Sally Hemings, Madison, and Eston as white, presumably to erase any trace of the crime of miscegenation attached to Jefferson's name, a crime which was punishable by fine and imprisonment at the time (in Virginia, until 1967).

In 1873, Madison published his memoirs in the *Pike County Gazette*. In them he revealed the fate of Harriet as he knew it:

> *Harriet married a white man in good standing in Washington City, whose name I could give but will not for prudential reasons. She raised a family of children, and as far as I know, they were never suspected of being tainted with African blood in the community where she lived, or lives. I have not heard from her for ten years, and do not know if she is dead or alive. She thought it in her interests, on leaving Virginia, to assume the role of a*

white woman, and by her dress and conduct as such, I am not aware that her identity as Harriet Hemings of Monticello has ever been discovered.

Edmund Bacon, the overseer at Monticello in 1822, had this to say:

He freed one girl some years before he died, and there was a great deal of talk about it. She was nearly as white as anybody, and very beautiful. People said he freed her because she was his own daughter. She was not his daughter; she was ————'s daughter. When she was nearly grown, by Mr. Jefferson's direction, I paid her stage fare to Philadelphia and gave her fifty dollars. I have never seen her since and don't know what became of her.

Harriet's elder brother Beverly, as far as we know, went west to California and passed for white, while Thomas Hemings changed his name to Woodson and remained, as Madison did, on the black side, from which scores of descendants, with tenecious oral histories, exist.

Thomas Jefferson never officially freed either Sally Hemings or his runaways, who would have been fugitive slaves up until the Civil War and the Emancipation Proclamation and thus the property of his heirs and subject to arrest or return to their owners or sale.

In 1974, Fawn Brodie, a professor of history at the University of California, included a chapter on the Hemings affair and their family relationships with Thomas Jefferson in her book *Thomas Jefferson, an Intimate Biography*. In 1979, the author of the present work published a novel based on the historical and psychological evidence in this biography, as well as on doctorate dissertations on the Hemings family at the University of Virginia, on the Jefferson papers at the Library of Congress, on previous research done by non-Jeffersonian historians, and on her own independent research in the United States and France.

The descendants of Eston Hemings came forward after the publication of Fawn Brodie's book. They all considered themselves white descendants of Jefferson.

On July 3, 1979, three months after the publication of *Sally Hemings*, the curator of Monticello tore out the staircase in Thomas Jefferson's bedroom mentioned in the novel, which had incited too many questions from tourists.

The staircase has never been restored. The rationale was that although there were "steps" there, the actual staircase was not authentic and to put *any* stairs back would be "misleading to the public."

In 1981, Virginius Dabney published *The Jefferson Scandals*, a rebuttal in which he attempted to defuse the issue by attacking both the Brodie biography and the Chase-Riboud novel—a strange thing for a historian to attack a novel. Dabney had a hard time even admitting that Sally Hemings was Thomas Jefferson's half sister-in-law, did not reprint Madison's memoirs, made no attempt to verify by date or location the accusation of the Carr brothers' parentage of the Hemings children.

In February 1993, the research director at Monticello discovered a letter from Thomas Jefferson to his son-in-law Francis Eppes, dated December 7, 1799, announcing that "Maria's maid" (according to the director, a euphemism for Sally Hemings) "produced a daughter about a fortnight ago, and is doing well." This hitherto unknown child was named Thenia and died at an early age. This is the first and only direct and poignant reference in writing to Sally Hemings by Thomas Jefferson himself, except his entries in his farm book. This extremely interesting letter raises the question of why Jefferson would share such news with his son-in-law if the daughter in question was not his.

Because of the notorious family resemblance of all of Sally Heming's children to Thomas Jefferson (guests were startled at seeing them) the "any old white man" theory of the origins of these children was, even in 1802, impossible and never attempted.

Instead, forty years after Jefferson's death and sixty years after the fact, by uncorroborated hearsay, Jefferson's granddaughter Virginia Randolph accused her by-now-dead grandfather's nephew, Samuel Carr ("a good natured Turk") of fathering Sally Hemings's children. The only trouble with this theory is that Samuel Carr had just turned nineteen when Sally Hemings's first child was born and this child had been conceived in Paris. Moreover, there is no explanation why Samuel Carr (and in some cases his brother Peter Carr) didn't come forward in 1802, when the scandal broke (and he was twenty-seven years old), to defend his granduncle's reputation. There would have been no social onus attached to such a declaration, even if he were married, except that it is obvious he wouldn't have been believed. If so, certainly Madison or Monroe, who were Jefferson's closest neighbors and his political allies, and who worked desperately to defuse the scandal, would have attempted it. Madison was Peter Carr's mentor. Also inexplicable is that if it was "well known" by the Virginia gentry that Thomas Jefferson was the father of Heming's children, why wouldn't it have been just as "well known" that Samuel Carr had been the father? Charlottesville was a hamlet "steeped in duelism sic [dueling] gambling, black dances and miscegenation,"[1] and Richmond a small southern village of some six thousand souls, one-third of them black and only one thousand of them white males over sixteen, where everyone, black and white, knew everything but maintained a wall of silence. It has been historically proven that Thomas Jefferson was present nine to ten months before the birth of all of Sally Hemings's children, including Paris, France, and that she did not conceive when he was not there. Virginia Randolph lied about this ("understandable" according to Virginius Dabney), but her other assertions about Samuel Carr are to be taken as the absolute truth. The Carr brothers never lived at Monticello after 1796, during Hemings's childbearing years. Moreover, it doesn't take a great deal of research to ascertain that not only were neither of the Carr brothers mentioned in 1802, but that Samuel Carr, for example, in order to have fathered Beverly or Thenia Hemings would have had to do so from Maryland and on his honeymoon.

Of course, in 1802 the story was exploited and renewed by Jefferson's political enemies and the abolitionists. On the other hand, despite his horrendous reputation, Callender had never been caught in an outright journalistic lie. There was always a basis of truth even in his most purple-prose accusations. He had spent over a year in the Richmond jail and environs and six months as the house guest of Richmond newspaper editor Meriwether Jones. Second, many of the newspapers that printed the story, especially the southern ones, made independent investigations of their own and pleaded with Jefferson or his representatives for a denial before going to press. Former President Adams, who had been a victim of Callender's excessive writing and the only historical political figure who had actually met Sally Hemings (in London), believed the story was true and said so. Although Callender is usually dismissed with one line as being "a disappointed office seeker, a drunkard, and a liar," whose declarations were suspect because they came from a "vengeful pen," Callender's own version, to a dispassionate observer, seems closer to the truth: Jefferson stood by and allowed the Republican press to attack him, Callender wrote, "when with one single word [Jefferson could have] extinguished the volcano of reproach, but with the frigid indifference which forms the pride of his character, the president stood neutral." When the Republican press attacked Callender through his wife, accusing Callender of infecting her with a sexually transmittable disease and thus killing her,

---

[1]Michael Durey: *With the Hammer of the Truth: James Thomson Callender and America's National Heroes* (Charlottesville and London: University Press of Virginia, 1990).

Callender attacked Jefferson through *his* wife. He later wrote that "If [Jefferson] had not violated the sanctuary of the grave, SALLY and her son TOM, would still perhaps, have slumbered in the tomb of oblivion."[2]

Of all the information published by Callender on the Hemings affair, only a suggestion that Harriet Hemings was a maid in Washington, D.C., has been proved to be incorrect and Callender had warned that this might be so and corrected himself in a later article. Most Jefferson biographers support their assertions about Callender's false statements with a denial of the existence of Thomas Hemings. But as proof, they cite Jefferson's own farm book as a "neutral," "independent," and "dependable" record. Against Jefferson's understandable omission, the newspaper war and its investigations of 1802 beyond those of Callender, must be weighed. The silence of Jefferson and his "sons," Madison and Monroe, the existence of Beverly, Thenia, Harriet, as well as Tom and the positive assertions of John Adams, John Quincy Adams, Governeu Morris, and various southern, neutral, contemporary newspaper editors of the times must also be weighed. Added to this is the fact that Jefferson was with Sally Hemings nine months before the births of all her children, including the most recently discovered child, that she never conceived without him, and that there is no contemporary evidence that anyone believed that either Peter or Samuel Carr fathered the Hemings children.

Of the four major accusations thrown at Jefferson by Callender, only the Sally Hemings story is in any doubt. No one at the time, including Jefferson himself, denied the existence of Hemings or her children, nor their shocking resemblance to him noted by numerous visitors to Monticello. Add to this the recent family publications of the Woodsons who claim descendence from this Tom and have a two-hundred-year oral history to back it up, which has been accepted by the Monticello Foundation as correct (although they deny Jefferson's parenthood); the living descendants of Madison and Eston Hemings; Madison Hemings's 1873 memoirs; the stubborn silence of Jefferson as well as the silence of the Carr brothers in 1802 and 1803; the discovery of still another Hemings child, Thenia, who corresponds directly to Jefferson's return from Philadelphia, and it seems that the balance of evidence is against the "defenders" of Jefferson.

In 1799, the birth year of Thenia Hemings, rumor of the liaison was known to the Virginia Federalist editor William Rind, but he failed to publicize it during the 1800 election. The sources of Callender's information were clearly,

---

[2] *The Recorder*, September 22, 1802; October 13, 27, 1802; March 19, 1803; May 28, 1803 as cited in Durey, *With the Hammer of Truth*.

and for whatever reason, the Virginia gentry itself, a person or persons living close to Monticello. Envy, political discord, vengeance, moral righteousness must all be considered. Callender himself, a product of a Scottish, Calvinist upbringing, who could be considered a "poor white" converted to slave holding and racism by his residence in Virginia, truly believed that the public had a right to know the character of the candidates running for or holding public office and therefore his prejudice against blacks would have made the Sally Hemings–Thomas Jefferson affair a particular affront. This was particularly apt in Jefferson's case since the President had used similar means to discredit Hamilton. At one point, Meriwether Jones accused John Marshall and Alexander Hamilton of leaking the story and then turned around and accused Supreme Court Justice Marshall of "not being invulnerable to accusations of miscegenation." My candidate is David Meade Randolph, a relative of Jefferson who hated him and who had been dismissed from his post as a federal marshal and was having difficulty settling his debts. Randolph had been Callender's jailer when he had served a term in the Richmond jail for sedition. Callender stated that he had moved out of Meriwether Jones's house where he had been a house guest for six months when Jones "modified his living arrangements" by moving in his black mistress. In other words, the newspaper war in which the Sally Hemings affair erupted was one of the most vicious, unprincipled, "nothing is sacred" wars in American history, which by far outstripped in scurrility the previous editorial battles of the 1790s. By the time it ended, the dark side of Virginia society had been dragged into prominence; even the most avid consumer of scandal and yellow journalism had been sated.

Callender was finally found dead in three feet of water under mysterious circumstances, on July 17, 1803. He was buried hurriedly the same day without autopsy or inquest, the verdict being that he accidentally drowned while inebriated.

If the claims in Madison Hemings's memoirs are to be ludicrously dismissed as self-serving hearsay "concerning things that happened before his birth," then Virginia Randolph's assertions about the Carrs are just as much hearsay and also must be dismissed as self-serving.

Harriet Hemings had one-sixteenth of "black blood" in her veins. This was enough to make her black in law and fiction, and therefore a slave. Passing for white in order to escape slavery and later racial harassment and discrimination is particularly American—although certainly mixed-bloods did so in every society, but not with such tremendous ramifications as in the United States, where the national punishment for being black was not only slavery or potential slavery or the threat of slavery, but an almost mystical denigration of any humanity and all visibility—as if the condition itself also struck people deaf, dumb, and blind.

Moreover the idea of "passing" offends both blacks and whites and is one of the most tenacious of American taboos.

The pathos of Harriet's dilemma and the tragedy of Harriet's enigma is just one more episode in the continuing story of love, race, and identity in America.

So, what should the reader gain from my Harriet? I hope an American heroine who embodies our central national obsession, and psychosis: race and color. For I have created, as I did with Sally Hemings, out of my imagination a historical woman who is a part of our national patrimony and a symbol of the metaphysics of race in this country. In creating her I took into consideration every historical reality, contemporary element, every document, attitude, and atmosphere available and viable to me. I also took considerable poetic license. In creating the many characters that surround Hemings, I have used as models and quoted historical personages of the epoch: for example, Alexis de Tocqueville for Maurice Meillasoux; Frederick Douglass for Robert Purvis, who is himself historical; Mary Wollstonecraft for Dorcas Willow-pole; Abraham Lincoln for Abraham Lincoln; Marie Bashkirtseff's diaries for Maria Cosway. The letters of John G. Perry for Beverly Wellington; the diary of First Lieutenant Frank Haskell for Harriet's battle of Gettysburg. Although the reader might consider words such as *colorphobia* and *negrophobia* anachronisms, both Frederick Douglass and William Wells Brown mentioned them as a social phenomenon as early as 1853. The most interesting chronology on fingerprints I established with the help of the French fingerprint experts of the Criminal Brigade, Paris. As early as 1820, the first scientific study was published by an Austrian, Johannes University Evangelista Purkinje (1787–1869), a Bohemian physiologist and professor of physiology at Breslau and later Prague. In 1858 an English functionary in Bengal, India, William Herschel, used fingerprints as a method of identification to pay out army pensions. In 1878, Faulds, an English doctor in Japan, published a study on the traces of fingerprints on lacquer furniture, and in 1892, Sir Francis Galton published his famous report, which inspired Mark Twain's *Pudd'n Head Wilson*. About the same time, Inspector Vucetich, an Argentinian policeman, discovered the criminal investigative uses of fingerprints. Abraham Lincoln did refer to the "electric cord between us" before the electric cord actually existed. And it was Karl Marx who stated that the American Revolution of 1776 freed the bourgeoisie while the American Revolution of 1861 freed the working class. "Any emancipation," he insisted, "is a restoration of the human world and of human relationships to man himself." This is what I intended when I placed Harriet at Gettysburg.

From the beginning, I wanted Harriet to find herself there, confronting her father's Declaration and Lincoln's Proclamation with the idea of juxtaposing or amalgamating, if not miscegenating, the two voices into Harriet's and our American credo. I had no idea how powerful that intermarriage would be until I actually did it by counterpointing the two texts directly. I therefore read Gary Wills's brilliant analysis of Lincoln's Gettysburg address and its relation to the Declaration with great emotion.

Harriet's insistence that she would think about her troubles later is not a *clin d'oeil* to Margaret Mitchell's Scarlett O'Hara, but to Leo Tolstoy's Anna Karenina, for whom he invented the phrase.

A bibliographical note: I used the *Official Government Records of War of the Rebellion of the Union and Confederate Armies*, of which I possess an incomplete set, found in a flea market in Milan, Italy along with a rare mezzotint self-portrait of Maria Cosway. I have used the standard and most popular Civil War histories: Bruce Catton's *Mr. Lincoln's Army, Glory Road*, and *A Stillness at Appomattox; The Civil War, a Narrative*, by Shelby Foote; and the awesome one-volume Oxford history, *Battle Cry of Freedom*, by James M. McPherson, as well as his *The Negro's Civil War*. I must of course acknowledge Fawn Brodie's *Thomas Jefferson, an Intimate Biography* and her archives on the Hemings children and descendants which remain for the most part unpublished. I refer you also to my own novel *Sally Hemings* and to Helen Duprey Bullock's biography of Maria Cosway, *My Head and My Heart*.

Civil War literature, Jeffersonian literature, Lincolnian literature, and literature on slavery and abolition are practically boundless. For source material, I must have touched on more than a thousand books and documents. Abolition and slavery historiographies and bibliographies run into the twenty thousands. In sifting through all this information, any errors or misinterpretations are, of course, my own.

There are great and rich and still, after two hundred years, unmined sources of our national history and destiny in the archives of the unwritten, the unexplored relations between the races of America waiting to be told.

About the Author

Barbara Chase-Riboud was born in Philadelphia and is a graduate of Yale University. She won the Janet Heidinger Kafka prize for the best novel by an American woman in 1979 for her first novel, *Sally Hemings*. In 1988, she won the Carl Sandburg Poetry Prize as best American poet for her second book of poetry, *Portrait of a Nude Woman as Cleopatra*. She has been awarded numerous fellowships, honorary degrees, and citations. A worldwide traveler, she was the first American woman to visit China after the revolution. She is married, has two sons, and lives in Paris and Rome.